Who are
The
Pretenders ?

The beautiful people you see in the columns, on the talk shows, at the openings . . .

The international swingers who hop from party to party, continent to continent, bed to bed . . .

The trend-setting crowd everybody wants to be part of—unless you're in it. Then you want to get out, get out before you're all used up—but you just can't quit while you're winning . . .

Other SIGNET Books You Will Want to Read

BOOK **1**

CHAPTER ONE

EVERYONE assumed the funeral would be held at Frank E. Campbell's. During his lifetime, Harry had worked too hard to get to the upper East Side for his memorial service to be held anywhere other than Madison Avenue and Eighty-second Street. Although the Riverside Chapel was becoming fairly fashionable for show business funerals, there was no getting away from the fact that it was on the West Side. Besides, Harry had long ago fought and connived and brainstormed in wider avenues than Broadway, becoming equally celebrated in the world of big business. So there was little doubt he would be laid to rest via Campbell's.

There was, however, some confusion about who would make the actual arrangements. Harry's attorney, Ron Abbate, was in Europe. One of the brothers was in Idaho, no one was exactly sure where; as Harry had long ago dismissed him as incompetent, the arrangements could not be entrusted to him. The brother he had tolerated was on Harry's private island in the Caribbean, with the four children Harry had never seen but allowed to vacation there in the height of the off-season. The main advantage of that island, especially when Harry went there with a girl, had been no telephone communication. Now it presented a distinct problem.

In the end, the decision fell to Harry's secretary, who was rather at a loss: she had never arranged a funeral before, except for her mother, who hadn't been important. But what with everybody calling to ask when the services would be held at Campbell's, the problem of where was eliminated. Considering the circumstances of Harry's death—the maid and butler were away on vacation, and Harry's secretary herself had been at home with a summer cold, so Harry had been dead for two days before anyone went into the town house and found him, and the air-conditioning wasn't even turned on—time was, as the mortician pointed out, of the essence. In addition there was the big holiday weekend coming up, and a lot of Harry's friends voiced concern that they would not be out of the city by Friday noon, and might get caught in heavy traffic. The funeral was set for 10 A.M. Friday.

Louise Felder was delighted now she had bought the black

9

dress. At the time of the purchase she considered it an extravagance: little black nothing dresses were always good, but this was strictly for summer and a hundred and twenty-five dollars for a one-season sheath, no matter how slenderizing, was too much money. She had worried about it for a week. When the bulletin came in on the Wednesday night eleven o'clock news, a great burden of guilt was lifted from her. She went to the closet, took the dress out from behind the gown she had worn to the last opening of the season, and hung it up in the bathroom to air.

The day of the funeral dawned clear, if not altogether bright. By eight o'clock in the morning oppressive heat clung to the asphalt pavements, like the curious onlookers beginning to gather in the vicinity of the funeral home. The police had cordoned off the Madison Avenue entrance; the *Today Show* had given Harry an extensive journalistic obituary, including a list of the great and near-great who had been his intimates and near-intimates, and who would probably attend the services, so people were waiting on the sidewalks as far as Kleiniger's Art Gallery on the south, and Les Elles Beauty Salon to the north.

Louise took a taxi, but even so the crawl of rubbernecks in cars made it necessary for her to get out of the cab a block and a half from the entrance. She walked slowly, avoiding the crush of people on the sidewalks, weaving her way carefully in and out of the stalled traffic, keeping her head high and her approach calm, so she wouldn't sweat out her hairdo. At the corner of Eighty-second Street a sudden swell of people caught her up for a moment in the movement of the crowd, and she pushed herself free with one arm, smoothing the black sheath with her right hand. A young girl in a pink miniskirt and pink net stockings stuck an autograph book under her face, but Louise waved it away.

"It's all right," the girl's mother said. "She isn't anybody."

"As long as you know so much," Louise said, "you might tell your daughter that light stockings are out."

A chauffeured limousine pulled up in front of the chapel and Luke Benjamin stepped onto the sidewalk. What directors did, much less most of their names, was foreign to most of the crowd. But even those who hadn't seen his portrait on the cover story about him in *Time* had heard about him, especially since he had become a frequent public escort of Countess Trejinska, and the word was passed back rapidly. He saw Louise and kissed her on the cheek.

Louise looked back over her shoulder to check whether the mother and her miniskirted daughter had seen. They had. She smiled and entered the chapel.

SIGNET TRADEMARK REG. U.S. PAT. OFF. AND FOREIGN COUNTRIES
REGISTERED TRADEMARK——MARCA REGISTRADA
HECHO EN CHICAGO, U.S.A.

SIGNET, SIGNET CLASSICS, MENTOR AND PLUME BOOKS
are published by The New American Library, Inc.,
1301 Avenue of the Americas, New York, New York 10019

FIRST PRINTING, APRIL, 1970

PRINTED IN THE UNITED STATES OF AMERICA

THE
PRETENDERS

by
Gwen Davis

A SIGNET BOOK from
NEW AMERICAN LIBRARY
TIMES MIRROR

The object of the game of *Careers* is to "succeed" but just as in real life, each player has his own idea of what success really means. In *Careers* each player decides upon his own success formula and writes it down privately before the game begins. The first player to achieve or exceed his own success formula is the winner of the game.

Fame Points are represented by orange ★s . . .
Happiness Points are represented by red ♥s . .
Happiness Points and Fame Points may not be traded.

. . . Rules for playing the game *Careers*
Parker Brothers, Inc.

For All My Roberts

   . . . and Don

"Where's Diane?" Louise said to Luke, but he had already moved down the aisle.

On the right of the entranceway two security guards flanked a man in a morning suit with a carnation in his lapel, who stood checking off a list. Behind them, Chet Oppenheim, his wrinkled face curiously rosy beneath a tan, gladhanded the mourners with a sad smile on his face, handling public relations for Harry in death as he had done in life. In the front of the chapel to the left of the casket, obscured by great banks of floral arrangements, an organist played a medley of hits from Harry Bell productions.

Louise's eye took in the familiar faces of those already assembled. They were all there: the very rich, the very beautiful, and those whose talent or wit had admitted them to the select arena where once only background and breeding had served. She could count three movie stars who were still too big to make the transition to television, two who had signed to do their own series, one whose anthology had already failed, making him a washed-up TV performer rather than one of the old greats, and four who were putting out feelers for guest shots. Rick Flinders, the most prominent of the new breed of cinema names, recipient of constant publicity as an escort of important ladies, was also present, having flown to New York for the funeral in the midst of shooting, in direct violation of his studio's insurance rulings.

The theatrical people present, including performers, writers and producers, lined up like the Sunday *Times* News of the Rialto. Another of Chet Oppenheim's clients, Rolf Orlovsky, rumored to be the wealthiest banker in America—even more important than Harry Bell (Chet was hired to keep his name out of the papers), sat shifting uncomfortably in wrinkled gray gabardine, trying to be inconspicuous. Next to him sat Dr. George Piner, Harry's personal physician, who had been away on Orlovsky's yacht so had been unable to pronounce Harry dead. Behind them sat the politicians, the older ones with their names not quite on the tip of Louise's tongue, the younger ones of that new era of statesman attractive enough to be remembered, and run with the celebrated. There was no doubt about it: it was an "A" funeral.

"Sweetie!" Maggie Bolin reached out her long slender arm and pulled Louise into her row. She was wearing a gay pink and white print, and open sandals. Louise could not help noticing her toes were dirty.

"Isn't it a disaster? his dying I mean, it's a lovely funeral. But so unexpected, he was full of life, he always said so. They've got the coffin closed, you don't suppose there was any foul play?"

Louise shook her head. "It was two days before anyone even found him. And what with the heat . . ."

"Ugh," Maggie said. "Say no more. Poor Harry, and he was always so fastidious about his personal grooming, he did so like to look his best."

"Which was hardly good enough," Louise muttered.

"*Perdone?*" said Maggie, who had just returned from Venice where she had bought several Puccis in the wrong size.

"He certainly did like to look his best." Once Harry had called Louise to the town house for a breakfast meeting to discuss a project he had in mind for her, he said, and when he had answered the door (the butler was conveniently off that morning), he had been wearing a satin-lapeled silk bathrobe which came to the top of his knees, with nothing underneath. She was sure of that, from the few strands of curly gray hair spotting his pallid chest and the clear definition of round belly beneath the loosely knotted sash.

"Baby . . ." he had greeted her, possibly because he couldn't remember her name, but knew that she was young and bouncy, and that made him hungry even if she wasn't a name or a real beauty.

"Harry . . ." she answered. "Why don't you slip into something more comfortable?"

That made him laugh enough so she could slip free of him, knowing that she could play him the same way she had been able to play college boys, because he was eager, like they were, to believe she was—and keep her—pure. It had come as a monumental surprise when he dropped her completely for a fading but brilliantly preserved amazonian chanteuse who everyone knew gave great head.

"Two days," Maggie said. "Can you imagine anyone like Harry Bell not being missed for two days. It's tragic really."

"It's . . . it's my fault," Louise said. "I should have known something was wrong the minute he didn't come to pick me up for dinner Tuesday."

"You were supposed to have dinner with him Tuesday?"

"And Wednesday." It was the first time of many Louise was to say it, and hearing how good it sounded she was surprised she had ever hesitated. It was certainly no longer open to dispute.

"Poor Louise," Maggie said. "I know how fond of you he was."

Actually Maggie didn't, and Louise knew it. But it wouldn't hurt to have Maggie think that Louise had had a shot at becoming the last Mrs. Bell, which, now that Louise came to think of it, might have been what she meant by "Poor Louise." Not that Maggie, up to her ears in inheri-

12

tances, ever had to give a thought to anything like marrying for money—and not that Harry, stingy son of a bitch that he was—had been—would have left anything to whomever he was married to at the time. One of the things Harry would brag about the second the occasion presented itself was the fact that all his wives had signed a premarital agreement, a document which was supposed to convince everybody that they had married him for love.

"Do I repel you?" he had asked her once in the back of his chauffeured limousine.

"What kind of a question is that?" Louise said.

"Then put your hand on my cock."

"How can I possibly turn you down when you approach things in such a romantic fashion, Harry."

"Don't be a smart-ass, Lou. I know how clever you can be. Put your hand on my cock."

"Go fuck yourself," Louise said.

"Then I do repel you."

"I didn't say that, Harry. But there are . . . ways to approach things."

"What do you want?"

"I don't want anything." What she wanted was at least some vestiges of a courtship, an evening with the few friends he had who weren't dying, perhaps even a winged invitation to that mythical island, something that could make a girl justify to herself touching an old man's shriveled thing.

"I don't give presents and I don't make promises, Lou. Anybody who has anything to do with me has to do with me because they care about me."

"I believe you, Harry."

"I don't have to take a girl fancy places."

"Well no one could accuse you of that." The last time they had gone to dinner it was at the Sixth Avenue Delicatessen, with the chauffeured Rolls waiting outside.

"Every time I've been married they signed premarital agreements because they cared about me. Sylvia married me twice and didn't get a fucking penny. She was crazy about me."

"Everybody knows that, Harry." They also knew about Sylvia's ski instructor and the diving champion, but Louise didn't say that.

"You don't marry a person twice unless you're crazy about them."

"She must have been quite a girl."

"She certainly is. I'm thinking of giving her a present."

"You going to marry her again?"

"Maybe," he said. "What if I told you I was?"

13

"I'd wish you every happiness."

"You're a good kid, Lou."

"Thank you, Harry."

"A little crude around the edges, but I could fix that."

"Don't make any promises, Harry. I wouldn't want you to spoil your record."

"Your mouth is just a little too fast for your own good, you know. If you'd just sit there and look blond and plump and pretty you'd be better off, you know, you'd get a lot farther."

"I'm sorry, Harry. I'll try to control myself. I'd certainly like you to approve of me."

"I approve of you. You're a cute kid."

"Thank you, Harry."

"Very cute."

"You're cute too."

"I don't repel you?"

"Of course not. I think you're adorable."

"Then put your hand on my cock."

She hadn't at the time, and now that he was dead she was sorry. To be Harry Bell's widow would have to be different from being Harry Bell's divorced wife, standing there waving a premarital agreement. The law would look out for the seemingly bereaved, no matter what they had put their signature to, she was sure.

What she wasn't sure of was whether or not Harry Bell ever considered marrying her; since he was dead she was convinced he would have. Her heart filled with a kind of sadness at the little foresight she had enjoyed, and the many millions (how many? nobody could guess, even) that were about to be flushed into the sod. When the organist segued into a slow-march rendition of "Hot-Shot Hooligan," the biggest lindy hop of the forties, she managed to work up a few tears.

The chapel was almost filled now. Above her handkerchief she spotted Harold Rankin, who had just been named Broadway producer of the year; she put her hand to her ear in pantomime of a phone call, which he promised to return. Louise was surprised to see that he seemed to be accompanied by Kate and David Waller. At one point in her life when she and Louise had been close friends, Kate had shown great potential writing dazzling lyrics that should have eventually brought her into the enchanted circle; but she had abandoned them for the security of advertising jingles, and David, and the baby that was now visibly swelling her belly. Louise was glad about the baby, she really was, she assured herself, knowing how hard Kate had been trying for one; but there was no reason, now that Kate was no longer golden with the right kind of promise, for Harold Rankin to be rubbing shoulders with her. She smiled warmly and beckoned to Kate and David to come sit beside her. They did, but without Harold Rankin. So they hadn't come together after all.

"It's a shame someone has to die for us to see you," Kate whispered.

"Don't be paranoid," Louise said. "I've been drowning. Everybody's going away for the summer, and it was all I could do before today to get enough names for a column."

"Little Lulu," David said. "You've come a long way."

"Not as far as I could have come," Louise said, shifting her eyes to the bier.

"You sorry?" Kate said.

Louise smiled. "Are you?"

Kate patted her belly and smiled. "Wracked."

They had both been dating Harry about the same time, they discovered in one of their girlie sessions, and he had pulled much the same stuff on Kate he had on Louise, though always on a higher level because he knew Kate was a Smith girl and had a family in the city. Right after they discovered Harry was pitching them both, they were sitting together at Sardi's, and he had walked in with the sequined chanteuse. "With us sitting there like the Dolly Sisters," Louise had said. "I want to die."

Now they were together again, not quite like the Dolly Sisters because Kate had sold out to the foes of Betty Friedan, and nobody knew who she was anymore, and everyone who mattered would eventually know Louise. Maggie Bolin already did.

"Oh I'm so sorry," Louise said, with her best cocktail party manners. "Kate, have you met Maggie Bolin?"

"I didn't see you," Kate said, leaning across Louise. "How are you, Mag?"

"Oh that's right," Louise said, suppressing a pang. "I forgot you went to school together."

"You're having a baby, Kate. How heaven."

There was a slight rustle at the front of the chapel, and conversation subsided, to Louise's great relief. When a person was out of it, it was best for them to remain out of it, and not suddenly find a place because of old privileged ties. She wiped around the back of her neck with her handkerchief, and then brought it around to her mouth in time to suppress a giggle as Andre (born Arnold) Sherman leaped to the platform. A glint of silver lamé shone above the gray weskit of his morning suit, and he pulled the four inches of starched white cuff that showed beneath the sleeves of his jacket. He tapped his silver-headed cane once on the microphone, and focused the gaze which *Playboy* magazine had characterized as hynoptic on the assembled throng.

"We are all here because we were friends of Harry Bell's," Andre said. "And, more important, we are here because Harry Bell was a friend to everything that matters to us: theater, art, individual enterprise, and, that most elusive quality in today's world, *chutzpah*."

"What's that?" Maggie Bolin whispered to Louise.

"Andre Sherman."

"No, I mean that word."

"So do I . . ." She turned, "It means nerve, only more."

Really what it meant was balls, but Louise didn't know if she should say that to Maggie. But balls it was, and balls she was surprised and gratified to see that Andre still had, after three of his latest building projects had been foreclosed. As far as she knew he had been only an acquaintance of Harry Bell's, as much as Andre wanted it to be otherwise, so it took colossal balls for him to be mounted up there on the platform, raging against the light that had gone out of the world, the disappearance of boldness and derring-do in modern society. In the confusion surrounding Harry Bell's death, how like Andre to step in and take over; and how fortunate for him that in his own lifetime he should have the opportunity to deliver what sounded curiously like his own eulogy.

"Initiative and guts are not the order of the day," Andre was saying. "But they were the order of Harry's day, and when Harry's day was over he wouldn't allow it to be. He kept those things alive by sheer force of will, even though the world told him they were outdated. And with his passing, not a man, but those qualities have left us.

"There is no fitting memorial to Harry Bell. Not the monument that has been planned, nor the great collection of his art treasures . . ."

The one time Louise had been sorely tempted, alone there with Harry in the great Fifth Avenue town house, she had paused on the landing of the winding marble staircase, and gazed smack up into the face of Michelangelo's "David," standing there for all the world like a coat rack in anyone else's apartment. He had paused behind her, Harry Bell had, and noticed her reverent silence looking at the naked masterpiece.

"I know what you're thinking, Louise."

"Do you?"

"You're thinking you'd like to ball him, right?"

". . . nor even the vast networks of cultural centers that he founded throughout the country are fitting monuments. Not even the acres and miles of limited-growth grass he and I

16

were engaged in cultivating will be a rich enough monument. There is only one monument that will be meaningful enough to have satisfied Harry Bell. And that is that those of us who knew him, and admired him, will keep those qualities alive . . . will fight for the continuance of brains, and guts, and daring, and initiative in a world that will have none of them . . . in a society so smug with its own leisured success that it covers its eyes and ears at the sight and sound of them." Andre took a deep breath and closed his heavy lids over his eyes, as if to renew their blue brilliance.

Louise cupped her hand over her mouth and whispered to Kate, "And Andre for one intends to keep those qualities alive."

"And I for one intend to keep those qualities alive. Let no man write my epitaph, someone once said. Let some men be my monument, Harry Bell would have said." He lowered his hands to his side, and waited for a moment.

"So be it," he ended.

Louise had the distinct impression she should applaud. It was incredible, even knowing Andre as well as she did, how he had managed to make himself a star of Harry's funeral. There was still a great deal she could learn from Andre.

A speech of tribute from Senator Kranet was followed by a poem read, in alternate lines, by Mulvaney and Karr, the songwriting team Harry had discovered in the forties. The chapel, in spite of the air-conditioning, was beginning to grow warm, and Louise shifted uncomfortably on the wooden pew. The services had already run well over forty minutes, and if she was to be able to move among the crowd she wished that they would get to the punchline.

It came sooner than she expected. The Reverend Mulholland, fresh from a brilliantly successful round-the-world tour which he had discussed at witty length on *Johnny Carson*, was launching into one of his warm anecdotal recollections. Like the good showman he was, Mulholland was working his audience into a peak of attention. Pocketbooks being waved as fans were set back in ladies' laps, handkerchiefs replaced in breast pockets, coughs wallowed. A quiet that surpassed silence set in, Dwight Mulholland took a breath to accentuate the spell he had cast. Nobody even noticed the short, wiry man at the doorway of the antechamber.

"What the hell is going on here?" the man said, and was immediately hustled by the security guards into the private family room adjacent to the chapel.

"God is with us everywhere," Mulholland said quickly, moving into the standard part of his sermon.

". . . by whose authority?" bellowed the voice from the anteroom before they closed the door.

"In the life of Christ, Moses and Mohammed there is but one message . . . and that is that man is God's noblest creation, the tool by which God manifests Himself."

"I wasn't even notified, goddammit!"

Chet Oppenheim managed to squirm out of the middle of the front pew with a minimum of commotion. He paused at the left of the dais, and crouched almost to a kneeling position, crossing like a viewer at a screening who didn't wish to cast his shadow on the projection. To the right of the bier he straightened up and strode with studied casualness over to the door of the anteroom, smiling vaguely at no one in particular. In a moment he was inside.

"The ancient Greeks, of whom Harry Bell was so fond, as witness his extraordinary sculpture collection, some of which he had so kindly consigned to our temple in New Orleans, believed in pantheism: God is everywhere in nature. A beautiful but incomplete philosophy. We, the members of a new church, of which Harry Bell was an avid follower, to which he contributed so generously . . ."

". . . And just who's supposed to pay for all this?"

". . . believe that God is everywhere in man. Men like Harry Bell. For it is not, as Milton believed, the task of God to justify His ways to man, but rather the task of man to justify his ways to God. The son showing the father how right He was to give him life. So there can be no sadness here . . ."

"Don't you tell me to lower my voice, I know it's a funeral. What I want to know is who made the arrangements, and why wasn't I notified? I don't care who's here—why wasn't his family consulted?"

"So there can be no sadness here, because . . ."

A drained Chet Oppenheim stuck his head out of the side door to the anteroom and nodded to Dwight Mulholland's secretary. The secretary raised his hand in the air and whirled his forefinger in a quick circle, giving Mulholland the speedup signal they had picked up around the networks.

"Because Harry Bell was hizzown tributeand hizzown justification. Wecan *mourn* hispassing, butwecanonly *rejoice* inhishaving lived. Godblessyouall. Rest, Harry." He stepped down from the dais, almost bumping into Chet Oppenheim, who mounted the platform and stuck his mouth too close to the microphone.

"The interment will be private," Chet said, and fled, as the organist began playing loudly to cover the buzz.

"How embarrassing," said Louise, when they were almost outside.

"Like the moment in the wedding ceremony when they ask if anyone knows a reason why these two should not be joined . . ." Kate said.

"I suppose the reference to forever holding your peace would be in bad taste in a funeral service."

"I don't think we ought to discuss it," Kate said.

"You're right," said Louise and smiled to the rest of the people standing around talking on the sidewalk.

"What do you suppose that was all about!" said Maggie, coming up beside them.

"It's bad taste to even discuss it," Louise said.

"I heard that was his brother Irving," Maggie said.

"Even his brother Irving would have to have more class than that," Louise said. "If you ask me, the whole thing was staged. You know Harry. All his productions had to have innovations in them, people jumping out of the boxes into the orchestra pit. If it had just been an ordinary nice funeral he might have been forgotten after the cemetery. This way people will talk about it for weeks."

"You don't really believe that?" Maggie said.

Louise shrugged. "It's certainly a sensational exit."

"Poor Harry," said Kate.

"We should all be so poor," muttered Louise.

"I guess private interment means we can't go to the cemetery," Maggie said. "I suppose I can send my chauffeur away. Luke and Harold Rankin and Chet were all supposed to come in my car, damn, and they closed their offices, yes?"

"It does seem a terrible waste," said Kate, and squeezed David's hand.

"Well, why does it have to be," said Maggie. "Actually I have a fab idea—I've got a zillion hors d'oeuvres left over from a little cocktail thing I threw Wednesday, and the staff doesn't go off until four. Why don't we all go back to my place, and we'll have a little wake thing. Louise, you go tell everyone."

"All right," said Louise.

"And let there be no moaning at the bar," Kate said.

"Exactly," Maggie said. "Harry would have liked that, don't you think he would have liked that, what? He never wanted to go to funerals because he said you should always think about people you loved as being alive, and not buried."

"Maybe we ought to bring him to the party," Kate said.

"You are wicked," Maggie said. "I'd forgotten how wicked you can be. Can you and . . . I'm sorry, I've forgotten your name."

"David."

"David, will you bring your wicked wife?"

"I'd love to, Maggie. Where's your apartment? Aren't you in the same building as Huntington Hartford?" David said.

"We've got to go back to the office," Kate said. "But thank you."

"All right, but now that I remember how wicked you are, I think you'd better come to something soon . . . I'm giving a little supper thing in three weeks for Algernon Reddy, have you met him he's sort of a disciple of Dwight Mulholland only much more liberalized, he thinks that the real domain of God is the Inner Man, and you can only achieve it by a fantastic stretch of inner consciousness, Harry was all set to give him a big donation you know, it's so sad, but Algernon doesn't really need money he's got such a huge following, and so many inner resources. Fantastically bright, you'll love him, yes? Actually it's a fund-raising thing for his new Function Center in Jersey, but I don't want you to contribute anything, you'll come as my guests."

"We'll call you," Kate said.

"See that she does, David, won't you, there'll be a lot of people there who can do you good in your business."

"You don't even know what I do," David said.

"It doesn't matter," Maggie said. "They'll be able to help you whatever it is."

"Actually I'm a stockbroker," David said. "Perhaps you're acquainted with my firm. It's . . ."

But Maggie had already gone.

"Why'd you say that about the office," David said to Kate. "We don't have to go back to the office, and you know it. It's a holiday weekend. Everyone's leaving early."

"She makes me nervous," Kate said. "I don't want to be with her."

"You ought to spend more time with people like that. What's the point of knowing people like that if you don't spend time with them."

"All right. But not today. I'm not up to her today."

"You shouldn't have said that about the office," David said. "She'll think we're not very important if we have to go back."

Maggie found Louise in the crowd. "Is everyone coming?"

"I can't find Diane Trejinska," Louise said.

"If you can't find her, she must not be here." Maggie walked toward her limousine. "Just make sure you tell everyone you should."

Louise had never been called upon to organize a wake before. Ever since her gossip column had begun to be carried by *Manhattan East* and a few minor magazines, in addition to the Long Island and Newark newspapers, she had imagined herself as one day being consulted to pass upon people's guest lists. Usually the fantasies would begin with the inclusion of the best possible people, on the order of Countess Diane Trejinska. Sometimes her own name would appear on the list, but she would not include herself in the end. Louise could not afford the gaffe of asking to come along, even in fantasy.

Today, though, was different. Obviously Maggie intended her to come to the wake. Harry, Louise could not help but realize, wryly, was giving her in death, the chance of a lifetime. Of all the admirable ones, Maggie was the most to be admired and Louise intended her to know it. The shortest distance between two points was a straight line: admiration was the quickest route into a circle.

When she was twenty-eight, Maggie Bolin, whom Louise so much admired, had embarked on a brief affair with the foremost faggot photographer of her day. It started with her inclusion in a magazine layout of five post-debutante heiresses; her own black and white and gray mood-portrait was headed "The Subtle Chic of Maggie Bolin," providing a few moments of amusement for everyone who knew her well: because as she stood there in the twelve-hundred-dollar Balenciaga afternoon dress, her slip showed.

She herself had never noticed that detail, anymore than she noticed Hugo's tendency to swish when he had a few drinks in him. When she could find him at the end of a party, and they went to bed, by some deft manipulation and clever cunnilingus he would bring her to a pitch of excitement she had never felt before. So the fact that they rarely had sexual intercourse more or less escaped her. The dull emptiness she felt inside from time to time she attributed to psychological hungers, and remorse at the suicide of her fiancé ten years before.

It was at that moment, when they told her that Gerald was actually dead, that the sense of vagueness had descended on Maggie. As heiress to one of the last great baronial family fortunes, her absent-mindedness became "madcap," her actions "eccentric" and her category around the cafés "nutty" until times and the language updated her to "kooky." The power of her income and the capital it implied were such that nobody recognized the fact for what it was: in the autumn of her eighteenth year, Maggie Bolin had gone quietly and totally insane.

Kate Waller of course suspected it. Kate's own income was

nowhere near Maggie's, but they had moved in the same circles in childhood, were both at Smith, and Kate felt some affection for her. When news of Gerald's hanging himself swept the campus, Kate had been the first to go to Maggie's dormitory room, expecting to find her wailing with grief, as she had been the night her father died. But Maggie was sitting there, her lanky legs twisted beneath her, yoga fashion, a pad propped on her knee, humming into the pencil pressed against her lips.

"Oh, hi," Maggie said.

"Hi," said Kate.

"You'll never believe what I'm doing."

"Oh?"

"I'm writing a letter to Gerald's mother. Again. Can you believe it? How come I never see you? The only times I ever see you I seem to be writing Gerald's mother. You remember last year, right about this time you came in and I was writing her? About not being able to marry Gerald, I mean. I don't know why I feel I always have to apologize to her every time I decide I can't marry Gerald. She ought to know better than I why I can't marry him, after all she's his mother."

"Are you all right, Maggie?" Kate said.

"If you mean do I know what I'm doing, of course I know what I'm doing. I've never been so clear. I can't possibly marry him, he's a very weak boy, and if there's one thing I need it's control, everybody knows that, it's obvious even to me. That's one of the reasons I run off so at the mouth. I talk fast because I haven't the least idea what I'm really thinking and I suppose I think if I get enough out I'll find out what I think. Either that or no one has enough guts to tell me to shut up. Certainly not Gerald. His mother does, but I won't be marrying her, I'd be marrying Gerald, and that would be a mistake. Don't you think so?"

For a moment it crossed Kate's mind that Maggie didn't know Gerald was dead. But then she saw the telegram lying half-crumpled on the floor, and the wet stains on Maggie's pillow.

"I really don't know what to say to her, that's the only thing," Maggie said. "I mean, I've written her so many times. You know how often I've slipped back into believing it would be all right to marry him, well, that's weakness on my part, she can't respect me very much for that. But he is lovely to look at, you will admit that, so long and lean, and he's very sensual. Nobody would think so to look at him, anymore than they'd think it about me if I hadn't sprouted the breasts." She brushed her hand absently over the front of her chest, as if it were an unimportant detail in a painting. "Actually I suppose I should be grateful for them, but I never had a chance at being a real beauty, all I could have been was a good lanky type, but they spoiled that, don't you think? They don't really go with the rest of me, and I'm terribly aware of them, so I keep caving in at the shoulders to make them disappear, but all it does is make me look like they're too heavy to carry. Gerald says I should be proud of them, they're lovely, but I can't listen to him, he's mad."

Kate sat down on the bed beside Maggie and reached tentatively for her arm, patting it once, ineffectually. "Can I do anything for you, Mag?"

"Actually, if you want to be a real friend you can help me with this letter. I don't like to look foolish to his mother, but I can't possibly go through with it. How would you phrase it if you were me?"

Shock and grief had probably unhinged Maggie for the moment, Kate reasoned, putting more alarming possibilities in the back of her mind. When Maggie left school shortly after, Kate assumed that time, as they said, would heal all wounds. They did not see each other often after that. As various stories of Maggie's adventures filtered down to her, Kate wondered if what had been in the back of her mind about Maggie was not indeed the case, and if so, why nobody had done anything about it.

Dr. Moynihan had tried. The spring Maggie joined a group of her young friends who were drying out at Golden Manors, he had suggested to the director that intensive psychotherapy might be better indicated in Maggie's case than the nightly glass of Ovaltine. But the director explained quite firmly that Golden Manors was not an institution for alcoholics, but a voluntary rehabilitation program for the very rich, among whom Maggie was the very richest. She had entered voluntarily, had been in no sense "committed," so it was not up to them to discuss or suggest more serious solutions. They would do their best, and if they failed, they failed.

They failed. Five weeks after she had entered Golden Manors, Maggie was found by an attendant, standing on her head in the shower, screaming with pleasure as the water beat between her legs. She was invited to go home, with the advice to her mother that she had no real wish for inner discipline. Her mother turned that knowledge over to the bank, where the trustees understood that inner discipline was very hard to achieve when one was worth over two hundred million dollars. They spoke to Maggie with some severity, however, and said they certainly wished she would try to exercise restraint. It was the least she owed the memory of her father.

"You're absolutely right," Maggie said, and promised she would never again drink to excess.

She was as good as her word. Shortly afterward she set up housekeeping in a Park Avenue apartment with a red-headed clarinet player named Arthur Landers, and his friend, Hoover Coolidge Gray, a graduate of George Washington Carver. Hoover Coolidge worshipped Arthur because he was an incredible musician, and also the source of most of the heroin on the East Side. Except for the time Maggie's mother rang the doorbell, and Hoover Coolidge answered the door buck naked, and the lawsuit, life in the ménage was comparatively free of incident. Maggie had given Arthur two hundred thousand dollars to start a record company, and the first singing group they signed were the Jujubes, four tiny Negro girls in different colored wigs. Although Maggie caught Arthur in the spare bedroom with the green Jujube, the lawsuit had nothing to do with revenge. It was simple business, Maggie's lawyers explained to her. The record company had lost all its money, and in order to make it a tax savings, she had to sue Arthur, with whom she was still living.

It was a friendly lawsuit. By the time the case reached the calendar, he had forgiven her. It required a deeper humiliation than she had yet submitted to, involving another girl and his clarinet, with him watching. But when it was over he kissed her. They might have continued quite happily like that if it hadn't been for the smart court reporter who looked into the case being hushed up in private chambers, and spotted the name on the calendar.

The next day the whole story was in the *Daily News*. Maggie's mother had feared the eventuality so long that she didn't even cut out the clippings. Arthur, however, had never before been subjected to public abuse, so he left her.

After that, Maggie gave herself to acting lessons, painting lessons, a course in faith healing, and an abortive study of the art of composing haiku. Her enthusiasms continued to be boundless, if undirected, and the major part of the mandatory charitable donations on her yearly tax return given to what her friends described as "lunatic" causes.

But no one listened to the adjective they used.

When Hugo the photographer met her, she was skipping in and out of the chilly waves at Southhampton, flapping her arms and chirping with pre-season delight. She looked at him at that moment like a big-breasted spindly-legged bird, all gangly wings and shrill cheeping.

"That girl is crazy," Hugo said to his hostess, lifting his jacket collar against the unseasonable late May cold. "The water can't be over fifty degrees."

24

"That's Maggie Bolin," Julie said. "Isn't she delightful?"

"So uninhibited," Hugo replied. "It's delicious."

When his hand was halfway up Maggie's leg after dinner that evening, he told her how impressed he was with her open nature.

"Are you?" she whispered, and slithered her hips farther down on the sun-porch swing.

"A photographer sees things like a lens," he said, bringing his hand up to his eyes to illustrate. "Light, glare, reflection, honesty. True radiance is a rare quality."

"I'm not very pretty," Maggie said, and reached for his hand.

Hugo swatted at a fly Maggie couldn't see. "You have a quality," he said. "It's rare."

"So have you, Hugo."

All his life Hugo had aspired to class. Distinction he already had in his field, and in the circle where accomplishment was fast becoming a compensation for social background. He could wear an ascot and the same turtleneck Anthony Armstrong Jones had donned with a tuxedo, and he affected a Noel Coward delivery of even the most sententious phrases so people mistook him for witty. He was a good man to have at a party or a weekend, and could get in anywhere he wanted.

That did not include Maggie's pants, but Maggie hadn't the least suspicion. He took her everywhere, and kept her aglow with more hugging and fondling than she had experienced since her father died. His displays of affection in public were overwhelming, and he was helping her select a new wardrobe to more precisely reflect the "real *her*," which involved a lot of touching. For a while she was almost satisfied.

Labor Day weekend they went back to Julia's house at the beach, to celebrate their having met. For a while they sat at the edge of the sea letting the tide ripple up to them, while he played with her toes. When he noticed her staring at the crotch of a newly arrived Italian who might or might not have been a prince, he hustled her inside the house, opened a split of champagne and took her up to her room, where he did with his tongue all the things he was so well practiced at doing, although not in quite the same way.

"Oh Hugo," she whispered. "You do care for me."

"You'll never know," he said.

When they got back to New York the theater season was just getting underway. Between opening night parties and backers' auditions to which Maggie was always invited, they were kept very busy and reasonably tired, and now that he was making her into a photographer's model, it was important she get her sleep, he usually told her at her door. When her incredible energy remained undiminished, he managed.

Maggie was terribly happy, she told everyone. She told her hairdresser, and her dentist, and the girl on Hugo's studio switchboard, and his receptionist, and many of his male models, including Peter, with whom she posed for a few pictures for a martini mix.

"I'm terribly happy," she said to Peter.

"That's nice to hear," Peter said. He was about six feet two, just a little shorter than Hugo, and had straw-blond hair that Hugo said would blend nicely in the shot with Maggie's, giving her a softer look than she ordinarily had because of the prominence of her chin. The width of Peter's chest would likewise diminish the size of hers, visually. With the wind that Hugo had set up at the right of the studio blowing through the soft blue chiffon, she would seem almost tiny and incredibly feminine, Hugo explained, especially as Peter was so male.

"I've never been happier with anyone," Maggie said as they posed for the pictures. "Hugo's a delight."

"He is that," Peter said.

"And so forthright and honest. He sees things like a lens, you know. He has a quality. Quality is rare."

"And how," Peter said.

"I like you, I really do, isn't that funny, Hugo said I would, most of the time I hardly have anything to say to people I don't know, but I can talk to you, you have something to say. You must come to a party I'm giving tomorrow night at Hugo's apartment, can you? It isn't very much really, just an intimate little thing for thirty or so, sit-down, black tie, do you think you can come?"

"I think I can."

"I hope so. I so admire people who can earn their own living, I'd give my ears to be able to do that, Hugo's so sweet to do this for me, I mean I know I'm not the average model type, but he says he can sell me for the right thing, and it would help give me a sense of personal pride if I could earn some money and not just be included in the snob gallery, in *Harper's,* did you happen to see that picture, Hugo did it."

"No, I—"

"Of course it isn't the same thing as being an actual model, like you are. I so admire people that earn their own living. At anything. Were you always a male model?"

"Well, no . . ."

"Oh really? How does a person become a male model, I mean what kind of background do you have, were you in some sort of related field before?"

"I suppose you could say so," Peter said.

"Well, what did you do? I mean I don't mean to pry, people's backgrounds mean absolutely nothing to me, I care what a person is, not what he comes from, what you come from means absolutely nothing, really. So you don't have to tell me if you don't want to, it's just that I'm so fascinated. I mean I imagine girls that are going to be models just become models if you know what I mean, someone tells them they're pretty and they go to an agency and either they make it or they don't, but I'm curious as to how it would happen to a man. I mean, it isn't as if someone tells you you're pretty."

"Yes it is."

"How funny you are, you're absolutely droll. Hugo told me you were droll. Those were his exact words, he said to me, you'll like Peter, he's very droll."

"Did he?"

"How did you get into it, really? What did you do before?"

"I was a whore," Peter said.

"You were so right about Peter," Maggie said to Hugo in the car on the way home. "He's absolutely droll. You wouldn't believe what he told me. I've invited him to come to the party tomorrow."

"I don't know if you should have done that, Maggie." Hugo looked very drained from the afternoon's shooting.

"Well why on earth not? He's very droll, and he's certainly beautiful to look at, we could use an extra man, and he'll look wonderful in a tux."

"Peter doesn't fit in with that group."

"Oh don't be such a snob, Hugo. Anybody fits in anywhere, you know that. All you have to do is make him feel comfortable."

"He knows how to make himself comfortable," Hugo said.

"Well, I think he's divine, and I want him at our party, and he is one of your closest friends, didn't you tell me, isn't he one of your closest friends?"

"I don't invite him to parties," Hugo said.

"You're really a snob, Hugo, I'm surprised at you. I don't want to talk about it anymore. I think he's very droll, and he'll look divine in a tux."

He did. The men all sat up taller in their chairs because of Peter's presence, and the women were enthralled, especially Maggie's friend, Julia White, who sat on his right during dinner, and hung on his arm through the latter part of the evening when the party moved into the living room. Maggie didn't get much of a chance to talk to Peter, trapped as she was in a group that were busy with money-raising plans to abolish fox hunting. But he seemed to be having a good time,

27

his white smile flashing on Julia, his strong square chin flung back as he threw his laughter over his shoulder. Hugo, Maggie was pleased to see, had made his way over to Peter, to put him more at his ease.

". . . Really shouldn't be monopolizing Julia . . ." she heard Hugo say to Peter. The rest of their exchange was lost in the drone around her.

"It's all so exasperating, isn't it?" said Darlene, a tiny brunette married to a stockbroker and tennis player who couldn't be with them that evening. "Isn't it exasperating, Maggie?"

"What?" She turned her eyes away from the group in the corner. "Oh . . . yes, madly exasperating."

"With all the progress made in the humanities, and they're still killing those poor little things in Virginia."

"And Maryland," the brunette's escort said. "You mustn't leave out Maryland."

"It's the ritual of it that's so barbaric," someone else said.

Maggie stretched forward in her chair to see past the people in the center of the room, but the brunette was restraining her arm. "What a shame your cousin York couldn't be here, Mag."

"Oh yes," Maggie said. "He'd be madly enthusiastic to help." York's outstanding physical characteristic was a great shock of orange hair and busy pink eyebrows, which had led an unkind colleague at the bank to rechristen him "Yoicks" —shorthand for "There goes the little red son-of-a-bitch." Ever since, York had despised fox hunting.

"Why don't I phone and ask him to come over?" Maggie got up from the chair. "He's always good for a few dollars, even if it's after dinner."

Her escape effected, Maggie made her way to the far side of the duplex living room. Julia was now standing alone in front of the floor-to-ceiling smoked-mirror glass of the fireplace.

"You didn't let him get away?" Maggie said.

"I assure you it was not my intention," said Julia, eyeing her gray reflection. "I thought I looked rather good tonight. This dress isn't even featured until the December issue. I took it out of my own layout."

"You look heaven, Julia. Have you seen Hugo?"

". . . went to powder his nose," Julia said into her brandy snifter.

Maggie kissed Julia on the cheek and dashed up the circular Lucite staircase to the bedroom floor.

Someone was throwing up in the master bathroom, and it didn't sound like Hugo. There was nothing but coats in the guest room, and no sound coming from inside the bath. She

28

went back to the master bedroom and pressed her nose against the intricate wrought-iron gates that had once led into a cathedral in Chartres, but now opened onto Hugo's terrace. The city sparkled behind and beneath Peter, who stood leaning against the railing, laughing.

Maggie opened the gates and reached for the handle to the sliding glass door. The sudden onrush of Indian summer that had overtaken New York that evening had swollen the metal sidings, and the door would not open easily.

". . . thought you were pretty smart coming here like this," she heard Hugo say.

"But my dear boy, I was invited."

"You didn't have to accept."

"I thought you'd be happy for us all to become great friends. Wasn't that your idea?"

"Very funny," Hugo said. "You know perfectly well . . ."

Maggie bit her bottom lip with the effort of loosening the door, and missed several words.

". . . falling all over that predatory cunt," Hugo said.

"Whew," Maggie laughed and bounded out onto the terrace beside them. "You're not talking about me, are you? although you'd have every right to, coming out here like this, I bet you think I haven't any manners, didn't your mother ever tell you to knock before leaving a room?" She laughed and hugged Hugo, pressing her cheek against his. He felt very warm. "Come, come back inside, you're right to want to escape from the party, it's a great bore, don't feel bad, Hugo, I'm giving it, not you, your parties are always lavish successes, everyone say so."

She reached up with her lips and kissed him on the nose. "It's all right, darling, I know you weren't talking about me, no one could describe me as a predatory cunt." The smile suddenly left her face, and her eyes. "Could they?"

"Of course not," Peter said, and hugged her from the other side, as they all went back to the party.

About an hour later as she sat with a newly converted Zen Buddhist in front of the fireplace, the anger that had been in Hugo's tone on the terrace struck her for the first time. The degree of his emotion was puzzling to her. Hugo was terribly contained, even in the act of passion. For him to expend that much passion in conversation was unthinkable. She tried not to think about it, and to listen to the words of the former advertising executive who had found peace. He had become quite boring as well as serene, so it was easy for her mind to wander.

The only time she had ever seen Hugo the least overwrought, an inept assistant had underdeveloped a series of his

29

pictures. Hugo's work was his life, he said that all the time, especially at parties. Whoever threatened his creations threatened him; he said that, too. A man, especially Hugo, did not speak with that degree of anger unless he was threatened.

But what threatened him? She recalled his discomfort when she told him Peter was coming to the party. Obviously he wasn't concerned with protecting Peter, so the answer had to be that he wanted to protect *her*. She was his creation, that was it, the statue in the centerfold of *Harper's Bazaar* to his Pygmalion, and he couldn't bear to have her threatened. By Peter, that was it, that had to be it: Peter was his good friend but Peter obviously didn't have the moral fiber of Hugo, so good friend or no he might have made a play for her, and Hugo didn't realize she wouldn't respond.

He loved her. It was as clear to her at that moment as if he had finally said so. She was so happy she had a few extra drinks to make the time fly and everyone else go away.

By the time the party dispersed at two thirty she had passed out on the couch. The butler and maid hired for the evening helped Hugo carry her upstairs before they emptied the last of the ashtrays and went home.

When Maggie woke up at four o'clock, the first thing that struck her was shame. Her hands and her mind were shaky, the way they had been in the old days before Golden Manors, before she had found out how important it was to dream. Dreams were the way you worked out your anxieties, and people who were awakened from dreaming couldn't cope with the realities around them. You could go back to sleep, but you couldn't go back to dream, that's what Dr. Moynihan had told her—and that was why alcoholics had the DTs. Alcohol sleep was dreamless, so spiders attacked them in the daytime.

She eased herself off the bed and stumbled into the bathroom, avoiding the glance of her own eyes. It was shocking, deeply shocking: there was no excuse for her. To drink as she had done because she was happy was no justification; the result was the same as if she had drunk because she was miserable. She deserved to be miserable, because she had deserted Hugo through stupor, on what should have been the happiest night of their lives. She washed her mouth out many times and went to look for him.

At the top of the circular staircase she took off her shoes: she felt that her feet, like most of her body, did not quite belong to her, and she was afraid of slipping on the Lucite, adding clumsiness to her sins of the evening. The living room was in darkness, except for keylight above a large red abstract, and the bulb inside a red-stained hurricane lamp. The room had a palely roseate glow; it was softening—flattering even to a drunk.

Halfway down the stairs she saw Hugo. He was standing naked in front of the smoked glass of the fireplace. She could not see his reflection in the mirror—the light was too indistinct—but even from behind she could tell he was masturbating from the direction and movement of his hand. She felt no repulsion or anger except at herself for deserting him in his need and leaving him no other recourse.

For a moment she paused, wondering if being caught at it like that would be too great an embarrassment for him. But it was her fault, she would make that clear. Most important, she wanted to have the erection he was holding in his hand inside her, before it was gone.

It wasn't until she was three feet away, when Hugo lowered his head to kiss the neck in front of him, that she saw there were two of them, and the face in the mirror was Peter's.

The next day she left for Acapulco to try and find Arthur Landers. He was untraceable, but she did bump into Harry Bell, and through him met Algernon Reddy, who decided to introduce her to God.

Louise could not help thinking that Maggie's wake was considerably less successful than Harry's funeral. The hors d'oeuvres left over from Wednesday's party were soggy. Although Maggie had telephoned Help! for two extra butlers to aid her regular staff, because of the short notice and the proximity of the holiday weekend the agency had been unable to provide their regular domestics and had sent two bartenders who were understudying in the off-Broadway revival of *The Blacks*. One recognized a great many of the show business celebrities at the party and was giving out his card with a list of his credits along with the drinks.

Maggie had forgotten to send out the laundry, so the canapés were passed with soiled cocktail napkins. The whole atmosphere seemed to Louise quite disorganized, although she could see that the napkins were the finest of Irish linen, complete with embroidered crest. The wrought silver candelabra, coffee services, wine decanters and trays in the breakfront next to the bar, the most elaborate, exquisite pieces Louise had ever seen in a home, were somewhat dulled by lack of polish and a fine film of dust on the glass of the breakfront. But, when you had these things, really had them, Louise supposed, you could afford to abuse them. Not like her mother whose one pair of Gorham candlesticks were shined religiously once a week and covered with Saran Wrap and kept in a drawer, so nothing could tarnish them.

In front of the fireplace where a fan had been set atop last winter's logs to abet the generally ineffective air-conditioning, a former Brooklyn poet recently returned from India strummed a funeral song on an electric sitar.

In the mirrored alcove bar on red-leather metalwork stools trellised with wrought-iron flowers, Chet Oppenheim sat in hushed conversation with Rolf Orlovsky, whose fingers absorbedly worried his heavy jaw, while his eyes from time to time darted about the room taking in the ladies. Louise leaned over to give the bartender her glass to refill, and her hand brushed Orlovsky's arm.

"Excuse me," she said, smiling warmly, but he did not turn to see. "Vodka and tonic," she said to the bartender.

"Aren't you Louise Felder?" he said, taking her glass.

"Yes."

"I read your column every other day. I live in Newark temporarily. Until I get my big break on Broadway."

"Wonderful," she said.

"I'm not really a bartender," he said. "I am currently understudying the lead in—"

"I know, Luke Benjamin already showed me your card."

"However, if you ever give a party . . ."

"You'll be the first to know," Louise said, turning, and met the glance of Rick Flinders, who was watching himself in the mirror behind the bar. He was still suntanned from California, a richer, deeper tan than the summer sun of the Hamptons afforded. With the sharp cut of his perfect profile, the controlled thickness of his shock of wheat-colored hair, and his tan sports jacket, he was so monotonedly handsome she thought he might still be wearing makeup. According to some of Louise's West Coast sources, he was currently waging a campaign, long-distance, for his newest target, the Countess Diane Trejinska. But that was not the kind of item that Louise printed, even blind. You did not mess with celebrities on the level of Diane Trejinska, who was too rich, too beautiful and too well connected to tolerate innuendo, no matter how cleverly veiled.

"Well, it's certainly no Miss Universe pageant," Rick said, surveying the girls in the room.

"What a shame Diane couldn't be here," Louise said.

He smiled, ivory on a field of topaz. "You look very well, Louise. I've never seen you looking better."

"Isn't that funny, Harry said that to me only Monday." She looked at her feet, and rearranged them on the trellis of the bar stool. "I was with him. You really think Lulu looks pretty?"

"For a fat girl." Andre Sherman came up to the bar beside her.

"God, it's getting so a person can't even go to a funeral in peace. They're starting to let anyone in," said Louise.

"Which reminds me," Andre said. "How did you happen to go?"

"Is everyone having a wonderful time?" Maggie said. "I mean under the circumstances, naturally, Andre you were magnificently poignant before, didn't you think so, Louise, I hadn't realized you were so friendly with Harry, Andre, what? But it was a heaven tribute, what a pity Harry couldn't have heard that elegy, it was divine, what? do you think he heard?"

"That's all there is," Andre said. "The one shot and then it's over."

"I've looked everywhere for more vodka," the bartender said. "But we seem to be out of it. I'm sorry, Miss Felder."

"That's all right. I'll have gin and tonic."

"I'm sorry about that," Maggie said. "I wish I had known this was going to happen and then I could've been better stocked. It'll only take me a minute to order up more whiskey." She headed back through the congested living room.

Andre hooked the fingers of his right hand in the pocket of his silver lamé vest. "How come you're here?" he said again.

"Who are you doing now?" Louise said. "Clarence Darrow or Napoleon?" She slipped from the stool and walked past him. "So many important contacts here, Andre, surely you don't want to waste your time with me."

"I couldn't ever think of you as a waste of time, Louise."

To her surprise Louise felt her eyes welling up with tears. Obviously she was not used to drinking, especially in the morning, and the events of the day had had greater impact on her than she had realized. The door to the bathroom was locked. "Do you have a Kleenex?" she said to a tall man standing by the armoire in the guest bedroom. He turned and smiled at her. She didn't recognize him, but he was tall and palely attractive in a conservative, dull way. He held out a linen handkerchief, and she felt very grateful.

"It's clean. How gallant can you get?" She wiped her eyes and smiled at him beneath the white linen. "Thank you."

"I suppose death is always more upsetting than we can anticipate," he said.

"I suppose. Will you mind very much if I blow my nose?"

"Not at all."

33

"It seems so tacky, somehow, blowing your nose in a clean handkerchief."

"It's all right. I'm a doctor." He smiled.

"Doctor who?"

"George Piner."

"You were Harry's doctor, weren't you . . ."

"I was away," George said. "I didn't even know . . ."

"I didn't mean anything by that, Dr. Piner, really I didn't. I know how much confidence Harry always had in you. We were discussing that the night before he died."

"Really," George said. "That's very kind of you to say. How was he feeling?"

"Fine. Just fine."

"These things just happen, I suppose. Still, it's always a shock, even to a man's doctor. You just can't help thinking there might have been something you could have done, Miss . . ."

"Felder. Louise Felder. I can't understand why we've never met before."

"Well, Harry never liked to parade his doctor. He prided himself so on being such a healthy man."

He smiled at her vacantly, and she sensed she was being dismissed. "I'll have this laundered for you."

"No please, it's quite all right."

"I want to," she said. "Are you listed?"

"Yes."

"So am I. I'll send it to you," she said and left him. She would include a note, polite but a little warm, so if he wanted the opening, it would be there for him. It was not that she was being pushy, she was sure. But the number of decent men in the world diminished in direct proportion to how long you waited and how selective you became. She had wasted too much time and gone blindly into too many cul-de-sacs, like Andre.

For a while Louise amused herself by joining in the conversation of the Senator, his wife, and his aide, an anxious young man named Rodney Drang.

"But they're all convinced of it, Ed," Rodney said to the Senator. "Whether or not you're running, you're the natural to win."

"I have no presidential aspirations," the Senator said.

"That's beside the point," Rodney said. "You could win."

"I have no wish to subvert my own party."

"Do you really think it's a question of subversion?" Louise said. "The Republicans have some glamour faces. You're the only Democrat who's attractive enough to get my vote. Even

34

Harry felt that way. We were discussing that only on Monday."

"Really?" the Senator said.

"I told you he was willing to give campaign money," Sylvia Kranet said. "You should have let Rodney speak to him last week when he wanted to."

"Oh drat," said Maggie, coming out of the dining room. "It must be an hour already and that wretched liquor store hasn't sent the delivery what? and everybody's feeling very let down, yes it's a terrible thing but I've got some heavenly pot—"

"If you'll excuse me," said the Senator. "I've got to leave for Connecticut before the holiday traffic really starts blocking the road—"

"Oh dear," Maggie said. "Must you? I was just about to turn everybody on . . ."

"Another time," Senator Kranet said, smiling weakly, and signaled his wife Sylvia, who came over and made her apologies, explaining that she had to attend a fashion show, for the benefit of SCLC.

In the sun room, papered in black, Dainty Lee Purbelow, in black culottes which her designer had promised her were appropriate for the funeral, stood with her arm looped through the restless elbow of Arnold Sussman, the political cartoonist, who was talking to Noel Gurion.

"You can hate me all you want for being a commercial success," Noel said. "But works of mine that you sneer at will become a part of American folklore, you'll see. I've been talking to the Guild about a musical version of *Heroes.*"

Louise giggled across the room, and Noel turned and caught her.

"Why are you laughing?" Noel said. "They're flying in Lindemeyer from the Coast. First class. He's Hollywood's highest ranked composer."

"I'm sorry," Louise said. "I thought you were making a wonderful joke. How can you do a musical about a concentration camp?"

"With stature, that's how," he said. "Does everything have to be *Doctor Dolittle?*"

"Listen, Noel," said Arnold, "I have a great idea for the second act. You could have a number called the Belsen Nova."

Noel looked blurred.

"Dainty Lee," Louise said. "Why don't you go into the living room? You've got to see Julia's Scaasi."

"Did she pay for it?" Dainty Lee said, heading for the living room, her hand still grasping Arnold's elbow.

"The only problem," Noel said to the bookcase, "is I'm not exactly sure how to end it."

"Why don't you ring down the steel curtain and gas the audience," Arnold said, as he was whisked out the doorway.

Noel looked thoughtful for a moment, and then downed the last of his drink. "I can ski better than Irwin Shaw," he said to Louise.

The phone on the Chinese table by the one slatted window in the sun room rang shrilly, and Louise ran for it. "It's for you, Mr. Oppenheim," she said, finding Chet.

"Thank you. Excuse me, Rolf."

"Mr. Orlovsky?" she smiled at him, seeing him finally alone, and slipped onto the bar stool beside him. "I don't believe we've met. I'm Louise Felder. I've heard so many marvelous things about you . . ."

"Don't gush," Andre said. "It isn't becoming."

"I'm terribly sorry, Mr. Orlovsky," said Louise. "Here I am trying to monopolize you with nothing but charm when Andre could be selling you something."

"He's already tried," Orlovsky said, and smiled at her. "You two go together?"

"Certainly not," said Louise, and started tracing water marks on the bar with her finger.

"I didn't mean to be nosy," Rolf said. "Only that kind of hostility, it's very good in bed. How come I never invited you on my boat?"

"Probably because we've never met before."

"That's true," Orlovsky said. "Harry was no dummy to hide you."

"Harry was no what to what?" Andre said.

"You did go together, you and Andre, didn't you?" Rolf looked at her carefully, and the wolf eyes narrowed, and he smiled. "I mean maybe not anymore, but you did used to be together, the two of you. And often."

"We did used to be together, yes," Andre said, coming to stand directly next to Rolf. "And often. Does that jolly you, Mr. Orlovsky?"

"Please excuse his lack of manners, Mr. Orlovsky," Louise said.

"It's all right," Orlovsky said. "I enjoy watching that kind of anger."

"I don't," Louise said. "If you'll excuse me." She slid from the stool and went back to the bathroom.

"She's still obviously crazy about you," Orlovsky said.

"Is she?"

"Perky little thing. I like plump. It's fresh, like fruit. How long did you go together?"

"A couple of years," Andre said. "She had a lot of glow on her then."

"You rub it off her?"

"Partly," Andre said. "Partly I did, yes."

"I'm sorry I never had you on my boat," Orlovsky said. "I would have enjoyed seeing you together."

"No you wouldn't," Andre said. "We weren't very good."

Their disappointment in each other had been all the stronger because for a while Louise believed in Andre almost as much as Andre did. No matter how often or how repeatedly his schemes failed, she, like he, had been convinced that the next idea he came up with would make him the success he was destined to be. When the second building project failed and he was trying to sell the city the idea of an inland waterway to connect LaGuardia with Idlewild, Louise had introduced him to the two politicians she knew personally. After all his old and new contacts had turned down his plan for developing a grass that would stop growing when it reached a height of two inches, she had encouraged him to go to Harry Bell.

"Two inches high?" Harry had said, plopping backward into the swivel chair behind his desk. "Two inches high, and then it'll stop, like magic."

"Like chemistry," Andre said. "It's got to do with this fixative in the seed. The chemist's been working on it for a year. We just need some capital for . . ."

"You told me," Harry said. "I am underwhelmed."

"You don't like the idea?"

"I love it," Harry said, and laughed. "Runt grass."

"But you're not interested."

"I'm fascinated. But I don't gamble, Sherman. Risks, yes, gambling—? Only morons gamble. Let me know how it comes out."

"I'm disappointed in you, Harry," Andre got up to leave the office. "I thought you had imagination."

"Not as much as you, Sherman." Harry buzzed the office door open. "Nobody has as much imagination as you. Two inches high," he laughed again. "You can't see the forest for the grass."

"He called me a moron," Andre said, when he met Louise for dinner.

"He's just jealous because you're taller than he is. And younger. And handsomer."

"And smarter?"

"And smarter," she said, and kissed him across the top of the menu.

No woman had had that much faith in him since his mother. From the moment her son was born, Yetta Sherman had known he was destined for greatness. Even when the Depression eased up slightly, she refused to let her husband buy new furniture or replace the cracking window blinds with curtains, because the money had to be saved for Arnold's future. By the time they had substantial savings, at least in comparison to other families in the block, she was convinced Arnold would be able to win a scholarship to any college in the United States. Even so she wouldn't consider moving to a better neighborhood: the money would go toward clothes, and a car, maybe, so he would look as good as anyone else on the campus, and none of the other boys would suspect how little he had come from.

When he failed to be accepted by any of his first four choices, Mrs. Sherman knew colleges were discriminating against him, and being unfair.

"You have wonderful grades," she said to him. "You're brilliant and a natural leader, your teacher wrote that, he told me."

"I didn't get such hot scores on the college boards," Arnold said.

"They wouldn't count that so much. They know some people can't work under pressure. They're just prejudiced."

That June he applied to Buffalo University, and on his application wrote his given name as Andre. He was accepted, although the university did not award him a scholarship. When he quit school the winter before receiving his degree, his mother accepted his explanation that it hadn't been challenging enough for him. She gave him money she was saving for his graduation gift to move into Manhattan and see if he couldn't get a little something going.

He got a great many things going. He was a runner on Wall Street where he actually got glimpses of some of the great financiers, and in the evening ushered at the Metropolitan Opera so he could bump into more of them. A few recognized him from the Street, and considered him very enterprising for a boy from a wealthy family, and very sharp even for a graduate of Harvard, which he let slip he was. Two investment firms offered him a job as salesman, and he accepted the one with the biggest profit potential.

It wasn't enough. Commissions were only commissions, and there was no way he could get rich enough quickly enough. For real greatness you had to speculate.

His mother agreed with him, once he explained it to her. And when things were a little slow, in between land deals and engineering deals and stock option deals, she gave him money to entertain the people he needed to get ahead, in the style to convince them they weren't needed.

By the time he was twenty-seven, and married for the first time, he had made and spent and lost what would have been a small fortune for his family, who were still living in the same beat-up apartment. His mother said she didn't mind. She knew he would become very successful and change everything overnight. She was an old woman, in an old dress. He couldn't stand to look at her anymore.

None of his wives bothered him the same way. When he made a score, they didn't say they had known he had it in him all along; when something fell through they weren't smart enough to be disappointed. They expected no more than good clothes and a fairly high style of living, which he always managed to give them. That, and a moderate display of passion which he also managed because he felt under no obligation to satisfy them.

When he met Louise, he was thirty-five years old. *Esquire* had just published an article on self-made American millionaires under thirty, and he realized with a pang that he was neither, and that was why he hadn't been included. But he consoled himself with an interview *Playboy* magazine had done on him and knew that if *Esquire* waited a year, and did the same article again, only on men under thirty-six, he would be among them. He had to be.

Louise believed that too. She was the first girl with whom he was seriously involved who was bright enough to understand even the most complicated of his schemes, although she usually smiled and told him not to try to explain, he was too brilliant for her little honey-blond mind. No matter how consistently he failed during their time together, she seemed to be convinced, as he was, that the next time would be magic.

She was the same way in bed.

To begin with she kept telling him he was wonderful, and it had been wonderful, but he knew she was lying. After a while he told her to stop pretending, if she would only learn how to relax, things would be fine. She loved him so much she felt sure he would be able to satisfy her; because she expected so much of him, he could not. She looked at him with such open-faced admiration his eyes began to burn, and he thought he could see disappointment eroding the edges of her trust. When it was about over between them, he began to punish her: for what, he himself was not exactly sure.

The night Harry Bell turned him down, Andre made her commit a sexual obscenity, and was not relieved even after she started to cry.

"You better move out," he said through her weeping. "You

better go back to your own apartment where you belong. I don't want you here anymore. You're too demanding."

"I never demanded anything," she sobbed.

"You expect too much of me," he said. "I can't work under pressure."

By one thirty there was almost no one at the party to whom Louise aspired but Maggie. Julia White, in her Scaasi, featured in that month's *Élan* magazine, of which she had just been made fashion editor, suggested, as the party was getting dull and there were only nine people left, that they play Lifeboat. Louise, politely but firmly, said that she didn't feel it was an occasion for games. It took a great deal of effort for her to say it and risk incurring Julia's annoyance, which could be more destructively powerful than most people's wrath. But it was a chance she had to take. Louise was very much afraid that if they played, she would be the first one declared superfluous, and condemned to be thrown overboard. Luke Benjamin left for a rehearsal, after telling Noel Gurion that he thought a musical version of *Heroes* was a fine idea, except that he had a minor switch that would make the property much more contemporary: with that he handed him the bartender's card, and told Noel that if he could get that actor to play the lead, Luke might consider directing it. Dainty Lee lost two curls from her Dynel hairpiece in the guest bedroom but was too embarrassed to look under the fur rug where she had been smoking pot and doing other things with Arnold. Maggie had given two sticks to the temporary bartender who was busily engaged in singing Hava Nagilah to Noel Gurion, to convince him that Luke Benjamin was right. Chet Oppenheim had left immediately after receiving the phone call, without saying good-bye to anyone except Rolf Orlovsky, who was standing at the door of the bedroom watching Arnold and Dainty Lee. All in all, Louise considered it as good a time as any to go.

"Thank you for having me," Louise said.

"My pleasure," Maggie mumbled from the pile of cushions in front of the divan. "May we meet again under happier circumstances."

As she passed from under the canopy onto Park Avenue, Louise ducked her head down, as if afraid that somebody would catch her being deserted. She was so intent in not seeming as though she were looking for anybody that she did not notice the black Lincoln, or the fact that the driver was sitting on the side of the car nearest the curb.

"Vell vell, Louize Velder, you cute peckitch."

She turned and saw Andre, and waved him away.

"You vere expectink mebbe Rolf Orlovsky?"

"You do a very bad Polish accent," Louise said.

"Is there any other kind?"

In spite of herself she smiled.

"Oh come on, get in," Andre said, stepping out onto the sidewalk. "It's air-conditioned and your hair's wilting."

"And you've lost your chauffeur," she said. "Nobody's perfect."

"Get in."

"You remember where I live?" she said as he slid in behind the wheel next to her.

"You remember where I live?"

"You're joking, of course. You don't expect me to go home with you after that display upstairs."

"Anything I said I said because it bugs me to see you with your anxiety showing. What do you want with those people?"

"Ho ho," Louise said. "The pot calling the kettle a climber. Just drop me at this next corner, please; I'll walk the rest of the way."

"I mean it. You deserve a lot more than you think you do, Louise. You're brighter and funnier and sweeter than most of the girls around."

"And prettier?" she said. "Is Lulu prettier?"

"If she took off a couple of pounds."

"You're not going to change my mind," she said. "How fast can you get to your apartment?"

In the two and a half years since Louise had been to Andre's, he had had the walls of the living room recovered with scarlet brocade, which also lined the drapes of pink herringbone tweed, shutting out the sun on the windows fronting Park Avenue. The portraits of Napoleon, Admiral Nelson, and Andre's three ex-wives in antebellum ballgowns still hung in their usual places on the wall adjoining the fireplace. Great brass keys were suspended from the gilded iron gates to the dining alcove, and a tiger hide complete with stuffed head and polished teeth covered the gold-painted piano.

"Your mother must love that," Louise said, pointing to the piano. "She must think it's the newest thing in Spanish shawls."

"Take off your clothes," Andre said, going to the telephone.

"Why don't you come straight to the point? Why are you always beating around the bush?"

"I've missed you, Louise." He kissed her.

"Oh shit," she said, and went into the bedroom and started undressing.

41

The bedroom too seemed to be in darkness, even with the lights on. Blackout curtains lined the gilt and ivory drapes. The sheets as she pulled back the tapestry bedspread were satin. He was still determined to play the freak scene, she could see that; but at the same time she forgave him a little, because nothing had happened to change him. He wanted to be interesting, and a conversation piece: he paraded his psychoses on the wall where other men hung their diplomas, and even in the closets, which she knew without checking were still lined with shoe bags, each shoe polished and buffed and stuffed with a ten-dollar tree, individually wrapped in a plastic bag, and set in spectacularly organized rows, all of it done by Andre himself, in case his psychiatrist should one day come and peek to check if Andre really had been potty-trained too early. She switched off the crystal chandelier lamp next to the bed and gave herself over to the blackness of the room, and the sheets chilling her body. The air-conditioner whirred underneath the window, and another Andre had had specially installed next to the bed threw a freezing draft across her naked shoulders. She knew better than to turn them down. She called to him to let him know she was ready, but she could hear from the clicking in the base of the telephone next to the bed that he was still dialing people, an endless series of calls that he could not come into a room without making. She waited, and closed her eyes, and set her teeth against the cold, and tried to think of something warm, like bright red.

"You all right?" he said, coming into the bedroom finally. "Shall I turn on the light?"

"No," she said.

"Christ, it's warm in here," he said. "I'll just be a minute. See if you can turn up the air-conditioner."

He went into the bathroom, and she lay still, trying to relax, but felt herself stiffen as she heard the whirring of the dial on the phone next to the toilet. His words were covered by the running of water. She had no stake in him anymore, so she had no right to be annoyed. That she had once been in love with him was beside the point. Love passed, and they were using each other like mature people had to learn to do, if they were going to survive, and live in the real world.

She tried not to kiss him too much when he got into bed with her.

"All right," he said after a while. "Turn over."

"But I want to hold you."

"You've held me enough. Turn over."

"Oh, Andre."

He was inside her, insistent but not very big.

42

"Now more. Move. Move, goddammit, don't just lie there."

"But I want to hold you."

"Oh for Christ's sake," he said, and collapsed on top of her.

She felt the warm sweat on his chest beading her back, and she kept quiet for a few minutes, waiting for it to build up again, not wanting to add stupidity to whatever she had done wrong. She tried not to recall the anxieties when she was in love with him, and it had all gone wrong. She had read all the books, and looked at all the pictures he had borrowed from Harry Bell, and studied the lives of courtesans with almost the gusto she had researched the history of Andre's ex-wives; not because she was a dirty girl, or a voyeur, but because she wanted everything to be wonderful with Andre, and it was not. A woman, a modern woman, who lived in the modern world and wanted to belong to someone had to give herself over to realistic problems at their root, and not be swallowed up by an outdated soul, streaked with innocence.

None of it had helped her then, and it was not helping her now. She did not want to let her feeling of inadequacy turn to an attack on Andre, but she could not help remembering what she had said weeping to Dr. Ehrens in the beginning of her analysis, tearing it all up inside herself, spewing it up at him.

"It wasn't my fault," she had wept on the couch. "They all looked like boys, even with their goddammed Gone-with-the-Wind ballgowns. They had no tits, and no asses underneath the goddamned hoops."

"Umm-huh," Dr. Ehrens said, puffing on his pipe.

"Well, doesn't it sound like that to you? Why else would he have treated me so badly?"

"Why do you think?"

"Because he wanted a boy. Even his wives looked like boys. All of them. And the shoes in his closet. He's a tight-ass. An anal compulsive. Doesn't it sound like that to you?"

"The way you describe it, I suppose it does."

"What are you saying, are you saying I'm distorting? Because I swear I'm telling it to you exactly the way it happened. I'm not coloring it at all, everything's the way it really was. What possible reason would I have for distorting it? Don't you think I would rather it was some other way? I loved the man."

"Did you?"

"What are you saying?"

"What do you think I'm saying?"

"I'm going to hit you," Louise said.

"And then you can punish me for not responding to you?"

"Like Andre, you mean. He was punishing me because he couldn't respond to me? If that's what you're saying, why don't you come out with it?"

"Because it isn't my saying something that's interesting. It's what you hear in my saying something."

"Do you think he was a fag?"

"What do you think?"

"Look at your watch," Louise said. "Tell me the session is over, I beg of you."

"Do you think he was a fag?" Dr. Ehrens said.

"What do you think?" Louise said, and caught him smiling.

"I think what's interesting is why, if a person has these problems, you would be drawn to him, and live with him for almost six months."

"Who else would I be drawn to?"

"There are plenty of other young men in the world."

"You're not a Freudian, you're Rebecca of Sunnybrook Farm. Where have you been? Who do you know? What circles do you move in that you think there's anybody else around? I'm thirty years old, for God's sake. Who else is there around that would want me? Married men, and dirty old men, and rejects . . ."

"And Andre."

"That's right. At least Andre's bright, and eligible, and a little spectacular."

"Why do they have to be spectacular, Louise?"

"Because I'm me. Because I'm choosy. Maybe I've been a little too selective, and maybe I've waited a little too long. But do you have to look for dwarfs and shrimps just because you're starting to feel a little faded?"

"Nobody said you should look for dwarfs and shrimps."

"Who else is there that would want me?"

"How about fags?" Dr. Ehrens said.

"So you do think he's a fag?"

"I didn't say that," Dr. Ehrens said. "But you seem to feel that the only people who could care for you have some crippling hangup."

"Don't they?" she said, and tears came to her eyes. "Do you think anybody decent and wonderful could care about me, really care about me? Are you going to try and sell me that middle-class Jewish dream about finding a nice young man and settling down to the ordinary unhappiness of day-to-day living?"

"It doesn't have to be unhappy."

"It does for me," she said. "I couldn't be ordinary. I haven't got the capacity to be ordinary. It takes more than I've got." She

44

laid her face down on the pillow and cried freely onto the Kleenex he had spread across it. "Oh God," she wept. "Oh God."

"You know what I think," Dr. Ehrens said. "I think you're a very lonely, unhappy girl."

"No shit," Louise said, and got up and left.

Lying in bed now, Andre sweaty and silent beside her, she wondered why she and Dr. Ehrens had never worked it out, so she would at least know what to do. "Freudian prick," she whispered, as her tears slid down the glaze of the pillow.

"People who live in glass houses," Andre said.

"I didn't mean you. I meant Dr. Ehrens. He hasn't helped me."

"I could've told you that the minute I saw you at Maggie's."

"Oh Andre," she said, and switched closed her lips so her words came out in the little-girl voice he had been so fond of. "Where did we go wrong?"

"Relax. It'll all be fine in a minute or so." He rolled over her and switched on the bed lamp, and looked at his watch.

"Is the session over?" she said.

He switched off the lamp. "It's hardly even started."

"I'm not having a good time."

"You will."

He let his hand move fleetingly over the side of her breast, and she felt a quiver of excitement and warmth toward him —great warmth. He was apparently learning patience. It was the least she could do to practice some of the same. She rolled slowly over onto her side, and let the fingers of her left hand fall gently onto his temple, and whorled them in happy cool patterns over his eyes, trailed down toward his ears, tracing the complexity of orifices, while her right hand played coolly around his belly, moving down to the inside of his thighs, trailing back over his slowly stiffening penis. His eyes were closed, but in response he flattened the back of his hand against her belly, pressing slowly, rhythmically with his knuckles. She felt herself growing more excited, and the old unaccustomed hunger started between her legs.

"Touch me," she whispered. "Please."

"In a minute," he said softly, and sitting up in bed on his elbow, blocked the sudden, surprising shaft of light from the hallway, so she could not quite see the silhouette in the door.

"Andre?" said the girl's voice.

"We're all ready for you, Dody," he said. "Close the door and come on in."

Even in the darkness, Louise could see the brightness of his smile. "Are you crazy?" she said.

"Don't be so bourgeois. You want to be touched, she's the best toucher in the business."

"You are crazy," she said. "Oh Jesus." She tried to get up, but he was holding her. The girl got into bed on the other side of her.

"Don't get excited," he said. "It's not as if I'm going anywhere. We'll all be together."

"Oh God," she said, and struggled against the pinion of his hands. "And to think I cared about you. I'm so ashamed."

"Nothing to be ashamed about, Lulu. She's a professional. Nobody will ever know. It's a professional confidence. Like a lawyer. Or a priest." He laughed.

"Let me go," she screamed, and brought her knee up sharply into his groin. He fell back, and she was free. "You pig. You terrible pig."

"I'm a pig." He sat on the edge of the bed, doubled over, his breath sounding squeezed. "You sit at that party sucking up to the biggest lecher on four continents and you call me a pig."

She fumbled in the darkness for her clothes. "Freak scenes. That's all that can do it for you is freak scenes."

"Well, at least something can do something for me. Don't blame me because you don't know how to be a woman."

"Whereas you do!" She ran into the living room, dressing while she was moving.

"You all right, honey?" Dody moved closer to him in the darkness. "Can I fix it for you?"

"Get your hands off me, whore," Andre said and went into the bathroom.

By the time she got to the street her face was so hot that the tears she had felt coming were evaporated by her anger. She told herself she would not even think about what had happened because she had asked for the humiliation, letting herself be with him, hoping, as she had always hoped, that things would be different. She walked very quickly down the sidestreet, and came out onto the brightness of Madison Avenue, already almost deserted in the holiday heat. She managed to catch a cab going uptown, and looked intently at the store windows, so she wouldn't have to think. As they passed Eighty-second Street, she was surprised to see a funeral cortege still parked in front of Campbell's, the lead silver-gray limousine racked high with flowers, wilting in the heat. She looked at her watch and saw that nearly six hours had passed since the fiasco of the funeral itself.

Louise frowned at the improbability of what she was thinking. But for all she knew, it was the height of the dying season, and somebody altogether new was lying in the chapel. Harry Bell, probably, like the meagerest of men, was in his final resting place.

CHAPTER TWO

(From *Time* magazine, July 8th, **Milestones**)
Died. Harry Bell, 66, much-married, multifaceted, minuscule multimillionaire, who ran his $18-a-week accountant's salary (1922) into one of the great personal fortunes of the century, parlaying economic know-how and theatrical instinct into some of the most raffish, spectacular productions of the thirties (*Whopper*) while acquiring a lion's share of the faltering real estate market in Florida (1936), in anticipation of the inevitable boom, then proceeded to corner International Network through a series of clever stock manipulations, selling short, marrying tall; of a heart attack; in Manhattan. (See: SHOW BUSINESS, BUSINESS, ART.)

"THEY certainly do boil you down to not very much," Ron Abbate said, setting down the magazine. He had arrived from Europe on Saturday night, and had slept very little all weekend. His dark eyes seemed deeper set than usual, and his craggy face, which so many of his clients considered prematurely reassuring, now looked merely old. "What do they say about him in the other sections?"

"I don't know," Chet said. "That was all the advance copy I could get, and I had a hell of a time worming that out of them." Chet got up from the leather lounging chair and walked to the window of his den, looking down at the hot morning hanging over the East River. "It took every ounce of influence I had to kill the story about the funeral. If they hear about Harry's body, we're dead."

"You press agents do have a way with words," Ron said.

"Buried is buried. A man is dead, he gets buried, that's it. You're in charge. You're the administrator. The executor. So bury him."

"The will doesn't have any provision for the funeral expenditures," Ron said. "It's supposed to be at my discretion, but if the beneficiaries think I'm allocating too much, they have the right to petition the surrogate court. They're the ones who have to make the decision on the distribution of monies."

"So what can we do?"

"If he had a specific provision in his will, which he didn't . . . Or even if we could ascertain with someone else that he had a specific wish at the end about burial, and the memorial building—that he didn't just discuss it with me. Corroboration might not mean anything in the event we had to take it to court, but maybe we could appeal to the family's sentimentality."

"Some sentimentality. You want a Scotch?" Chet poured himself another one.

"No. I'll just wait for the call from my office and then I'll take off."

Chet sat back down in the leather chair, and studied the liquor in his glass. "A specific wish about burial voiced to somebody else. That might do it?"

"If you're thinking of telling me he expressed a specific wish to you, forget it. The Bells aren't about to buy something he supposedly told a press agent. Nobody would."

"How about a girl? A sweet-faced, smart young girl. Not one of the flashy show-types Harry usually ran with, but a bright one that Harry genuinely admired."

"What girl?"

"Louise Felder. You know her?"

Ron shook his head.

"He was with her the night before he died, she told a couple of people. Right after the funeral at Maggie's. I heard her talking. She was supposed to be with him Tuesday, and Wednesday too. Poor kid, she was genuinely broken up."

"Who is she?"

"A would-be something. She used to be Art Phillips' secretary, then he made her a junior partner, then she quit and went out on her own."

"Harry didn't like press agents."

"She's not a press agent anymore. She's got some little column, Limelight by Louise."

"The whole purpose of my coming here was to figure out how to keep it out of the papers. And you want to tell a columnist?"

"Listen, this thing isn't settled fast, there's no way you're going to keep it out of Radio City Music Hall. Louise is smart, and she's ambitious. And Harry was crazy about her, Maggie Bolin told me so. If he had lived, they would have been married."

"Oh come on . . ." Ron said.

"Well, why not? He hadn't been married for a while, and she was young, and bright. Brains were getting to be important to him, he'd had enough empty-headed cooze."

"You expect me to believe Harry was going to marry some girl I never even heard of?"

"No. But his family might. They might even like to believe it—a nice, bright girl, from a *heimisch* background, like Harry. Maybe they'll even figure he was finally coming to his senses. Maybe they'll even forgive him for whatever it was they're mad at him for. Maybe when they hear her tell how it was Harry wanted to be remembered, and where, they'll go along with the burial plans."

"And maybe they'll laugh in your face."

"True," Chet said. "But it's a better shot than we have now."

"Even if she goes along with it, you sure she'll keep it quiet?"

"No," Chet said. "But if she cared about Harry as much as she seemed to, she will. And if he cared about her, she will." He took a long drink of his Scotch. "Or if she really wants to be somebody as much as I think she does, she will."

He turned to Ron and smiled. "And then when this whole burial thing is settled, she can tell the family how very deep was Harry's wish that you and I get paid for handling the memorial."

Chet Oppenheim had not started out in public relations; nor had he always moved in the best social circles. However, several times during the course of his undergraduate career at Princeton, Chet had had the opportunity to have sexual relations with society girls. He was almost six feet tall, and working out in the gym, where he could meet many of the young men whose eating clubs were closed to him, had gotten his body into excellent shape. His light-brown hair was cut short enough so it didn't curl, and the glasses he chose were horn-rimmed, in imitation of the editor of the *Tiger*. By the time he was a junior his handwriting was a close facsimile of the prep school, feministic semi-printing style, as his manner of speaking was an approximation of the long-voweled, slurred-consonants delivery. All in all, he made a quite presentable picture when a few of the better friends he had made invited him home for weekends or occasionally a vacation. At the parties or dances given on these occasions, his way of fitting in completely without really fitting in at all was irresistible to the hungrier and more defiant of the young ladies.

"I've never known anyone like you before," Odalie Wyceth said in the back of the new '39 Buick Chet had borrowed from his uncle. "You're so passionate."

She placed his warm big hand inside the fold of her pink chiffon blouse, and lowered the strap of her slip. She wore no brassiere, and the breast that tilted easily into the cup of Chet's hand was firm and hard. "That's it," she whispered. "Don't try to hold back. I know how passionate you people are."

The same instinct (and mother) that had told Chet that going to an Ivy League college was his admission ticket to the upper middle class also advised him that slipping it surreptitiously to a pale, upper-class blonde would not provide an entree to that milieu. "We mustn't," he whispered, gently extricating his hand from the porcelain trap. "I have too much respect for you."

"But I want it to happen," she said. "It's going to happen anyway, why can't it be with you?"

"I have too much respect for you," Chet said again.

"Everybody has respect for me," Odalie said sullenly. "I thought you at least would be different. You have no reason to worry about me. It isn't as if you're bound by any of the stuffed-shirt rules of this group."

"You mean because of how passionate we people are?"

"You know what I mean. You don't belong here and you know it. Bob only invited you for the weekend to show how liberal he is. He isn't, you know. He only pretends to be liberal. But I am. I really am. I like you, and you're very attractive."

"So are you, Odalie."

"Then why won't you make love to me. We don't have to go all the way if you don't want to, but it isn't like we'd get caught. I know a way to do it where we couldn't possibly get caught. Coitus interruptus. Do you know about that? I read it in Krafft-Ebing."

"It doesn't always work."

"You see? That's why I knew I could depend on you. Reading about it in books isn't like having all the experience you must have had."

Actually his experience had been a great deal more limited than Odalie imagined. Sex was subsidiary to accomplishment; his mother had been very explicit about that. The first time in her life she had forgotten her higher purpose and lowered herself to the animal level of Chet's father, she had been impregnated, bringing to a stunning and permanent conclusion her plans to rise above her origins. That it hadn't been worth it, she was quite definite about impressing on Chet. She loved her son, so didn't for one minute, not for one minute mind his being born. But her husband's pawings and fevered plungings had continued long after the spell that made her a willing participant was gone. All that lived on was regret that she had lost her chance for becoming more than she was destined to be, even after Chet's father was speeded mercifully to his lower middle-class rest.

"These feelings pass," Mrs. Oppenheim said. "The only thing that lasts is what you are, if you haven't been a damn fool."

Chet had no intention of being any such thing. Even with Odalie's warm little hand groping between his legs he could manage to deal with his excitement. You didn't do it to nice girls because they didn't really enjoy it. You especially didn't do it to Odalie because if she did it with an outsider she could pretend it had never happened, unless she saw him again, and she wouldn't want to do that. There would never be another invitation to this particular part of Pennsylvania.

"Look Chet," Odalie whispered. "Look how stiff my nipples are. You've done that."

"Cover up. What if somebody comes into the parking lot."

"Why are you so worried about other people? You don't care about me at all."

"I care about you too much, Odalie."

"Really?"

"Of course. Cover up."

She twisted her mouth into a wry pout and tucked her breasts back inside the blouse. "They still show. I have buttons on my blouse where I didn't have any before. Everybody will see. You know how satin is."

"They'll go away. Let's just don't touch each other for a while."

"But I want to touch you. And I want you to touch me. All over. Don't you want to?"

"Of course I do, Odalie, but not now. Not here, in the back seat of a car."

"You know someplace we can go?"

"I want everything to be right between us, Odalie." He kissed her sweetly on the lips, pulling his head back as she tried to work her tongue into his mouth. "I have too much respect for you."

"I don't want you to have respect. If you really had respect, you'd respect my wishes, and my wishes are that you shouldn't have so much respect."

"All right," he said. "But not now."

"When?"

"There's a dance at Princeton in two weeks. Will you come for the weekend as my guest?"

"Can we be together? Have you got a place?"

"Well, I'll have to reserve you a room at the Inn, for the sake of appearances. But we can be in my room part of the time."

51

"You have a private room?"

"Ahctuahlly . . ." He pronounced it with the long, thick emphasis he had mastered so completely, copied from the graduates of Lawrenceville and Andover. "Roger Ormsby's my roommate, but he's very discreet. He'll go away whenever we want him to."

"I know Roger. We used to play mixed doubles together in Tarrytown. He's a pompous ass."

"Really? He speaks very well of you."

"He does?"

"Very well. When I told him I was coming down to Bob's for the weekend he said I should be sure to keep an eye out for Bob's cousin Odalie, that she was a winner."

"He meant at tennis."

"I don't think so. He seemed genuinely fond of you." Actually, Odalie's name hadn't even been mentioned. But Chet had minored in Shakespeare in order to get close to the boys with no need to earn a living, and the ruse of Beatrice and Benedick had impressed him. "How is it you two never got together?"

"He's not my type," Odalie said.

As it turned out, Roger was a much better type for Odalie than Chet. That became obvious when the three of them were sitting in the room together drinking neat Scotch with beer chasers, talking about F. Scott Fitzgerald's undergraduate days at Princeton, and the tragedy of his turning out a drunk.

Odalie was clearly not used to drinking. That, in combination with her brilliantly healthy kidneys, led to repeated quick retreats to the bathroom, so Chet had many opportunities to tell Roger how much Odalie admired him. "It's a shame you only think of her as a tennis player," Chet said. "I know how attractive she thinks you are."

"Really?"

"Can't you see it?" Chet said.

"Well she certainly does seem a little softer-eyed than I remember, but I thought that was the hooch."

"I don't think so," Chet said.

"Anyway, girls like Odalie don't play around."

"Not just with anyone, they don't, but with someone they really cared for they might, Roger."

"She's your date, Chet."

"I don't like to lie to myself," Chet said. "Now that I see the way she's been watching you, I realize she only accepted me because she thought it might be a way of getting nearer to you."

"You serious?"

52

"I've never been more serious in my life."

"Where are you going, Chet?"

"I just remembered some books I was supposed to get out of the library. They're in the rare book room, I think, so it'll probably take a while. You'll take care of Odalie while I'm gone?"

"Well, Jesus, fella . . ."

It was all Chet could do not to hold up his hand in benediction. "If the right man comes along and a girl is ready, another man would be a bastard to stand in the way."

Another man would also be a fool to blow up with one preternatural act something he had been constructing all his life, just because a girl was ripe and thought he wouldn't count. "See you later, Roger," he said. "Much later."

As easily as that, Chet Oppenheim became a pimp. Naturally they did not consider him that at Princeton, because his style was undergraduate and cleanly collegiate. In his gratitude at the unexpected bonanza tossed onto his lap, Roger felt it was the least he could do to invite Chet home for Christmas. With all the holiday dances Chet managed to collect four more ladies no one had ever suspected were in waiting, they were in turn invited up to Princeton and placed quite circumspectly with four other horny young men in whose circle they belonged. Each of the four then proffered a similar invitation to Chet. Eventually the word got around that Chet Oppenheim really had a way of sniffing out hitherto-undreamed-of pussy. He became a welcome guest at the homes of even the best families, so long as they had a scrofulous son.

When the war came, and Chet, the young graduate, was deferred because of fallen arches, he was one of the few attractive men available. He became the perfect escort for waning debutantes, managing always to have them suppering in 21 when one of his officer friends came in on leave to dine. Gradually his sphere extended to include young models, and would-be movie stars, who noted that Chet, besides being attractive and available, also numbered among his acquaintances Hollywood producers and millionaires, who were friendly with Chet because he numbered among his acquaintances models and would-be movie stars.

The thought of procuring for a living never entered Chet's mind. In the first place, there was no conceivable way he would be able to explain it to his mother: to her way of thinking, a job was a job, and getting girls for men, no matter how high the level of people involved, was at best a questionable calling. More important, he did not have to consider a career as panderer because his talent fit so well with his role as customer's representative in a banking house on Wall Street, owned by Barnett Otis, father of one of his Princeton friends.

"What does that mean exactly," Chet's mother said. "Customer's representative?"

"That means you service the people who are interested in buying stocks and bonds."

"What does that mean exactly, service?"

"You counsel them about their investments, tell them what it would be wise to include in their portfolio."

"What kind of portfolio?"

"Their collection of stocks and bonds. Certificates. Holdings."

"I don't know," Mrs. Oppenheim said. "That all sounds very Republican. I wanted a lot for you, but I don't know that it included being a Republican."

"That's all propaganda, Mom. Everybody in the business world doesn't have to be Republican."

"Nobody has to be a Republican. President Roosevelt is a true aristocrat, and he's a Democrat. If he can afford to be a Democrat, you can afford to be a Democrat."

"I'm a Democrat, Mom." He could say that without lying. During the only two elections in which he had been old enough to vote, the bars had been closed, and his friends decided to throw the party at Chet's apartment, so he had never actually cast a ballot. "You don't have to worry."

"I don't worry. I never worry. But I wish you would get in a business I could explain to my neighbors. It's time you made something of yourself."

His mother was quite right, Chet realized. The most he could ever hope to attain at Otis and Son was the position of a highly paid inferior. Otis, Jr., would be president of the company someday, if he lived; if he got killed in the war that seemed about over, Senior would ring in a nephew, fondness for Chet or no fondness. He was still an outsider.

The entire problem was solved for him with the growing importance in his life and on the entertainment scene of Bertram Lester. Bertram had started out making some low-budget horror pictures that pulled the audiences in during the last year of the war ("They're acting out their anxieties," Bertram explained, having grown rich enough to require analysis). Once the war was over he had enough dollar profit to make a folksy picture about wounded combat veterans, with a big-star cast and an implicit hint of adultery. It was a stunning audacity for a Hollywood postwar movie, everyone having temporarily forgotten the Barbara Stanwyck vehicles of the thirties where such things went on all the time.

"I need representation in the East," Bertram said to Chet at lunch at 21. "They're saying I'm the biggest man in the industry, but it's mostly industry people that are saying that. I need other people to say it. The business is changing. The stars are fading from the sky, even as we speak. It's the producers that are going to become the stars soon, you mark my words. It's going to be a 'Bertram Lester Production,' like *Gone with the Wind* was Selznick, that's what's going to mean everything. That's what's going to pull in the stars and the audiences, you see if I'm not right."

"I'm sure you're right," Chet said. "Nobody knows more about the business than you, B.L."

"But there's no doubt that I need some kind of representation back here in the East. It's too big a market to ignore just because Fred Allen says California is the only place for oranges."

"Excuse me, B.L., I don't think he said that exactly. What he said is that California is a great place if you're an orange."

"It comes out the same, doesn't it?"

"If you say so," Chet said.

"No doubt about it. I need representation here." Bertram crossed his pudgy hands on the tablecloth, and then maneuvered his napkin up to his mouth. "I tell you what else I need. I need two girls. Young, great bodies. Not whores, though, I don't like watching whores. There's something cheap about them."

"What about Sukie?" Chet said, mentioning the name of the last girl to whom he had introduced Lester.

"Not Sukie. She started getting all nutsy last time we had a party, on the yacht, went ding-gy on me. I don't want anything to do with disturbed girls. But no whores either."

"I don't know any whores," Chet said, which was the truth. He did, however, happen to know one ex-fashion model named Athena who had soured on men after her last abortion, and it seemed to him he had seen her cast a wistful eye on Mary Elizabeth, who wanted very much to get into pictures. But they weren't whores, anymore than Chet was a pimp.

"I don't want to go to bed with any woman," Mary Elizabeth said in the cab on the way to Bertram's penthouse hotel suite.

"Did I say you were going to go to bed with a woman?" Chet said. "All I said was that Bertram wanted you and Athena to spend the evening with him. And she isn't just any woman, she's Athena. I thought she was a friend of yours."

"Well if you ask me she's gone all dykey. There's nothing dykey about me."

55

"We know that, Mary Elizabeth. Everybody knows that."

"I'm a very healthy girl. I like all kinds of sex, but I'm no dyke."

"You're doing Lester an injustice. He's a fabulous man. What makes you think the evening has anything whatsoever to do with sex?"

"You know Sukie?" Mary Elizabeth said.

"I know Sukie." Some instinct warned him it was wiser not to tell Mary Elizabeth he had introduced Sukie to Bertram.

"Poor Sukie went with that bastard on his boat, and he tied her spread-eagled on the deck and smeared her all over, and I mean *all* over with beef stock and then he brought out his lap dog. I mean a for-real lap dog." Mary Elizabeth shuddered. "The man is a complete freak."

"Sukie's crazy. You shouldn't believe what Sukie says, she's unbalanced."

"Well, he had a lot to do with making her that way," Mary Elizabeth said. "He must really despise women."

"Don't be silly," Chet said, as he paid the driver. "He adores women. Otherwise how could he enjoy seeing them together?"

They got out of the cab.

"Then that is what he wants." She paused underneath the satin-monogrammed white and black canopy of the apartment hotel. "I don't think I'm going. I'm no freak."

"Nobody said you were, and nobody wants you to be, Mary Elizabeth. Especially me. You know how much respect I have for you. Too much respect to let you throw yourself away on an ordinary life. Not with all your potential."

"You mean as a lez?"

"I mean your potential as a full, rich human being. Very rich. I look at your face, and you know what I see? I see a very important personage, with incredible bone structure, who ought to be able to make something very big of herself. You understand this isn't a line, Mary Elizabeth. I have too much respect for you to hand you a line. I'm not doing this for myself. If I wanted to do something for myself, I would have gone to bed with you a long time ago."

She narrowed her eyes, reflecting yellow-green in the fading sunlight, and brushed a renegade strand of auburn hair from her forehead. "Why haven't you?"

"I have too much respect for you."

"So you'd like it better if I did it with another woman?"

"I would like anything that got you what you ought to have, Mary Elizabeth. I think Bertram could mean a big future for you."

"He's a freak," she said.

"I think you're doing him an injustice. Bertram Lester is nothing more nor less than a man who has been fortunate enough to be able to afford a great deal of experiences. If he were living in another century, say the Renaissance, he would be considered a voluptuary."

"And that's good?"

"It was the only thing to be in the Renaissance. I don't think we ought to stand here like this, on the sidewalk. I'll take you home if you insist. But it would be a great mistake."

"You think so?"

"Considering how much I want for you, a great mistake."

"Well, maybe I'll just go upstairs and meet him," Mary Elizabeth said. "I can always change my mind."

In the private foyer outside Bertram's apartment, she placed her hand on Chet's arm, restraining him gently as he reached for the doorbell. "I'm a little afraid," she said, smiling crookedly, wetting her lower lip with her tongue. "I guess that's silly, my being nervous meeting such a big man."

"It's the most normal thing in the world," Chet said.

"I'm shaking," she said, putting his hands to her shoulder. "Can you feel how I'm shaking?" She stepped close to him, into the quiet circle of his arms, and placed her cheek against his chest. "Feel."

"You're going to be fine. You're going to be just fine." He patted her shoulders soothingly, fraternally.

"I don't know why you and I never did it," she said against his throat. "I mean it's very gentlemanly and all, but you're silly to have this old-fashioned thing about respect. It isn't as if we were kids or I'm a virgin, you know. I like sex."

"Good," Chet said, as he reached for the doorbell. "Then tonight won't be any problem for you."

The motion picture debut of Mary Elizabeth Craig did not take place until the spring of 1950, in Bertram Lester's Technicolor epic, *Lot's Wife*, a modern-day parable of wife-swapping in the suburbs, in which she had the ingenue lead. Actual production on the picture was delayed for a year in order to enable Bertram an around-the-world yacht honeymoon with his third wife, Athena, a tall, slender brunette, with a look of great sadness in her extraordinary black eyes, especially when she smiled. She wore clothes with the authority of the fashion model she had been, and delivered short, witty jibes with the éclat of the cynic she had become. She also knew when to remain aristocratically silent at big dinner parties for business, and how to charmingly hostess the small ones for pleasure, all of which made her the perfect wife for Bertram. Besides, she made the most perfect love to another woman Bertram Lester had ever been privileged to observe,

57

working her partner into a state of incredible excitement without for a moment losing her own imperious reserve. There was a coolness about Athena, a deliberateness in her exploration of the female body that transcended passion, because of the passion it evinced. Never for a moment did she seem other than detached, but Bertram Lester could tell how deeply she was involved, because of the almost devotional nature of her ministrations. The tableau of the two perfect bodies, Mary Elizabeth's rounded like a prematurely voluptuous child's, Athena's long, almost curveless feminine fluidity, writhing beneath the mirrored ceiling of his playroom, had been overwhelming to him, the more so as Mary Elizabeth, so obviously reluctant at the start to participate, became first willing, then eager. It was a performance that superseded the need for artificial objects, or for that matter, man, relying mainly on Athena's brilliantly practiced tongue and gently fluttering hands on Mary Elizabeth's breasts and genitals. Bertram Lester was so excited he had enough for both of them, but not, of course, until they were finished, as he had no wish to interfere with the pure spirituality of the moment.

They did not take Mary Elizabeth with them on the honeymoon cruise. There were other girls in other places where the yacht stopped to refuel. Besides, it was Athena, really, who was the great talent, working, Bertram thought, like a genius director, getting a first-rate performance out of an only mediocre star. Occasionally when they hit a Mediterranean resort off-season, or didn't know anybody in the crowd, Bertram could cable Chet, who was very busy running the newly opening New York offices of Bertram Lester, Inc. Chet had kept up his contacts, knew where everybody was, and always managed to come up with the name of a girl, which he would wire back to Bertram. Bertram was very pleased with Chet. It was quite a present for a man, making him eastern representative for such an enterprise. But Chet deserved it. He had, after all, introduced Bertram to Athena, with whom he had fallen in love at first sight, so to speak.

The transition from customer's representative to personal representative in the East for Bertram Lester, Inc., was made very easily by Chet. The offices were comfortably lavish, and anyone of importance from Hollywood who visited New York could be assured of temporary headquarters, and all the little niceties Chet knew how to provide. Chet went to all the movie openings, where he met distributors who were most gratified to know that the Hollywood people were starting to realize the sun didn't rise and set in California.

Opening nights of legitimate productions on Broadway, where he had often gone in the normal course of affairs, he was now welcomed officially because, it was rumored, he was scouting properties for Lester. On the whole, it was an enviable and highly satisfactory position to be in: Chet's desk was strewn with the daily trade papers, and his social schedule blossomed. It continued so for about two years.

"What's that mean, exactly, eastern representative?" his mother said.

"Well, it means what it says, Mom. I service all aspects of Bertram Lester enterprises in New York."

"The same kind of service from before?"

"More or less. I see that everyone involved in his productions, the people he has business dealings with, have headquarters, their appointments in order, set up business lunches, reservations, that sort of thing. I try to see that everything is to their satisfaction."

"Like a maître d'," his mother said. "You're thirty-four years old and you went to Princeton. You should make something of yourself."

"Oh Mom, how can you say that. I earn two thousand dollars a week."

"Doing what?"

"I told you. I work for one of the biggest producers in the business."

"You make movies?"

"Not exactly," Chet said. "But I'm very involved with product, and the people who are involved with that product."

"That shouldn't be worth two thousand dollars a week. That's a hundred thousand dollars a year. What do you do that's worth a hundred thousand dollars? President Eisenhower gets seventy-five thousand a year, and he's a general."

"I'm in a very important position."

"I understand that," his mother said. "But what do you do?"

"I think," Chet said during cocktails the next afternoon at Bertram's penthouse. "I think we're going to have to make a slight change in my status."

"You don't like your job?" Bertram said. "Or is it money. You been getting feelers from Spiegel? Goldwyn?"

"Nothing like that. I'm very happy, Bertram. It's just that I feel my function should be a little more specifically delineated."

"I don't get you."

"There really isn't enough for me to do, Bert. We all know you're the world's greatest producer, and it's going to get even bigger after *Slice of Life* is released. But an eastern headquarters for you is a luxury. You deserve a luxury, and you've earned it. But I've got to have a more definite function."

"How about Eastern Executive Vice-President."

"It's not a title I care about, Bert. It's what I'm really doing."

"You're doing a hell of a job at what you do best, Chet. No man should be ashamed of doing what he does best."

Chet did not feel like examining what that was. "I'd rather be my own man. Working for you, of course, but with a career of my own."

"Like what?"

"I'm not sure."

"How about press agent?" Bertram said. "You could take over half the offices just as they are, get your own staff, that kind of thing. Send out releases. You know everybody, the columnists would print your stuff, especially if it was about me. Of course I'd still expect you to service me whenever I was in town, that kind of thing."

"I wouldn't mind that," Chet said. "I'd want to do that."

"Fine, then it's all settled. You're a press agent. Congratulations. Chet Oppenheim, boy press agent."

"Public relations," Chet said. "I wouldn't want to do anything that sounded undignified."

He never tried to explain his business to his mother in detail. He did send her newspaper columns with items ringed in red, and a marginal note saying "I planted that." In a world that was growing constantly more disappointing, one of the last things in which Mrs. Oppenheim believed was the word of Walter Winchell. Her son's association with that by-line, no matter how vague and indirect, was enough to sustain her. Eventually she started making a scrapbook, so when neighbors asked her what her son did, she could bring it out to show he was successful. "He plants things," she said. "This is his garden."

The actual business of press agentry was one for which Chet showed a definite flair. Working in conjunction with the studio that was releasing *Slice of Life*, a picture dealing with the horrors of the Chicago stockyards, and a war-weary veteran rebelling against the butchery of the industry and its men, Chet managed to uncover a story of a thirty-two-year-old war hero employed in the yards who had gone berserk and killed his wife and four children. It was a neat tie-in: Chet managed to get a picture story in *Life*, of the yards, the slaughter pens, the house where the family lived, and the rooms where the murders took place, and a picture of the veteran with some quotes from his psychiatrist in the V.A. Hospital, facing a full-page pictorial interview with Bertram Lester.

"Horror exists," Bertram Lester said. "There is no doubt about it. I'm not one of these mealy-mouthed producers who's afraid to show truth. The world has seen enough of sequined tap shoes. Let's show things the way they are. Hard-hitting. Honest. If the pressures of the day are brutality and blood-lust, we can't just make musicals. Unless you bring me a script for an honest hard-hitting musical, then we'll talk."

It was a brilliantly successful campaign. The picture surprised everyone by being commercial as well as controversial, due in major part to the performance of its star, Jason Stone, who won an Academy Award. Bertram also won an Academy Award, but he was in Switzerland, making arrangements for Athena to enter a hotel-sanitarium for wealthy drug addicts, so he could not accept in person. Chet accepted in his place. He kept his speech brief, explaining how humble and grateful Bertram was, and how sorry not to be there: but he was even now in the Far East scouting locations and feeling the pulse of the times for his next movie, in which he would further establish the tradition of the great, new kind of picture-maker.

"That's my son," Mrs. Oppenheim said to the four ladies who were gathered in her apartment watching the building's only twenty-four-inch television set.

"I'm sorry I never saw him in a picture," one of them said. "He must be some actor."

"He's no actor. Actors don't count anymore. The nature of the business is changing," Mrs. Oppenheim quoted the *Newsweek* interview with Bertram Lester her son had sent her. "The stars are fading from the sky, even as we speak. The future, dear Brutus, is not in our stars, but in ourselves."

"I'm sorry. I thought he was an actor. He's good-looking enough to be an actor."

"He's losing his hair," Mrs. Oppenheim said. "But thank you anyway."

"Bing Crosby is losing his hair," another lady said. "And it doesn't make any difference. He's still handsome, with that voice."

"I wouldn't want him to be an actor. The nature of the business is changing."

How much the nature of the business was changing even Bertram Lester could not imagine, much less Chet's mother. The bankers were beginning to move in from New York, treating the motion picture industry like any other business. A number of the studios, with production beginning to level off after the first panicky threat from television, had no objection to independent financing of a diminished yearly number of pictures. Budgets were getting bigger, because people would leave their houses for big pictures, the studios knew that now, so they were no longer terror-stricken that the party was over. But bigger budgets required bigger hunks of cash, and the fewer number of bankable stars there were, the fewer number of big productions would be forthcoming. So the studios had no grievous objections when people like Rolf Orlovsky of New Jersey Security and Trust showed interest in motion picture financing. People like Orlovsky wanted only a stake in the financial growth of a studio: they wanted no fuss, no publicity, about their role in the making of motion pictures.

The job of no publicity fell quite easily to Chet Oppenheim. The studios liked his style, as did Orlovsky who, preferring to remain inconspicuous, had noted how inconspicuously Chet managed to get him to the right type of parties —not thrown in his honor, and not even advertised in advance as promising his presence. But the people that should have known he was there reacted with proper enthusiasm when he was introduced; these included young ladies.

Now that he was public relations man for Rolf Orlovsky, Chet had less and less time for Bertram. Bertram's two follow-up pictures to *Slice of Life* were mildly successful, if overbudgeted, but the spectacle he had promised in the middle and early Fifties seemed to have diminished. Still he continued to pay Chet a token retainer fee, and was glad to do so. The episode of Athena in Istanbul, where she set fire to her own hotel room, tried to escape and was pinned under debris for two days before she was discovered, was known to only those few people whose mail Chet had been unable to intercept. Fortunately the debris had been metal, and the fire had not raged completely out of control, so she did not die immediately. Chet arranged for a European plastic surgeon to do skin grafts, and the surgeon assured Athena it would take no more than a year or two at the most, by which time she might also have regained use of her legs. Chet also managed to keep the details of the divorce out of the papers. When Athena committed suicide three years later, only the *New York Times* obituary made mention of the fact that she was Bertram Lester's ex-wife.

There was no doubt that Chet was worth a retainer, even if he could no longer devote himself to Bertram most of the time. There was still the possibility that Bertram would make another big picture, and in the meantime he was invited, occasionally, to the parties Chet was giving for Rolf Orlovsky. At one of these dinners Bertram met Sylvia Bell, who had recently been divorced from Harry Bell. She didn't like to do anything fancy, but she reminded him vaguely of Athena, and because he was such a sentimental man, he married her.

Chet knew Harry Bell only slightly, but a few weeks later when they were both dining at the Colony, Harry came over to his table.

"You got a minute?" Harry said to Chet, his eyes on the face of the girl beside Chet on the banquette.

"Of course," Chet said, and excused himself to his companion.

"I owe you a T.L.," Harry said, when they were seated at his table.

"I beg your pardon?" Chet said.

"I mean you did me a big favor. Introducing Sylvia to Lester, I mean. Saved me a couple of bucks."

"That's nice to know."

"Not that I had to pay alimony, you understand," Harry said. "All my wives signed premarital agreements. Sylvia was crazy about me, you know, she married me twice. I didn't have to give her a fucking penny."

Chet kept quiet.

"But I'm a generous man, and I liked her, she's a good kid. So I've been sending her a little something every month for she and Shaney. Nothing flashy you understand. Just eating money, so she shouldn't have to go out with somebody she wasn't really nuts about just to have a meal, you know what I mean?"

"I think so."

"He hasn't been so big lately, but Bertram Lester's well fixed, isn't he?"

"He's built some good tax shelters, if that's what you mean."

"Is it true he's some kind of freak? With women, I mean."

Chet smiled. "No more than you or I."

"So I don't have to worry about her anymore. Or Shaney."

"I guess not," Chet said.

"That means I got a hundred dollars a week to play with."

"That much?" Chet said.

"You have contempt for a hundred dollars a week? Maybe if you had earned eighteen dollars a week when you were a kid nineteen years old instead of hanging around with those stripe ties, you'd have a little more respect for a hundred dollars."

"I have a lot of respect for a hundred dollars, Harry. I certainly didn't mean to imply I disrespected a hundred dollars."

"But you get more, is that what you mean?"

"I get a great deal more."

"How much for instance. How much from Orlovsky for example?"

"I don't discuss what my clients pay me, Harry. I'm sorry, but that's one of the things that's privileged between a man and his publicist."

"I'm in four deals with plastics with Orlovsky. I could call him right now, he'd tell me what he pays you."

"Then I suggest you call him."

"More than a grand?"

"Yes."

"Fifteen hundred?"

"More," Chet said.

"Well what does he give a shit, it's the bank's money. Every penny I got is my own."

"That's great, Harry. I suggest you keep it."

"My money isn't good enough for you?"

"Not at all," Chet said. "But I have a young lady waiting at my table, and I don't want to waste any more of your time."

"I decide what's waste," Harry said. "She's a very pretty girl, close friend of yours?"

"An acquaintance," Chet said. "She's new in town, I thought I'd show her around."

"That's very nice of you. Maybe you'd like to come to dinner tomorrow at the house. She'd probably like to see an authentic New York town house."

"She might. I'll have to ask her." He started to get up from the table, but Harry took his arm.

"I'll tell you what I'll do. I'll give you two hundred a week for four weeks, and if you work out, I'll double it."

"No good, Harry. I haven't got the time for that kind of account."

"Don't you turn your nose up, I didn't even tell you what kind of an account it was."

"It's a two-hundred-dollar account. I haven't got time."

"You know, I don't need a publicity guy, Oppenheim. I make my own news. I always have."

"Then there's no point our talking, Harry."

"The only thing is I'm setting up this new foundation, and it's very important to me I get a new, what are they calling it now, image, that's what I need is an image."

"You make your own publicity, Harry, you said so yourself. Why don't you make your own image."

"I'm sixty-two years old," Harry said looking down at his empty plate. "I can't start sucking around art magazines and the *New York Review of Books* like I'm hungry. I need to be talked about in the papers I can't stand to read because they're so boring."

"You want class."

"Class I don't need. I'm too rich to have class. Anybody with the money I've got has to be vulgar. I need a new image."

"Seven-fifty a week," Chet said.

"Three-fifty. We'll double it after a month if it's working out."

"You have a deal," Chet said, and offered his hand.

"Dinner's at eight o'clock," Harry said.

Chet slid into the banquette next to the tiny brunette, and patted her hand. "Sorry I took so long, Vicki. But I just got Harry Bell."

"To do what?" Vicki arranged the last of the scallops from her Coquilles on her plate to form a V.

"For a client. At seven hundred a week."

"Congratulations."

"I would have taken him on for a hundred, just to be able to say I handled him."

"That's terrific. You want my cream sauce?"

"No thank you. I don't like rich sauces."

"Neither do I," she said, setting the shell in the ashtray. "I just like scallops."

"Why didn't you order them plain?"

"What's the point of eating in a French restaurant?" she said.

"Harry Bell has a French chef," he said.

"Good for him."

"We're having dinner there tomorrow night."

"I thought you and I were going to the country, Chet."

"We can do that another time."

"But I thought tomorrow had a special meaning. You going to pull that again about having too much respect for me?"

"I do have respect for you, Vicki."

"You ask me, I think you don't like sex."

"I don't dislike it," Chet said. "It just doesn't make that much difference to me, one way or the other."

"I'm very good both ways," Vicki said.

"Well don't tell that to Harry. I told him you were new in town."

The day after the funeral, Louise awoke with the groggy conviction that there was something she had to do. She rolled over on her back and tried to ferret out a clue from the clustered plaster grapes at the corners of the high baroque ceiling, but she couldn't remember. Her left hand automatically reached for the package of cigarettes on her bed table, and as she struck a match the realization of what it was she had to do came to her: nothing. Her hand shook even after she had waved out the match, and she fanned the smoke away from the front of her face, coughing once in disgust as she reached around blindly on the floor for her ashtray and stubbed out the cigarette. She had only started smoking recently, in defiance of all the people she knew who were trying to give it up, and she couldn't stand the taste of it, especially in the morning before she had brushed her teeth. But it was something to do with her hands, lovely hands they were, with their fingernails almost to the length of a Chinese war lord's, to show she didn't have to work in the field with the coolies, or do her own typing. That they were shaking now filled her with momentary panic. Obviously she was tired. She had slept ten hours, but the funeral and the people she had seen had taken more out of her than she realized, and that was why her hands were shaking. It was in no way connected with the fact that the long holiday weekend stretched in front of her and she had nothing to do.

She shoved her hands under the covers and curled her upper torso around them in the posture of warm comforting sleep, and stayed that way, fighting to drift, until well past noon. In the window facing Eighty-sixth Street the air-conditioner whirred vaguely, doing only a dilatory job of cooling the bedroom; but that was one of the minor disadvantages of living in the best neighborhood, in a building that was still seedy enough to be within her price range. When she had been a secretary paying ninety-seven fifty a month for the apartment on West End Avenue she imagined that a two-hundred-dollar apartment would be the end in luxury; once the two-hundred-dollar apartment had been achieved on West Fifty-fifth Street (convenient to the office, she had told herself), she knew that she would not be content until she was living in the East Eighties, on a sidestreet, maybe, but certainly no farther east than Park Avenue. She had imagined that some of those probably went as high as three hundred dollars. Now she was paying four and a quarter a month for a one-bedroom between Park and Lexington with cracked glass in the diamond-shaped panes of the dust-clogged bathroom windows, and an ancient electrical system that would not accommodate more than a half-ton air-conditioning unit in each room.

If she had granted herself the leeway of freer boundaries, she might be shuddering in modern central air-conditioned splendor somewhere between First and Second Avenue at this moment, looking at freshly painted ceilings instead of peeling plaster grapes, twice as many rooms for the same rent. But she knew better than to expose herself to the people she would meet in slick self-service elevators; second-string faggots, like the ones who didn't even make the designs, but put them on the lathe; stewardesses with two hours in between planes, sharing a one-bedroom apartment with four other stewardesses on different schedules, so that at any hour you could hear them humping, in shifts, through the paper walls.

She was living the only possible place she could live, and if her hands were a little moist against her belly, that was just too bad. She had no business being under the covers in the middle of the afternoon, especially as there was no chance of getting back to sleep. She got up and went into the bathroom, and did what she had to do as quickly as she could do it, because the air-conditioner didn't have enough power to blow all the way across the bed, much less to the bathroom, and she thought she would faint from the sticky heat.

She went to the mirror above her dresser and stood looking at herself. There were the beginnings of circles under her eyes, but that was only because she hadn't slept enough, she was sure. The face was still young, and shiny, with none of the wrinkles she had noticed on those who admitted being thirty-three. She was juicy and bright and delicious, and Harry Bell had been a goddam fool. Andre she would not think about at all.

A sudden spasm touched inside her rib cage, and she wished that her body was not such a shameless index to her feelings: people did not go around actually feeling pangs of remorse, or regret, or despair. But she did, and she hated her physical self for it and wished that Dr. Ehrens would come back from his vacation. She cursed all New York psychiatrists for going away for a full month in the summer when she could not. A wave of nausea swept over her, and she steadied herself against the dresser, and then smiled as she recognized the feeling as hunger. How very obvious, and how very stupid of her not to have known at once that that was all it was. Hunger. She did have a tendency to overcomplicate everything, just as Dr. Ehrens said. All the way into the kitchen she gave herself over to adoring him for being so much smarter about her than she was about herself, and she hoped he was having a wonderful time.

She turned on the burner underneath the pan of water, for instant coffee, and in the moment before she opened the refrigerator door hoped that she was wrong about not having any food. When she was six years old she had seen a movie or thought she had seen a movie where Shirley Temple was very poor and lived in an attic or a garret or with poor people of some sort, and Shirley had gone to bed with a prayer and during the night a rich man had sneaked in, and in the morning the garret was flooded with cakes and turkeys and toys. She told Dr. Ehrens about the picture, but if he had seen it he would not admit it to her, just as he never admitted knowing who even Elizabeth Taylor was, or having seen any play or movie, ever.

"Why is it so important to you whether I saw it or not?" he said, the first time she asked him about the picture.

"We could just save a lot of discussion if you knew the plot, Dr. Ehrens."

"What is it about the plot that's important to you?"

"I wish you would tell me, just tell me yes or no, if you saw the picture."

"Why?"

"Oh for Christ's sake," Louise said, and lapsed into silence.

After a few minutes, pulling on his pipe, he smiled at her. "Actually in the time you've been quiet you could have told me the plot of the picture."

"You already know the plot."

"What makes you think so?"

"You just don't want to tell me if you've seen the picture because then I'll have something on you. Then I'll know once when you were a little boy or a medium boy or maybe even in college you went to a movie, and that'll be an admission that you're maybe as vulnerable as I am, and then I'll know you're a human being and you won't be able to help me."

"Is that what you think?"

"Listen Dr. Ehrens, anybody could go to the movies, even Jesus Christ or Sigmund Freud. I guarantee you nothing you say will be used against you. Did you see the picture?"

"Why don't you just tell me about it."

"Goddammit!" Louise sat up on the couch. "I can't afford to sit here for thirty-five dollars an hour and tell you the plots of movies."

"All right. Then what would you like to talk about."

"I would like to talk about your being a pompous orthodox ass."

"All right. As long as you can afford it."

"If I tell you the plot of the picture will you tell me afterward if you've seen it?"

"Why don't you tell me and then we'll discuss it."

She noticed that she was on the point of biting one of the nails it had taken her so long to nurture to its startling length, so she decided to tell him just to have something to do. She couldn't remember anything past the point where Shirley Temple woke up and found the wonderful things. But she was sure that the movie had had one of those sad-happy endings, because the recollection filled her with wistful longing, and her throat actually became heavy with the words.

"The only thing is," Louise said, "I don't remember what it was called. Do you know?"

"No."

"Really no, or are you just saying no so I won't have anything on you?"

"Why don't we just talk about the picture."

"I told you about it. I don't remember the rest."

"Well what's important about it to you?"

"Nothing's important," she said impatiently. "It was just a nice movie."

"You mean a little girl waking up and finding everything she's always wanted . . ."

"It was only a movie," Louise said.

"And in movies desires are very simple. Cakes and toys. The simplest kind of wish fulfillment."

"That's right, the simplest kind of wish fulfillment," she said, annoyed. "What's wrong with remembering a scene from a movie?"

"Nothing," he said. "What's important is why you remember it when you do. It's a lot like dreaming."

"Are you implying I made it up? Because if you weren't such a stiff-neck, you might have gone out sometime in your life and seen a movie, and then you'd know what I was talking about, and we'd save a lot of time."

"I didn't say I didn't see it," Dr. Ehrens said. "I only asked why it was so important whether I saw it or not."

"Then you did see it?" Louise asked, and her body rose with hope. She asked him because she wasn't really sure if *she* had seen it. A lot of the people she ran with nowadays played parlor games with an intensity she could not believe, panicky lest their parties or evening dinners leave too much opening for conversation. But even the most sharp and faggotty among them, those most versed in the newly popular pastime of Trivia, who recalled the theme songs from *Jack Armstrong* and *Let's Pretend* in their entirety, and could tell you who played Mr. Keane, Tracer of Lost Persons, and what Claire Trevor had sung in *Key Largo,* seemed blank during the discussion of Louise's Shirley Temple picture. Andre had told her she meant Little Miss Marker, but she knew she didn't mean Little Miss Marker at all. It was another picture, with a name she couldn't remember but would recognize the instant she heard it. And then she would be off the hook, then she could be sure it wasn't just a fantasy of hers from childhood, because that was too embarrassingly obvious a fantasy to have. "Did you see it?"

"If I did, I don't remember," Dr. Ehrens said.

She despised him because he had answered her almost directly, and she still had no way of knowing if he was dodging or not.

"I don't suppose you saw *Gone with the Wind,* either," she said angrily.

"Why is it so important to you whether I saw it or not," they both said together. For one of the few times she had been with him, Dr. Ehrens laughed aloud.

Louise had been seven years old when *Gone with the Wind* first played the neighborhood theater in Great Neck; in spite of the fact that she was allowed to go to the movies every Saturday afternoon, her mother wouldn't let her go see it, because they used the word "miscarriage." Mrs. Felder had just had an ectopic pregnancy, which would leave Louise her only child, and she had enough trouble without having to answer questions about Scarlett O'Hara. By the time it was revived, Louise was fifteen, and as she sat in the theater crying and eating Goldenberg's Peanut Chews, she knew her life would never be the same.

That night, as she undressed for bed, in front of the Salvation Army armoire that held her five skirts and blouses, she leaned over and picked up her bobby socks, and shook them angrily at the ceiling, or God. "I'll never go hungry again," she said with controlled ferocity. "I'll never go hungry again."

She caught a glimpse of her reflection in the streaked, graying mirror, the thick little waist and dumpling belly beneath the slightly burgeoning bra. Reddening, she had dropped the anklets to the floor beside the Hollywood bed.

"I know I'm not Scarlett O'Hara," she wept to Dr. Ehrens. "I haven't got the plantation or the Civil War. I'm not even Vivien Leigh. I'm too tall."

"And you're blond," Dr. Ehrens said.

"And fat, why don't you say I'm fat?" She rolled over on her stomach and buried her face in the pillow. "I look pretty when I get dressed up, everyone says so, very pretty. And I don't look fat in clothes, I look all honey blond and cuddly."

"Almost like Shirley Temple."

She whirled on him. "Are you trying to say I made it up? You think that's all the fantasy I have for myself."

"I don't know," he said. "You tell me."

She was glad he was on vacation. He was a prick and a boor and she despised him, and no one had come into her house during the night and filled the refrigerator. There was nothing for her to eat except leftover Chinese food in yellowing sticky containers. She stood over the sink and spooned it cold into her mouth, not even tasting. Then she went to phone Kate.

"Lulu's blue," she said mournfully, in her little-girl voice.

"My God, David, it's Louise," Kate said. "Why are you calling? Is someone else dead?"

"Don't pick on me. Lulu's depressed," Louise said. "Where did I go wrong?"

"I don't know, Lou." Kate was spoiling the fun of it by taking the question seriously. It had only been a fun question.

"Oh shit," Louise said, and started to cry.

"You want to come over?"

"You have anything to eat?" Louise said. "I'm starving in this goddam apartment. You can't send out when you live on Park Avenue. It isn't like you have a deli downstairs that delivers, or you can run around in jeans looking for a greasy spoon. I've got to put on a full theatrical makeup including eyelashes to go to the fucking drugstore, and they're probably closed."

"We have food," Kate said. "Come over."

"Where do you live?"

"Same address."

"Tell me again, I can never remember addresses." She could of course but it had been almost a year since she had visited their apartment and she had replaced it in the confines of her memory bank with more vital numbers, like Otto Preminger's town house.

By the time the taxi let her off outside their building she had recovered herself completely. She blew her nose in the elevator, noting it had been inspected for the last time in May by Bruce Wayne and his ward.

"There are a lot of kids in this building," she said, kissing their cheeks. "Your child will not grow up a misfit. I had a better opener, but I forgot it."

"You don't have to do lines," David said, hugging her. "We're happy to see you."

"I see he's still got a big glib mouth on him," Louise said. "No wonder you're always offending people, David."

He excused himself, saying he would be in the den if they wanted him. Louise followed Kate into the pantry.

"Why did he leave; do you think he took me seriously? I was only kidding about his offending people. You don't think he really thinks I meant he was offensive. He didn't."

"I'm sure not."

"Then why did he go away. Do I offend him?"

"Not at all. It's just . . . *Boy's Day,* that's all. There's a ball game on, and Charley's coming."

"Who?"

"Charley Radnor, our friend from California."

"Oh Christ, I don't want to meet anyone, look at me, I didn't even brush my hair. Why didn't you tell me, I never would have come over if I thought there was anyone else coming. I thought the whole world would be in East Hampton. I better go."

"He won't be here for a while."

"You sure?"

"Yes."

"Is he attractive?"

"Very. Warm. Straight."

"A nice guy, huh?"

"A nice guy."

"Fuck him," Louise said, and started on the cheese sandwich Kate had put in front of her. "So what's new besides you're pregnant. Are you living happily ever after?"

"What's happening with you, Lou? Why are you so down?"

"I'm not down. I'm just tired and hot, and I'm mad because I didn't go away for the weekend. When I was really poor, people invited me to Fire Island and now that I can afford a place on Fire Island I wouldn't go anyplace but East Hampton, and all my friends in East Hampton invited me for other weekends during the summer, but I guess they all assume I'm so popular I couldn't possibly be free the Fourth of July."

"Why didn't you just go to a hotel there for the weekend?"

"Then they'd think no one wanted me and they'd all cancel me for the rest of the summer. It's like not having a date New Years."

"You remember when you called us and said if we had any class we'd get married New Year's Eve so you'd have someplace to go?"

"Did I really say that? That's kind of darling! No wonder everybody's crazy about me. Are you glad you did it? After all, you could have had Harry Bell, the shriveled Adonis."

"I don't think he was interested in getting married. Certainly not to me."

"My God, he's dead, why must you be so realistic?"

"I feel sorry for him," Kate said.

"Why? He was a mean old man and he didn't care about anybody."

"He was very sweet about David. I told him there was a young man, and we were having problems, and Harry said I should shack up with the young man for a little while, there was no way to fake a hard-on."

"What beautiful imagery," Louise said. "How is it that he never became a poet?"

"I admit I was a little shaken at the time, but Harry said it was what he did whenever he was trying to work out a problem. If you can manage to see through the shock effect, it's kind of a sweet wisdom."

"Except that every girl that ever let Harry do it to her was lying, and he didn't say it to help you, he said it to shock you and maybe excite you a little bit, besides which he was bragging, trying to make you think he could still get it up. Which I happen to know he only could when he was raping somebody, the old fart."

"And how is it that *you* never became a poet?" Kate said.

"You're right." She reached over and cut a hunk from the salami. "I've gotten so sloppy with my mind. It really is easier to talk smut than to have to think what you're saying. I'm sorry. Apologize to the baby. Do you think it heard?"

"He's sleeping."

"You think it's a boy?"

"It has to be. The dominant one always wins."

"You believe that, huh? That's great. You're going to have a boy."

"You interested in babies?"

"I can hardly think about anything else," Louise said wryly. "Andre said once I would probably eat my young."

"I bet you'd surprise yourself how good a wife you'd be."

"We are not in imminent danger of finding out. You'll be astonished to know that Michael Caine and Jean Paul Belmondo were in town last week and neither of them asked for me."

"Do you know them now?" It had been a long time since Kate and Louise had played that game.

"I'm starting to know them," Louise said. "It isn't like when I was a press agent's secretary or even when I became a junior press agent, when my living depended on meeting these people. I mean, my column is starting to build, so eventually I'll get to them all. But that doesn't mean that ones I would want will be tripping over themselves to fall at my feet."

"Well how about just guys? Just nice guys."

"I have no use for just nice guys. Oh I don't mean that the way it sounds, Kate, honest to God I don't, but just nice guys . . . I meet fairies and married men and cocksman celebrities, and none of them are really interested, not in just a bright, funny girl with a big mouth, no matter if she does have a column. They want some young glamour girl, and I'm not twenty-two anymore, don't tell anyone that, I'll deny it.

Christ, if I had thought when I was twenty-two that in eleven years I would have my own column and be rubbing tits with the greats I would have died of pleasure. But the greats don't want Lulu, as adorable as she is."

"Don't you want to get married?"

"Of course I do, but not to a just nice guy. I'm not like you, Kate. I don't have the capacity to be ordinary. Shit. I don't mean that the way it sounds—but it's something I tried to explain to Dr. Ehrens. People like you can blossom with things like being loved, and having something grow inside you. You've made your decision, but it takes more discipline than I've got."

"It doesn't take discipline," Kate said. "It takes . . . oh, I don't know, wanting to lean on someone."

"It takes more than that," said Louise. "When I was twenty-five I wondered if I was making a mistake being a theatrical secretary, that maybe if I worked on Wall Street my world wouldn't be so limited, maybe I'd get smarter and with wider vistas, all that garbage, and if worse came to worst I could get lucky and meet a young stockbroker. So I went down to the telephone company where they give the lessons to operate the teletype, so I could send those goddam orders to Alaska or Detroit or wherever. There were seventy girls in the room, and not one of them was over seventeen, and they were all morons, they didn't have a thought in their head, I could tell that right away. But they could touch-type like maniacs, and I had never really learned to touch-type. I could type, but mostly what I had to do was answer the phone at the reception desk and say clever things to clients, and pick up the right attitudes. So the lady at the front of the room gave us two minutes to send the fucking sell order, and by the time I found the plus key every girl in the room had been finished for an hour. Morons, but they were done. I excused myself to go to the ladies' room, and I never went back. Twenty-five dollars it cost me to find the plus key. All the way home on the subway I cried, and to top it all I got caught in the rush hour, and all those peons were pushing me, and you know what I realized in that moment? I was not meant to be one of the masses. I screamed that out at the top of my lungs, right there in the middle of the subway. You have any Coke?"

"Maybe you'd rather have coffee."

"And then again maybe I'd rather not have you counting my calories. When the right time comes I will go on a diet, you know I will, but I have to be in exactly the right frame of mind, otherwise I always end up fatter than when I started, and this is not exactly the right frame."

"I'm sorry," Kate said, and went to get the Coke.

"I was at a party last month at Dainty Lee's, and I met the Countess Trejinska, that phony cunt, but she is really beautiful. Anyway, she was mad about me, she kept telling everybody how funny and bright I was, and then she took me into the bathroom and asked how I could let myself go like that, with her fucking size-eight mouth, she asked me. She asked how come with my face and my brain and my pretty legs I could let myself get so heavy, and why didn't I just masturbate to keep my weight down like she did."

"I really miss those people," Kate said.

For a minute Louise studied Kate to see if she was being sarcastic, or if there wasn't just a note of wistfulness there.

"I guess that's what it is to have the security of being born with real money," Kate said.

"Maybe," said Louise. "I don't know if I would ever have the guts to play with myself, but if I did I certainly couldn't talk about it."

"I wish you'd stay and meet Charley."

"Why?"

"He's a funny, attractive, earthy guy, and he's straight."

"So what made you bring him up at this particular point in the discussion."

"It might just raise your spirits to know that there are straight nice people in the world, who aren't faggots or married."

"And you've already told him I was an emotional charity case, and he should throw me a friendly fuck."

"Go home," Kate said. "I don't know why I even try talking to you."

"I was with Andre yesterday after the funeral. He made Lulu cry." Louise's lip quivered. "Lulu's depressed. Where did she go wrong?"

"I'll get you a Kleenex."

"Don't bother." She reached into the pocket of her shift and took out a wrinkled handkerchief. "I got this from a doctor at the wake. George Piner. You should have seen him. Tall, attractive, unmarried, educated." She blew her nose. "He's probably a transvestite."

Kate laughed. "I want you to meet Charley."

"What for? What's the use?"

"Because he's lovely," Kate said. "Because he's clean and he's funny and he's healthy and he's sexy and he's in a business, a normal business, like a normal young man."

"I hate him already," Louise said. Even so, she planned on spending the day, and meeting Charley. But when she phoned

75

her service, there was a message from Chet Oppenheim who asked to see her right away. Louise was so nervous and excited, she left without saying good-bye.

"Louise said to say good-bye," Kate said, going into the den.

"She's gone?" David put his feet up on the ottoman and smiled. "That's good."

"You weren't very nice, David. We haven't seen her for a year, and then you hide in here. You're the one who's always saying we ought to spend more time with 'those' people."

"Louise isn't really one of those people. She's not in a league with Maggie Bolin."

"Well neither am I," Kate said.

"You have more of a right to be with her than Louise does. You went to school with her."

"That didn't put me in her league. Not Brearley, not Smith . . . I didn't fit in at the debutante balls. I was never that rich, or that pretty . . ."

"I won't have you denigrate yourself," David said. "You have more of a right to be with those people than Louise."

"I don't want to be with them. I feel uncomfortable with them."

"Well I want you to get over that. It's important for you, and it's important for me. Are you planning to call Maggie Bolin?"

"I don't know," Kate said.

The doorbell rang. "It's Charley," Kate said. "Please don't say anything nasty to him about Louise. I want them to meet."

"What for?"

"I think they'll like each other. I think he'll be very good for her. Please don't put her down in front of him."

"Are you going to call Maggie?"

"I'll call her. You won't say anything nasty?"

"I won't," he said. "I have no cause to denigrate Louise."

Louise crossed her legs at the ankles, the way Diane Trejinska did when she was holding court, and leaned forward in the Savonarola chair. Chet's apartment was not at all the lush functional bachelor pad she had imagined, and had been in so many times around town, and categorized as early Ross Hunter. It was decorated with quietly expensive and rather dreary antiques, the colors running to deep russets and browns; in spite of the insistent floor-to-ceiling glassed sunshine beaming in from Sutton Place South, the atmosphere the decor created was one of genteel gloom, the more oppressive because it was obviously in imitation of apartments like Maggie Bolin's. Maggie had at least come by that taste honestly, through inheritance, having no choice other than to strew her many cooperative rooms with old family possessions. For a man to deliberately set out after acquisitions that would make his domain a showcase of clutter was beyond Louise. But as Chet had made the transition to Louis Quinze from origins which had probably been Jewish McKinley, without anybody knowing for sure that he hadn't sat in eighteenth-century love seats all his life, she had to give him credit. Everyone knew the candy store Andre Sherman had sprung from, Andre's furniture was so brazenly expensive and uncomfortable. Chet's living room at least gave the impression that that was the man's taste, and as everyone knew, there was no accounting for taste; and not, like Andre's, that a man was trying to prove something and consequently disproved everything, except that he had come from a candy store.

If Chet Oppenheim wanted to play lord of the manor, he had at least chosen his props with discretion. There was probably a great deal she could learn from him.

"You have lovely things," Louise said, fingering the carved arm of her chair. "It's so interesting the way you've mixed French with Italian. I adore antique furniture, but I'd be nervous about trying to collect any; I'd probably end up with fakes because I know so little about it. Maybe now that I live so close to Parke-Bernet I should start going to auctions—not to buy anything, really, I wouldn't have the nerve—but just to try and learn what's good."

"I'm sure you'd learn very quickly," Chet said. "I'm sure you could pick up on anything in no time at all. You're a bright little girl and you'd know a good thing when you saw it. Drink?"

"No thank you. I don't drink."

"Or smoke either?" Chet held out the red leather box with its neatly martialed lines of filtered, nonfiltered and mentholated cigarettes compartmentalized inside.

"Not really," Louise said. "I just started to try and learn a couple of weeks ago, but I don't really enjoy it."

"Good," Chet said, closing the cover of the box. "Leave it that way."

"Really, Mr. Oppenheim," she flashed him her most cunning smile. "I thought Rolf Orlovsky was one of the largest quiet owners of Consolidated Tobacco. Aren't you discouraging one of your most important accounts?"

"I'm not concerned with my accounts at this moment. I'm concerned about you."

"My health, you mean?"

"In a way," he said.

Louise smiled, and cast her eyes down, not so much from

77

a wish to be coy as avoid the scrutinizing stare of Ron Abbate. Except for an abrupt hello when they were first introduced, he had said nothing, retiring to a wing chair in the corner, watching her. For what reason she wasn't yet sure; but she was glad she had crossed her legs at the ankles.

"How did you meet Harry?" Abbate said.

"At a party, I suppose it was."

"You suppose?"

"It was a party. Harry was interested in one of the actresses Phillips handled, and I was with her."

"And were you introduced to him?" Abbate said.

"How else do you meet people at parties? You're introduced or you introduce yourself." Louise sat up straighter in the chair. "Mr. Abbate, I know you have a reputation as a brilliant attorney, but do you always start conversations like this? I have the impression I'm on the witness stand."

"I'm sorry," said Abbate. "Force of habit. Why don't you just tell us about you and Harry?"

"But for what reason? When Chet asked me to come over here, he said it was important, that he had something interesting to discuss. He didn't say I was going to be questioned about Harry Bell. What business is it of anybody's what went on between me and Harry?"

"Then something did go on?"

"I don't think that's any of your business."

"Didn't you tell a few people you were with Harry the night before he died?"

"I said I had a date with him Tuesday and Wednesday."

"And did you?"

She crossed her legs again, and held her hand out, trying to look coolly at her long, long fingernails. But her hand was trembling, so the effect was not the one she wanted. She lowered it again, and placed her palm on the carved surface of the wood.

"Go easy, Ron," Chet said. "This is a darling kid. I have genuine respect for her. There's no reason to act like you're cross-examining her."

"Exactly," Louise said. "What's the crime if I was supposed to be with him? He was a dear friend of mine, and he's dead, and if I was supposed to be with him, what difference can it possibly make to anybody? What's the crime?"

"No crime," Ron said, and got up to get a drink. "Just as there would be no crime if you admitted you were with him the night before he died. Harry was alone in the house that evening, as far as we know, the servants were away, nobody saw him. Nobody we know of. He died a natural death. No one would have to be afraid of admitting they were with him

78

the night before he died. It couldn't hurt them at all to admit it. Maybe it could do them a great deal of good."

"I don't think I understand you," Louise said.

"I think you do," Chet said. "I think you could if you wanted to. You pick up quickly."

"All right, what if I admitted I was with him the night before he died? So what?"

"Well then," Ron said, "you might be able to tell us if by any chance Harry expressed a wish to you as to how he would like to be buried. You might tell us about the memorial buildings he wanted, for housing his charities, and his remains. I know it's not something that people talk about over supper, but Harry was getting on, and he was frightened. Everything he gave to institutions and various groups in the last couple of years were by way of being memorials to him while he was still alive. It would follow that he might very well confide to someone he really cared about, someone he thought enough of to plan on seeing three nights in a row, how it was he hoped to be remembered."

"But you're the one who said people don't talk about that over supper. Especially Harry. Harry wanted to be young and vital, and death would be the last thing he talked about. You knew Harry. You ought to know better than that about him."

"I ought to, but men are very different with their attorneys than they are with the girl they love."

Louise looked up and met his glance directly.

"Nobody knows anything better than the last girl a man loves. The woman a man plans to marry."

"I never said that," Louise said. "I never even implied that." Louise took a deep breath, and closed her eyes, and all the possibilities paraded through the front of her brain. "Regardless of the plans that Harry and I might have made, they don't matter anymore, because Harry's dead, and the plans are dead, too."

"Good girl," Chet said, and smiled over at Ron. "I told you she was a bright one."

"Don't you dare talk about me like I'm not here," Louise said. "If you have something to say, say it directly, and to me. What do you want, and why?"

"We don't want anything," Abbate said. "Anything that you don't feel it's right for you to say. But as the last girl Harry loved, the one he would have married if he had lived, you're the only one who can help him now—and maybe help yourself. You understand, nobody's promising you anything. But you would really help yourself if you knew that the man you were going to marry was laid to rest the way he would want to be laid to rest."

"He isn't buried?" Louise said. "That's what this is all about. He honest to God isn't buried?"

Chet turned around. "You tell that to anyone, you're going to blow your whole future, I promise you."

"Are you threatening me? You call me up here and nance about what you really want, and then you have the nerve to threaten me?" Her voice was quavering, but she held her hands firmly on the armrests and steadied herself, so her torso at least would have enough support to fight the vibration, and then perhaps her voice would stop shaking.

"Nobody's threatening you," Chet said. "I certainly didn't mean it to sound like that."

"Well, then maybe you ought to phrase your words more carefully." There was no doubt about it: she could be a lady and ballsy at the same time. Harry would have been proud of her.

"I only meant that you might be hurting your own opportunities," Chet said.

"What opportunities?"

Ron got up from the chair. "As I said before, nobody's promising you anything. It's important that you understand that."

"You understand it," Chet said. "I'm sure you do. Just as I'm sure you understand the kind of life you would have led as Harry's wife, the people you would have met. Harry was very proud of you. He told me so often. As far back as when you first met him . . ."

"Three years ago,"-Louise said carefully.

"That's right, three years ago. And he took you to . . ."

"Mostly the Sixth Avenue Delicatessen."

"I like that," Chet smiled. "No pretension, no big deal, very warm and down to earth, the way someone would be, no matter how rich he was, with the girl he really cared for. I suppose the waiters knew who he was, and remember."

"Of course. I could never go in there again without them asking me how Harry was. It's one of the reasons I moved out of the neighborhood. I always move out of neighborhoods. It's easier than not going into delicatessens. So?"

"So it's a shame he never got to take you to the places you might have enjoyed. Not that you didn't enjoy the Sixth Avenue Delicatessen, because you were with Harry, but you might have enjoyed something a little more glamorous."

"He took me to one movie premiere," Louise said. "Formal, invitational kind of thing."

"And when you were there you saw a lot of people Harry knew."

"Yes."

"So many of his friends knew about you?" Ron said.

"They met me, if that's what you mean. And once he took me to dinner at some dying magazine editor's. I can't remember his name, some refugee. But there were a lot of casual celebrity friends of Harry's."

"And they'd recognize you again if they saw you."

"Probably," Louise said. "Cut to the punchline."

"No punchline," Chet said. "But it really is a little sad, I mean aside from the enormous sadness of losing Harry, I find it a little regrettable that you never had a chance to do so many of the things Harry would have wanted you to do once you were married. The people, the places, that sort of thing. Naturally he kept your relationship more or less hidden these past few years, because he'd lost a couple of girls who got a little drunk from all that publicity and spotlight, but I'm sure once you were married, he would have taken you everywhere, and introduced you to everyone."

"I'm sure," Louise said. "Most regrettable."

"But it doesn't have to be," Chet said. "After all, I think the least I could do, as Harry's close friend, is take the little girl he was going to marry under my wing, help her cultivate real relationships with people like Diane Trejinska, introduce her to everyone she might have met, get her the wide newspaper syndication her column would have had, if Harry had lived. Once he's properly buried. With the fitting memorial building, of course."

"I see," said Louise.

"I certainly hope so."

"Was he really that close to Diane Trejinska? She wasn't even at his funeral."

"The summer theater manager wouldn't let her out of the last performances. That's why she's planning the party in his memory. I'd like nothing better than making sure you were there."

"You must be mad," Louise said. "Stark staring mad. Do you imagine for one minute that I would have anything to do with this . . . thing, just for the sake of going to some . . . party?"

"Well no, I never . . ." Chet started to say.

"Still . . ." she dimpled. "I don't see what harm it could do, really, meeting those people under the right auspices. I know it's what Harry would have wanted." She sat back in the chair and looked at them coolly. "He was talking about that very thing the night before he died, when we were discussing his memorial building."

"Good girl," Chet said.

"Lulu always tries to be just that," said Louise.

CHAPTER THREE

DIANE Trejinska had not been born beautiful, all the magazine articles notwithstanding. As a child there had been only an indication of the tall regality that was to come; at the time she was only a long, skinny girl, who sat a good saddle in that sport her mother considered most suitable for an heiress. Her mother was tiny and chic and smelled of jasmine even in the mornings, while Diane was sure she had about herself the faint odor of the stables, no matter how often she bathed. She continued riding daily because it was expected of her, holding her long back straight and her head tilted slightly, so her thick red hair, her best feature, fell in heavy folds around her shoulders, and blew in the Greenwich winds. At six o'clock every morning she would ride along the paths that ran through their Connecticut estate before leaving for Rosemary Hall; at four o'clock she would practice jumping before returning to the house for afternoon tea with her mother and her two half-brothers. And three times a year she would ride in the Westport show, and take the blue ribbon, because it was expected of her.

She had no particular interest in boys. Her two half-brothers, the children of her mother's first marriage to a man Diane had never seen, though he lived less than ten miles away, were almost painfully handsome; yet her mother showed no greater affection for them than she did for Diane. Diane's own father, whom Diane thought of in her mind as her mother's husband, was a distinguished-looking man in his late forties, about whom her mother spoke with the deepest regard in his absence, but whom she never touched in the children's presence, not even to hold his hand. There was, therefore, in Diane's mind, no particular wonder or mystery about men, certainly nothing that would justify all the whispers and gigglings that were starting among her classmates in the tenth grade at Rosemary. But when she was fourteen her mother began drawing up a list of "suitables," those whom Diane might consider inviting to the small parties that would be given at Christmas and the prom at Rosemary Hall, preparatory to making the final selection for those to be included at Diane's debut.

"After all, Diane, three years pass more quickly than you

want to believe when you're young." Her mother sat at the big oak desk in the west library, writing on blue-bordered notepaper bearing her same faint jasmine scent. "We must think about your future."

"I'm not worried, Mummy."

"Well I'm not worried either, dear, but we must acknowledge the realities and make a list. Have you given any thought to which of the boys you'd like to ask to the dance?"

"No."

"Maybe one of Tony's friends. Or George's?"

"No."

"Well, don't worry about it. There are plenty of suitable young men. We can take our time."

Her mother's voice was calm and measured, as it always was; nonetheless her words filled Diane with a faint sense of alarm. She had never deeply considered the realities, as her mother had put it, and the realities were that she would grow up and get married and go away. Maybe not far away, maybe she could find somebody who lived within a few minutes' ride of the house. That thought suddenly upset her even more: within a few months she would be expected to go to a dance, to let a young man hold her; and all the time she smelled of horses.

She went upstairs and had her second bath of the day, lingering long enough to make her almost miss the private bus that came to take her to school. All through her classes that day she felt vaguely distracted. At her best, Diane was only an adequate student. Several of her teachers for the first time that day considered the possibility that Diane might not be terribly bright. When she came home from school she dutifully changed from her navy and white uniform into jodhpurs and riding jacket and made her way to the stables. Her mother's horse, Festa, which Diane always preferred when she was riding alone, was behaving with unaccustomed bad temper, so Diane took Salutary, a gift from three Christmases before. She rode him automatically along the bridle path surrounding the estate. When she came to the gate bordering the sound end of the gardens, she drew him suddenly to the left, and out onto the private street standing off the Round Hill Road exit of the Merritt Parkway.

There was never any traffic at that hour of the afternoon, everyone said so later. It was the most understandable thing in the world that a young girl who knew her part of the country, and everyone who lived and moved in it, could have felt sufficiently secure to give her horse his head when he wanted to canter along a quiet country road. The man driving the car was a stranger, naturally, a radical, many were to suggest, deliberately flouting the stability of a sign that read PRIVATE ROAD. She could hear the whirr of the autumn wind through the leaves, and somewhere in the back of her mind, she heard the engine. But that was easily confused with the sounds she was accustomed to. She saw him turn the corner at the moment he saw her, and as he veered to avoid her, she pulled the reins up tight, so the horse's hindquarters were right in his path.

She was only slightly hurt, a miracle everyone said. But Salutary, with two broken legs, hemorrhaging from the rectum, had to be put away, instantly. Diane wept for a week until her eyes were bloated closed. But she began to notice after a while when she blew her nose, she could detect only the faintest odor of horses. Within a month it was gone completely.

Only once after that did her mother suggest Diane might like to try riding again. But seeing the expression on Diane's face, she immediately withdrew the suggestion.

"I suppose," she said to her husband later that evening, "she is just too deeply touched with shock and grief over Salutary."

"Really?" Diane's father said. "I always wondered if she even liked the animal."

"What a peculiar thing to say, John. He was her favorite. Oh of course she liked Festa, I know she rode him when she wasn't riding with us, but she loved Salutary."

"Did she?"

"Of course."

"I don't even know if she really liked riding."

"What a ridiculous thing to say. Since she was seven years old she's been out every morning at six. She's a champion fourteen times. Why would she do that if she didn't adore riding."

"Maybe because you wanted her to go riding. Maybe she thought it would please you."

"For a bright man, John, there are times when you show absolutely no understanding."

"All right."

"All right, what?"

"You're right, I show very little understanding."

"You don't have to speak to me in that conciliatory tone, John."

"I didn't mean to sound conciliatory, Barbara. I was only trying to get you to consider another possibility besides the one . . ."

"Anyway, I suppose it's just as well, in a tragic way of

course. It's time she started thinking about other things besides being so devoted to horses."

"Like what?"

"Like young men."

"Don't push her, Barbara."

"I have no intention of pushing her. But she's a pretty, normal girl, and she should start showing interest in the things that will ultimately govern her life."

"Like sex?"

"I didn't say sex," Barbara said. "I meant the social graces. You don't have to be so coarse about things at times, John."

"If I weren't so coarse about things at times you'd still be married to Mr. Ashland, Barbara."

"Don't do that. The children might come in."

"It's two o'clock in the morning, Barbara. For Christ's sake, we're in our own bedroom."

"Turn out the light, then."

She waited, eyes closed, until she saw the light disappear through her eyelids. "Nothing elaborate," she said. "It's very late."

"All right," he said, and climbed into bed beside her.

"You really didn't mean that, what you said before, John. You don't think I've ever given her the impression that sex governs her life."

"Oh for Christ's sake, Barbara, now?"

"Well I have to get these things off my mind, John. Don't you want me to enjoy it too?"

"Of course," he sighed.

"Well, have I?"

"Have you what?"

"Have I ever given any of the children the impression that sex governs a person's life."

"Right now I'm finding it difficult to believe you consider sex important at all."

"I have an obligation to my children, John."

"One of them's also mine."

"That's right, John. And if she's got you in her, then I don't have to tell her about sex, she'll have a natural bent for it."

"I hope so."

"Really, John. Sometimes I wonder why I married you."

"Maybe this will help."

"You're vile."

"Good."

"Sometimes I wonder why I even . . . try . . . to talk to you."

"Then shut up," he said, and made her be quiet. It was

only when they were away alone in a hotel, where there was no one registered whom they knew even vaguely, that she would allow herself to scream.

"But don't you think she'll take to it nicely," she said the moment it was over.

"Sex?"

"Oh stop," she said. "I'm not in the mood for teasing. You know what I mean. The social life proper to a girl of her age and background."

"She'll be fine," Diane's father said. "Just be careful you make clear to her what it is you want from her, Barbara. I'd hate to see her try and sit such a good saddle in too many directions."

Diane began attending parties with the same obedience and grace with which she had ridden horses, being just charming enough and smiling just wide enough to be considered best in her class by anyone who might be judging her. Young men were more than willing to escort her because of the elegance with which she handled herself at parties, and in the parking lots of various country clubs and cotillions afterward. It was then that she first discovered she had the power to hurt boys, not by doing anything to hurt them, but by refusing to do.

"Touch it," one would whisper. "Please. Just touch it."

"All right," she would say softly, reaching for his fly. "All right, I will." Her fingers lowered the zipper, and then she pulled her hands away. "No, no, I don't think I should. You're liable to get excited."

"Please. Please. Just touch it."

"Like that?"

"Oh yes. Oh yes. Like that. Please."

"I think we shouldn't do any more," she would say, and pull her hand away.

The boys did not seem to hate her for it. On the contrary: the boys behaved toward her as if she had some cool dominion over them, and they pursued her at parties as if there were some hope of finally attaining heaven in the parking lot. It made her feel quite like her mother, possessing a regality which made people worship her that way.

Her mother considered that Diane had made the transition from girlhood to young womanhood beautifully. It was only her father who suggested, out of her hearing, that Diane might be a little cold.

"I don't understand what you mean by cold, John," she said after she had closed the door to their bedroom.

"I mean cold, Barbara."

"But she's terribly popular, John. She's turning out a real beauty, you can see that, and all the boys seem to be very

86

eager to be with her. Granted she's a little light on humor, but everybody can't be hearty like you are."

"If you ask me, my heartiness is an embarrassment to her. That's your fault, she's taken the cue from you, Barbara. You always turn your nose up at my little jokes . . . except in the bedroom."

"That's the proper place for your little jokes."

"Why not in the bathroom? Isn't that where sex belongs?"

"Of course not. You know I don't really feel that way."

"That's fine, but does Diane? You've done a very good job of hiding your real feelings from your children, Barbara; I don't know if it's because you think you were doing penance for your adultery . . ."

"I've asked you never to use that word, John. We were in love and you know it."

"Nooky is nooky, no matter how you cover it up."

"My father was right about you. He always said you had no class, no matter how much money you had to disguise it with."

"You mean because I didn't sit on my ass and live on inherited income, because I went out and worked for a living, and built up a communications company . . ."

"Oh, don't start rattling off your—"

"That's right, Barbara. Horses and children, with their long blue lines. Just take care you don't end up with a frigid, joyless daughter."

"I despise you," she said.

"Fine." He turned off the lights and got into bed.

"Aren't you coming over here," she said in a few minutes.

The next day as she sat with her daughter going through the revised list of young men for Diane's debutante ball to be held a year from the following Christmas, she looked at her daughter carefully. "Is there anyone I haven't included, that you'd like to have on the invitation list?"

"No, Mama."

"I mean maybe there's some nice young man who wouldn't ordinarily be included that you'd like to have? I don't want you to feel you have to stay with what everyone else considered suitable."

"It's a very big list," Diane said. "There are plenty of boys already. After all, the party has to stay within bounds, Mother, you did say that."

"I was talking numbers, Diane."

"So was I, Mummy."

"Well maybe when you go off to Vassar in September you may meet some young man or men you'd like to have included. You will let me know?"

"Of course, Mother, but I doubt it. I think what's there is fine."

"Is there anyone on the list you like especially?" her mother said, trying to keep her voice from sounding unusual.

"They're all all right."

"I mean someone you really like."

"I like them all," Diane said. "Boys are boys."

"No they're not, Diane. There's a great difference between them. A happy wonderful difference. Some of them exist, and some of them are full of life and laughter and love, like your father."

"Like Daddy?" She tried to keep from giggling.

"There's nothing wrong with being a lady, Diane. It's what every woman should try and be. But sometimes, happily, more often than people think, it's possible to behave like a lady, and still feel something deeply passionate and outrageously human for another person."

"Oh I know he worships you," Diane said. "Why shouldn't he."

"I'm not discussing how he feels about me. I mean the way I feel about him."

"Really?"

"I don't want you to think of it as weakness, or sickness. It can be the richest area of a woman's life if she's lucky. If I've led you to think otherwise, I'm sorry."

Diane was silent.

"Do you understand what I'm saying?"

"I think so, Mother."

"I don't want you to confuse being a lady with having no feelings. Naturally I expect you to behave with dignity and restraint, but I don't want you to lose what is the happiest part of a woman's nature in choosing a husband."

The next evening she had a date with Tucker Randall, who was on Easter vacation from Brown. They parked on the bridge by the brook in Darien. Instead of reaching out her hand as she usually did, she offered the happiest part of her nature, after first making sure that he had a contraceptive.

"What do you mean, a thing," Tucker Randall said.

"You know, a thing. A rubber."

"Are you kidding?"

"Why would I kid about something like that?"

"What do you want to know if I'm carrying one for?"

"What do you think, Tuck?"

"Are you serious? You mean you'd really . . . ?"

"Why else would I ask you if you had one."

"I don't know, maybe you want to know if I'm the kind of guy who carries a thing in his wallet."

"Are you?"

"Maybe you'd think I had it there because I thought I could score with you. You wouldn't think very much of me if you thought I thought that."

"Yes I would, Tuck. I wouldn't think anything bad about you at all. I'd just think you were very farsighted to be prepared."

"Yeah?"

"Yes."

"I don't believe you."

"Do you have one?" she said impatiently.

"I'm not that kind of guy," he said.

"All right," she said. "Let's look for a drugstore."

They drove over to the Boston Post Road, and looked at all the shuttered store fronts in Darien, then checked the highway en route to Stamford. All the while they were trying to keep each other interested with their hands.

"Everything's closed," she said, sighing. "Damn."

"It's all right," he said, pulling off the main road. "I have a thing."

They were together several times before he went back to Brown, and his farewell present to her was the name of a gynecologist he knew in Manhattan who didn't ask any questions. Because she wanted to act with dignity and restraint and had no wish to become pregnant, Diane went in on the Stamford Local, telling her mother she had to have an interview with her adviser from Vassar. After her fitting she felt comparatively free, and although she got little or no pleasure from the several young men who gratefully accepted her bounty, she blamed only herself for not being a tenth of the woman her mother was. She thought perhaps it would come in time, and meanwhile she kept herself in practice, disappointing them occasionally, to make sure she had not lost her touch.

Her sophomore year, after Thanksgiving vacation, she discovered, to her horror, that there was a hole in her diaphragm. She anxiously communicated that news to her current beau, a graduate student in business administration at Harvard. They telephoned each other nightly, never mentioning that what they really were doing was waiting out the month.

The month never ended. When she had not gotten her period five weeks later, she and Hal Pembroke met in Greenwich to break the news to Diane's parents. Her father was away in Washington for the weekend, but that didn't matter to Diane. It was her mother who mattered. After she and Hal had picked their way through a rather formal luncheon of egg in aspic, she told her mother that they had some news for her.

"Yes?" Barbara said.

"I'd hoped your husband would be here," said Hal.

"Yes?" said Barbara.

"Your daughter and I would like to be married."

"Well that's very nice, Hal. Diane had written us about you several times the past few weeks. I suspected something like this would be coming. You seem like a very nice young man, and I believe my husband is acquainted with your father—he is the Pembroke on the Street, isn't he?"

"Thirty Wall, yes ma'am."

"John mentioned he thought he knew him."

"After I graduate from Harvard Business I plan to go into the company with him."

"After you graduate, Hal?"

"Yes, ma'am. Naturally I plan to complete my studies."

"Naturally, Hal. It's quite natural for a man to plan to finish something."

"Mother . . ."

"Just a minute, Diane, I'd like to be allowed to complete a thought. You may regard this as odd, Hal, but in this family we've always considered it important for the women to finish something as well. Diane is only in her sophomore year, and . . ."

"We've talked about that, Mrs. Braddock, Diane and I, and we thought that possibly she could transfer her credits to Radcliffe . . ."

"Diane isn't bright enough for Radcliffe, Hal; if you want to marry her, you ought to be aware of that."

"Mother . . ."

"Well, it's true, darling. You're lovely and sweet and bright enough and I'm very proud of you, but we oughtn't to deceive ourselves, ought we." She turned her frozen smile on Hal. "No Hal, transferring isn't the solution. You're both nice, handsome healthy young people, but I think in this instance you ought to exercise some restraint. If you love each other, and I'm sure you do, you want what's best for both of you, and each of you, so you can certainly wait another two years."

"We want to be married now," Diane said.

"I'm sure you do, but everything has its time. Hal will be that much prouder of you as a woman if you can stand on your own. In my day a diploma wasn't necessary to show a woman's wit, but nowadays that's changed, after all this is 1951, and we must move with the times. I want Diane to have the most of a woman's opportunities. We had a hard enough time getting her into Vassar, Hal. I'm sure you understand why we don't want her to throw it all away."

"But this is different . . ." Diane said.

"It's always different," Barbara said. "Every young man you've been seeing for the past two years was different and there have been many of them, Hal; I don't want to give the impression my daughter is flighty, but she is interested and curious, and as she grows, her attitudes change, and it's possible that in another two years you might discover you don't have that much in common."

"Is that it, Mrs. Braddock? Don't you think I'm good enough for her?"

"Well I'm sure you are, Hal, more than good enough for any nice young girl. But my daughter isn't any nice young girl. She's exceptional. She should be able to have any young man she wants."

"She wants me," Hal said.

"Well, that's right now, Hal. Let's see if she still feels that way in two years."

"In two years your grandchild will be a year and a half old," Diane said.

Barbara got up and closed the door to the servants' pantry. When she returned, her face was the same color it usually was, but there were patches of white around her mouth. "You did this," she said to Diane. "You did this to me?"

"Mother . . . it happened. It's happened to a lot of people . . ."

"Not my daughter. How could my daughter . . ."

"You were the one who said . . . you told me it was the richest area of a woman's life . . ."

"And did you take that to mean—did you think this would make me *proud* of you?"

"I don't know!"

"This is all your father's fault," Barbara said. "He was the one who made me have a talk with you."

"Would you excuse me a minute, please," Hal said. "I want to go wash my hands."

"Well," Barbara said after a few minutes. "What's done is done. He seems like a very nice young man. I'm sure you'll be very happy."

"Will that make you proud of me?"

"I've always been proud of you, Diane. I always loved you, and I've always been proud of you. I only wanted . . . I only wanted you to set a value on yourself. To enjoy life, yes, but to set a value on yourself."

From that point on, before and after the honeymoon, Diane rarely allowed Hal to achieve completion, at least one which included her. It was the only way she knew to punish him for what he had done; besides, it made her feel very smart, outwitting a graduate at Harvard in such a basic way. She was much brighter than her mother thought. She had to be.

They were married less than four weeks later, in a small church ceremony in Greenwich, with a lawn supper held afterward behind the Braddock home. Diane's mother told Diane not to worry about anything, she was slim by nature; except for the new roundness of her breasts there was nothing unusual about her figure at all, and there were many families whose babies were born prematurely.

"I want you to be happy, darling, really I do. Just remember to put a value on yourself."

Twelve years later after she had been divorced twice and her children were in boarding school, Chet Oppenheim told Diane that Harry Bell was willing to give her ten thousand dollars to go to bed with him. Well, not exactly give her ten thousand dollars, Chet explained, as Harry didn't like to think he was paying for anything like that. But Harry had just taken over an automobile company and he was willing to have the sports model delivered to her town-house apartment the next morning if she would say the word tonight.

Diane was thirty-one at the time, and she knew only two of the men in her party, none of whom particularly interested her. Harry Bell she did not know at all, other than to cut him politely from time to time at a gathering to which they were both invited for different reasons. In the purse she was carrying, which she realized now was really much too big for the cocktail hour, was a savings book which contained over half a million dollars in insured deposits, and a checkbook, the balance of which showed twenty-two thousand and some odd dollars. But ten thousand dollars for a single night. That would have to be considered value, even by her mother's standards.

She told Chet Oppenheim he must be mad, covering it with one of her most elegant smiles so the censure wouldn't be impressed on his memory. She watched him cross the restaurant to Harry's table, where, after Chet had spoken to him, the little man looked more crestfallen than usual. After dinner she went with her group to El Morocco, excused herself to them, pleading a sick headache, and took a taxi to Harry Bell's town house.

He answered the door himself. "Hello," he said, and the awe in his voice made it almost as hushed in tone as Diane's.

"Is anyone here?"

"Only my servants. They're sleeping."

"You'll have to get rid of them," Diane said.

"They have a whole separate quarters. Their own entrance. All that garbage."

"Fine," Diane said, and followed him inside.

"It certainly is wonderful meeting you finally," Harry said. "At such long last."

"It's a thrill for me too," Diane said. "Why don't we just go upstairs."

"Sure," Harry said. "Suits me."

When they were in his bedroom she insisted he pull down the shade.

"You don't have to worry," Harry said. "There's no way anyone could see in here unless they were robbing the Metropolitan. It's closed at night, you know."

"Pull down the shade anyway."

"Sure, Diane, sure. But I promise you I am the soul of discretion."

"Pardon?"

"I mean there's no way anyone could know. This is very private here, you know, being such a solidly built town house, and I'd never tell anyone."

"Really?"

"Never. Nobody has any idea of half the people I screwed."

"That's terribly gallant."

"Not that I'm including you with them, even. I've had movie stars, you know about the movie stars I've had, not that I told in most cases, it's just that movie stars have big yaps, they like to brag and a lot of them were stuck on me, so they told, it kind of built up their stock . . ."

"I can understand that," Diane said.

"And a lot of them were in the columns, you know, their press agents planted it that we were humping because it made them look good."

"I can see where it would," Diane said, pulling her slip over her head.

"And of course the world knows about the beautiful women because in a lot of cases I married them. I'm a sucker for beautiful women."

"Cleverly put."

"But I wouldn't include them with you. I mean you're as beautiful as any of them, even Sylvia, but you're not just a beautiful woman. You're an aristocrat. No shit. I've never known anyone like you. Intimately I mean."

"I know what you mean, Harry."

"So you don't have to worry about a thing. I'll never tell anyone you were here. I swear. You have my word."

"I'm not worried," Diane said.

"But you really have my word." He kissed his pinky up to the ceiling. "I'd never tell anyone."

"It really wouldn't make any difference," Diane said. "Even if you told anyone they wouldn't believe you."

"Oh," Harry said.

In a moment he followed her over to the bed. "Do you mind if I just look at you for a minute?"

"If you like."

"You have a beautiful body."

"I know."

"You know I'd heard that about redheads, and I've had a couple but I've never seen such pink ones before."

"That's probably because I'm an aristocrat."

"I guess so. Do you mind if I suck on them for a minute?"

"If you like."

"Jesus. You even taste different. I'll only be a minute."

"Don't go."

"I have to take off my clothes. I don't think it's right, I get undressed in front of you."

"You don't have to take off your clothes."

"Huh?"

"Not for what you're going to do."

"I don't get it."

"Sure you do." She held firmly to the back of his head and pressed him toward her belly.

"You crazy? What are you doing."

"Go ahead. Do."

"Cut it out. I don't go down on anybody."

"I want you to do it to me."

"I wouldn't even do that for Sylvia, and I was nuts about her."

"But she wasn't an aristocrat."

"That's true," Harry said, and flicked his tongue once tentatively across her belly. "There."

"Come on Harry. Come . . . on." She opened her legs.

"I . . ."

"Go ahead. Go."

"But I don't do this . . . it's degrading for a man."

"It's all right," she whispered. "I won't tell anybody you did it."

He raised his head briefly before his tongue swept burningly between her legs. "You know, even if you did tell anyone, they'd never believe you."

In spite of how curiously inexpert he was, it was the most sexually exciting experience of her life, because every dart of his coarse warm tongue reminded her that he wanted her ten thousand dollars worth, and was ready to pay in a number of ways. At the end, because he acted as though he were being accorded a royal favor, she let him be inside her for a moment. It was over quickly. He was so tremblingly grateful, she could not help but whisper to his profuse thanks, *"Honi soit qui mal y pense,"* all the while meaning to say "Noblesse oblige."

They never spoke directly to one another again, no matter how often they were at the same parties, or in the same restaurants. He accepted his dismissal with a dignity that surprised her, and more often than not she was the first one to avert her eyes. When she married the Count she added Harry's name to the invitation list for the wedding. He had the graciousness not to attend, and to send a $1,500 carved crystal paperweight from Steuben. She knew the price because she had tried to return it, and finding out that she would receive no refund, but only a credit, thought it might be just as well to have the gift itself in the house, in case he should ever come by, although she had no intention of inviting him. The last few times she saw him, she felt something she was sure was almost affection for him. At the news of his death, she wept for an hour. It was not until the next morning she realized it was from relief.

Being glad somebody was dead made her feel almost as guilty as what she had done when he was alive. Her behavior since the incident with Harry Bell had been above reproach, even in her own mind. The marriage to the Count had received considerable publicity, but all of it in good taste. There were countless parties, charity balls and premieres at which they were the handsomest and most glittering celebrants, raising a great deal of money for the very best causes. None of it was phony: they were very happy together, on the few occasions yearly when they were both in the same city at the same time. Since their discovery of their happy mutual quirk, they even delighted each other sexually. For the rest of it, she surrounded herself with amiable and talented fairies, all of them, in their own words, "gifted," and in her ears incredibly articulate. There could not be the slightest suspicion about her, publicly or privately. Her escorts demanded nothing more of her than that she be beautiful at all times, which there was no longer any doubt she was, even in the eyes of the most captious magazines; she made no demands of them at all, except that they be brilliant, and not nance too much in public. She dressed magnificently, and paid retail for all her clothes, in spite of the fact that her escort was often the designer of the gown she was wearing. In all, she was a symbol of her times, there could be no doubt about that, especially in her own eyes. There was no one living who could say a bad word about her. Especially now that Harry was dead.

She was so overcome with fondness for him, she realized how very much she had hated his being alive, and that made her feel guilty. That she had missed the funeral was irreparable and tragic, but as she discussed it with Maggie by phone, the important thing was to get back to New York as quickly as possible. It was not that she considered her summer-stock tour a failure. She had played three tents in an in-the-round presentation of *The Student Prince;* and of her performance *Women's Wear Daily* wrote that she lacked grace and majesty even in comparison to Mario Lanza. The critique did not bother her, she assured Maggie. What bothered her was that Harry hadn't had a proper send-off. Not that Maggie's wake hadn't been a huge success, Diane was quick to add, but she wanted to be a part of his final farewell. It just wouldn't seem right to her otherwise; she would never forgive herself. She left it up to Maggie to be her advance squad, and start rounding up the people so they would plan on being at Southampton the following weekend.

"I'd call from here, Mag, you know that, but I think it would be too degrading to get a long-distance call from Steubenville, or wherever I am."

"Love to call for you," Maggie said. "I have a madly empty day. Anyone in particular you want to invite?"

"The usual people. And anyone fun and attractive you think ought to be there. Oh, and of course people that were especially fond of Harry."

"Isn't that funny. I never even knew you were."

"I was what?" Diane said.

"Fond of Harry. I didn't even know you knew him that well."

"I didn't know him well," Diane said. "But he was one of our people. You didn't have to be that close to a Viking to load up his ship for the big launch, did you, sweet?"

"What a wonderful idea," Maggie said. "Will we have a fire? Algernon would love that, fire is so purifying, shall I speak to the fire commissioner at Southampton, it shouldn't be too troublesome if we keep it on the water, what? Are you on the ocean or the bay side, I forget?"

"Don't make any plans for the program," Diane said. "Just get the people. If you don't mind."

"How could I mind," Maggie said. "It's the least I can do for Harry."

"Yes," said Diane. "I feel exactly the same way."

According to the card on the revolving door of Bonwit Teller, the fragrance in the air was Madame Rochas, but Louise was too nervous to smell it. She had never before bought a dress for over two hundred dollars, even reduced, as she had just done. But she had told the saleslady she was going to Diane Trejinska's party on the Island, and the saleslady, only mildly impressed, explained that Maggie Bolin had bought a twenty-five-hundred-dollar Norell in the department only that morning, and for the same party. So she and the saleslady had both agreed she had to buy the pink beaded dress. She would just have to make financial sacrifices in areas that didn't count, like Dr. Ehrens.

As the gates opened to the ground floor, Louise tried to look as comfortable as the bare-armed deeply tanned matrons, standing coolly in crisp pastel linens and chambrays. They could afford their semi-smiling detachment. They had husbands to pay their bills if they overstepped themselves. Louise did not. Because Harry, poor Harry, had died too soon.

Naturally she was not pretending to herself that she believed it; but it was a fun role to play. As long as she was enjoying the role, she might as well dress for it. The morning's extravagance was justified and dismissed. A smile pulled at the corner of Louise's mouth, and quite inadvertently her face assumed the detached complacency of the rest of the ladies stepping out of the elevator.

As she passed the perfume counter, Louise heard someone call her name. She turned and saw Maggie Bolin, who was hunched over a saleslady's wrist, sniffing. Maggie was dressed in white lace culottes with a white body stocking on underneath. It was probably a very pretty outfit, but as the body stocking was turning an indeterminate yellow, it was very difficult to tell for sure.

"Help me," Maggie said. "I can't decide."

"What do you want?"

"I'm mad for the Rochas, that's what's in the air-conditioning smell, but I'm so used to Fleurs de Rocaille and Joy, I'm not sure it would be divine on me, what? The Rochas is on my left wrist and the Joy is on hers, and the Rocaille is here. What do you think?"

"I'm not very good on smells," Louise said. "Taste and vision, fine, but smells not so good."

"Try," Maggie said. "What do you think?"

"I like them all," Louise said. "Why don't you get all three?"

"You're joking," Maggie said. "I can't possibly afford all of them."

Louise said nothing. She just stood there and smelled while Maggie sniffed and thought and finally decided on one of the bottles. The saleslady went to have it wrapped. "Stay with me," Maggie said. "I've got to meet Algernon at the Plaza, have you met him yet, well, you'll meet him at Diane's party, you are coming? I'm sorry about the last-minuteness of the invitation but I've been madly disorganized. I'm so glad you're coming to the party, it'll help get your mind off things, but of course that isn't until day after tomorrow. Why don't you come with me to the Plaza and meet Algernon. You'll adore him, he's a saint, you know, he was a great friend of Harry's." Maggie squeezed her hand. "I'm sorry I didn't know how deeply you were involved. Chet's told me all, I would've tried to make things a little easier for you at the funeral. Has it been very ghastly?"

"Not really," Louise said. "I suppose it's been about the way these things are."

"I've been very lucky in a way, I suppose, I've never had to bury anyone dear to me except my father, and that was inevitable I suppose, but never someone I was going to marry, except if you count Gerald. But then I don't know if I would have gone through with marrying him, it was one of those crazy college romances but I think I might have had too much sense to go through with it. I don't know. But this must all be so awful for you. Poor Harry. You would have made him so happy."

"I like to think so."

"But it's true." Maggie squeezed her hand. "You will come to lunch with me and Algernon, won't you, it's only a block to the Plaza, and I know he'll be able to help you."

"You're sweet to offer, but I don't really need help."

"Everybody needs help," Maggie said. "Even me. Algernon knows that, he's one of the few people in the world I ever let know that, and he hasn't used that information and vulnerability for any other purpose than my own flowering love. Not for Algernon, really, that was all over between us some time ago, but he has helped me to grow inside, and all through myself with love in general, and I think he could be enormously helpful to you."

"I think I ought to go back to the office," Louise said. "I'd like to get a few columns ahead so I don't have to rush back from the weekend."

"You can go back to the office after lunch. First you'll meet Algernon."

The saleslady handed Maggie her receipt and her package, and they left the store. When they were a half block from Bonwit's, Maggie took Louise's arm, and giggled. "I have a

98

present for you." She opened her purse, and pulled out a two-ounce bottle of Rochas. "I want you to have this."

"Maggie, you didn't."

"Of course I did. I do it all the time. You mustn't be shocked, there's actually a great deal of morality involved. I only do it in the places that overcharge me, where I spend a great deal of money. Sort of a free-enterprise Robin Hood, I like that, what? Doesn't that strike you as fair?"

"It strikes me as funny," Louise said. "I know that much. I've never considered stealing anything in my life."

"Why how silly of you, darling, that must be because you've never been easy with money, you must learn to be, what? You would have been terribly rich when you married Harry no matter what everybody says about how stingy he was to his actual wives, and then you would have had absolute license to be light-fingered."

"I don't think I could," Louise said. "Not that I'm criticizing you, I don't want you to think that. But I couldn't do it."

"Don't be such a prig, I bought a Norell dinner dress there this morning, and you wouldn't believe what I paid for it, they won't be hurt by a little gift of Rochas. Here, I'm giving it to you," Maggie said.

"Thank you, but I just couldn't accept it."

"For God's sake," Maggie said, and put it in her hand. "Of course you can. It isn't as though I were after your virtue. Come. Cross with the light. There's Algernon."

The fountain in front of the Plaza, protected with zeal by the various committees devoted to the salvation of attractive New York landmarks, pitifully dwarfed by the superstructures that were taking over all but the southeast corner of Fifth Avenue and Central Park South, did not appear in the summer afternoon as exactly the oasis of quiet and beauty its defenders proclaimed. The water spurting from the top of the statue at the fountain's center blended grayly into the ancient smoke-faded stone, and in the round pool at the statue's base paper cups and dead cigarettes floated. The colorless pigeons that strutted in the square seemed to find it a pleasant sanctuary, as did the New Yorkers and out-of-towners who sat in an erratically ordered circle around the asphalt wall edging the pool. People paused for a moment of respite and solitude, their arms barely six inches away from the shoulders of the person next to them. But it was, after all, someplace to sit down in the hub of Manhattan. The park just across the way, filled as it was with lush green beauty, still carried the dark promise of incident, even in the daytime, so some preferred to stay away.

On the edge of the pool a man sat, stretching his face up to an obscured sun, his eyes closed against the radiance that would have been forthcoming were it not for the clouds. To anyone who noted the deep color in his cheeks, it might have seemed he was simply reinforcing his tan. He was a slim man, well built, and if his posture had been good, he might have appeared quite tall, even sitting as he was with one leg crossed under his buttocks. He was dressed neatly, if somewhat too youthfully for his years, in a blue cotton knit pullover, open at the throat, and blue chinos, tight in the hips, made all the tighter by the enormous erection to the left of his fly. He opened his eyes and smiled. Then he picked up a discarded copy of the *New York Times* and placed it across the obstreperous bulge on his lap.

Maggie Bolin made her way across the square, laughing with delight as her sandaled feet avoided the pigeons. "They've gotten so bold, Louise, isn't it wonderful, what? they don't even fly away anymore, they've started to understand people."

"Any messages?" Louise said to the pigeons.

But if Maggie heard, she didn't think it was as funny as Louise meant it to be. "Look, there's Algernon," Maggie said. "Have you ever seen such a blue serenity in the midst of ugliness? Isn't he wonderful-looking, I've always thought he was wonderful-looking, isn't he?

"I didn't think he was so old."

"He's not, darling, he's only thirty-seven but inner exploration takes something out of one, what?"

"I don't know," Louise said.

"You will," Maggie skipped over the the man in blue at the fountain's edge and squeezed him warmly around the neck.

"Careful," he said as the paper was almost knocked from his lap by Maggie's ebullient greeting. "I'm right in the middle of something. I don't want to lose my place."

"Nonny darling," Maggie said. "I want you to meet my friend Louise. Louise Felder, this is my dearest friend, Algernon Reddy."

"Excuse me if I don't get up," Algernon said. "I have a crick in my back."

"That's perfectly all right." Louise extended her hand and smiled at him. The very pronounced strength of his bone structure, especially his cheekbones, almost Slavic in their prominence, emphasized by contrast, the watery grayness of his eyes. Louise had always assumed that if a person were fortunate enough to have a strong, square chin, there was no way his mouth could seem weak. She was wrong, she could see that now. The overriding impression he gave was that of a carved stone statue wrought by a sculptor who had run out of patience by the time he got to the features.

"I've heard so much about you, Louise." He paused, as if to listen to what he was saying. "Louise. Felder, did you say? She is the one, Maggie?"

"She's the one," Maggie said.

"Dear girl," he brought his lips briefly down to her hand, and raised his eyes. "Soul child."

"Oh, come on," Louise said.

"That is what you are, and that is what I call you. Don't be embarrassed. You weren't embarrassed to love Harry Bell. And he wasn't embarrassed to love you, I know that. Harry was ashamed of love, almost all his life. But it didn't shame him to love you, and his values were first forming just before he died. He could have only loved you as he did, at that time of his life, because you were a soul child."

"Harry was a very down-to-earth man," Louise said. "I appreciate the compliment, but I'm afraid you're overstating it a little."

"I didn't say that soul contradicted body, Louise. You mustn't be confused by outdated doctrine. Purity exists in a whorehouse, every writer knows that."

"I don't remember there being a whorehouse in your novel," Louise said.

"My book was an allegory. It didn't need a whorehouse. The world is a whorehouse."

"Such profundity so early in the day," Louise said, smiling. "And in front of the Plaza."

Algernon Reddy laughed. "You mustn't be embarrassed by emotion, soul child, even if it comes to you on Fifth Avenue. Come, Maggie, we'll all have lunch, and we'll talk of ordinary things so our Louise will feel comfortable."

"That's very thoughtful of you," Louise said.

"The basket is right over there, under that bench. Will you get it, Maggie, my leg is still a little stiff. Come Louise, you sit here beside me, I'll spread my newspaper so you don't dirty your dress on the stone. No, come to think of it the print might come off and that's harder to get off. You won't mind sitting on the stone, it's only a little dusty?"

"I thought we were lunching at the Plaza," Louise said.

"But we are, darling," Maggie said, bringing over the basket. "Isn't it wonderful? Nonny had my cook roast some little guinea hens, and we've got potato salad Niçoise, and white wine in a thermos. What could be more heavenly? Isn't it heavenly, Nonny?"

"Heavenly and earthly," he said.

101

"I really don't want to horn in on your picnic," Louise said.

"Are you embarrassed?" Algernon smiled at her, so deeply that for a moment all the flaccidity and looseness seemed to have been pulled into the crevices of his face, and swallowed up by them, leaving only the fine flint covering of his bone structure. "Are you that frightened of indulging your wonderful appetites anywhere else but in the privacy of your own kitchen."

"I'm just not hungry," Louise said.

"Well, that's honest." Algernon reached into the basket and pulled out a small foil packet. "Unfortunate, but honest." He unwrapped the small, neatly trussed bird, and pulled at its orange-coated wings. "Apricot glaze," he said. "Apricots and wine and bitters. There's nothing more wonderful in the external world, except love, of course."

Maggie spread the tablecloth covering the basket on the walk in front of Algernon, sat down cross-legged at his feet, and started wolfing down pieces of hen which she ripped loose with her fingers, wiping her hands in little staccato motions on the cloth underneath her as she ate. Then she licked her fingers, as hungrily as she had eaten the game, and resumed ripping again. The potato salad she ladled into her mouth with the lid of the thermos, and after licking the lid, and her fingers again, started back on the bird. Louise watched, fascinated.

"Louise can't understand your appetite, Maggie," Algernon said. "I watch her face and I see that she has no understanding of true zest."

"I'm hungry," Maggie said, swilling some of the wine into her mouth. "I hope you'll forgive my not waiting." A piece of hen escaped her teeth and fell onto her chin with the words. "Oops."

"Divine," Algernon said. "Heretically divine."

"It looks fantastic," Louise said.

"Eat," Algernon said. "Aren't you even a little hungry?"

"I suppose I am, vaguely," Louise said. "I'm usually vaguely hungry."

"We are all of us vaguely hungry," said Algernon.

"I never am," Maggie said, licking her fingers. "If I have the slightest appetite, I eat."

"You can afford to," Louise said, and reached for a piece of chicken. "You have such a great figure."

"Really? I never used to think so. I was always embarrassed about my breasts."

"Sit down, Louise," Algernon said, smiling.

"I really prefer eating standing up," Louise started to say, and then sat down beside Algernon.

"We must have Louise down to the Function Center, mustn't we? Perhaps cloaked in freedom and anonymity she can afford to have a complete hen."

"I'll have another piece," Louise said.

"And some wine?" said Algernon.

"I'm a bad drinker, I better not. Not in the noonday sun."

"Have you always been so guarded," he said.

"It's the way Harry would have wanted me to be," Louise said.

"But my darling, you're wrong." Algernon was tapping her arm with a leg. "He was getting freer all the time. He very much wanted to bring you to the Function Center."

"He told you that?" She wanted to laugh in his face, to throw back her head the way really womanly women did in the movies and let out a great Mercouri-like guffaw, to show that she had been part of and seen life. But she did not have a first-rate laugh. She had practiced a good deal in front of her mirror, but it still came up more hollow and annoying than lusty. She had compromised by developing a campy, semi-spoken "Tee-hee," delivered usually in her tiny Lulu voice, so everyone would know she was kidding. "Tee-hee" would hardly do now; and if she knew she was kidding, that was enough.

"He said the Function Center was a revelation," Algernon said. "Naturally he would have brought you in time."

"Naturally," Louise said. "One more sadness that he had to pass so soon."

"I have a wonderful idea." Algernon closed the foil packet around the cleanly picked bones. "Why don't we close up shop on the picnic and I'll take you and Louise to the Museum of Modern Art and buy you coffee and dessert in the garden. You don't object to open-air lunching, Louise, surely you could eat off lovely plates in a garden freckled with statues . . ."

He started to get up, and a slight wince crossed his face. He sat down again and patted the *New York Times* on his lap. "On second thought, do you mind if we take a rain-check? I've still got this funny pain in my foot."

"All right, another time," Louise said. "I hope you feel better."

"Oh I will, I will, I assure you. It'll go away. It always does."

He had not always been called Nonny by those particularly close to him. In the old days, around the Acapulco circuit, Algernon had been known as "Ever" Reddy, because of his ability to get it up as quickly as a battery turned on. The slightest touch or even a suggestion of carnality resulted in the instant ability to perform sexually, which in combination with his extraordinary equipment, made him almost legendary on a local scale. The fact that he did not enjoy sex, that he never achieved orgasm, was beside the point, as it eventually became to the ladies who were the objects of his affliction, as he called them, sometimes adding the tune. He also made jokes about being hoist on his own petard, knowing that he was the only one of his group who had trafficked enough with words to understand the root came from breaking wind and bouncing, the word itself was linked to exploding, and as that was exactly what he could not accomplish in the bedroom or indeed on fiesta floors, the expression was far from apropos.

His activities went beyond the mere exploits of a swordsman, and even past the usual definition of satyriasis. He could service the divorcées, the ingenues, the renegade ladies and the locals with dispatch and when it was called for, discretion. That he never achieved orgasm was for a while troublesome to him. But after he had spent some time in analysis and hypnotherapy, resulting in little or no greater understanding of his problem, he decided it would be easier, as he said at the time, to fuck everyone, including his doctor.

The last, of course, was by way of a joke. There was nothing homosexual about Algernon Reddy, as almost all the ladies in Acapulco could tell you. The men could tell you that too: he was a great favorite among them, and hardly a day began at the beach club or on the golf course without a summation of "Ever" Reddy's exploits of the previous evening. He was extremely generous about sharing accounts of his adventures with them. Indeed, if such was their bent, he was more than willing to share the adventures themselves, as he did several times when Rolf Orlovsky's yacht anchored in Acapulco, and Reddy was a guest on board.

All of his performances did not have to do with the sex act itself; once he served himself up on an hors d'oeuvres tray which he passed around a cocktail party given by an expatriate movie star, garnished with parsley and rosebud radishes in between the Italian salami and deviled eggs. If the Senator's daughter had not reached without looking, bringing him to immediate attention, the merriment might have continued for hours. As it was, it became the best story of the season, which only newcomers and old friends dared to suggest was apocryphal.

Old friends were mostly those from the academic community who had not seen him for a long time: professors and other writers in residence as he had been, who were unaware of his problem. As an undergraduate he had assumed he was preoccupied with sex as most healthy young men were. As a graduate student he had been married, and attributed his prowess cum failure to his wife Rosalind's coldness, to his need to subdue her all the while understanding he never could, because it was in her nature to be a castrating bitch, and this was his nature's way of abhorring the would-be vacuum. When he took mistresses, his failure to come was put down to middle-class guilt because he was being unfaithful to his wife. It had always been easier to think in terms of a temporary problem, all the more so as the erection would disappear as soon as he became deeply engrossed in something, which was probably why his first novel ran to over a thousand pages.

His reception by the critics had been excellent. Dealing with a futuristic prisoner-of-war camp, in which too much creature comfort, and television-filled leisure time, was the means for vitiating all free will, the novel followed the one man who struggled to escape his captors, robots programmed by IBM. It was viewed as a fresh indictment of modern-day society and so-called authority, and enjoyed a moderate commercial success. The critical pronunciamento that he was one of the few novelists of the Fifties about whose future one felt curiosity ensured him of a seat at a good university. Many were offered, and one was accepted at a private college in Carmel, close enough to Big Sur for Reddy to spend frequent weekends and unscheduled leaves of absence at the thinning feet of the Mahatma of modern sexual letters, Sheldon Davis.

Sheldon was extremely helpful to him. Sitting on a bar stool in Nepenthe, an inn jutting from the edge of a cliff road designed for those with a death wish, he explained that America was crap, critical appraisal was crap, and the modern preoccupation with sexual exploits was crap. While he talked, a seventeen-year-old junior from Berkeley licked his big toe, and his wife did a bare-topped barefooted tarantella on the terrace, where the temperature was forty-two degrees. Sheldon paid no attention to either of them; it was Halloween, the big night at Nepenthe, and he had more important things to think about.

"What are you going to do with yourself, Reddy boy? I don't want you just hanging around, getting breast-fed on all this crap."

"I don't intend to, Sheldon," Algernon said. "I just have to decide what my next project is."

"You going to stay with that cunt you're married to? Is she still putting it to you about the Catholic doctrine and no divorce? I don't want you drowning in the cesspool of that crap."

"We're splitting," Algernon said. "She keeps pestering me about kids. We may be able to get an annulment. There's some technical hangup."

"Good. You have too much talent to suck at the teat of that crap."

A group of barefooted children in levis and sweatshirts ran through the bar of the inn, shrieking with the pleasure of some unnamed game being played at one o'clock in the morning. "You ought to think about settling here, Reddy. Even the kids are fantastic. You know what's so wonderful about them? Their sexuality. It develops so early. Look at them, you wouldn't even know they were eight years old."

"I don't suppose you would," Algernon said.

Their friendship became all the closer as it had been thirty years since Sheldon had written his last book, and three since Algernon had written his first. Sheldon blamed the fact that critical acceptance had come too late, Algernon the truth that it had come too early. That which the critics expected from Sheldon was a shattering return to lust, and it had been a long time since it interested him. The only type of writing he did not consider crap was scatological, and it was difficult to imagine stretching that out to novel length. As for Algernon, the more he thought and the more he talked and the more he gave himself over to the study of modern communication, the more evident it became to him that the novel was dead, and the future of literature was in the tape recorder.

His view was applauded and shared by the other members of the community, especially those who were also using peyote and marijuana. He was in no way dependent on drugs, or even enamored of them. Of course he enjoyed the colors, the great stretches of time that were pleasurably shortened by their very lengthening, and the vast inner avenues that were open for him to explore. But he did not use it for escape. True, reality was dull and at times unbearable for him, while with the help of peyote and marijuana he could even achieve the orgasm that had so long eluded him, or, just as important, be convinced he had achieved it.

But like everything else, including Big Sur and Sheldon, orgasm was overrated. Eventually he became bored with his role as seer in waiting, as Sheldon gave no sign of being ready to give up what little was left of the ghost. Reddy's ex-wife, having recently been released from the hospital where he had taken her after breaking one of her arms, had decided to press charges, and the Narco police were starting to raid various houses along the cliff coast with regularity. All in all, it seemed a propitious time to move to Mexico. He left with no regret.

For a while he lived in border towns, scratching his food and lodgings from other Americans who fancied themselves fugitives, if not from the law, at least from confining principles. As he moved farther south, into the choicer expatriate communities, his reputation as nonconformist novelist did not serve him in quite as good stead, so it became necessary to call on his other abilities. In short order he was established as "Ever" Reddy, and invited to all the best parties.

The De Revignys made him their official house guest and mascot. As two of the social leaders of Acapulco, they had tired of the usual water-skiing and dinner parties, and had flown in at great expense a two-way mirror which was installed in the ceiling of the guest bedroom. For the duration of Algernon's stay with them, the money they had spent seemed minimal: they had never been so consistently entertained, and, realizing they were being selfish, began inviting friends whose company was once again tolerable, since the floor show, as it came to be called, eliminated the need for conversation.

At the moment Algernon lay under the undiscovered mirror with Gloria Stanley, exquisite star of screen and screen, whom all the world loved because of the passionate nature beneath that darkly angelic face, the lustfulness martialing to break through the little-girl voice. All the world did not suspect what Algernon was finding out for himself: that Gloria had never before had a decent fuck. Algernon gave it to her as often and as well as he could. Above his room, unseen happy faces mirrored their newfound amusement. Gloria, with the right coach, delivered a far better performance than she had thus far exhibited on the screen.

"Isn't that funny," Gloria said, putting her hands up to his chest and stopping his movements. "I fell so self-conscious. As if I were being watched."

"Why should that make you self-conscious?" Algernon said. "You're used to that by now. More Americans per annum etc., top ten rising to top two."

"But it's different knowing they're going to watch you on the screen. Even when the grips watch you on the set, you're not really doing anything . . . intimate. I mean, all the world knew that Bart and I were lovers, but nobody ever saw us do it."

"Did you?"

"Not really. But I was in love with him."

"I heard he was a fairy."

"Oh no. Not Bart. Just frightened. And respectful."

"Like both your husbands."

"Not at all like either of them. Randy was nervous, that was all, he was weak and young, and he worshipped me, so he used to come too fast, that was all, and Lloyd was older than I thought, and he worshipped me too."

"From afar," Algernon said.

"Usually."

"And you, you pitiful romantic, you victim of your own medium, pretty people only do pretty things, you never even noticed they couldn't get it up."

"I noticed," Gloria said, and began to move again under him. "I noticed. But not the way I would now that I know you."

When she was finishing she cried, a fervent little mewing sound like a sound-track recording of a cat, and she touched him, hoisting her hips high and reaching between her legs for his soft underpinnings. She pleaded with him and tried to bring him along with her. "I'm sorry," she said. "I wanted to wait for you."

"No need," Algernon said. "Spring when you feel like springing, that's the point."

"But you didn't come with me. You're still hard."

"Not still," he said. "Again. That's what you do for me, Gloria."

"Really?" she whispered into his neck. "Am I really good?"

"You're wonderful," he said.

"I didn't ask you that. I asked you if I was good."

"You're very good."

"I mean in bed."

"I know what you mean."

"I don't know why I have such a terrible need for approval. Dr. Sharpe says it goes back to being a child actress. I was always terrified that when I got to the awkward stage, my parents wouldn't want me anymore. Of course they always did, because I never had one, but I couldn't know that in advance, could I."

"What?" he said. "I find it a little difficult to follow your pronouns."

"Oh wonderful. You're going to teach me. Everything, I mean."

"If you're a quick study."

"I'm a very quick study," she said. "Can't you tell already, I mean how quickly I've come along. Is that really for me? Is it really all for me."

"All for you, America's softheart," he said, and entered her again.

The second time it was over for her he rolled quickly onto

his stomach and panted, assuring her it had been equally wonderful for him. "Are you sure," she said, and tried to reach between his legs.

"Don't do that, I'm sore."

"Did I hurt you?" she said. "Did I do anything to hurt you?"

"No, goddammit, but don't try to check me out."

"I'm sorry," she said. "It's just that I really care about you, and I couldn't bear it if you weren't getting as much out of it as I . . . as me?"

"As I. It all goes back to your terrible need for approval. You need verification all the time. I'm sure Dr. . . . what's his name would tell you that."

"What do you think he'd tell you?" Gloria said.

"I couldn't care less."

"Maybe you should, Algernon. Maybe he could help you. He is my personal psychiatrist, you know, and he worships me."

"From afar?"

"You don't have to be fusty . . ."

"Feisty . . ."

"But maybe there's something wrong if I can't satisfy you."

"Because you would have to satisfy anybody? Is that why all your men have been impotent and fags?"

"Please don't turn against me," she said, and her voice was very soft. "Please don't be antagonistic just because I care and want to help."

"Help what? What is there to help?"

"Well there must be something wrong. I know it could be me, I've been eating myself up so these past few weeks that it could be me. Maybe it all goes back to my need for approval, maybe that's why I have the feeling someone is watching, like you were judging me even while we were in bed together, I'm aware of that possibility, I examine my own motives, honestly I do. If I was as selfish as you think I am, I wouldn't care in the least, you know I wouldn't, because it's been wonderful for me. In bed, I mean."

"I know what you mean."

"But there must be something wrong that you've never gotten rid of your hard-on."

"What a beautiful language is American," Algernon said. "What an inspiration to the soul, the ear, and to the loins. I have a hard-on, so I must get my rocks off because I'm horny and need to get laid. What a feast of imagery. Is it a wonder we're a nation of lovers."

"I'm sorry," she said. "I was only trying to show you how you've liberated me."

"Go fuck yourself. And other love words." He put his face into the pillow and snored.

"Avoiding the issue doesn't mean it doesn't exist. The issue I mean."

"I know you mean the issue. But the issue of my cock, the issue of my sperm, or the issue of my issues's issue?"

"You don't have to try to fight me with words."

"To issue or not to issue, that is the issue."

"Putting me on the defensive isn't going to solve anything."

"What is?" He lifted his head and rested it on his elbow. "Tell me the solution, my princess. After all the years of enlightenment and study to which you've devoted yourself."

"You can make fun of me as much as you want . . ."

"Thank you." He kissed her nose.

". . . but I still think Dr. Sharpe could help you. He is my personal psychiatrist you know."

"I know, you told me . . ."

"And he'd be happy to fly down here and talk to you . . ."

"With all expenses paid?"

"Of course. That's always been our understanding. Why not? It's deductible." Gloria smiled and touched his lips. "I don't want to do anything to degrade you. Honest to God I don't. Not after everything you've done to uplift me."

"Literally." He reached between her thighs.

"Stop."

"But I thought you liked it that way. Uplifted, I mean."

"I do. You know I do. But not now. Please. I'm trying to be serious."

"So am I, lady. So am I."

"No, please. Don't . . . Al, don't, oh don't, please. Not . . . no, I won't let . . . not until you promise. Promise . . . oh promise you'll at least . . . oh, please. At least . . . talk to him."

In the end he agreed to meet with Dr. Sharpe, whom Gloria had flown to Acapulco. After two hour-sessions in between cocktail parties, during which Dr. Sharpe at least established that Algernon Reddy had no wish to marry Gloria, making him selfless enough to be worth saving, they agreed that Algernon should continue therapy with the prominent hypnoanalyst Harry Krieger as a parting gift from Gloria. Krieger's specialty, when he had been located in Los Angeles, was weight-reduction and hysteria. Now that he was settled in Acapulco, his main practice was alcoholism. But he was glad to take Algernon on as patient.

"Tell me the first thing that comes into your mind," Dr. Krieger said.

"Charlatan," said Algernon Reddy.

"I haven't started yet."

"Are you trying to inhibit me, Doctor?"

"My colleague George Sharpe says you have a problem with impotence."

"Hardly." Algernon laughed. "Not a bad pun, really, it's a shame you have no humor."

"There are all kinds of impotence, Mr. Reddy. Because a man has a superficial tumescence does not mean he is able to achieve fulfillment."

"How delicately you put it, Doctor. You must have been reading Harold Robbins."

"Why are you so hostile, Mr. Reddy? Don't you want to be helped?"

"No. And if I did, I don't think you could help me."

"Then why did you agree to come?"

"Are we speaking sexually or socially."

"Why did you agree to be my patient?"

"It's a scholarship," Algernon said. "I could never turn down a scholarship."

"Academically oriented," Dr. Krieger said. "All the world must serve as your diploma."

"How perceptive, Doctor. Maybe that's the solution. A cap and gown for my whang."

"I didn't mean to sound glib."

"Then maybe you ought to think about what you say before you say it."

"Are *you* trying to inhibit *me,* Mr. Reddy?"

"Somebody should. A person could do a lot of harm jumping to such tumescent solutions."

They both realized that direct talk and word association would be pointless. Krieger tried a few sessions of hypnosis, but Algernon was a difficult subject. For a while they experimented with narco-synthesis, but as relaxed as Reddy was under the influence of sodium pentothal, once awake, he was totally resistant to the thought that the words on the tape recorder were truths. There was no denying the voice was his, but the words were false, he was sure.

"Even that business about your father being a faggot?" Dr. Krieger said.

"I just said that to throw you, because I wanted to see you dancing. My father was six feet three, and he weighed two hundred and forty pounds."

"And we've never seen a big fat fairy. All the wee people have blond hair and blue eyes, and they carry a wand, like in Walt Disney."

"I said it to confuse you," Reddy said. "Go fuck yourself."

"The usual form of punishment in your mind. Coitus is an

obscene act, the grosser part of the obscenity being that a woman would want it, the man pummels her with a literal battering ram, refusing to ejaculate, because that would be a form of surrender, losing his manhood, and making him a weakling like his father."

"Why don't we go back to the Walt Disney parallel, and regard it as my wand."

"Exactly," Kreiger said. "You're beginning to see."

"Oh for Christ's sake," Reddy said, and put his head in his hands.

After a few more weeks Krieger agreed with Reddy that further narco-synthesis would be a waste of time. "The important thing is that you be aware of the truths as they're being revealed."

"Huzzah," Algernon said.

"You must try to control your resistance or I'll never be able to help you."

"Have you ever really helped anyone, Doctor? I mean, beside that vast army of fatties who substituted the oral compulsion of talking for the oral compulsion of eating."

"Now who's being glib, Mr. Reddy."

"I am."

"Exactly."

"Do I get a gold star for knowing the answer?"

"That gold star is very important to you, isn't it?"

"Go . . ." he stopped himself.

"It just so happens that I am the only American doctor who had eighty percent success with obesity cases. I had the only foolproof solution. I used to tell my patients they could eat anything they wanted, only they shouldn't swallow."

"Brilliant," Algernon said.

"It just so happens I was making a joke. You insist on regarding me as humorless, I was showing you otherwise."

"Well you certainly did show me otherwise. If there's anything wise about you, it's assuredly other."

"I don't have to put up with this, you know."

"Of course you do. You're being paid."

"I could get other patients."

"Not who'd pay you the full forty, like Gloria. Not in *los dólares*. Why are you being so defensive, Doctor? Surely my judgment isn't important to you."

"Of course it isn't."

"It just so happens, as you always say, that I have incredible respect for you. That's one of the most astonishing dictums I've ever heard. Eat everything, only don't swallow."

"It happens to work, even if it is a joke," Kreiger said.

"I believe you. So why can't we apply the same dictum to me. Fuck everyone, only don't shoot."

"Very funny."

"But I was being serious," Algernon said. "After all, it is a terrible problem. Aren't you glad you don't have it, Doctor?"

"You needn't sound so contemptuous, Mr. Reddy. The contempt is because you think you're kidding, you think I'd really like to have your problem, relentless tumescence . . ."

"And unrelenting pussy, wouldn't you just hate to dig into that."

"I certainly wouldn't enjoy it if I couldn't ejaculate."

"I don't know how you could enjoy it at all if you think about it in those terms."

"Thinking about it is different from experiencing it."

"You bet your ass, old thinker."

"All right, so you've proved yourself superior to me, as you're superior to all men. You have the weapon, but you never lose your ammunition. Superman. Just like the hero in your book. The only man alive with the *cojones* to resist the institution, to fight authority. What wish fulfillment, what an idealization of yourself and your problem, Reddy."

"*Cojones,*" Algernon said. "How quaint, and how delicate, Doctor. I'm tickled to death you didn't say scrotum and penis. *Cojones*. You are cute. You must have been reading Hemingway."

"Is it a threat to you, my reading these other people?"

"I think it's a threat to you that you can't say balls."

"We're not here to discuss my problem."

"What a shame. I think I could really help you."

The second month of Algernon's treatment, Dr. Krieger began trying mescaline. He had read about the experiments that were being conducted in Redwood City, and although he did not have full clinical details, he thought hallucinogens might be the answer. Algernon was more than receptive to the idea. His use of marijuana and peyote had been sporadic since living in Acapulco, because of the demands of his social schedule, and only when there was a big party in which everybody blew did he allow himself hashish.

"You understand there's no reason to be afraid," Dr. Krieger said as he injected the needle into his arm. "If at any point you feel it's becoming too much for you, let me know and I'll bring you back immediately. I've got the chlorpromazine. Don't be afraid of anything, no matter how convincing the hallucination. Remember I'm here."

"That's the only part of it that makes me nervous," Algernon said.

By the fourth mescaline session, Algernon was masturbating openly, and by the fifth, Krieger was happy to report, he had observed an emission. "As long as I'm helping you, Doctor," Algernon said. "Did you get a nice close look?"

"I take no pleasure from this," Krieger said.

"If you mean you didn't ejaculate I don't believe you."

After the sixth session Krieger increased the dosage and Algernon's fantasies ceased to be sexual in nature. He was able to enter the heart of a rose, and he found inside the soft center petals the gentle nakedness of his mother, her body still warm on the crucifix.

"Oh my God," Algernon wept. "Oh my God."

"Typical Catholic hallucination," Krieger said, once the chlorpromazine had taken effect. "The symbol of the rose, deeply religious in nature."

"Not to mention socio-economic and political."

"Don't try to couch your guilt in contempt. Not after you've revealed yourself so clearly."

"Revealed what?"

"The mother-martyr figure. Surely you can see it. You're angry because you're coming so close."

"You mean ejaculating in such proximity," Algernon said, got up. "You're up to your orifices in feces, Dr. Kreiger," he said, and left the office for the last time.

There was no doubt that Algernon was shaken. To have shared such intimacy with a quack like Krieger was inexcusable, and an insult to the memory of his mother. To screw or even masturbate with people watching was more than tolerable, it was amusing, because it degraded the voyeurs as much as the participants, made them as contemptible as those who committed the vile act. But to have paraded the pale vision of her naked body before the depraved eyes of that pervert was a blasphemy. He could not be sure Krieger hadn't seen. Even as the drug was wearing off completely, he could not shake from his mind the conviction that the doctor had been inside his brain with him, and had seen what was in the center of the rose. He was deeply ashamed, not only for the iniquities visited on that saint in her lifetime, but for the indignity to which he had exposed her that day.

He did not intend to violate his inner privacy again. Mescaline could be had, and easily, without a fraud for a connection.

After a time, Acapulco ceased to amuse him. He had known about the two-way mirror for several months, ever since he had become aware of light footfalls and distant subdued giggling, and explored the locked room above his own, bribing the maid for the master key. Even stopping his activities in medias res and turning over to stick out his tongue, or something more insulting, at the ceiling gave him little pleasure. For a while he tried fornicating while under the influence of mescaline, but he usually got sidetracked on a pleasanter, sadder fantasy if he used it alone, and if the partner of the moment were using it too, reactions were unpredictable. Either the women cried because they thought he despised them, or they became convinced that Algernon was not actually servicing them, or some other hallucination with which he could not deal, interfering as it did with his own fine time. Eventually he began receiving complaints from upstairs as to the quality of his performances. He told them they were all freaks and paranoids and they should take a flying jack off Dr. Krieger. Then he thanked them for their hospitality, and went down the Yucatan peninsula.

He did not enjoy Merida: like all one-time havens in the throes of being discovered by tourists it was rife with new corruption. The Meridans did not have the ancient, splendid degeneracy Algernon had found during a collegiate foray to Rome: the Italians had been taking advantage of tourists for so long that they practiced it as art: but the Meridans, like the Spaniards, were new at the game, and childishly obvious, with none of the grace of the Romans. It was innocence in the process of being lost. Algernon, for one, did not care to watch.

It was on his way north, trying to get back to Acapulco that he reencountered Ladslo Sillis, who had once occupied the anthropology chair at Carmel. Ladslo was conducting some research into the habits of the Otomi Indians, who had been doing some remarkable thing with, as he put it, local bacillus. He invited Algernon to join his party, and as Algernon had no place better to go, he was pleased to accept.

With all that he had heard about the mushrooms, and all he had experienced with drugs, Algernon was not prepared for the actuality. The first time he ate them he felt a euphoria beyond the most manic reaches of his experience and imagination. He was shot into his own vein, and his arteries became the yellow brick road, and he hopped and skipped along it as he had never done when he was the age of Judy Garland. It was a very pretty picture, with every stripe of a fifteen-color rainbow breaking into a song, and no wicked witch to threaten the excursion. He lay on his back and watched his own troublesome root grow skyward, higher and higher until he climbed it like his private beanstalk and got into heaven, where the giant was no larger than six feet three and weighed no more than two hundred and forty pounds, not so big for a giant, especially as he was a sissy and could

115

be pistol-whipped with a beanstalk root into giving up the golden goose, who wore a rose around her neck, inside which was a crucifix, hanging in which was (thank God) only Jesus.

"I can see into my own coal-black heart," he was sure he said aloud. But if Ladslo heard, at the far side of the starlit tree-ringed circle of mud in the center of the universe, he gave no sign.

"My own coal-black heart," Algernon said, as it broke and splintered into heaving, ventilating chunks, which, when penetrated, yielded a perfect shining diamond. "I'm pure," he said, and wept for the priest he should have become.

"I saw God," he said to Ladslo late that night.

"Perhaps you only think you saw God."

"I saw him. He was inside me."

"Not a new hallucination. Not even a new religious philosophy."

"But it wasn't a hallucination. It was truth."

"I hope so, Algernon. These drugs are very powerful. Sometimes pleasant, sometimes horrible."

"So is the truth."

After that, there were those around Acapulco who said that Algernon Reddy, on his return, had become a bore. True, he still participated in an occasional party, house-guesting aboard Orlovsky's yacht when it was anchored in the harbor. Some people insinuated that was only to suck Orlovsky in so he would put up some cash for experimentation and chemical manufacture of the stuff Reddy was so whacked up on and maybe a program to bring it to the states. Orlovsky wasn't about to become involved, but through Orlovsky Algernon met Harry Bell. Harry had read a review of Algernon's novel, and the cover copy, and he was very impressed with his talent. But what really impressed him was what he had heard about his ability in the sack.

"I heard you take on maybe four, five ladies inside an hour," Harry said on the verandah of the racquet club.

"They're putting you on, Harry."

"Yeah, well, people exaggerate."

"What they meant was I can take a lady maybe four, five times."

"Inside an hour?"

"It depends how much they want."

"You bee-essing me? Never bee-ess a bee-esser."

"I could show you."

"No. I'm not a watcher. I'm a doer. Four times an hour? No ess."

"No ess at all."

116

"How old are you?" Harry said.

"Thirty-three."

"That's not so young," Harry said sadly, his eyes on his tiny hands. "It's not like you're seventeen."

"Not like it at all. It's got nothing to do with age."

"How do you explain it then? You always been able to do it like that?"

"Only since I made my discovery, with the Otomi Indians."

"Cut it out, Reddy. Orlovsky told me you've been touting some mushroom stuff. You want to be a weird-head, do it, but don't try to sell me a bill of goods."

"Nobody's selling you anything, Harry."

"I'm not interested in becoming a junkie, or supporting some junkie project."

"It's not junk, Harry. There's nothing habit-forming about it. It's a wonderful experience that frees a man's inner consciousness, and helps him explore what he never knew was there."

"I'm not interested. I got nothing to hide from. Reality has been very good to me, I like it."

"It also helps you get hard."

"No shit," Harry said.

"Not even bee-ess," said Algernon.

As it turned out, Harry was afraid to try it after the first time, even though Algernon told him he had been in the hay for three hours with a local senorita Algernon had provided. Harry couldn't remember, and he said if he had been doing it, he hadn't gotten any pleasure, as most of the time he was sure he was drowning. But he was grateful for Algernon's efforts in his behalf, and the fact that he had set it up with a girl. Naturally he didn't give money to projects that people couldn't walk around, sit in, listen to, or look at, but he figured it was the least he could do to introduce Algernon to Maggie Bolin, who didn't care what she did with her cash as she hadn't made it, every penny, like he had. Maggie was hanging around Acapulco looking for some junkie musician and she was always giving to looney-bird causes. So Harry figured it was almost, like they said in the musicals, fated to be.

"You've abused yourself, my darling," Algernon said to Maggie. They were lying together naked in the bed of her room at Las Brisas, the door of the cottage flung wide to catch the wind from the sea, and Algernon was pleased to notice that it was over an hour they had lain together that way, and his organ was still at rest. One of the wonderful, lingering side-effects of the drug on him was that it drained almost all his sexual energies so he was free to dance down more important avenues, like raising money for a cause. She was a dear girl, and he was fond of her, and she was so vulnerable while under the influence of the drug that he could bring her around with only the vocal suggestion that he was inside her. "I won't permit you to go on abusing yourself."

"What do you want me to do?"

"I want you to enter the spiritual part of yourself, and find all the beauty that is inside you, and inside the universe. It's all there. Inside you."

"Inside me," Maggie said, and began to writhe on the bed.

"No Maggie, not now."

"But I have to . . . Inside . . . Oh."

"There. Is that better?"

"I love you, Nonny."

"I know you do, sweetheart. And one day, if I get the money to go back to America, and do the work I know now is the only work important enough for me to do, we'll be together."

She started to cry. "You're going away."

"No, sweetheart. I'm here. Right here."

"If you're here, why can't we be together?"

"We are together. But one day soon you'll go away."

"Oh dear," Maggie said, and a tear ran down the side of her face. "Don't make me go."

"I wouldn't dream of making you go. If I could, I wouldn't let you go. But go you must, and I must stay behind."

"Why?"

"Because I have my work."

"Why couldn't you do it in New York?"

"You can't live in New York the way you can here. Not for the money. I'm a poet, a novelist. I can't attend to the freeing of minds and souls if I must worry about my bread."

"I have bread," she said, and giggled. "I mean I really do. All kinds of bread. Real and jazz kind."

"I couldn't take money from a woman."

"But I wouldn't give you money."

"Oh."

"I've got a wonderful old house in New Jersey, it's just sitting there, and you could use it for your headquarters and have people come work with you or live with you, whatever you wanted, and then you wouldn't have to worry, would you, you could do whatever you wanted what? and I could help you spread the word, or have contemplations, whatever it is you want to do, what is it you want to do, Nonny?"

"Good things," he said. "Especially to you."

They came back to New York together in the spring of '64

after Maggie had paved the way with a few small matters like having her attorney pay off Algernon's ex-wife to drop the charges. Their affair continued through the summer. At least Maggie was convinced it continued. She had never felt so sublimely fulfilled, and told him that all the time. Eventually he explained to her that spiritual desires were taking a deeper hold on him. Maggie said she understood.

What she didn't understand, because Algernon never tried to explain it to her, any more than he tried to explain it to himself was that the longer he took the drug, the less sexual ability he demonstrated. He was relieved and proud when, at the end of three years, he hardly ever had an erection at all, and those few remaining only when there was no woman around, and he thought of his mother.

CHAPTER FOUR

JUST before she left for the country Friday afternoon, Louise received a phone call. She picked up the phone without thinking, and answered it herself, not even waiting in silence for her service to intercept. The only people who knew she was in New York, Louise was sure, were those who were supposed to drive her out to Diane Trejinska's party, so the person calling Louise was automatically someone to whom she was willing to talk. She had forgotten about Kate. All week long she had been avoiding Kate's call, knowing that the purpose of the communication was to get her together with the healthy hulk from California, Charley whatever his name was. Kate, poor Kate still tried to make believe that the solution in life was finding somebody; not being somebody, as Louise realized.

"Oh my God," Louise said into the phone. "I just this minute remembered. Oh Christ."

"You just remembered what?"

"It was tonight, wasn't it? I was supposed to come to your house tonight for dinner. I'll kill myself."

"You don't have to do that, Lou," Kate said. "Just slip into something and come over. We don't care how you look."

"It isn't that. I look gorgeous. I'm all honey blond and my suitcase is bursting with things pink and beaded. It's Diane Trejinska's party. I forgot all about it. I mean, I didn't forget all about it, I forgot . . ."

"About coming here," Kate said.

"Oh please don't sound so martyred, Kate, what do you want me to do? Do you want me not to go to Southampton? Do you want me to skip the Trejinska party? Can you hold on a minute while I go inside and open my veins?"

"It's all right," Kate said. "Have a good time."

"Will it ruin your party?"

"It isn't a party," Kate said. "It just would have been the four of us. Us and you and Charley."

"Is he still around? How great can he be if he's been here all week and he's still looking forward to meeting me."

"Have a good time," Kate said.

"Oh stop. Don't be mad at me, please. Lulu's depressed. Where did I go wrong?" Louise said, just before Kate hung up the phone. She started to call her back but the buzzer rang from downstairs and she realized it was Bunyan Reis, with the limousine.

When she got to the street, a tall, dark young man with ringlets peeking from the edge of his chauffeur's cap was waiting for her. "Mees Felder?" he said, tipping cap and ringlets. "Thees way, *per piacere.*"

Bunyan Reis waved tiny butterfly fingers at her from the back seat of the silver car, and motioned her inside. "We're delightfully air-conditioned," he said. "Otherwise I would've lowered the window to greet you. Is that all you've brought, the one suitcase, did Alfredo help you like a good boy?"

"The one suitcase and a little stretch wig," Louise said.

"Oh, wise, wise, the salt breezes of the bay do kink one so, the only disadvantage of the seashore." He touched his own feathered, silver bob and smiled. "I always take two."

"You're looking marvelous, Mr. Reis. I never would have guessed."

"Mr. Randolph cut and set it for me," he said. "I'm not supposed to tell anyone. He only did it as a concession to the lovely Diane, but I know I can trust you. You've met my secretary?" he said as Alfredo got into the front seat.

"Hello, Alfredo."

"*Ciao, bellisima,*" Alfredo said, and grinned white, as he adjusted the rear-view mirror.

"*Avanti,*" said Bunyan. "Leave the city to the poor people and the rioters."

Louise leaned back against the soft pearl-gray upholstery, and did not try to press conversation. Bunyan Reis, even in a strata silted with celebrities, was one of the few creative artists in America whom the public knew almost as well as it did the movie stars, mostly because the stars flocked to know him. His reputation as party-giver, connoisseur of wine, people, and antiques was only slightly eclipsed by his popularity as an artist; his current collection of noncollated collages, composed of sticks, ribbons and gingham fabric from Raggedy Ann dolls from around the world, were being sold at three thousand dollars apiece.

As the car moved onto the East River Drive, Bunyan pressed her hand through her white cotton gloves. "I suppose it's all been a dreadful ordeal. Diane wanted me to be sure to make you feel warm and welcome, she can imagine what you've been through."

"Excuse me?"

"Chet's told us everything." He squeezed her hand again, and she could feel, even through the cotton, that his palms were slightly clammy. "Diane was beside herself, naturally, that she couldn't get to the funeral, and she's asked me to proffer her most heartfelt apologies. But that bastard manager wouldn't let her out of the contract, you know how greedy people are about exploiting the Trejinska name."

"I understand," Louise said.

"That's why she's giving the party, don't you know, to try and give Harry a proper send-off. She's especially happy you can come."

"You're very kind."

"Stop stop stop," said Bunyan Reis. "What else are friends for."

The drive to Southampton took nearly three hours, and during the elapsed time, Louise did her best to speak only when spoken to. It was a bit of a strain for her, but seemed to be none at all for Bunyan Reis, who brought her up to date on world events, art news and gossip over the previous six months.

"But it's flown," he said, as the highway narrowed into tiny country roads, and the car approached the Hamptons. "What a lively companion you are. Shall we go direct to the Trejinskas', or do you want to drop your bag off at Julia's and change? Diane told me to be sure and tell you there's a dressing room and bath set aside for you at her house to freshen up in, so there's no need to stop at Julia's unless you're thirsting for pre-party intimacy with the fashion cunts. We wouldn't want you to miss the thigh of the evening. She's come up with an absolute drumstick, has our Diane. Not that she needs to gloss up her own party list, with those who would kill just to be with her. But I think it is a bit of a coup, what with all the burning, baby burning, don't you know. Hoover Coolidge Gray. How's that?" Bunyan's little gray eyes were glittering, shining through the night darkening the roadway. "He's gotten quite glossy since he stopped being a celebrity athlete who was maybe in music, don't you know. Truth to tell, they've just set a deal for him to write, produce and direct a picture about the first Negro astronaut at Marathon. I only hope it's not too dinge-y." Bunyan giggled. "Have you seen him recently?"

"No," said Louise, not bothering to add that she had also never seen him before.

"He's become very priss-elegant," Bunyan said. "He was the celebrity coon all winter in England, with several of the boys, and he's really started to speak the Queen's English. In every sense of the word." He tittered again. "I understand that vocally he's a ringer for Princess Margaret."

Louise laughed, and he patted her hand. "Still," he said, "it was a little bit of foresight, don't you think, getting him out

122

to the party. Just in case the fires spread to Southampton.
Diane said he can always greet them at the door, in case they
want to break in, to show that we embrace their own. What
say? Direct to Diane's?"

"Direct to Diane's," Louise said.

"*Avanti!*" Bunyan Reis yelled into the front seat. "*Dretti-
simo à la casa de la Contessa, Alfredo mio.* Wasn't that good,
Louise? I love Italian. I'm not sure if I really speak it, but
Alfredo is very kind about not correcting me. Everything
sounds so much more romantic in Italian, don't you know.
And elegant. *La Contessa,* isn't that divine? It makes her
sound so Ava Gardner."

"Isn't she?"

"You don't know her very well, do you?" Bunyan smiled,
and his small pink face bulged with cherubic knobs. "That's
all right, you will."

From the outside, Diane Trejinska's house seemed more
suited to New England than a resort area of Long Island.
White-painted widow's walks fretted three separate gray-shin-
gled steeples, although the front of the house faced away
from the sea. The inside of the house, however, owed little to
tradition or Nathaniel Hawthorne. Remnants of old porticos
and some white wood lacework clung to the ceiling at irregu-
lar intervals, as if old more traditional rooms had been gutted
to make the vast entrance hall that greeted them. The living
room, where several people were already gathering, was completely glassed on the bay side of the house, so Louise could
see through to the tented garden, the crew of bartenders at
white tables, and red-jacketed butlers shucking clams in front
of vast blocks of waist-high ice. The few guests outside, even
from a distance, were dazzling. She followed the butler upstairs.

In her dressing room, she could hear the music seeping dis-
creetly from the tent in the garden below her window. At the
water's edge, some early but apparently heavy drinkers were
maneuvering on the trampoline, to the accompaniment of excited laughter and whoops of approval, mostly from the
trampoline jumpers themselves. In the Christmasy-lit darkness, candle-bulbs of celebration splashing the water-edged
night, Louise could not tell whether the boat anchored at the
end of the dock was a yacht or only a cabin cruiser. She
smiled, and brushed the last strands of honey-blond hair into
soft place across her forehead. Only a cabin cruiser. Poor
things.

She gave herself a final inspection in the mirror. She was
shiny and pink, perhaps not as dazzling as the lights outside,
but with glow enough to qualify. She was ready for them.

123

Coming down the winding marble staircase, the only remnant of the old-fashioned interior that had been, she looked up slowly from heavy lids, as if expecting a swarm of suitors, softly southern-accented, with eager faces. Instead, she saw Hoover Coolidge Gray. "Hello," she said, Miss Scarlett of the new sixties, and extended her soft pink hand toward his dark one. "I'm Louise Felder. You must be Hoover Coolidge."

"Clever guhl," he said, and clicked his heels together. "Howevah did you guess."

The accent, coming through the perfectly spaced and shatteringly white teeth, was astonishing, but Louise did not laugh. He clearly did not mean it to be amusing.

"I'd like a drink," she said. "Won't you come outside with me?"

"Into the gahden? Love to, luv, but I'm waiting for my date."

"Well, then I guess I'll see you outside."

"It would be difficult to miss me, in this crowd."

The damp of the seashore at night was settling around them, Louise could feel as she moved through the white-furnitured glass living room. But once outside, under the vast blue and white striped tent, she felt suddenly warm. She looked up at the vast rainproofed covering and saw radiant heaters speckling the inside of the striped canvas like stars, interspersed with huge hanging chandeliers, brightened with candle-bulbs.

"They're plastic," Rick Flinders said, coming up to her. "They look very convincing, don't they, but it's very tricky, hanging real chandeliers on the inside of a tent. What the hell. Artificial elegance is better than none."

She smiled automatically, and looked at him. Wheat-colored hair fell shaggily across his forehead. The turtleneck silk shirt he wore was the same color as his hair, and the tan mohair jacket blended with the tan deepened since his arrival from Hollywood. In the midst of the deliberately luxurious atmosphere, he looked more the movie star than she remembered him; to her embarrassment, she felt genuinely thrilled.

He seemed to sense her approval: his sullen, brooding lips pulled back slowly to reveal his smile, like a curtain raised teasingly to show the most ingenious opera set of the season. He caught her with the smile and held her with his eyes. "You look very nice. How is it I never did it to you?"

"We all have our crosses," she said.

His eyes darted away as he sighted Harold Rankin, the producer. He raised his hand and voice in greeting. "I tried to phone you twice when you were in Acapulco."

"I tried to phone you eighty times when you were everywhere," Rankin said, making his way with elaborate care through the barrels set six in a circle around tiny white-clothed dinner tables, each piled high with elaborate yellow summer bouquets.

"So when are you coming to the Coast," Rick said. "When are you going to give up this local rat-race and start some real producing?"

"Well maybe if I have the property and the star. . . . I have a script I've been thinking . . . maybe you'd like to . . ."

Louise's eyes moved around the portable dance floor, set up at the far end of the huge round tent, and she waved to Dainty Lee Purbelow, who was boogalooing with Arnold Sussman to the electrified strains of the Illusionary Four. The Four, plugged in to various machines set up beside the dance floor, were singing, gyrating and hip-swiveling with as much energy as if they were playing to the two hundred expected that evening, instead of the few arrivals who had begun dancing. Besides Dainty Lee and Arnold, these included Diane Trejinska and Bunyan Reis. Louise skirted the edge of the yellow and white plastic harlequined floor, and walked over to one of the three bars set up at the edge of the tent.

"Vodka and tonic," she said to the bartender.

"I certainly would have done it differently," said someone behind her. She turned and saw William Meister, appraising the red-jacketed waiters shucking clams and setting them atop the huge rectangles of waist-high ice.

"I mean it's pretty enough, with the blue and white and yellow flowers and the rest of that garbage, but you can't trust the catering firms in Long Island. They only live for summer, so what do they care if they antagonize you."

"Are you talking to me?" she said, and smiled at his gleaming bald pate, which seemed to be aimed in her direction, a bull about to butt. He was standing alone, so she assumed his conversation had to be directed at her.

"I would have set up cocktail frankfurters and sauerkraut, that was Harry's kind of New York, for the hors d'oeuvres, and not this clam garbage, even if it is summer. Maybe even a couple of Sabrett stands, that would have been cute, Harry would have liked that."

"Sabrett stands," Louise said. "What a charming idea. Maybe when I have my next party . . ."

"You talking to me?" William Meister said, and raised his head and aimed his eyes at her. They were quite cold, and very blue, and seemed to look directly through her, as if there were a more important personage standing behind, waiting for a table.

125

"Hello," she said, "I'm Louise Felder."

"Of course," he said. "You're the one. Harry used to bring you around to my place all the time."

"No, he never brought me there," Louise said. "Naturally I very much wanted to go, but he usually . . ."

"Oh, certainly, I forgot. The last few years he preferred Meister's East. But you ought to come to the West Side more often. There's much more action. You'll ask for me? I'll make sure you're taken good care of, it's the least I can do for Harry. He was my best customer. Sometimes he would come in very late at night and just sit there for hours, to get the feel of the place, not even order anything. You come in, I'll see you get a table up front. Can I get you a dish of clams? They're nice this time of year, but I still would have done frankfurters."

"Thank you," she said.

The band took a break, and merciful silence flooded the tent, mingling with the sound of cocktail-party laughter and conversation as more guests began to arrive. Rolf Orlovsky and Chet Oppenheim, in identical turtleneck sweaters over navy-blue slacks, with blue blazers, strode in from the dock. Dainty Lee, in flowing chiffon Pucci pajamas, rushed by them to take her turn on the trampoline, kissing their cheeks as she passed. Algernon Reddy in a Nehru suit and Maggie in her beaded Norell strode through the far flap of the tent into the garden area beyond, holding little fingers. From the trampoline came the sound of giggles as Arnold Sussman joined Dainty Lee, and the two of them bounced, embracing.

Sylvia Kranet, wife of the Senator, told Louise she read her column all the time. Two cows turned slowly on an enormous wooden spit in the fire-spattered darkness. Rolf Orlovsky put his hand on Louise's buttock and smiled.

"How pretty you look," he said.

"In a pink dress," muttered Andre Sherman, and passed them, running toward the trampoline.

"Stop," shrieked Dainty Lee. "Stop bouncing."

"It's you who's bouncing," Arnold Sussman shouted. "Lie still or we can't."

Near the bar Hoover Coolidge Gray stood talking to Bunyan Reis and Diane Trejinska. Seated on one of the barrels, her long red hair flowing free to her naked shoulders, Diane held her head on a slightly inquisitive angle, emphasizing the extraordinary grace and whiteness of her throat, and making her seem to be paying attention.

"When she came out on stage at the Palladium, there were ebbsolute ovations," Hoover Coolidge said. "Four of them.

Before Marlene evah sang a note. Four stending ovations. I nevah heard sech applause."

"She still has the magic, don't you know," Bunyan Reis said.

"Ebbsolutely ear-shattering applause. Before she evah sang a note."

"Maybe they were applauding her for being alive," Louise said, coming up to them.

Bunyan laughed, squealingly. People at tables around joined in his laughter, although most of them had missed what Louise said.

"Oh isn't she funny," Bunyan said. "Can she sit with us, Diane, or have you made other seating arrangements?"

"It's all terribly informal," Diane crossed her legs under her skirt of white organza and seed pearls. "You can sit wherever you like."

"Right now?" said Rick Flinders, directly behind Diane. "Can I sit wherever I like, right now? You look good enough to sit on, to change a phrase slightly."

"Did you get that dialogue from your last picture?" Bunyan said.

"It's a cinch I didn't get it from yours."

"Oh really. Look who's learned to retaliate."

Rick turned to him. "May I have this dance?"

"Very funny. They must consider you a true wit in Hollywood."

"Only in the places where they consider you a true painter."

"Excuse me," Louise said, and moved away in the direction of Hoover Coolidge, who was already making tracks.

"Diane, may I get you a drink?" Bunyan said. "I would hesitate to leave you alone with Rough Trade Ralph here, but I understand when the chips are down you have nothing to fear."

"On your way, Sybil," Rick said.

"That's enough." Diane put her hand on Rick's arm. "I'll have a Scotch and water, Bunyan. Try to exercise a little restraint, Rick. Remember why you're here."

"Oh of course," Rick said. "God Bless Harry."

When Harry Bell first met Rick Flinders, Rick was twenty years old and had had the lead in seventeen major motion pictures, and the leading lady in sixteen of them. The seventeenth had declined only because she had just recovered from a hysterectomy and was afraid Rick would see her scars and suspect that there was more separating them than the twenty-five years to which she admitted. The scars would have been impossible to hide, as by that time he was so well practiced at what he did best that he could no longer perform in a simple, usual manner. Especially with the lights out.

He had not meant it to be that way. As late as his fifteenth year, in spite of his early physical development, and his remarkable beauty, he tried to keep a romantic view of life. All during the run of the Broadway play in which he received excellent reviews, he managed to cling to his virginity, fencing with the obvious hunger of the seventeen-year-old girl who played opposite him, and the actress he so much admired who played her mother. It was not until he got to Rome, to make his first picture with Gloria Stanley, that anything happened. He had such wonderful rapport with her and her third husband that they invited him to Viareggio where they locked him in their villa and had him repeatedly for three days. It was then that he came to understand what was expected of him. He was hospitalized for a month with what Italian physicians were reluctant to label a nervous breakdown; but it gave him the chance to repair physically as well. His recuperative powers were such that a year later he had forgiven Gloria, and even spent the night in her cottage at Malibu, although he would not allow the Colonel to use him in the same way again.

By this time Sidney Skolsky and Sheilah Graham and the rest of the surviving columnists had recognized in him a new breed of teenage movie star, one who cut a more impressive swath off-screen than he did on. He was happy to comply with their image of him, comporting himself publicly with each of his leading ladies, taking adjoining rooms with them on location and vacations alike, making no attempt to veil the arrangements, sometimes even holding press conferences in the ladies' suites, with the lady of the moment on his lap.

All of it was quite a shot in the arm to the gossip columns, and the atmosphere of Hollywood itself, where glamour alone was no longer enough, and sexual indiscretion was needed to garner national attention, and the front page of the New York *Daily News*. It also did no harm to Rick's financial position: in spite of the uneven quality of his performances, and the vehicles being offered him, with each new tiny *scandale* his salary increased.

What it did injure somewhat was the sense of mystery he tried to preserve even after Viareggio. As each new lady opened her arms and her legs to him, he began to despair of ever having a conversation with a woman, about life, perhaps, or art, or religion. Sometimes he would put on a disguise in the makeup department before leaving the studio and go out to the UCLA campus and pick up a coed, or Dolores' to pick up a waitress, depending on whether or not he was feeling intellectual. But always before the evening was over he would inadvertently let slip who he was. The results were inevitable. Those who did not want secretly to be movie stars, wanted to have been to bed with one so they could tell their friends. Especially one with his reputation.

By the time he went around the world with Robin McKay, there was nothing he hadn't done, with considerable variation. All of it suited Robin quite well, as the aging enfant terrible of Hollywood, she had long ago run out of things that could keep her interested. The first time they left the set together she drove to an abandoned house she had once owned in Coldwater Canyon, and broke in, and made love in her old bathtub, to try and recapture her youth. But nostalgia did not work for her. After that they had to be more inventive. Anything sweet and simple they did, like touching tongues, had to be saved for Chasen's and Sardi's.

They were quite a popular couple, though not terribly animated. Rick was by nature a little sanguine, and it was difficult for him to loosen up in public, particularly restaurants where they would not serve him liquor because he was underage. But they were very attractive together, and invited everywhere, and all of fan-magazine America was a little saddened when he left Robin and joined the English lady in Acapulco.

Including Harry Bell. When he met Rick for the first time officially at the De Revignys' in Acapulco, Rick was sunning himself by the pool. Harry studied him for several minutes before speaking.

"You don't look all that good," Harry said. "You shouldn't have dumped that what's her name."

Rick looked up and smiled. "How do you do, Mr. Bell."

"Why'd you do it? This one looks like a boy."

"She has a lot of elegance."

"You're mixing up talking English with class, kid. If you'd been in London as often as me, you'd hear the difference in accents. You shouldn't have dumped her. She had something, that kid. Spirit. A lot of spirit. And you were great together."

"Maybe that was just publicity."

"No," Harry said. "I saw you."

"I would have remembered meeting you, Mr. Bell."

"Harry. We weren't exactly introduced. I looked through the ceiling."

"Huh?"

"Oh, I'm sorry. I didn't know I was talking out of school. I figured you knew. You been the main attraction since Reddy went spiritual."

Rick laughed. "What a shame Robin didn't know. She would have gotten a real jolt."

"So what's the story on you and her. Was it, like they say, an amical parting?"

"Fairly."

"So you could maybe call her and tell her you had somebody you want her to meet."

"I didn't think Robin was your style, Harry."

"Who knows what's my style anymore. I'd like to give her a shot."

Rick paused for a minute. "I don't think it's such a good idea. Robin's a little . . . tough."

"Listen, who are you to tell me, for Christ's sake. Twenty. I didn't even start getting good till I was around thirty-six, and by that time I'd had maybe a dozen women."

"That many?" Rick said.

"You had more?"

"Not this year."

"Don't you play worldly with me, kid. Believe me, anything she got from you, I could give her. You're not so good."

"I thought you saw."

"I didn't really stay long. I'm a doer, not a watcher."

In the end, Rick agreed to introduce them. He called Robin in Hollywood, and didn't tell Harry how long or loudly she laughed at the idea of coming to Acapulco to meet Harry Bell. He said only that she was unavailable.

"Maybe it's just as well," Harry said. "I just had a hunch she'd be spunky. Different."

"They're all the same," Rick said.

"It's a shame you feel that way, kid. You're missing a lot in life if you really believe that."

"I don't believe it, I know it. Only their legs change, and I'm not a leg man."

"Jesus Christ," Harry said. "Twenty years old. Maybe you ought to get rid of that cockney garbage and try getting stuck on somebody special."

"There is nobody special."

"Jesus. What are you going to have to look forward to when you're my age." Harry cleared his throat. "Not that I'm that much older than you."

The conversation stayed with Rick and from time to time he would try and conduct a sentimental, romantic relationship with some woman, but in short order they would accuse him of being a fag and he would have to go to bed with them. By his twenty-eighth year he had almost despaired. That was the same year the studio asked him to see *Man of La Mancha,* which they were considering buying for him.

They realized he was a little young for the part, but they had just hired a great makeup man, and Rick had been taking singing lessons, and there were no longer too many bankable stars. He sat through the performance enthralled, and knew he could never play it on the screen, but thought he could do with a little of that idealism in his life. He went to the Beverly Hills library, incognito, and read *Don Quixote* in stilted translation, and knew, as surely as he had ever known anything, that he would find his Dulcinea, and dedicate himself to her.

Then he met Diane Trejinska. She cut him dead at the first party, totally unimpressed with him. She was quite aloof at their second meeting. Something burned in his soul that he had despaired of ever feeling, and he knew that he loved her. He also knew that it was inevitable they have each other, but it would be an act of love, and that was something he had never had the chance to make it be. He wanted to be worthy of her when it happened. He launched himself on a program of total asceticism, working out regularly in the studio gym, reading a great many out-of-print books, and putting only classical music on the stereo by his pool. He also abstained completely from any and all sexual relations even for health purposes, for more than eight months. He wanted to save himself for her, and regain the innocent, easily satiated appetites of his adolescence.

When she didn't appear at Harry Bell's funeral, he had thought his head would burst. When he saw her, with her long red hair flowing over her white shoulders, covered with seed pearls, in the middle of her tented garden, he thought his heart would.

"Why are you so hostile to Bunyan, Rick," Diane said, after Bunyan went off to get drinks. "He never did anything to offend you."

"It offends me your being with him. Such a waste of good womanhood. Why didn't you call me when you were in California?"

"When was I in California?"

"Last November and this March. I must have left thirty messages at the hotel."

"I didn't realize you kept such an accurate record of my whereabouts."

"I don't do very much else," Rick said.

"I suppose I should consider that sweet, if I believed for a minute it was true."

"You can believe it," he said.

"Even if it were, Rick, there are two things you're not considering. Aside from the fact that I'm married, I'm not interested in you."

"Well maybe not yet. But you will be."

"Why?"

"You have to," he said. "You just have to be."

In the corner of the glassed-in hothouse at the bottom of the garden where the Count Trejinska liked to grow flowers on the occasions when he was home, Algernon Reddy stood talking with a sociologist from Harvard.

"It's not law, it's tribal prejudice, man," Algernon said. "The custom of the reservation. Souls must not be too free."

"You make unintellectual generalizations," the sociologist said. "You sew too big a bag out of your own hangup."

"It's a valid bag," Algernon said. "You know that in this country Indians were not permitted to drink until Eisenhower repealed an old law? Eisenhower, of all people. That's why they always got so drunk. Because if they got caught with a bottle they went to jail. So they drank it all the minute they got out of the store. We punish the living, the aware, for the prejudices of the Custers. So today we refuse to free freeable spirits, because of the witch-hunting Salems of the American soul."

"Too broad," said the sociologist. "There's just a time and a place, and the right circumstances when it should be allowed, that's all. Hopeless situations, maybe, when reality is too much to bear. Terminal cancer. The inmates of death row."

"We are all on death row," Algernon said.

In the den, Julia White was organizing a game of Truth. "It's too many girls," Dainty Lee said. "You don't have as much fun asking girls questions about masturbating."

"Are we doing it with or without numbers?" Louise asked.

"Well, with numbers of course," Julia said, handing out paper. "Maggie, you're number one, two, you, and so on around to Louise, who's number six. Write your hideously personal question to the person's corresponding number, and don't forget, everybody, you must answer the whole and complete truth. No kidding around now. No evasions."

"But everybody will know who it is answering the questions if you read the numbers," Louise said.

"Well, of course we won't read the numbers," Julia said. "We'll erase them before we hand in the answers."

The first of the five written questions directed to Louise was "What are your fantasies when you masturbate," which of course had to have been asked her by Dainty Lee. Relieved, she wrote: "None, I don't." The second, "Do you

132

really think you have any talent," she answered misleadingly, so everyone would think it was Julia's question: "Of course. Otherwise why would I take magazines so seriously." The third question was a bit more difficult, and had to be handled well. "How big was your last love's pecker?" Obviously whoever had written the question would recognize it and know the answer was coming from her. They also were assuming her lover was Harry Bell. The easiest thing would have been to lie, but she wanted to tell the truth because otherwise she had no right to be in the game.

"Nothing to get choked up about," she wrote, giggling. Then immediately she crossed it out. It was too disrespectful: she was still presumably in mourning, and, after all, the party was in Harry's honor.

"Dinner," one of the butlers announced at the door of the library.

"Thank God," Louise said, and got to her feet, ripping the paper.

Dinner was served under the tent on two long, white-linened buffet tables, each of which held a platter of the roasted cow, sliced up into oversized slabs of beef, a bubbling cauldron of corn on the cob, salad and bread. The waiter filled Louise's plate. She looked around blindly for a moment, then saw Bunyan Reis, waving to her and patting an empty barrel next to him. The others seated at the table were Harold Rankin, Peter Daisy, with the subject of his first and most celebrated portrait, Elizabeth Merchant Slade, whose eyes Peter had cast in moving mercury, and her most recent husband Hanover Slade the IVth.

"I'm so happy to meet you, Mrs. Slade," Louise said. "I understand Peter's done a very exciting portrait."

"Oh but he has," Elizabeth Merchant Slade said. "Oh but you must come and see it. Oh but you must let Peter do you."

"I don't know how you can sit here talking about paintings and good times," Harold Rankin said, biting into his corn on the cob, "when America is in flames."

"Really?" Elizabeth said. "I'm so sorry, what's happened now?"

"St. Louis. Cincinnati. New Orleans." He waved his hand, and the ear of corn, and some of the butter from it spattered in Louise's eye. She tried not to pull away too sharply. "Flames."

"It's always worse in the summer," Hanover said. "It's the heat."

"Is Hoover Coolidge very upset?"

133

"We're all upset," Harold Rankin said. "We've asked him to say a few words after dinner."

"And he's agreed?" Louise said.

"He'll be ebbsolutely enchanted," said Bunyan, and tittered.

When the waiters were removing the dinner plates, and refilling the silver tankards of wine and pewter mugs of beer, Harold Rankin rapped on his glass with his fork. The rest of those at the table joined him, and the tent was tinkled into silence. Harold got to his feet.

"Ladies, gentlemen, charming and respected guests, and our most beautiful and generous hostess. Sitting here, enjoying the fruits of this great society, which was so good to Harry Bell, whom we are honoring tonight, and to us all, we cannot help but realize what is going on in the rest of the country this evening. So your gracious hostess and I thought we might call on our most distinguished guest to say a few words. As you know, Hoover Coolidge Gray has just contracted to do his first picture in Hollywood, after a distinguished earlier career as a champion athlete, and next season I hope to be presenting his first play on Broadway. Meantime he has been gracious enough to offer us some insight into the sad events now taking place. Ladies and gentlemen, our most distinguished guest, Hoover Coolidge Gray."

"Thenk yew, Herold," said Hoover Coolidge, softly, and got slowly to his feet. He cleared his throat. "Ah's Sambo," he said slowly. "Now ah don't want to make you feel guilty fo' bein' rich people, and influential people, an' white people. Ah's just Sambo. But a lot of yo' cities is buhnin', an' a lot mo' is goin' to burn, becawz we got nothin' to lose, an' you got everythin' to lose. An' you gonna lose it. Ah thanks you."

He sat down. A few stunned handclaps broke the frozen silent air.

"Jesus," Bunyan said.

Everyone looked at Harold, who turned a deep pink. "Well, that's what happens when a people is suppressed," he said.

"At a dinner party?" Louise said. "He's suppressed at a dinner party?" Nobody laughed, or even reacted. She excused herself and went outside, as Diane signaled the orchestra to start playing.

On a lounge chair on the grass Andre sat, the moon glowing yellow behind him. To her great chagrin, Louise found herself moving in his direction. The night air was cold on her shoulders, and she remembered how warm his hands could be. And it was, after all, a party.

"Fat girls shouldn't wear pink," Andre said.

134

"You're just jealous because you couldn't wear it. Honest to God, Andre. A sequined turtleneck."

"But they shouldn't. Not pink."

She turned and started back for the relieving noise and confusion inside the tent. The rest of the evening did not go well. Hoover Coolidge got into a violent argument with Arnold Sussman, and was invited to leave for his own protection. People, generally, seemed inclined to leave the party early. Louise was losing one of her false eyelashes, and no one was carrying surgical adhesive. Rather than embarrass herself, she left at midnight for Julia's house, thinking she would get up early in the morning and work on her tan.

When Louise awoke the next morning, at six, she could hear the rain, relentlessly battering the Cape Cod roof. "Shit," she said, and tried to go back to sleep. But she could not. A resort in the rain. Her luck. She felt restless and angry, and knew she could not survive until five o'clock without the sun. It should have been the greatest weekend of her life, but already forces had conspired to spoil it for her: Andre Sherman, Stokely Carmichael, and God.

She got out of bed, packed, wrote a note of apology to Julia, phoned the weather bureau recording to make sure it was going to rain all day, and called a cab to go to the station.

By the time Kate cleared away the last of the breakfast dishes and put away the smoked salmon and leftover bacon, it was almost noon. She was ready for sleep again, but when the bell rang she was neither angry nor surprised.

"Am I too late?" Louise said. "I took the only morning train back from Southampton and I came straight here. If you're mad I'll go home."

"No, it's okay, Lou, you might as well come in."

"Must you be so effusive, Kate? How often do I have to tell you to learn to control your enthusiasms."

"Wasn't it a good party?"

"It was a great party, why are you so defensive, the party was fantastic, I could hardly tear myself away. Do you think the only reason I'd come here is because I wasn't having a good time?"

"Yes."

"You're right," Louise said, and sat down on the couch. "Lulu's depressed."

"Didn't you like all the pretty people?"

"I loved them," she said. "But I don't know if I was pretty enough. Andrew said fat girls shouldn't wear pink."

"You were probably the prettiest one there."

135

"You're just trying to build Lulu up because Lulu's blue."

"Tell me about the party. Who was there?"

"You don't mean you're curious. I thought you didn't care about that sort of thing anymore."

"Let me tell Charley you're here," Kate said.

"No, please, I can't, I'm not up to meeting anyone. I didn't think he'd be here again." A great booming laugh emanated from the library and Louise shifted her legs on the couch. "He certainly has a deep enough voice. Is it any index?"

Kate nodded.

"Maybe I'll just go in and brush my hair," Louise said.

"Louise is here. She's brushing her hair," Kate announced, closing the library door behind her.

"Should I get my trumpet?" Charley said. Charley's face was that of an aging cherub, blue eyes set in unending laugh lines, his cheeks stubbornly rosy in spite of his deep tan. His body was long and lean, contemporary Californian, long-legged and big in the chest, but with a tight bottom that could fit into impossibly small pants.

"Now you be nice to her," Kate said. "No raunchy stories for at least five minutes, no funny insults for ten."

"Listen, I'm nice to everybody, but what kind of bullshit is that, I have to wait a week to meet a close friend of yours. I have to skulk around New York until the lady decides if she wants to receive me? Since when does anyone have to be protected from me? I've been with a lot more important people than some Leonard Lyoness and they seemed to enjoy my company."

"Don't get angry," Kate said. "She's a warm, darling girl, but she's got problems. And I don't want her to think this is a setup."

"Poor Kate," David said. "She takes this all so seriously. Just because we're so happy she thinks she has to fix everybody up. Right, sweetheart?" He hugged her gruffly around the neck.

"Don't be mad," Kate said to Charley.

"I'm not mad." Charley stretched his legs over the ottoman, and slouched down in the chair. "But I don't know why you're protecting her. Especially from me. I'm a normal American boy who takes vitamin E every morning in case something comes up, to make sure it can. But I'm not eager. The fact that there isn't a girl I know in the city right now and I pole-vault around my room every morning doesn't mean I'm anxious to get laid."

"God, you're gross," Kate said, laughing. "Just promise you won't come on too strong."

"If you want I won't even whip out my pu pu."

"You are the vilest. Don't you dare scare Louise. Go easy on her."

There was a knock on the door of the den, and Kate excused herself and slipped into the hall.

"Is Lulu pretty?" Louise said. She had brushed her hair so it fell in soft waves around her eyes, and her face was shiny from scrubbing. "Is she all honey blond and rosy?" She didn't wait for an answer. "Let's go into the living room. I don't know why this is so embarrassing for me, I guess it's just that I'm so used to running after people at parties or restaurants I don't know when was the last time I just met someone at a friend's house. I feel like I'm eleven years old." She arranged herself on the couch, fluffing a cushion over her stomach so only her legs and the upper part of her torso showed. "You won't be hurt if I don't like him? I mean you won't take it personally?"

"Of course not," Kate said.

"All right." She stretched an arm out over her head and posed. "Lulu's ready."

Kate started back for the den, and stopped when she heard Louise whisper her name.

"Kate?"

"Yes?"

The voice was very tiny. "Isn't that funny? I feel actually shy. A nice boy. Imagine."

"All right," Charley said, striding into the living room. "Where is she? Where is this adorable girl?" He was all confidence and ease, and he caught sight of her, and smiled with his dazzling California teeth. "Hello," he said softly.

"It'll only take me a minute to get my clothes off," Louise said.

"Huh?"

"Actually we can do it with our clothes on if you're pressed for time and you don't really care about the preliminaries."

Charley turned to Kate. "I shouldn't come on too strong, you said?"

Louise giggled. "But Lulu hasn't seen such a sun-browned body in a long time, and she genuinely wants to fuck."

"Huh?" Charley said again.

"Oh come off it." The little-girl tone had left her voice. "You West Coast people are all the same. Blow into town with your suntans and checkered sports coats and just because all the boy starlets are fairies and the girls out there are so grateful, you think everybody wants to get you in the hay. Well you know something? You're right. Let's go into the bedroom and Lulu will make you a star."

"Hamburger," Charley said. "She wants to grind me into hamburger." He started for the door. "Call me when you haven't got company."

"But I was only kidding," Louise said, an expression of genuine dismay on her face.

"I'm from California. I haven't got your quick New York wit. I'm slow, but I'm not so slow I want to become hamburger."

"Kate said you were earthy," Louise said.

"That's right, and it might be cute on me but I'm a boy; it's not very cute on you, toilet-mouth."

"Didn't I tell you they'd get along?" Kate said to David.

"Please don't go." Louise held out her hand. "I'd get up and pull on your arm only I don't like what I'm wearing and you look so pretty I'd feel inferior."

"Call me, David."

"Don't let him go. Tell him Lulu's sorry."

"Lulu's sorry," Kate said.

"He doesn't like Lulu," Louise said mournfully. "Lulu should have put on makeup."

"You happen to have a very cute face," Charley said. "And I have a weakness for little blond butterballs, but not when they have a mouth like a sewer."

"I'll try to change, really I will. But don't go home. I'm really a nice girl," Louise said. "Come into the room again, please, Charley. Let's start over."

"I don't like games."

"Please." Louise looked at him very wistfully. "I'm tired of playing too. Just this once."

He went into the den and came out again, awkward and angry. "Hello," he said.

"How do you do," Louise said. "I've heard so much about you. How nice that you're here."

"It's lovely to meet you, too," he said, and went to sit beside her.

"And how long are you going to be in New York?"

"A week. Maybe ten days."

"And then you'll be getting back to . . . What is it you do?"

"Real estate," Charley said.

"Real estate. That is down to earth. I know so few civilians, I hardly know what to say to you."

"I'm sure you'll find something."

"I certainly hope so," Louise said, and stared into her lap.

"It's all right," Charley said, and patted her hand. "You can relax now. I like you."

"Really?" she looked at him hopefully. "You really do?"

"Yes."

"Why?"

"Because you have a sweet little face and when garbage doesn't fall out of it, it's very pretty, and you're obviously sharp, and with a little effort you can behave like a lady, and that's very appealing."

"You *do* like me."

"Yes, I do."

"Okay," she said. "Let's fuck."

"I'll go make drinks," Kate said.

About four o'clock Sunday morning Louise turned on her bedroom lamp and pulled the covers back from Charley's sleeping torso. With all the lovemaking they had done in the past day, she had not really looked at his body, turning away when he got in and out of bed, to go to the bathroom or switch on the television, or bring them each a sandwich from the big bag of delicatessen they had bought on Madison Avenue on the way home. Averting her eyes was not done out of distaste for a man's body, or a false sense of shame: she had looked away in the faint hope of preserving some sense of delicacy, some hint of maidenly modesty as foolish as she knew that pose to be.

For all that Dr. Ehrens had assured her that the same standards no longer applied as in her twenty-first year, when she had clung to her virginity like barnacles at the end of a pier being swept away by a changing tide, it still disturbed her that she might be thought easy. She was thirty-three years old, no matter how the realization stung her, and she was unmarried, and it was normal and excusable to have appetites. The nice boy from Forest Hills wasn't going to sweep her away to Levittown if she was still a good girl. To sustain the mystique of a meaningless membrane even in her head was immature and unrealistic. She was frustrated and Charley was attractive, so if she wanted to hump him she should do just that, and she had told him so in no uncertain terms.

She had still been embarrassed when he actually brought her home. There was a moment just as they paused outside her door when she nearly told him to go away, with his beaming face and his thoughtful, presumptuous bag of groceries. But then he was inside the apartment, and he was kissing her long and sweetly on the mouth, his big hands reaching gently for the small curve of her breasts. An unaccustomed feeling of tenderness mixed with the growing excitement inside her, and she had told him to cut the shit and just get into bed.

They had been there for the duration of the weekend, and

in all that time she hadn't really looked at his naked body until now. Stretched out in the careless posture of sleep he seemed longer and more vulnerable than she had thought him. His chest, for all its thickness, seemed almost like a little boy's, hairless and soft-skinned, and the line of hair starting softly down below his navel was pale brown with red highlights, almost as if he had been sunbathing naked. But he hadn't, he wasn't that bold no matter how much he pretended. She ran her hand along the white line across his hips, and smiled as she felt the movement against the back of her wrist.

"Poor tired thing," she said softly, taking his penis gently between her palms, warming it and watching it grow. "Lovely," she whispered, and reached over to turn off the light in case he should awaken and see her naked.

Protected by the darkness, emboldened by it, she cushioned her face in the softness between his legs, rubbing her cheek slowly back and forth against the velvet casing of his hardness. Quite without her planning it, her tongue began to explore the sudden length of him. She felt cheeks growing flushed, and assured herself it was embarrassment and not excitement: it was something she had only done with Andre, because he insisted and she was sure she loved him, and that was the only way he could get a complete erection; but it had to be gotten over with as quickly as possible, so they could get on with it. Now though her ministrations were gentle and luxuriant, and she told herself it was because she didn't want to wake Charley. It was too delicious an idea to have him while he was sleeping; she would be one up on him, so to speak, and he wouldn't even know.

It was simply the idea of exciting him again, after all the times they had had intercourse, and he had said he was too exhausted to manage it again, that was all that was making her do it. There was no conceivable way that she could be enjoying the obscenity. As if to prove to herself that she was thinking the truth, she pulled her head abruptly away, and positioned herself above him, straddling his motionless hips and thrusting him inside her.

His breathing became less regular, as her pelvis whipped in more insistent patterns; she reached over and touched his eyes. They were still closed. But as her fingers traced downward to his mouth, she felt it set in a grin.

"You phony," she said.

"Easy. Go easy. I want to do something nice for you."

"Just do it to me. Please. All the way inside me. All the way. Yes. Deeper. Please."

"Easy, Lou. I'm very ready."

"So am I . . . So . . . am . . . I!"

She felt him breaking inside her, and she groaned, and raked her nails once against his shoulder, so he would know she was fulfilled. "Lovely," she whispered against his chest.

"You didn't make it."

"Of course I did. I did every time."

"You didn't make it once."

"I always do."

"Why did you have to rush me? I could have brought you along."

"But I loved it. I loved it as much as I ever have."

He was quiet for a moment. "Then you've never really made it."

"Oh that's ridiculous. How do you know if I made it or not? What am I supposed to do, faint?"

"If you don't know, there's no way I can describe it to you."

"That's right, Charley. There's no way."

"But I could have shown you. Somebody could show you if you'd only give them the chance. Why don't you give anyone a chance, Lou."

"Oh for Christ's sake," she said, and went into the bathroom.

When she came back he was smoking a cigarette. She lay down as far away from him on the bed as she could, and pulled the blanket up to her eyes. But she could hear him inhaling, and visualized his big, smooth chest moving up and down, a little boy smoking a cigarette.

"I thought all men were interested in was their own satisfaction."

"A lot of the time that's true."

"Didn't I satisfy you?"

"In a way."

"In what way?"

"Well I got off my rocks if that's what you mean."

"But you didn't really enjoy it?"

"I enjoyed it," Charley said. "I would have enjoyed it more if you were with me."

"And how do you know I wasn't with you."

"Moaning and fingernail-scratching do not orgasm make."

"You really think I've never made it?"

"Not if what you just had was as good as you ever got."

"So what if I told you I never had made it, that I only enjoyed it, but whatever this . . . mysterious thing was that supposed to happen hadn't happened. So what?"

"I'd think it was a shame."

"And you could do something about it."

"I think so. I'd sure as hell try. But you'd have to give me a chance, Lou. You couldn't keep jumping on me and rushing me. You'd have to let me make love to you."

"And you'd want to?"

"Why not."

"Why, more important? Why would you want to take the trouble?"

"Oh I don't know. Maybe it's just the hunch I have that there's a lot of woman there if you'd let it come out."

"And you're the one to do it? Don't you think that's a little arrogant."

"No. I think any man who cared about you at all could do it if you gave him a chance."

She was quiet for a moment, and then she turned over and cuddled him with her best little-girl voice. "Okay."

"Okay, what?"

"Okay, I'd like to give you a chance."

"Oh sweetie, not now." He reached over and stroked her hair. "You take a lot out of a man. I need time to recover."

"How long?"

"A couple of hours, anyway."

"Can we make a date, Charley?"

"Sure," Charley laughed. "We can make a date."

"Lulu's so excited." She snuggled into the warm curve of his body. "She probably won't be able to sleep a wink."

The date they agreed upon was for twelve noon. But at ten forty-five the phone rang and the call came from Chet, so they never got a chance to keep it.

CHAPTER FIVE

THE man who should have signed Harry Bell's death certificate, if he hadn't been vacationing at the time, was Dr. George Piner. In recent years, George had functioned mainly as a diagnostician, a better category for the East Side than mere general practitioner. But at the start of his career he had considered specializing in obstetrics and gynecology. And, as Harry Bell once quipped about him, he liked to keep his finger in.

That was how George met Maggie Bolin. Or rather, it was the way he met Maggie when they were both aware of each other. There were many who were later to take credit for that particular courtship; if Harry Bell had still been alive, he would have been among them. Harry had always urged Dr. George to get a rich one, and, of all the availables, Maggie was without a doubt the richest. Harry had meant to get them together, but somehow, he never did. But still, paths had a way of crossing; as *Town and Country* was later to acknowledge, George and Maggie were meant for each other, so they *had* to meet.

The first time they were introduced was at a party given by Chet Oppenheim. After four martinis, George sat playing the piano. His eyes were closed, his breathing heavy and regular, the only detectable movement in his hands, and that fitful, and in no way to be confused with the way Chopin intended. His right hand fell heavily on the arpeggio, and made of it all one chord; his foot rested unmoving on the loud pedal. A few people in the living room made faces of protest. Maggie Bolin, standing next to the piano, only halfway down from a trip Algernon had taken her on that morning, was able to break down the sound into its components inside her head. It sounded exactly as it should have to her.

"Lovely," she half-whispered, about the pictures in the front of her brain.

Without missing more than three or four beats, George took the cue from her word, and shifted into "The Way You Look Tonight," only with the wrong harmonies.

"How long have you been playing," Maggie said, wondering if it was polite yet to leave.

"Two years," said George, without opening his eyes.

Maggie could not imagine that she had been standing by the piano that long. "Two years?" she repeated thickly.

"That's all the formal training I've had, but I play whenever I can."

"That's good," she said. "You keep it up." She saw that he was not looking at her, and seemed to be asleep, so she started to move away. But her right hand had melted into the dark wood of the piano, and she was literally stuck. Algernon had taught her never to panic when such things occurred, to flow with them until the moment when they, and you, drifted. She did not give in to alarm. She just looked at the man playing the piano, as he became a black and white illustration in a magazine, surprising his friends at parties, and being the most popular man in his group, and all because he had sent the enclosed coupon with his two dollars.

"Oh good," Chet said, coming over to where she stood. "I've been meaning to get you two together. Dr. George, I see you've mesmerized our Maggie."

"Umm," said George, his head nodding, his eyes still closed.

"Can you believe it?" Maggie said. "He's been playing for two years, and his fingers are still moving."

"Can I get you anything?" Chet said.

"Maybe another two dollars," Maggie said. "Then he could send away for the colored keyboard and not be stuck with the black and white ones. A red one," she said. "Play something red."

"Divine girl," Chet said, patting her on the head, and moved away.

"I have always loved music," Maggie said. "I once owned a record company, and we had a group. The Jujubes. You may have heard of them."

"Umm," said George.

"I was madly enthusiastic about them, but then fate took a hand, you might say if you weren't being terribly original. We were strangled by a green Jujube."

"I'm sorry," George said.

"Not that I have anything against a green Jujube. Some of my best friends are green Jujubes. Boss they are, truly, madly boss. I've never been a bigot. Algernon would tell you that in a minute, he says in my mind color fades into sound, and that's where it's at, that's how it should be. Have you heard that about me?"

George said nothing.

"But certain things just stick in one's craw, what? and if it sticks in one's craw, one must spit it up, even if it is green. Yes?"

"Umm," said George.

"You're a doctor?" Maggie said.

George nodded.

"Precisely what is a craw?"

He did not answer, but Maggie did not mind. A breeze from the East River shattered the piano, and her hand came loose, and she was free to go. She wanted to leave the party before anyone else noticed the piano had fallen apart and called the police. She was much too groggy to answer questions, and they might just suspect she was on something. Neither did she have any wish to implicate the piano player. It was not his fault that he had spent the two dollars for nothing. It was very hard to be the life of the party, no matter what the ad said, when the restful quality of your own music lulled you to sleep.

She left without saying good-bye to the piano doctor and didn't think about him again. She did not remember him the second time they were introduced, in the Oak Room of the Plaza, where she was having cocktails with Louise and Julia White, who was organizing a fashion show for *Élan* magazine.

"Oh here's someone you ought to know, Louise," Julia said, waving George over to the table. "George, what are you doing here, and in a tux at five thirty. I know, you're making a house call on J. Paul Getty."

"Not quite," said George. "I've got an opening at seven."

"Are you a surgeon?" Louise said. George did not smile. "I'm sorry. I suppose you've heard that before. It was a bad joke, but I'm supposed to be witty."

"Oh?" said George.

"I guess he told me," said Louise.

"George . . . Maggie Bolin, Louise Felder, I'd like you to meet Dr. George Piner."

"How do you do," said Maggie, and shook his hand.

"We've already met," said Louise as their palms touched. "Right after Harry's funeral. I owe you a handkerchief. Don't you remember?"

"I'm afraid not."

"He's crazy about me," Louise stage-whispered. "He just doesn't want to let anyone know how much of an impression I made on him, for fear he'll be compromised. You can let go of my hand now, George, or everybody will find out about us."

"Find out what?" said George.

"Is he putting me down?" said Louise.

"George is an authentic straightforward gentleman," Julia said. "The last of a vanishing breed.

Louise put her hands over her eyes. "I'd better cover my eyes or I'll be struck blind." She lowered her fingers into her lap when she saw none of them was paying any attention.

"I can't understand how you and George never met each other, Maggie," said Julia. "George was at your apartment after Harry's funeral."

"So many people . . ." Maggie waved her hand.

"Oh see how quickly the object of interest is now switched to Maggie. I guess I've blown it, huh," Louise said, and dimpled deeply.

"Well, now we've met," Maggie said.

Nevertheless she did not remember the next day that she had met him the day before. She had a vague feeling of familiarity when they saw each other on a few different occasions, but never connected it with a name or a formal introduction. George was not hurt: people seldom remembered him at first, while at the same time they assumed they knew him. He reminded everyone of someone. He had the kind of face that blurred immediately into semi-recognition: the features were good enough, but vaguely rubbery and washed-out, so whatever fair gentleman was in social or political vogue the week people first met George was the man he resembled. He was tall and blond and carried himself well when he was not at a piano, and had a pleasant enough manner, but nothing that would make him indelible on someone's mind, unless they were in need of him. Maggie was introduced to him on three other separate occasions, and only the last time, when he took her hand, and said "We've met," did she think to say "Oh, yes, of course, how are you." Because she did not really know who he was, it did not strike her as curious when he began turning up more and more often at the places she frequented.

It was not until her mother's Papanicolaou smear came back suspect, and Kate Waller was about to give birth, that Maggie began seriously thinking about the womanly part of herself and how she had abused it. It was then she had occasion to remember Dr. George Piner, and to call on him. She made an appointment for the fifth of September, her birthday, on the theory that life renews itself on birthdays.

"I suppose you're wondering why I didn't go to my regular doctor," Maggie said.

"No such thing," said George, leaning back in the leather seat behind the great English desk, laden with all the latest in medical journals, most of them still in their mailing wrappers. "I'm just delighted you wanted to see me."

"That's very nice of you, Doctor." She looked at him carefully. As often as she had seen him, and he made no mark on memory, she was quite sure she knew now who he was. He was very clean and positive-looking in his white jacket, little silver pens clinging to his breast pocket. With the sun shining in the window behind him, silvering his blond hair, there was a certain fatherly radiance. They would have pink and white and yellow children, which was what Algernon had told her she could have, and soon. "I didn't go to Dr. Wilcox, because he's my mother's doctor, and very old. He delivered me, you know."

"I see."

"One can't always tell one's oldest family friends and servants what's on one's mind, what?"

"Of course."

"They think my mother has cancer. Uterine cancer."

"I'm so sorry," said George. "But Dr. Wilcox is the best in his field, and surgery nowadays . . ."

"I'm not worried about my mother," Maggie said. "I'm sure she'll be all right if it's possible for her to be all right. I'm worried about myself. I'm not madly hypochondriacal or anything, and I've had Pap smears regularly since I was twenty or so, but there is one thing that worries me, what? and it's not exactly anything I can discuss with Dr. Wilcox."

George waited.

"I've never been pregnant."

"I see," said George.

"Well no, you don't, what? you don't see at all, it's terribly odd, really. I suppose some people would consider it madly lucky never to need an abortion or to rush into the wrong marriages merely for the sake of the blooming fetus, but to tell you the truth, Dr. Piner, I haven't been exactly a saint."

"There's no need to apologize."

"Well of course not, I wasn't apologizing, my dear, a person would have to be a freak if she hadn't done a little something by my age, yes? I've never used anything, before, during, after; not even a tissue, and it's just never taken hold. Don't you think that's madly odd?"

"Not necessarily. There might be a perfectly simple explanation."

"Like what?"

George slid his chair back from the desk and stood up. "Why don't you go into the examining room, and I'll have Miss Valley help you . . ."

"I don't want a nurse. I'm perfectly capable of undressing alone."

"But I always have the nurse when I'm examining . . ."

"I trust you," Maggie said. "You can examine me without witnesses."

"Very well," George said. Opening the door into the sterile white and gray examining room, he told her to remove her panties and stockings, and sit on the table when she was ready for him. There was a sheet on the table to cover herself.

When he entered the room five minutes later, she was standing by the window, completely naked. He did not show his surprise. "You want to sit on the table, Miss Bolin?"

"I was thinking of jumping," she said, and laughed.

"Put your feet in the stirrups, please," George said.

"Don't you think it's peculiar to have a window without a shade in your examining room? I mean even if it does face a brick wall, the whole thing seems too exhibitionistic."

"Press down," he said.

"All right."

"Don't be nervous."

"I'm not nervous."

"Relax your knees."

"They're relaxed." She tried to sit up. "Maybe it's you. Maybe you're not relaxed."

"Lie back, please."

"You see, you're not, you're not relaxed. You're frowning, and your face is all twisted up, what? Do I make you nervous?"

"Lie back," he said again. "How does that feel?"

"A little impersonal."

"This doesn't give you any discomfort?"

"Not really. Try it again, please."

"Well?"

"No, it felt a little . . . funny, but it isn't a bad feeling. Why? Shouldn't it feel funny? Have you found something?"

"Nothing to be alarmed about. Just the simple explanation I suspected. Get dressed and come inside and we'll talk."

"You can talk to me now, Dr. Piner, I won't be embarrassed. I know there's nothing the least bit sexual when you're being examined by a gynecologist. I used to wonder how a doctor could ever become sexually excited with all the poking around he has to do, he must become fairly inured to any kind of sex play, what? I mean surely you don't have any sexual feeling involved in an examination, it's just like an ear doctor poking around a canal, what? Aren't you going to examine my breasts?"

"When was the last time you were examined?"

"A long time ago," Maggie said, and lay back on the table, her eyes fixed on his face.

She was embarrassing him deliberately, and George Piner knew it. Her look was so frankly interested that he had to try

148

very hard to pretend her body belonged to just anybody, and not to a woman whose influence and capital could be so valuable. Not that Dr. George was a climber: he was a very easygoing man who just went along with the tide, and the tide had begun to carry him to very high places. He liked what he glimpsed there, and saw no reason why he should not stay.

The first important place the tide had carried him was to a cocktail party three years before, where he met Harry Bell. Dr. George was not invited, but went as a guest of his nurse-receptionist, Wendy, a startlingly beautiful black-haired girl with enormous breasts, who moonlighted as a call girl. Wendy did her double-duty not out of immorality, but from a generosity of nature that a doctor's office could not contain, in combination with an apartment and wardrobe a receptionist's salary would not pay for. At no point did she consider abandoning either role: she liked working for Dr. George because wearing white uniforms made her feel crisp and benevolent, and the other made her feel soft and benevolent, even though she did not exactly give it away. Everyone who had had her said she was a great lay, but they meant it with respect. The fact that she was a nurse besides was reassuring to those who thought they might have a heart attack in the middle, like Harry Bell.

Harry never knew Wendy expected to be paid for her favors. He called her "the Florence Nightingale of Fuck," and because he prided himself on never having to give a woman anything, Chet Oppenheim slipped her some cash every time she was "nice" to Harry.

The quotation marks were Harry's. The first time Chet brought her around to Harry's house, Harry took her up to the second floor library, opened the safe behind the Da Vinci, and showed her his less-publicized art collection, comprised of prints and photographs of people being "nice" to each other, in every possible combination and position.

"Do you like that?" he said. "Do you think that one's nice?"

Wendy shrugged. "If it's what he wants, it's nice."

"Would you be 'nice' to me like that?"

"I don't know. Should I be?"

"You be nice to me, baby, and I'll be nice to you. You want to get ahead in this business, you got to be nice to the right people."

"What business is that, Mr. Bell?"

"Show business. You got a pretty face and a great body, but there are a million pretty faces and bodies in show business."

"I'm not in show business."

"You're not? What do you do?"

"I'm a nurse."

"No shit," Harry said.

"Well not exactly a nurse. I didn't finish nursing school but I work for a doctor, I'm his receptionist. He lets me help with the patients when it's not too serious."

"I'm not too serious," Harry said. "You want to help me?"

"That depends. What kind of help do you need?"

He turned over the second stack of pictures. "This kind. You think you could help me like that."

"I might."

"Let's go upstairs," Harry said.

He started to put the pictures back in the safe. Just before closing the door, he took one from the top of the pile, and put it under his arm. Then he slid the Da Vinci back in place and led her to the door. His arm was around her waist, slipping with the undulations of her walk onto her deep, full buttocks.

"So you're a nurse, huh?" he said, the hand holding the picture resting on her hips, his other hand clutching the balustrade of the winding marble staircase. "Is that where Chet found you? I mean he came into this doctor's office and you were working there? How about that guy, he can't go anywhere without falling into a vat of honey."

"I knew Chet first. He was a patient of George's."

"George?"

"Dr. Piner. My employer. George was looking for someone to work in the office and Chet knew I had gone to nursing school for a while before I came here from Canada."

"Canada," Harry said. "I like that. I like girls from out of town."

"So I got the job."

"You like it?"

"I love it. Dr. Piner is a terribly decent man, very kind. He can't pay too much money, he hasn't built up a very big practice yet, he's still a young man. . ."

"How young?"

"Thirty-eight."

"That isn't so young," Harry said.

"Well, it is if you didn't graduate medical school until you were thirty-one. George had to work his way through, you see, he couldn't get a scholarship and he was very poor."

"You stuck on this guy?"

"Am I what?"

"Stuck on him. You know. Nuts about him."

"George?" Wendy said. "Nobody could be stuck on George. He's very sweet, that's all."

150

"Because if you're stuck on him, maybe we should forget about this whole thing. I don't like to fool around with a girl if she's stuck on somebody else."

"Are you all right, Mr. Bell?"

"What do you mean, am I all right?"

"Your face is a little red. Maybe you shouldn't talk while you're climbing the stairs. Don't you have an elevator in this house?"

"Of course I have an elevator," Harry said. "I don't need to use the elevator. I'm in shape like a young man, full of beans, you'll see." He stopped at the landing and tried to cover up the shortness of his breath. "Better shape than your doctor, I'll bet you that."

"I'll bet you that, too," Wendy said. "I think George is low thyroid. I've never known anyone so sleepy. He falls asleep at the oddest times."

"Yeah?" Harry grinned, as he led her toward the bedroom. "Well you won't catch that happening with me."

He watched her undress from the bed, so impressed by her body as it was revealed to him that he kept an unaccustomed silence, breaking it only once.

"You got sensational knockers, kid."

"That isn't all," Wendy said, and slipped off her pants.

She came over to the bed and he closed his eyes while she began undressing him. He reached up to the headboard and flicked a concealed switch so that all the lights in the room were turned out except the one soft red bulb in the bedside lamp that his last wife had insisted upon. He held in his belly as she snapped open his shorts.

"Not bad for an old man, huh?"

"How old are you?" Wendy said.

"Not so old," he said, and pulled her to him.

After a few minutes she raised her head. "Maybe we should take it easy for a few minutes, huh Mr. Bell?"

"What do you mean, take it easy?"

"I mean maybe we should just rest for a little bit."

"I don't need any rest. What do I need rest for?"

"Maybe it just took a little more out of you than you thought, climbing those stairs."

"You go to hell. It didn't take anything out of me. If you did what you're supposed to do there wouldn't be any problem at all."

"I've been doing it."

"Well maybe you haven't been doing it good enough. Take a look at the picture and see what's she's doing."

"I don't need to look at any pictures."

"Well I do," Harry said. "Pass it over to me and I'll look at it."

After a few minutes he dropped the picture to the floor and closed his eyes. "Good," he said. "Very good. Now use your tits."

Wendy did as she was told, and in a moment when he told her to climb on, because he wanted to make her as happy as she had made him, she did that too. Afterward he hugged her and asked her if it had been wonderful, and told her it was before she had a chance to answer. "You're a good kid," he said. "I like you. I'm going to do something for you too."

"That's very nice of you, Mr. Bell."

"I'm going to make a date with you for next week."

"Thank you very much," Wendy said.

"I tell you that right now because I know how nervous you girls get all alone by the telephone, wondering if a man like me could want to see you again. Well I do, and I'm letting you know now so you won't get insecure."

"How thoughtful," said Wendy. She waited until she was alone later with Chet to let him have the full brunt of her anger. But he explained about Harry's liking to think women only did it for love, and he slipped her a hundred-dollar bill, so all in all she felt kindly disposed toward Harry.

After that she saw Harry about once every other week, except when he was courting somebody special and explained to her that he wanted to save himself, but she shouldn't be hurt, he'd see her again soon. When he started getting shortness of breath every morning after jumping off the exercycle in the gym next to his bath, he stopped being alone with her. The thought of dying in the saddle, as glamorous as he had always thought it would be, now threw him into a panic. But he did invite her to a cocktail party to show he wasn't just dismissing her. He told her to bring a date, so she wouldn't be too shattered when he didn't take her upstairs.

The date was Dr. George Piner. Harry's first impression was that Wendy had hooked up with one of those celebrity fags that designed women's clothes and went to openings escorting some celebrity dyke; but on closer inspection Harry realized the doctor wasn't anyone he resembled at all. He was just a nice-looking fair-haired man in his late thirties, who looked like a lot of people, but wasn't any of them, and was probably sorry about it.

"I had a whole different picture," Harry said, as he shook George Piner's hand.

"Really?" George said.

"I thought you'd be taller."

"I'm six one."

"You don't look that tall."

"I'm afraid I have a habit of slouching."

"Yeah," said Harry. "Me too."

Because there were only eight other people in the small library bar, most of whom George didn't know, and no piano for him to play, he stood quite awkwardly. Finally he concentrated on listening to Harry breathe.

"I hope you're doing something for that asthma," Dr. Piner said.

"Asthma? What asthma?"

"Haven't you ever been treated for asthma?"

"I've never been treated for anything except the clap. And that was the biggest dose my doctor had ever seen. When I do things, I do them big. But there's nothing wrong with me, I'm full of beans."

"Haven't you noticed any shortness of breath?"

"Who, me?"

"I'm sorry," George said. "I didn't mean to speak out of line. I'm sure your doctor takes care of whatever's necessary."

Harry lowered his head. "My doctor died six months ago."

"I'm sorry."

"Just keeled over in his office. Didn't smoke, didn't drink, he lived so clean he didn't even fool around. And snap, just like that, his heart. Can you imagine?" Harry put down his drink. "He was practically a kid. Fifty-seven years old. Nowadays that's nothing."

"That's true," George said. "The life expectancy for a man nowadays is eighty years."

"You really believe that?"

"If he takes care of himself."

"Maybe I ought to come in and see you," Harry said. "You really think I got asthma?"

"I don't like to do a superficial diagnosis without examining a patient."

"But if it's asthma, that's simple. You could probably clear it up, huh?"

"There's a lot we can do."

"Thank you." Harry turned and rested his cheek against the grainy side of the bookcase and closed his eyes. "I thought it was my heart," he whispered.

After a moment he opened his eyes again, and saw the bookcase full of leather-bound first editions. "What color's your office?"

"Color?"

"You know, the decor, the motif?"

153

"I'm afraid it's just a doctor's office. Gray metal, white walls, black chairs."

"None of those fairy decorators get their hands on you, huh? That's probably just as well. I let one of them come down to my Wall Street office and I'll never get over it. I got Oriental rugs and elephant tusks up the ass. Here's a red one. Red goes good with black and white." Harry turned the volume on its side. It was *The Great Gatsby*. "I'd like you to have this."

"Well Mr. Bell, that's certainly . . ."

"Only it's about a Golden Girl. Every man ought to aspire to a Golden Girl. Man's reach should exceed his grasp, or what's a doctor for, huh?" Harry grinned.

"Thank you," George said. "That's certainly very kind."

"Kind, schmind, you want to look out for me, I want to look out for you. A Golden Girl. That's what you should get. And rich. Rich is very important."

"I always thought the man should be rich."

"That's very naive. A man doesn't have to be rich at all."

"I thought you were very concerned with being rich."

"That's *me*. But I assure you if I was some nice, tall, good-looking goy I wouldn't have to worry. They're just lying around, waiting. That's the most surprising thing. Women are just as hungry as men. Nobody falls into a tub of butter, not once they're past twenty, so women start getting desperate when they're a little older. Not even a lot, just a little, like Sylvia. You know, now that she's divorcing Lester, that poor bitch doesn't know where to go. She may be coming back to me."

"Really," George said, not very interested.

"Not as a concession, mind you. She was always stuck on me. We had something going that was deeper."

"I'd heard that," George said.

"But if I was a tall good-looking goy I'd have had my choice, without even lifting a finger. They're just lying around waiting, you'll see. Like a tub of butter."

Maggie Bolin was far from a tub of butter. Her body was long and lanky, and lying on the table now in front of him, a nervous smile pulling at the corner of her mouth as she watched George, she resembled nothing more than that Golden Girl, at least to George. In her own way, she was attractive, especially if you considered who she was. George Piner tried very hard not to show he was doing just that.

Slowly he worked his hands from under her arm, around her right breast, pressing gently, moving his hands in small circles funneling her nipple up into the cone of his palms.

His breathing was steady, but she could see his forehead beading up with small drops of perspiration.

"Have you found anything?" she said.

"Just relax."

"Tell me what you found inside me. Please. It isn't fair to keep me waiting like that."

"Your uterus is slightly tipped." He moved around to the other side of the table, starting the manipulations on the left breast.

"What does that mean exactly?"

"It's nothing to be alarmed about, but it could and probably does account for your failure to conceive. Unless you had coitus in a certain position, it's doubtful the sperm could reach the ovum."

"What position is that?"

"Wouldn't you rather wait till I'm finished?"

"Don't be silly. There's nothing embarrassing about this. You're a doctor. You couldn't possibly touch all those breasts and reach into all those lady parts day after day if there was anything sexual involved, or you'd go mad. I know there's nothing the least bit sexual involved about what's going on right now. The body just reacts in a certain way, that's all. You have a gentle touch, a very gentle touch, so my nipples are stiffening, but that's automatic, what? It has nothing to do with sex. What position?"

"Your hips would have to be tilted up very high to allow maximum penetration."

"Oh well, I've done that, Doctor. Why haven't I gotten pregnant?"

"Do you use that position all the time?"

"Hardly."

"Then that's most likely the answer. You'd have to have intercourse at the right time of month, in the right position. You can get dressed now."

"Don't you like me with my clothes off? Wouldn't it be funny if there was a gynecologist who had a deadly fear of naked women because he was afraid of being aroused?"

When he finally had her, it was on the living room sofa of her apartment, with her clothes on. At the last she stopped him for a moment, to lift her skirt above her waist, so she could raise her hips high in the air.

CHAPTER SIX

THE overcast sky disintegrated into one of those splotchy fitful summer rains serving neither to clear the air nor cleanse the sidewalks. For a few moments, Louise, hurrying along the sidewalks of East Fifty-fourth Street, amused herself trying to dodge between the water falling in visible clumps around her; but she was not as young as she used to be (how young was that—had she ever been that young?) and her hair with the coloring job had run her twenty-two fifty, even with the professional discount. She raised her arm as a taxi neared the curb closest to her.

"Taxi dear," she said, waving. He switched on his off-duty sign and leaned over to lock the rear door. "Prick," she said, as he went past her.

The rain was beginning to fall more consistently now, and she held her small cobra pocketbook over her head, waving it back and forth as if to outwit the rain. She could feel the body beginning to leave her hairdo. "Damn." She ran into a small arcade between a jewelry store and an Indian rug merchant, and stood there, hating the rain, and despising cabdrivers. It was twenty to four and she was due at Chet's office at three thirty, and it was feminine, maybe even cute to be ten minutes late; any later would be presumptuous. She didn't have the right to be presumptuous. Not yet. She touched her hair, very lightly, not wanting to make the moisture a permanent ruination of the line. It was all right, she was still pretty, she could tell that with her fingers. Fortified with that security, she turned to look at the mirror on the arcade wall. It was dark glass, and badly in need of a cleaning but even so she could not mistake the reflection outside the arcade.

"Charley!" she said happily.

He kept walking, head down, toward Fifth Avenue, his big shoulders hunched against the rain. His tan had almost faded, the luster she had been sure he always carried with him when they first met not so obviously in evidence. But he still looked wonderful, moving with a scowling grace against the intemperate day; all the more remarkable in that she knew for a fact that nobody walked in California, and he looked like he'd been doing it all his life.

"Charley?" she said again.

He stopped. "Well, well. Brenda Starr."

"Please don't be funny. You have to save Lulu. Lulu's very late for an important appointment and she can't get a cab."

"It's nice seeing you again, too," Charley said. "But enough about me, let's talk about you."

"I'm sorry. I really don't have time for manners. I'm so late."

"See you."

"Oh, please, don't be angry with Lulu."

"Charley isn't angry with Lulu," Charley said. "Charley just thinks Lulu is a pain in the ass."

"You do not," she said coldly. "You're just mad because I didn't take any of your calls."

"Then you *were* in the office. I love that bitch secretary telling me she would see if you were in. I guess you're too big a man to take my phone call."

"I was busy, I swear. Why didn't you call me at home?"

"Lulu's unlisted," Charley said.

"So why didn't you ask Kate and David for my number?" She looked at him carefully. "Tee hee. You didn't want them to know you still cared for Lulu. Tee hee."

"Tee hee your ass. You give me one more tee hee, I'll kick you in the balls. I'll get you a cab." Charley started moving along the sidewalk, toward Fifth Avenue. She hung back in the arcade for a moment, flirting with the rain, touching her hair over and over again. She bit her lip, and ran out on the sidewalk, hurrying to catch up with him. "Hello," she said. "I'm Louise Felder . . ."

"Go back there and wait. I'll bring the cab."

"I want to be with you," she said.

"Dummy," he said, and smiled.

He pushed her gently back to the awning of Mark Cross, and hurried out into the rain-slowed traffic of Fifth Avenue, trying for cabs with no one inside, or without an off-duty sign. After ten minutes, he shook his head, and came toward her.

"I'm not having a good time," Louise said, biting her lip.

He laughed and took her arm, turning her around the corner, toward the front entrance of the store.

"Where are we going."

"To get an umbrella," Charley said.

"Why don't you just make it stop raining?" Louise said, as he pushed her inside. "What kind of hero are you anyway?"

The smell of leather, fresh, new and expensive, flooded her nostrils, and she imagined she understood what it would be like to be born to security and wealth. "It's a nice store," he said.

"I come here all the time," Louise said, touching one of the wallets on the counter, feeling the smoothness beneath her fingers.

"Hooray for you."

"I didn't say I bought anything. I just come here all the time."

"Okay." He went over to a rack of umbrellas and drew out one with a long leather handle.

"Charley, please. This is a very expensive store. You don't have to buy me anything, really."

"I know that."

"You've been gallant enough as it is. Really. I feel like a fucking princess."

"You sound like one. How much is this?" he asked the well-dressed clerk hovering near them.

"Forty-two dollars, I believe."

"Come on, let's go. My hair is already ruined. It only costs six fifty to have it reset. It isn't worth forty-two dollars."

"I don't know. Sometimes it's worth forty-two dollars to save something that's already there." Charley turned to the clerk. "We'll take it."

"Now you're making me mad. What are you trying to prove?"

He gave the clerk forty-five dollars, ignoring her.

"Big man," Louise muttered. "Big fucking cavalier. Big fucking gentleman."

"Why is it so hard for you to let anyone do something for you? Why can't you learn to accept something with grace, instead of opening your cesspool?"

"Why does it matter to you?"

"Because you're upset, because you said in the rain you weren't having a good time."

"Did I say that? That's really kind of darling, no wonder you're crazy about me."

"I'm not," he said.

"Of course you're not. I don't know if you've got enough money to stay in a hotel, and you're spending practically fifty dollars on a lousy umbrella that I'll probably lose. Have you got enough money to stay in a hotel? Or is that it, do you think because you're making this gesture you can move in with me. Is that it? Because if it is, you can take your umbrella and . . ."

"I was about to suggest that very thing to you," Charley said.

"Have you?" she said, when they were out on the sidewalk, and he had opened the umbrella against the soft-blowing rain.

"Have I what?"

"Have you enough money for a hotel?"

"I do, but if I didn't, it wouldn't matter. I'm leaving tonight."

"For California?"

"For California."

"Oh," she said, confused at how upset she felt. "But you'll be coming back soon."

"I don't think so. Once every two years, that's enough."

"You're trying to scare me," Louise said.

"Why should that scare you?"

"Stop fishing."

"I'm not fishing. Lulu's too busy. Lulu's too caught up in Lulu's fucking fake phony idea of where to be when. Lulu doesn't know how to enjoy."

"So why do you bother? Why did you get me this stupid umbrella?"

"Because I like to give presents."

"You're full of shit," she said.

"Besides I love how gracefully you can accept things, how sweetly you say thank you."

"Thank you," she said, furious.

"Didn't anybody ever give you anything before?"

"Why do you care?" she said exasperatedly. "If you're not trying to prove anything, why do you care?" She stopped walking. "I mean nobody's going to drop dead because they meet me, I got over thinking that a long time ago. That's for movies and true confessions, it doesn't happen like that. Does it?" She tried to swallow the panic inside herself, mixing with the hope she was sure she had long ago banished. "Does it?"

"Stop fishing," he said.

"Please don't play, Charley. Do you care about me?"

"No," he said. "Not the way you are. But I'm very excited about what you could become."

She squeezed his hand and started walking, fast, so she wouldn't have to listen to what was going on inside her. "You want to come home with me?"

"I thought you had an appointment."

"I do. But maybe I can call and postpone."

"Till when."

"Till after you're gone," she said.

"Why don't you just cancel."

"Oh, I couldn't do that," she said. "It's . . . it's not just an unimportant appointment, Charley, you've got to understand that."

"I understand," he said.

"But we do have time for a quickie," she said.

159

"You mean like one umbrella's worth."

"You think I'm worth fifty?" Louise said.

"I'm sorry if you think it's all you're worth. Here's a cab," he said, and whistled it down with his fingers.

"Where were you when I needed you," she said, smiling and winning the driver, as she got inside. "Come," she patted the leather seat. "Get in."

"Fuck off," Charley said.

"You're kidding. Or were you just kidding me about everything else you said."

"Lulu has important business," said Charley, slamming the door. "Up Lulu's!"

The distance to Chet Oppenheim's office was less than four blocks, but with one-way streets and the traffic congestion in the hot, wet afternoon, it took the taxi another fifteen minutes to get here. All the time in the cab Louise chewed on the handle of the umbrella, cursing Charley to herself, cursing the rain, cursing the taxis that put on their off-duty signs at three thirty when they weren't due in till five. If she hadn't seen him again, she would have been fine. Even if she had seen him and a cab had come right away she would have been spared the confusion. He had shown her tenderness.

"Big fucking deal," she mumbled, and the cabdriver turned his head.

Everything was timing, being in the right place at the right time, with the right people of course; seeing Charley at that moment was the worst timing imaginable. Charley, whom nobody in their right mind in the right position would invite to anything, had made her feel like a daisy.

Obviously she was not as mature as she gave herself credit for being. People didn't throw away everything they decided they wanted and run into the pastel sunset because someone said something tender. That, too, was movies and true confessions and to have even been tempted to cancel Chet was teen-age time.

When she was eighteen, acting like a teen-ager had been consistent and apropos. When she was eighteen, she had stood in front of the mirror, her hair not yet golden, as Eddie said he would like it to be, Saks being far away and expensive and only cheap girls going so far as to peroxide their hair.

"Is Lulu pretty?" she asked Eddie, steadying herself against the rocking of the boat which her mother had reminded her just before she left for the weekend was rented. Of course his parents were rich, but that was only *by comparison.* For "by comparison" a girl shouldn't make a mistake, especially as a girl because of her sweet face and a good sense of humor had already been invited many times to Fire Island.

"But don't get carried away because you think they're so much better than Rockaway," Mrs. Felder had said, as she watched her daughter pack her bag for the weekend. "Those Fire Island people aren't all that they're cracked up to be. I've talked to people. I saw *Season in the Sun* on Broadway."

"Yes, Mama, I know."

"Don't call me Mama. You know I don't like to be called Mama."

"I'm sorry, it just slipped out."

"My experience isn't just limited to Great Neck, you know; I could have been many places, done many things in my lifetime, if I hadn't been such a fool about my family. I could have been more. Much more."

"I know, Mother."

"That's why I want more for you. You can be more, Louise, if you don't make a fool of yourself because of some phony from Fire Island. Just don't be so impressed because they want you. You're very bright, and you have a sweet face, and nice legs, why shouldn't they want you. God knows if you lost weight everybody would want you."

"I'm dieting, Mother. I'm down to a hundred twenty-eight."

"You're a wide-hipped, short-waisted girl. On a wide-hipped, short-waisted girl a hundred and twenty-eight still looks like a pig."

"I'm trying, Mother. I haven't eaten for a week."

"You didn't eat for a year, it wouldn't hurt you. Look at the people in the concentration camps. I just want what's best for you. I want you to be the most you can be. I just know for a fact you can be more if you're thin."

"I'm trying, Mother, please."

"It's all right," Mrs. Felder said. "Some men like fat girls."

"Thank you," Louise said. "I feel much better."

"Don't you open up a mouth with me," Mrs. Felder said. "After what I've been through for you. My insides. Just don't pay me back by doing anything to make me ashamed of you, Louise, just because his people rented a boat. For all you know they're as phony as the ones on the Island who are just plain pansies, otherwise why wouldn't they have invited us to their home to see how they lived."

Actually, Eddie's parents had suggested having the Felders out for a visit, but Louise had quashed the suggestion, because when her mother was around for some reason she felt very self-conscious. "They're very busy people," Louise said.

"They're always entertaining important buyers from out of town."

"When I was twenty-two years old I was in the same restaurant as Herbert Marshall, and he couldn't take his eyes off me, as much of a gentleman as he was, he couldn't take his eyes off me. If I hadn't been such a fool about my family, I could have been with anyone."

"I know, Mama. You could still get anyone you wanted, if you weren't so loyal to Daddy."

"He makes me sick," Mrs. Felder said. "What I've been through for that man."

"I know," Louise said.

Mrs. Felder moved to the mirror, and touched her upper lip, where vague puckers were beginning. "You really mean that, or are you just trying to get on my good side? Do I still look that good?"

"Fantastic," Louise said.

"Well you look all right too," Mrs. Felder said. "There's nothing you couldn't have if you lost a few pounds. Is she pretty, this Eddie's mother?"

"Not like you. She's a little heavy."

"Well, that's good," Mrs. Felder said. "That's all to the good. If his mother's fat, he probably leans toward fat girls."

Standing now, in front of the mirror on the boat, Louise caught Eddie's glance in the mirror. "Do you think Lulu looks pretty?" she said again.

"You always look wonderful in the summer," he said, getting up from the cabin bunk, coming up behind her so she could see his hand in the mirror, cold against her shoulder. "I'd love to see you as a blonde. With your teeth, and your coloring, you'd make a sensational blonde."

"Does your mother have false teeth?" Louise said.

"What kind of a question is that?"

"I just wondered."

"You'd kill me as a blonde. You've got great color."

"So do you," she said. He had reddish hair and pale skin which never became more than thickly freckled, but she didn't mind. She had always preferred Ashley Wilkes to Rhett Butler, except for the rape scene, and she still wept occasionally at Leslie Howard's being shot down during the war. She hadn't been aware of his death when it happened, but once having seen the picture, she was grateful for all the stories that he had been, variously, a spy and a Hungarian Jew. So it was possible to be both that and elegant; sudden certitude gave her great hope, along with sadness that she never got the chance to meet him.

"I'm not brown like you are," Eddie said, touching her collarbone. "Not that wonderful shade you get."

"Thank you."

"Let me see the line . . ."

"Eddie . . ."

"Please, I just want to see the white line . . ."

"Eddie, your brother and Karen . . ."

"They know better than to come down into the cabin. I told them we were going to take a nap."

"I don't know if that's nice."

"Well for God's sake, I won't try anything. My parents have probably got their binoculars trained on us this very minute."

"They aren't worried," Louise said. "They don't have to worry. They know I'm a nice girl."

"Don't you think I know you're a nice girl."

"I wonder sometimes."

"For God's sake, Louise, I only wanted to see the line."

"All right," she said, loosening her straps. "But stand over there by the bunk."

"You're so white," he whispered. "You're so white underneath . . ."

"Eddie . . ."

"Please . . . Please let me just see them . . . Please."

He was standing behind her, close to her, looking over her shoulder into the mirror, her fingers on her upper arms, trailing gentle light tracks. He leaned over and put his tongue in her ear.

"Don't . . ."

"I just want to see them."

"They're not very big," she said, after a moment.

"They're beautiful," he said, and cupped his palms tight on her breasts, rubbing them until they were pink, only the nipples as dark as her skin.

In all the times that he had touched her, working his fingers inside her brassiere, even taking it off on the few occasions when they were sure his parents were asleep, he had never seen her breasts, and she had never seen him watching her. They always made their limited love in darkness, and seeing how excited he was made her breath come faster, she could see that happening in the mirror, too. She turned, and pressed herself against his chest, so she wouldn't see how excited they both were, and be able to calm down. "Oh Eddie," she said, and opened her mouth wide against his lips, so he would know it was all right to use his tongue, even though it was only two o'clock in the afternoon.

"Why do you think nice girls don't make love?" he said,

when he had pulled her over to the bunk, and drawn the bathing suit down to just below her waist, and she told him to stop.

"They don't, that's all. Everyone knows that."

"Don't you think there are nice girls at Cornell?"

"I'm sure I don't know," Louise said, reddening beneath the tan.

"Well there are, believe me. From some of the best families in the country. And they make love."

"Good for them," Louise said. "I'm sorry I'm not in their league."

"You are in their league. Of course you are."

"Only I'm not a college girl, is that it?"

"Oh Louise, you've got to get over these terrible middle-class prejudices, like people that go to college are better. I admire you for going to work. Really. I know you could have gone to college if you wanted to. But you wanted to accomplish something, get out and be something right away, that was it, wasn't it?"

"Was it?"

"Of course, I know that. I don't blame you for being in such a hurry. I'd get a job myself if what I wanted to do didn't require a college education. I can't tell you how useless I feel sometimes, taking those asinine courses I'll never be able to use—but if you want to be an architect, those are the rules. If I could just go out and start building without having to get those dumb requirements out of the way, I'd do it in a minute. As it is I spend most of my time sitting on my duff."

"Making love to those nice college girls."

"Why do you want to be so narrow-minded. All I mean is that the world is different. Ideas are different. Just because a woman has natural appetites and the sense to know it isn't wrong to satisfy them doesn't make her not nice."

"You really believe that?"

"Of course I do," he said, and kissed her, wet and warmly, as his hand circled her waist.

"Don't do that."

"Don't you want to?"

"Of course I want to, but I can't stop believing what I believe is right."

"Then just hold me."

She hadn't noticed all the time he was talking he had been taking his zipper down. He turned, slightly, and she could feel him against her thigh, as he tried to push her hand down.

"Don't."

"Just feel," he said. "Just hold it. Please."

She closed her eyes so she wouldn't see it, but she could

hear him moving against the pressure of her hand, moaning. In a moment his fingers were reaching under the elastic of her pants.

"Don't, Eddie, please."

"But it's so warm, you know you want me to, it's . . . oh God Louise you're so warm and . . . wet, you're wet, you want me to, you know it, I can feel, just touching, you're all . . . hold tighter hold me tighter, move, move your hand, don't squeeze, just hold . . . hold . . . HOLD!!"

He broke against her and she could feel the stickiness on her hand and on her leg, and she knew that even if she swam to shore, it wouldn't all come off her new bathing suit, and his parents would know immediately. She hated him in that moment because whenever they had done that before he had always given her a Kleenex first to hold in her hand; besides she had never let him touch her so much, not inside her pants, and he had never even asked her if she wanted him to stop, and once he was touching her she didn't. For the rest of the summer she never let him touch her like that again, and always kept Kleenex handy.

The next summer he was a little harder to handle, but she had picked up some smart lines in the agency where she was working, and people liked him to bring her along for week-end parties. She brightened up the place, they said, always ready with a funny crack and a good gossipy story, so she managed to keep him in line. The next summer he told her she was a cock-teaser and he didn't want anything more to do with her. So she became a blonde, even though her mother knew for a fact Jean Harlow had died from peroxide. By the time he graduated from architectural college, she was twenty-one and wondered what she was holding onto it for anyway. He loved her, and he was going to marry her, there was no doubt of it: why else would he have kept coming back for four years with all he was getting from the college girls?

"Sweetheart," he said, when they were alone together in the beach house his cousin had rented for the summer. "Let me look at you."

She was ready and he knew she was ready.

The college girls had done their job a little too well. "Do you like that?" he said, swooping down as he bit her nipples sharply, first one, then the other, while his finger jiggled the nipple not between his teeth. "Doesn't that feel good," he whispered against her breasts, tongue flashing out in impersonal starts as his hand worked her legs open. "Isn't that good," as his fingers found her and tightened as he began a rhythmic unrelenting tweaking. "Do you like how that feels, is it good, is it the best thing you ever felt, or do you like this

165

better," as he moved toward her. "Just let me know when you think you're ready, oh you're going to love it . . . or do you like it better this way"—when all the time she only wanted his silence, or, at most, a whispered "I love you" as he moved on top of her and entered.

"How was it?" he said. "Was it great for you?"

"I give you an 'A.'" Immediately she regretted having made a wisecrack. But he apparently had become as insensitive to her disappointment as he was to her stored-up sense of wonder, and said nothing. They spent the rest of the summer, now that they could be "relaxed and open" about it, copulating whenever he found a place where they could be alone, while he taught her not to be so passive, showing her how to raise and move her hips, and telling her not to be so middle-class conservative, just because they weren't engaged yet was no reason to refuse to let him put it in her mouth.

After Labor Day, the first fall in all the time she had know him when he was not going away to college, she persuaded her mother to begin taking the Sunday *Times* in addition to the *Daily News,* so they would be able to have something to talk about when Eddie came to dinner. In the first Sunday paper that came, Louise read of his engagement to Ellen Feinblatt, of 90 Riverside Drive, who had just returned from vacationing abroad.

Louise did not go to pieces as she imagined she would. She spoke to her boss about a raise, and moved into Manhattan, taking her own furnished apartment on West End Avenue. She thought it beautiful, but realized objectively it was neither large enough nor grand enough to entertain young men, unless they were just humps that pass in the night, as she learned to say. As for Eddie, she did not mourn him at all: she had no doubts that he would be only moderately successful and be bald and fat by the time he was thirty. When Eddie was thirty she bumped into him at a concert where Andre Sherman took her: he was as good-looking as ever, and had made over a million dollars. He told her she looked well, even if she had put on a little weight.

There was no such thing as love. If you were important, where you didn't depend on it, you might find affection and companionship. But nobody really cared about you just because you needed them. She was glad she had not been so adolescent as to let Charley throw her. The days of standing in front of the mirror asking someone to tell her what she was, to promise her she was someone, were long gone. Upstairs Chet Oppenheim was waiting to see her, and she had no time for Charley, and whatever game it was he was playing.

She stopped at Chet's reception desk, as a courtesy, because by now she was sure everyone in the office knew who she was. "I'm Louise Felder," she said.

"Yes, Miss Felder. If you'll take a seat."

"But he was expecting me at three thirty. I couldn't get a cab in the rain, and if you'll tell him I'm here . . ."

"He has someone with him at the moment," the receptionist said. "If you'll take a seat . . ."

"Oh." She started to sit down in the wing chair by the elevator, but stopped. "Are you sure he's not waiting for me? I'm very late, and I know he was expecting . . ."

"I'm sure. If you'll take a seat, he'll be with you shortly."

"May I use your telephone?"

"There's one on the magazine table in the corner. I have to keep this one clear for messages."

"All right," Louise said. She went to the phone and dialed information for the number of the advertising agency where Kate worked.

"Mrs. Waller please," she said into the phone. "Kate? You answer the phone yourself, you don't even have a secretary with your brains and talent? I'd demand one immediately or threaten to quit." She laughed nervously. "How are you."

"Fine, Louise," Kate said. "What's up."

"Oh nothing, I just thought I'd call to ask you how you were."

"That's very nice."

"Do you happen to know where Charley is staying?"

"Charley." There was a silence. "Why."

"Oh I don't know, I was just curious, I thought it wouldn't hurt to call and say good-bye. Listen, what's the story on him anyway."

"No story, he's a lovely guy, I told you."

"I mean does he like to hang up frustrated ladies, or what."

"Or what," Kate said.

"Oh. Where did we go wrong?"

"I don't know, Lou."

"You think I should call him?"

"You can't. He's checked out of his hotel."

"Oh. Do you know where I can get in touch with him?"

"I might be able to reach him. Do you want him to call you."

"Please. I'm at Chet Oppenheim's. LT 1-2244. Tell him I'm willing to cancel."

"I'll tell him, Lou."

"He bought me an umbrella, Kate. Why did he do that?

167

No man ever bought me anything before. If you don't count the furs and jewels I got from Harry Bell. Tee hee. Please. Ask him to call."

"I don't understand," Chet said, when Louise was seated in the big leather chair beside his desk. Ron Abbate was hovering nervously around the liquor cabinet lighting cigarette after cigarette, stubbing them out the moment they were lit. "What do you mean, you're resigning from tonight. You know I have a party planned for you."

"I don't feel like being the queen of the Harry Bell Memorial Prom. I changed my mind. Sue me."

"But you were telling the truth about your relationship with Harry, we all know that. A lot of people know that. Nobody can say otherwise. And you're not putting yourself in any jeopardy."

"I just don't see what's to be gained."

"Don't offer her anything," Ron said quietly from the corner.

"Oh screw," Louise said. "I'm not looking for anything. I don't want to be involved. I feel stupid."

"I agree," Chet said, and she looked up, surprised. "It would be stupid if all you were going to get out of . . . publicly exposing your relationship with Harry . . ."

"Exposing?" Louise said. "Since when did we talk about publicly exposing."

"Not now, Chet," Ron said.

"You better let me have it all," Louise said.

"I planned to have a little surprise for you at the party this evening. The usual crowd, Countess Trejinska, Luke Benjamin, Rolf Orlovsky, Bunyan Reis, and of course the press people."

"What press people?"

"All the ones who have been running the blind items about the girl Harry left behind. I planned to introduce you to them as the lady."

"You've got to be out of your mind," Louise said. "I said I would go along with it on a private discreet basis. I didn't say I was willing to expose myself to public ridicule."

"I assure you it will be very tastefully handled."

"How can it be? What can you possibly hope to gain?"

"Harry's family isn't interested in your version of Harry's wishes. They've refused to even meet with you."

"All right, so forget it. You made a try, it didn't work. Finish. End of tale."

"Not exactly," Chet said. "If we can work this up into the

kind of story I think it can be, the public pressure alone . . . might embarrass the family into . . ."

"That's the worst thing I've ever heard." She got up.

"I've already spoken to your publisher, Louise," Chet said. "He's really delighted with the kind of readership your column is going to get after this kind of publicity. He's talking about syndicating you in . . . maybe twenty more markets."

"So he won't be so delighted."

"It would be a shame if I had to expose your little story as a hoax. Not that I realized it. How could I. I believed you. But how would it sound—that you'd lied to me, and degraded yourself and Harry by this immoral callous lie. Trading on a dead man. I'd never have expected it of you, Louise."

"Oh come on," Louise said. "You don't have to play melodrama. It isn't as if you've cornered me. This is the twentieth century, like they say. This is America. You might know enough people to blackmail me around town, to make it very tough for me here. But I could go someplace else."

"Could you?" Chet said.

The intercom on Chet's desk buzzed, and he walked over and flipped the key. "I thought I told you no calls."

"It's for Miss Felder. A gentleman."

"Shall I ask who's calling?" Chet said to her.

"I know who's calling." Louise stood silent. "I don't suppose the Lady in Black could bring an escort?" Chet shook his head.

"Tell him I'm not here," she said.

She walked to the window and leaned over the broad, dust-covered sill. At the top of the airshaft there was a small square of light, and she could see the sky was clearing. "All to get that little man underground," she said quietly.

"Did you say something?" Chet released the intercom.

"I only hope there's an afterlife," Louise said. "I never gave much thought one way or the other to heaven, but I hope now there is an afterlife, so he can see how much he was hated."

"I'm shocked," Chet said. "Those are hardly the sentiments one would expect to hear from Harry's fiancée."

"Don't worry, I won't say it to anyone outside of you two, loyal, caring friends. You must have an enormous stake in this funeral—of loyalty, I mean, naturally."

"Naturally," Chet said. "Do you want a drink?"

"No." She started toward the door. "If I'm to meet all these people I'd better go have my hair done again. I had it done once today already, but I got caught in the rain." She smiled. "I don't suppose that's of earthshaking interest to you."

"Not really," Chet said.

"Not to me either," said Louise.

BOOK 2

CHAPTER ONE

HARRY Bell had not believed in an afterlife. When he was a little boy, his mother had tried to instill in him a fear of God, and along with the fear of God had gone the hope of heaven. But whenever someone died in the neighborhood, there was too much clutching of hearts and hands, too much moaning and weeping as the family sat around in grieving circle. Whenever the dead person was young, there was so much *schreiing* about the injustice of it that Harry figured out very early that there couldn't be anyplace so wonderful to go to, or people wouldn't be making such a fuss about leaving where they were.

Where they were at the time was Hester Street. Even two blocks uptown would have been an improvement, so heaven had to be nothing not to be desired. And for heaven to be nothing, it could not exist: it was something fizzy, like the Brioschi his father took after too heavy a meal, to make death go down easier, like stuffed cabbage.

The stuffed cabbage was not made by Harry's mother. In a building where food smells hung like badges in the hallway, Harry's mother did not feel that her worth or her love had to be measured by the success of her *cholishches*. It was for her sister-in-law Sarah to roll up chopped meat and rice in leaves. Sarah liked that kind of hanging over the stove and suffering, even in summer, and as long as she lived with her brother and his wife and their three sons in the two-room apartment for nothing, it didn't hurt her to cook a few meals.

In Harry's view it was absolutely right that his mother was not doing the cooking. Miriam was an unusual woman in many ways: tiny and fragile with a cool regality that had no place on Hester Street. If she had to be there, it was right someone else should labor over the stove, and do the sweating. Harry had never seen a drop of perspiration even on his mother's upper lip, and he adored her for that. That and her misplaced brilliance, the knowledge between them that she had no place in that crowded apartment on that crowded street. She bore her poverty-ridden misfortune with none of that stoicism that typified the attitude of the ladies on the block. She yelled at Harry's father and told him to make something of himself, it wasn't enough to be earning a living as a barber, it was no big accomplishment just to be alive even if one had escaped from the Cossacks. So he was alive. So what. So now be something.

Harry shared her enthusiasm for accomplishment. He also shared her eye for beauty, and thought it was only right that she devoted the major part of her time to redoing old embroideries on blouses she had managed to salvage from her mother's trousseau, and making doilies for the backs of the two stuffed chairs they owned. He also joined in her love of the wonderful things in nature, and sat for many hours on the roof of his building at her side, looking at the sky readying itself for evening. In all, there was nothing she rejoiced in, as little as she seemed to rejoice, that he did not take joy in too. That was why it was so surprising that she couldn't stand him.

The realization came slowly. When he got the best grades in school, and part-time jobs in the afternoons and weekends to help bring money into the house, she would praise him enough, as mothers were supposed to do. But when he would move against her in the evenings, as she sat doing her delicate needlework, when he would sit on the arm of her chair and sidle over with his face poised for a chance brush against that soft, hairless cheek, she would shift her position subtly and get out of his way. After a while, when he did not seem to understand, she told him there was more room on the sofa-bed, why didn't he sit over there, he was blocking her light.

When he saved five dollars, he bought her a floor lamp, with a powerful bulb, and set it up behind her left shoulder. She thanked him, smiling slightly; that evening when he came to sit by her she said nothing. But the next night the lamp was on her right, and when he joined her, she told him there was more room on the couch, he was blocking her light.

The other brothers were out in the evenings, playing, and maybe getting into trouble the father said. But Miriam was not worried. "They're boys," she said. "Boys are trouble. Be glad they come home at all." Only Harry stayed close to where she was. But not too close, as she was careful to remind him.

When he was fourteen years old, Harry apprenticed himself to a junior ward heeler named McLuskey, who was looking for a bright young Jew kid who would help him make inroads politically in the Manhattan ghetto vote. Harry canvassed his neighborhood with aggressive energy, getting people out to vote who didn't know what voting was, greasing those who couldn't care less, and all but singing "Yankee Doodle Dandy" for potential patriots. When he tried to ex-

174

plain to his mother what he was doing that was different from the part-time chores of other "good" boys, how far above aiding pushcart peddlers and delivering for the tailor he was, she seemed unimpressed. All she knew was that McLuskey liked Harry to do his running at night, late, and go to political meetings, especially Fridays, and that meant Harry stayed in bed all of Saturday mornings, and a good part of the afternoon. As he slept on one of the sofa-beds in the living room, it meant that the bed and the room were unmade for most of the day.

Miriam could not stand disorganization. As little as she did around the house, what had to be done she got over with as early in the day as possible, so she would be free to tend to pretty things. The sight of Harry making his small lump in the living room weekend after weekend was more than she could bear. The only thing that made her life tolerable was losing herself in the small pieces of beauty that were available to her, like intricate embroidery. Harry obtruded the sadness of her reality late into her Saturday afternoon. It was bad enough that a woman had not been given daughters to resurrect her with a future better chance, at a more beautiful, richer marriage. That such a sad apology for a son should be there to scald her eyes at three o'clock Saturday was beyond endurance.

"Get out of bed," she said, finally, one Saturday afternoon at three thirty. There was no one else in the small apartment. Max the husband was in the shop, *shabbis* or no *shabbis*, Sarah was shopping for dinner, and the two boys were God knew where. "Get out of bed," she said again, as Harry stirred. "Get out of bed," her voice raised to a shriek.

Harry, startled, jumped up from sleep, his eyes still closed, pajama rope clutched to his middle, holding up his pants. Slowly he opened his eyes, and saw her. A smile spread across his face.

"Oh get back into bed," Miriam said. "I can't stand to look at you."

Sigmund Freud might never have been born for all the good or understanding he brought to the Lower East Side denizens of that day; but forty-some years later when Harry finally went into analysis he told his doctor about that afternoon, adding that he did not think it had particular significance.

"Then why do you remember it?" the doctor said.

"Because she kills me. She's an extraordinary woman."

"Who couldn't stand to look at you."

"Can you blame her?" Harry said. "A woman who looked

175

like that, to have a son who looked like me. It must have been a knife in her heart, every time she saw me."

"Why a knife in her heart? Don't you think she put a knife in yours saying that?"

"Don't be silly, Doctor. I'm not as sensitive as she is."

He did not remember, forty-three years later, that he went into the bathroom beside the third-floor landing and cried like a girl. Nor did he remember, even at five o'clock the same evening, what it was that pressed his eyes with weights, as if he were a dead man. That night McLuskey paid him a bonus for the good job he had done in October, and the first thing Harry did was go out and look for a woman. He knew instinctively there was no way he could get it free, and aside from an Irisher with little tits pointing up to the sky and pink around her eyes, there was no one in the neighborhood he would have wanted it from even as a present.

There was a Romanian lady named Wilma who lived on the corner of Mott Street above the fish store, and some of the older boys in school made jokes on the way home about how many ways there was to smell fish, so Harry went to Wilma's apartment. He wasn't sure what he was expected to do when he got there, but Romanians were very industrious when it involved profit, so she could probably direct him; as long as he hid the rest of his money someplace safe, like in his socks, there was no way a Romanian could hurt him. He climbed the stairway in the fishy darkness, feeling his way along the wall next to the railing, listening to nothing, not even his own thoughts, conscious only of the darkness and the sound of his own breathing. When he reached the landing, he knocked. He was surprised when a man's voice answered.

"Wilma?" he said. The man stood there in his long underwear and trousers opened at the waist. He smelled of tobacco and beer, and the hair on the side of his bald head was matted with graying curls. "Does Wilma live here?"

The man narrowed his eyes, and chewed on the cigar in the corner of his mouth. "She know you?"

"I was here once about voting," Harry said.

"You old enough to vote?"

"Is she here?"

"Hold on, I'll find out." He turned and walked up a short flight of stairs, and disappeared onto a second landing. "Someone wants to know if you're here."

"So?"

"So are you here, or not?"

"Who is it?"

"I don't know. A voter."

"Tell him I'll be down."

"Tell him yourself. I don't run your errands."

The woman appeared in a moment, silhouetted against the dull light behind the open door at the top of the stairway. Harry could see her legs through her dress, the same as if she had no skirt on. But they were thick legs, almost together at the top, not long and slim with space for walking and movement like his mother's. "Yes," she said.

"Can I come up?"

"Who is it?"

"I was here once before."

"I don't remember you," Wilma said, coming closer. "You sure it was me."

"We didn't do anything," Harry said. "I talked to you about your councilman."

"How old are you?" Her breasts were very large underneath the cotton print of the fabric, and he could see where the nipples bulged the material.

"Sixteen," he said.

"You're lying," Wilma said. "You have money?"

"Plenty."

"Come on up."

She turned around and he started up the steps so quickly that his eyes were on a level with her behind. He grasped the railing to stop himself from hitting against it, and waited for her to precede him. Her skirt hiked up her legs as she climbed, and he could see a faint trail of hair, darkening and thickening as it grew up the inside of her thigh. Harry had never seen a naked woman, except for his aunt Sarah. In spite of the crowded proximity in which they lived, her mother kept herself private, dressing at all times behind the one door that closed inside the apartment. He was sorry now he had even watched Aunt Sarah from behind the cover of sleep. He had hoped to find a veil of sweet mystery at the top of that dusky trail, but he knew from secret peekings there was only a clumpy bush, and he wondered what all the excitement was about, at the same time that he found the heat rising in himself. Wilma's scent drifted back to him across the few inches that separated her mysteries from his nose, as he followed her up the stairway. It was heavy, but not unpleasant. He could feel the heaviness between his own loins, and the tide of excitement flowing from his neck to his penis, and he wondered if she could tell, even with her back turned like that.

She could. At the top of the landing she stopped, and turned, and reached between his legs. "Cute," she said, and tweaked it as easily as Aunt Sarah did his nose.

The man in his long underwear sat in a chair by the window, looking at a newspaper folded in his lap. He did not look up as Wilma led Harry to the bed at the far side of the room. She reached up and tugged at the fabric hung with rings like a shower curtain, and pulled it across the rod, separating them from the rest of the small parlor.

"Is he going to stay there?" Harry said.

"He can't see anything."

"He can hear," Harry said, remembering the stories all the boys had about listening to parental mattresses squeaking in the close-quartered darkness, recalling the times he had strained his own ears for familiar repulsive signals on the other side of the door.

"He's deaf," Wilma said.

"Then how come he answered the bell?"

"I told him it was ringing."

"He heard you tell him, though."

"You want to do something, or you want to have an argument."

Harry lowered his head.

"That's what I thought," Wilma said, pulling her skirt up to her waist. "Take off your pants."

He turned his back to her and unbuttoned his fly, and slipped his knickers down to his knees. "Close your eyes," he said.

"You close yours," Wilma said. "Then you won't be able to tell if I'm watching."

Harry closed his eyes and reopened them instantly to check if she was joking. She was lying on her back, her hands folded against her neck, and she was smiling, but not at his face.

"It is cute," she said. "Like a little soldier standing at attention."

"You said you wouldn't look."

"No I didn't. I said you should close your eyes so you wouldn't know if I was. What's so terrible if I see? It's all right to stick it inside me, but not to look at it. Why don't you take your pants off, not just down. It isn't like going to the toilet."

But in a way, it was. She got him on top of her, and guided him inside, and in spite of not liking her, and the man breathing on the other side of the curtain, Harry was so excited he thought he was going to pee.

"I can't," he whispered.

"Sure you can," she answered back, clutching his buttocks with her two big hands, moving his hips in an easy circle as if he were a lazy Susan. "Let go. Just relax and let go." She reached her hand down on the inside of his hip and felt beneath him, scratching gently along his scrotum with the tip of her fingernail.

A wave of exquisite pain shot through him, and he shuddered.

"Good, huh?" she said.

"I have to go to the bathroom," Harry said.

"There's a sink in the closet over there. Anything serious the toilet's out in back."

He unstraddled her and walked over to the closet, turning once and waving, like a politician, but she was already turned over with her face on the pillow, not looking at him. Harry stepped inside the closet and shut the door behind him, reaching over his head to pull the light cord. To his surprise he did not have to pee at all. But looking down at the part of himself he held in his hand, he wondered if he had hurt it by what he did. His mother had not cautioned him about disease, as his mother did not discuss any physical matters; but Aunt Sarah had warned him never to sit down on a strange toilet seat, and he knew from his friends with part-time jobs it was easy to pick up a dose of something if you didn't choose your company.

He narrowed his eyes against the yellow dimness and tried to sort through the bottles and jars on the glass shelf above the sink without touching any of them. There were unmarked apothecary jars of crystals and toothpowder and a tube of some greenish jelly with the cap missing. A straight razor and some shaving soap were placed upright in a cup at the right side of the shelf, and right behind it Harry could see a bottle that looked like what his father used after shaving. He reached carefully around the cup and drew it up and over the rest of the objects on the shelf, and read the label: Lilac Vegetal. If anything would purify him, that should.

He poured a dollop of it into the cup of his left palm and lifting his penis with his right hand, splashed it on himself, rubbing briskly.

The scream of pure agony that echoed from the water closet made Wilma clutch at her heart. None of her customers had ever died in her place, and it was hard enough keeping up a nice trade above a fish store, without a kid kicking off in your closet. For a moment she was afraid to open the door, but by that time her husband was already over there, and the closet was flung open.

"Jesus," Harry said, hunched over himself. "Oh my God."

"What happened?" the man said.

"The lotion." His teeth were clenched so tight there was hardly room for the words. "I put . . ."

179

"On your pecker?" Wilma said, peering over her husband's shoulder.

Harry nodded, his face flaming, little spots of white sweat on his forehead.

Wilma leaned over and turned on the cold-water tap, full. "Dunk it," she said.

"But . . ."

"Shut up and dunk."

He was not tall enough to reach over and have anything more than the tip of himself reach the water. Pain took precedence over the embarrassment he felt, as he climbed up and straddled the sink, lowering his behind into the flow of the water. "Christ," he said, washing his injured member under the cold-water tap. "Oh Lord."

"Is that better?" she said, as he nodded mutely. "What a damn fool thing to do. What did you do a damn fool thing like that for? Don't you know it's full of alcohol."

"I wanted to . . . didn't want to . . . I thought . . ."

"You afraid of getting dirty?" Wilma said, and smiled. "If you're so afraid of getting dirty why don't you just burn it off ahead of time, and then you don't have to worry about burning it off after."

"Will I have scars?" Harry said, but could not hear her answer through the running of the water, and the man's laughter.

For a long time Miriam Bell suspected her son had been going to a woman. The one thing in the house she was careful about, besides her embroidery, was the laundry, which she would change regularly and sort for her sister-in-law Sarah to wash. She hated any kind of filth or debris, and was always checking Harry's undershorts to see if he wasn't wiping himself carefully enough, and his sheets to see if he was playing with himself in bed, or having wet dreams. She knew about those because her husband continued to have them at forty-one years of age, with her lying there right beside him, even on nights when they had had relations, and she fully expected her son to be cut from the same soiled cloth.

Twice, she noted, in the space of two weeks, Harry had not turned in a dirty pair of shorts in the morning, as he was supposed to do. When she asked him if he was wearing dirty pants he only stammered and avoided the question; so she assumed, correctly, that he had taken them off somewhere and been too embarrassed to look for them again in the dark. As for the sheets, there was not even the hint of a stain. Unless he was playing with himself in the toilet down the hall, which was unlikely, what with the four families who had to use it, and the cry that went up if anybody stayed in the closed cabi-

180

net for more than five minutes, he had to be getting rid of it someplace.

"You have a girl, Harry?" she said, when he got home from running errands for McLuskey one afternoon.

"Don't be sil, Ma," Harry said.

"Don't get smart with me, mister."

"I didn't mean to get smart, Ma. I only meant . . ."

"You don't call your mother silly. And not in that cute language you talk. Where did you learn that cute language?"

"That's how everybody talks around school, Ma."

"Well you don't speak that way in my home. In my home we speak English. Good English. No refugee, and no street language. Understand?"

"Yes, Mother."

"Now what about the girl?"

"There's no girl, Mother."

"Are you seeing a prostitute?"

"How could you think that, Mother."

"I think it because I know what you are. You're old enough. God knows you aren't big, but you're old enough. And you are your father's son."

"I'm your son too, Mother."

"I suppose."

He tried to come close to her and embrace her. But she had already grabbed up the embroidery needle and stationed herself in her usual position on the sofa, her velvet dark head turned away from him.

"I'm going to make you very proud of me, Ma."

"Are you?"

"I'm going to make a big success."

"Really?"

"A very big success."

She turned her head slightly and looked at him directly, appraising. "You're going to have to," she said.

Twenty years later when he gave out his first national magazine interview after becoming a millionaire for the tenth time in the midst of the Depression, the reporter for *Life* magazine asked him what had been his impetus for becoming such a success.

"I'm a little ugly man," Harry said, "and I like to be with tall beautiful girls. I had no choice."

The first of the tall beautiful girls was Rona Jean, who worked as a secretary in the law offices where Harry was an accountant. He would have preferred being a lawyer, but the night-school course in accounting had been quicker and more manageable, with his political errands still being run in the afternoons, and his normal high-school career having been completed during the day. He had accelerated everything so in case the Army wanted him he would still have credentials if he lived.

The Army rejected him. He was ready to conquer life in America on the peaceful side.

One of the councilmen Harry's group had helped elect had a brother who ran a law firm that employed some CPA's, and McLuskey owed Harry a favor, and thought he was smart besides. As soon as Harry got his certificate, McLuskey got him into the firm: Radwell, Honeker and Geer. The only one of the three who by the furthest stretch of the imagination might have had Jewish antecedents was Geer, but nobody ever mentioned it, because he had a Main Line accent and was by far the most brilliant member of the firm. Even supposing there might have been that in his background, he stood well over six feet tall, so there was no way Harry Bell could conceivably be related to him. Harry's becoming Geer's favorite, then, had nothing to do with nepotism: the only other explanation had to be that Harry was really as bright as he seemed, and Geer, who was never so happy as when he was pontificating on the philosophy of the law and free enterprise, really liked the way the little fellow listened, and learned. He took Harry into his confidence on the most complex of trust setups and will probates, explained to him point by point the most elaborate details of the country's great banking fortunes. Geer knew them all, the railroad families, the third-generation industrialists. Everyone of great financial stature at some point touched on Geer's life or experience, and eventually, touched on Harry's imagination.

"Listen, General," Harry said one afternoon. Barnaby Geer had enjoyed a short military appointment by President Wilson to help formulate the legal tenets of the League of Nations, and Harry had shrewdly intuited that he had enjoyed the title more than the actual work. "I want to discuss something personal."

"Go ahead," Geer said.

Harry paused for a moment. His mother had told him that the reason Gentiles were so distinguished was they never discussed personal problems during business hours. Harry had no way of ascertaining if Geer really was Jewish. "No. Forget it," he said. "Another time."

Rona Jean was five feet ten, and walking past the glass cubicle down the corridor as she was doing now put her buttocks on a level so that Harry could see them moving, one two, one two, like some heavenly feminine corruption of an army marching. It was all he could do to keep his mind on the inheritance program he was working on with Geer. By the time Rona Jean reached the water cooler and bent down to reach for her cup, Harry lost the battle.

"I want to be very rich," he said.

"There's nothing personal about that," Geer said smiling. "It's social and economic. And it's also very American."

"So how do I do it, General?"

"Personal thrift. Economy."

"Begging your pardon sir, but I wasn't asking you to be Benjamin Franklin. You've tripled your personal fortune in the last eighteen months. I was hoping you'd give me some sort of practical tip."

Barnaby Geer raised his eyebrows. "What do you mean trebled, Harry?"

"Tripled," he said. "I checked into the personal file from the bank. Don't get mad at the bank, sir. I had your authorization. On the Hendricks' inheritance appraisal, only I typed a different audit order over Hendricks' name and substituted yours."

"And why are you telling me this?"

"Because you'll either fire me for being a punk, which I think you know I'm not, or reward me for my industry."

"And what if I fired you?"

"It wouldn't be too terrible a loss, sir; I'm a good accountant—eighteen dollars a week I could earn almost anywhere. It's certainly worth the risk if it could mean I'd end up with money."

"You really think that's industry? Sneaking into somebody's personal affairs."

"There's nothing personal about that, sir. It's social and economic."

Geer smiled slightly. "And American?"

"If it's American to have *chutzpah*, yessir."

"To have what?"

"*Chutzpah*. You don't know what it means? I don't know why I thought you would."

"Probably because of the various hushed whispers that I have a Jew hiding behind my family tree. I'm sorry to disappoint you, Harry."

"Oh I'm not disappointed, sir. It really wouldn't have made any difference. When you've become what you are sir, nobody would dare say a word about what you were."

"And is that what you want, Harry? To be so rich nobody cares that you're a Jew?"

"Oh no sir," Harry said, as his eyes trailed Rona Jean back to her office. "That isn't what I want at all."

As it ended up, Harry turned over nearly a thousand dollars to Geer, consisting of his hoarded salary, his accumulated savings from high school, everything that he could borrow from members of his family, plus a small loan from McLuskey. They went partners on a block of new railroad stock on which Geer had a tip from his brother the Senator, who knew the new bills that were coming up in Washington. Within five weeks, the bill had been passed, and postwar prosperity had thrust Harry into a profit position of nearly seventeen hundred dollars. He began studying the stock market as carefully as he had studied the double entry system in night school, and tapping into Geer's line to Washington. At the end of six months he was still living at home, and, telling his family nothing of what he was doing, had accumulated nearly ten thousand dollars.

"I'd like to turn this over to you, sir," he said to Geer, giving him nine thousand dollars.

"What's this for?"

"It's all the profits I've made, minus my original investment. It's because of you that I have it, so I want you to do with it what you like. Your brother's campaign fund, or whatever you think worthy."

"Well Harry, I'm slightly stunned by your sentimentality. You have that much admiration for me?"

"Yessir, I do."

"So you want to give me everything you've made so far."

"Why not, Mr. Geer. Ten thousand dollars is a lot of money for me, but it's hardly going to make me a rich man. And it's not as exciting as I thought it would be, accumulating money so slowly."

Barnaby Geer laughed. "Harry, you're an anachronism."

"Beg pardon, sir?"

"You are out of your time. You should have been around with Richelieu. Or Machiavelli."

"I'm not trying to do anything devious, if that's what you mean."

"I'd be disappointed in you if you weren't," Geer said. "All right. I'm going to call my broker. There's a new municipal bonds roadway issue coming up in Chicago—a bridge they're supposed to be building, and my information is it's going to go through almost immediately. But my information could be wrong. I can buy eighty thousand shares on margin with your nine thousand, and if it goes through, you could make, oh, upward of fifty thousand dollars, if the price goes high enough and we resell immediately. If it doesn't go through right away, they'll call for the rest of the cash, and you're dead. I won't come up with the money."

"There's no reason why you should," Harry said. "Go ahead and invest it. And thank you sir."

Within three weeks Harry had made seventy-six thousand dollars. The bonds sold for one hundred and fifty-six thousand dollars. Out of the profits Harry paid the seventy-one thousand he owed. He moved his family to a five-room apartment on Fourteenth Street, where he decided to keep living for the sake of his working capital, bought himself three seventy-five-dollar suits, six custom shirts, and asked Rona Jean for a date.

"I'd love to, Harry," she said, her big brown eyes sparkling down on him.

Harry went home to dress for the evening. Stepping into the elevator, pressing the button for the fifth floor, he hummed contentedly to himself. Vague food smells permeated the new hallways, but they did not bother Harry. The toilets were inside the apartments and there was carpeting in every room, even the one that his brother Seymour, the mechanic, shared with Irving, who was going to be an English teacher. There was no way any of them could emerge a hero, except him. He was very pleased with himself.

"I'm going out, Ma," he said. She was sitting by the window, doing her embroidery, on the couch he had brought over from the old apartment. "I won't be home for dinner."

"Tell your aunt Sarah," Miriam said. "She's the one who's cooking."

He went into his bedroom and opened the bureau drawer, pulling out the pale blue striped shirt with the HB embroidered on the pocket and took it into the bathroom. Although he could not detect much of a beard, he shaved for the second time that day. He splashed his face and under his arms with shaving lotion, and put on his shirt and went back to his room, covering his bottom half with a towel so his mother would not have to glimpse him in undershorts. When he had finished dressing he went into the living room.

"I'm going out now, Ma."

"Fine."

"How do I look."

Her head was slightly bent over her embroidery, and she did not turn to look at him. In the lights from the strong lamps he had bought for the living room, her hair shone with illusory gold highlights, only serving to emphasize by contrast the rich, deep darkness. "You look fine," she said.

He moved closer to the sofa, watching her slim long fingers flying deftly over the intricate design, and saw to his surprise that it was a pattern she had completed the month before. "Didn't you do that one already?" he said.

"I didn't like the way it looked. I took it out and started over."

"If you'd like me to get you some more patterns, Ma, I'd . . ."

"If I want some I'll get some." She looked over the top of the embroidery. "I've got a rich son."

Harry grinned. "That's right, Ma, you have."

"Just how rich are you?"

"Not very rich yet. Rich enough. But I'm going to get very rich."

"From playing the stock market?"

"Not playing it, Mom. It's not a game. Not like the horses. It's not like I'm gambling."

"I wasn't criticizing, Harry. You can play as much as you want to. It's your money."

"But I'm going to take care of you with it, Mom."

"I don't want you to take care of me. I want to make my own money. The same way as you."

"You want to play the market?"

"Why not?" she said. "I have a rich son. And he didn't get his brains from his father."

He would have laughed at that moment, Harry would have laughed with delight at the extent of the conspiracy that was about to be launched between them, but his brother Irving came in the front door, home from teacher's college. "You know what you are, Mom," Harry said, all but winking. "You're an anachronism."

"Hi, Mom. Harry," Irving said.

"Irving," said Harry.

"You look great. New suit?"

Harry nodded, his eyes still on his mother. "That's what you are. You're a contradiction in your own time. A Jewish mama who doesn't like to cook, doesn't even care if her son goes out with a *shicksa*. A true anachronism."

"I think you mean anomaly," Irving said.

"You going out with a *shicksa?*" said Miriam.

"You mind?"

"I don't mind. Just be careful with your money. They're not ashamed to take money, the *goyim*."

"Rona Jean's a lovely girl. She's Radwell's secretary."

"She's pretty?"

"Beautiful," Harry said. "Almost as beautiful as you, Ma."

"I don't want compliments, Harry, all I want to know is what kind of girl. All this time you knew her, and she's only now going out with you."

"I only just asked her out. She would have gone out with me a long time ago if I had asked her."

"Really?" Miriam said. "Look in the mirror. Your tie is crooked, you better fix it."

Later that evening as Rona Jean glowed at him across the top of her orchid corsage, candlelight softening the brick-red walls of the speakeasy and flickering through the thick redness of her hair, he reached for her hand. Her hand was not as graceful or as cool as his mother's, and a few freckles marred the white perfection of her wrist, but she was the loveliest girl he had ever been with and he was sure he loved her. She had such a small, sweet voice for such a tall, overpoweringly pretty girl, he was not the only one who had fallen victim to it, Harry was sure. Even the man at the door of the speak had admitted them instantly, although he didn't know Harry, because he had recognized Rona Jean. Or, if he hadn't recognized her, he had recognized what she was, and that was pure feminine grace that would add sparkle to any assemblage. Harry's fingertips touched hers and he felt a shudder go through him.

"I hope you don't think I'm being forward," Harry said.

"Don't be sil."

"You don't know how long I've waited for this. To be with you, I mean."

"Have you, Harry?"

"But I didn't think you'd go out with me."

"Why not? I like you. You're loads of fun."

"I haven't been loads of fun this evening. I suppose that's because this whole thing is so serious to me. Being with you I mean."

"Why?"

"You're very beautiful, Rona Jean."

"A lot of girls are very beautiful."

"Not like you. Not any that I know."

"You'll meet plenty of beautiful girls, Harry. I hear around the office you're going to be very rich."

"I'm going to have to be."

She looked at him blankly. "What for? I mean it's nice to be very rich, but nobody has to be."

"I do. You want to know why?"

"If you want to tell me."

"Because I want to be with you." He squeezed her hand tentatively.

"Let's go," Rona Jean said.

"Have I said something to offend you."

"Not at all, Harry. Get a taxi. You'll take me home."

In the cab he sat silent, his hand held palm upward on the seat between them. She did not move her hand into his. There was no doubt he had said something wrong, but he could not bear to ask her and be confronted with his own stupidity. He had never had a happier time in his life, being shown to prime tables, the admiring glances of all the other men in the room directed at him. Now he had blown it, like a true dummy, as his mother had always suspected him to be. There was nothing about him that was handsome, and he had no chance at class, and apparently he wasn't rich enough yet for anyone to overlook what a colossal ass he was capable of making of himself.

"Do you live with your mother?" he said finally, miserably, not wanting to live with the thoughts of his silence.

"My mother's dead," Rona Jean said.

"I'm sorry."

"Why. You didn't know her."

He hung his head, and did not speak for the remainder of the taxi ride. When they arrived at the small brownstone on West Seventy-fourth Street he stood on the sidewalk and extended his hand, hoping she did not hate him too much to shake it. "Well, I guess I'll say good night to you here."

"Don't you want to come up for a nightcap?"

"You want me to?"

"Of course I do, Harry. You're such a sil."

He followed her up the small stairway; the silk of her short skirt clung to the silk of her stockings, and he could see a faint trace of reddish gold where her stockings pulled away from the white skin of her inner thigh and he detested himself for having an eye of a twenty-one-year-old lecher, for placing her, even physically on a staircase, in the same category with a Wilma. He averted his eyes, and strengthened his heart against degrading her, and tried to look at his own feet as he climbed, and at the ceiling as he passed behind her down the corridor.

"Well, here we are," Rona Jean said.

Harry had not been prepared for the suddenness of her stopping, and he collided with her back. The warmth of her through her clothing rushed into him. She smelled of lilacs and talcum powder. He felt his face and his soul blazing. "I'm so sorry," he said.

"Stop apologizing so much," Rona Jean said laughing, and unlocked the door of her apartment.

It was a small bed-sitting room wtih a kitchenette behind a cord hung with gingham. For all the lack of space there was about the room no feeling of clutter, and not even the vaguest hint of food smell. The decorations were simple, dark velvets and pictures of flowers, with fresh flowers in two vases.

"You like flowers?"

188

"I love flowers," said Rona Jean.

"You're going to have them every day."

"Thank you," said Rona Jean. "But I have them every day now."

"I guess you want me to leave."

"Relax, Harry. Do you want to take off your jacket?"

"If you want me to."

"You always this easy to get along with, Harry? I would have guessed you had to do a little more asserting yourself around the office."

"This isn't the office, Rona Jean. What I do around the office I did so I could be here, if you get my meaning. But I told you that before, didn't I. When you got mad at me."

"I didn't get mad, Harry. Come, sit down. Over here, on the couch, beside me."

"Am I blocking your light?" Harry said.

Rona Jean laughed and put her hand through his arm. "What a beautiful shirt," she said. "Such soft material."

"I had it custom-made."

"I'm sure you'll have everything custom-made before you're finished, Harry." She pressed her wonderful head against his shoulder and he could smell lilac in her hair, although he was not sure how lilac really smelled. Before he could stop himself he had turned her face with his hand, and his fingers were on her thick beautiful eyelashes, and his lips were on her luxurious mouth.

"Oh my God," he said. "I'm sorry."

"Why?" she said, and the tip of her tongue pointed at him between her teeth.

By the time he had kissed her twice his mouth was so swollen he was convinced he would choke from his own shame. "I better go home now."

"Why?" she said.

"Rona Jean . . ."

"Harry, how old are you?"

"The same age as you. I checked the insurance records at the company."

"I suppose twenty-one in a woman is older than twenty-one in a man," she said, and turned her face away.

"Have I done something wrong?"

"Well what's the matter with you? How dumb can you be?"

"I have offended you," he said, and covered his eyes against the light. "Everything I've done so I could be with you, and now you're offended."

"Oh for God's sake, Harry. Wise up. I told you once and I tell you again. You don't have to get rich to be with me."

"Really?" he said. "You really care for me."

"Of course, I do," she said, reaching for his fly. "You never needed more than twenty-five dollars."

After that he knew that all women were whores, and all he wanted from life was never again to know their price. He still decided to get very rich, so he would never have to put his cash on the line. But he knew they would be there from then on, waiting.

Marilyn, his first wife, was almost as rich as he was, but her price was she needed an escort that people wouldn't say married her for her money. Harry knew a lot of her crowd and could take her to the right places. Right after they got divorced he bumped into Rona Jean one night, and she looked tired and the luster was gone from her hair, and his heart moved with long-dead pity for dreams people didn't have anymore. They went out and got drunk together.

"Why twenty-five?" he said sloppily. "Why'd you ask twenty-five."

"That was what I got paid a week," Rona Jean said. "I thought it was kind of a kick getting the same thing for work I was getting for play."

"I would have married you, you know. If you hadn't told me, if you'd played me along a little, I would have married you."

"I know," she said. "That's why I told you."

"It would have been so terrible marrying me?"

"I like to screw around," she said. "I really do. I mean I know people are supposed to talk about it in whispers, and nice girls don't enjoy it, but I've been jumping since I was fifteen just because I love to do it, that's all."

"And I wouldn't have been enough for you."

"You're sweet, Harry," she said. "Let's not go into it."

She was willing to give him a free ride for old time's sake, but he didn't want it, now that he knew exactly what it would cost him (he couldn't bear to ask her if her price had gone down, because he suspected between the stock market's crashing, and the shine leaving her hair, that it had). At the outside staircase of her brownstone, the same one on Seventy-fourth Street and West End, he took her hand, and kissed the inside of her palm and pressed it to his cheek.

"Call me if you need anything, kid."

"I will, Harry. Sure."

He knew of course that she would never call him again, for anything, and he was grateful because he didn't want her to call. On the way home he had the cab stop at the flower store on the corner of Broadway and Seventy-ninth, and he told Spiro to send fresh flowers to her house, every other day, and send the bill to his office.

That spring he got a call from Geer, who was visiting with the Senator in Washington. Geer had a tip that Prohibition was going to be repealed, and if Harry wouldn't mind taking a trip to London, there were a couple of people over there that Geer could put him in touch with, through whom Harry could get the American franchise on a few of the better Scotches. Naturally Geer would like a share in the profits from the franchise, but he didn't insist on having it. It was a favor for a friend who was smart enough to handle it, that was all.

"Why don't you go over there yourself?" Harry said.

"It might look funny," Geer said. "Almost as if I had had advance information from my brother. Undue senatorial influence, all of that."

"Well we certainly wouldn't want that to happen, would we, General?"

"No, we certainly wouldn't. No share of profit is worth besmirching a fine senatorial reputation."

"What share of profit did you have in mind?" Harry asked.

"Thirty-three and a third."

"No, that certainly would be too risky. A third of all that money. That's a regular besmirching amount. Five percent, nobody could even accuse you of getting a finder's fee."

"Five percent isn't very much, Harry."

"It's plenty for remaining unbesmirched," Harry said.

He sailed for England the next afternoon, on the *Queen Mary*. Three weeks later he returned with franchises for four of the best brands of Scotch in his pocket. When Prohibition was repealed, liquor dealers all over the country could deal only with him. He was an incredibly rich man, even in his own eyes. So rich that he could consider being remiss with the payments on his bills. It was the privilege of only the very rich not to pay their bills on time, and the privilege of the debtee to be owed by a very rich man.

The one account he paid promptly, the first of every month, was Spiro the florist. Spiro was too small a business to sustain without being paid, and if he didn't have operating capital, he might start sending Rona Jean wilted flowers. Ten months later Spiro sent Harry a note saying the occupant of that apartment was deceased. By that time Harry was already so involved with Celeste he did not even bother to inquire into the cause of Rona Jean's death. Instead, he commended Spiro on his honesty in not padding an account that no longer existed, and ordered the flowers instead to be redirected to Celeste's apartment, which was down the hall from his.

If it hadn't been for Harry's mother, Celeste would have been living right in Harry's apartment, because she was so crazy about him, she told him all the time, and didn't give a rat's ass what the world said about her. Harry didn't like her to talk that way, except in bed, and he said so, but very gently, because she was so lovely he didn't want to do anything to offend her. She was not the run-of-the-mill showgirl, but had had a featured tap dance in a nightclub revue in Miami, where Harry had gone to close the first of his numerous real estate deals, buying up a four-or-five-miles-wide strip east of the city that some anxious promoters wanted to make into a resort area, and needed capitalization for. In the end Harry squeezed the rest of them out of the deal, and brought it in himself, with the aid of some excess capital from Geer. But even if it hadn't worked out to such enormous profit, it would have been worth the trip, because he met Celeste.

The first time he saw her, her long blond hair piled up in ringlets twirled gently around the glass bubbles on top of her head, he had thought his heart would break, she was so ethereal. When she shuffled and tapped in her silver shoes, every spangle and sequin on her body shimmered. But the muscles of her thighs were solid, unquivering, even on the inside, where women got hit the earliest and hardest. "She's in great shape," he said to the proprietor, who was sitting next to him at ringside. "It must be the dancing."

"Yeah, well, she gets a lot of exercise," Maury said.

After that Harry shut his ears to everything but the music, and the solid tap tap tap of her feet on the nightclub floor. When she was through with her number, he was standing up, clapping his hands loudly, even after the rest of the audience's polite applause had ceased. People were staring at him, including Celeste, who peered nearsightedly through the spotlight on her pink and white face, and finally smiled blindly in the direction of the applause, doing a little half-curtsey before cartwheeling off the stage. Harry sat impatiently drumming his fingers on the marble top through the rhythm of the rhumba band. He started to go to the men's room during the production number, except that he followed the direction of the male production singer's hand: at the eye's extension of that tuxedoed arm, among the feathered headdresses and masks, as the man sang "Bird of Paradise," he recognized the thighs at the top of the stairs. They were golden white against the bright kelly green of the feathers.

"Would that I were a feather, to rest against that," said Harry softly.

"Excuse me?" Maury said.

"Shakespeare," Harry said. "My brother teaches English."

Maury let Celeste skip the second show, so Harry could take her down the peninsula to Nestleman's Wharf, a big converted-trawler houseboat where diners could fish off the top-deck balustrade for their appetizers, which were swimming around in a big net Nestleman had attached to the bottom of the boat. The main course was almost always lobster, and Nestleman had them displayed in a glass tank by the gangway. "You pick one for me," Celeste said, averting her yellow-green eyes. "I can't stand to look at them."

"Those two," Harry said to the man with the big pliers. "The fat lazy ones in the corner. You make sure you cook them till they turn pink."

"They all turn pink the minute they hit the boiling water."

"I don't want to hear about it," Celeste said, and covered her ears.

By the time he had threaded her hook with bait, so she wouldn't have to see, and lowered her line over the side until the action was under the surface of the water, raised the struggling mackerel and handed it to the waiter while she turned away and powdered her nose, not using a mirror for fear she might catch a glimpse of the fish, Harry knew he could be served up on a plate along with the entree. In spite of her height she was the daintiest girl he had ever been with, except for his mother, who did not count because she was tiny to begin with, besides which this was purely a social situation. He wanted to know everything about Celeste. Once she told him she was nineteen, he understood she could not have very much of a history. Mainly they talked about his ex-wife Marilyn.

"I used to see her pictures in the papers a lot," Celeste said. "She was very glamorous."

"Not pretty," Harry said, "but glamorous, yes. She knows how to wear clothes."

"I didn't read her book, but everyone who read it says it was wonderful."

"It was a wonderful book," Harry said.

"I can't imagine a woman sitting down and writing a novel. She must have a lot of patience."

"And drive," Harry said. "Plenty of drive."

"You have to really want to be somebody to have drive."

"I suppose so," Harry said, and signaled for some wine.

"Was it very hard being married to a celebrity."

"Not really," Harry said. "Of course the novel was such a big hit with women that she became kind of a national heroine like Daphne, in the book you know, the one who goes crazy in Paris . . . so they hung all over her wherever she went, the ones who didn't really know her, but I didn't mind that. And of course our friends were *both* our friends, they all know who I am. I guess you could say, in a minor way of course, I'm a bit of a celebrity myself."

"I suppose," said Celeste. "But it isn't really the same thing, is it, really being somebody and just making money."

"I guess you could say that," Harry said.

"So how come you married her?"

"I didn't really marry her. She married me. I was only a kid, not really that much older than you are now, but she liked me, she liked how I handled myself, and I wasn't impressed by her, she liked that, and there was no way I could be impressed by her money. And she was lonely. The very successful are very lonely."

"I hear that a lot," Celeste said. "Especially around Miami."

At the end of three days he had not been to bed with her, and he was going crazy. The insanity was more or less of his own creation, because he had never actually asked her if she would sleep with him, mainly because he was afraid of her answer. Once he kissed her good night in the back of the limousine he hired to bring her home nightly from the club. When he took her to the beach the next day he spread oil on her back, and she turned over, unintentionally, and he touched her breast where it pressed against the top of her bathing suit. He thought his hand would burn off.

"I'm going back to New York tomorrow, kid," he said when he drove her home that night.

"I know," she said. "I heard."

"You going to miss me, kid?"

"What do you think, Harry?" She turned to him, and in the speckled light from the lamps along the causeway, he could see tears in her eyes. He was sure they were tears.

"I'm crazy about you, Celeste. You know that."

"Really, Harry?"

"I'd like to take you back with me, only I know what you'd say if I asked you."

"Asked me what, Harry."

"To come back to New York with me."

"Oh."

"I'd like to do the right things by you, Celeste. I'd like to show you the town, and to show the town you . . ."

"That's nice, Harry."

"And I'd like you to meet my mother."

"She must be a very sweet old lady."

"She's younger than anybody, and she's a shrewder busi-

194

nessman than I am. You should see her studying the *Wall Street Journal* like it was the *Racing Form*. Shrewd. She plays company owners like some people bet jockeys. I got her an observer's seat on the Stock Exchange, so she can run up there and watch the action. She gives me some of my best tips."

"That must be very nice for you," Celeste said.

"She's a great woman."

"You sound really crazy about her, Harry. It's nice you'll have somebody you like so much to be with when you get back to New York."

He sat, silent, watching the lights go by the car window, holding her hand, and trying not to think about the inside of her thighs. Pressed as close to him as her upper leg was, it was very difficult. "I wouldn't even ask you to come back with me," he said, finally.

"Okay," said Celeste.

When they were a block away from the hotel apartment she shared with three other girls from the show, Harry turned to her, and, careful to put his arm across her lap so she wouldn't think he was trying for a feel, kissed her. She opened her teeth to him behind her lips, and sat up very straight and tall next to him. Harry realized that her skirt must have slid up from the shiny leatheriness of the car seat, because the next thing he knew he could feel the naked tops of her legs against the heel of his hand, and then the car must have jolted, because her legs slipped apart and his hand was caught between her thighs, and he could feel the tight silkiness of them, and the warm furriness above.

"Come to New York with me," he said.

"You know what I want, Harry."

"You can have it," he said. "Anything. Just don't tell me no."

"I want to be somebody. Not just belong to a rich man, Harry. I want to be somebody."

"You'll have it," he said. "You're beautiful and you're talented. So beautiful and talented. I'd like to see anybody try and stop you."

"Thank you, Harry," she said. "You're good. You're so good." She slid down in the seat to embrace him so suddenly that he did not have time to adjust his hand and without his even knowing how it happened, his finger was inside her, drowning in warmth.

"Oh baby," he said. "Oh my goodness." It was all so quick and enveloping to his senses that she didn't even have to touch him, and it was over. "Oh my goodness," he said, and rested his head against her breast. "You sweet thing."

195

The next day they left for New York on the Silver Meteor, each with a separate compartment, because he did not want her to feel she was trapped. They had two martinis apiece in the club car. He took her back to the observation car and sat in the last chair with his arm around her, their seats turned away from the rest of the occupants, their eyes trailing the scenery they were leaving behind.

"It isn't that I don't want to get married," Harry said. "But I know too many guys got rich too fast got hooked by girls who weren't really nuts about them. That's the only reason I'd insist on a premarital agreement."

"I didn't even say anything about getting married," Celeste said. "Who said anything about getting married."

"I know you didn't, sweetheart, but I just wanted to lay it out in the beginning so when and if the time was propitious you wouldn't think I was throwing up a roadblock or anything."

"I wouldn't even consider marriage at this point in my life. I want to be somebody."

"I know that, angel."

"What exactly is a premarital agreement?"

He told her. In turn, she told him she thought that was absolutely the right thing to do, with all the money he had, to make sure the girl didn't get any part of it.

"That isn't what I said," Harry said. "Naturally my wife would have everything she wanted. I just want to make sure that nobody marries me so when they get out they can be a rich woman."

"How could anybody do anything like that? To you of all people."

"Well, it takes all kinds."

"I guess so," said Celeste.

That night, after they had had dinner in the dining car, he showed her to her compartment, and waiting until the corridor was clear, kissed her good night. "Good night, kid," he said.

"You're so sweet."

"I'm not sweet," Harry said. "I'm not sweet at all. It's easy to be sweet to you, because I'm nuts about you. You're such a great kid. Nineteen. Jesus Christ. It's only seventeen years since I was nineteen and I feel like it was a million years ago. I'm an old man."

"You're young," she said. "You're like a little boy."

"I wish."

"I'm going to show you," she said, and slipped inside her own door.

Harry got into his best pajamas and turned out the lamps

in his compartment, raising the shade so the light from the moon would illuminate love's own glow, in case there were any. He lay on his back, the sheet drawn halfway up to his chin, wondering if she was really coming to him, or if he wasn't being a naive sucker waiting there for her, hardly daring to breathe, even. He was immediately ashamed of himself for having such thoughts: Celeste was the best thing that had ever happened to him, and the finest, in a social situation. She was coming to New York. He could presume nothing except that she cared enough to come along. What would ensue, would ensue, and it had to come in its own time, in her own time. He had no right to demand anything, unless it was in due course. To insist that she volunteer was presumptuous. He chewed on his little fingernail in the moon-speckled darkness and wondered if he should take off his pinky ring, just in case she had meant what he thought she meant.

He got up and brushed his teeth for the third time that evening, sprayed a little men's cologne into his hand and patted it into his cheeks, the hollow of his throat, and under his arms. He was just about to loosen his pajama string and freshen his privates when he remembered the incident with Wilma, for the first time in years.

"Jesus," he said, and stared at the would-be offending hand, turned on the cold water and rinsed it clear.

"Harry?" came the gentle longed-for voice from outside.

"I'm only washing my hands," he said quickly. He dried himself and opened the door.

She was standing, tentatively, shyly, he could see, by the door to the corridor, which was slightly ajar. The moonlight, or maybe it was rushing presences of cities outside, made her white-gold hair a halo, and standing there in her white-negligeed private illumination she could have been a goddess. "You want to close the door?" he said, and his voice was thicker than he remembered it ever sounding.

"If you want me to, Harry." She turned, slowly, not a single staccato motion jarring the gracefulness of her flow. In that split second he violated the dreaminess of it, running behind her and jumping into his bed, pulling the covers up to his chin so she would find him as he had intended. He was not at all sure of the effect he had planned, but whatever it was he hurt it a little by being out of breath.

"Harry . . ." She came toward him, her arms outstretched.

"Baby . . ." He reached up for her, wondering if he should try for it, like a schoolboy, in stages. But her robe came apart and she was naked underneath. His hands were on her velvet breasts, and he could see that the pink around

197

the tips was lightly freckled, like the skin on the back of her hands, and the nipples were darkening and growing under the touch of his fingers. "You lovely thing," he whispered, his lips nuzzling her throat, so he could continue to watch from the corner of his eye the magnificent progress of her breasts. "Beauty girl."

"Harry," she said.

A sudden motion of the train hurled her backward and he was lying almost on top of her, and her knee was between his legs, probably to slow him down, Harry reasoned, but having the opposite effect, what with the gentle warm pressure through the silk against his vitals, and the way she moved her foot back and forth. The string of his pajama came untied, and he lay there, exposed, with no way to conceal the extent of his longing, pressed as it was against her thigh.

"Oh baby," he said. "I want you so bad."

"I see, I see how you do."

And he was plunging headfirst into the warm bath of her kisses while the rest of her accepted him, yieldingly, hotly, and there was such motion beneath him as he had never experienced in his life, and had to be, he was sure, the curiously sensual vibrations of the train. No woman could know that much, least of all a nineteen-year-old angel. Even if she knew, there was no way to translate the knowledge into the incredible undulations that shot him from his loins headfirst, out of his own brain.

"Oh Jesus, oh God. Oh baby. Oh. Kid," he whispered, and collapsed inside her, and belonged to her for good, until she was finished with him.

That did not happen until nine years later, although as far as Harry's mother was concerned, it should have happened right away.

"Where's the whore? Down the hall?" Miriam would say, when she came to her son's apartment for her weekly dinner, cooked by his French chef.

"Why Mom, anyone would think you were jealous of her."

"To be jealous I would have to love you," Miriam said, and then laughed to let him know she was kidding. "After all, you are my son, Harry, and you're very smart. Everybody on the Exchange says so. They treat me with nothing but respect because I'm your mother, and also I'm smarter than any of them. That's why I hate to see you being played for a fool by such an obvious little floozy."

"She's a lovely girl, Mom, and I love her."

"And she'd be crazy about you if you weren't rich, wouldn't she." Miriam set down her cocktail glass and refilled it with sherry.

"Well, we'll never have a chance to find out, will we, Ma. After all, it's your fault I'm a rich man. You told me I'd have to be, to get what I wanted, didn't you."

"I didn't mean a whore. I figured if you were going to pick on a whore, you'd at least have the discretion to find one with a little more class."

"She has a lot of class, Mom."

"You confuse her with a horse, Harry. Good legs don't mean breeding."

"You are jealous. You lovely thing."

"You're in my light, Harry." She leaned her head down over the *Wall Street Journal* and pursed her lips, in exaggerated thoughtfulness. "Well? What are we playing this week?"

"You're a little more au courant with the market right now than I am, Ma. My mind's on other things."

"Au courant? You're getting very grand. Irving the English teacher wouldn't have the nerve to drop an au courant. What *other* things?"

"I'm thinking of investing in the theater. I think people want a little more spectacle. I think I could bring the theater some flair. Besides, there's a friend of McLuskey, a real old-fashioned showman type, who's up to his ears in IOUs and I could take them over and get his next production for almost nothing. There's a lot of money to be made from the theater, Ma, the only thing is nobody's thought of it in terms of big business. Spectacle is a commodity, like anything else, and I could give the people what they wanted, a spectacle."

"How long have you been rehearsing that speech?" Miriam said.

"I was just thinking about it very seriously this afternoon, and I made a few notes."

"What do you mean by spectacle," Miriam said. "Tap dancing?"

"Of course if there's a spot for her, I'd love to have Celeste do a number."

"There'll be a spot for her," Miriam said sadly.

"Oh, Mom, I don't know why you're so down on her. She's a genuinely talented girl."

"She must be, if she could make such a smart man into such a stupid boy. Is she coming to dinner, the whore, or what. I'm hungry."

"Would you like her to eat with us?"

"I couldn't swallow a mouthful without her."

Harry went to the phone and started to dial.

"Don't make everything so elaborate for my benefit," Miriam said. "Just press the button and let her come through her usual hole in the wall."

"Please don't talk like that, Mother."

"Well this whole thing is too stupid, going through all this roundabout for me. Let her move in here. Save the rent on the other apartment. I know you're sleeping together. Calling her on the phone to invite her here for dinner isn't going to turn her into a virgin."

"She was a virgin when I met her."

Miriam started to laugh.

"Well it's true. A man knows things like that."

"You're right," Miriam said. "I was wrong to call her what I did. She isn't a whore. She's a hypnotist. Don't just stop with a tap-dancing number. Give her a reflecting mirror and a wand."

Halfway through the Dover Sole Meunière Harry was still trying to remember. His mind and his senses were blurred by Celeste's nearness, and his mother smiling across the silver tapers, sharing her unspoken joke with the fish in front of her, as the butler refilled her wineglass. Of course Harry was clear enough to know Celeste hadn't bled on the train, but some women didn't bleed, several of the girls he slept with had assured him of that. The brilliance of her subsequent sexual performances he knew he could attribute to his own tutelage. She got better all the time, but that was good, that was natural, because they loved each other. The only question, then, was that first time, on the train. Even remembering the train, he could feel himself getting hard and he straightened the napkin in his lap, and tried to keep the color out of his face, for fear that his mother would know. Then he remembered. Of course. The time on the train hadn't been the first time for her. There was the night before that, in the limousine, when he'd gotten his hand in, and oh God, come in his pants like a twelve-year-old.

"You're wrong, Ma," Harry said. "I was there."

"Vass you dere, Charley?" Miriam said to Celeste.

"Pardon?" Celeste said.

"It's a vaudeville routine," Miriam said, smiling sweetly, the tines of her fork twirling a piece of lemon. "I don't suppose you'd be familiar with it. After all, you haven't been around show business very much, have you."

"I only had the one specialty in Miami," Celeste said.

"So I understand," Miriam said, and laughed.

"How's your fish, Ma?"

"Not so hot," she said. "I don't know why you think it's such a triumph, getting that Frenchman to come cook for you. You wanted a refugee, your aunt Sarah is available. She cooks better and I'd give you half my kingdom to get her out of my house. And take her brother with her."

"How is Dad?"

"His back."

"I'm sorry."

"He's not. He's enjoying it. He can sit with the pad, and go to the steams, and then come home to the apartment and have Sarah moan around with him, while she cooks. They make a lovely couple. I wish they had found each other years ago."

"You ought to spend more time with him."

"Why?" Miriam said. "I didn't like him when we were young and had children and had to be with each other. Why should I like him now? I'm in business and my children are grown and I can go anywhere. Why should I go home, except to sleep?"

"Why did you marry Dad?" Harry said.

"Because he asked me. Because everybody was poor and running everywhere on cattle boats, and I was afraid, and he asked me."

"You were a beautiful woman. You still are. You could have had anybody."

"Maybe," Miriam said. "And maybe not. Maybe a woman wasn't allowed to tippytoe around with her destiny in my day. Maybe a woman did what her people expected her to do, and maybe if she was a good girl she didn't wiggle herself around a resort looking to catch a better one than her mother had."

"May I have some milk, honey?" Celeste said. Harry rang the little silver bell in front of him on the white damask cloth, and the butler appeared in the doorway. *"Du lait,"* Harry said.

"Oh for Christ's sake," said Miriam. "Speak English."

"Were you married when you were very young, Mrs. Bell?"

"Very young," Miriam said softly. "Very young. Young enough to breed three marvelous sons, a mechanic, a teacher, and a multimillionaire who wants to make a spectacle. Maybe that's the reason, maybe that's why I was born, and that's why I married your father, so I could fulfill my destiny of raising these remarkable boys, the most successful one of whom can't even speak English."

"Mama always wanted a daughter," Harry said, reaching over the napkin ring and squeezing Celeste's hand. "That's why she sometimes gets mad at us for being sons."

"My own daughter," Miriam said, and the heat rose in her face, so for the first time in his adult recollection Harry could see blue veins in her forehead. "My *own* daughter. Don't you dare try and palm this one off on me. If I couldn't have one, you're not going to pick one for me."

"I didn't say—"

"Don't you try that with me, Harry Bell. Don't you try to play on my sentiment, because I don't have any. Not anymore. It dried up a long time ago. You couldn't dish that goo out to me with Marilyn, and I'm not going to listen to it now. Here she is, Ma, the daughter you always wanted. I won't have it, Harry. Make your own mistakes. Don't offer them on a platter to me."

"I didn't even say anything."

"You're getting ready," Miriam said. "Don't tell me you aren't getting ready. I know all the signs, and they make me sick, so don't say you're doing anything for me." She took a drink of her wine, and set the light crystal glass abruptly on the table, shattering the stem. "I'd apologize but I know how much it excites you to have to order crystal from Denmark."

"Would you care for some more wine?" the butler said, taking away the broken glass.

"I'm potted," Miriam said. "Bring me coffee."

"I'm sorry you're upset, Ma."

"I'm not upset. Don't apologize. Apologize to the tap dancer, or whatever she is."

"I'm sorry, Celeste."

"What for?" Celeste said.

Miriam narrowed her eyes. "He's right. You're smarter than I think you are. Nobody could be that stupid."

"Thank you," said Celeste.

The show opened, and with its circus atmosphere, bit players jumping out of boxes, the orchestra running through the aisle, and moving picture opulence, was an enormous success, although, in Harry's words, nobody liked it but the people. The critics were amused, but unimpressed, except with Celeste, who had been costumed by Davigny and mounted in a tableau of six exceptionally handsome and nubile young men to get the hungry-lady trade, as Harry put it. The men wore white jersey leotards stretching and straining and revealing every inch and lump of their parts—and sometimes, Harry was sure, a little stuffing with towels. So the show also did a large fairy trade. As the critics at that time were neither hungry ladies nor homosexuals, they averted their eyes, made notes in their programs, and found in Celeste "that singular piece of Americana: the girl who steps out of the cake at the stag party, elevated to goddess." Celeste thought the critic who wrote that didn't like her so much, but Harry assured her it was a great sell quote, and he ran full-page ads in all the New York papers with her picture, with that line above.

For the trade papers he shortened the message to read "That singular piece of Americana." Within six weeks of the opening, there was no doubt in either of their minds that she was a celebrity.

"A real somebody," he said, in the front banquette at El Morocco. "They saw the papers. They'll all be sucking around now, the columnists, the gigolos, the fancy boys."

"And what about your mother."

"My mother doesn't read the newspapers. She only reads the *Blue List* and the *Wall Street Journal*."

"She hates my guts."

"How could she. I'm her son and I love you, so she has to love you too."

"You ask me, she hates your guts too."

"Listen, Celeste, please don't try to understand my mother. My mother's a wonderful woman. She just doesn't know how to show affection too easily, that's all."

"You're telling me. Here's Leonard."

"Hi Leonard," Harry said, waving slightly, but not motioning him to sit down. "I believe you know the star of our show, Celeste Hart."

"Pleasure," Leonard said. "You're even lovelier off the stage."

"You have no idea," Harry said.

"Well what's happening with you two? The rumors true, or what?"

"We're just good friends," Celeste said.

"You hear the one about the couple that froze to death in flagrante in Shubert Alley?" Harry said.

"Yeah, very funny, but I can't use it in my column. Maybe tell Walter. What kind of ring is that, Miss Hart?"

"Just an aquamarine," she said. "I wear it in the show. The company manager let me borrow it because I'm wearing light blue."

"You certainly are," Leonard said. "Or I guess you could say almost wearing light blue."

"Don't crack wise, Leonard," Harry said. "You're a nice guy. Don't spoil what you got going for you by cracking wise."

"Sorry, Harry."

"S'okay."

"You sure that isn't an engagement ring, Miss Hart?"

"You think he'd give me an aquamarine?"

"Good, good," Leonard laughed. "I can use that."

"I got something better you can use, you need an item," Harry said. "Celeste's had offers from four of the studios."

"You going to Hollywood to test?"

203

"If Harry wants to produce pictures, maybe."

"You want to produce pictures, Harry?" Leonard said.

"I'm not sure. I could probably do it as good as anybody, but I like it here, this is my town. From what I hear about the Coast, it's all tinsel and glitter."

"I heard that too," Celeste said.

"You think you'll get married before you go?" Leonard said.

"Why would she want to marry me for," Harry said, and squeezed her hand under the tablecloth. "She's a very big celebrity."

She squeezed his hand back in return greeting, and then as an added fillip, trailed her fingers across his crotch, the heel of her palm coming to rest pressed against his penis.

"If you'll excuse us now, Leonard, we have some personal business to discuss," Harry said, reddening.

"Of course."

As soon as they had been left alone, Harry turned to her. "Let's go home, kid."

"Why?" she giggled, her little finger scratching against his scrotum. "I'm having a swell time."

"Come on, stop. I won't be able to stand up."

"Why do you have to? Nobody can see under the table. Let's just sit here and smile politely at everybody and they'll never know what we're doing."

"In El Morocco?"

"Why not," she said, reaching for the zipper on his fly. "It's your world, Harry. Yours and mine. We can do anything we want to. And it's a kick."

"I don't need any extra kick with you, kid. Let's go home. You're making me crazy."

"That's right, Harry. That's what I make you is crazy. You'll never find anybody like me, ever again . . ."

"Please . . ." the color drained from his face as her fingers closed around him.

"Now smile, Harry. Chester Morris is waving at you, and the rubberneckers are looking."

"Oh God," he said. "Oh Jesus, kid. I want to kiss you."

"Well, you can do that, Harry. People do that in Elmer's all the time."

"Oh kid," he whispered, and reached for her mouth. "Oh my sweet kid."

"Hold it a second," she said. "I dropped the napkin."

The next day the news of their engagement was given out to the newspapers, and Harry personally telephoned Leonard to tell him the decision had been made right in the middle of El Morocco. They were married in Luchow's, three weeks from the following Sunday. The restaurant was closed to the public, and the two hundred and fifty invited guests included the cast and crew of *Whopper*, Geer and his partners from the law office, the Senator, Harry's investment staff counselor, the lawyer who had drawn up the premarital agreement, a few celebrities from Hollywood who were in town, and Harry's family. His mother was wearing a black dress from Bergdorf Goodman, which she had bought especially for the occasion.

When the summer slack hit Broadway, Harry let Celeste's understudy take over the part. She was not nearly as pretty, but her tap dancing was impressive, and Harry said the show was such an established hit Celeste's absence would not make that much difference, except artistically. They boarded the Twentieth Century for Hollywood, and Harry's imagination watered with recollection and anticipation, but Celeste had her period for the length of the trip. Mostly he read books that were being made into pictures that year, to try and get the hang of the kind of properties people were looking for. He enjoyed *Gone with the Wind* because it took up most of the United States, and he could see Bette Davis in the part, but *Wuthering Heights* he couldn't get into at all, and thought Goldwyn was making a mistake for the sake of looking artistic. When the train reached Los Angeles, Celeste told him she still didn't feel so hot, so on the way to the hotel he had the limousine stop at a bookstore. "What's good," Harry asked the lady behind the counter. When she didn't seem to have much of an opinion, he ordered all the current sellers and told her to send a couple of English books over to their suite at the Beverly Hills.

"Grammar and composition?" she asked.

"Stories from England," he said. "Sad ones. On the moors."

"What are those?" Celeste said, when the books were delivered as the bellboy unloaded the parcels in their rooms.

"I figured since you weren't feeling good I'd do a little reading."

"I never saw so many books."

"Well, we're going to be here for a while. I might as well have something to chew around the studios with. While you're making your screen test and everything."

"It isn't like you're just hanging around me. They want you to produce *Whopper*."

"I already know I can do that. That wouldn't be any fun. I want to see how good I can bullshit these people. They're all fakes and phonies, and Goldwyn's making some arty English job, so I figured I'd find some arty English job and see how many lunches I can bull my way through with how many producers. They're all fakes and phonies."

"I've heard that," Celeste said.

"But don't let it bother you, kid. It's your world. You've got them all by the balls."

"Yes," said Celeste. "Yes I do."

Harry couldn't sleep that night, because of the change of climate he imagined, and Celeste had a headache. He sat up, skimming through the books. About six in the morning, his eyelids got very heavy, so he settled on *Tess of the D'Urbervilles* as his talk-shot for the trip. It was boring, as far as he could tell, but the title was as weird as *Wuthering Heights* and there were plenty of moors in it, so he figured it would be good for a number of luncheons.

At the end of four months, when Celeste was two weeks away from starting her first picture, he decided the time had come to get out of Hollywood. "But Harry, they're crazy about you," she protested. "They all think you're a genius. It's in all the columns that you're being considered to head three different studios."

"That's why I got to leave," said Harry. "You know I had six firm offers this week for me to produce *Tess?* These *putzes* don't know where their asses are at. I mean the worst of it is I'm starting to believe it would be a great picture."

"Who are they talking about for the lead?"

"Carole Landis."

"She'd be very good."

"What do you mean she'd be good. You didn't read the book. Nobody's read the book. I'm the one who's supposed to be selling it, and I couldn't even get through it."

"So screenwriters can do wonderful things. You should see the script of my picture."

"I saw it," Harry said. "Just keep dancing."

"What's the matter with you, Harry? Why are you so down on everything. We have this beautiful house. Twenty-two rooms. Everybody is crazy about us. We go to all the parties. It's just like in the movies."

"That's the whole trouble," Harry said. "Tinsel and glitter. Everything shouldn't be so perfect. Nobody loves everybody the way everybody loves us. Not when we're not doing anything to earn it. My whole life I've done everything I wanted, only I've done it well, Celeste, you have to try and understand that. I did things that were over my head sometimes, but I always came out smelling like a rose, because even when I didn't know what I was doing, I learned, you understand, I learned fast and I did everything with éclat."

"What's that mean?"

"Style. That's what they said in *Life*. I learned and I did everything with éclat. If I stay here I'm going to turn into a phony like everybody else, and I'm going to fall on my ass. I see it coming."

"So don't do it."

"I can't stay here and do nothing."

"So why don't you go back to New York for a while. I'll be finished the picture in eight weeks, and you can come here or I'll go back to join you."

"Will you miss me?"

"I'll be working so hard," Celeste came over and sat down on the satin stool at the foot of his bergère. "I'll just be falling into bed at night, Harry. I probably wouldn't even have the energy to do anything. Maybe it's just as well you'll be back in New York, busy. Then when I come back we can have a real honeymoon." She moved over to the arm of his chair, and put her arms around his neck, and her cool hands on his forehead. "Where do you want to go, Harry?"

"The same place I've been going for years," he said against her satin-negligeed breast. "Up the canal to paradise."

"Don't sweetie. Not now. I have to give out an interview in a half hour."

"Okay," he whispered, and put his hands back in his lap. "Where do you want to go on your honeymoon, princess."

"Someplace different," she said.

He decided to buy it for her, without telling her about it. By the time he left Hollywood three days later, he had already been on the phone several times with real estate agents in the East all the way from New York to Florida, asking them to come up with something unusual that was a good investment, for possible conversion to a vacation site.

"Be good," he said to her at the station, as she kissed him good-bye.

"Haven't I always been?"

"The best," he said. "The best."

Celeste's conduct during the weeks Harry was away was exemplary. Although her costar, Wheeler Wright, was one of the most notorious and charming cocksmen in Hollywood, Celeste refused to have so much as a drink with him off the set, and it was reported so in Louella Parsons' column. Opting out on the lavish Hollywood parties where she might be seen with someone the world could construe as a fit adulterous partner, Celeste preferred, instead, at the end of the work day, a simple dish of spaghetti with her stand-in and a few of the bit players in the cast. All this was faithfully recorded by columnists, who marveled at her down-to-earth good humor, and her deep love for Harry, not wishing to upset him with even a trace of suspicion. And once set down in print, that news was read by Harry over and over again on the plane. From Miami to Cuba.

Harry had never flown before, and he had a great deal of trepidation. He could not afford the time to go by boat to Cuba, then to the private island the real estate agent in Miami promised him was exactly what he was looking for. If it was what he wanted, he needed to see it as quickly as possible, so he could make it ready for Celeste in time for the great surprise. During the flight over in the wobbly craft, he closed his eyes several times and silently told God he knew He didn't owe him any favors, because he had a terrific amount of blessings so far, but he would appreciate it if He could let him have a little more time on earth to enjoy Celeste, His greatest gift to His faithful servant, Harry Bell.

The island was everything Harry had dreamed of, and more. The main house had been built to entertain customers by a pharmaceutical corporation that had failed during the Depression. There were eighteen rooms, sparsely but nicely furnished, everything paneled in deep, dark wood except for the fireplaces, one of which was in each room in the house, except for the baths. There was an open hearth in the kitchen, and a rocked-in lagoon pool which had gone to slight disrepair. But otherwise the grounds were in excellent condition, considering no one had tended them in eight years. Harry had the real estate dealer take pictures, and he had them developed that night in Miami, because he could not hold the surprise for Celeste until she was free to join him. He concluded the deal the next morning, and had the agent make arrangements for a staff from Cuba, linens, groceries, a gardener, wood for the fireplaces, and everything else that would be necessary to set his house in order for the coming of his bride. Then, because he was such an experienced air traveler, he chartered a plane to take him from Miami to California, with stopovers in New Orleans and Houston, so he could take the picture of his honeymoon castle to his bride. He dropped her a postcard from Miami, saying he might be coming out to California sooner than they expected, laughing to himself all the while because of the deliciousness of the surprise that he would probably get there before the card.

"When you're rich enough," he chuckled to the pilot, "you can make your own time."

"That's probably true, sir."

"And your own weather," Harry said. "You realize everybody will be freezing their asses in New York this winter, and we'll be lying in the sun."

"That's nice, sir."

"Your own time, and your own weather. It's a little like being God." Realizing what he had said, Harry closed his eyes, and explained it was only in a manner of speaking, and he had nothing but the utmost of respect, and would be grateful for a few more years so he could be with Celeste.

He did not phone her from the airport, but hired a limousine to drive him directly to their estate in Bel-Air. He was about to ring the front doorbell when he remembered the servants were off Thursday evening, so he used his front door key. He made his way carefully up the heavily white-carpeted stairway. He bit his lips against whistling, as happy as he was, and did not even call her name as he went down the hall. He wanted to see her face when she saw him. But that would have been a little difficult, with her head in the position it was.

The young man, however, was sitting up on the edge of the bed, and his face was toward Harry as Harry switched on the light, so Harry could see his expression clearly, and it certainly was one of surprise. Surprise, and hanging lip-bloated lust, stupid, the way Harry must have looked when she did that to him. Celeste raised her head slowly from between the man's legs, and peered at Harry in that nearsighted, drunken way she had when she was making love.

"You think that's something," Harry said. "She gave me a hand job in the middle of El Morocco. Getting blown in a bedroom with the lights out, that's nothing, believe me."

He did not divorce her right away. He waited for her picture to come out and be a bomb, which it was. Then he hired a detective to watch her and advise Harry of the moment when she was completely on her ass. That was when he intended to set her adrift, in every sense of the word. Meanwhile he pursued his business activities in New York with a fervor unusual even for him. His money luck was running so that even things he invested in to flood his brain with issues and numbers were giving him an enormous return. From time to time he would closet some ambitious, pretty girl in a hotel for ten days at a crack, and send all her clothes to the cleaners, so she would just be there, naked, to service him. He never gave them anything, and they were all too hopeful because of who he was to ask. When it was over and they had received nothing but their meals from room service and their clothes back from the cleaners, they were too embarrassed at their own stupidity and lack of foresight to tell anyone what they, or he, had done.

He was over forty years old, and the truth of the matter was he didn't feel so much like screwing around anymore.

Psychological truths were not yet raging rampant around Broadway or Broad Street, so he did not give much credence to his own intuition that Celeste had struck where he was most vulnerable, and that was why he could hardly get it up. Every once in a while he would talk long-distance to the detective, who advised him that the bit player Harry had caught her with, Biff Clintock, was being "groomed" for stardom. What the studio wasn't doing for him, Celeste was, hiring a dramatic coach to work on his Mid-West diction, setting up a little gym for him in the Bel-Air house so he could strengthen his already powerful frame.

"Well what do you think?" Harry said into his office phone. "You think he'll make it?"

"As a big star?" said the detective. "No chance."

Harry remembered that even the drugstore clerk in Hollywood was so caught up in industry bullshit he was also a full-time critic, so the detective's appraisal was probably as good as anyone's. Still, Biff was handsome, Harry remembered, shuddering. His appearance in Celeste's picture had been brief, but impressive, like his appearance in the bedroom scenes burned into Harry's brain.

"How old is he?" Harry said.

"Nineteen."

"Legitimately nineteen or for the studio releases."

"Maybe twenty at the outside."

"So even if he makes it, he'll probably dump her."

"I don't know, Mr. Bell, I haven't been spending time with them. Only checking."

"Something will happen," Harry said. "There's God."

What happened was World War II. Biff Clintock was drafted into the Navy. Although Harry did not have the presumption to think the Almighty would plunge the United States into a great conflagration merely to wreak revenge for Harry, he did consider Him thoughtful enough to include personal justice in what had to be done anyway. A sailor's pay would not even keep her in Kleenex, Harry reasoned, so the timing was exactly right. And if there really was God, Biff Clintock would be killed, although Harry wished him no real harm.

He advised his attorneys to institute immediate divorce proceedings, wired the owner of the Bel-Air house that he was no longer responsible for the rent, and did the same for credit with all California merchants, foodstores, and even the bottled-water vendor who had been supplying their kitchen cooler in Bel-Air. He wrote letters to all their personal and fake friends in Hollywood, including heads of studios, advising them not to lend her any money, as it was not Harry's intention to be of any help in making restitution, and Celeste liked nothing better than spending somebody else's cash with no thought of paying it back.

"I don't know why you're being so hard on her," his mother said. She had just come back from Harry's island, where she had spent the winter, and her skin was deeply tanned, and her hair, which still had not the slightest trace of gray, was streaked with gold around her face. She had stopped in Curaçao before her return and her wardrobe was spiced with pale soft silks and beautiful Dutch laces, exported before the Germans entered Holland.

"You look beautiful, Mom," Harry said. "Who made up the clothes? Davigny, or your dressmaker?"

"Well you are being hard on her, Harry. You act as if it were her fault."

"Oh Mom, come on." He got up from the swivel chair behind his big oak desk, and crossed the Persian carpet toward the couch where she had settled herself, next to the ticker tape, the issues of which were confettied across her lap. "You're kidding. You always hated her. You knew what she was."

"But you didn't," Miriam said. "Or if you did, you didn't allow yourself to believe it. Self-delusion is a terrible sin, Harry, much worse than being what you really are. Celeste was a whore. I told you that all along. So you shouldn't get so spiteful merely because you caught her behaving like a whore."

"What kills me, what really kills me, is that she did it at the first opportunity. The first opportunity."

"She would have done it sooner if she had the chance," Miriam said, and reached into her pocketbook for a cigarette. The case she extracted was thin, pressed gold, hammered into a slim rectangle, with her initials. Her long tapered fingers, browned from a souvenir sun, pressed a hidden spring and the case opened. "Cigarette?"

"When did you start smoking?"

"On the island. It got very dull after a month or so, especially after Seymour and the children left. It was dull with them there, too, but the girls are cute. You can have some pleasure from little girls."

"Next year we'll make it a party. I'll invite some of the top people down, Geer, and Stuarti, and Mulvaney and Karr, they're brilliant, Ma, a baby songwriting-team, but you should hear their rhymes, how sophisticated, and maybe Clifford P. and his wife, you know how much you enjoy listening to him on the radio, he's a genuine wit, believe me, even in person. And Mulvaney and Karr can do all their numbers from Cornell—she's a hell of a performer, Ma, you'll love her. What kind of shape is the piano in?"

"I don't really know. Millie tried playing 'Heart and Soul' but it sounded tinny. Maybe it's her. She is only four."

"And she plays the piano? That's something."

"She isn't a prodigy, Harry, she's just a nice little girl. I don't know why Seymour has such sweet children when I always had such rotten ones." Miriam laughed, to show she was kidding.

"We can fly somebody over to tune the piano. Maybe there's somebody in Cuba. Won't that be a party? Won't you love that party, Ma?"

"It's nice thinking about it, Harry, but you don't have to promise me anything you won't be able to deliver."

"You don't think I can get those people to come? They're good friends of mine, Mother, all of them. They'd love an invitation to the island."

"I'm not saying you don't really know them, Harry. I'm sure you really know them. When you have enough money, you can know anybody. All I mean is by next year you'll probably have a new tramp, so don't make any plans that include me for the island."

As it turned out, they did not go to the island the following winter, as Harry had planned. In the first place there were a lot of submarine scares in the Caribbean, because of the naval base being built up in Key West, and in the second place, Harry was a little bit in love.

He was being very mature about it this time, he was sure. He recognized in Sylvia a woman who was elegant but most likely a little worldly. She was dark, and in contrast to Celeste, almost sedate in her appearance. But there was a sparkle in her eye that made up for the conservatism of her dress, a serenity in her bearing that he had never encountered in a young woman before. He was aware that, in spite of her youth, she had probably been to bed with a man. Especially as she had just been divorced.

They met in El Morocco, where Harry had taken his mother after the opening of Mulvaney and Karr's first Broadway musical, in which Harry was the silent partner. He would have produced it himself, with his name on the marquee, but the mood of the world even around New York was not one of unremitting gaiety, and he thought it might be considered a little shallow of him to be openly profiting from people's need to forget the war. Harry remembered it with a fierceness unusual for him, turning over four of his plants, hitherto devoted to the manufacture of small parts and yachting equipment, to the defense industry, only reluctantly accepting the government contracts to run the new businesses. When Treasury restrictions let him buy only fifty thousand dollars' worth of Defense Bonds a year, he strode into Defense Bond headquarters in Manhattan, gave them a check for one hundred thousand dollars and said to save him fifty thousand dollars' worth for 1943. What had happened to him could have happened to him only in America, and besides, nobody else could win the war.

The opening of the musical had gone quite well, but after the party upstairs from Sardi's Harry didn't feel tired, and neither did Miriam. She was wearing a long beige dress, of Alençon lace, molded to her remarkably slim frame, and a fingertip-length jacket of Russian sable Harry had given her, and for which she told him he paid too much. She was, he said, the prettiest woman in El Morocco. That was before he noticed the group in the corner banquette.

"I don't know how you do it, Ma," Harry said, his eyes narrowing against the darkness, trying to determine if the profile across the room was really that lovely. "You don't look a day over forty."

"That's probably because you're not looking at me," Miriam said. "Who is it, Brenda Frazier?"

"No, that's Brenda over there," he nodded his head in the direction of the dance floor. "With Shipwreck Kelly."

"Amazing," she said. "It must really be true love. They've been married at least six months by now."

"You shouldn't be so cynical, a young woman like you."

"Go ahead, ask the headwaiter who she is, it makes me crazy, your sneaking around with your eyes."

Her name was Sylvia Doff Rowan, and it was seven years before she became Sylvia Bell, for the first time. In the interim Harry wooed her, but with caution, because he didn't want to be hurt ever again, and besides he didn't really believe she was interested in anyone else. His mother assured him Sylvia was only testing him, trying to hook him, telling him she would go to California if he couldn't make up his mind.

"After all," Miriam said. "How much could she be. A dental assistant from Philadelphia. Married to a dentist."

"I thought you liked the idea that she wasn't in show business."

"It's just a clever switch, that's all. This one is no dummy. She has too much sense to try and pass herself off as some debutante divorcée, so she gives you this solidness in her background. But how do you even know she was a dental assistant? Just because she has good teeth."

"I'm not going to check on her, if that's what you're trying to make me do."

"I'm not trying to make you do anything. A dental assistant. A dentist is the garbage can of the white collar professions."

"So why would she make that up?"

"Exactly what I said," said Miriam. "How much could she be, coming from that."

"Why don't you like her, Ma? She's crazy about you. She still doesn't believe you're my mother. You know how beautiful she thinks you are, how much she admires you."

"I told you this one was no dummy."

"So why don't you like her?"

"I don't *dis*like her. I just don't think you should rush into anything, that's all."

"I've been seeing her for over a year."

"So if she really cares about you, she'll be willing to wait."

"She's crazy about me, Ma. That's why she doesn't want to wait any longer. That's why she says she's going to California. She says she doesn't want to just be here anymore, if she can't be here as my wife."

"She said that to you?"

"That's right. She isn't like any of the women I've known, Mother, believe me. She's stuck on me."

"Here," Miriam said, and reached into her handbag, drawing out a hammered gold compact, opening it, and holding it away from herself, turned the mirror toward Harry. "Look. You have something on your cheek."

"You don't have to do that. You don't have to do that to me." He closed the double doors to the front of the apartment and came over to the stool at his mother's feet. "You don't have to rub my face in it."

"Why are you shouting?" Miriam said.

"You don't have to keep showing me what I look like. You don't have to keep telling me the truths of what I am."

"You had something on your cheek," Miriam said, paling.

"You're smarter than that, Mother, but so am I. Just because I love you, just because I respect you more than I respect any woman in this world, that's no reason to keep rubbing my face in it. I know I'm not pretty, but I'm someone. I've made something of myself. More than most people, even the handsome ones. And it isn't just money. That isn't all I have to recommend myself."

"I never said it was," Miriam said.

"It isn't just the money. The money alone doesn't do it. A lot of people come from money and their families give them money and that doesn't make them important, it only makes them rich. I'm more than rich, I'm important. Because of how I made the money, that I made it and how I made it. That makes me admirable. Most women go through their whole lives, and they never find anybody admirable."

"That's true," Miriam said.

"So why couldn't a woman like Sylvia look up to me. And don't you dare make a joke. It's too obvious, Mother, it's not worthy of you, a joke like that."

"I didn't say a thing," Miriam said.

"So? So do you think it's really impossible, a hundred percent impossible, that a woman like Sylvia could have genuine admiration for me?"

"There's always that possibility, Harry. I never said there wasn't that remote possibility. I just don't think you should allow yourself to be pressured, that's all. You are a remarkable man. You've made a great deal of yourself. I think you can do a lot better than Sylvia, but then, I'm only a mother."

"I love her," he said. "I would marry her tomorrow but I can't afford another mistake. I have to be sure."

"Then wait," Miriam said.

"What if she goes to California?"

"She's not going to California so fast. She knows a good thing when she sees it."

The next evening when Harry went to the Algonquin to pick up Sylvia, the desk clerk informed him that Mrs. Rowan had left for California that morning. Harry was frantic, but Miriam managed to soothe him, telling him the worst thing he could do would be to run after Sylvia like a crazy man, because then she'd have him in exactly the position she wanted. The wise thing to do would be to wait for a few days, and give her time to be lost and lonely, as everyone was when they arrived in Los Angeles. Then he could go out there and get her on his own terms.

He agreed with the wisdom of his mother's advice, and managed to suppress his own anxiety, mostly by reading books and taking over a company that was perfecting a way of manufacturing artificial tinfoil which all of Harry's advisers agreed would have to become enormously profitable, whether or not the war ended. He managed to kill six days, and on the seventh boarded the Twentieth Century for Los Angeles, just to make sure she would have an extra three days to get good and lonely, like his mother said.

By the time he arrived in Hollywood, Sylvia had married Warren Key, the producer. They had already left for a honeymoon in Mexico, so Harry never got a chance to see if he was tall.

"So isn't it better that it happened now," his mother said

when he returned to New York, "instead of *after* you married her, like Celeste. You needed that aggravation twice."

"It wouldn't have happened after I married her. She loved me."

"So much she ran off with another man four, five days after she met him."

"It was a rebound, Mother. Pure and simple."

"Those are funny words to use about Sylvia," Miriam said.

They were in Harry's new duplex on Park Avenue, and while he had been away he had instructed the decorators to make two of the rooms into a princess' palace, so Sylvia would be enchanted when he brought her back with him. He floundered now in canopies and drapes of prewar silk, hitting his fist against chairs that were so overstuffed with down in satin casings that there was only a sigh as his hand beat futilely against them. His shoulders heaved in empty accompaniment to the screams that were not coming from his lips, and only the faintest echo of a squeal escaped from his mouth.

It was a spectacle, restrained and restricted as it was, unlike any that Miriam had observed in her limited life with her sons, and the extent of the pathetic, little-boy anguish in a man forty-six years old brought something almost like compassion into her. For the first time in many years she reached out with her hand toward his shoulder.

"Don't you touch me, you old bitch," Harry said. "Don't you dare play mother with me after you've done everything you could to ruin my life."

"Harry," she said, and shook her head slowly back and forth. "Oh my poor Harry. Is this what she's done to you, this terrible woman, to turn you against your own mother." Tears sprang to her eyes.

"What mother?" he screamed. "What mother?"

"And you never had a quarrel with her?" the psychiatrist said. "You never expressed any of the anger she made you feel?"

"I was never angry," Harry said. "How could you be angry with a mother? You should have seen, Doc, she was a fantastic-looking woman, and charming, you know, the kind who would walk into a room and every woman there would look down to see if her slip was showing."

"You think that's charming?" the doctor said.

"You bet your ass," Harry said. "Any woman that's that sure of herself she makes everybody else unsure, that's something very rare."

"You could say that," the doctor said.

216

"You don't understand, you really don't. You should have seen her. You should see her, even today. She's great-looking. Like a little lady Dorian Gray."

"Do you know how Dorian Gray stayed young?"

"If you're talking about that inner corruption shit, forget it. She doesn't have any of that. First of all she had her face lifted right after my father died, I guess she was about sixty-four, but even before that she looked, oh on a bad day, maybe forty. She looked younger than I did, and I was her son."

"Why do you have to tell me you were her son. She was your mother, it's obvious you're her son. Is it so hard for you to believe you were her son, because of how she treated you?"

"Listen, she just wasn't your average mother, that's all. I'm glad about that. It made something of me. I couldn't allow myself to be lazy and sloppy, because she wouldn't love me if I was. It wasn't enough, that I was just her son."

"And she never looked like your mother."

"But she could act like a mother when it really mattered, that's what you don't understand. When Sylvia married the producer I thought I'd go crazy, but Miriam told me if it was meant to be, it would be, and if I would just be patient the marriage would probably end, like all Hollywood marriages, and she would come back to me. And she was right."

"When did you start calling her Miriam?"

"Oh I don't know. I guess after my father died, right after the war, when she had the lift. She was very young-looking, even before that . . ."

"Yes, you told me."

"But now she really looked sensational. We used to go on double dates sometimes, and believe me, her escort was luckier than I was most of the time. Until Sylvia came back. She asked me to call her Miriam, because of the double-dating."

"Did you enjoy having the double dates, more than you would have enjoyed having a mother?"

"Oh come on. I was almost fifty years old. What did I need with a mother?"

"How about when you were a child?"

"Oh for Christ's sake, I told you. She was an anachronism. She just wasn't made like that, that's all."

"And you never felt angry, or deprived? You never felt loss or anxiety because you didn't have a mother?"

"I had a mother, goddammit. She just wasn't like other people's mothers, that's all. She never read your friend Erich Fromm, so she didn't believe that horseshit that mother-love is unconditional. I had to earn it, and that's a good thing. I had to earn her love, and that's a lot of what went into making me a *mensch,* believe me. It was right that she couldn't stand my just being there, like a lump. A woman that looked like that. With a life like that."

"Then you forgive her?"

"For what," Harry screamed. "I was never angry."

The child was two years old. The child was a girl who looked so much like Sylvia it was almost as though there had been no man involved, so when Harry took her up into his lap he could whisper against her hair with all the affection he intended to lavish on her mother, and not feel even the slightest trace of resentment that she was not really his. Her name was Shaney, and she had straight-falling thick hair, cut in deep bangs that framed her eyes with black satin, so even when she was two, she could be put on the list as a certified heart-breaker. That's what he told her mother, and that's what he whispered into Shaney's hair, as it wisped against his nostrils, and astonished him with its perfume. "She smells like a woman," he said to Sylvia in awe. "That's scary."

"It's only scary if you do something about it," she said, smiling at him with dark gray eyes.

"Go for a walk, kid," he said to Shaney, patting her rounded little behind, and setting her down on the rug. "Beat it. You. The big one. Come here."

"You can't talk like that to a kid," Sylvia said, laughing. She went down the hall to call the nanny Harry had hired to stay with them.

The house was not yet everything Harry wanted it to be, for her, for them. Right after the war, when he had gone into prefabricated housing, he had decided for personal contrast he was going to have the most lavish town house this side of Doris Duke (the "right" side, Harry chuckled from time to time, adding verbal ammunition to his decision to make uptown chic-er than down). But he had bought too quickly, and paid too much, considering the amount he would have to spend in making it into Little Versailles. Only half the staircases were marble, and the one he had had brought over from Venice was cracking in obvious places, and he did not consider that there was enough majesty in wood, no matter how highly polished. The main balustrade from the ground floor to the first floor (he had recently returned from France where he had bought two fireplaces, one for the formal dining room and one for the master bath, and he had decided to keep to the European tradition of things, so the second floor was the first) was carved alabaster, mounted with fleur de lis rosettes, repeated in the fleur de lis motif etched in subtle gold threads through the beige brocade of the wallpaper in the entrance hall. There was much Harry intended to do with the entrance hall and the foyer, besides leaving it empty and huge and impressive, so that it wasn't just for Shaney to go roller-skating through, if she ever got her balance well enough to skate. There was much he intended to do with the whole house, installing an elevator to take care of the six huge flights, a dumbwaiter from the second-floor kitchen to the first-floor breakfast room and pantry, and a second one so that snacks could be sent from the servants' quarters kitchen on the sixth floor down to the master bedroom, late at night, so nobody had to be inconvenienced just because they were hungry. All these things were to be major improvements, like the Louis XV furniture he was collecting, bit by bit, to be sure of value and authenticity. But in the meantime he loved his house, and felt a great sense of relaxation for having achieved it, no matter how haphazardly. He felt exactly the same way about Sylvia.

"Oh kid," he said, after the nanny had dressed the little girl and taken her out to the park, and they were alone in the den. "Oh kid, I'm happy to be here with you."

"Me too, Harry." She snuggled against him on the tiny red velvet love seat, and put her head in his lap.

"Was it very bad with Warren?"

"Not all the time," she said. "Some of the time we had a lot of fun. Great laughs. You know the Acapulco crowd, he was very big with them, and he got a great tan, so it was pretty, being with him. Hollywood was unbelievable, though. That's why there's so much screwing around and divorcing and everything there I think, there's nothing else to do but go to bed. Even on the set there's so much time for the technical people to take charge in between shots that the cast and the directors and all have no choice but to run back to the bungalows and ball . . ."

"I don't want to hear about it," Harry said.

"Okay."

"Did you have a lot of affairs."

"Only two," said Sylvia. "And not until I realized he was screwing Pauline. I mean, it was really ludicrous, because the whole world knew she was a dyke, and the first time he was away on location she came over to the house and started pitching me. She was really something, I mean to tell you, with her long, lovely body undulating to some tune in her head, while she gave me the good propaganda."

"What."

"Oh the usual stuff, how if all your life someone keeps scratching the top of your hand, and then finally someone tickles your palm, it can be excruciatingly lovely—and that anyone who ever has a wonderful woman lover is never satisfied with anything else. The usual recruiting speech."

"What did you do?"

"Nothing. I just listened. And smiled. In a way I felt sorry for her. She is so beautiful, after all, and she isn't stupid. But obviously she's never had a man go down on her or she wouldn't be so high on ladies."

Harry blushed and moved his hand gently across her ear, bringing it to rest on his own lap. "A man has to be a pretty weak sister to resort to that."

"Why."

"Because if he's any kind of man he can satisfy a woman the normal way. You'd have to be pretty missing on self-respect to do that. I'm over fifty years old and I've never done that to anybody, and they've always been satisfied. Aren't you satisfied."

"Of course I am, darling." She sat up and ran her fingers around his lips. "You know I am."

"There's plenty we can do that's normal," Harry said. "We don't have to resort to that."

"Of course not, darling," she said, and reached inside his silk dressing gown, as he toyed with her nipples through her blouse.

"Any woman that loved a man would never want him to degrade himself like that."

"Of course," she said, and slipping the belt free from his dressing gown, raised herself against the swelling in his lap.

She did not say anything of that nature again until a year later. As soon as her divorce was final, she and Harry were married. They were on their honeymoon, in the house on the island.

"Why do you think it's degrading?" she whispered, the second night, very late.

"What?"

"Making love to a woman that way."

"Because it just is, that's all. Among other things it just shows that a man hasn't got enough to offer the regular way, that he has to resort to that."

"You don't mind when I do it to you. You love it."

"That's different. You're a woman."

"So you think it would be womanly?"

"I think it's disgusting," Harry said, and went to sleep.

They did not discuss sex at all after that, until several years later when she was in analysis, and her doctor told her not to be afraid to bring these things out into the open. "That's what he said," Sylvia said. "He said we shouldn't be afraid to bring these things out into the open."

"Those shrinkers are all crazy. All they want to do is talk about sex. Sex should be done and not talked. None of them probably ever had a decent lay."

"What about you, Harry? Have you?"

"Are you kidding?"

"Then why are you so inhibited about it."

"Inhibited? Me? I once had a hand job in El Morocco. They don't make them much freer than that."

"Why do you call it a hand job? Why do you make it sound so crude? Were you so embarrassed that you have to make it sound ugly?"

"Listen, I call it a hand job because that's what it was, a hand job. She was a whore and she loved giving hand jobs. And blow jobs."

"Is that why you're so inhibited."

"Listen Sylvia, if you want to know the truth, I liked you better when you weren't so busy getting aware. Why don't you put on your gown and look pretty and get ready. We have twenty people coming to dinner in a half hour. Stop worrying about sex so much and check your table settings."

"Since when did you stop worrying about sex?"

"I never worried about it," Harry said. "I just did it."

Once he said that, of course, it was as if he had unleashed a giant curse upon his own head, as if God, caring about sex as much as the shrinkers, struck him down for being presumptuous. There was a period of almost two months when he could hardly do anything, and even managing to do it, didn't think it had been worth getting all that excited about. Sylvia went on a vacation to Switzerland with Shaney, and it never occurred to Harry to be sad that he couldn't go with her, or try and change his business plans so he could join her, so relieved was he at the prospect of going to bed without feeling obligated. He thought it would be a nice rest for Sylvia, too, and that maybe the separation would bring on some of the old excitement. It did, at least two times the first week of her return. The second week he was back to abstinence, but for a different reason. He could hardly pee without feeling his mind was exploding, so the prospect of sex was physically unbearable. Sylvia persuaded him to go to the doctor eventually, after managing to convince him that it wasn't necessarily cancer because it burned.

What it was, according to the doctor, was the biggest dose of gonorrhea he had ever encountered. Even when he got clap, Harry could not help thinking, he got it a little more and a little better than anyone else. He was quite puffed up,

221

even among his male friends, regarding it as something of an accomplishment, especially at his age. It was not until a while afterward that he remembered he hadn't been with anyone but Sylvia.

He said nothing to her about it. He had his doctor phone her and say she better come into the office to see him, and assuming it was some critical news about Harry, she went with an excitement she did not quite understand. The doctor told her what Harry had, and suggested she might need some treatment herself. That night they stared at each other, just the two of them, tight-lipped, across dinner in their formal dining room. Halfway through the entree she had the butler move the elaborate silver candelabra out of the way, so she could stare Harry down. He did not avoid her gaze, and even when she looked at him with the contempt she felt, he did not lower his eyes.

"You ought to be more careful who you go to bed with," she said finally.

Harry wiped his lips with his napkin, and got up from the table. "You're right about that, kid."

He took a taxi to the Latin Quarter, and told the maître d' to give him a ringside table, but not to make a fuss about his being there. "No mentions to the press," he said, "or tomorrow I go to the Copa."

There was one girl in the line of dancers who looked a little like Celeste, and one who reminded him of Rona Jean, but he told himself he was not one of those sad sacks who was going to end up living in the past. So instead he asked the captain to invite the tiny brunette from the right end of the line to come to his table. She was pretty enough, Harry decided, as she moved toward him from the dressing room, and she carried herself well enough to make up for the lack of height. He did not stand up as the waiter pulled out the chair, and she joined him.

"Hello," she said.

"You got a boyfriend?"

"Huh?"

"You got anybody you run around with regular?"

"No, Mr. Bell."

"You know who I am then."

"Of course, Mr. Bell."

"So if you know who I am then you know how smart I am, so you wouldn't try to put anything over on me."

"Huh?"

"Do you have a boyfriend or not?"

"Well no, sir, I don't. I just moved here from Peoria, so I haven't met a lot of people yet, and . . ."

222

"You're going to meet them all," he said, and snapped his fingers for the check. "Come on."

"I have a second show to do, Mr. Bell."

"No you don't," he said. "I took care of it."

On the way out he stopped and made a phone call. He did not take her arm until they were inside the taxi.

"You wouldn't try and put anything over on me. That business about Peoria, you wouldn't make that up."

"Why would anybody make up that they come from Peoria?"

"Good, good," he said, and pinched her thigh.

The tower apartment Harry kept for his mother was locked up while Miriam was in Cannes, but Harry had his own key. The doorman told him the other gentleman was waiting in the foyer, upstairs.

"What other gentleman?" the little brunette said, as Harry pushed the button for the penthouse.

Harry did not answer.

"Listen, I don't want to get involved in anything funny."

"What do you call the line at the Latin Quarter?"

"I don't think that's very nice of you. A man like you that's been around so much certainly shouldn't have such old-fashioned ideas."

"You mean you're still virtuous even though you dance half-naked in a nightclub."

"I don't go in for parties," she said.

"Neither do I," said Harry.

"So what other gentleman? Why is there another man here."

"He's my doctor," Harry said. "I asked him to meet us here."

"You sick?" she said, and went a little pale. "Maybe you shouldn't do anything if you're sick. Are you?"

"No," he said. "Not anymore. And I just want to make sure you're not either."

A few of the girls he had checked out in the next few years objected, some of them strenuously, but almost all of them let the doctor examine them. Harry left a lot of magazine articles around the apartment, collected by his research staff, underlined and with red-penciled margins, about terribly rich and famous men who had fetishes about germs. The clap was as potent a germ as any, and if some of the big guys were afraid of touching their fingers to money, a woman would have to understand about a man dipping his wick in an unsafe vat. Either understand or get her ass out of his apartment.

He had an apartment of his own now. His mother still had

the tower, but Harry figured it was easier, getting a place on the next floor that was a hundred percent his own, so he didn't have to keep checking his mother for schedule. Miriam was getting very liberated, what with the new airline schedules, going to the casinos of Europe as often and easily as she had once gone to the island. The reports of her prowess trickled back to him: he was amused by anecdotes of her regal coolness at the gambling tables, while compulsive gamblers from all over the world lost fortunes around her. Once he received the news that she had personally staked Bertram Lester, after Lester had publicly threatened suicide, and, as his benefactor, was now half-owner of Lester's soon to be produced *Slice of Life*.

"Is it true, Miriam?" Harry said. "You a secret movie mogul."

"I don't like motion picture entertainment," Miriam said. "I don't like books and I don't like plays. I like living lovely things, and I don't enjoy seeing them abused."

"Bertram Lester is lovely? I hear he's a real loud-mouthed Hollywood type, very crude."

"Well we can't all have your polish, Harry. Lester is a very arrogant, boisterous type, but he has a lovely wife, a real lady, and I didn't enjoy seeing her humiliated while he blubbered around the casino. It was all very simple, really. Athena asked me if I would stake him, and I did. I couldn't have cared less. It was the house's money."

"You win that much?"

"I win enough," Miriam said.

"I never had the nerve to gamble," Harry said. "Not really gamble."

"It doesn't take nerve, Harry. There are times when you have to pull back, when it's going against you, there are times when you have to just enjoy killing time, clicking your chips, staying alive. That doesn't take nerve. It takes elegance."

"I'd have to wear a tuxedo, huh?"

"I'm very tired," Miriam said. "Would you mind locking the door on your way out?"

She did not approve of his arrangement with Sylvia. She told him many times that if the marriage were over, he should end it, instead of sneaking off to the hotel-apartment like a middle-aged alley cat with every slut he thought could soothe him. Miriam was also genuinely fond of Shaney, and she resented the loss of her company at the dinners she had been used to having at Harry's house. She had Shaney over to tea at the tower once or twice a week, but it was an unnatural situation, even the child felt that. She had hardly grown comfortable giving Miriam the appellation of Grandma, before her surroundings were changed, her emotions uprooted. It also didn't help seeing her stepfather, whom she seldom saw at home anymore, going up in the elevator with some whore.

"She isn't a whore, goddammit," Harry screamed at Miriam when Shaney had been sent home. "How many times do I have to tell you. Not everybody is a whore. Mary Elizabeth is a very nice girl, from a fine family. Just because a girl made one movie, doesn't make her a whore."

"She was in the elevator with you and that little girl saw. I will not have that child upset and punished because her stepfather is a pea-brained adolescent in a middle-aged pod."

"Listen, I'm as fond of Shaney as you are . . ."

"You're fond of nobody, Harry, you haven't got the capacity to be fond of anybody except yourself, and you're an honest enough man to know how unworthy of any affection you are. So if you're really honest, you can't really like yourself."

"You mean I have a face that even a mother couldn't love."

"Oh, Harry. Why are you hanging around me. I haven't got too much of life left. Why don't you let me live it in peace and pleasure."

"What gives you pleasure? For Christ's sake, what can I do to please you?"

"Move away," Miriam said.

"Isn't this something, Doctor?" Harry said. "Look at me. A man fifty-seven years old, a man like me, crying because his mother doesn't love him. Have you ever heard of anything so ridiculous?"

"It's taken long enough to get to it," the doctor said.

"Oh don't be such a horse's ass, Doc, this isn't something I've worried about all my life, for God's sake. I'm just upset because of what she said yesterday. It doesn't have any bearing on what we've been talking about these past months."

"Doesn't it?"

"Listen, what is it with you? I come to you to find out why I haven't been able to do so much lately, even with Mary Elizabeth, and you start asking me was my mother mad when I shit my diapers."

"Was she?"

"What difference does that make now? Who could remember. And why shouldn't she have been, a woman like that, having to clean up after me."

"What were you supposed to do? Hold it in?"

"You're all sick," Harry said. "First you guys fucked up Sylvia, and now you're trying to do it to me."

225

"Who do you think did it to your mother?"

"Nobody did anything to my mother. She's a fantastic, beautiful woman. You wouldn't believe, a woman her age, how she looks. You'd think Shaney was her kid before you'd think I was. They even look alike, with the great dark hair, and the big black eyes. That's the kind of kid she should have had, a pretty, tight-assed little girl."

"Who'd be fifty-seven years old by now."

"Hard to believe," Harry said. "Hard to believe."

"Is that why you're not getting a divorce from Sylvia? So your mother can have Shaney?"

"What a cluck," Harry shook his head. "All those years you went to school, and you're a real cluck. I'm not getting a divorce from Sylvia because I don't want to get married again. A man in my position can't afford to be single. If I was single, they'd all want to marry me. Mary Elizabeth. I'd have to shit or get off the pot with Mary Elizabeth."

"You'd have to what?"

"Shit or get off the pot," Harry said. "It's an expression."

"Why do you use it with respect to love?"

"What a cluck," Harry said.

"Is that what your mother taught you love was?"

"My mother didn't teach me love was anything. My mother doesn't fuck herself up with 'love.' She knows better."

"And you think that's admirable? You think that's normal?"

"I don't want to discuss what's normal with you, cluck." Harry got up from the chair and reached for his hat. "See you in the funny papers," he said.

That week Harry reorganized all of the radio and television stations over which he had control and negotiated a contract with Continental Network to become affiliated, and eventually, to be absorbed. His name was in the newspapers a good deal, because, as a celebrity, business deals in which he was involved became more glittering, and hence a greater source of public interest. News that was usually relegated to the business pages of the papers was set in a more prominent place, sometimes even on the front page. Conversely, the page-one scandal about Harry that hit all the headlines shortly thereafter was continued on the business pages, so when people were finished shaking their heads over the story they could check whether or not it had affected the stocks.

Mary Elizabeth Craig, as Harry had pointed out to his mother, was a nice enough girl. She had made one picture with Bertram Lester, and had been married as many times as Harry, with no happier result. When she met Harry, she was very tired, and it showed in her eyes; but otherwise she looked as young and pretty as any of the girls Harry had been seen with, and tried to behave with similar vitality. It was only after she came to understand how tired Harry really was that she allowed herself the luxury of collapsing.

The nature of the collapse was not dramatic or startling. One night, after they had been seeing each other for over a year, when Harry began his tri-weekly series of phone calls, trying to find a restaurant where they would not be seen, where there could be no danger of anyone's reporting to Sylvia, Mary Elizabeth suggested it might be just as easy to have dinner in the apartment.

"You mean that?" Harry said.

"Of course, Harry."

"But I don't want you hiding your light under a bushel."

She did not explain to him that everywhere they went, there was enforced darkness and obscurity anyway. She only smiled, and touched his hand. "It's enough if you see it."

"I like that," he said. "That's terrific. Only don't feel you have to cook. I'll send for something to the Sixth Avenue Deli."

"I'm not hungry," Mary Elizabeth said. She was wearing the negligee he had bought her for Christmas, peach chiffon with shrimp-colored ostrich feathers twisted around the neck, and extending between her remarkably high breasts. She had giggled when he gave it to her, and said she felt she had to wear it only if she was lying on a white satin bed, eating a box of chocolates, reading movie magazines, and waiting for her lover. That she was wearing it on tonight, of all nights, with what he was going through, filled him with a vague sense of alarm.

"You want to fool around?" he said.

"I just want to be with you," she answered. "As if . . ."

She hesitated, and he knew from the hesitation that he was in a lot of trouble. Seeing the look in his eyes, she was smart enough not to continue what she wanted it to be as if. She kept it up for approximately three weeks. Then she took off her brassiere underneath the peach robe, and stepped out of her pink silken panties, and came and stretched out beside him on the chaise longue, watching the picture on the television tube, with her legs slightly parted, absently toying with her pubic hair.

"I wish you'd stop that," he said.

"Stop what?" she said.

"Stop playing with yourself."

"I'm not playing with myself, Harry. Haven't you ever seen anyone twirling their hair before."

"Not that hair," he said. "Cut it out."

"Why? That part of me's become as impersonal as any other part of me, haven't you noticed that? For all the sweet and loving attention it gets."

"I told you I was trying to work it out, Mary Elizabeth. For God's sake, isn't a man entitled to be tired?"

"Of course, darling. And a man's also entitled to be fifty-seven years old. And his wife has to understand. I'm sure Sylvia would understand."

"I don't want to be with Sylvia. I want to be with you."

"But we never do anything!" Mary Elizabeth screamed. "We never go anywhere, and we never make love. We sit and watch television, and hold hands. What kind of a mistress does that make me. If I'm going to sit and hold hands, Harry, I don't mind, but I'll do it as your wife."

"Don't overplay your hand, kid," he said.

"I love you, Harry."

"And I love you."

"So?"

"Sylvia would never give me a divorce."

"Ask her." She turned on her side and brought her naked thighs next to his hand, catching his fingers in the warm triangle. "Ask her."

"Don't get yourself all worked up for nothing," he said, but even as he said it, he felt himself moving and growing beneath the dressing gown. Her desperation was the most exciting thing that had happened to him in a long time.

"What do you want me to do," she whispered against his chest. "I'll do anything."

"For what, kid?"

"For you to marry me."

"Have you had to do a lot to get the others to marry you?" Harry said.

"What do you mean?"

"What have you had to do?" His mouth was dry, and the thought of her writhing there inside herself shot between his legs and strengthened him; but not enough. Not yet. "Tell me what you've had to do."

"What's the matter with you, Harry?"

"Nothing's the matter. I love you. I want to know what you've had to do."

"I haven't had to do anything."

"Why'd you tell me you'd do anything, then."

"Because I want to marry you. You know that. Don't make me degrade myself."

"But you offered to degrade yourself, right, so it must be something you've been through before."

228

"I didn't mean it. I just . . . I want you to love me, Harry. I want to be exciting to you. And there are some people who . . ."

"Don't stop now, baby, please," he said, and gave a reassuring pinch to her breast. "You are exciting me, you really are. See."

She started to climb on him, but he held her off. "No, not yet. Some people who what . . ."

"You know."

"No, you tell me."

"You really want to know?"

"Look at me," Harry said, and opened the belt to his robe. "Can't you see how much I want to know?"

"Make love to me, Harry," she said.

"First tell me. Didn't you used to go with Lester. Was he one like that?"

"I didn't go with him," she said. "He just produced my movie. But he was like that, yes. He liked to watch his wife."

"With other guys?"

"With women," she said.

"And you were one of the women."

"Not really," Mary Elizabeth said. "You couldn't really say that."

"What could you really say?" Harry said.

"Well, it's what I was trying to tell you. Some men get very excited at a woman's body. You know. The way a woman looks when she moves, when she has a really great body, and she's getting excited. When you're involved in making love to her, you don't see all that. I mean if she really has a great body."

"Show me," Harry said.

"You mean it?"

"You said you'd do anything," Harry said. "I wouldn't want to miss out on that."

"Then come inside," she said, and took his hand, leading him to the bedroom. "It's a shame not to make use of all that white satin."

She did not take off her robe, but let it slip away from her, as she ran her hands slowly from her throat over her breasts, down to the gentle roundness of her belly, and then slowly up again. Her eyes were closed, and her head slipped gently back over the pillow, so her back was arched and her breasts seemed even more prominent as she gently rubbed her nipples into full buds. Slowly, deliciously, her tongue appeared between her lips, wetting them. Even as he watched Harry could feel his own tongue moving across his lips, and his hands moving to himself.

She bent her knees up on the bed, and with infinite patience, silken-fingered restraint, moved her hands along the inside of her thighs, back and forth, trailing across herself, touching almost, but not quite, on the pale rosy mouth that was blossoming, opening, in the dark jungle between her legs.

"Jesus," he whispered hoarsely, hating the soft outburst, fearing it would disturb the exquisite rhythm of what was taking place. But if she heard, she gave no sign, so intent was she on what she was doing.

Her legs bent outward and down, and her index finger softly circled the shining pink marble between her legs, circled and rubbed it until it grew bright and flaming in front of his eyes, and her hips began moving in undulating circle, and she moaned softly, and reached for herself with her other hand.

"No," Harry said. "No, don't. Me." He plunged into her with a ferocity he had been convinced he could no longer feel, and there was no need to worry if he could wait long enough because she was exploding around him, and he thought that was what it meant, in the old love stories, about dying together. "Oh baby," he said. "Oh sweetheart. The best. The best it's ever been."

"I love you, Harry," she said.

"Yeah, I see."

"So you will marry me, won't you?"

"What for?" he said. "You don't really need me at all."

"You son of a bitch," she said, and wrenched herself free of him. "You miserable son of a bitch."

"You watch what you call me."

"Goddammit, Harry, you marry me or it's over." There were tears in her eyes, and she covered herself with a sheet, modestly. "I mean it. That's it. You marry me or it's all over. Tonight. Finished. You call your attorney and tell him to start the divorce proceedings, or you don't come back here ever again."

Harry propped his head up against his palm. "You ever watch a dog chasing a car? Barking and yapping. Did you ever wonder what would happen if he caught it?"

"I don't get you."

"So you wanted to threaten me, you wanted to catch me in a bluff. So you caught me. I'm not having any. Now what do you do?"

"You prick," she whispered. "You miserable prick." She got up and ran into the bathroom.

Harry got up and dressed, using some of her cologne under his arms. For some reason he felt very good about life, knowing they were all pigs. He went into the living room and poured himself a Scotch and toasted himself in the formal way of a non-drinker becoming a sophisticate. At the end of two Scotches, when she still hadn't come out of the bathroom, he went inside and knocked.

"Mary Elizabeth," he said. "What are you doing in there so long, playing with yourself again?"

When there was still silence, he felt a vague clutching at his heart, and reached for the knob, expecting the door to be locked. It was open, but the rest was the way he was afraid it would be. She was seated on the toilet, naked, not a very graceful position to choose for dying, but at least the lid was down. Her head was resting on the sink, and he could tell from her breathing that the pills hadn't taken that deep an effect yet; but as the bottle was empty, he had no way of knowing how many she had taken.

He wrapped a towel around her, so that her breasts and her pubis were covered, and went inside to call the police. He stopped, as he realized what that would mean. Instead, he picked the white satin quilt off the bed, and spread it on the floor, neatly. He went into the bathroom, and half carried, half dragged Mary Elizabeth over to the rug, placing her in the center of the quilt and closing the edges of it around her. He pulled it across the apartment, to the corridor, looked both ways in the hall, and rang for the elevator, careful to check before entering that there was nobody inside. Then he pressed the button for the tower.

His mother's apartment was the only one on the floor, but he still looked both ways in the corridor before pulling his burden out of the elevator. He took the spare key out of his pocket, and opened the door. As an afterthought, he rang.

"What, are you crazy?" Miriam said, coming out of the bedroom in her bathrobe, seeing him prop Mary Elizabeth up on the couch.

"Call the police. Tell them to bring an ambulance."

"You're insane." She dialed the phone. "How could you let this happen."

"What, let. She was chasing a car, and she caught it. She was a dog catching a car."

"You're crazy, bringing her up here," she said, as she directed her voice into the phone, and told the police the address, and to bring an ambulance. "What if she dies?"

"She's not going to die. How could I have the police come to my apartment. You realize the scandal? You know what Sylvia could do to me."

"You stupid, ugly little man," she said. "What about me? How am I supposed to explain a naked girl in my living room?"

"Oh you ought to be able to handle that, Mom. Just like you handled Lester's wife. You must be used to naked women by now. Athena Lester's a dyke. Everybody knows she's a dyke."

"Well she was always very lovely to me," Miriam said.

"I'll bet," Harry said. "I'll just bet."

"I want you to get your trash out of here," Miriam said. "I want you to take your naked garbage and get the hell out of here."

"It kills me," Harry said. "It just kills me, thinking of all the years and all the times I broke my balls to please you, and all along you're some kind of a freak, and that's why you always tried to make me into one."

"Get out of here," Miriam said. "I won't be responsible for what I say if you stay here."

"Everybody must have known. Everybody must have seen it but me. My poor father, he wasn't sophisticated enough to understand it, so he just collapsed in his back so he wouldn't have to fight you."

"I was faithful to your father," Miriam said. "I never let anyone touch me while he was alive. You're overwrought, Harry. You can't be thinking clearly. Dragging a girl through the hall up to my apartment when it might have meant the difference between her living and dying, not calling the police like that, and now you come here and call your mother names."

"Is is true?" Harry said.

"For heaven's sake, Harry. I'm seventy-five years old."

"It's hard to remember that, because of how you look," Harry said, and chucked her under the chin.

"Don't do that," she moved his hand away.

"You can't stand it when I touch you," he screamed. "You've never been able to stand it when I touched you. My shrinker tried to tell me that. The son of a bitch wouldn't speak up, but he tried to tell me you weren't normal."

"What's normal, Harry," Miriam said. "Being able to stand touching you, is that normal? That girl on the couch, is she normal? Sylvia? Celeste? That poor love-starved butch you were married to in the beginning."

"Butch?" he said. "Butch. You have an amazing vocabulary for a mother. You must have hung around some pretty interesting bridge clubs."

"Get out, Harry," Miriam said.

"What about her."

"I'll take care of it for you. I always have. What else is a mother for."

When the police arrived, Miriam told them and the crime

reporter that the girl on the couch was the mistress of her son, Harry Bell, she had attempted suicide in Harry's apartment and he had carried her upstairs in order to avoid a scandal, as he was hoping for a reconciliation with his wife, Sylvia.

It took a few weeks for Sylvia to secure her divorce from Harry; she received a handsome settlement, in spite of the premarital agreement. Shortly afterward Miriam moved permanently to Biarritz, and Cannes, buying a home in both cities, with money she had made with no help from her son. She invited Shaney and Sylvia to come visit her as often as they liked, until she heard that Sylvia and Harry were remarrying, when she rescinded the invitation. Sylvia and Harry were married once more afterward, and even when they were divorced the second time, she continued to stay in his house when she was in New York. But he never spoke to Miriam again as long as he lived.

After the funeral, Seymour and Irving wired their mother in Cannes, asking her what she wanted done with the body. Her two-word reply was undeliverable according to the rules of Western Union.

CHAPTER TWO

WHEN the first contractions gripped her, Kate had the nightmare sensation that she might not have a son. She laughed about it even on the way to the hospital in the taxi, telling David he must have something in him of the Oriental potentate. "I thought you were supposed to worry about dying, and here I am afraid I won't produce the heir."

"Nobody dies in childbirth anymore," he said.

"Would you hate me if I had a girl?"

"Why don't you just have a baby so you can stop being pregnant." He leaned over in the seat and kissed her. "I'd just like to have my wife back."

"It'll be a boy, I just know it."

"It doesn't make any difference to me."

"It does to me," Kate said. "It'll be a boy."

Her terror was not because she disbelieved David: she was the one who needed a son. She had to prove to herself, unalterably that she had been right about him. She had surrendered herself so completely to the marriage, making it a refuge from all the avenues she had walked on so unsurely, the bright gaudy places girls like Louise needed so much to be, she could not entertain for a moment the possibility that she fled because she was afraid. She had given up that life because it was the mature, womanly thing to do, and had turned to David because he was man enough for a mature woman. As strong as he was, he could only generate a son.

She believed that with as much fierce emotionalism as she disputed it intellectually. All the facts of sex determination, slow and fast sperm, time of ovulation, were totally beside the point. He was in command: their son would be the proof.

She stopped worrying about it in the labor room. Wracked with a pain for which there was no preparation in knowledge or experience, she stopped thinking about the baby's sex, and thought only on death, fearful of it, wishing for it. There was no way for the baby to get out. Dr. Rady wouldn't be there in time because New York obstetricians were all too busy and she didn't want to be delivered by a stranger. Not that the baby would be delivered: it would just rip her to death, stretch by stretch, from inside.

"I intended to be brave," Kate said, and clawed at the

breast of the nurse in the labor room, before blacking out for a moment.

"Listen," she said to the anesthesiologist, when she came back, too soon, and he was there, finally. "Forget what I said about no anesthetic."

"We already gave you Demerol in the hips," he said.

"It's not enough."

"You've forgotten your breathing," said the nurse. "Breathe through the contractions."

"You breathe. Oh. Damn. Oh God. Give me sodium pentothal."

"We don't give that here. It hurts the baby."

"Then give me something. SOME-thing. Oh God."

When she was fully dilated they gave her scopolamine, so she wouldn't remember the pain. She remembered only a deep sense of humiliation, and wondered where she could get some five-dollar bills to give to the nurses whose hair she had pulled, to make them forget.

"Bear down," said Dr. Rady.

"I've got to go to the john."

"That's the baby."

"Oh please." She started to cry. "I don't want to shame myself. Let me go to the toilet."

They moved the gas mask toward her face and she knew they were going to kill her for being a coward. For a moment she fought them, until she realized she deserved to die, defecating in public like that, with her legs up in the air. The cold rank rubber touched around her mouth, and she breathed in.

"Congratulations," Dr. Rady said. "You have a fine baby girl."

"Don't be ridiculous," said Kate, and tried to make her way back on to the delivery table. "There's been some mistake."

"Here she is." Dr. Rady held the baby up.

"You better try again. I'm having a boy."

When they wheeled her back to her room she cried for the few minutes she was conscious, because she knew she had lied to herself all along about David. She knew she was being irrational, but she knew she was right. The important thing was never to let him find out that she was the stronger one.

"You don't mind?" she said when she saw him.

"I don't mind," David said. "I like girls."

"Is she pretty?"

"Not particularly, but none of them are. The whole nursery looks like little old men in glass baskets. Especially the girls."

"You're not mad?"

"Why should I be mad."

"It hurt. I need some five-dollar bills or they'll tell everyone," she said, and went back to sleep.

By the time she was up to talking rationally, she received a call from a girl in her office who was pregnant. "How was it," the girl asked. "Was it very bad?"

"Oh it was uncomfortable," Kate said. "You certainly have a great deal of discomfort. But it's over before you know it, and you forget it as soon as it's over. You forget that kind of discomfort." She had not forgotten at all. But in that moment she had joined the club, the mysterious sorority, the secret rules of which were transmitted from mother to mother instinctively from the moment of giving birth: never tell the truth about exactly what you go through to a woman who has not yet had her child. Pain became "discomfort," an unendurable passage of time became "over before you know it." Without Kate's meaning to let it, the final cliché slipped from her lips. "Anyway, it's all worth it, you forget everything the minute you see the baby."

They had brought the baby to her at five in the afternoon and she had looked at the swollen, eyeless, red-faced thing, and counted all its fingers and toes. All up and down the corridor she could hear women saying "How long, please, don't take him away yet—let her stay a little longer," and she reached up and rang the bell for her nurse.

"You can take her now," she said. "I've seen her."

On the third day her stitches were giving her a great deal of trouble, but even so she managed to get off the bed and walk straddle-legged to the nursery, not waiting for them to come collect the baby, holding it out in front of her. "She's finished eating," Kate said. "You can have her back." She made her way back to bed and sat for a moment on the edge, feeling the tenderness in her breasts, making sure that the shots and the pills were really taking effect as the doctor had promised they would, and that there would be no milk.

When it was time to take the baby home, the baby nurse appeared at the hospital. Mrs. Hanner was a fiercely efficient little Irish woman with great arthritic hands that bound the baby in a grip that surprised Kate, who had held her like an uncooked egg. "Obviously she knows what she's doing," she said to David, when the four of them were home from the hospital. "We have nothing to worry about."

She sat at the blue silk, embroidered bench of her dressing table, receiving with laughter the fevered affection of Albert, their German shepherd, who was licking her face excitedly. "He really missed me," said Kate. "That's lovely. I always thought he was your dog."

"He was afraid you weren't coming back," said David.

"So was I."

After the two o'clock feeding the baby started to cry. David had already gone back to his office, and Kate was alone in the bedroom, watching television, and writing thank-you notes to the people who sent flowers to the hospital. She closed her bedroom door, and finally the nursery door, but she could still hear Mrs. Hanner trying to soothe the baby with shrill Irish song, and the sharp persistent wail.

"I'm going in to the office for a while," she said to Mrs. Hanner. "The number's above the phone in the kitchen if you need me, and the doctor's number if anything's wrong. But I'm sure you'll be fine. Won't you?"

"I'll be fine. But should you be going out so soon?" Mrs. Hanner said.

"There are some things I left on my desk on Friday I ought to finish up. What's wrong with her?"

"Nothing's wrong," Mrs. Hanner said, rocking the baby back and forth with a dizzying rhythm. "She's a baby. Babies cry."

Everybody in the office congratulated Kate on the birth of her daughter, and marveled at her quick recovery. "You're quite something, Mrs. Waller," her secretary said. "Having a child over the weekend and back at your desk on Wednesday. If I hadn't noticed your stomach on Friday, I wouldn't have known you had had a baby at all."

About four o'clock the executive vice-president in charge of copywriting made a special stop by her office. "My God," he said. "Wonder Woman. You know you're entitled to a month's maternity leave."

"I had some copy I didn't have a chance to finish on the NCA presentation," she said, smiling. "Maybe when I'm satisfied with it I can take a little time off."

"You're really something else," he said. "I can't tell you what a pleasure it is to know somebody nowadays who isn't afraid of responsibility."

About three weeks later the people at NCA accepted the new campaign for their shaving lotion without qualification. As a matter of fact, they were so pleased with Kate's presentation that they offered the agency the advertising contract on their new toothpaste, to reach the market the following spring. Kate was given a bonus, her second in two months, and she and David agreed it did call for a small holiday, by way of celebration. They rented a small house in upstate New York, and even though they wanted very much to be alone, they took Albert with them in the station wagon, because the country was wonderful for dogs.

Maggie Bolin could hardly wait to see the baby. As little as she had seen Kate in the past few years, she was delighted Kate had called, she told Kate on the phone, and thrilled about the baby. Kate's having a baby was the most exciting thing imaginable, short of Maggie's having her own.

"Can I see her, when? You do want me to, yes?" Maggie said.

"She's home most of the time," Kate said. "Except when Mrs. Hanner takes her to the park."

"But of course I'd like to see you, too."

"I'm at the office until six thirty," Kate said. "And she's asleep for the night at seven."

"What a good baby, aren't you lucky, when can I come over, now? I'm mad to see her."

"Well, David isn't home yet, Maggie, and I know he'd like to see you too. Maybe you can have dinner with us one night later this week. Thursday is our best night. How is it for you?"

"Oh drat, I have the cancer dance, and then I'm going to Georgia for skeets. How about a week from?"

"That's fine," Kate said.

"I can't tell you how thrilled I am you called. I had the feeling last summer after the funeral that you were avoiding me, but I suppose that was just the big pregs, yes? I can't wait to see the baby."

Maggie felt suddenly so close to Kate that she even decided to use Kate's gynecologist. Now that she and George Piner were in love, Maggie wanted him to have no ambivalence or medical approach to her insides, so she had decided to use someone else as a doctor. Dr. Rady agreed with George's findings: there was nothing wrong except a slightly tipped uterus, which had served over the years as a natural contraceptive. There was no reason she couldn't conceive. Kate, too, had had the same fear and considerable difficulty getting pregnant, Dr. Rady said, and had had one miscarriage. But now that she had a beautiful little girl all that was forgotten.

"I can't thank you enough, Dr. Rady, you're an angel," Maggie said, as she got off the examining table.

"Of course there is one pronounced distinction between you and Kate," he said. "Kate is married."

"Oh tush," said Maggie. "You are a stick, what? You needn't sound so disapproving, you're not my father, did you know him?"

"No, I didn't."

"He was a heaven man, terribly free even in his day, and he certainly never lectured me about sex, of course I was

238

twelve when he died. You must have read about him though, Archie Bolin. He was a stunning personality."

"No, I don't think I did."

"Well, I'm not that promiscuous, and I am thirty-four, so how many years of childbearing do I have left, so you can understand my worrying that I've never had to have an abortion, it does make me a standout in my crowd, what?"

"You're pretty lucky if you ask me." He washed his hands. "I'll want to see you again in about three months."

"Really?" Maggie slipped into her underpants, and let the sheet fall from her shoulders. "I don't think I want to see you."

"I'm sorry if I've offended you, Miss Bolin, but I think if you're serious about wanting to have a baby . . ."

"For all you know, I might already have one. Could you tell? Could you look at someone in the very beginning and tell?"

"Usually it's about six or seven weeks before we can run accurate tests. When was your last period?"

"I don't think I'll tell you," Maggie said. "You're not the sort of man I think I want to deliver my child."

"If you change your mind, my secretary will give you an appointment anytime you call."

"That's very reassuring, Dr. Rady."

"Miss Bolin . . . I think . . . I think if you are this anxious to have a baby, you might be wise to see someone. A lot of times anxiety alone can make it difficult for a woman . . ."

"Someone?" she said shrilly. "What do you mean by someone."

"Have you ever consulted a psychiatrist?"

"I'd like to get dressed now," she said. "Would you go, please?"

The moment she left his inner office she was furious with herself for having gone to him in the first place, just because he had given Kate a whole baby. In another four or five days she would know herself for sure, more than he could know for seven or eight weeks, by his own confession, so how smart could he be?

But in the reception room on the way out of the office, as she paused to put on her coat, all anger left her. She smiled benignly at the other expectant mothers, nodding and signaling them with her eyes that she was one of them, if not yet in actuality, at least in potential.

She was lacking nothing that would make her a full woman, if she wanted to be a full woman. But she hadn't before, it was that simple, and that was why her body had cooperated in keeping her out of trouble.

Only lately, once or twice in the past few months, when Algernon had guided her deeper back into innocence than she had ever been, did she begin to see the child waiting there, trapped and crying, each vocal cry breaking visibly into crystal tears, a shattered chandelier in a deserted ball-room. The child was not her, she knew that for a certainty, no matter how hard Algernon tried to convince her it might be herself. The child was beautiful, and she had been homely, in spite of how lovely her father insisted she was. This child was pink and white and golden, except for its lips which were purple from suffocating so long inside her. It had caused her many days of anguish, wondering if she had so abused her capacity for pleasure that her body would punish her, and not yield up the child. But Algernon had promised her that if that was what she wanted, the child would come forth, though it was beyond his religiosity of the moment to plant the seed. And then she had found George.

Smiling, she nodded to the race of women in Dr. Rady's waiting room, and waved a companionly good-bye, as she slipped into her coat and walked out onto Seventy-second Street. A cold wet wind from the river whipped the wide pavements. From time to time she had to steady herself against the sides of the apartment buildings, avoiding the little traps of ice puddles and squares of frozen earth surrounded by ankle-high fences of metal, hundreds of little croquet wickets soldered together to ward off the careless footsteps of New York. It was all she could do to walk and not run, careless in her exhilaration. But she would not tramp on any form of life: not seeds of grass encased in winter, not beads of water suspended in a slab of cold. Everything would flow again, in season; that which was meant to grow, would grow. All of existence was Snow White—sleeping, but never dead, unless you withheld the kiss.

"I'm going to be a mother," she said to the doorman of the building on the corner of Park Avenue.

He looked at her a little oddly. "May I get you a cab?" he said.

"Yes, thank you. I feel a little dizzy." She did, actually. It was the excitement, of course. That and anxiety to begin buying the layette for her baby.

She had the cab to go uptown, although it was out of her way, because the moment was too big, too full, not to be shared. Aside from the fact that she had a tentative lunch date with Louise, Maggie felt she would genuinely enjoy her company. "Hello," she said over the house phone. "It's me, I'm downstairs, I know it's a little early but it's a blustery terrible day what? and I thought you might have trouble getting a cab."

Maggie settled back into the taxi, humming softly to herself, doing a little tap dance with her feet against the jump seat in front of her, musing at the beautiful simplicity of life. She opened the door excitedly as Louise came out of the building.

"We're going to do a fun thing, a tribute to life, hurry up," Maggie said. "How pretty you look."

It wasn't altogether true. Louise was wearing a white wool dress underneath her dark mink coat, and a black ribbon tied beneath her chin kept her hat in place, framing the gold hair with dark mink. But attractive as the outfit was, it served to emphasize the lines around Louise's eyes, lines that Maggie had never particularly noticed before.

"F.A.O. Schwartz," Maggie said to the driver.

"Oh for Christ's sakes," Louise said. "You're in one of those moods. I have to get dressed up like this to go to Toyland."

"Now now, Lulu, mustn't play stone-heart, it's on the way to Côte, our reservation isn't until one, and I have to pick up a few things."

"Whatever for?"

Maggie looked at Louise carefully. For all the friends she had made in the past months, for all the acceptance, even welcome she had enjoyed, Louise was still a newcomer to belonging. She would relax in time: security and Algernon would see to that, Maggie was sure. But in the meantime, it would be wrong to tell her the entire truth of why it was Maggie had to go baby-shopping. "I'm mad for layettes," was all Maggie said.

"God, what a dreary day," said Louise, looking out the window. "On a day like this, I wonder why anyone wants to live in New York."

"Everybody else is here. We have no choice."

When they got to Schwartz's, Maggie went directly to the second floor, and asked the lady to show her everything adorable for babies. Louise wandered around the back of the store for a while, looking at parlor games to introduce at Dainty Lee's next dinner party. In a few minutes she was bored.

"Are you almost through?" she said to Maggie, "or are you going to buy out the whole store?"

"I suppose that's about it. Maybe just those two pairs of booties." She pointed them out to the saleslady.

"Who are you getting all this for?"

"Oh," Maggie said. She looked at Louise carefully. "Kate Waller. She's had a baby."

"I'd heard that," Louise said quietly. "I didn't realize you were such good friends."

"Well we go back a long time," Maggie said. "And I'm mad for layettes."

"I know. You told me."

"You don't have to sound so down, darling, you can get her a present too if you want to, you are close friends with her, what? I'm not trying to make you feel badly."

"I don't feel bad. I haven't even talked to her for months. A present at this point would seem hollow."

"Babies are wonderful, don't you think?" Maggie said.

"Babies are babies. Let's have lunch."

In the end, Maggie decided to let Kate have some of the presents after all. She went to dinner with Kate and David at Le Voisin Thursday evening, and it turned out to be quite a pleasant evening when David wasn't urging Maggie to discuss her portfolio.

"I really don't have anything to do with my investments," Maggie said. "All that is handled by my trustees."

"That's sort of an old-geezer way of running things, isn't it?" David said, signaling the wine steward. "Maybe if you had someone who was more your contemporary, to apprise you of the changes and the action in the market . . ."

"I don't understand any of it."

"Well that's what I mean, maybe someone who was more your own age instead of these eighty-year-old banking types, a real investments counselor could explain . . ."

"I don't want to understand," Maggie said. "It's all too confusing for me."

"Yessir?" the wine steward said to David.

"There's a taste of cork in this bottle. Give us a fresh one."

"Your baby's so lovely, Kate," Maggie said. "I wish we could have spent more time with her."

"They're very tight here about people being on time for their reservations," David said. "Not everybody can get a good table. Why don't you come over to the apartment some day and spend more time."

"But you both work during the day. I envy you so, being that clever and industrious."

"Maybe over the weekend. Why don't you plan on spending Saturday with us."

"I thought we were going to the country this weekend," Kate said.

242

"I have some business that will probably keep me in town. Do you think you'd like to come over Saturday, Maggie?"

"I'd love it," she said. "Playing with baby, what fun."

"Why'd you do that?" Kate said to David when they got home. "You know I was counting on going away."

"I think you ought to spend more time with her," he said.

"I already called her when I didn't want to. We had dinner. She made it very clear she wasn't interested in your handling her account."

"I don't think Maggie Bolin's that clear on anything. She can be brought around."

"If you understand that about her, if you see how mixed up she is, why do you insist on my spending time with her?"

"I didn't say she was mixed up. I said she was unclear. When you have that much money, it's forgivable that you're a little vague."

"She isn't vague. She's crazy."

"You overstate everything," David said. "If it makes her happy hanging around you and Tracy, let her hang around. It doesn't hurt being kind to someone like that. You're always so worried about being kind, you wasted so much time being kind to Louise, what's the harm in being kind to Maggie."

"I like Louise," Kate said.

"Well I didn't. Louise can't do anybody any real good, including herself. A friend like Maggie Bolin can be invaluable."

"She already told you you weren't getting her account. That isn't going to change, believe me."

"She has a lot of rich friends," David said. "You never can tell when someone like that will come in handy."

"We're both making plenty of money," Kate said.

"Day to day," he said. "It isn't the same level. There's nothing wrong with getting to that other level."

"I don't like being with people because they might come in handy."

"Well you better get over that," David said.

David himself had gotten over it his sophomore year at the University of Pennsylvania. By that time he understood he had neither the intellect nor the patience to pursue any of the loftier professions, like law or medicine; the arts, being both effete and inconsistently profitable, were also out of the question. The only career that would provide both financial and social rewards, quickly, was business. So he stayed on to attend Wharton, where he had learned all his lessons well.

Saturday afternoon, Maggie arrived, her arms laden with baby presents. After lunch Maggie insisted she and Kate walk the baby carriage to Central Park. They made their way along Seventy-second Street, Kate awkward and unsure.

"That's such a big carriage," Maggie said. "I don't wonder it's hard to handle."

"I can handle it," Kate said. "It's just that some of the curbs are higher than I thought, that's all."

"I shouldn't have made you bring her out if you didn't want to, but it's such a beautiful day, I thought it would do us all good to go to the park. Isn't it wonderful out? The kind of crisp fall day that's a terrible tease to New Yorkers who have to move to California or Acapulco, I could never live there, could you, do you think? What will you call her for short?"

"I think Tracy's short enough."

"What ever happened to Patsys and Mary Janes?" Maggie said, starting to skip across the island in the middle of Park Avenue. She noticed that Kate was trapped by the light back at the intersection, and ran back to help her, holding her hand up toward a car making its legal way along Park. "Oh, Katie, I'm so sorry you're having such trouble. I should have let her go out with Mrs. Hanner, the way you wanted."

"I'll manage," Kate said. "Don't make such a fuss."

"She seems quite nice, Mrs. Hanner."

"I'd die without her," Kate said, as the light changed.

The boat lake at the park was surrounded by darting, laughing toddlers, dodging in and out of baby carriages and strollers, while middle-aged and elderly men, kneeling by the pond, gave their miniature boats full sail in the brisk, sun-warmed wind. Maggie reached over and held the handle of the carriage, and rocked it slowly.

"The handle's cold," she said. "Maybe Tracy should be in the sun." When she looked up there were tears in her blue-gray eyes. "I hope David didn't mind my asking him not to come. I wanted to tell just you. I'm going to have a baby, too, Kate."

"Oh, Maggie. What does Algernon want you to do?"

"But it's not Algernon's, Kate, I'd love it to be his, but that was all over between us a long time ago. I've met a nice man, a doctor, and he loves me, and I'm going to have his baby. Imagine me, of all people, marrying a nice New York doctor, great grief, they might even let me stay in the Register. I don't know if I could tolerate that. George and I will make a good balance for each other. Not like Gerald when we were still in college, do you remember all that, what I went through trying to decide whether to marry him or not?"

"I remember," Kate said.

"It's really just as well," Maggie said, and looked down at

244

the cement beneath her sneakers. "Not that he hanged himself of course, that never solves anything, does it, I didn't mean that was just as well."

"I didn't think you did."

"If I had married him I never would have gotten over it, his killing himself I mean." She kicked at a fallen leaf. "I don't want to talk about death, life is the issue, that's what Algernon says. Literally the issue. We get over everything else. No matter how terrible it seems to us at the time. These things have a way of balancing out, in the cruel fairness of nature. Even my breasts. Don't you remember how I always used to hate my breasts in school, because they kept me from that starving debutante chic, I thought it was some insidious punishment inflicted on me, because I didn't want to be like my mother, but now look, just think about them, coming into a life of their own, fulfilling a beautiful purpose. Are you breast-feeding Tracy?"

"No," Kate said.

"Oh of course. Well, necessity, you're working. That's nothing to feel guilty about."

"I assure you I don't feel guilty. I think women who make a career out of the birth process are as pathetic and obsessed as women who want nothing to do with their babies at all."

"I can't imagine anyone being like that," Maggie said.

"Neither could I," said Kate.

The opening that George and Maggie went to that night was a comedy about a couple with a retarded child, and Maggie was angry and uncomfortable all during the first act. She was more uncomfortable, because she could not tell George why she was uncomfortable; she did not want to tell him under those circumstances the happy truth she suspected, because then it would not be a happy truth at all. She rushed up the aisle the moment the lights went on after the first-act curtain.

"Are you all right?" George said, puffing up the aisle behind her.

"Maggie," the tall beautiful redhead in silver lamé with crystal said, reaching out from one of the rows. *"Ciao,* hello."

"Diane," Maggie said over the marble railing. "Diane, this is Dr. George Piner; George, the Countess Trejinska."

"Just Diane," she said.

"Where's Tzigie?"

"In the *piccolo uomo.*"

"George is a doctor," Maggie said. "Is Tzigie still having his bladder trouble?"

"Actually, I'm not a urologist."

"But he's a marvelous diagnostician," said Maggie. "Maybe Tzigie could come in and see you and then you could send him to the best possible specialist."

"I could do that," George said.

"Somehow it's always more reassuring to go to someone you know and trust than just any specialist," Maggie said. "I know Harry Bell swore by George."

"Really?" Diane said.

"I didn't even know you knew I knew Harry," George said to Maggie.

"Of course I did. Harry used to talk about you all the time. He swore by you. Said you had given him a new lease on life. Naturally that was before July."

"Poor Harry," Diane said. "Have they settled that burial thing yet?"

"I'm afraid not," Maggie said. "According to Louise . . ." The buzzer sounded in the outer lobby, and the lights dimmed twice to signal the end of intermission. "Drat, we have to fly, you will have Tzigie stop in and see George, won't you? Ta."

During the second act when the couple in the play were averting their eyes from the crib, Maggie averted her eyes from the couple, and let her glance wander to the wings and follow a trail of smoke from a stagehand's cigarette.

The first place the smoke went was in small circles toward the top of the proscenium, and she followed it, slowly, with her eyes until she felt concentration increasing. She went with it out through the ceiling of the theater, and along Forty-fifth Street where it hopped into an empty cab to Penn Station and caught a late commuter local to Deal, New Jersey, where it could be with Algernon, as she had been the night before.

He had lain on his back, against a sofa of light green, the white warrior, barefoot and pale in his white chinos, lasciviously holy, the smoke coming from between his lips as he spoke, and puffed on the water pipe.

"Why do you smoke it through water?" Maggie asked.

"To cool it," Algernon said, and laughed.

"I'm having his baby," she said.

"That's beautiful, Mag. I'm really happy for you."

"Are you? I wanted it to be your baby."

"Then it is my baby. I adopt it in my heart."

"Oh Algernon," she said and threw her head across his lap. "We could have been so happy."

"But sweetheart," he whispered, patting the top of her head. "We are. We are the happiest. The world falters in the death of the sun, and we are the only ones who can see it rising."

"Yes," she whispered against him. "Yes, I think that all the time."

"Poor baby," he said laughing quietly, and then stiffened as he felt her mouth against his loins. "Don't do that."

"I'm sorry," she said. "It was only . . ."

"If you have to smoke something, smoke this." He passed her the water pipe. "Love girl," he patted her head, pushing it away from the vicinity of his crotch. "The only ingenue in the frontier movie that is life. You and Walter Brennan."

"Thank you," she whispered. "Not just for saying nice things, Nonny, I mean for finding me. You know, for a while I almost stopped believing in God, because everyone went away right when I needed them, but you won't do that, will you, you'll be here."

"As long as I have this house," Algernon said.

"Yes," she whispered. "That's what I told my attorneys. They're very reluctant to let me sign it over to you permanently, but when I get married they'll have to stop giving me an argument. When I get married they'll have to turn over at least control of the property from the estate."

"I wish you every happiness," Algernon said.

"Especially with Mother dying."

"Are they sure?"

"Very sure. They got out as much as they could, but it had already gone too far. She's all black inside."

"Poor lady," Algernon said. "So when will you marry him. The pale yellow knight."

"When do you think I should."

"As quick as you can, my Maggie. For the sake of the baby."

"Oh yes," she said. "The baby. I almost forgot."

Sitting now, in the theater, she remembered it quite clearly and the stupidity of being where she was, in her condition, hearing words about defectiveness of infant life that insisted on seeping in through her happier reveries, struck her with a force that was nearly physical. Her breathing became heavy as her anger at the poor choice of play increased, and by the time the curtain fell on the second act, she felt dizzy. "Is it over," she whispered to George. "Is that the end of it?"

"There's one more act, I think," George said.

"Please," she whispered, as they moved up the aisle. "Go get me something to drink."

"I knew I should have made you eat dinner before," George said, as he hurried in front of her. "I'll meet you at the back."

George elbowed his way to the crowded, ceilinged alley

outside the rear doors of the theater. Without waiting to see if he was treading on the toes of anyone he knew, or might like to know, he urged himself forward and to the front of the concession counter, and insisted on an orangeade. Twice he asked politely, nicely. The third time he spoke louder than he had spoken in public during his entire adult life. The man behind the counter handed him a slightly damp, cold, wax container.

"Piner!" Chet Oppenheim said, from behind him. "I thought that looked like you. How are you enjoying the play?"

"Fine, fine," George said, caught for a moment in the crush.

"Do you think it would make a movie? My friend Bert, oh I'm sorry, do you know each other, Bertram Lester, Dr. George Piner, Bert's thinking of bidding on the rights, what do you think?"

"Bert!" a woman said from behind, and Lester nodded his round balding head, excused himself, and turned away from George.

"I'll tell you what else he's thinking," Chet said softly. "He's thinking maybe he needs a complete physical. You still got Wendy working in the office?"

"She's visiting her family in Canada. I really have to go, Chet."

"Get her back. Maybe he'll make you medical adviser on the new picture."

"I don't know if my fiancée would like that," George said. "See you."

"Fiancée?" Chet said. "Fiancée?"

"Maggie Bolin," George smiled and passed through the red velvet curtains draping the doorway, to the outer lobby, holding the orangeade high in gentle palms, looking for a glimpse of golden hair. But there were too many, all the same shade, and none of them natural like Maggie's.

A murmured "Oh," went up from the outer lobby, through the glass doors, and people leaned and craned their necks around a hole that seemed to have formed in a swirling whirlpool of gawkers.

"Stand back," someone said. "Give her air."

"Stop pushing in like that."

"Someone get a doctor."

For a moment George was frozen, listening to his own heart pounding. It was something he had always hoped for, on an opening night, to have someone say "Is there a doctor in the house," enabling him to share in the theatricality of the evening, coming forward, so implausibly handsome in his dinner jacket, to heal, to help. But it had never happened before, much as he had always waited for the cliché.

"Is there a doctor in the house," someone actually said.

George started to raise his arm to step forward, but saw what he was holding in his hand. Maggie was waiting for him.

"What happened?" he asked a woman in a beaded gown.

"Somebody fainted," the woman said.

"Oh." There was very little you could do for people who fainted, except wait for them to revive. Fainting involved a simple drop in blood pressure, and there was nothing you could do about it once it had happened except wait for it to right itself, so there was little point in his rushing to the aid of the fainter. They might not faint again for years. On the other hand they might faint again next week. You could never tell. Some people were just fainters. Only a charlatan would make it into a big deal and try to develop a patient-doctor relationship or a house call out of a simple faint.

He held the orangeade like a sword, and cut through the people pushing toward the outer lobby, moving back toward the aisle, his eyes canvassing the heads in theater rows. He stopped, and leaned over the back balustrade.

"Diane," he said. "Countess Diane."

"Oh Dr. Piner," she looked back delighted. "What a pity. You just missed Tzigie. He's in the *kleine mensche*."

"Did you see Maggie?"

"Well yes, as a matter of fact I did, she didn't even stop to say hello, just rushed past here. She looked so pale, doctor, is she all right?"

"Oh my goodness," George said, connecting, and turned around. "Oh my goodness."

He pushed through the crowds, saying "Let me through, I'm a doctor. Let me through, I'm a doctor."

But by the time he reached the place where she would have been lying, he could see the cab door closing. He could see her pale golden head resting on the back of the seat, and beside her (oh God!) a pushy young internist from New York Hospital.

He tried to hail a second cab. But even as he stood there, waving his orangeade in the bulb-lit night, he knew that there was no way he could be there in time.

CHAPTER THREE

BY the end of October, Louise had moved to a bigger apartment, far more sensible, she and Chet had agreed, in view of all the entertaining a woman in her position had to do. There was a full formal living room, a dining room that could accommodate either catered buffet service or a simple sit-down dinner for eight, and a combination den-study where she dictated and wrote her columns, which were now syndicated in eighteen papers. The second bedroom fortunately was big enough to accommodate the pool table with which Chet had gifted her, so there would be no problem of what to do with the heavy thinkers who weren't interested in playing games. On any one of the alternate Saturdays that came to be Louise's regular "evenings" those standing around the table, cue stick poised, might be found to include Arnold Sussman, the political cartoonist, at least one author from the nonfiction best-seller list, Harold Rankin, who was trying diligently to get back his sixteen-year-old pool-shark eye, Peter Daisy, the portraitist who had finished casting the eyes of eight other wealthy young matrons in mercury, and, when he was in town, a Hollywood actor who had recently married into society, for the fifth time. The only regular in the game who was not legitimately a celebrity was an apple-cheeked hooker named Sally, included because she played sensational pool, and because several people were convinced she was the original model for Holly Golightly, and maybe even Sally Bowles, although she hardly seemed old enough.

The walls of the room had been covered with green felt, studded sporadically with gold and crystal sconces, sporadically, because shortly before completion the decorator had questioned the wisdom of doing an apartment gratis because everyone who visited would be touted onto using him, and wondered if he couldn't have a little cash. Louise had filled the gaps by covering the walls with framed eight-by-ten glossies of the professionally theatrical people who visited the apartment, and some charity ball-posed informal portraits for the *Times* women's page of the non-theatrical celebrities, such as the one of Elizabeth Merchant Slade shaking hands with Ronald Reagan. She called it her "Vogue's Gallery," and considered it fitting the slightly Dinty Moore's atmosphere of the poolroom. At the same time she was sure that no one could think it pushy because none of the pictures was autographed, although any number of the faces were in the apartment at any given alternate Saturday.

The wall made her particularly happy because sometimes after all of them were gone, and the apartment was empty, she could look at it and reassure herself that she really did know most of those people. She had never had a "mush" collection; not even during her early teens, when the best of all possible worlds seemed to be Hollywood, had she mounted any of her favorites on the wall. The only pictures she had ever hung above her bed were the glossy photos of her mother in a sequined gown at the captain's ball, and in a white shorts outfit playing shuffleboard on the cruise ship on which she had run away when Louise was thirteen.

Her mother had looked sensational in that picture, white teeth flashing against the dark coat of tan, the cynosure of all eyes of everyone else photographed. She was as good-looking as any movie star, and Louise's only regret had been that she had to hang the pictures underneath a poster because if her father had seen them on the wall he would have had a heart attack.

Mrs. Felder was the only woman in her neighborhood who had run off and deserted her family (except for the *goyim*, the ladies of Great Neck said, who did that kind of thing all the time). Louise did not consider herself deserted, as once a week she received a present from a far-off mysterious place, like Miami Beach, care of her girl friend Corinne. Mrs. Felder knew better than to send anything home, what with Louise's father intercepting all mail and ripping things up like a madman. Twice Louise received pictures, which she secreted beneath his very eyes, and once she even received a loving explanation. "I couldn't go on like that," Mrs. Felder wrote. "I had a chance at life with this job and I couldn't resist it. Your father is a beast. Forgive me."

There was nothing to forgive as far as Louise was concerned. Her mother was tanning and brilliant beneath a tropical sun, dressed all in white, like a dark-haired Lana Turner, so it was only right she should be with John Garfield or John Hodiak, and not with the dentist in the bedroom.

"You know what your mother is?" he said to Louise one evening, as they sat at the table by the kitchenette, eating the meal he had cooked.

"She's a cruise director," Louise said.

"She's a whore," said Dentist Felder. "I don't say this to upset you, you understand, I just don't want you to bow

251

down before any false idols. A spade is a spade, even when it's a Jewish woman."

"She's a cruise director," Louise said.

"And what, pray tell, is that?"

"It's the person who organizes games and activities, tournament and social events for those who are spending their happy holiday on the sun-swept *Princess of the Isles,*" Louise quoted from the brochure her mother had sent her.

"And what, pray tell, would have qualified her for such a position? The only jobs she ever held in her life before I married your mother were as secretaries. Secretaries. What background is that for this sudden transition to cruise director." He bit into the title with teeth fashioned by himself.

"She could have been many things in her time, if she had given herself the chance. When she was twenty-two . . ."

"If you're going to tell me about Herbert Marshall, I happened to have been there. He didn't even turn his head to look at her, although God knows she did everything she could to make him turn, including lifting her skirt up to her pupick. Plenty of people turned to look, it's no trick to get people to look at you if you do something vulgar enough, but among the people who turned to look was not Herbert Marshall."

"Did you look?"

"I was a fool. I loved her. I was such a fool that I permitted passion to outweigh good judgment, so I discarded my perfectly reasonable jealousy and married her. I would not be guilty of such stupidity again, believe me. I know how she got this job. She's sleeping with one of the owners of the line. I don't say this to upset you, understand, I just want you to know why it is so important we cling to each other."

"Why is that?" Louise said.

He paused, fork poised above his mushroom omelet. "We are all we have."

Louise genuinely hoped not, but she did not say so to him. From time to time she would write her mother a letter, care of the cruise line, suggesting that a thirteen-year-old girl might fit in very inconspicuously on a cruise ship if she brought her schoolbooks with her, and stayed below decks most of the time. Once her mother actually answered the allusion directly, saying that nothing would make her happier than to have Louise along, but that life aboard the ship was not as glamorous as she had heretofore led Louise to believe; that she was indeed in the thick of things at parties and tournaments, especially ring toss, at which she had become somewhat of a champion. But when the lonely night was through she had to descend to a tiny cabin far below-decks which was hardly large enough to contain the few outfits she had managed to buy wholesale, so it was not the place for a growing girl.

Louise was certainly growing. Her long-awaited breasts began to blossom slightly, and the period she had been waiting for since the sixth grade when the world got the curse and she was left out, came to her in the middle of her first night as a freshman. She had to run home and tell her father, and for one of the few times since her mother had gone away, she despised her for not being there, and leaving the business of explanation to him.

"You know what this means?" her father said, after he finished giving her the basic details about Kotex.

Louise sat back and waited for the poetic truths about the wonderful task and responsibility of being a woman, and bringing new life onto the earth. Her father had written a great deal of poetry when he was in high school, before he decided that the one thing people always needed was teeth, no matter how easily they turned their backs on soul. He could seldom resist romanticizing in crucial situations, often in ballad meter. "You know what this means?" he said again.

"I think I do, Daddy."

"It means if you do anything dirty, you're going to get in real trouble now, because you can get caught."

Louise averted her eyes, and tried to counter her disappointment with reason. "Don't be silly, Daddy. If I haven't done anything up to now, I'm certainly not going to start."

They lived together at arm's length from then on; Dr. Felder did not understand that her reserve came from his approach to the one moment she would have welcomed his sentimentality. He attributed the distance between them to the influence of her mother, whose pictures he had discovered on the wall behind the poster, but had not dared to take down, for fear it would make her a martyr as well as glamorous.

"What have you heard from your mother?" he said to Louise casually, as they sat eating the brisket he had made.

"Nothing, Daddy. Only the letters in the beginning, that you opened."

"And she hasn't sent you anything else? Like the candy in your bottom drawer, or some pictures maybe?"

"Have you been going through my things?"

"Your mother is a whore," Dr. Felder said. "I don't say that to hurt you, I just don't want you to have illusions."

"My mother is a cruise director," Louise said angrily. "Probably the best in the business because she's been offered jobs on two other lines."

"Aha!" he said. "You've heard from her."

"I've heard from her," Louise said. "What did you think, she was abandoning me?"

"In a minute, in a flash of a second of lightning of an elephant's eye, if she could land somebody rich enough who didn't want a woman with an almost grown child. Why else do you think she went on such a job, if not to find."

"Maybe to get away from you," Louise said, but not aloud.

"And how pray tell would she get such a job, if she was not whoring around with one of the owners. You're old enough to tell you these things, but not so you will be upset, so you will grow with some sense of values, better than hers. How else would she get such a job."

"With charm," Louise said. "She always had a great deal of charm when she wanted to, and she knows how to handle people."

"Not me!" he said, coughing on some meat lodged in his throat. "For me she has no charm. No. Nevermore. Quoth the raven."

"She may be coming home soon," Louise said. "I got a letter."

"Not here," he said, and stamped his fist on the table. "Not my house. She will not be welcome in my house ever again. Why is she coming home, the whore, does the man's wife know?"

"She misses us," Louise said.

"Hell hath no vengeance," he said. "She doesn't fool me. She won't come back here. I'm finished. Finished. For me she has no more charm."

When she came back, he was waiting at the dock at Pier 55 on Twelfth Avenue, with two dozen roses in his arms, and tears in his eyes. Her own eyes teared for a minute in the bitter cold of a winter-swept dock, and then she gave him a Kleenex from a wax-paper container marked "Compliments of the Princess Lines," and told him not to cry, she was back for good, and he better blow his nose because there were a lot of important contacts she had made on board who were interested and excited at the prospect of having him for their dentist. He smiled at everyone she introduced him to, including a man with a hearty handshake whom he was sure was the One, or certainly one of the ones, because he didn't believe for a minute that crap about her going back to her cabin alone.

"So how did you come to get such a job?" he said to her, when she was unpacking, laying the things out on the bed, neatly—clothes, towels, hangers marked "Happy cruising on the Princess."

"What does it matter, Ralph, I'm home for good."

"I'm thrilled, Dolores, thrilled. How did you come to get such a job?"

"Here, Louise," Dolores said. "These are for you." She handed her a stack of photographs, and some cakes of perfumed soap, wrapped with the compliments of the Princess Line.

"Thank you," Louise said. "You look beautiful."

"I'm tired," Dolores said. "I'm not well."

"You're sensational," Ralph said. "How did you come to get such a job?"

"My old boss, you remember, Aaron Frolizy, the attorney, I worked for before we got married? I kept up contact from time to time, with his wife, you know, letters, so when I got so nervous and bored and started writing away for these jobs I saw advertised in magazines, I asked Aaron for a recommendation, and it turned out one of his clients owned the Princess Lines."

"Well that was ingenious of you, Dolores, really ingenious," he said, and when he was finished he mouthed to Louise, "You see? You see?"

"Aaron said I would have gotten the job even without his help, once I had the interview, the thing that sold them was my interview. But it was certainly helpful his making the recommendation because the one thing that might have put me out of the running was my lack of experience."

"I wouldn't say that," Ralph said. "The experience you needed you certainly had, and what you didn't have I bet you made up for plenty on that boat."

"Leave the room, Louise."

"Why?" he said. "She's heard all those phone calls you make to your lovers."

"I'm getting out of here," Dolores said, and started to throw things back in her bag. "You haven't changed at all. I came back because you wrote me you'd changed, but I should have known you'd never change."

"And you, whore? Did you change?" He picked up the clock on the bedstand and hurled it at her. She moved her head so it struck the wall.

"You've killed me!" she screamed. "You've killed me. Louise, call the police."

"You call the police, I'll break your arm, this is between your mother and your father, Louise. If I *am* your father."

"MURDERER," Dolores screamed.

He ran into the living room and pulled the phone cord out of the wall.

"He's crazier than ever," Dolores said. "You better run

downstairs and call the police. He'll never let me leave here alive."

"I'll stay here with you," Louise said.

"Go, run, here's a nickel," said Dolores, turning on the hot water in the bathroom, looking for a pitcher to fill up to throw at him. "You'll do more good."

Louise called the police from the Rexall pay phone, crying openly so they wouldn't ask too many questions. When the police arrived Louise stood in the hallway behind them, and she could see her mother's swollen face, through the crack in the door, the black eye starting above the bulging cheek. In the background she could hear the shower running, and her father singing.

"I don't understand," Dolores said, smiling through swelling lips. "She said what?"

"She said that her father was beating up her mother. That is you?" the policeman said.

"My daughter's crazy," she said, and smiled. "Look at me. Do I look like I'm upset?" She didn't. Louise could see that. She had never looked happier in her life.

After that Louise went to stay with her friend Corinne for three days so her parents could have a proper, private reunion. She took the pictures she had had hung on the wall with her so Corinne could see how pretty her mother looked on the cruise.

At the end of the three days Dolores Felder went to her gynecologist and found out she was not pregnant, as she had suspected. But he did find a questionable situation, so before it was over she had a hysterectomy. Her youth and her beauty and her womanhood were over with, at thirty-eight years, she was sure. She had no more stomach for conquest.

"It's up to you, baby," she said to Louise, as the two of them went over the photos of the year's cruises, putting them away in the cedar chest off the living room, because there wasn't enough space in the apartment for clutter. "You're going to be the one who does it all."

"Who's this?" Louise said, looking at the picture of the man standing by the railing. He had his arm around a blond woman, and was not exactly looking at Dolores in the photo, but Louise could tell he wanted to, that he was controlling himself for the sake of appearances.

"That's Morton Downey, the famous bandleader."

Louise had never heard of Morton Downey, but after that he became her favorite bandleader, and she told everyone at school that he was even more famous than Tommy Dorsey. "You look beautiful in this picture."

"You'll be even prettier when you lose your baby fat, Louise. Maybe when you get your period."

"I've already gotten it."

"Did your father talk to you about life?"

"He certainly did," Louise said. "If he *is* my father."

"Don't be too hard on him. He had dreams. He wanted to be a poet."

"I know."

"You can't survive in this world being a poet. It's hard enough being a dentist, especially when you won't move into Manhattan. You don't know the people I cultivated on those boats to be his patients, but they're certainly not going to come to Great Neck to fix their teeth. Bum."

"Why did you come back?" Louise said.

"I'm tired," said Dolores. "My insides. You're the one. You'll do it all. You can have everything in the world you want, you know, if you meet the right people. You'll know them all. As soon as you lose your baby fat."

In spite of Ralph's increasing trouble with bursitis (he claimed it was the direct result of Dolores hitting him in the neck with the ironing board) which cut his work schedule down to half the normal dental day, the Felders managed to save enough money to send Louise to Elizabeth Arden's Maine Chance for Teen-age Weight Week. She met a number of teen-agers who were going to come out the following year, all of them as fat or fatter than she, none of them with as pretty a face. She lost only ten pounds, but on party night, which included as refreshments, among other things, lime buttermilk sherbet and Sucaryl strawberries, the entertainment consisted of an old gypsy woman who rode onto the estate by donkey cart, and read all the girls' fortunes with a deck of playing cards. Louise had never been particularly superstitious, but she watched with a sense of growing anticipation as the old woman hit with unfailing accuracy some truth about each of the girls. When it came her turn, she felt a sense of great excitement.

The gypsy turned over ten face cards in a row. "Important people," she said. "You are going to be with important people. Headlines. Celebrities. Big stars."

It wasn't until an hour afterward, with her soul still fluttering, that Louise penetrated the disguise in her mind, and recognized Renee, the assistant makeup counselor. She made her way slowly up the hill from the lake, across the darkened green, through the pine trees, lit only by stars and an occasional floodlight, and entered the help's quarters of the old estate. Renee was sitting at the dressing table in her converted attic room, wiping off the last traces of makeup with her cold cream. She saw Louise in the mirror.

"Caught me, you dog," Renee said, and smiled.

"No wonder you knew so much about everybody."

"But I only cheated with them," Renee said. "Honest to God, kid, I read your cards for true. I never saw so many honor cards in my life. You saw. All face cards. I didn't set that up, really. I read them for true."

"What does that prove?"

"All face cards. Honors. Royalty. What else can it mean, kings and queens and jacks. I'm not a real gypsy but I do know a little something about telling fortunes, I swear. You're going to know a lot of important people."

When Louise came home her mother was very disappointed that she hadn't gotten thin, at those prices. "It was only two weeks, Mama. It was a start, anyway."

"At those prices," Dolores said. "Who did you meet, and don't call me Mama."

"I met a gypsy."

"Oh for Christ's sake. Three hundred dollars a week and twenty debutantes, and you meet a gypsy."

"She read my fortune, really, she's a great fortuneteller, and she said I was going to know all celebrities."

"How many coming-out parties did you get invited to?"

"Really. It came up all face cards."

"Six hundred dollars for face cards. You didn't get invited to any of them."

"They're going to call me," Louise said. "Really. I made some good friends."

"Gypsies," Dolores said. "I might have known."

A few of the girls did call her to have lunch in Manhattan, but none of them mentioned anything about their debuts. Eventually Louise lost contact with everybody from Arden's except Renee, whom she phoned from time to time. In the fall she and Dolores decided that as long as Louise could only afford a city college, where there was no chance of really improving herself, except intellectually, she might as well get a job. She had gotten considerably slimmer over the summer, and with the secretarial skills learned in high school, and drilled into her at home by Dolores, she managed to get a job with Phillips & Rose.

"Guess who I saw today, my dear," she said to Renee on the phone. "Gregory Peck. He was standing a half a foot away from me, and naturally he was dying to take me into his arms, but he's afraid of what people will say. Tee hee."

She learned to do her hair in a soft, flattering pageboy that would serve to outline the warm darkness of her eyes, and she set her mouth in a smiling pout, and showed important clients her perfect teeth in the dazzling way she had practiced before the mirror. She was not too secure about her manner of dress, but her mother took her shopping wholesale, and she had several dresses of the same style in different colors, which convinced her she had a varied wardrobe. Within a few months she had picked up some of the slyer mannerisms of her immediate superior, a twenty-eight-year-old publicist named Phillip Cook, who grayed his hair at the temples and said he had gone to Cambridge, meaning Harvard.

"I'm going to take you to a Christmas party, Louise love," Phillip said. "Very high tone. Donald and Julia White. She's *Élan*, and he's East Coast Twentieth-Century Fox."

"Am I in show business?" Louise said.

" 'Scuse?"

"Well don't you think I know that, for heaven's sake, Donald and Julia White, how would you feel if I told you who Kazan was?"

"Who?"

"Fun-nee," Louise said. "What'll I wear."

"Something very dressy, love. The World will be there."

"Lulu is so excited," Louise said.

It was clearly not an occasion for one of her mother's wholesale numbers. Louise took her two-week paycheck and went to Russeks, where she bought a red velveteen dress with a low-cut square neck and puffed sleeves. She had shoes dyed to match at A. S. Beck, which also provided her with a matching velvet headband. The night of the party she stood in front of the armoire, with the fading mirror on it, and tried to see herself clearly.

"Is Louise pretty?" she said to her mother.

"You've never looked better in your life," Dolores said. "I'm proud of you. Now if only . . ."

"Not tonight, Mother, please."

"I only want you to watch yourself at the party. There'll probably be a lot of fancy food, and a good time doesn't mean you have to stuff yourself."

"I know that, Mother."

"Many times on shipboard I was tempted, believe me, you've never seen such spreads, the chef was an artist. But every time I weakened, I remembered that the momentary pleasure is passing, but the fat stays with you forever."

"I'll keep that in mind at all times," Louise said, pinning a sprig of holly on her headband. "You think that's too much?"

"It's perfect. There's nothing religious about holly. It's just festive."

"How do I look?"

"Like a present," Dolores said. "Like an adorable Christmas present."

"Really?"

"Just stand up straight and suck in your stomach. I want you to have confidence in yourself."

She had on her coat when she met Phillip at Pennsylvania Station, so he could not get the full impact of how she looked, but he told her she smelled nice and her hair looked lovely. "Thank you," she said, and held his hand in the taxi going uptown because she needed reassurance and knew he wouldn't mind as long as she was wearing gloves.

That evening was the first time Louise saw Harry Bell, but she had no wish to make any impression on him, because she thought him very old, and the whole world was stretching out before her. There were several movie stars, three famous stage actors, and many peripheral celebrities at the party, but she did not have the chance to make an impression on them either.

"Whatever you do," Phillip warned her, "don't come on too strong with Julia. She despises gush."

"You don't have to tell me how to handle myself," Louise said. "For God's sake, Phillip, I've been places before, you know, this isn't my first party."

After getting her a drink, and introducing her to a few people who nodded vaguely and smiled, Phillip left her alone by the buffet table in the living room, and went off into a corner with a playwright the office was trying to sign. Louise stood for a moment, smiling at the room in general, and then, looking down, noticed that she was picking up a ham sandwich. She put it back. Looking around her for someone she knew, even for five minutes, she found Julia White.

"Hi," she said. "I'm Louise Felder, I met you by the door?"

"Yes?"

"I can't tell you how kind it was of you to invite me, it's a perfectly beautiful party, I suppose you could say that everyone here is a celebrity in one way or another, couldn't you?"

Julia stepped back and eyed her, slowly, starting at her red shoes, moving up to the holly in her headband. "And who are you supposed to be, darling, the mother of the bride?"

It struck Louise that if she had gone to college, which is what she had genuinely wanted to do, she could have been at this moment drinking beer with some nice freshman at an NYU fraternity house, singing carols maybe, which were not so much religious as festive. She got her coat without even telling Phillip she was leaving, and avoided looking at herself in the foyer mirror.

260

"Where do the college girls go this joyous season?" she asked the cabdriver as they headed downtown.

"The Biltmore," he said. "Lot of the time. Under the clock."

"Of course. I knew that all along. I don't know why I even bothered to ask."

She was in the lobby for only six minutes when Eddie came over and introduced himself. She had no particular penchant for redheaded men, but he was wearing a tweed jacket and striped tie, and was supposed to be meeting a girl from Sweetbriar, so she found him fascinating. He confessed, in very short order, that he was drawn to her, and saw no reason why they shouldn't skip off together into the night, and go dancing at the Harwyn, where she probably went all the time. She didn't tell him she had never been there, and after that evening didn't have to. When he brought her home at four o'clock that morning, he said he had known—even before she told him—he had guessed from how glamorously she dressed, that she was in show business.

During the year she went with Eddie, nobody ever told her she was dressed wrong, mostly because his friends considered her very stylish, or at least knew that Eddie did. After he married Ellen Feinblatt, Louise never felt completely pretty again, no matter how happy she thought she was with the dress she was wearing. Every once in a while she would find herself at the same party or opening or restaurant as Julia White, and would get out of her way without knowing why she was so upset.

The first time Louise met Harry Bell officially was at Harold Rankin's first anniversary cocktail party for *Platinum!*, a musical comedy loosely based on the lives of Jean Harlow and Zelda Fitzgerald. Harry had recently been divorced from Sylvia for the second time, and all of Broadway knew he was at loose ends. Louise whispered to several people that she wouldn't mind picking a few of them up (tee hee). By then she was thirty, and working as a press agent for Paul Harris, Limited. Her list of suitors was limited to married men whose suits were limited to a quickie in her apartment, and an occasional movie star whom Harris was representing in the East, and whom Louise was assigned to "service," though not always in the way she would have liked. More often than not the handsomer the star, the more handsome was the star he was seeking. She laughed to her friends on the phone, and told them she was becoming a faggot's moll, and was thinking of having her tits removed to increase her appeal. But she was selective about making the joke to close friends like Phillip Cook, who was now also graying his eyebrows, as she suspected he was more than a little enamored with a few of her escorts.

The night of the *Platinum!* party, Louise was assigned to a tall, red-headed defector named Petra Orloff, recently put under contract by Bertram Lester. There was no doubt that Petra was an astonishing beauty, in the sullen tradition of Garbo, but the office wasn't at all sure she was really going to happen, what with Lester's fortunes turning. So they figured there was no harm in letting her go around town with Louise. Louise had no particular objection to touring around with girls, as she had long ago decided that reflected glory was better than none.

The star of *Platinum!* did her famous tabletop dance and then swam around the replica of the Plaza fountain which Harold Rankin had had set up in the middle of the hors d'oeuvres table. The press took pictures and friends of Harold Rankin applauded. Louise paid little attention to the official festivities, as she was very busy watching Harry Bell watching Petra Orloff. His jaw was slack, and his eyes were watering, almost like a little boy's at the sight of a birthday cake, and it did not occur to her until later that perhaps he was not so much lusting as ill. By that time it didn't matter.

He came over to them eventually, as Louise knew he would. Louise whispered in Petra's ear to be nice to the little gentleman, he was very powerful, in the European sense.

"You got a boyfriend?" he said to Petra.

"I beg pardon . . ."

"I'm Louise Felder. I don't think we've met, Mr. Bell."

"Now we have. You got a boyfriend?" he said to Petra.

"I have many new friends in this wonderful country of freedom."

"I guess she told you," Louise said.

"You're a refugee, huh, how'd Lester find you, you his girl?"

"Pardon."

"You sleeping with him?"

"Mr. Lester has been very kind, like an uncle."

"I had an uncle like that once. They put him in jail," Harry said, and laughed.

"I do not understand."

"It's just as well, darling," Louise said.

"Have you seen much of this beautiful country?" Harry said.

"I have seen Hollywood."

"Tinsel and glitter. Maybe you'd like to see the real America. You ever been in an authentic New York town house? I have a French chef."

Louise was fast losing interest, in spite of how tall everybody said Harry was when he stood on his money. But then she looked up as a waiter offered her the champagne tray, and saw Julia White watching them.

"We'd love to," Louise said, and linked her arm through Harry's. "Come, Petra."

"I do not understand."

"Mr. Bell has kindly invited us to have dinner with him at his home."

"What are you, the duenna?" Harry said.

"I am the good fairy," Louise said. "At her birth the fairy of darkness predicted that Petra would die from a prick when she was twenty-three, and it's my job to see that the prophecy doesn't come to pass."

"A smart-ass," he said. "What do I need with a smart-ass."

"It might be a refreshing change for you," Louise said. "You never can tell."

The chauffeured Rolls was waiting outside the Americana, and all the way uptown, as Harry made stilted conversations with Petra, Louise held on to the velvet-covered arm loop that hung by the window, and felt how much softer it was even than her own honey-silk skin. Sitting beside him, with his face turned away, she saw that their shoulders were almost level, and realized that he was not, after all, as small as she had imagined at first. It wasn't standing on his money that made him taller, it was sitting in his Rolls. She smiled and told herself she would have to remember that line for the next day when Phillip Cook called for details, as he certainly would. Half the room had noted their departure.

The car pulled up in front of the Fifth Avenue house. For all the homes that she had seen from the outside, and all the expensive apartments she had visited, Louise was unprepared for the richness and the beauty. Black and white marble (not tile, Harry noted, anyone can get tile, or terrazzo even) harlequined the entrance hall, the arch was striped with rectangles of sculpted stone; recessed cavities that had once held the holy founts of European churches offered up bronzed busts of Caesar, Balzac, Shakespeare, and Churchill.

"That last was a favor," Harry said. "It doesn't fit in, but I always admired him, so I commissioned this poor starving bastard to do it, in the style of Rodin, of course."

"Of course," Louise said, looking up at the ceiling. It was vaulted, and the dome was inset with infinitely precise biblical scenes of birth, and death, and damnation, in stained glass, through which streamed a constant sun of Harry's own

263

design, a floodlight on the roof four stories above, in case of night, or bad weather.

"It's like the Vatican," Louise said.

"You been to the Vatican?"

"I've seen photographs."

"It's better than the Vatican," Harry said. "I told the Pope that, my last audience, and he promised to come see, maybe, one day."

"I hope he won't be too envious," she said. But just at that moment Harry turned on the light in the living room, and she looked. After that she kept more or less quiet.

It was splendor. That was all there was to it, was splendor. Dinner was served on gold-leafed trays on a table set up by the butler in a corner of the living room, in front of a fireplace from a Venetian castle. They would have eaten in the dining room, but the three of them at a table for forty, Harry explained, might have been a little lonely. Louise didn't think so. She would not have minded eating alone in a room with dark-paneled walls inset with portraits of Borgias. Nor would she have minded in the least being the poor bereft widow of Harry Bell, solitary in that vast room, picking at the quenelles in golden-tapered candlelight. She did not say so aloud. As it was she enjoyed every mouthful of the food, served on Crown Derby China (Harry had bought it at auction, and paid only forty dollars a plate, he told them proudly). Although she did not as a rule drink wine, she lifted the leaded gold goblet to her mouth until it was drained of every drop of Lafite-Rothschild 1945, from Harry's private three-room cellar, which he showed them after dinner. In the cool Hitchcockian darkness divided with checkered slots of rare champagnes, she saw him reach for the less public cheek of Petra Orloff. When they came upstairs, and she sensed that he wanted to be alone with Petra, Louise went home without protest, because it was in the Rolls, and if she played her cards right, which she had every intention of doing, she knew she could cut out the Russian in a minute. Before she went to bed, she called her mother, and told her she had had dinner with Harry Bell. At his home. Alone. Except for a girl she had let come along for the sake of appearances.

The next morning she was in the office for twenty minutes before the call came in from Phillip Cook. Her own office space was one of ten glassed-in cubicles, with a green metal desk covered with papers, press releases, items of supposed personal and topical nature about clients of the firm, including one memo marked in red and penciled "KILL" about a food poisoning that supposedly occurred in a new Italian restaurant the firm handled. There was a small pullout leaf on the right of the desk that held Louise's ancient typewriter, and beside it was a phone, with three pushbutton extensions. Louise shared her extension with another girl and the agency photographer. When it rang she always let one of the others pick up first, so people would assume she had a secretary.

The phone jangled beside her, but she didn't answer, finishing up some copy, for the miscellany editors of various newspapers, on a juggler who had just ended a tour of European army camps. "The world loves Rudy," she wrote, "and would welcome a feature story on him. Not only is his background unique and fascinating, but there is his marked resemblance to Yul Brynner, from whose native city he also comes. Next Sunday will mark his thirtieth appearance on the Sullivan show. How about a feature, kids?" The phone kept ringing, and she figured maybe the others were out of the office. She answered in a husky voice.

"Miss Felder's wire," she said.

"Miss Felder, please. Phillip Cook calling."

"Who are you calling?"

"Louise Felder."

"No no, sweetheart," she switched onto her little-girl voice, so he would know who it was. "Louise Bell. You mean Louise Bell."

Phillip started to laugh.

"Lulu must have him. Lulu could never do it with that little man, but Lulu must slide down that bannister, you wouldn't believe that bannister, Phillip, it's two stories if it's a day, and Lulu must slide down it and play with those statues."

"You mercenary," he said, still laughing.

"How can you say that. Lulu is in love. She really is. She is in love with his paintings, and his furniture. Phillip, you wouldn't believe the dinnerware. His silverware is gold, can you imagine, gold silverware. I could learn to live like that, I swear I could. Lulu Bell, I've decided."

"But he's so ugly."

"How can you be so concerned with externals," Louise said, and laughed. "And he's not as short as everyone thinks. He's very tall when he sits in his Rolls. Besides, why should all those tall beautiful *goyim* get all that money. Why shouldn't it happen to a short cuddly Jewish girl."

Her appointment with Dr. Ehrens wasn't until three o'clock that afternoon, by which time she had spoken with almost everyone she knew in New York, and told them about Harry Bell's house. When she went into Ehrens' office she thought she might as well tell him too, as there were times when she genuinely considered him her friend.

"Guess who I went to dinner with last night? Harry Bell."

He just sat there, looking at her, waiting, so she picked up the fresh white cloth on the pillow and held it across her nose, like an Arabian veil. "Well? Aren't you going to say anything?"

"What do you want me to say?"

"Well, aren't you excited for me, for God's sake, a man like Harry Bell, interested in me, don't you see what it means?"

"What does it mean?" Dr. Ehrens said.

"Oh are you going to start that psychiatric shit, because if you are, I don't even want to go into it, I was trying to talk to you like a real person, and I thought in my innocence, I thought maybe as a real person you might be happy for me. A man like Harry Bell, for God's sake."

"What exactly is a man like Harry Bell?"

"Do you live in this world? I mean, I know you're a Freudian, but even so, don't you sometimes visit the real world."

"Why don't you tell me about it?"

"What? The real world, or Harry Bell, my nights among the paintings and furniture, by Louise Berenson."

"You pick," Dr. Ehrens said.

"It isn't as if it was a movie," Louise said. "You could admit you knew about it."

"What, the real world, or Harry Bell?"

"When I marry Harry I'm going to see that he gives you several million dollars in research so you won't have any more private practice so you can stop driving people crazy. Do you think I could?"

"What?"

"Get a man like that to marry me."

"Why would you want to?"

"I want to punch you," Louise said. "Honest to God, you don't even know the man, and look how prejudiced you are. He happens to be very sweet."

"I wasn't discussing him. I was asking why you'd want to marry him."

"Why? Just because he's old? He's very young when he sits in his Rolls." She waited for him to laugh, but he didn't. "You have no sense of humor, did anyone ever tell you that?"

"Why are you so concerned with my reaction?"

"Well, you're a human being, for God's sake, at least I always figured deep down there was a chance you were a human being, and you do like me, you like me a little bit, don't you, and you know what I've been through with fags

266

and Andre and there isn't anybody around, and at least he's single, and he's rich. I never knew anybody was that rich. I used to figure it was enough just to be beautiful and famous like I am, tee hee, but now I saw it and I want it. It isn't just the glamour, seriously, Dr. Ehrens. There's an aura about people that have that much, even when they're not as rich as Harry. But when they're that rich, my God, you could never be insecure about anything, ever. And don't give me that bullshit about the rich not always being happy. My God, I'd love to be unhappy like that, don't you dare say anything so corny."

"I haven't said a word," Dr. Ehrens said.

"You're skeptical, huh," Louise said. "That's why you don't want to discuss it, isn't it. Because you know I'm lying."

He lit his pipe, and said nothing.

"I don't mean I'm lying about meeting Harry Bell. I did have dinner with him last night. My mother almost peed when I told her. That cunt Julia White."

"Who?"

"I don't want to discuss it, it isn't important."

"Then why did you mention her at this particular moment?"

"You know the thing about you, you never say anything and then when I'm about to have a moment of real insight, you keep interrupting me, Dr. Ehrens."

"Why don't we go back to what you think you wanted to tell me."

"What was that?"

"About lying."

"Oh. Well, I don't mean lying so much as fantasizing. I mean I know it's a fantasy, playing with the idea of someone like Harry Bell marrying me. A man like Harry Bell would never marry me. Would he?"

"Why would you want him to?"

"Then you think he could, don't you. Phillip said that too. It doesn't matter that I'm not beautiful and famous like he's used to. The fact of the matter is I'm bright and cuddly and that might be a new kick for that shriveled old man. Ugh. How could anybody go to bed with him."

"How about Julia White?"

"What? Go to bed with him? Julia White is one of the most attractive, successful women in New York. She's the editor of *Élan*, for God's sake. She dictates the styles, she doesn't have to adapt to them. She doesn't have to do anything she doesn't want to."

"How about your mother?"

"How did my mother get into this?"

"You said she 'almost peed' when you told her about Harry Bell, and then you mentioned Julia White."

"And what are you saying, you saying there's any comparison between them? Because if you are, you're not really very perceptive, and if you don't go to the movies maybe you ought to at least read a few magazines and columns and find out who people are."

"Then there's no similarity between them."

"Are you kidding? Julia White is one of the beautiful people. She has an aura. A radiance."

"Doesn't your mother?"

"Of course not," Louise said. And then more quietly: "At least not anymore."

"Then why did you keep her pictures on your wall."

"Oh for God's sake, sometimes I wonder why I tell you anything. I was a kid. What has that got to do with anything. You think I think my mother's a movie star."

"You must have thought she was glamorous, or you wouldn't have kept her picture on your wall."

"I was thirteen. Big deal."

"There's a reason why people chase after celebrities."

"My mother is not in the least like Cary Grant, tee hee."

"Is she like Julia White?"

"You poor Freudian bastard. Next you'll tell me I have a weight problem because I wasn't breast-fed."

"Were you?"

"Who remembers," Louise said, and got up from the couch. "This is a waste of time. I have to go to Saks and get my hair done, so when my fiancé calls, I'll be ready. Lulu Bell. How do you think that sounds?"

"Very cute," he said. "Tee hee."

"Oh!" she said and threw her arms up in the air, and brought her hands down over her eyes. "Oh if only there was a God I could get hysterical paralysis and then you could find out that I'd been raped by my father when I was eight, and things would be much easier, but I don't suppose you saw that picture either."

"No, but I read the case," Dr. Ehrens said, and smiled. "Would you really have liked that?"

"It just would have made our whole relationship so much easier."

"How about your relationship with your mother?"

Louise picked up her coat. "I'll have Harry send you a check."

When she got back to the office there was a phone message for her from Harry Bell, with his unlisted number. She copied it down in her personal phone book before she called him back.

"That was a nice telegram," he said, when she got him on the line. "I'm glad you liked the house, and the dinner."

"And the company," she said. "You mustn't leave out the company."

"Most people wouldn't think to send a telegram. Most people write a note, by the time you get it, you forget what you had them there for. Either that or they call."

"Well I didn't want to seem pushy," Louise said, thinking it just as well not to tell him that Celebrity Service had only his office number.

"Except for refugees. Refugees send flowers."

"I never send flowers to an unmarried man," Louise said.

"Anyhow, thanks for the telegram."

"Thanks for the dinner."

"So where's the refugee?"

"Pardon."

"The long red-headed drink of water. I called her hotel, she's out."

"She's doing *Les Crane*. They're taping late this afternoon."

"You think she'll be finished in time for the opening?"

"What opening is that, Mr. Bell?"

"Some big movie premiere Columbia is having."

"*Ship of Fools*?"

"I wouldn't know. Maybe. I don't want to go, but I got a good friend, she's a dissident stockholder wants me to come in with her, so I have to see what's shaking. You think the Rusky'll be through in time."

"Let me check her schedule," Louise said, and turned to her memo pad. The taping would be over at seven. "What time is the premiere."

"Eight fifteen," Harry said.

"She won't be finished until nine."

"Oh. You have a long dress?"

"I even have a pumpkin," Louise said.

The picture was boring, but it was graced with a long intermission which gave Louise a chance to stand at his side, hunched only slightly, and smile back at everyone who was smiling at Harry. Most of the people who greeted him she did not recognize, as there was an older crowd at the movie premiere than she usually saw at a theatrical opening. Harry did not go out of his way to introduce her to anybody, but that was all right, Louise thought, he was probably possessive about her, and that was good. It was even charming. The only person there that Louise genuinely wanted to meet, whom she recognized instantly, was the Countess Trejinska, who whipped past them in the lobby in a floor-length coat dress of white brocade. Harry seemed to turn away at her passing, almost as if he were embarrassed by that much radiance.

"She is beautiful," Louise said.

"Who?"

"Diane Trejinska."

"Yeah."

"You think those were real diamonds?"

"They would have to be," Harry said.

"Oh, then you do know her."

"Not to talk to," Harry said, taking Louise's arm and guiding her back into the theater.

Just before the lights went down Louise caught a glimpse of Julia White, and craned her neck hoping that Julia would see her and note who she was with, for the second night in a row.

She was immediately ashamed, and looked at Harry Bell in the diminishing yellow light, and realized that the thing to be most envied about him was his position of not being embarrassed to run into anybody.

Afterward he did not feel like going to the party. He said maybe they could have an intimate little supper, just the two of them.

"At your house?" she said.

"No. You're all dressed up. You should go out."

When the Rolls pulled up to the Sixth Avenue Delicatessen she tried not to say anything. "I guess you're right," she said, losing. "Anybody could go to Sardi's."

"They have good food here. That's all supper should be."

She managed to control the anger, biting through her corned beef sandwich, by reminding herself what a good story it would make in the morning. Thinking it over, she realized he must really like her, or he wouldn't be so intent on keeping her to himself.

"You really like me, don't you?" she said as they sat back in the limousine.

"You're cute," he said, and put his hand between her legs.

"It's all right," she said, pinching them closed. "I wasn't asking for a testimonial."

"Can I come up?" he said, as the car pulled up to her apartment building. "Or you want to play that nitsy-poo stuff about it being the first date."

"Why Harry, it's all I can do to keep from pleading with you to have me right here, but we might wake my roommate." There was no roommate; nor was it a ploy because she was afraid she couldn't handle Harry. What she was afraid of were the four flights of stairs up to her apartment. She wasn't ashamed because he might realize she was poor. She was nervous he might have a heart attack before he could help make her a little richer.

"A girl or a boy roommate?"

"Do you think I'm the kind of girl who would live with a man?"

"Somebody's fucking you," he said, "or your skin wouldn't be so good."

"You sweetheart." She leaned over and kissed his cheek. "You really know how to pay a girl a compliment."

In the next few weeks she saw him a number of times, but it was always to go to the Sixth Avenue Delicatessen, or to some aging friends of his for dinner. The overtures, like the evenings, were not particularly romantic in nature, being restricted to asking her to put her hand on his cock in the back of the Rolls, and meeting her once half-naked at the door of his house. The seventh time they were together (she marked the number on her calendar) he invited her to a party at his home. She borrowed a dinner dress from Kate Waller, but did not tell her what it was for, because she suspected that Kate, unlike most of her friends, would not consider it such a big accomplishment, dating Harry Bell. She also canceled her afternoon appointment with Dr. Ehrens, because she saw no reason for her euphoria to be marred with his perverted truths about why she was going. Why she was going was she loved parties, and she had just had her head gilded, and she looked as pretty as she had ever looked (didn't she?) and she loved the way she felt about herself when she was in that house. She enjoyed the prospect of seeing the paintings and the sculptings and the furnishings at her leisure, a leisure granted by the fact of other people being there, diminishing the fear that if she turned her back to gaze, he would have time to whip out his wizened thing.

She was the first to arrive at the party, a gaffe she would have considered unforgivable in herself if she hadn't noticed by the eighteenth-century clock in the second foyer that she was an hour later than he had specified. "So it's to be that kind of party," she smiled. "You gay dog."

"Don't treat me like a college boy," he said. "I'm no college boy, and I resent being treated like one."

"But Harry darling, how could I have known, when you act so young and . . ."

"Stow it," he said, and opened up the guest closet. "You want to hang up your coat?"

"Not even a butler tonight?" she giggled. "Tee hee. You want to be alone with Lulu?"

"If I was so hungry to be alone with you, I'd invite you to the island."

"Why haven't you?"

"You get invited when I'm sure that all you want isn't to get invited. You want a drink before everyone gets here?"

"Then somebody else is really coming? In a way, I'm kind of disappointed." Safe, she started to climb the stairs, her fingernails clicking on the marble of the bannister.

"Where are you going?"

"I just want to see the statue close up," she said. "It's so beautiful, and I didn't really have a chance to look at it before." She stopped on the first landing, and looked up into the incredibly wrought face of David, and in that moment realized that it might not be so terrible after all, that she had thrown herself away on creeps and wise guys and had let herself be used all her life by those who had nothing to offer her, or if they had something to offer, had no wish to give. This man at least could offer Michelangelo. She could survive the weekly (how often could they do it, sixty-four-year-old men—biweekly maybe, or not even) indignity. So much of her life that she had considered romantic had added up to humiliation, it would not be so humiliating accompanied by Michelangelo. In his own way, Harry was sweet, and he was probably not so unattractive when he lay on his money.

"I know what you're thinking," he said. "You're thinking you'd like to ball him."

"Of course. That was the first thing that came into my mind."

"Don't be a wise guy," he said, and he was behind her, his hand cupping her breast through the black crepe. She could feel every one of his fingers pressing against her.

"Oh for . . ."

"Shut up," he said, and his other hand was on her shoulder, and he was turning her around with a strength surprising in such a small man. His face thrust against hers, and his lips pressed coldly against her mouth, straight on, so their noses touched. She would have giggled except his tongue was in her mouth, so she couldn't breathe, much less laugh. "I'm nuts about you," he whispered against her mouth, and squeezed her breast as if to give the words authority. "Get upstairs."

"But the people . . ."

"They won't be here for an hour. I told them it was going to be a late dinner."

"And what am I, the hors d'oeuvre?"

"Wise guy, wise guy," he muttered, and his arm was

272

around her, bending her toward him. She tried to step away but his grip was too strong, and she slipped on the Indian carpet and the two of them were on the floor. "Okay kid, that's how you want it, that's how you'll get it," and he was on top of her, his knees between her legs, forcing them open.

"Harry, for Christ's sake, it's a fitted skirt," she said. If he heard he gave no sign. His knee probed, and his right hand held both her wrists, while he reached down to his trousers, and she heard the zipping sound, in a moment she felt him against her leg, hard and bigger than she would have imagined.

"Couldn't we talk this over?" she said, but his mouth was on hers, cold lips, with a thick warm tongue.

"Bitch," he said. "You think you can pull that ingenue shit with me, don't you think I've learned anything since Miami?"

"Huh?" she said.

His hand slapped across her face, and she felt him grow even harder against her and he reached down and pulled her legs apart.

And then they heard the ripping.

"Oh my God," she said. "Oh my God."

"Now you see what you did?"

"What I did?" she shrieked. "You think I ripped the dress."

"Well if you weren't playing your stupid games . . ."

"Games? Who cares about games? What am I going to do?"

"I'll get you another dress."

"It isn't mine," she said, and started to cry. "I borrowed it from my best friend because I didn't have anything that was classy enough for an evening at your house. Classy enough, for Christ's sake. Rolling around on the fucking staircase in front of your goddam statue. How's that for a feature in *Town and Country*. An evening at home with Harry Bell."

"I'm sorry, kid. I really didn't mean to hurt your dress."

"Oh, tuck yourself in," she said, sniffling.

He looked down at the gap in his trousers, from which his erection protruded, an angry red sentinel breaking ranks. "What a waste," he muttered, and pushed his extension inside his trousers, and zipped up his fly. "I guess you better go home and change. I'll send you in the car."

"That's very thoughtful of you," she said.

When she got to her door she told Harry's chauffeur that she would not be going back to Mr. Bell's house, that he was free to leave. It would serve Harry right, she thought, as she climbed the stairs to the fourth floor. Let him know that he couldn't get away with something like that. Besides, she had nothing else to wear. She opened the door to her apartment and flung herself across the sofa bed, reaching for a Kleenex, and wept angrily. The dress could be fixed, probably, the rip straight up the seam, but the evening was gone. The first evening when he was going to show her to other people. Most of them famous, probably.

When she got to her office the next day, there were two dozen roses on her desk, and a gift certificate for a dress at Macy's. "Piker," she muttered, and put the certificate in an envelope and addressed it to Kate. She told the phone operator that if Mr. Bell called, she was out of the office. When the New York *Post* came in at noon, she turned to Erlam's column, and saw a list of the people who had been at Harry's party the night before, and she started to cry all over again.

It was three days before she answered his call.

"Didn't you get the flowers?" he said.

"I got them."

"Didn't you like them?"

"They were all right if you like roses."

"How about the gift certificate. Did you get yourself something pretty?"

"I sent it to my friend. The one whose dress I ripped."

"Well, you got another long dress?"

"What for? I have to decide if my wardrobe can take the strain."

"I got tickets for Harold Rankin's new opening tonight. His own house seats. Will you go with me?"

"And afterward I guess it'll be another candlelit dinner at the Sixth Avenue Delicatessen."

"I made reservations at the Oak Room for dinner. Or we can go to Sardi's afterwards, if you'd rather."

"I don't know," Louise said, as she looked at the clock to see if there was time to get her hair done, and go to Ohrbach's both.

"I said I was sorry," he said.

"No you didn't."

"Well I sent roses, it's the same thing."

"Is it?"

"So I'm sorry."

"Pick me up at six thirty," Louise said.

She took a cab to Ohrbach's, and picked out a long beige chiffon with imitation tourmaline mink at the cuffs that had been reduced to fifty-nine ninety-five, and taxied uptown to Saks and told her hairdresser to give it a golden beigey tone. Then she phoned a furrier friend and told him that she was going to a premiere with Harry Bell, and needed to borrow a tourmaline stole. He promised to have it up to her apartment by six.

At six fifteen she looked at herself in the mirror, and she was lovely (wasn't she?), as honey beige as she had ever been in her life. Harry Bell would be a fool not to love her. She genuinely hoped.

The buzzer from downstairs sounded at exactly six thirty. She smiled one last time at herself in the mirror, picked up the stole, and went downstairs.

"You look very nice," he said, as the chauffeur opened the door for her.

"So do you."

"We have an hour before the opening. I thought maybe you'd like a drink."

"That would be very nice," she said.

"I thought so too," said Harry, and without a moment's hesitation lowered venetian blinds on three sides of them and pulled down the shade that separated them from the chauffeur.

"What the hell is this all about?" Louise said.

He pressed a button behind the chauffeur's glass, and a portable bar opened in front of them, completely stocked with ice cubes and every assortment of liquor, "How about that?"

"Terrific," Louise said. "Now let's go to a bar."

"But I got everything here, and a drink is a drink."

"I'm a social drinker," Louise said.

"I'm prepared to be very social," said Harry. His hands were on her breasts, and his mouth was pressing hard against her.

"Harry, for God's sake . . ."

"Don't start pulling that crap again," he said, and his fingers bit into her breast. "What do you think I wanted to see you for?"

"You invited me to an opening."

"We got an hour till the opening."

"You said you were sorry."

"I was sorry last time. This is a whole other time."

"Harry please . . ." She held out her hand to try and pacify him, but she had not judged wisely, or at least had not watched him move, because he slipped something pulsing and warm into her outstretched palm and it did not feel anything like his hand. "Harry, for God's sake, we're in the back of a car."

"This is a custom Rolls," he said. "It's not like a rumble-seat." And he threw himself on top of her, and pinioned her hand and its lengthening burden against her.

"Harry . . ."

"Shut up," he said, and pressed his mouth against her, and kneaded her breasts angrily with his hands.

And then they heard the ripping.

"Oh for Christ's sake," she said. "Oh for Christ's sake."

"Well if you wouldn't put up so much of a phony goddamned struggle . . ."

"I just bought this dress this afternoon. I paid three hundred dollars for it at Bendel."

"So you'll sew it," he said.

"You can't sew chiffon," she said, and started to cry, genuinely, because the only other long dress she had she had worn three times already and everyone had seen her in it, including Harry, at Rankin's party. There was no way she could go to this opening in a short dress.

"So maybe you could get a pin or something."

"And do what. Stick it in my tit? Look at me, I'm just hanging out, like a goddam Italian movie."

"So I'll take you home and you'll change."

"You'll take me home, but I won't change," she said. "Goddammit. Goddammit!"

"Well don't excite yourself, kid."

"Oh, screw," she wept.

She did not hear from him the next day, or the day after that. She did not hear from him for a week, and her mother did not understand it. She told Louise that on the phone, and again when Louise went home for Friday night dinner in Great Neck. She was clearing up the plates from the pot roast while Ralph was inside giving his gums an after-dinner massage with his Water Pik.

"But he was crazy about you," Dolores said. "A man like that doesn't take you to such places unless he's crazy about you. Why would he just drop you like that?"

"He wanted to go to bed with me, Mother."

"But that's perfectly normal, what else should a man want from a woman he's crazy about? I suppose you think Herbert Marshall's interest in me was spiritual, the way he looked at me with those eyes."

"I'm sure it wasn't, Mother."

"So what would have been the harm? You're not going to tell me you haven't been to bed with anyone, Louise. You're thirty years old, though God knows you wouldn't look it if you took off a little weight. How could you throw away an opportunity like that, how could you lose a man like Harry Bell?"

"He's sixty-four years old," Louise said.

"Sweetheart, I'm not one of those mothers who doesn't

care if her baby has a happy sex life, I read articles. But a man like Harry Bell, he's been around, believe me, he'd know tricks that would make up for his not being a young man. In the dark anyone can be handsome, if he knows tricks. I want you to be satisfied, believe me."

"He likes violence."

"Who doesn't?" Dolores said. "There are worse things in life than marrying an older man." She nodded her head in the direction of the bathroom, and the noise of the running motor. "Listen to that. Three times a day. Blood all over the sink. As if the world would crumble if his gums got soft."

When she got back to the city, Louise phoned Harry. Her mother was right, as her mother was usually right; he was crazy about her, or he wouldn't have gone to all those extremes. The reason he hadn't called her since was because of his embarrassment at the second ripped escapade. She had probably gone too far, telling him the dress was from Bendel's. She should have said Best's, and then he could have lived with himself.

"Harry?" she said into the phone. "It's Louise. Louise Felder. I want to thank you for sending me those beautiful flowers."

"Flowers?"

"The two dozen roses you sent to my office. They were exquisite. I realize it's been a while since you sent them, but I just remembered I never said thank you, and I don't want you to think I have bad manners."

"Okay," he said. "So you're welcome."

"Oh. Well, how have you been?"

"Fine. I've been fine. How's yourself?"

"I'm fine too, Harry."

"That's good." Silence.

"I've missed you," Louise said.

"I'll bet."

"No really, I have. Why haven't you called me?"

"You're a smart girl. You figure it out."

"Don't you like me anymore?"

"I like you," he said. "I just don't need that kind of aggravation, life's too short, you know what I mean?"

"Yes it is, Harry, you're right. I don't need that kind of aggravation either. It's silly and juvenile."

"You sure?"

"I'm sure."

"Well tomorrow's Saturday. I was planning to go away for the weekend, but if you'd like to get together . . ."

"I'd like to get together," Louise said.

"There's nothing opening."

"We don't have to go to an opening, Harry. Why don't we just have nice dinner, the two of us."

"You want to go to Twenty-One or Colony or Sardi's or what?"

"Why don't we just have dinner at your house," Louise said, with no little effort. "Another time, you can take me those places."

"You sure?"

"I'm sure."

"I'll send the car for you at seven," Harry said.

She spent most of the afternoon in the bathtub, soaking, because she felt less than clean. She had never deliberately planned going to bed with anybody before, always pretending to herself that it was an accident, or the spontaneous loss of innocence. Even when she was first going with Andre and staying at his apartment for two weeks at a time, she would always pretend surprise when he took her into the bedroom. But she was right to be doing what she was doing, there was no doubt about it in her mind, or her body either. Harry was not the nicest man in the world, but that was probably just a defense mechanism, because he wasn't sure of himself with her. And, in a strange way, she felt sorry for him. It was undoubtedly humiliating for a man with his track record to have failed twice. Besides, she probably would have gone to bed with him long before, if he hadn't been so goddam grabby.

All the same, she put so much jelly on her diaphragm that she could feel herself squishing when she walked, because the thought of any little Bell seeds getting into her was really more than she could bear. Marrying him would be one thing, but popping some miniature Harry (was it still possible at sixty-four? could there be any such thing as an even littler Harry?) was too much to contemplate.

She wore something that was easy to get out of. It was also a dress that she didn't mind losing, just in case he was feeling rippy.

The preparation was all unnecessarily elaborate. He greeted her in his study more meekly than she imagined he could be. He was wearing a smoking jacket, and his attention was centered on the floor. He took her hand when she offered it, but shook it only, and let it drop to her side.

"You want something to drink before dinner?" he said. "I had the cook set out some hors d'oeuvres."

"I've already had the hors d'oeuvres," she said. "Why don't we just cut right to the main course." She walked over to the sofa, and put her arms around his neck, and bent to kiss him, closing her eyes, but not out of romantic impulse.

He pulled her down abruptly beside him. She reminded him that they were in his house, and at her suggestion, so there was no need for discomfort, or unnecessary rude haste. She suggested they go upstairs.

"What made you change your mind?" he said.

"I just realized how I felt about you."

"How's that?"

"Friendly," she said.

"I'll buy that," he said, and led her upstairs to the bedroom.

She took her clothes off in the corner of the room, turning her back less out of modesty than a wish to avoid seeing him take off his. Then she made her way in the darkness to the bed, and stretched out beside him. And waited.

And waited.

"Is anything wrong?" she said finally.

"Why are you always talking," he said. "Why don't you do something?"

"I have been."

"Well shut up and do some more."

She tried.

"Maybe if I put my dress back on, and we started all over."

"You're a wise guy," he said. "I should have known all along you were a wise guy. Why don't you get the hell out of here?"

"But I didn't mean anything," she said. "I swear. I was only trying to be helpful." She reached for him in the darkness and felt how limp he was, and turned away embarrassed for him, and for some reason she did not understand, curiously ashamed.

"I'm sorry, Harry. I really am."

"Go fuck yourself," he said.

And without meaning to, she said, "You don't leave me much choice."

"Get out of here," he screamed.

And she did.

"You know I didn't mean that about the dress," she said to Dr. Ehrens the next day. "I mean, I didn't realize until I was home much later that I had hit the nail on the head, so to speak. Violence is the key. Both times he had a hard-on, excuse me, it was because he was clawing me and ripping my clothes, and that's what got him excited. The minute I was quiescent, and I went to him naked and ready, in a manner of speaking, he couldn't get it up, if you'll forgive me."

"Why all the apology?"

"I don't know. I guess real sex embarrasses me. If you can call that real sex. The poor bastard."

"Because it embarrasses you, what makes you think it embarrasses me?"

"I like you today. I don't want to offend you. I don't know. I really don't want to offend anybody. I'm only offensive when I think people can handle it, you know that. Poor Harry."

"Why?"

"He must feel so humiliated. He probably doesn't even want to look at me."

"That's his problem."

"Is it?" Louise said.

"Do you think it is?"

"I don't know. Jesus, all those people he's screwed, why does he strike out with me?"

"How do you know he's been successful with everyone else?"

"He must have been. A man can't face that kind of humiliation with those beautiful showgirls, and still go on seeing them. Do you think?"

Dr. Ehrens said nothing.

"You mean you think it may not be my fault? That's interesting."

"Is it?"

"Isn't it?" Louise said.

"What I think is more interesting is why you assume it's your fault. Why are you the one who's making apologies and feeling guilty?"

"I don't know," Louise said. "Shouldn't I be? Wouldn't you?"

"You mean if I were a girl, and I had had two dresses ripped and missed a party I very much wanted to go to, and a play I wanted to see . . . and then I finally went to bed with a man, and he . . ."

"That isn't the worst of it," she said. "He was so angry and so abusive I didn't even get to stay for dinner."

"And for that you feel sorry for him, and apologetic."

"I should be angry, shouldn't I? I'm the one who was offended, so I should get mad. Shouldn't I? Shouldn't I?"

"What do you think?"

"The nerve of the cocksucker," she said.

She saw Harry twice that same year in Sardi's, and once the following year at an opening. All three times she tried to seem inconspicuous, in case he wanted to pretend she was not there. But in each instance he did not seem to notice she was there so she could pretend she wasn't, what with the girls he was proudly parading on his arm. The first was a Hungarian chanteuse, the second a starlet from Washington state. At the opening he was with Julia White, who was enjoying a brief separation from her husband who had just been fired from Fox. That time Louise actually ducked out of sight, because she was afraid if he pointed her out, Julia would say, "But, my dear, what would you expect? She once wore red velvet with matching shoes. What else could she possibly be but lousy in bed." Louise did not relate this last imaginary conversation to Dr. Ehrens for fear that he might think her paranoid, which she conceded there was a good possibility she was.

After that, she never saw him again.

He hung now, on the green felt wall of her poolroom, wedged among the greats she was starting to number among her friends, in eight-by-ten glossy. He was in his favorite pose, head cocked to the right, fingers spread making a little glad-handed Hi! to the left of his face, almost as if he were shielding himself from some radiance from above, while greeting his friends. There was in his face not the slightest trace of embarrassment. She tried to look at him in exactly the same way.

The photo was given no special prominence in the growing ranks of the elite coterie on the poolroom wall, but it stood out just the same, because of the sepia tone of the print. It was the most well-known photo of Harry extant, the only one he had ever sent out to personal friends, or for publicity releases. It had been taken when he was twenty-seven years old.

Checking out the poolroom to make sure that everything was neat and ready for the informal party to be held that evening, Louise could not help noticing that the wall with its glossy uniform hangings had a fairly sterile look. Everyone in her new, expanding circle owned paintings, not just pictures, and the reproductions she had hung on various walls in the apartment were clearly not enough. Peter Daisy had offered to do her portrait for a hundred dollars provided she told everyone she paid him two thousand, and gave him a few mentions in her column. But the vanity required to hang herself above her own fireplace was as yet beyond her; besides which her best feature were her eyes, and she was damned if she was going to have them done in mercury.

There were still several hours before she had to get ready for the party. Now that she was in a position to have her little "evenings" with great regularity, she found that there was really very little she had to do to prepare. The food was brought in by a catering service, which charged her only fifty dollars for the services of the two butlers and maid, in return for her promise to urge everyone she knew to use that service. Liquor was provided for her by Chet Oppenheim, who got it at cost from one of Rolf Orlovsky's distribution companies. Curiouser and curiouser, Louise had started thinking, that when you finally could afford to give parties, you hardly had to pay for them anymore. It was exactly the same with gossip items for the columns. In the old days (how old? even now it seemed hard to believe that it was only last July, four months before, when Harry had given her the great gift of dying) she had gotten vicious and juicy rumors from two unemployed male press agents, Glinda and Margaret Hamilton, as she referred to them, at the cost of five dollars per scandal. Naturally all rumors had to be checked out, with increasing care according to the degree of slander. But even those that could not be verified could be cloaked under the guise of "blind" items, mentioning no names, but rife with insinuation of the principals involved. At five dollars per, she could scarcely afford not to use the information. As a matter of fact, the item that had stirred up the most comment and attention for Louise was more or less an invention. The Wicked Fairy of the West had telephoned her with a hot scoop: one of Hollywood's biggest movie stars was involved in an affair with one of the Wilson brothers.

"Which one?" Louise had asked.

"Senator Wilson."

"Which Senator?"

"Artie."

"And who's the movie star?"

"Oh come on, Louise. You know you won't be able to name her."

"I have to know for my own protection, Jack. I won't mention her by name, but I have to know."

There was a pause. "Marilyn Monroe."

"What is it, six or seven years she's been dead?"

"It's still a great item and nobody ever printed it."

"Everybody knew it, Jack."

"Not the civilians, angel. The public never knew about it, and it seems such a waste of a great scandal."

"Anyway, nobody wants to read about a dead movie star."

"So don't tell them she's dead."

"You mean keep it a secret about Marilyn Monroe."

"I mean update her. Make it another movie star. The Senator is such a swinger he must have humped another one by now. Just leave it vague who the girl is. And throw in another guy, people like it better that way, and who can sue if it's vague."

The article finally reached the paper under the heading "Pyramid Club: Insiders are all a-giggle over the oddest triangular build-up in a swoon's age. SHE is the star of many a Technicolor to-do. HE is torn between television activities and movie locations. The final (but maybe not ultimate) HE is a member of one of America's top families, in the headlines almost every day, but not necessarily in the entertainment section. If this one ever hits the fans, you can count on bigger repercussions than at the box office."

Louise knew nobody would make a fuss. Shirley MacLaine reading the item would be convinced the girl was Barbra Streisand, and Barbra Streisand would think it was Shirley MacLaine, unless it was Julie Andrews, who never read gossip columns. The only one whose identity was fairly unmistakable was Senator Wilson, but he was hardly likely to make a fuss, dignifying the insinuation. On the whole it was a triumph for Louise, whose phone rang more than it had in all her time in the business, with people wanting to know the real story. Even her hairdresser gave an extra fillip to her blond bob and whispered to her that she could tell him who the people were, it would go no further. As a matter of fact, in return, he could give her a tidbit about *the* Republican and the maimed automobile heiress. But she averted her eyes, and smiled, and squeezed his hand, and said, "That would be telling. Besides, there are principles involved."

There certainly were. The story had more results than anything she ever used. Even though as a lie it could not be legitimately classified as a piece of information, she paid Jack the usual five dollars.

In those days, five dollars had been very important to her: she could not afford to part with it so easily. Now, as with everything else, now that she could have afforded to pay ten and even twenty-five dollars per juicy item, people could not wait to give her the inside story on almost everything, and free. A chicquer grade of pansy, like Peter Daisy and Bunyan Reis, who were everywhere with everyone, liked nothing better than "dishing" with Louise. It was not, perhaps, all that she had contemplated wanting from life, but it did count for something to be so well thought of as to be given so much of value, for free.

She looked down at the gold Mod watch that Dainty Lee had given her for a house present, and seeing that she had at least five hours before getting ready for the party that evening, thought she might go down to the neighborhood galleries and browse among potential art purchases. There was no doubt that a girl in her position ought to own something besides photographs, no matter how beautiful the subjects.

The art gallery on Seventy-seventh Street off Madison garnered each Saturday a share of drifters, some grown bored with the auction of Parke-Bernet, some apartment-hunting with their prematurely acquired Sunday *New York Times* real estate section already under arm, and some just strolling, because it was Saturday afternoon. Madison Avenue on a sparkling day was infinitely more appealing than Central Park. There were also those who came specifically to see the exhibition, such as the one now on display of the new paintings by Bunyan Reis. The show ranged from two collages labeled "Remnants," appropriately patched with gingham and small squares of drapery silk from Scalamandré, to several currently avant garde paintings spotted with bright reds, or partitioned with rough gray slabs.

One of the other visitors in the white terrazzoed, glass-and-white-walled room was a pale, paint-stained young man with pastel hair, who wore his leather-patched corduroy jacket like a cloak, and stood in front of the somberest of the gray paintings with a look on his face of almost mystical bliss. Behind him were two well-scrubbed high-school girls in navy blue tunics underneath identical tan polo coats, who held hands and giggled in between taking notes. There was also a middle-aged woman of indiscriminate appearance wearing a purple hat with three fresh violets tucked in the brim, who might have just come in on the Stamford local. She wandered from painting to painting, murmuring, "Isn't it breathtaking, isn't it breathtaking."

And behind her was Charley. Tall and tan. The boy from Ipanema.

"Charley," Louise said. "Charley."

"Well, well. Well, well."

"You're thrilled to see me, you are, you're overcome, otherwise you'd think of something clever to say."

"I didn't know this was an audition," he said. "I thought I came here to look at paintings."

"What do you think of them?"

"It's terrific if you like crud."

"I've missed you," she said, laughing. "I really have."

The moment she said it, she realized it was true. "I have," she said. "How about that."

"Do you mind lowering your voices?" said the young man in the corduroy jacket. "I'm trying to look at paintings."

The cool whiteness of the marble floor, the flat white of the high-ceilinged walls streaked with November sunlight through the glass fronting the street gave the gallery a medicinal crispness, a startling black and white reality in the midst of the Technicolor world outside. Lining the center of the gallery were block-mounted metal sculptures of square, sectioned aluminum rods, the cut ends of which created a glittering mosaic over the shaped surfaces of a metal field. Around them wandered a few stragglers mouthing impressions to themselves, all except the woman in the hat with the violets, who muttered aloud: "Breathtaking. Breathtaking."

"What are you doing here?" Louise said.

"It was on my way east and my feet were cold."

"I mean what are you doing in New York? You said once a year, that was all you came, or were you just trying to scare me."

"They flew me in about a commercial."

"What do you mean, a commercial?"

"They want me to try out for spokesman for some cigarette."

"You lied to me," she said. "You told me you were in real estate."

"I am in real estate," said Charley. "When you sell a house in Hollywood to the head of an ad agency, he tries to tell you what a great voice you've got, what a nice appearance you make, and have you ever thought about doing commercials, because he thinks if he vaselines your ego it'll help him with his price."

"But naturally you're above such things."

"Why?" said Charley. "I'm a human being, and I was brought up in Hollywood. Some of my best friends are egomaniacs."

"You cute thing," she said, and squeezed his hand. "You'd make a great announcer."

"It's a way to pick up a few extra scrobs."

"Do you mind?" said the young man in corduroy.

"Do you?" said Louise, putting her arm through Charley's, pulling him toward the glass entrance and the sunshine outside.

"You didn't even get to look at the paintings," Charley said when they were on the sidewalk.

"I don't have to. I know the painter."

"Of course. I should have known."

"Well it's true. Bunyan Reis is the In painter of the day, but nobody really takes his work seriously except people who read his publicity, and a few of the toney critics. His friends buy him because they can afford him. Not necessarily because they like his paintings."

"Then they're stupid," Charley said. "The collages and sculptures are terrible, but the gray paintings are something else. He's got great skill as a craftsman you know, he understands paint and textures for the sake of ornament and expression."

"My goodness." Louise narrowed her eyes against the sunlight and peered at him. "Who did you say you were?"

"Don't let it throw you," said Charley. "I read the *New Yorker* this week."

"I don't believe you. You really know about these things. Aren't you full of surprises."

"I tried to tell you that, but you didn't have the patience to wait and find out."

"Oo, you still want me," she said, and her voice became very tiny. "Lulu is all excited."

"Good," said Charley, and held her elbow as they stepped down from the curb. "I'll buy you a hamburger."

The Stark's on the corner of Seventy-eighth and Madison was known to some as the Separation Center, sheltering as it did divorced neighborhood fathers entertaining their weekend children, on despairingly long Saturday afternoons. Unnaturally neat little girls in frilled pastel dresses, navy blue coats with velvet collars and wrist-button white gloves sat at formica-topped tables, opposite young middle-aged men who were tieless and sport-shirted, smiling a great deal.

Charley and Louise sat in a leatherette booth at the far corner of the inside room. She had had enough of sunlight for the day, and was in no mood for all the scenes of domestic bliss, she told him. For a while they talked of little but the weather, what a mild and lovely fall it was, and the sun in California. Then they fell silent. He reached over and took her hand, because he said he had forgotten what a pretty face she had, and besides, it made him nervous the way she was toying with the relish pot.

"They never come in these places," she said, looking around. "Where's the waitress?"

"Why don't you just relax. You in such a big hurry to get someplace?"

"I can't stand to just sit," she said. "There are a lot of things I could be doing."

"Like what?"

"What are you doing here?" she said.

"Why are you so nervous?"

"I hate to just sit."

"You told me that. Why?"

He was looking at her with his dark, intense eyes, and he was smiling, even inside them, she could see that, and she hated him because his hand was so warm. A few blocks away at the auction gallery across the street cold-fingered ladies in black suits with pearls were signaling the auctioneer for another bombé chest for their overcrowded country houses in Tarrytown, and here she was wasting her time when there were so many things she could be learning.

"I think I love you," she said. "Do I really have a pretty face?"

"I always thought so."

"I do love you," Louise said. "I'll have a rare cheeseburger."

As they ate, she asked about Kate and David because she was mildly interested in how they were, and it would keep the talk away from her and Charley. He told her they were fine, that the baby was rosy and blooming, and they had been spending a lot of time in the country place they had rented upstate.

"Without the baby," Louise said.

"What makes you say that?"

"I heard. With all Kate's talk of domestic bliss, and love being the solution for everything, and as hard as she tried to get pregnant, now that the kid is here she doesn't want it."

"I think you're being a little unfair," Charley said. "She loves the baby, she's just a little frightened of it, that's all. Everybody's different, and it's a lot of responsibility, all of a sudden having another human being who's completely dependent on you."

"She should have thought of that before."

"I'm sure she did. But thinking about something is different from the reality. Leave your potatoes. You're being unfair."

"I can afford to be. I never waved any flags about home and motherhood. Don't tell me what to eat." She lifted three French fries and stuffed them in her mouth.

"Well, it's nice you know where you stand."

"I think so," Louise said, and shoved the plate toward him. "Here, you finish. Kate settled. She could have had a lot more. She settled for somebody who wanted her, and all those tacky fantasies about home and babies. She was so frightened she couldn't make it herself, she settled for the first person who seemed strong. Because he wanted her."

"You think that's so terrible?"

"Why?" she said, and looked into his deep dark eyes, and studied the square set of his still vaguely suntanned chin and the line where a vague remnant of sun stained his throat. "Do you want me?"

"Maybe," he said. "Nothing permanent, you understand. Just a warm roly-poly in the hay."

"That's healthy," she said. "There's nothing wrong with

287

that. I mean everybody has to grow up and call a spade a spade. Except if you've read the new Riots Commission Report."

He asked for the check, and then turned to Louise. "You still live in the same apartment?"

"No," she said. "But it doesn't make any difference. We're going to your hotel."

"Why?"

There was no way to tell him there was preparation for the party going on without her having to invite him. "You're nice. You're much too nice. I want to feel dirty."

There was about it, Louise could not help thinking, a vague hint of adultery, an elusive, forbidden quality. Everything had become too free, in general, what with the pill, and everyone having their own apartments, and nobody having to sneak off into the back seat of a car: there was no proper way to build up hungers. For Louise specifically, this particular assignation was almost wholesome. Charley was unmarried and not a fag and she had been with him before which took it completely out of the realm of one-night stand. The image of adultery was certainly a more exciting one than just traipsing off hand in hand into a matinee sunset. In the first place, she had only three hours, three and a half at most, before she had to get back to her apartment, which gave it at least a furtive fleeting quality. If she were to keep the two entities separate, hidden from each other, Charley, the lover, from her friends (husband?), there would be about it the aura of cheating. That would make up for the fact that he had nothing to offer.

Nothing.

Walking along the avenue, he had a way of handling sunlight without flinching, or even seeming to squint, moving his head slightly so the glare was deflected onto his temples. She supposed that was a trait indigenous to people from Hollywood, who had to know how to handle too much light in order to survive. She watched him out of the corner of her eye, because she was not like him, and could not handle all that cool sparkle. He was, she realized, as attractive as any man she had ever seen, more attractive than any of the ones she would be with that evening. The realization annoyed her.

He raised his hand to hail a taxi, and she pressed it back down against his side. "I want to go in here for a minute," she said, and started toward the great, double, glass doors of Parke-Bernet.

She turned, and he was standing motionless at the curb, half-smiling at her, but not in a pleasant way. "Aren't you coming?" she said.

"Apparently not."

"But Charley, sweetie, procrastinating a little makes it even more exciting."

"Really?"

"I read that someplace," Louise said.

"You must have. It's a cinch that you don't speak from experience."

"Are you going to be masterful?" she said, and giggled. "Are you going to seize me by the wrists and throw me onto the floor of the taxi?"

"Get in," Charley said, as the cab moved up to the curb. "Get in or go away, whichever you want, it makes no difference." He moved inside the yellow door, and sat. For a minute Louise was afraid he would close the door behind him.

"That's what I said," she sprang inside to the seat beside him. "You're mad for me, you're forcing me to come." She turned to the driver and smiled. "We're going to his hotel," she said.

CHAPTER FOUR

THE elevator at the rear of the marbleized banklike entrance to Parke-Bernet was fairly empty, as it always was in the midst of Saturday afternoon auction. Those who were seriously interested in the day's possible acquisitions had been in their seats since two thirty, almost martialing in the rows of chairs, in spite of the studiedly social air of Saturday afternoon. Weekends were not like evening sales, which had lately taken on the aura of the high-stake chemin de fer tables in the grander casinos of Europe, where most of the buyers were well-known dealers with international reputations, connoisseurs and collectors of high standing, who had little in common with the average auction-goer, except a certain shortness of breath when the object or painting on which they were bidding seemed about to be eluding them. Saturday auctions had more the atmosphere of the blackjack tables or roulette wheels in the spicier casinos, where women played to pass the time while their husbands were off gambling for higher stakes.

Lately, however, some of the tone of high competition of the evening sales seemed to have filtered down to Saturdays. People who had not previously been regulars, who had read about the free-for-all Rembrandt prices on the *New York Times* front page, had seen the sale of Impressionist painters on the seven o'clock news report, and had read the cover story on Norton Simon in *Time* magazine, and Rolf Orlovsky in *Newsweek,* had begun to come to the auctions. It was no longer a matter of just buying a painting for the foyer, or a fauteuil for the entrance hall. When a man who owned Hunt's foods and Ohio matches wanted something, there had to be enormous profit involved. As Parke-Bernet was still America, anybody could play. Those who didn't have nerve enough, or cash enough, could certainly watch. Watching excitement was exciting and there was always the chance of a silver tea-service going cheap.

One of those who was watching was Andre Sherman. He stood at the rear of the gallery, behind one of the red velvet ropes, in a suit of bronze gabardine, with a vest of bronze brocade that matched his lining. Although he had no need of glasses, a pince-nez was strung around his neck: a thin thread of gold made a better mounting for a Phi Beta Kappa key than a watch chain across his vest would have. The pince-nez had been purchased in a pawnshop in Philadelphia where he had gone on business the week before. So had the Phi Beta Kappa key.

Directly in front of him, to the left of the auctioneer's rostrum with its microphone, he could see several shiny societal heads that, looking through his pince-nez, he could assume from their shape and style belonged to Maggie Bolin and Diane Trejinska, or any one of the clientele of Mr. Randolph's salon. Casual drifters from the rug exhibition passed the door. A few ladies, seeing the crystal, diamond and Lucite collection of a prominent beauty-cream manufacturer who had died at eighty-two, wandered by.

There were numerous society matrons, distinguished, but indistinguishable one from the other, in dark suits with pearls at the throat, their leather gloves gripping tightly on blue-veined hands, even as they raised them to make bids. There were also some professional dealers, whom Andre knew by sight and reputation, because he had made it a point to find out.

If you watched the dealers, the subtle ways they had of bidding, scratching an eyebrow, fanning themselves with the program, you could tell the important objects by what they were after, those which had a big profit in resale at the professional shops and galleries. Andre had to smile. Professional shops and galleries, resale value indeed. If he could pull off what he was here to pull off, he could afford to laugh out loud, and long, at their purportedly professional status, putting them all forever in the realm of amateur.

He had done his homework well, and carefully. For ten weeks, Saturdays and evenings, he had been attending the more important auctions, watching bidding techniques, studying the paintings (and the furniture, as long as he was there: it couldn't hurt to make sure his living room was still authentic), to see what period was bringing the best price. Then he found out what buyers were fronting for actual purchasers, Hartford, Simon, and a mysterious European nobleman who disappointingly turned out to be the Prince of Liechtenstein. The most important discovery he had made was that the inconspicuous little man with the bald head and the white monk's fringe, in a lint-specked gray pinstripe, was acting on behalf of Rolf Orlovksy. Orlovsky had grown weary of the publicity about his growing art collection, and had no wish to have the prices jacked up because he was the purchaser. Orlovsky was not at all like Harry Bell had been. Orlovsky did not hang his paintings where anyone could see them. Those he did not donate temporarily to museums, he stored in a fire-proof, bomb-proof, moisture-proof cellar outside Ardsley, New York, where no harm could come to them as well as no light, and no appreciation of beauty. He was a greedy man, Andre had decided, and that was why he deserved what Andre was going to do to him. He was also a very rich man, so he could afford it.

Harry Bell, at least, had loved his art, once he began to understand what it was all about, aside from the prestige of owning priceless objects. The fact that he continued to call his paintings pictures did nothing to change the truth that he loved art. He had told Andre that, in no uncertain terms, the one night Andre had succeeded in staying in Harry's good graces long enough to be invited to his home. Mostly he stayed in Harry's good graces because Harry had very big and obvious eyes for Andre's second wife, who had just had her hair cut into blond scallops and looked like a minuscule Venus rising from the half-shell that was her head.

"I love art," Harry had said, turning on all the lights in his den, the walls of which were strung with masterpieces as other people would hang Christmas cards from friends.

"It's certainly obvious that you do," Andre said.

"My yes," said Bitsey Sherman.

Harry went from painting to painting, switching on supplementary key lights, giving a running commentary on the artist and subject of each, while Bitsey stared, wide-eyed, and Andre tried to remember everything Harry said. He also tried to figure out how to get a little of it to rub off on him, without wanting to seem obvious.

"So how'd you get so rich?" Andre said.

"I started by buying on margin, selling short." His words were directed at Andre, but his eyes on Bitsey. "You know what that means, little lady?"

"It always says that in the magazines, that you started building your fortunes by selling short," Andre said. "We understand . . ."

"Do we?" Harry said, and smiled. "I'm not so sure we all do, do we, little lady? Do you know what it means?"

"I guess not," Bitsey said.

"It means you get what somebody else wants, badly, before they even know they want it, and then you make them know they want it, and you've got it, and it doesn't really cost you anything, but you can take it out of their hide." Harry laughed loudly and chucked her under the chin. "You get it?"

If Bitsey got it, she made no sign to show she got it. She just shifted her weight on her tiny perfect legs, twisted up under her on the red velvet sofa.

"You get it, don't you, Sherman?"

"You have any more paintings upstairs?" Andre said.

"Smart boy," said Harry, and led him up the winding marble staircase, after first refilling Bitsey's brandy snifter. In the upstairs den, Harry pointed out the Da Vinci, and then opened the safe behind it and pulled out his secondary collection.

"I thought I had seen most of the great collections in New York," Andre said, scanning the photographs and prints. "These are unbelievable."

"Some of them are from Pompeii, I mean, really from Pompeii. You understand why they got the lava job."

"Fantastic," Andre said.

"Well maybe we ought to do a little trade. You're a trader, aren't you? Just temporarily?"

"Maybe we should," Andre said. "I'd like some time to look these over."

"You got time. Take it." Harry started to leave the library.

"How do I get rich, Harry?" Andre said.

"I already told you."

"No, you told me how you got rich. I asked you, how do I?"

"I gave you the basic ingredients. You got to figure out how to put it in application. If you're at all smart, you'll find your spot."

"I think . . . I think I need a little something more than that."

"Okay. So tomorrow I meet you at my office, I drive you around Wall in my limousine, I shake hands with you and hug you around the shoulders in the middle of Broad Street. If you can't parlay that into something in banking circles, you got no business wanting to be rich."

"Will you let it be known we're talking deal?"

"People know I'm too smart to get involved in spec deals. Hey, don't go through them so fast. You like that one? I call it Andy Hardy sucks up."

"Cute," Andre said.

"The boy can't be over twelve. I never could understand it with little boys. It's probably an Arab dick, don't you think?"

"I don't know. They all look alike to me."

"I was in Tangiers once, in the Casbah, and believe me, there were no Hedy Lamarrs. I met two Englishmen, very fahncy, and about three thirty in the afternoon, in the middle of tea, the door opens and these two little boys, with big dark eyes, maybe nine ten years old, in Buster Brown collars, lace yet, and fancy knickers come in the door, and go skipping up the stairs, like regular kids. And I said to these two, I said, cute kids, you know, I wanted to be polite, and the important one, the novelist, you know who I mean, the Nobel Prize who lives in Tangiers, says to me, 'They're ours. We bought them.' I guess it takes all kinds."

"I guess," Andre said.

"Maybe that makes me peculiar, I don't like little boys. I like little girls. Or big girls. Tonight it's little girls."

"Will you let it be known we're talking deal?" Andre said.

"I told you . . ."

"You don't have to name a specific deal. Just a deal."

"I don't know," Harry said.

"I guess I've seen enough of these," Andre said. "I might as well go back downstairs with you; Bitsey must be getting lonesome . . ."

"All right," Harry said. "I'll say we're talking deal. After all, that's what we're doing, aren't we?"

As it turned out, Harry did none of what he promised, except lend Andre part of his pornographic collection. It wasn't exactly a welsh. After three years of marriage, during which time she had jumped into bed with anything that moved, Bitsey suddenly developed principles, and refused to have anything to do with Harry. Andre divorced her soon after, and she married a man Andre understood had made several million dollars. But Andre didn't like to think about that.

What he liked to think about, over and over again, was the evening he had spent with Harry. Somewhere, concealed in that scene, was the secret of how to do it. It had been, in his life, a visit with some high lama of finance, in which the mystery was contained, but unrevealed. He studied it in his mind, over and over again, a Persian carpet, with the clue contained somewhere in its complicated pattern, obvious, but camouflaged. Because he had looked at it so much, he could not see it.

And then, when Harry died, and the dispute began among his heirs and representatives over the disposition of the estate, it all came clear.

Art.

Among the disputed legacies of Harry Bell were the statues and paintings he had prided himself on collecting. "Buy on margin," he had said. "Sell short. Get what somebody else wants badly before they know they want it. It doesn't really cost you anything, but you can take it out of their hide."

The lack of imagination of most art collectors, as Andre saw it, was waiting until they could afford things before they started buying. The history of finance was rife with people who had made great killings, by buying before they could afford to buy, and then selling to those who were richer, before getting caught. Wall Street was loaded with men who regularly "kited" checks, depositing one amount in a first bank, depositing a check for that amount in a second, drawing a check on the second bank and putting it in a third—writing the amount over and over in different banks when there was only the money in the first. Naturally it was illegal, but nobody ever got punished for it if they covered themselves in time so they didn't get caught. That way they could stay alive for weeks. But all they were buying was money.

Andre was more creative. Andre was going to buy art. And be rich. The way Harry had told him, only Andre hadn't realized it at the time. Such was Harry's oblique wisdom.

Andre studied all the back stories available in newspapers and magazines about prominent collectors, and their preferences, and began attending the art auctions with great regularity, watching for the secret signals, finding out who the bidders were acting for. He had taken his time, an admirable trait in an impatient man. But it had been worthwhile waiting for the propitious moment. Propitious. That had been in an article quoting Harry Bell, who said, "Great paintings, like great men, will emerge when the time is propitious."

Well if anything, propitious was what you could say the time was.

Orlovsky had his yacht anchored at a spa in Florida for the weekend, and he was on it. Andre had checked that out. He had also discovered that Orlovsky's wife was on the boat, and his mistress was registered at the spa. But Andre had no intention of using that. He was not a man who would resort to anything dishonest, like blackmail.

Orlovsky would not be back until the following Tuesday. The little man in the lint-specked suit, bidding for Orlovsky, would not be there that afternoon to pick up the paintings Orlovsky was after. Andre knew which ones they were, because he had watched the little man at the exhibition Thursday afternoon, examining the various lots, making notes, moving with his magnifying glass, verifying, authenticating. After the exhibition Andre followed him back to the Adams Hotel, and waited a minute before going into the lobby, giving the man time to get past the desk clerk.

"The gentleman who just came in," Andre said, to the desk clerk. "Could you tell me his name?"

"Pardon," said the desk clerk.

"He looks quite like an old teacher of mine from Harvard, but I'm embarrassed to say I've forgotten his name. You know how these things will happen."

"Of course," said the desk clerk, and looked carefully at

Andre's attire, the royal-blue boating blazer with the insignia on the pocket, and the sword-cane. "It's Mr. Edwards."

"Edwards?" Andre said.

"Penn Edwards," said the desk clerk.

"No," Andre shook his head. "That isn't him. Thank you anyway."

Friday night Andre telephoned a friend of his in Miami Beach and told him to send a night letter to Penn Edwards, Adams Hotel, New York City.

DISREGARD PREVIOUS INSTRUCTIONS. MEET CHET OPPENHEIM 3:30 SATURDAY ST. REGIS BAR FOR FURTHER WORD.

ORLOVSKY

Andre looked at his watch. It was three thirty-eight. It would be at least another twenty minutes before Edwards, with his Boston calm, would begin to get impatient and telephone Oppenheim; to be told that Oppenheim was away for the weekend (Andre had checked that out in advance, too). By the time Edwards realized he had been set up, the paintings would have already come up for sale, and gone, going going gone to Andre. Of course there had been the chance that Orlovsky might have telephoned Edwards some time during the day, for a last-minute confirmation. But a man juggling a wife and a mistress probably didn't have a chance to worry about phone calls to his art buyer, especially such an indefatigably reliable Bostonian as Edwards.

Andre had to smile, he certainly did. Objects bought at auction on Saturday did not have to be picked up and paid for until at least the following Thursday, by which time he would have resold the paintings to Orlovsky, at a profit of at least a hundred, maybe two hundred thousand dollars.

"The next item," said the auctioneer from the rostrum, "is lot number three-oh-nine. Antique French cupid clock, on Grecian pillar, with ormolu mountings." Two colored men in khaki fatigues carried it onto the proscenium platform. In the second row on the right a well-dressed very neat little woman in a Norell cape-suit sat nervously twisting a handkerchief, which hung out slightly from her black alligator bag. Andre thought he recognized her from the auction two weeks before. She was a good deal handsomer than the clock, with much svelter lines. Watching the expression of mild panic on her face as the dealer opened the bidding at fifty dollars, Andre was sure he remembered her. She had been in a swivet of compulsive bidding the day of that auction, and the clock had been one of her more blatant mistakes. Probably she had gotten it home and seen what a horror it was, and hadn't even shown it to her husband, who was probably inured to the grossness of her errors. Parke-Bernet was likewise passive to the mistakes of its female patrons, the bored ladies who bought without meaning to, just to have something to show for their wasted day. The policy of the gallery was a firm "no return"; but Andre was sure they stretched it a little for their regular patrons. Obviously she was here to have the clock re-sold, and intended to bid it up to make sure she recouped her original investment, plus the commission she would have to pay the gallery. The little larcenies of the privileged.

"TWO hundred twenty-five dollars. Do I hear two-FIFTY. Two-FIFTY."

Desperation whitened the handsome features of the woman, and her hand came away from the twisting handkerchief, and waved briefly, apologetically, in the air.

"Two seventy-five," the auctioneer said. "Two seventy-five once . . ."

"No, I didn't mean it as a bid," the woman said, shattering the attentive silence.

The man on the rostrum swallowed. "Two-fifty, Mr. Mendel's bid. Do I hear two seventy-five. Going for two-fifty, two-fifty."

"Two seventy-five," said the woman, gnarling her handkerchief.

She bought it again, Andre thought. She bought it again because she doesn't want to be out fifty dollars, so in order not to be out fifty dollars she makes the same mistake twice. If there's a God she'll have to pay the commission again on this sale.

He was really disappointed in her. From all outward appearances she had taste, and grooming and, maybe even—outdated word—class. All that should have amounted to privilege. Privilege, in Andre's view, was the ability to afford costly errors. Maybe, if it was true privilege, to turn costly errors into a triumph of taste.

He could not afford to give her any more of his thoughts. It was time. There was a restless rustle, and the dealers, who had simply marked time before the next item, started sitting at attention, moving up toward the front of the rows of chairs to better see the lot of paintings, and watch the bidding. Porters hurried to the men's room to summon those who had asked to be notified when the Impressionist paintings came up for sale. Through curtains of red velvet draping the alcoves, underneath crystal sconces that were part permanent fixture, part display for future sales, came those who had been biding their time, or passing it among the tapestries and furnitures to be sold the following week.

Class or no class, Andre thought, an arena is an arena. Ladies and gentlemen, the main event.

He fingered the chain of his pince-nez and drew it out into the triangle of a slingshot, David about to shoot down all the Goliaths. The bidding began.

At first he was silent, like the most experienced of bidders, giving everyone else the chance to show their hand, or in some cases, wave their programs. Lot number 310 was two watercolors and a small still life in oil by Utrillo. When the bidding was cut from twenty-five hundred a bid to easier jumps of one thousand, and stopped at thirty-eight, Andre raised his head, and then deliberately lowered his jaw into throat, giving the auctioneer the full benefit of his electrifying, eyebrow-shadowed stare.

"Thirty-eight thousand," repeated the man on the rostrum, apparently missing the powerful gaze.

"Thirty-nine," said Andrew, annoyed.

After that, the auctioneer knew Andre was there. From then on, before he made the mistake of closing the bidding, his glance would sweep back to where Andre stood, and Andre would nod, into his eyebrows, and sometimes even smile, slightly, deepening his cleft. The Utrillos he got for only forty-three thousand, but two of them were watercolors. As soon as the bidding was closed, a man in morning suit came over and asked for his name, and his signature on the form. Andre gave it; the man went back to the platform and spoke to the auctioneer.

For the rest of the sale in which Andre participated, the man on the rostrum closed the bidding with "Sold to Mr. Sherman." Like the best maître d', the auctioneer knew how to recognize and greet important customers, to get them coming back, and to make the rest of the gathering appreciate the important presence, Andre saw. After Andre got the Cézanne still life for only thirty-seven thousand dollars, Maggie Bolin turned to him and smiled. He blew back a kiss.

The Corot he had planned on getting he let go, because he was in no position, even lying, to compete with the tomato-sauce foundation for a figure above three hundred thousand. Besides, his palms were still sweating from his having bought the Cézanne portrait for two hundred and fifty thousand dollars. A commitment for a quarter of a million dollars was still a commitment for a quarter of a million dollars. In spite of the brilliance with which he was operating, he felt the slightest bit shaky.

In all, he bought ten paintings, for a total of five hundred and eighty-six thousand dollars. He told himself he was not in the least unsettled at the thought of that much money, even though there was only forty thousand in his account, most of which belonged to an escrow department of a bank. That didn't really disturb him, as he now saw he had made a low estimate on his potential profit; Orlovsky taking the paintings singly might even give him as much as a quarter of a million in profit.

Still, he fingered the chain of the pince-nez continuously as he stood by the cashier's window in the rear of the gallery. In front of him stood the woman in the Norell cape-suit.

"But it was a mistake," she said to the cashier. "I didn't mean to buy it. Couldn't they put it up for resale on Wednesday."

"This is the fifth time, Mrs. Stern."

"But it's only the second time for this clock. Oh please. My husband will kill me. We have no more room in the apartment."

From the corner of his eye Andre saw Maggie and Diane Trejinska leaving the auction, pausing at the glass counter by the elevators to look at the jewelry collection. He waved to them, but they were absorbed in the Lucite and diamond display.

"Yes?" said the cashier.

"I'm Andre Sherman," he said. "The man who took my name said I should come back and talk to you."

"Oh yes, Mr. Sherman. The paintings are still out on the floor, but you'll be able to have them picked up on Thursday."

"All right," Andre said. "Thank you." He started to walk way.

"Mr. Sherman, one moment please."

"Yes?"

"It's customary in the case of such a large purchase to put down a deposit."

"Yes, of course." Andre took out his checkbook from his inside breast pocket, lined with beige brocade. He wrote out a check for a thousand dollars.

"I'm very sorry," the cashier said. "But for a purchase this large by someone we don't know, we require at least ten percent."

"Who has sixty thousand in a checking account?" Andre said.

"People who buy six hundred thousand dollars in paintings."

"Well, I guess you've got me there," Andre said, and smiled, taking up his pen. The check would probably be put in for collection clearing on Monday, the deficit found by Tuesday, and Orlovsky wouldn't be in town long enough to start negotiating on the resale. Beads of sweat broke out on Andre's forehead, and moisture started under his high starched collar. "I seem to be out of ink," he said.

"Use my pen," said the cashier.

"I'm superstitious about this one," he said. "Excuse me a minute." He made his way across the thickly carpeted floor to where Maggie and Diane Trejinska stood, looking and laughing at the jewelry in the case.

"Beautiful ladies," he said. "Greetings."

"Huntington Hartford," said Diane. "How you've changed."

"I'm so impressed," Maggie said. "I never realized you were such a collector."

"Well they're not all for me," Andre said. "One of them is for you, Maggie."

"I don't understand."

"I read that you're being married next month, and I'd like you to have one of the Utrillos as a wedding gift."

Maggie paled. "You can't be serious."

"You've always been one of my favorites. Why not."

"But you paid a fortune."

"Be quiet and say thank you," Diane said.

"Oh I couldn't," Maggie said. "I'm too madly embarrassed."

"What reason have you got to be embarrassed," Andre said. "I want to give it to you, that's all that should concern you."

"But the wedding," she grew even paler. "You understand, Andre, I meant to invite you, but the list was starting to get out of hand, and there's only so many seats on a Boeing."

"Oh dear Maggie, I'm not pumping for an invitation if that's what you think."

"Oh I didn't think that, really, I never thought that, I just thought . . ."

"I want you to have the painting," Andre said. "There's no need to get too excited. It's only a watercolor."

"That's right," Diane said. "It isn't as if it cost over five or six thousand." She leaned over the case and peered inside. "Diamonds set in Lucite," she said. "I'm surprised she didn't die sooner."

"Come," Andre said. "Let me take you to the cashier, and you can tell him where you want it to be delivered."

"I can't, I just can't."

He led her over to the cashier's window. "But why should you do this for me?"

"If I can't do it for you, who can I do it for?"

"Oh," Maggie said.

Andre told the cashier to have one of the Utrillo watercolors set aside and delivered to Miss Bolin, Miss Margaret Bolin, naturally he knew Miss Bolin. Naturally the cashier did. He looked at her, and then he looked at Andre Sherman, his arm around Maggie's slender neck. He looked at Maggie again.

"Where would you like it delivered?" the cashier said.

"Oh I don't know. What should I do, Andre? We're closing up the apartment, but we're not sure yet when we can move into Harry's house. You did know we were buying Harry Bell's house, didn't you, it's sort of a mutual wedding present from me, should I have it sent to Harry's?"

"You have it sent wherever you like," Andre said, squeezing gently on her collarbone.

"I'm sure we can find one extra seat," Maggie said.

"Don't worry about it," he said.

The cashier looked at them carefully. "Miss Bolin, if you'll forgive me, you know Mr. Sherman?"

"Well who doesn't know him," Maggie said. "He's one of the most prominent art connoisseurs in America."

"I'm sure he is," the cashier said. "I didn't mean to question that. It's just that we haven't done business with him before at this gallery, and I wondered if you knew him well."

"You must be joking," Maggie said, and linked her arm through his. "He's one of my closest friends."

When Diane got home there were three messages and a calling card on the silver tray placed on the drawing room table. The table, like the drawing room, and the custom of leaving calling cards on a silver tray, was more outdated than antique, but with a twelve-room apartment and the children away at boarding school, one had to do something with the extra space. It was not Diane's penchant to give overlavish parties in Manhattan for which two or three receiving rooms, with ample clearing space for a dance floor, were necessary. She preferred to entertain, or even better, be entertained, outside the apartment. If she did decide to have people at home, they were never more than twelve, and not invited for anything more or less than a suitably elaborate dinner, with seven courses, and appropriate wines. Coffee and one brandy only were served at the table, and if the conversation was particularly lively at the end of the formal meal, and she felt up to it, the guests were invited into the living room for one after-dinner drink more. As a result, most of the decoration money (Tzigie still had limited funds coming in from Liechtenstein) had gone into the dining room and the main living room, which mixed Victorian with French provincial. The other rooms in the front of the apartment had been deliberately furnished in the gallery style, with formal benches and high tables, to discourage settling in. She did not mind that her apartment did not look or feel cozy. Because she was who she was, nobody had ever questioned her taste, and several people had gone so far as to imitate her style. In many of the costlier cooperatives on Park and Fifth Avenues, there were rooms that looked like nothing more than the week's exhibition at Parke-Bernet, wanting only a red velvet rope to keep out loiterers.

She picked up the card from the tray, and leaving her brown kid gloves and her alligator pocketbook on the table, proceeded through the archway to the library, avoiding the two Kirman area rugs, because the click of her Gucci heels on the parquet floors made her life seem more spirited. She sat on the wood-backed Savonarola chair by the built-in, dark-wood bookcase, filled from twelve-foot-high ceiling to floor with expensively leatherbound editions of the Harvard Classics, and the Chicago Great Books Series, with one row of selections from the Book of the Month Club, which she had joined for one year, for color. Although it was only four o'clock in the afternoon, because of the thickness of the green velvet drapes, there was no sunlight whatever, and she had to switch on both eighteenth-century candle lamps to see the messages. The darkness of the room was not only to dissuade people from using it as a library. (She and Tzigie did read, and copiously, but it was usually in bed, with the aid of individual lamps that had been built into the headboard, so as not to offend a possibly sleeping partner.) It was deliberate, because the place that had most impressed Tzigie when he first came to New York had been the Knickerbocker Club, with bookshelves at a level so high that no one but a professional librarian could have attempted to read anything contained therein, and a general feeling of gloom so deep that Tzigie considered it the one true bastion of conservatism in an otherwise flailingly liberalized city, and he had wanted his library to be done accordingly.

The first message was from the buyer at Farquard's department store, reminding her of the showing of French imports the following Tuesday at three o'clock; the Senator and his wife would receive at cocktails in the Farquard's own suite, atop the store, after the collection. The second was from Louise, saying that the party that evening was informal, and just "any one of your imported numbers will do." The third was simply "a gentleman called." Diane turned over the calling card. It was hand-embossed, from Tiffany, and it read "Yours Truly. Room 186. The Regency."

302

She went to the phone, dialed the hotel, and asked for the room. When he answered, she knew from the deep deliberateness of the voice who it was, instantly, but she still asked.

"Who is this?" she said.

"It's my own true love," he said.

"I mean, who are you?"

"Yours truly."

"Rick?"

"None other than. In person."

"How could you be so bold as to leave this card, Rick Flinders?"

"I thought it was kind of sensational. You don't know what lengths I had to go to, to get Tiffany to print it up in one day. And the suspense. Never knowing if I would lose the room before I got the card, and vice-versa. I love you, Diane."

"You're crazy. What if Tzigie had seen it first?"

"He did. He already called. I told him the same thing."

"You told him you loved me?"

"Don't be silly. I told him I loved him. He's on his way over here, this very minute."

"You bastard," she said, and laughed.

"Please come," he said, and his voice got very low, and she could feel it in the small of her back. "Please. You're breaking me into pieces, you know. You're breaking my heart, and you're breaking other things, and they're practically the last pair left in Hollywood."

"That's your problem."

"Only for the moment," he said. "What if they go, and we've never had each other, then you'll be sorry."

"I don't want you to come here, or call." She hung up the phone. In spite of herself, she found her breath coming heavier, and a vague feeling of hunger at the base of her belly. A few times in her life Diane had received obscene phone calls, especially after the layout of her waterskiing in Acapulco with that unfortunate crotch shot. Each time she had felt frightened, but strangely excited. She worried about it at first, until she realized, quite objectively, that obscenity was exciting. Especially in someone like Rick, who prided himself on being so cool, but was willing to jeopardize his attitude wanting her so badly, all that came through was the wanting.

The phone rang. She started to walk by it, and leave him just hanging there, it would serve him right. But she realized that Tzigie might be in the back of the apartment, and might answer it if the servants didn't pick it up first.

"I'm sorry," he said, the moment she picked up the receiver.

"You're not sorry, you're crazy. You don't even wait to see if it's me answering. You're a madman. What if it were Tzigie?"

"The sorry would still apply. I'm sorry for him. I'm sorry for him because he can't satisfy you, I'm sorry because he has you and doesn't know what to do with you."

"You are crazy. You don't know anything. You don't know what goes on between us. You don't know what you're talking about."

"If there were anything, you wouldn't talk to me."

"I'm trying not to. I hung up, and you called back. Why don't you let me alone."

"Because we want each other. We've always wanted each other."

"You're an arrogant son of a bitch," she said.

"I have every right to be. The woman I love wants me. Why don't you cut the pretense and come over here, and jump into bed with me. I have pink satin sheets," he said.

"I'm not surprised," said Diane, but she made no move to hang up the phone.

"Room eighteen-oh-six," he said.

"You're crazy."

"I love you."

"I couldn't walk through the lobby without bumping into twenty people I knew."

"So for all they knew you'd be there to organize a charity ball. You're always doing that. Why are you so generous with everyone else, and you won't be charitable with yourself, and the people who really love you."

"Do you?"

"Do I what?"

"Do you love me?"

"Of course I do."

"A lot of people love me," she said. "And even more say they do. Why should it be you?"

"Because of what I want to do to you. For you."

"Like what?" she whispered.

He started to tell her.

"Wait a second," she said. "Let me call you back on the other line."

She dialed him on the number for which there was no other extension except the library. "Yes?" she said.

"And then I would make of you a meal."

"You think nobody's ever done that before."

"They may have. But it would have been like devouring a side of beef. I would make you seven courses, and distill my own wine from your sweet juices."

304

"You make it sound very poetic."

"It might sound poetic. It wouldn't feel poetic."

"Why not."

"Because of how I would do it."

"How?"

He told her.

"I'll be right over," she said, and hung up the phone.

She put her leopard coat on a hanger in the guest closet, and put her bag and gloves away. Walking toward the rear of the apartment, she smiled to herself. It would be a while before he realized she wasn't coming; by the time the realization came he would be sick with wanting her, and that was only just. He had no call to speak to her like that, to even think of her like that. She had no objection to admiration, or even desire from people. But no one had a right to be gross. Love was still a delicate matter. An extremely delicate matter.

She hummed as she opened the door to the master suite, and heard the noise of the shower running. He was home, and he was making himself clean. That was good. It was more than good, it was wonderful. In spite of her dismissal of Rick, he had succeeded in exciting her, and she didn't want to waste it. She walked through the hanging wardrobe closet into her bathroom, turned on the golden fish faucets in her bathtub, and leaned over so the first gush of hot water lightly steamed her face. Then she walked back through the closet, hung the width of the bedroom with clothes: evening gowns, evening pajamas, floor-length evening coats, and fingertip furs. No. Nothing evening. She wanted it to feel like evening, but be very much late afternoon. A special kind of late afternoon.

She walked to the other side of the closet, and started going through her at-home outfits and negligees. Nothing too frilly, something opalescent, but still soft. The blue. Blue was the best color for home, he always said that, especially for the bedroom.

She started to undress, cupping her breasts with her hands as she slipped out of her brassiere, holding them as if afraid they would sag if left to themselves. But she was foolish to worry, she knew that even as she caught a glimpse of herself in the full-length mirror. Twice a week at Kounovsky, working out with the rest of her friends, and her own natural resilience had kept her body as young and lithe as it had always been. She stretched an invisible cord at the back of her neck, the way they taught her in class, and swung on an imaginary trapeze. Except for the faintest blue stretch-marks under her arm where her breasts had pulled slightly during the two

305

pregnancies, the body was the same. Exactly. The belly was as flat, the hips as slightly rounded, the soft curve of buttock as subtle, and good for wearing the severe fashions as ever. She reached for the pale blue negligee and held it against her pink skin. Her hair, loosed from the twist at the back of her neck, fell in titian Rapunzel rings across her shoulders.

Superb. The negligee looked superb. It was perfect for the hour, the mood, and what she wanted. She carried it over her arm into the bedroom, and laid it on the chaise outside his bathroom door, where he would find it easily the moment he came out. She loosened the voile belt, and opened it slightly, and smiled.

It was a beautiful negligee. There was no doubt about it. It would look almost as good on him as it had on her.

In the beginning, of course, it had come as rather a rude surprise. She and Tzigie had been married a little over two months, and their marriage, like their courtship, was rather stilted. His approach to her in bed had a formal, reluctant quality, which she attributed to his European background and training. His wit, which their friends characterized as dry, escaped Diane, who considered him rather boring. But he was sweet, and attentive, and he appreciated her place, which was in the spotlight of every affair they attended, and as the cynosure of whatever group they chose to be in. In the same way, she appreciated his title, which, though hardly overwhelming, was authentic. He was not disconcertingly attractive, but he was nice-looking, with dark red hair and a whimsical moustache that made him look a little like Igor Cassini, whom she found amusing but would not seriously consider as an escort. Although he was contemptuous of parlor games, Tzigie enjoyed opera, and he was used to traveling, so together they could do many things without getting on each other's nerves.

It seemed as good a basis as any for a marriage. That it was not exciting, especially when they were alone, did not surprise or discomfort Diane. She had always assumed from her parents' marriage that passion was not meant to be part of a marital relationship, and if people enjoyed each other's company most of the time, that was enough.

They went to openings together, and parties together, if he was in town and the hosts promised not to play charades. They also went shopping. He took enormous pride in her appearance, and as she grew under his tutelage from the rather spectacular but overstated beauty she had been in the early sixties to one of the most subtle women on the Best-Dressed list, they both glowed. He would fly with her to the Mainbocher collection in Paris, and the new Valentino showing in

Rome; he was not above sitting with her through the viewings of the entire French line at Alexander's. He also enjoyed skipping over to Splendiferous when she felt like something Mod and "kicky"; and even encouraged her to buy there, as long as the fashions she chose were genuinely "her."

The night of Julia White's big Camouflage game, he pleaded a headache and insanity, and she laughed and kissed his moustache and told him it was all right, he could stay home. At the last minute, because of the intensity with which Julia's games were usually played, Diane decided against the vinyl jumper and boots she had been wearing, and slipped into a little white Zuckerman dress with buttons down the front in case she started to perspire. Tzigie expressed disappointment with the change, telling her she had looked adorable, and young, and very wizzit.

"With it," Diane said.

"That is what I said. Wizzit."

"It isn't if I wizzit or wozzit, it's how I play the game," she said. "What are you going to do about supper? Should I have cook set out something?"

"I'm not hungry," he said. "I'd just as soon do wizzout, I've been putting on a little weight."

He took her to the door and reminded her to make sure to ask if everything was on eye level. They kissed, with dry lips.

After the buffet supper at Julia's the game players assembled in the den, which had recently been redecorated, giving Julia many more ingenious places to conceal things. It was the usual crowd of intense players, as opposed to the fun people who played to pass the time: Andre Sherman, Dick Dussman who had just completed his latest score for a show to star Stephen Ryder, who was still trying to pretend he and Dick weren't lovers, Luke Benjamin, who would direct the musical, and the rest. For some reason Diane did not feel the usual stimulation she felt with these people. There was a vague airy feeling under her ribs, and she wondered if she had been wise to eat the salmon mousse.

She and Andre were paired up, as they usually were at Julia's, because Andre was the best and quickest at games, and Diane knew she was being protected from feeling she was the worst. There were twelve items on the list.

"Are they all on eye level?" Diane said.

"One is above," said Julia, "and one is below. The rest are on eye level."

"I've already spotted the one above," Andre whispered into Diane's ear, covering his lips with his hand. "Don't look up, Luke is watching us, and he'll look where you do, he's such a cheat, but the toothbrush is in the chandelier."

"Marvelous," Diane said, but felt no enthusiasm.

Six found items later (she had found none of them, Andre had found all), she felt actually faint.

"Julia, dear," she whispered to her hostess, who was sitting on the leather hassock, giggling with glee as everyone rushed around the room, peering and meeting, and whispering. "Forgive me, I must go."

"You can't," Julia said. "It'll floor you when you see where I stashed the Tampax. It's the best game I've ever set up. What's wrong?"

"I took some pills for a headache before I came, and I'm afraid I shouldn't have drunk the wine with dinner."

"You poor thing," Julia said, her eyes on Luke Benjamin as he saw, and tried to pretend he didn't see, the deflated balloon in the middle of the tulip. "Well I guess we'll have to stop."

"Oh please don't stop on my account," Diane said.

"But what about Andre?"

"I found the Tampax," Andre said, coming over to them.

"Where?" said Julia.

He leaned down and whispered to her.

"That's right!" she squealed, and clapped her hands together.

"Here, I'll tell my partner," he started to come toward Diane.

"I don't feel well," she said. "I have to go home."

"It's in the silver candelabra," he whispered. "With its wick hanging out, and half burned down."

"But don't let me break up the game. I'll just slip out, and afterward you can apologize to everybody, all right?"

"Fine," said Julia. "But what about Andre, will he be able to play alone, it hardly seems fair . . ."

"I can do as well alone as anybody with a partner," Andre said. "I'm sorry you don't feel well. No reflection on you, Diane, it's just I'm a great game player."

"Of course, darling," she said, and kissed the air between their cheeks.

When she got home, the lights were out in the foyer. The servants had all gone to bed, thinking she was in the bedroom with Tzigie. That probably meant that Tzigie was sleeping. She slipped out of her Valentino shoes, made her way quietly across the apartment floors, and gently opened the door to the master suite.

He was standing in front of the full-length mirror by the marble-topped console. He had on one of her black chiffon scarves and a necklace of imitation rose quartz from Kenneth Lane, with matching earrings. His dress was the black and white vinyl she had discarded before the party.

"Oh," he said, and brought up his hands, as if to shield himself from his own reflection.

She closed the door and locked it, behind her back, watching him the entire time. He did not move.

"I'm sorry," he said. "I'm really sorry."

"It's all right," she swallowed. "If it makes you happy."

"I didn't think you'd be home so early."

"It isn't as if you're hurting anyone, is it."

"I didn't want you to know."

"Why not?" Diane said. "People do all kinds of things. As long as you don't hurt anybody. You make a very good-looking woman."

"You're laughing at me?"

"Not at all."

"You don't feel like laughing?"

She looked at him in the reflection, and then she looked at him directly. "As a matter of fact, I never realized until this very moment how much like me you really looked."

"I take that as a great compliment," he said.

"So you should," she said, and went to him.

That evening they made love with a ferocity they had never had before, she wanting him more than she had ever done, and he hungering to please her. Shortly after that he shaved off his moustache. From then on, she never went shopping, even for a brassiere, without his coming along. And whenever she wanted him, she had only to set out something of hers on the bed, or the chaise, so he would know, and make himself ready for her.

She lay back in the tub, and let the hot water play over her remarkable body, and smiled. Rick Flinders was a fool to say Tzigie couldn't satisfy her. And the world was foolish to assume she wanted her husband only because it was convenient for her. Just as foolish as she had been, for all those wasted years, to have considered him dull. The truth of it was he was as fascinating a man as probably existed.

The lobby of the Warwick Hotel was, for the moment, empty of those passing through; even those passing through the Warwick would have been strangers to Louise. Where she might have been caught or embarrassed meeting someone she knew would have been a likelier mating ground, like the Plaza, or the Drake, or the St. Regis. Certainly not the Warwick. But all the same she took her dark glasses out of her purse, and slipped them on while Charley went to the desk to get his key.

Filtered like that, through the oversize light-tinted blue frames, he was not as great-looking as he had been in the sunshine. But catching a glimpse of herself in the mirror by the elevator, she realized that neither was she.

"Come," Charley said, coming across the lobby, and reached for her arm.

"Do you have to make an announcement, for God's sake," she muttered hoarsely. "You go up and I'll meet you there in a few minutes."

"I hadn't realized your husband was having you followed," Charley said.

"Very funny. Ha ha."

"What's the matter with you?"

"Lulu's embarrassed. She's never done it in somebody's hotel room. Honest." She lifted her glasses away from her face to show him she was, and he saw the pleading expression in her eyes.

"Okay," he said. "Room eight-oh-four. Don't be too long."

"Getting there is half the fun. Isn't it?"

"I'll see you," Charley said, and went up in the elevator.

She walked to the newsstand in the corner of the lobby, and bought the *Cosmopolitan* featuring the article about Diane, and two candy bars, one of which she put in her purse. The other she unwrapped quickly and ate in three bites, with her back turned to the lobby. Then she bought a package of Certs, and popped one in her mouth, as she moved toward the elevator.

"Eight, please," she said, and didn't look at the operator, in case he knew why she was there.

She rapped gently on Charley's door. When he didn't open it immediately, she looked up and down the empty corridor, rapped loudly, and said, "Hooker service."

He opened the door immediately, laughing. "So how embarrassed can you really be if you say something like that."

"More than you know," she closed the door behind her. "Can we pull down the shades or something? There's a dazzling view of the courtyard."

"I'll pull them down."

"Do you want me to get undressed, or do you want to undress me?"

"I want you to stop asking questions."

"Why?"

"I want you to relax, and just see what happens."

"Why?" she said. "What's going to happen."

"As little as possible, if you have anything to do with it."

"You really think that? You really think I want to spoil it?"

"Don't you?"

"I don't know." She sat down on the bed, and slipped off her shoes. "Is that too aggressive?"

"Give me your hand."

"Really?" she said. "You really want to start there?"

He reached for her hand, and pulled her slowly, gently to her feet. Before she could say anything, his lips were on her mouth, soft, loosening the tight corners of her surprised smile. She waited for the onslaught of his tongue, but there were only tentative little reachings, darting silken fires into her mouth. And his hands came up cool, to cradle her chin, and touch the cap of her hair.

"My goodness," she said, and started to reach behind his back to pull his shirt out of his trousers.

"Shh," he whispered against her lips, as his hands stopped hers in mid-motion. "Shh."

And he stood there, kissing her, kissing her only, for what seemed a heady, curious length of time, and she wondered if that was to be her punishment, to be teased to death barely in her prime, for all the bad things she had done. And then his lips were on her throat, and her neck, as his fingers quietly worked open the front button closing of her dress, and slipped it down from her shoulders. His tongue traced little circles across her collarbone, down to the tiny valley between her breasts.

She reached behind her to undo her brassiere, anxious to get it off, because she hadn't expected anything to come of the afternoon, and had worn an old washed-out cotton. But his hands were already behind her back, slapping her wrists out of the way.

"I'll do that," he said.

"Oh. Okay."

His fingers worked at the hooks while his lips continued the warm peregrinations. She found herself seated on the edge of the bed, and he was smiling at her.

"I'm out of high-school condition," he said. "In the old days I could undo one of those backhanded, blindfolded, in a single fell swoop."

"May I help you?"

"Just turn around," he said, and she did. He knelt on the bed beside her, and quickly sprung the hooks free from the eyes, and wiped the brassiere straps from her shoulders like a light coat of dust. He clung to her, kissing the back of her neck where the blond hair curled damply. And his fingers were on her breasts, fleetingly, tracing the sparely rounded contours with velvet.

"Please," she whispered. "Let me turn around. I want to kiss you."

She was afraid for a moment that he would say no.

"That's nice," he whispered, turning her gently. "I want to kiss you too."

And she was holding him, pressing him close, so close against her face that she had the drunken sensation that if she probed deep enough, and pulled hard enough, she could lose herself in his mouth. She pressed her hands against his back, and opened her mouth wider, and struck into him with her tongue, reaching in the afternoon darkness for his thigh.

"Easy," he whispered. "Easy. Let it be someone else's turn."

She looked up into the warm dark face, and felt the cool, expert fingers drawing her dress down over her hips. And she realized even as he moved against her, and played the flesh of her belly like a guitar, that there was no one, absolutely no one that he could tell if she was terrible.

"Okay," she said. "Okay I will."

"My goodness," she said. "My goodness. It really is, isn't it. Like they say in the books, I mean. I never knew it could be like this, and did you feel the earth move, and everything. Did it move for you, English?"

"Well, you felt mine moving inside yours, so it's kind of a dopey question, isn't it?" He traced his hands across the moisture of her breasts, and smiled. "Dumpling," he said.

"Only it isn't just the romantic crap, is it, I mean it's really kind of basic, it's so inevitable. Like a sneeze, really. I mean you feel it starting to happen, and the tickling is there, and there's that big gathering of breath and you know if you don't get it out, you're going to die, but you don't have time to worry about it, because it's there, it just happens, you explode, you sneeze. I mean, I don't mean to minimize, I had a wonderful time. Did you have a good time?"

"I had a fine time," Charley said. "Thank you."

"My pleasure. Do come again."

He laughed, and stroked her arm. "You're cute. You really are."

"But did you enjoy it, I mean. Was it worth all the effort? You really went to a lot of effort. I mean, was it worth all that for me?"

"It wasn't so much effort, Louise. I enjoy my work."

"You do that all the time? For everybody."

"Why don't you just shut up and put your arms around me, and let me feel your pudgy little ass."

"Am I too fat, naked I mean? Do you think it cuts down on my active sex potential or anything."

"I think you're cute," he said, and touched the inside of

her thigh. "I told you. You have lovely legs, and lovely skin . . ."

"So do you. You have skin like a baby, did anyone ever tell you that?"

"My mother."

"You really do. I mean your belly feels just like a baby's. If I told that to Dr. Ehrens, he would probably say your skin feels like a baby's to me because of how I feel about you. He can't deal with reality, poor man. If I ever go back to him, will you come in and let him feel your belly?"

"I don't know. Is he cute?"

"Not very. But he means well."

"Then why don't you just feel it, and tell him about it."

"You wouldn't mind?"

"Not at all."

She ran her fingers through the slight divide next to his hip bone, along through the darkening rings of hair starting down at the base of his stomach. "It is like a baby's. Your skin I mean. This isn't like a baby's, is it. I mean, if it was, the mother would have a lot of problems, wouldn't she."

"I don't know. It would depend on what she wanted from her kid."

"Isn't it amazing. How it grows before your very eyes. My very eyes. It's like magic, isn't it. I mean, Dr. Ehrens always said you should never expect something to change in a minute, that there were no purple flashes where your whole life changes in an instant, but that's certainly an instantaneous change isn't it, look how big you are, why Grandma, what big . . ."

"The better to what you with, my dear?"

"Do you think we ought to? I mean I'm so flushed with success, aren't you, it would be a shame to spoil it with only a pale imitation, so to speak. I mean, when you've got a great punchline, you shouldn't try to top it, as it were. Do you think?"

"Why are you sure it wouldn't be as good?"

"Well how could it be. I mean, there isn't that much time, you couldn't go to all that elaborate preparation, and . . ."

"I wouldn't have to," he whispered against her throat. "The pump is well primed."

"You think so," she said, kissing the side of his face. "Isn't it just the opposite, isn't it the more recently you've had it, the more you have to . . ."

"Why don't you stop being a running commentary and just be a girl."

"I can do that, can't I. I mean, just be a girl. I am a girl, aren't I."

"Let me check," Charley said, and his fingers found her. "Oh yes," he whispered. "Oh yes. You certainly are."

He was on top of her, entering her more brusquely than he had before, but with that same insinuating gentleness. He moved slowly, circling her hips with slow, steady rhythm. He was bending her legs back with his arms, his elbows, raised her higher and higher. All the time she wanted to tell him not to move too fast, that she wasn't ready. But he didn't. And she was.

He slapped against her like the waves of an ocean gone violent, and she felt the breaking of her own personal tide. She pulled at him, and tried to reach his face to kiss him, but he was straining against her, and battering her repeatedly.

"I'm there," she said. "I'm already there. Come with me."

He thrust, once finally, into her, and she could feel his spasms inside as he let her fall, gently. And his face was on hers.

"Oh my," she whispered against his mouth. "My darling boy."

"Sweet thing," he said, against her hair. "Thank you."

"You're putting me on," said Louise. "Thank you."

"Okay," he said. "You be both of them. Alphonse and Gaston."

"It's really incredible. I mean, isn't it. How everything can be changed, so quickly. Oh Charley, I don't mean to bore you with analyzing everything, but if you only knew how long I waited, without even realizing I was waiting, I mean. I mean I really wouldn't acknowledge that nothing was really happening, you know?"

"I know."

"Well so what do we do now, do I love you or what?"

"Why don't you just relax and wait and see."

"Good." She smiled. "I like that. I mean it would be wonderful if we could both make some kind of declaration, and then we lived happily ever after, but real life isn't like that, is it?"

"Why don't we wait and see," he said.

"Oh yes, you already said that. Okay."

She turned over on her side, and rested her head on her hand, smiling at him. "I'm waiting."

"Well, for openers, where would you like to go for dinner."

"Dinner?" She sat up abruptly. "Oh my God, how late is it?"

He switched on the lamp and looked at his watch. "The little hand is on the six . . ."

"How did it get to be so late. Oh Jesus." She jumped out

314

of bed and started getting into her clothes, not even stopping to think he could see her pulling on her girdle. "I'll never be ready in time."

"Ready?" he said. "What have you got to get ready for?"

"I can't stop to explain now. There's something I can't get out of. Really. I mean it's not as if . . ." She looked at him, lying there on the bed, the marvelous length of him golden brown against the whiteness of the sheets. It would be the easiest thing in the world to invite him; but if she asked him to the party now, there would be no way he wouldn't know she hadn't intended inviting him before. Besides, it was ridiculous. He wouldn't fit in.

"I mean, don't you think if I could get out of it, I would?"

"I don't know," he said, and got up out of bed. "I really don't know." He started past her toward the bathroom, and she reached for his arm.

"It isn't as if you've said anything." Quietly.

"I've said more than you've probably ever heard in your life. Your problem is you don't listen."

"Then you do?" she said. "You do care for me a little. I'm not so terrible in bed."

"You're not terrible at all," he said. "You're very warm and juicy when you relax."

"You really think so?" she said, grinning.

"Nothing to get smug about. You need practice."

"How fast can you pack a bag." She laughed. "I mean it does seem kind of silly, you are going to be in New York for a while and I do have that whole enormous apartment and I'd feel very dirty skulking around hotel corridors. Assuming you'd like to see me again. Would you?"

"I'd like to very much."

"So would you like to come and stay with me? It certainly makes sense, doesn't it. I mean it's much more practical, isn't it?"

"Much more practical," Charley said and smiled.

"Oo, Lulu is so excited. I've never really lived with a man before, at least not in my apartment, if you don't consider . . ."

He put his fingers across her mouth, gently.

"I'm not interested."

"I thought men liked to hear confessions."

"You thought wrong."

"Well that's good, because I don't want to hear about your past either. I don't even want to know about the girls you've been with. Who were they, I'll kill them." He laughed and kissed her, gently.

"Thank you," she whispered. "For not letting me tell you, I mean. It helps me keep up the illusion I'm an innocent."

"I have news for you. That's exactly what you are."

"I won't tell if you won't," Louise said, and pressed her head against his throat.

"Hey, better go get dressed. I wouldn't want to check out in my underwear."

"Maybe . . . Charley, maybe it would be better if we held off until tomorrow. I mean, I'd spirit you off with me this minute, but . . . but my mother's coming to dinner and I might have a hard time explaining your luggage, she goes through my closets looking for signs of sin. Would you mind waiting until tomorrow."

"Okay," Charley said. "If that's what you want. I'll call you in the morning."

"No, don't call me," said Louise. "I'll call . . ." She laughed, and got a lipstick out of her purse, and scrawled her unlisted number on the mirror above the dresser.

"Yes. Please. You call me."

CHAPTER FIVE

THE chartered plane for Paradise Island, and Maggie's wedding, left Kennedy Airport at Friday noon, thus allowing last-minute passengers from Europe to make the connection without any undue hardship. The Principessa Firenze, Adriana and Nando Zimbatelli, and Gianconda, the designer, arrived on the ten thirty from Rome and were directly escorted, by TWA cart, to the Bolin excursion, or, as the bridegroom-to-be tried to refer to it, Dr. Piner's plane. Alfie Gerard, author, publisher, guest lecturer and sometime cameo star of the new earth breed of British pictures, came on the eleven o'clock from London, with Rosamundy, a skeletal, pale model, who had already had a ten-column story in *Women's Wear Daily* as Alfie's latest "bird." Also making the deadline with them was Julia White, who had been doing a five-page layout on Rosamundy and Alfie, "People Are Looking At: (LOVE—Old and New)" for *Élan* magazine, and somewhat enjoying a brief reconciliation with her husband, recently appointed European sales representative for Marathon Pictures. The eleven five from Paris disgorged Pierre Olphant, a career diplomat who had gone to Harvard with Maggie's father, and his wife, who had been three years behind Maggie at Smith. With them was nineteen-year-old Ysabel Duvivier, daughter of a former Parisian prostitute who had six years before become the Duchess of Medwin. This in combination with what *Vogue* called Ysabel's "shamelessly graceful arms" and her "intoxicating mane—acres and acres of chestnut slung on a willowy tree," had led to her inclusion in the "young goddess" section of that magazine.

Also on the plane from Paris was Rolf Orlovsky, coming in from an emergency meeting of the Banque du Cosmopole of which he was vice-chairman of the board. The European trip had kept Orlovsky from returning any one of the twenty-four phone calls from Andre Sherman, whom Rolf was surprised to see was aboard Maggie's junket.

Those coming directly from town, by private limousine, were Maggie's hairdresser, Mr. Randolph, Bunyan Reis, Algernon Reddy and an officer of the Mitsaki Bank of Tokyo whom Algernon had suggested Maggie invite when the Negro they had been counting on was arrested for inciting a riot in his latest off-Broadway play. Louise Felder, Rick Flinders and Chet Oppenheim came by Carey Cadillac, which was in caravan following Maggie's car. Maggie's mother was too ill to come, but Maggie was accompanied by Mary Elizabeth Craig, the former movie actress, whom Maggie had hired as a social secretary for the duration of the wedding party to get Mary Elizabeth's mind off the suicide of her third husband, a cousin of Bertram Lester. Assorted golden couples, from the pages of *Town and Country,* and the Social Register, whose lines were as unblemished as Maggie's own, came in the Fun Bus especially bought and done up for the occasion by Dainty Lee Purbelow, who had temporarily abandoned her career in the theater in favor of painting, and had begun with the outside of the bus. Diane Trejinska was driven from Manhattan by her husband, who could not attend the wedding because of an estate foreclosure to take place over the weekend in Connecticut. The Mayor sent his regrets, but loaned his city car to Senator and Mrs. Kranet, to take them to the airport. Dr. George Piner, Maggie's fiancé, took a Yellow Cab.

Finally settled aboard the plane, the wedding party numbered the bare minimum of fifty-eight to which Maggie had been able to reduce the list of her closest friends. Luke Benjamin had to beg off on Tuesday because of a crisis with the orchestra conductor of a musical he was trying out in Boston, as did Harold Rankin, the show's producer. The cancellation had enabled Maggie to issue an invitation, couched in flowers, to Andre Sherman, with a personal note accompanying the engraved one, reading "It's all right, we decided not to take the pilot." The fifty-eighth seat had been offered to Kate Waller, whom Maggie decided at the last minute she really loved, and would Kate mind coming without David. Kate said she would come only if David could. There was no way Maggie could make room for him, besides which she didn't care for him much. So the last place on the plane went to George's brother, who was fine as long as he didn't open his mouth. He promised to relate all details of the ceremony to his parents, who George had assured Maggie didn't like to travel.

The stewardesses for the trip were wearing maxi-length afternoon dresses of yellow lace, designed especially for the trip by Gianconda, who had also designed the clothes for the bridal party itself. They moved up and down the aisles, a piece of bright island afternoon, offering champagne cocktails to the passengers, and giving them the luncheon menu, which consisted of caviar, vichyssoisse and quiche lorraine followed by a choice of quenelles, roulades de veau, lobster fra diavolo or frog's legs. The PA system played a privately recorded tape of the last concert conducted by Thomas Schippers, and the individual television sets in front of each chair carried the last David Wolper television special concerning George Plimpton's most recent charming masquerade, among the bullfighters of Mexico.

Andre Sherman tried not to fidget. It had not been his intention, in spite of how awkwardly pushy he must have appeared to Maggie, to try to be invited to the wedding. He had intended to spend this weekend gloating over the enormous profit from the resale of the paintings to Rolf Orlovsky. But by Wednesday, when all attempts to contact Orlovsky failed, and he finally extracted the information from Orlovsky's secretary that Rolf was in Paris, Andre began to suffer a little anxiety. It was too late to try and unload the paintings to other collectors—pictures in the six-figure range could not be sold overnight—and Thursday he was due to pay Parke-Bernet.

When the wedding invitation came from Maggie, he reaffirmed to himself the fact that there was a God. He telephoned the credit manager of Parke-Bernet, after first having his secretary imitate the long-distance operator, and said he was phoning from Providence, Rhode Island, that he had been unexpectedly held up on important banking business, and would not be back to New York until Friday morning, at which time he would have to go directly from one plane to another in order to join Maggie Bolin's wedding charter flight. He was sure that under those circumstances, a slight delinquency would be indulged, and that the postponements would not be viewed as the machinations of a promoter.

God had also sent Rolf Orlovsky to the wedding, as Suzy Knickerbocker and Limelight by Louise had both assured Andre weeks ago God would. If Andre handled himself right, if he didn't act frantic, which there was no need to be, because this time he really had it, the foolproof, huge-return plan, he could dispose of the paintings over the weekend.

Andre wiped his hands on the orange voile handkerchief that matched his silk-lined orange voile tie, and reached out to receive the champagne cocktail offered him by the stewardess. As she handed him the menu, Andre neatly avoided a few drops tipped into the air by his seatmate, a tall, pallid, young man from Pennsylvania who was telling the stewardess he was the brother of the groom.

"Sorry," said the brother of the groom, and tried to offer his hand for shaking, but it was still wet with champagne.

"That's okay," said Andre.

"I'm Harold, the brother of the groom," he said, offering his hand after wiping it on his trousers.

"Congratulations," said Andre.

"Is that right, is that what you say to the family, or do you just wish them every happiness, like you do the bride."

"Whatever's right," Andre said.

"Oh yes. Yes, of course." Harold opened his menu. "It's so early in the day, isn't it. Everything sounds so fancy, for so early in the day, doesn't it. What is that, quenelles?"

"Hot gefilte fish," Andre said.

"Oh fine," said Harold. "That's what I'll have."

The plane landed at Nassau at three thirty in the afternoon. Senator Kranet's wife said she was feeling a little drunky-wunky from the champagne and the altitude, so she was put in the first limousine. There were nineteen cars in all, including three with trailer trucks attached for the extra luggage. Mr. Randolph insisted that the bags containing the hairpieces were to travel inside the car with him, and not on any truck or the trunk of any car either. Aside from that, nobody made a fuss about how or when they would get to the hotel which the travel agent promised them was merely a whisk away.

Everyone seemed in excellent spirits. It was a perfect tropical afternoon, with lengthening palm trees and a few painted-backdrop clouds spotting an otherwise spectacularly blue sky, and the wind was from the south, which Algernon said was a wonderful sign. Bunyan Reis exclaimed at the natural radiance of the causeway, and said he hoped to capture it in oil, with sequins. Rick Flinders feeling, he said, more the fortunate observer than the narcissistic observed, whispered warm words of greeting to Diane as he put on his photographer's cap and started focusing the lens of his camera to better capture for fond memory, and possibly *Look* magazine, this happy time with his friends.

Only Maggie seemed a little out of it, tentative, and somewhat more fidgety than usual. She blew a few kisses to George, who was in the car behind with his brother and Mr. Randolph. Then she turned to Algernon, seated beside her on the pearl-gray upholstered back seat of the Rolls, and squeezed his hand.

"Hello, Nonny." She squeezed his hand.

"Don't worry if you're feeling a little unsure, Mag. Everyone feels a little unsure, and nervous, before they get married."

"Yes?"

"Of course. It's normal."

"You're so beautifully wise, that's the lovely thing, yes? Do you have the feeling I'm avoiding George, actually I'm not avoiding George, you know, it's just so many things have to be taken care of, I have to be thinking about details all the time, I can't just sit there and be in love, can I? I really am, you know, do you think George thinks I'm avoiding him?"

"I'm sure he's as nervous in his own way as you are. You'll both be all right once it's over."

"Really? Do you really think so? Oh I know I love him, Nonny, if I had any doubts they were all dispelled, flash, the night he came home and found me with the internist from New York Hospital, isn't that mad, I can't even remember his name anymore. I never knew there could be such calm rage in this world, Nonny, filled with passion, but controlled, he just stood there, white, with this orangeade in his hand, and he told him to get out and then he crushed the wax container in his fingers, and the orange juice oozed down his arm and his pants and everything, like blood, that's just what it looked like, only dark yellow, and you knew he would do that to him, like some yellow-blooded insect, just ooze him to death if he didn't get out. Of course I told the other one not to leave, I was being perverse you know, just testing George. He knew the other one would go away, and then I told him to, and he did. And I went to George and he looked at me with those gray eyes of his, they were almost black he was so dark and accusing that night, and he said to me: 'You will never be with another man again. You belong to me!' "

"Really?" Algernon said. "Did he say that? You told me the rest of the story before, but you never told me that part of it. Imagine George saying that."

"Are you insinuating that I made it up, because if you are, Nonny, you must realize that there are some things I will not forgive, even in you." She turned away and looked out the window at the blue waters beside the bridge to Paradise Island, and her voice became very low. "I'm sure he said it."

"Well, that's beautiful, love girl. You must feel very secure about a man that could be so strong about you."

"I do," Maggie said. "You really think he's the one?"

"He fathered your child, Maggie. That's the most important single act of your life, and your life with anyone else." He leaned over and patted her slightly rounding belly. "That's the great truth that emerges. Life is the issue."

"I still didn't tell him about the baby," Maggie said. "I don't want him to feel trapped."

"Oh yes," Algernon leaned his neck back against the pearl-gray headrest, and smiled. "Yes, that's true. It hardly seems fair to use pressure."

"You do like him, don't you, Nonny?"

"He is the father of your child," Algernon said. "I pinch his cheeks."

Diane unpacked slowly, dismissing the chambermaid the hotel sent, as they sent a chambermaid or valet to unpack each of the guests of the Bolin party. Diane thanked the girl, giving her a tiny gift-wrapped vial of perfume, from among the fifty half-ounce perfumes she had received the previous Christmas from the buyers of New York department stores, and told her she would ring if she needed help with anything.

Once the maid was gone, Diane put the latch on the door and drew the drapes against the still-warm tropical sun. The leaf-spattered blue silk of the fabric that faced the room was backed with thick muslin, to shut out whatever it was that potential occupants wished to ignore, thus making it possible for them to create their own nighttime, even in the middle of day. It was more darkness than she wanted. Much more. She walked to the floor lamp behind the white silk, round-backed love seat, and switched it on, low. Then she started hanging her clothes in the closet, pausing first at the full-length mirror to hold the clothes up against her body.

Silks, organzas, crisp white linens, wildly splattered Pucci pajamas flashed underneath the remarkable face, clung to the mannequin body like the most understated but complex sauce by a master chef in love with his main course. She realized with a flash of pleasure that Tzigie had helped her become almost as beautiful as people had always considered her to be. To her surprise she thought she could detect a faint sparkle of tears in the eyes that looked back at her from the mirror. Being pleased with oneself, even thrilled, could cause no such phenomenon, she was sure, so she assumed it was because he could not be with her to share. Everything.

She went to the phone and asked the operator how long it would be before she could get a call through to New York, and gave her the number. The operator said she would get right back to her and let her know. Meantime, Diane drew from the bottom of one of her suitcases a pair of his silk pajamas that she had brought along in case she missed him, which at this moment, she very much did. She was halfway into the sleeve when she heard the door.

"It's all right," she whispered, half against the frame. "I said I'll call you when I need you."

"When will that be?" Rick said.

She tucked Tzigie's pajamas under the pillow of the bed, and slipped into her least attractive robe. "Really," she said, opening the door. "What is all this whispered urgent carrying on? 'I've got to see you!' Why have you got to see me?"

"It's been over a year and a half I've waited," he said, coming inside. "I can't wait anymore."

"You are a child," she said, and closed the door.

"No, I'm not. Children have no persistence. I won't give up on you no matter how hard you make it for me. We're meant to be together. My astrologer says that's why you went out on the road, so it wouldn't be so obvious when you came to Hollywood."

"I'm waiting for a call from New York."

"Okay." He was wearing white flannel trousers and pale blue moccasins with no socks. His pale blue shirt was open at the throat, draping the three gold charms that glimmered from the center of his tanned chest. "You are coming to Hollywood?"

"Maybe. There's been talk of some offers."

"Then we can be together all the time."

"I want to take a bath," Diane said. She walked into the bathroom and leaned over the deep marble tub, turning the metal stopper and letting the first gush of water warm her skin. Then she started to get up, but he was standing over her, smiling.

"Oh do stop being such a fool," she said. "Get out of my way."

"Okay," he said, and pulled up a white marbleized stool. "I'll be completely inconspicuous." He sat down, and folded his arms, and smiled.

"What do you want from me?" she said.

"I want to give you myself."

"What an incredible present," she said.

"Everything that happened to me in my life was because of you, so it would be really wonderful with you, so it all makes sense, finally, do you see that?"

"I don't see anything," she said and went in to call the operator back.

"You still here?" she said as she went back into the bathroom.

"I love you," he said. "You have to try and understand."

"You insist upon staying?"

"I insist."

"All right. If that's how you want it." She slipped off the bathrobe and let it slide to the floor at his feet. Then she walked by him, close, so her nipples almost brushed his face.

"God, you have a beautiful body."

"Yes," she said. "I know."

"I always thought you'd be completely flat-chested, because of how you look in clothes. But your breasts are a modest groove."

"Yes, I know that too." She stepped into the too hot water. But because the timing was so good so far, she did not want to spoil the rhythm by stepping out again. She lowered herself cautiously, turned off the hot water and let the cold keep running. "Would you mind handing me the soap."

"Not at all." He reached over to the sink, and unwrapped the perfumed rectangle, and held it to his nose. "It'll go great on your skin."

"Thank you."

She drew the soap into the water, and moved it back along her sides, across her stomach, and up between her breasts. Rick watched.

"May I kiss you?" he said.

"I don't like kissing."

"Oh. Have you ever done it in a bathtub?"

"If that's your way of courting euphemism, Rick, I would say that if by 'it,' you meant fucking, I would say no, I had not ever done 'it' in a bathtub, nor had I any wish to do 'it' in a bathtub. People drown in bathtubs, and even if they do not drown, they ruin their hair." She drew the soap slowly back and forth across her breasts, and watched, with quiet amusement, as the pink nipples seemed almost to darken as they grew hard and firm. "Well mercy me," she said. "What do you suppose made them do that?"

"Come out of there," Rick said.

"But I can't, darling. I'm not clean. You want me to be clean, don't you?"

"Then let me come in."

"But I just told you. I'm too young to die. And Mr. Randolph is here, hairpiece in hand for Maggie. It wouldn't do for me to intrude my little fall on *her* occasion, would it, and I have no idea how the beauty salon is in this hotel, so I have to keep myself unstringy, don't I." She slid the soap slowly down her stomach, holding it briefly at the darkening rise above her pubis; then, with the other hand reached up from underneath her and drew it down between her legs, where it disappeared.

"Then let me . . . let me do that for you." His voice was hoarse and strained, and the look of casual insolence had left his face. "Please."

"Do what for me, darling? You mean wash me, soap me up and down all over and in between, oh isn't that sweet. That's rather like having a nanny again, isn't it. I like that. That's very thoughtful, isn't it. Here." She handed him the soap, and let her fingers trail his wrist.

"Maybe it would be better . . . would you mind **very** much if I . . . my shirt is silk, and water spots . . ."

"You want to take your shirt off? Oh well, by all means. Please. Take your shirt off. And your shoes. Pale blue leather waterspots too, don't you think? Nanny always used to take off her uniform when she bathed me, I did so love to splash around, but then of course she always wore a bra. You look very handsome, Rick, all barefooted and naked to the waist, sort of my very own male geisha. However did you manage to get so tan already, and we've only been here for an hour."

He folded a towel and knelt on it, by the side of the tub, and reached over into the water, soaping her easily, from her collarbone to her waist, with one hand, lathering with the other. He did not look at her face, but knew she was watching his, and he could feel his cheeks reddening.

"That's nice," she said. "That's very nice. Down a little further. Oh yes. That's lovely. Now further down still. You're not nervous about anything, are you?"

"It's a very deep tub," Rick said, with some difficulty. "It's hard leaning over like this, and my pants . . ."

"Well, maybe you'd like to take off your trousers," said Diane. "I wouldn't want you to get them all spotted."

"Thank you." Rick got up and dried his hands on the towel. Then he turned his back and got out of his trousers. He was not wearing any shorts.

"Oh I think that's very smart," Diane said. "Especially in pants that are cut so tight, shorts would kind of spoil the line, wouldn't they. Even a jock strap . . ."

"Be quiet," Rick said, and stepped into the tub.

"But my dear," said Diane. "I thought I had made myself perfectly clear. I have no wish to die in a bathtub with stringy hair."

"You said I could take off my pants."

"So you could wash me better, that's all I meant. I didn't want you to soil yourself, but I only wanted you to wash me."

"All right," he said. "Then I'll wash you." He reached underneath her for the soap, and drew it up slowly between her legs, and back and forth across her mons veneris.

"Oh that's nice," she said. "It really is. There's something so clean and velvety about soap."

"I'm glad you're enjoying it."

"I am," she said. "I really am. I think that the least I could do in return, because you're being such a good boy, is wash you."

"All right," he said, and raised himself on his knees, handing her the soap.

"No, I didn't mean for you to stop. Isn't there another cake on the sink?"

He raised himself to his feet, and reached over, unwrapping the fresh soap. As he started to sit back down, she raised herself for a moment, and kissed the tip of his erection.

"I'm so sorry," she said. "I certainly didn't mean to be so bold."

"That's perfectly all right."

"Oh no," she said. "I'm a woman of my word, and my word was that I would wash you." She brushed the cake back and forth in her palms, until they were covered with lather. And then she reached for him.

"Oh," he said, closing his eyes.

"Squeaky clean," she said. "We're going to make it squeaky clean. Now don't be so forgetful, Rick, just because you're enjoying yourself doesn't mean you can't keep washing me too."

He soaped the inside of her thighs, beneath the water. She opened her legs to him, and he rubbed her more and more frantically with the soap, as her hand lathered his penis.

"That's good," she said. "Oh yes, I think that's fine. I'm clean enough now." And in a moment she had slipped past him, up and out of the tub.

"But what about me?" he said, looking down at the ridiculous spectacle of himself, body half out of the water, his pubic hairs like a lathered beard, with the red soapy erection protruding.

"Finish yourself off," she said, and ran into the living room. "It was your idea in the first place, you work it out."

"Cunt!" he screamed, as she shut the door.

The courtyard outside the bar of the Ocean Club, where tables had been set up for the cocktail hour, was so covered with flowers of such brilliant hue that Maggie was convinced Algernon had put something in her drink. "But it's so splendid," she murmured. "So much red, and all of it so bright, did you ever know there was so much red in the universe, Nonny."

"Living is always red," he whispered. "Especially in the tropics."

"But there's so much green, too, have you noticed that, I don't just mean the grass, Nonny, although the grass is magnificent, not like regular grass at all, but all the foliage around the statues, and aren't they white, all those Cupids in marble, the foliage around them is so green. And the sea."

"You're excited," he said, patting her hand. "That's good. I want you to be delighted with the place you're getting married in. Emotions recollected in fertility."

"Yes, of course," Maggie said, and lifted her head as the waiter took their order for a drink.

There was a path through the middle of the courtyard, coming from the tennis courts, punctuating the gardens with stone, darting around the rococo statues set on their pedestals. Down it came a few of the couples, who had been, according to their own account, not being able to believe their eyes. They were already slightly flushed, as if the mere idea of the dazzling sun to rise the following morning had already started their menalin flowing. H. Reynolds Tracy (the H. was for Helen, but nobody ever mentioned that anymore, except in the *New York Times,* when they wrote of his father's finance company) and his wife, Jennifer, bolstered between their matching, striped, yachting outfits the still-languid Mrs. Kranet. The Senator was napping in his room, but Mrs. Kranet, in spite of feeling a little hungy-wungy, said she didn't want to miss a minute of the happy festivities.

"After all, Maggie dear," Sylvia Kranet said, and leaned over to kiss her cheek, "how often does a woman get married in her life, three, maybe four times." She giggled at her joke. "I hope you'll be so happy."

"It was nice of you to come down. I hope you're feeling better after the plane."

"Oh I'll be fine, as soon as I get a little hair of the doggy."

"Woggy," said Algernon.

"Pardon?" said Sylvia, but she was already whisked off into another group.

Andre came through the lobby of the hotel to the courtyard, in a madras jacket with a matching madras cap, with a visor shading his eyes from the sun. He stepped aside as someone brushed by him. It was Rolf Orlovsky.

"I've got to talk to you," Andre said.

"I don't want to talk to you now," said Rolf.

"We could make a date for later."

"Yes, we could, but I have other plans."

"Then when?" Andre said.

"I'll just have to let you know."

Rolf went on the patio, and leaned over Maggie, kissing her hand, clicking his heels together. "You look lovely, Maggie. You have never looked lovelier."

"Thank you," she said. "I'm so madly happy you could come. Won't you sit down with us?"

"In a moment," he said. "I see they have caviar on the hors d'oeuvres table, and I have the happy suspicion it's Russian."

"Can they do that?" she said. "Can they truly get Russian caviar?"

"Only from Cuba," he said, and laughed to himself as he moved to the table in the middle of the garden.

A marimba band came out of the French doors from the bar and started playing their island music, while at the opposite end of the garden, a steel band started playing rock 'n' roll. "It is lovely here," she said.

"Lovely," said Algernon.

"Nonny—please, I hate to keep bothering you, but . . ."

"Speak," he reached for a ringlet of her yellow hair, trailing across her naked shoulder.

"The ceremony's at twelve thirty."

"So I understand."

"Well do I . . ." She reached for his fingers, tangled in her hair. "You better not do that, the whole thing's liable to come out, and Randolph is asleep for the evening. He hates flying, it knocks him out for days."

"I'm so sorry," said Algernon, and pulled his fingers free. "I thought it was yours."

"Yes, doesn't he do a wonderful job?"

"The ceremony's at twelve thirty," Algernon prompted.

"Yes, so?"

"You wanted to ask me something. Did it have to do with George?"

"Did what have to do with George?"

"What you wanted to ask me."

"I'm not insecure about George, if that's what you mean."

"No," Algernon said. "No, I'm sure you're not."

She got very close to him, and whispered, behind her hand. "Do we spend tonight together?"

"Love child, that was over so long ago . . ."

"I mean George and I. He's been staying in my apartment in New York, of course, on and off, but I wondered about tonight. Randolph is coming up to do my hair at eight thirty in the morning, and I thought maybe . . ."

"You're absolutely right," Algernon said. "Under no circumstances should you spend the night before your wedding together. Rosalind and I were living together for seven years, and the night before the wedding she made me go to a motel."

"And were you glad you did it."

"It made all the difference," he said. "I was never happier I did anything in my life."

"I'm glad," she said. "Because I really do love George. I want everything to be perfect between us."

Just then George Piner came out onto the patio, with his brother. They were both wearing white dinner jackets. And

328

between them stood Julia White, smiling nastily in Pucci pajamas.

"Oh God," Maggie said, ducking her head. "Oh God, I should have told him it was casual."

"It's all right," Algernon said. "I'll go up and dress."

"No," Maggie said, and reached for his arm. "Don't leave me alone with him."

The bridal dinner was held at nine o'clock in the Martinique Restaurant, the most elegant the island had to offer. Guests were taken from the hotel across the bay by motorboat and water-taxis, chartered for the evening. Everyone had gathered on the dock below the hotel at eight forty-five, after first going back to their rooms to change into more formal tropical attire. George and his brother, who had been in dinner jackets since five, had used the extra time to consume two extra Planter's punches apiece, and stood on the dock, their arms entwined, singing the song with which their mother had lulled them to sleep, according to their best recollections.

When the guests were seated at the tables, arranged in the shape of an enormous rectangle so everyone could see everyone else, through elaborate floral arrangements, Rolf Orlovsky arose and proposed the first champagne toast of the evening, to the bride and groom. Maggie, in a one-shouldered Scaasi of pale blue chiffon, nodded her head and smiled, and pressed her hand against George, who was about to get up and give a speech of acknowledgment.

"Did you think I wouldn't know what to say?" George whispered angrily, when there was enough conversational hum to cover his words. "Do you think after all these years of attending functions I don't know how to handle myself."

"It's just that it's going to be such a long evening," Maggie said, and kissed his ear. "I thought you might want to pace yourself for later."

"Oh, good thinking," he said, and attacked his first course.

The restaurant had prepared a cuisine that Mary Elizabeth Craig ordered especially, according to her remembrances of the food served during the bacchanal scene in *Lot's Wife*, in which she had made her motion-picture debut. Pompano in a paper bag was followed by hearts of palm salad, chicken à la Kiev, and pheasant under glass, each served with an appropriate wine. The chef had been unable to secure any sheep's eyes, but Mary Elizabeth was just as glad. They had tasted better than she thought they would, hearing about them. But even at the time the picture was shot she considered them inappropriate for a wife-swapping community in Babylon, Long Island, and they were the symbol of Bertram

Lester's tendency to go overbudget for the sake of too much Technicolor reality, which had later led to his downfall as one of the great producers. The main course, beef Mirabeau, was accompanied by a Chateau Margaux, and champagne.

Neither Rolf Orlovsky nor Chet Oppenheim ate anything more than the pompano. They rearranged the rest of the food as it was served them, cutting into the Kiev and letting the melted butter squirt out onto the plate, lifting the anchovies and olives from the Mirabeau and cutting into the beef. To all appearances they were eating as much as anyone could, considering the quantity of food. But since four o'clock in the afternoon they had known about the midnight supper not on the wedding agenda, which one of the divorcées who lived year-round on the island had arranged for them, and they did not want to spoil their appetites. Any of their appetites.

Louise, too, was not eating very much of the food, although she had not been invited to the midnight party, and the gnawing inside her was easily confused with hunger. She looked around her at all the unbelievable faces, with their prominent cheekbones and high sweeping foreheads and dazzlingly simple hairdos, and tried to be as thrilled as she had always known she would be, to be securely among them. She was thrilled, she was sure she was.

It was just that Charley was confusing her. They had been together for less than a month, and she felt odd about leaving him. In New York she could go any number of places without him, and did, without feeling guilty; but it was not the same as going away.

"You know I'd take you with me if I could," she had said. "I take you to as many of the parties as I can. But it is Maggie's wedding. I can't ask to bring you. Not to Paradise Island."

"I know that," he said. "You don't have to apologize. I don't want to go."

"Then why'd you say that?"

"I only said I'd miss you," he said, handing her her freshly pressed underwear. "That doesn't mean I want to go."

"I'd stay home in a minute but it's the wedding of the year, the decade maybe, Charley. It's my job. I can't not go."

"I know that. I want you to go."

"Then why'd you say you'd miss me?"

"Because I will."

"You're mixing me up," she said.

Fortunately he hadn't mixed her up so much that she made the mistake of staying away. There was no doubt about it: it was an "A" wedding. Even an A Double Plus.

Her eyes and her little gold pencil linked to the jewel-encrusted notepad took in all the details of the guests' clothes, the Mainbocher summer dinner-dresses, the caftans, the naked-seeming chiffons over the body-hugging crepe underslips. But except for the elegance of cuisine and attire, and the obvious gentility (Gentile-ity?) of feature she might have been attending a bar mitzvah in Great Neck. The table was arranged in exactly the same way, so that everyone could see, but nobody could talk across. There had always been too much food there, too, though not of such a high order. For her own taste, she preferred hot Chinese hors d'oeuvres and unending trays of delicatessen, so you could at least move around a lot before the main dinner, leaving you the illusion of room to breathe. There was, of course, one other distinct difference: these people did not seem to be having as good a time as the bar mitzvah crowd.

She smiled at her own foolishness, and touched the coral dinner-jacketed arm of Rick Flinders, marveling at the granite perfection of his profile, as he stared at the table opposite. "Isn't it a beautiful party," she said, and yelled across at Maggie, "I love it, I love it, what time are we meeting here next month?"

Rick was still watching something or someone at the side table, and Maggie, holding her hand up to her ear, mimed the impossibility of catching what Louise said. "We must do this every December," said Louise. Maggie shrugged her despair.

Louise set down her pencil and picked up the ornately carved, well-shined silver spoon, and held it a little in front of her face. She squinted her eyes to see herself better in its reflection, and turned it around.

"You look great," Rick said. "Just great. You've never looked better in your life."

"Oh, then it must be the spoon," she said, relieved, and brushed a honey-blond wave back from her forehead.

The dinner plates were cleared, and the lights of the restaurant were suddenly extinguished. Except for the glimmering of boat lights and moon reflection across the waters outside, there was darkness.

"Rick," Louise said loudly into the silence. "Control yourself."

"I didn't lay a finger on you."

"You have to tell everybody?" said Louise.

The waiters entered from the kitchen with trays of flaming crêpes suzettes, and collective "Oohs" and "Aahs" came from the gathering. In the blue-seared darkness, Maggie reached for George's hand. But she couldn't find it. When the lights came back on, his place was empty.

"Where do you suppose George went?" she said to Algernon, who was seated on her left, while the waiters served the pancakes.

"I don't know."

"Maybe he's left, do you think, do you suppose that could be it?"

"He couldn't leave you, Mag," said Algernon, and ran his fingers up her arm.

She leaned closer to him, and met the gaze of Harold, George's brother. "I was just wondering about George," she said.

"I don't think he was feeling too well," said Harold, whose own face had gone a little gray.

"Poor George," said Maggie. "Oh dear."

"You want me to check the men's room."

"No, I don't think so, Harold," Maggie said. "George is such a private person, he must be especially so about illness, he must really despise it, you know, find it very degrading, the idea of being sick, I suppose that's why he went to medical school, what? I read an article in the Sunday *Times* magazine a few months back that the people who study medicine are almost always those who are most concerned with dying, don't you think that's interesting?"

"George isn't going to die."

"Well I didn't mean tonight," Maggie said. "Maybe you ought to check on him, Nonny."

Algernon was halfway out of his chair when he saw George coming back toward the horseshoe of tables. George's face, above the white lace ruffles of his dinner shirt, was flushed, but he was smiling.

"Are you all right?" Maggie said, as he sat back down.

"I had a bit of a rough go, but I'm all right now. It must have been the food and the excitement."

"It must have been," Maggie said.

"But I'm fine now. I took a Compazine suppository."

"Oh," Maggie said, and set her fork down.

"I don't usually vomit, but I had them with me just in case. Not that I anticipated vomiting, but in moments of extreme excitement and anxiety it's a typical reaction. That and a spastic colon. So I brought them just in case. That and Lomotil."

"That certainly was farsighted of you," Algernon said.

"Are you feeling all right, Maggie?"

"Fine."

"You look a little . . ."

"I just had too much to eat," she said. "I'll be fine as soon as I get some air." She stood up and walked in the direction of the screened porch, where the musicians were playing tender music against the balmy star-flecked night.

George was still standing where he had risen for her departure. "Go with her," Algernon said, nodding.

"Maybe she wants to be by herself."

"Why don't you ask her?" Algernon said.

"All right," said George, and then stopped in his tracks. "Do you happen to have a lifesaver, or a piece of gum on you?"

"Here," Algernon handed him an after-dinner mint, from the gold-leaf basket on the table.

"Thank you," said George.

Maggie stood on the patio by the water, her back whitened with moonlight, the light breeze from the bay riffling the soft folds of chiffon. He came up next to her, and put his arm around her shoulders, and she settled her head into the bend of his arm.

"You sure it's going to be all right?" she whispered.

"I'm sure. Compazine never fails."

"Oh. George."

"Would you care to dance?" He opened his arms, as some of the other couples started sifting out from inside the restaurant.

"I'm so tired, George. I must have overeaten."

"Well maybe we ought to go back to the hotel, and you could lie down. And I could rub your back. And your neck." He started working the skin behind her ears, slowly.

"George . . ." she pulled away slightly. "Do you mind very much, I know it's a little late to be conservative, what? but I think it's best, just because it's our last unmarried night, the way it should be, please don't take this in the wrong way, but we oughtn't stay together, not tonight, anyway, Mr. Randolph will be coming at eight thirty."

"I could leave at dawn, couldn't I."

"I don't think so. Not tonight. I know it's a little late for me to wax all over traditional, but that's just the way it's done, what?"

"All right. If that's what you want."

"Well it isn't what I want, darling, it's just for the sake of custom. For the last time."

"The last time." He reached his arm around her neck and bear-hugged her to his chest, and she could hear the words coming through his breastbone. "We'll have the rest of our lives together. Never again, one without the other. Isn't it wonderful."

"Isn't it," Maggie said, and closed her eyes.

About twelve thirty when the third pill had failed to put her to sleep, she slipped into a negligee and dark glasses, and made her way carefully along the hotel corridor to Algernon's room. There was no answer to her cautious knocking, so she hit the door louder, and louder, until, with all strength, and uncaring about the noise, she pounded. Nobody came.

And then she remembered Andrea de Revigny, and the midnight supper party to which a small number of the wedding guests had been invited. She returned to her room, dressed, and went to join Algernon by water-taxi in the house across the bay.

Andrea de Revigny had lived in Paradise Island ever since closing up her house in Acapulco, after catching the Baron de Revigny at Las Brisas with the Pinckney heiress. The Baron's title had been fake, but the Pinckney fortune luckily was not, and little Daphne Pinckney had been more than glad to give him two million to settle on his wife, so he would be free to pursue his little peculiarity, which Daphne apparently found irresistible. Andrea had never much cared for it, except as a way to pass the time, and with two million dollars, time passed quite as pleasurably in Paradise Island. She had her share of local talent, and interesting transients, some of whom were moved to stay longer than they intended after enjoying one of her evenings. She also continued to obtain as fine a quality of pot as she had ever enjoyed in Acapulco, and the acid supply provided more consistently delightful trips.

When she went somewhere in actuality, it was usually to New York, at which time she would be beautifully entertained by Chet Oppenheim, so she considered it only good manners to set up this little party for him and his special friend Rolf Orlovsky now that they were on the island. Algernon Reddy she knew as "Ever" Reddy, from his old reliable days in Acapulco. She was not aware of his new role as philosopher and religious leader, except for those articles she had glanced at in magazines, articles she was immediately able to dismiss, because she had known him better, and under more honest circumstances, than any interviewer possibly could. Other invitees from the wedding party at the hotel were the Senator and his wife, Dainty Purbelow, whom Andrea found particularly adorable in her press releases, and Diane Trejinska, who had declined, with regrets, saying she was exhausted from the trip. For the rest of the assemblage, Andrea had relied on the local talent, a few fascinating couples who had easily adapted to the ways of the island, and two astonishingly handsome beach boys who preferred to work in twos, in water-skiing instruction and other matters.

When Maggie arrived at the party it was nearly one o'clock. She saw immediately that she was overdressed in her tight-fitting white linen dinner dress, in the swirl of wildly colored Puccis around her, just as she was especially pale in the sea of tanned beautiful backs. But she was not concerned for more than the moment she took to apologize to her hostess for intruding.

"But my dear," Andrea said, reaching a warm tan hand from beneath her red silk caftan. "If I had dreamed you would have considered coming, I'd have invited you in a moment. Somehow I imagined, the night before your wedding . . ."

"I couldn't sleep," Maggie said. "Yes, that was it, I couldn't sleep."

"May I introduce you to my other guests."

"No, please," Maggie said. "I'll find my own way."

She started with the back of the house, the sun deck built out on cantilevers over the water, where two swaying couples locked in vague embrace moved slightly to the sound of the marimba band. Algernon was not among them. A girl in turquoise evening pajamas leaned against the railing, drawing deeply on a pipe being held for her by Chet Oppenheim. But Algernon was not outside.

Maggie made her way across the thick white carpeting, along the hallway past the atrium, glassing in rows of tropical plants, her hearing so acute she thought she could make out the sound of her own footsteps trampling the plushness underfoot. But she could not hear his voice.

When she found him, he was standing by the door of the master suite, with Rolf Orlovsky. The door was slightly ajar. On the white satin bedspread, a woman lay, her naked body outstretched, legs apart, a towel covering her face. The vague sound of giggling came from beneath the towel, as the two beach boys knelt, naked from the waist down, on the bed. One, his buttocks toward the towel, straddled her waist, and leaned over to further separate her legs, as the other, purple-tipped erection protruding from the bottom of his gaily colored tropical shirt, entered her from the front. The boy holding her lifted her thighs into the air, and leaned his face hungrily into the triangle of dark pubic hair, his tongue flashing across clitoris, touching penis. The woman giggled, and moaned. The boy inside her shuddered. Then the two boys switched positions.

"But it is," Rolf whispered. "It is Sylvia Kranet."

"Don't be absurd," said Algernon. "The Senator turned down the invitation. He's sleeping back at the hotel."

"So she came without him. But that's her."

"She has a towel over her face. How do you know it's her?"

"I know. I just know. I recognize her."

"At night all pussies are black," said Algernon, and turned to find Maggie.

"Love girl," he said, "why aren't you sleeping?"

"I couldn't sleep."

"Well, that's as good a reason as any for not sleeping." He took her arm and led her back down the hall, toward the sunken living room.

"Come back with me, now," Maggie said. "Please. Let's go to the hotel."

"Andrea's an old friend of mine, from Acapulco. It wouldn't be right for me to leave her party. Not when she's having it especially."

"Especially for what?"

"Especially to have a party."

He sat her down on the white and gold brocade couch by the smoked-mirror fireplace and cupped her chin in his hands. "I understand, Mag. I understand. You're afraid. It's not a new truth, it's not a new fear. Everyone experiences it when they are about to step into something permanent, and unknown. Getting married. Giving birth. Dying. Commitment to a changed state is the most frightening alternative a human being has."

"You can't go back on dying, or having a baby," Maggie said. "But you can on getting married."

"Why? Because you are the first person who ever felt doubt, indecision, trepidation? How many times have we been there, on that avenue, and you saw the road ahead as dark and full of knives, and I told you, no, turning back that was what would rip you into shreds; trust me, trust me, the way ahead is clear, it only seems frightening and fraught with peril—move, move, my hand in yours, that's where the great freedom lies."

"Can you get anything?" Maggie said.

"I've already gotten. Andrea has the best supply east of the Archipelago. But I'm not sure you should. There's enough perception and awareness in the very act of marriage in a courtyard fraught with flowers . . ."

"I don't love him," Maggie said. "I love you."

"I'll get you something," Algernon said.

At one thirty Andre Sherman, after searching the hotel for Orlovsky, arrived at the landing of the De Revigny home. A butler asked him if he could help, if he was expected, and Andre said no, and apologized, but it was very important that he see Mr. Orlovsky, he had urgent business to discuss.

Rolf Orlovsky was very annoyed at being taken away from his own rather urgent business, of trying to get a glimmer of the face underneath the towel, or waiting until they were finished, so he could be sure. When he was called out to the sun deck, he looked at Andre with all the darkness he could muster, and told him he was a damned fool.

"This is a vacation for me," Rolf said. "I don't relish being disturbed by the same issues I avoid in New York."

"You'll be glad you've talked to me, I assure you," Andre said, assuming Orlovsky's own tone. "I have in my possession . . ."

"Not in your possession," Orlovsky said. "You have in your alleged promise to pay and then get possession, yes?"

"All right," Andre said. "I have ten paintings that I believe you would be interested in buying, and at the same time I find myself in the position of having overstepped myself a little financially."

"A little," Orlovsky said, and laughed. "Five hundred and sixty thousand dollars is scarcely a little."

Andre paled. "How did you . . ."

"My dear boy. I own the bank you keep your money in. And if I didn't own it, I would surely know the people that do, and they would tell me your questionable assets."

"That's illegal," Andre said.

Rolf laughed. "You are amazing. Pointing a finger at me. Really amazing. It's a shame you're not a little brighter, because with your gall, if you were a shadow more intelligent you might really make something of yourself."

"I don't have to stand here and be insulted by you," Andre said.

"That's quite true. Why don't you go home."

"All right," Andre said. "So you've called my bluff. Now that I think about it, I suppose I should be flattered that a man as busy as yourself went to all the trouble of having my accounts checked. I guess that makes me very important to you."

"I went to no trouble, I assure you. When somebody gets something I very much want, and I am suspicious about his ability to pay, running a check is quite simple. A matter of only a few minutes. Everything, dear boy, is very simple. Your sending the telegram to poor Mr. Penn Edwards, who has never failed to be reliable. Tracking him, I suppose, like some adolescent James Bond, to find out his hotel. Stalking him through the gallery to see those pictures he paid especial attention to. Crafty, yes, but crafty juvenile."

"I'll let you have them, all ten of them, except for one watercolor, I already promised that to someone, I'll let you have them all for seven hundred thousand."

Rolf smiled. "When I want something, I do not let myself be outmaneuvered by Norton Simon or Huntington Hartford. You don't for a minute imagine I would put myself in a bidding position with you."

"All right then. I'll let you have them at a little more than cost."

"I'll get them at cost or less than cost, when they come up for resale, after you've been exposed as unable to pay."

"Dinner," Andrea de Revigny announced from the sliding glass doors. "Come, you have no idea what treats there are in store. Oh, I'm so sorry, I had no idea you were with anyone. I don't think I know you, Mr. . . ."

"Sherman," Andre said. "Andre Sherman."

"What a coincidence, my name is Andrea, you suppose that has any significance?"

"I'm not sure," Andre said, bowing over her hand, and clicking his heels together. "But I would be delighted if it did."

"How charming," said Andrea. "It'll take a moment to set an extra place and make some arrangements, but if you're a friend of Mr. Orlovsky's . . ."

"He's not."

"Oh. Oh, well in that case . . ." She turned her back to Andre, and took Rolf's arm, leading him inside. "I'm sure you'll excuse us."

"Yes," Andre muttered to the empty sun deck. "Yes. Of course."

In the living room, Maggie sat with her head between her knees, as Algernon gently manipulated the golden hair at the nape of her neck, and told her to cool it, and just swing free.

"There are no birds," he whispered softly. "It was only the leaves in the atrium, and the rush of wind, that's all. You looked up and caught the suddenness, so there seemed to be birds."

"They weren't there," she said. "They were in here."

"Birds are gentle, fluttering creatures. They want nothing with you. Just go ahead, that's all. Don't clutch. Move ahead."

"I love you," she said.

"George is under pressure, too. He's just as nervous about all this as you are. If he said certain things or behaved in a way that seems foolish, it's because we all say and do things under pressure we don't mean. He is a fine man, and you are going to have his child."

"Oh," Maggie said, and raised her head slowly, and looked at him. His lids lifted and parted and fled his face completely, leaving only his naked eyes. And they were emeralds. "Oh yes. I forgot."

"Dinner, you two," said Andrea from the steps.

"No. Couldn't," Maggie said. "Already so much. Not another thing."

"We had a very elaborate dinner earlier on," Algernon said.

"I assure you you'll be able to manage this one," Andrea said. "Believe me, it's all been very carefully arranged. And you can always—in a manner of speaking—toy with your food."

"Excuse me, angel child," Algernon said, letting go of Maggie's arm. "If you need me, I'll be inside." He left her sitting on the couch.

The dining room, unlike any of the other rooms of the sparkling modern glass and white and tropically casual house was refurbished with the decor of an old European mansion. The ceiling was covered with friezes, thick and crusted and baroque, and what patches of paint were visible were a faded cream shade.

"It's from an old Austrian castle," Andrea said to Dainty Lee. "My husband, the maybe Baron, had the ceiling brought over piece by piece to our home in Acapulco, and then when we separated, I had it transported *entière* here, to me. Naturally I had to have the whole wing restructured, but a dining room is such an important room in a house, don't you think. Dining does so set the tone."

"Yes, it does," Dainty Lee said. "It's really fab."

The walls of the room were hung with crimson velvet, fastened with crystal light sconces and elaborate bronzes. Some were in the shape of cupids, some were satyrs, and sometimes there was no easily discernible form at all.

"René used to be heaven at auctions," Andrea said. "When we were in New York we absolutely scavenged every hotel that was being torn down."

"Fab," said Dainty Lee. "Absolutely."

In the center of the uncarpeted, darkly lustrous parquet floor was a large oval dining table, draped with heavy cream linen, hanging to the floor. Six chairs were placed at wide intervals around it, and the total absence of any other furniture made it seem even more baronial, in the deceptive smallness of the room. Candles flickered in elaborate six-pronged candelabra. Gold and white china glittered in the place settings, and fluted silver and crystal surrounded each plate.

"You've outdone yourself, Andrea," said Chet. "It's absolutely Borgia."

"I would have said De Medici," Andrea said.

"Borgia," said Chet.

"We'll see," Andrea said, and smiled.

"What about the other guests," asked Rolf Orlovsky, as Andrea indicated his place. "Aren't they dining with us?"

"They're all doing their own thing," Andrea said. "Dinner was planned for you."

"What about Sylvia Kranet? Isn't she here?"

"Not that I know of," Andrea said. "The Senator was too tired to come."

"That doesn't always stop Sylvia," said Dainty Lee.

"I'm sure that was her," said Rolf Orlovsky to Algernon as Andrea signaled them all to be seated.

Algernon was designing ski tracks on the top of his eggs in aspic when he felt the light pressure between his legs. At first he thought he had dropped his napkin, the touch was so fleeting and gentle. But when he reached to check if it was still in his lap, he touched a hand.

He glanced quickly over at Andrea, wondering if she would do anything so sophomoric as grope him at a dinner party. But he realized at once that the distance between them was far too great.

"Everyone's certainly very dull tonight," Algernon said, as the phantom fingers unzippered his fly.

"No pressure," Andrea said smiling. "Good food was meant to be enjoyed. Talk is superfluous. I think you'll all love the next course."

"What is it?" Rolf Orlovsky managed, as clever hands sprung free his erection, and he felt the first deft maneuverings of a warm, considerate tongue. Expert fingers gently massaged his scrotum.

"I don't want to spoil it by telling," Andrea said, and rang her little silver bell. "Enjoy."

The most remarkable thing, to Andrea, was the blankness of all their faces. Not one of the guests gave any sign that there was anything the least unusual going on, except for their silence. Dainty Lee got quite flushed during the fish dish, and almost toppled the bottle of wine the butler poured.

"Excuse me," Dainty Lee said, with more emotion than the situation warranted, and cheeks flaming, got up from the and fled the room.

For a moment, Andrea was afraid the party would be

spoiled. It had been a mistake to invite her, not knowing her well. Dainty Lee might make a priggish scene, or tell the others, when the whole game was meant to be everybody sitting there not saying a word, thinking they were the only ones it was being done to.

But Andrea's fears were unfounded. Dainty Lee returned in time for the crown roast. Andrea could see from the line of her gown that Dainty Lee's abrupt departure had been only for the purpose of removing her girdle. She settled in again, revitalized, eager, at her place.

"It doesn't look like anybody's eating very much, except me," Andrea said. "Aren't you enjoying it?" she smiled at Chet.

He nodded, glazed.

"And you, Mr. Orlovsky?"

"Lovely," he whispered hoarsely. "Lovely."

"It's what I always said," Andrea bit onto the tines of her silver fork. "There's nothing better than a good meal served in attractive surroundings, and eaten in precisely the right manner."

"Oh God," Dainty Lee moaned.

"How nice," said Andrea. "Sincere appreciation."

"There's just one thing," Dainty Lee said, following Andrea into the powder room. "Were they men or women? Under there, I mean."

"Why, my dear," Andrea turned to her, and lifted a strand of red-streaked chestnut hair off the glossy face. "What difference does it make?"

They did not return to the hotel until after four in the morning. On the boat ride back, Algernon let Maggie nestle her face into his neck, and he patted her golden shining hair, and cradled her shoulders from the wind.

"I love you," Maggie said.

"And I love you. Who wouldn't love you. Seeking angel face. You will make him a very happy man. Your child will have a beautiful home."

"Oh," Maggie said. "You still want me to marry George."

The wedding went off as beautifully as all the guests, and several magazines, had anticipated. To supplement the natural red and white floral beds of the courtyard, huge baskets of yellow flowers were piled up all along the path etched in the garden for the bride. Six bridesmaids, halves of golden couples, all in yellow, all with the same high foreheads and early sun-browned high cheekbones, all with their hair pulled back from noble brows and held with tight bands of stephanotis, ringed the bride and groom like pastel fairy godmothers.

The Right Reverend Dwight Mulholland flew in by seaplane to perform the ceremony. Maggie had wanted Algernon to officiate, but Algernon questioned the validity of such a ceremony in certain parts of America, until the new religion was made official by Congress. So Mulholland, who was giving the official benediction for the Florida Kiwanis convention, had arranged to come in from Miami.

Julia White and Rick Flinders took a great many color pictures of the ceremony. A free-lance photographer for *Vogue* and *Town and Country,* who had not been officially invited but was not asked to leave, took constant pictures of the guests, who asked for copies if any turned out especially well.

After the champagne brunch wedding guests were left on their own. Most of them went down to the beach to begin their weekend tan. Bunyan Reis, with a small portable pallet of oils, painted Julia White's bellybutton into an eye. Diane Trejinska arranged to go waterskiing with the two boys recommended by Sylvia Kranet. Others hired fishing boats, though it was clearly much too late in the day to expect to catch anything good.

In the evening, people dined with their own particular friends, wherever they chose. Some went back to the Martinique, some to he Bahamian Club, and some just had sandwiches sent up to their rooms before going over to try their luck at the casino.

Rolf Orlovsky avoided Andre Sherman.

Louise did a lengthy interview over dinner with Rick Flinders, so she would not have to be concerned about Wednesday's column (Monday's, already air-mailed, special-delivered to New York, was all about the wedding). Rick seemed a little preoccupied, but when she asked him if he was upset about anything, he said he wasn't going to start with all that Actor's Studio garbage about inner conflicts, that wasn't his bag, and why didn't they just talk about his new picture, and afterward, if she behaved herself, maybe they could fool around.

There were four bottles of champagne in the bridal suite. By eight thirty that evening, Maggie had consumed three of them, along with a little something Algernon had slipped to her the last minute, just in case.

At nine forty-five she came dancing out onto the balcony of their room, naked, shuddering at the stars. She threw her body in cataclysmic starts, and screamed something about Acapulco. George managed to get her inside, before anyone saw, except the boogaloo band that was playing on the patio below.

And she received her groom.

BOOK 3

CHAPTER ONE

IN a curious way, Louise was looking forward to meeting Miriam Bell. At first, when Ron Abbate had called Louise to tell her Harry Bell's mother was coming to New York, and had agreed to meet with her, Louise was slightly discomfited. But the more she thought about it, the more the prospect amused her: to keep up the masquerade for a doddering old lady (how old was she?—she would have to be in her eighties at least) would be infinitely simpler than fooling the chic members of the In crowd. Other people's mothers had always loved her. Other people's mothers would chuck her under the chin as late as her thirty-second year, remarking on the prettiness of her face, the sweetness of her smile, the astonishing clarity of her complexion. Every fairly nice boy she had ever dated had provided a mother who became Louise's champion, starting with Eddie, and ending up with—Harry Bell? Well, why not? It was conceivable that at some point in his life even Harry had been a nice Jewish boy. Undoubtedly he had the typical Old World mother. There was no way Louise could fail to win her. She began visualizing their meeting as the recognition scene from *Anastasia*, with different accents.

"I don't suppose you saw that either," she said to Dr. Ehrens. She had begun seeing him again, erratically, when she could work him into her schedule in between parties and her questionable contentment with Charley. Mostly she saw Ehrens because she wanted to be told it was all right having her cake and eating it too, and he never came out and said she was doing anything wrong. "Naturally I don't think of myself for a minute as Ingrid Bergman, she's much too long and lovely with that bone structure, but then the old lady won't exactly be Helen Hayes, will she? Probably a shriveled Molly Picon, but I can handle that in a minute."

"Why would you want to?" Dr. Ehrens said.

"Well, why not? It's the least I owe Harry, trying to get this thing settled."

"Why?"

"I don't want to go into it. We were a lot closer than I ever let on, even to you. Let's not discuss it. I didn't tell you when I started to see him again because I didn't want to look foolish in case it didn't work out. And then when it started to, you were on vacation. Will you buy that?"

"Do you want me to?"

"I don't want you to do anything but start going to the movies," Louise said. "Anyway, I'm going to meet Harry's mother next week. It ought to be amusing."

"Haven't you got enough in your life to amuse you?"

"I don't know," Louise said.

Actually, she did. It frightened her sometimes how much real and imagined happiness she had in her life. She had worked out what she considered to be a brilliant compromise, not committing herself completely to Charley, but not exactly hiding him either. He had his own phone in the apartment, and his own answering service, so that no one calling her would know he was actually living there. His name was not on the mailbox, but he was allowed to have letters sent care of her, so the doormen knew, but she didn't mind that. To especially close friends like Diane she let it be known that she was seeing somebody, but it was nothing crucial, so if they wanted Cary Grant to be her dinner partner they could go ahead and invite him. (Tee hee.) When the parties were large enough, and the theatrical openings were fairly unspectacular, she would take him as her escort. It always surprised her how good he looked, and how secure she felt with him holding her arm, even when they saw people like Bunyan Reis, who seemed to find Charley charming, but always had to be reintroduced. The rest of the time she excused herself to Charley, cuddling him with her little-girl voice, explaining that it was business: she was, after all, writing a column.

"It's all right, sweetheart," Charley said, stretching out his long legs. "There are some places I'd just as soon go without you."

"There are?" she said, vaguely alarmed.

"Of course there are. We're both grown-up people, aren't we? I have interviews to go on, I have to meet agency people for drinks, I can't always drag you along with me just because I like to see your shiny little face. You understand."

"Of course," she said, surprised at how upset she felt. "So it all works out very well, doesn't it?"

"It does," he said, and kissed her.

"You understand," she said, a little later. "It doesn't have anything to do with my not wanting to take you. Bunyan said I could take you anywhere."

"Well, doesn't that make me just terrific."

"You don't like Bunyan? He's crazy about you."

"Even though he can't remember my name?"

"You mustn't be offended. He's a little feather-brained, that's all."

"I'm not offended," he said. "I understand. Char-Ley. It does kind of slip off your tongue. Not an easy name to get hold of like Diane Tre-jin-ska and Rolf Or-lov-sky."

"You don't like them?"

"What's not to like? They're all very rich, attractive people. And Bunyan is a pussycat. If I had a big enough den I'd stuff him and pin him to my wall. He'd love that. Especially if I did it hard enough."

"You're terrible." She laughed, and kissed him. "But I love you."

"Don't say anything you'll be sorry for," Charley said.

Sometimes, when she would return from a party where she had gone alone, she would loathe Charley for being in the apartment waiting for her, and wonder if he really did have the spine she thought he had. A few times when she came back, he wasn't there at all, and she worried about his having too much spine. Once she stayed up until four o'clock in the morning, with the lights out, and didn't even pretend to be sleeping when he got into bed beside her.

"Were you with Kate and David?" she said.

"No," he answered.

She waited, but he said nothing else. "Where were you?"

He let it hang on the air, so she heard how foolish and hagridden it sounded. "I'm not trying to check on you, Charley, it's just that I was worried."

"There's no need to worry," he said. "I'm a big boy."

She reached for him across the coolness of sheets, but he moved her hand away. "I'm tired," he said.

"I've never been unfaithful to you," she said.

"That's nice."

"Well, I haven't. I'm only doing my job. There are places I have to be where I can't always take you, but I haven't gone to bed with anyone else since we were together."

"Okay," he said. "I believe you."

She scuttled tentatively down under the covers, and brought her face slowly across to his belly, and let her lips roam across the smoothness there. He stopped the movement of her head with a firm hand.

"I want to make love to you," she said.

"No you don't. You want to check if I was with another girl."

"Were you?"

"No."

All the same she kept at it until he responded, so she could be sure. Even after it was over, and as good as it always was,

347

she wondered if she had proved anything, or if he wasn't enough man to be with two different girls in one night.

"Am I woman enough for you?" she said.

"In bed?"

"All right. In bed."

"In bed, yes."

"And in other ways?"

"Some other ways."

"What other ways?"

"Oh come on, Lou. It's five o'clock in the morning. I have an interview at ten."

"But in other ways? Am I getting there or what?"

"Well, you're fighting getting there, but I think you'll get there."

"If it's so unsatisfactory for you, why do you stay?"

"I didn't say it was unsatisfactory."

"You're happy with me?"

"Most of the time, yes."

"And the rest of the time?"

"I have to go to sleep," Charley said. "We'll talk about it tomorrow."

"We have a cocktail party tomorrow at Hanover Slade's, for Senator Kranet."

"Okay," Charley said.

"You can make it? You don't have any other plans?"

"Nothing I can't get out of," Charley said.

"Oh. I see."

"Good night, butterball," he said, and kissed her.

They divided the time that was just their own, when neither of them had any obligation to be anywhere, between quiet evenings alone at home, and going out to a movie or dinner with Kate and David. The evenings alone were increasingly pleasurable to Louise, who was gradually starting to feel under no obligation to be bright and amusing. He insisted she always have her hair done, because he liked her better when she felt good about herself, and she felt better when she looked pretty. But she didn't have to get dressed. The two of them wandered around half-naked and relaxed, while they took turns cooking dinner, which they sometimes took directly to the bedroom on trays. When she really wanted him badly she usually put a robe on over her brassiere and panties, because he still looked prettier in his underwear than she did, even though his tan by now was quite faded. After dinner they would watch television, or talk, until it was time. They no longer felt obligated to make daily love, although she usually felt better about herself when they did, because it gave her a sense of accomplishment, and meant the day hadn't been wasted.

They quarreled a little, usually on nights when they had been with Kate and David. Louise had noted in Kate an increasing irritability, a tendency to be short with David, especially when he showed too obvious a curiosity about the people Louise had been seeing. Louise made little jokes and called them the Bickersons, and that would embarrass them into silence, to Louise's great relief. Not that she really believed they weren't happy with each other. A little quarreling didn't mean that people were unhappy. She was fonder of Kate than she was of David, as most people had to be; but he had made Kate happy, so Louise had to be fond of him for that.

"I mean, a little quarreling doesn't mean people aren't happy with each other, does it?" she said to Dr. Ehrens. "Charley and I quarrel, but we care about each other, we really do."

"Why do you suppose you and Charley quarrel mostly after being with David and Kate?" Dr. Ehrens said.

"You don't have to point that out to me, I've already pointed it out to you. It's perfectly obvious to me, so you don't get extra points for being perceptive. If they weren't really happy together it would be a threat to me and Charley, wouldn't it?"

"Would it?"

"I hope you don't think I'm as simple-minded as that. We're not the same people. I'm not Kate, and David certainly isn't Charley. Besides which, I don't have to do anything so melodramatic as make a choice, do I? It isn't domesticity versus the gay life. Things aren't that black and white, not in real life. I have the best of both possible worlds. Nobody's asking me to give up one or the other."

"Do you want somebody to?"

"Real life isn't such desperate alternatives," Louise said. "Desperate alternatives are in movies, and you wouldn't know about that, having never seen one." She chewed on her lip. "Do you think he'd want to marry me?"

"I don't know."

"Well, I'm certainly not going to ask him."

"Why not?"

"Girls aren't supposed to do that. What if he said no?"

"What if he said yes?" Dr. Ehrens said.

"Oh. Then you mean I'd have to decide."

"That's what usually happens."

"Do you think he loves me?"

"I don't know," Dr. Ehrens said. "I don't know him."

"He certainly acts as if he loves me. But why shouldn't he? He has it very cozy, living in my apartment, eating my food. Oh sure, he grocery-shops when I'm too busy, and buys me presents, but why shouldn't he, he has it very easy. He doesn't have to spend a nickel on living expenses, does he, and he's going to get more than twenty thousand for the commercials he's done already."

"Then he doesn't really need your apartment, does he?"

"Oh," Louise said. "But it's a very unsure business, that spokesman kind of thing. They could get bored with him or he could supersaturate with that big deep voice and he'd be out of work tomorrow, and then where would he be?"

"In your apartment?"

"You agree with me then, that he's using me."

"I didn't say that."

"I really think he loves me," Louise said. "I really do. The charming and articulate Harry Bell said there was no way to fake a hard-on. Is there?"

"Not that I know of."

"Of course you haven't known many gigolos or male whores."

"Do you think that's what Charley is?"

"Of course not," Louise said. "I know better than that." She sat up on the couch and looked at him. "I do wish you'd wear longer socks, it's very upsetting when you cross your knee like that and your calf shows."

"Why?"

"You don't have to wax all analytical about it, it's just tacky, that's all. I like you well enough to tell you. If my slip was showing at an elegant party I'd expect you to tell me."

"You want me to tell you you shouldn't take Charley to a party?"

"Oh come on. That's too silly. As anxious as I am to have you make a direct statement, I didn't expect it to be so moronically pat. It isn't like that at all, I told you. It isn't a question of choices. I'm not doing anything wrong, am I? I mean, there's nothing wrong with enjoying him for what he is, and still doing the rest of it without him, is there? Please. Tell me. It's not as if I were having two affairs at the same time."

"What if you were?"

"You think that would be all right?"

"I think if you've been very cold for a long time, and you can finally afford a good coat, there's no harm in trying on a few before you pick out the one you want most."

"Well, thank you for that," Louise said. "That's really very kind. Finally almost saying something direct, I mean. But you're wrong, you know. I don't have to make a choice."

"All right."

"But I don't. Really. Bunyan Reis said I could take him anywhere."

"Did you tell Charley that?"

"Of course," Louise said. "I don't know why he was so offended."

The day Maggie returned from her honeymoon, she started shopping for maternity clothes. It was a little difficult to fit in, what with all the excitement about moving into Harry's house. Details of the move itself had been difficult to work out. Because of the quarrel over Harry's estate, between the family and Harry's own executors, there had been some doubt up to the last moment as to whether or not the sale would go through. But Maggie finally offered a price so high that neither party could object to it. Her attorneys placed a half million dollars in escrow for the purchase, and Ron Abbate, representing the estate, arranged for all furnishings, paintings, miscellaneous works of art, tapestries and carpetings to be placed in storage until details for their disposal, at auction or through private sale, could be arranged. The only thing that Maggie demanded remain in the house were the built-in bookcases, the chandeliers and the equipment in Harry's private gymnasium, next to the master bath, and the sauna.

The last she had done as a surprise present for George. About the third day of their honeymoon, when the pressure on her eyes had begun to lift a little, and she could see how sweet and attentive he was really trying to be, they had begun to talk a little of the future. For a long time he had considered going into heart research, he told her, and if he could manage to get all the proper equipment, was considering opening a private clinic. Naturally the latest, most advanced equipment was outrageously expensive, and just as naturally, he was quick to tell her, he had no intention of allowing her to get it for him. But they had so many new and good friends, all of whom were concerned with prolonged life, like Rolf Orlovsky and the Count Trejinska, that raising the money should be no problem. He had, however, made no definite decision that heart research was what he should choose. He was also fascinated with the problem of overweight, and thought that there was much room in New York for a spa, on the order of the one in Palm Beach, or the Rice Institute at Duke University, where patients were put on a diet and at the same time were provided with some sort of healthful activity, possibly even exercise. All of this they discussed as he drank his morning juice in the honeymoon suite.

"That all sounds wonderful," Maggie said, rolling over on her stomach, so her breasts pressed into the floral pattern of the chaise. "You're going to be a very important man."

"Naturally there wouldn't be live-in facilities at the spa, not if we had it in the middle of Manhattan."

"Naturally."

"But I think if you let people spend the day there, and take their meals, and have some sort of a workout, and a steam, and you put them on their honor for the evening, they can go to the theater or opera or a movie, or even home without cheating on their diets."

"It certainly sounds reasonable," Maggie said, watching the points of her breasts being swallowed into the center of an aquamarine rose.

"The same holds true for a heart clinic. You can run your tests, and put people on a program, and then, warning them, of course, according to the serious nature of their potential illnesses, put them on their honor to take bed rest, and not to drink too much or take in cholesterol. It isn't so hard, really. A man can have champagne and caviar in moderation, and still have a healthy heart, if he restricts himself to plain caviar, and skips the eggs and sour cream."

"I prefer it plain, myself."

"Then you'll never have a heart attack," George said. "Or, even if you do, with today's advanced equipment we could prolong your life by twenty years, maybe even more, depending on the seriousness of the attack. The equipment is really astounding, Maggie. I could show you pamphlets . . ."

"I'd love to see them."

"Naturally I wouldn't expect or want you to get any of the equipment for me."

"But I'd want to, George."

"I appreciate that, but I just couldn't let you, Maggie."

"That's so sweet, George. Really I'd want to, but it's just as well you have other people to go to, because I doubt very much that the administrators of my trust would let me touch another penny, not after I bought the house, and with all the money I spent on the wedding and all. We'll probably have barely enough to live on for the next year."

"They couldn't do that," George set down his orange juice, and wiped his mouth slowly with the pink linen napkin. "Not to you, surely. Not that I'd let you spend another penny, and certainly not on my clinic, but they couldn't *really* keep your cash from you, could they? Not all that cash."

"Oh yes," Maggie said. "Oh yes, they could."

"Not really," said George. "That hardly seems possible. After all, you're a big girl now. You're a married woman."

"Well, that means the property falls to me, all the actual physical property I own, according to the terms of the estate, falls to me when I get married. So I can do whatever I want with the Function Center, you see, I can give it to Nonny irrevocably, and they're powerless to do anything about it, and that's why I could get away with the house, yes? We have to have someplace to live, so I talked them into letting me buy it, and it became my property, what? So that much is irrevocable, wasn't that clever of me, Georgio?"

"Very clever," he said. "Is that all the property you own?"

"Well, there's a few hundred acres in western Pennsylvania but I've always hated that part of the country, haven't you, it's so madly . . . country, what would I do with it, anyway, so that's why I decided to turn it over to Essex, my grandfather went there. Not that I love the university less, but that I hate the country more, yes? Besides, it made a good tax deduction, so my executors explained to me."

"You generous thing. I wouldn't take that equipment from you if you begged me."

She turned over on her back and touched the top of his head, as he kissed her navel. "I wish I could beg you, Georgio, but I'm not in that position."

"I'm glad," he said, and nuzzled his head against her breast. "What about the property near Deal, you ought to be able to pick up a pretty penny with that, it's good property, that part of Jersey."

"But I promised it to Algernon, you know that. I couldn't go back on a promise."

"No. No, I suppose not. Well, you won't have to worry about a thing, Mag, I'll take care of you. A man could make a lot of money with a spa in the middle of New York. Of course, there might be a little bit of a problem, without the proper equipment."

"I'm sure you'll get it," Maggie said. "It's such a madly brilliant idea, you ought to be able to get all kinds of support."

"Thank you, Mag. You're a great encouragement to me. And I know it's all going to work out beautifully."

"We'll manage," she said. "Very nicely, what? And then of course, there's the money that comes due when I'm thirty-five."

"Let's not even think about that," George said, and kissed her between her breasts. "After all, that's not so far away, is it?"

"A year," she said.

"A year," he said.

"But of course, there's the other thing," she said, and her voice became a whisper.

"Other thing?"

"There's the trust that comes due when I have my first child."

"Do you want a child?" George said. "I love children."

"That's good. Because we've already got one."

"What do you mean?"

"You're not very observant for a doctor, are you, Georgio? Haven't you noticed my breasts?"

"How could I help it?" he said, and rubbed his nose back and forth against her nipples.

"I mean, they're even bigger than before, George, haven't you seen? And haven't you heard me in the mornings? I mean I know I try to cover it up with running the shower, and you're madly sweet about pretending not to listen, but you know I've been being sick."

"I thought it was the tension and the anxiety," George said, and hugged her to him. "You're going to have a baby, Maggie, that's wonderful, just wonderful. How far along?"

"About three months."

He pulled his head away and looked past her gray-blue eyes. Then his own glance came back into focus, and he smiled. "But that's when we first met, when we were first together."

"Exactly."

"Then it's mine!" George said, and hugged her even closer, rubbing her back in hard-palmed circles.

"Well of course it's yours, did you think I would make a baby and marry you if it wasn't yours, what a terrible thing to say, George, how could you say anything like that."

"I didn't say that," George said. "You're mixing up what I said."

"You said it was wonderful that I was having a baby. You said that and you didn't even know that it was yours." She looked at him accusingly. "What kind of a woman do you think I am."

"A wonderful woman, a darling woman."

"Why didn't you scream at me if you thought for a moment that it wasn't yours, how could you think it was wonderful if it wasn't yours."

"You're my wife! What was I supposed to say? I told you, I love children, and I love you. So I said it was wonderful, that's all. And it's mine. That's even better."

"All right," Maggie said. "Then I forgive you."

He took her into the bedroom and started making love, and she closed her eyes and tried to pretend it was Algernon.

But there was too much light in the room, even with the backing on the drapes. She stopped the movement of his hand, and asked him to tell her some more about the clinic. The heart clinic, and the fat clinic, as George called it. Either one would be easy to set up, once he had the equipment, which he knew wouldn't be a problem. He told her that several times.

"That's what I really want to do, is the clinic," he said. "For a while, anyway. Till things are really, well, secure, you might say. Then maybe I'll go into something else."

"Like what?" Maggie said.

"I'm not sure," said George. "I've been seriously thinking of giving up medicine and devoting myself to studying the piano."

"That's nice," Maggie said.

"You're nice," he said, and started tracing his fingers along the milky inside of her thigh.

"No. No, don't."

"Don't you want to?"

"I want to very much," Maggie said, getting up from the bed. "But I have to throw up."

"I want you to go to the best man in Manhattan," George said, when she came out of the bathroom. "There are a lot of good ones, but I want you to have the best. Not that there will be any problems. Childbirth nowadays is as simple as pissing into a hole."

"As simple as that," said Maggie. "Imagine."

"But there's no point in taking any chances. I want you to see the best man in Manhattan, the minute you get back."

"All right," Maggie said. "All right, the minute we get back."

"Come here," George said, and held out his long, fair arms.

She started toward him, and then the nausea seized her, and she darted toward the bathroom.

"Again?" George said.

"I shouldn't have had the juice," she said, as she closed the door.

Kate had left several phone messages for Maggie, at David's urging. Now that she was settled and married, David said, Maggie would have even more in common with Kate, so there was no reason they shouldn't spend time together, the four of them.

Thursday afternoon the doorbell rang. When Kate opened the door, Maggie was leaning against the corridor wall. She was bundled in lynx, her high Cossack fur hat at a jaunty angle above her still tanned temples. But her face, against the fur, beneath the tan, was curiously pale.

"Maggie," Kate said. "Come in. How was the honeymoon? Are you feeling all right?"

"I'm fine, I never felt better, except for the queasies, but you had those, didn't you, it's just par for the heavenly course, yes?" She threw herself down on the sofa, her high tan leather boots hanging over the edge of the couch, and pulled the fur tighter around herself. "You were darling to leave all those messages. I would have called to tell you I was coming, but I didn't know I was, what? Do you mind? I'm totally bushed, how's the babe?"

"She's shaping up. How was the honeymoon?"

"Can I see her? Is she doing anything exceptional, or is she exceptional enough, just being a baby?"

"She's having her bath. You can see her in a minute. How's George?"

"In an absolute whirl of activity, we've taken over Harry Bell's house, you know, and he's started a kind of spa, you might call it, a program for general health and the slims. I've got Harry's whole gymnasium still in the house."

Maggie went into Kate's bedroom and opened the closet door, as Kate followed.

"Where did you get your maternity clothes? I haven't been able to find anything without a bow over the belly."

"You want to borrow my old dresses?"

"Oh, could I, Kate, that would be heaven, I never would have asked, but they are dreary, all the clothes I've seen. I'll make it up to you, I swear, I'll get something wonderful for the baby." She flopped on the bed, clapping and hooting as Kate pulled dresses from the back of the closet. "Oh pretty, you are clever, Kate, how did you find that, you always were the tasteful one."

"Some of them might be a little too summery," Kate said.

"No, how? I'll still be pregnant in summer, yes?"

"When's your due date?"

"Oh, sometime in June or July, I would imagine."

"Your doctor didn't give you a definite date yet?" Kate looked at Maggie carefully. "Maggie, you are going to a doctor? I mean a medical doctor."

"Oh tish, of course I'll go, I just haven't been yet, I have been a little busy, getting married and all, and trying to furnish the house. It's empty, you know, just my old bedroom furniture and George's office stuff, and the gym. I must start going to auctions and looking for sofas and things."

"Is George taking care of you?"

"I wouldn't let him examine me, darling, it would kill the

romance, have to keep the illusion alive, yes? But I'm fine. As soon as I have a minute I'll go to someone."

"Who are you going to use?"

"Wilcox, I suppose, he's been in the family for years, he's taking care of my mother, she has uterine cancer."

"I'm so sorry."

"So am I," Maggie said. "But life must go on. Is the baby finished, do you think?"

"Maybe you shouldn't use Wilcox, if it has an unpleasant association." Kate started along the corridor to the baby's room, Maggie at her heels, darting and giggling, like a furry child. "Why don't you go to my OB? Matthew Rady. He's wonderful."

"I've been to him, darling. I hated his guts. Nothing personal, you understand, he just isn't for me. Oh, look. Oh, look. Just look at her."

The baby, warm and pink from the bath, lay on top of the basinette, half out of a large blue towel with which Mrs. Hanner was rubbing her. Her legs kicked toward the ceiling, her arms reached out from the towel.

"Oh please," Maggie said. "Let me hold her." She grabbed the baby up with the towel, and held it tight against her. "Isn't she lovely. Oh what a sweet girl."

"She isn't diapered," Kate said. "She might pee on you."

"Who cares," Maggie said, and laughed. "And she wouldn't, not on me, oh look, Kate, look, she's laughing, she loves me, she's a real girl, she loves the fur, that's it, I'm her furry godmother."

"Mrs. Hanner," Kate said. "You know our friend Miss Bolin."

"Of course," Mrs. Hanner said. "How are you?"

"I'm sorry," Kate said. "I mean Mrs. Piner. Forgive me, Mag."

"For what, dear?" Maggie said, and held the baby a little away from herself, and laughed into the red-cheeked face. "All that love. All that pure love."

"Mrs. Piner is expecting a baby too, Mrs. Hanner."

"How nice. When is that?"

"Summer," Maggie said, crooning against the naked chest.

"Maybe you could talk Mrs. Hanner into taking care of your baby, Maggie. If we can ever bring ourselves to let her go."

"Oh no," Maggie said. "Oh no. I'm sure you're a wonderful nurse, Mrs. Hanner, but nobody's going to lay a finger on my baby but me. I want to do everything. Everything."

"You'll be sorry," Kate said. "They're a lot of trouble in

357

the beginning, especially. It isn't a game, Maggie. They require constant attention."

"I know," she murmured into the baby's flossy hair. "Constant attention. Isn't that a wonderful thing."

On the way home, Maggie danced. Her arms were full of maternity clothes, but she still managed to dance. She waltzed in Kate's elevator to the electronic beat of the Muzak that serenaded her in between floors, and when a little boy got on at seven and stared at her all the way down to street level, she smiled at him, and said: "Well if they didn't expect you to dance, why would they make music?"

There was no radio in the taxi. So she hummed to herself, and clacked the wooden heels of her boots against the jump seat in front of her, doing the time step she had learned as a child at Barclay's dance studio, where she wasn't sure she would send her daughter. She was almost sure now that it would be a girl. A pink and white and yellow girl.

When she arrived at the front door of the town house and climbed the four steps up from Fifth Avenue, she fumbled in her pocketbook, the dresses pressed beneath her chin. But she could not see over the clothes. She had lost her gloves, and her fingers were cold in the December day; she could not feel metal. She leaned against the bell with her right shoulder, thinking perhaps George was finished his appointments for the day. She was only a little surprised when Wendy opened the door.

"I thought you'd gone back to Canada," Maggie said, with no trace of malice. "George said he was going to have to find a new receptionist. And I knew how long you'd been together, so I was sad for him, what? What made you decide to come back?"

"I missed New York," Wendy said, and reached for the clothes in Maggie's arms. Wendy's dark hair was piled in a coronet above her head, and her remarkable breasts strained the sterile whiteness of the uniform.

"You can just put those in the master bedroom closet, if you would. It's on the second floor behind . . ."

"Oh I know," Wendy said, starting up the stairs. "I know this house quite well. I used to come here all the time."

"Well how nice," Maggie said. "Then you must try to feel at home here."

"That's very kind of you, Mrs. Piner."

"Not at all, Wendy. Anyone who worked with George all these years is entitled to feel one of the family, yes? So I insist you make yourself comfortable. Of course it might be a bit difficult with so little furniture, but I'm sure you'll manage."

"I'm sure I will," Wendy said, and walked down the corridor toward the master bedroom.

Outside George's office, Harry's old second-floor study, two patients were still waiting, reading back issue magazines that George had brought over from the old office, along with the black bench they were sitting on. The first was an older woman Maggie had never seen before; the second, Harold Rankin, who was wearing a tuxedo in readiness for the opening, that evening, of his new musical.

She greeted him warmly, and found out that he had put on a few pounds, because of the aggravation in Boston. Dr. George had promised to get it off in a couple of days, provided Harold checked with him about what to eat after the opening, and took his shot. She wished him good luck with the opening, and he wished her belated congratulations on her marriage. Then she went to the bedroom to lie down.

It was twenty-five minutes before George came back to the bedroom. By that time it was getting late, and he was afraid they might have trouble getting a cab, and might be late for the opening. Especially if they didn't hurry up and get dressed.

"I don't mean to rush you, dear," George said. "But hadn't you better change."

"I need to rest a few minutes." Maggie stretched her neck back, and let her head fall slightly over the side of the bed. "I've had a madly hectic day."

"Did you go to the doctor?" He was half in the closet, looking for a fresh dress shirt.

"I told you I'd go the first free moment I had, why are you checking up on me, George?"

"I saw Wilcox at the hospital this afternoon. He said you hadn't even called him."

"I decided to use Matthew Rady. Kate Waller's doctor."

"And what did he say. Is everything fine?"

"Everything's perfect. I'm healthy as a horse."

"What made you decide not to use Wilcox?"

"It's got an unpleasant association. He's an old man, and he's ushering my mother into death. I don't want him to usher me into death. Any objections?"

"I can understand that," George slipped out of his shirt, and sprayed under his arms with an aerosol deodorant before putting his dress shirt on. "If you're happy with Rady . . ."

"I'm very happy."

"I've heard he's a good man. Naturally he doesn't have the important practice that some of the East Side OB-GYN people have, but then, of course, he's young. He delivers at New

York Hospital, doesn't he? I don't know him myself, but I hear good things about him."

"Then we don't have anything to worry about, do we?"

"I guess I can make a few calls in the morning, and check him out, and then I'll call him direct, and see how everything is."

"I told you how everything was," Maggie said, sitting up. "Dammit, George, everything's fine, and I'm fine, how dare you start checking on me, I'm not a child."

"I'm not checking on you, Maggie. I'm a doctor."

"Don't you think I know that, for God's sake, I know you're a doctor, you don't have to start showing off to me that you're a doctor.

"How do you think he'll treat me with you looking over his shoulder? Other husbands don't call their wife's obstetrician, George, they stay out of it, they're happy to stay out of it until after the delivery, is that what you intend to do, to come into the delivery room and poke your head in there, too?"

"I haven't got privileges at New York Hospital," George said. "I do at Doctors'."

"And I expect you'd like me to have my child there, so you could give cocktail parties."

"I'm satisfied for you to have the baby at New York."

"Well that's very generous of you," Maggie said, and lay back down on the satin pillow.

"I didn't mean to upset you." He came over to the bed, his bow tie hanging open around his shirt collar. "There's no need to get worked up about it, Maggie."

"I won't be treated like a child." She turned her head away as he reached out to touch her cheek. "I'm perfectly capable of choosing my own doctor, who is perfectly capable of delivering my baby, with no interference from you."

"I won't interfere," George said. "I promise."

"And you won't call him?"

"I'd just like to telephone and introduce myself so he knows I'm your husband, and a doctor."

"He already knows that, George. He recognized your name the minute I told him."

"Really?" George said. "He knew who I was?"

"Of course," Maggie said. "That's why I wouldn't want him to be resentful that you had any reservations at all about his taking care of me."

"But I don't."

"Then don't call him," Maggie said.

"All right." He leaned over and kissed her cheek. "If you tie my tie."

"I'm not good at those things. Why don't you ask Wendy, is she still here?"

"Well yes, I suppose she's inside, cleaning up."

"She certainly is handy to have around," Maggie said. "She hung up my clothes and everything, we certainly are lucky she decided to come back from Canada, it's so hard nowadays to find any kind of decent help. It must be twice as hard to dig up someone with medical training, especially anyone attractive."

"You don't mind her working for me, do you, Maggie?"

"Not at all," Maggie said. "I thought she was gone for good, giving up her apartment and everything when she went back to Canada, where is she staying?"

"At the Winslow, I think. Chet Oppenheim is trying to find her an apartment, but I think she's temporarily at the Winslow."

"Well that's silly, that's just plain silly, when we have all this space. Why doesn't she just move in here? It would be madly convenient for the clinic, don't you think?"

"You're so generous," he said. "But it really isn't necessary. After all, it is your house."

"Our house." Maggie smiled. "And Harry's. Did Wendy know Harry? She said something madly provocative about being here many times."

"She knew Harry very well. Very well. As a matter of fact, that's how I met Harry, through her."

"Imagine," Maggie said. "Then we really do owe her a great deal. I insist on it. Let her move into one of the upstairs rooms."

"You're being too kind."

"Oh, I don't think so. I think it's just being practical, what?"

"It certainly would make everything easier for my practice. Especially if we move ahead with a full program for the spa."

"Well that's what I want to do, Georgio, is make everything easier, for the spa."

"We don't even have an extra bed."

"I'll call Hertz," Maggie said, and laughed. "Go ahead. Tell her, and have her fix your tie."

"And while I'm gone, you get dressed."

"Oh I don't think so," Maggie said. "I'm madly weary, and I'm sure all my long dresses will be much too tight on me, and I haven't got a maternity evening. Maybe they would fit Wendy, one of my regular gowns, I mean, do you think she'd mind going to the opening in my place?"

"If you don't feel well enough to go, I'll stay home with you."

"Oh I feel well," Maggie said, and caressed his ear with long slender fingers. "I feel wonderfully well, I'm just tired, that's normal isn't it, all the books say it's perfectly normal."

"Well yes, but . . ."

"No buts," she said. "You run along and tell Wendy."

"It wouldn't look right," George said. "How would it look, with us married less than three weeks, and my going to the opening with somebody else. Wendy."

"What do we care how it looks, darling." She sat up, and for the first time since the beginning of the honeymoon, kissed him on the lips without feeling fear or anxiety or the vague sickness that had oppressed her. She felt nothing except his lips.

"We don't have to care how anything looks, or what anybody thinks, what? Because we know how we really feel about each other, don't we?"

And George was moved to agree.

"People tend to think of me as papier-mâché," Rick Flinders said, settling himself more firmly inside his cocoa brown Nehru jacket. "Because of the movies I've done, because of the image the columnists have given me. Papier-mâché profile, and papier-mâché balls."

"I must say I've never thought that," said Bunyan Reis, setting down his glue. "Certainly not the last." He stood by the easel of his latest collage, a depiction of Maggie's wedding, done from snips and scraps of the bridesmaids' gowns, which some of them had been kind enough to let him cut from beneath the hems, a few faded tropical flowers and a stuffed tiny tropical bird in brilliant blue. The collage was set up in the corner of Bunyan's studio, a high-ceilinged, glass-encased room on the roof of the penthouse Bunyan shared with his secretary, a nineteen-year-old boy from Spoleto, where Bunyan had been exhibited in two Festivals. Because of the glass, the studio had somewhat the same atmosphere as a hothouse, so often in the midst of winter it was necessary to have the air-conditioning on, as it was now. Vague whirrings punctuated his conversation with Rick, at the same time that the mechanical breeze served to whisk away the smell of glue.

"But they do. Papier-mâché," Rick said. "And anyone that I try to show that I am a person, that I am flesh and blood, I end up offending them."

"Not me," said Bunyan. "You've never offended me. Except before I got to know you, perhaps a little, but that was because you were so perfect. Perfect does rather turn one off unless one is participating in the perfection. Hmm?"

"I am flesh and blood, that's the hell of it, Bun."

"Please. Bunyan. As much as I am coming to know and love you, I will not abide the foreshortening of my name, unless it's in England, where the abbreviation is a little kicky. Hmm?"

"We should have become friends a long time ago," Rick said, crossing his left ankle over his right knee, the cocoa pants tightening across his firm, slightly rounded buttocks. "Then maybe I wouldn't be in all this trouble now."

"Trouble?" Bunyan said, and set aside the pasty brush, lifting a flap of yellow organza from his fingers. "What trouble could you be in, a tall perfect boy like you?" He tried not to talk too quickly, for fear that Rick would see how anxious he was to know, and punish him with silence. Bunyan loved nothing so much as a good piece of gossip, and as glittering as was the circle he had orbited in for the past few years, there was still nothing like having something on a movie star.

"I'm dying, Bunyan. Inside, I mean. All those things they write about. Sleeping, eating, working. I can't do any of them. I had to tell my agent to try to postpone the start of my new picture. I'll probably get sued by the studio if I don't pull myself in shape by the end of December."

Bunyan waited to see if Rick would continue by himself, if the confession would roll off the tongue without any prodding. But Rick had worked consistently if not spectacularly in films: he was obviously waiting for a cue. "But what's wrong?" Bunyan said.

"It's Diane. I'm in love with her."

"Oh come," Bunyan said, and turned his back to the easel. "That's old news. You've been stalking her forever."

"But that was before. It was a game, something to do at parties. But I've changed, Bun . . . yan. Something happened to me at Paradise Island. I really love her."

"You mean you never knew you could feel like this."

"Exactly," Rick said. There was no trace of a smile on Rick's face, nor any sign that he had picked up the irony in Bunyan's voice. "It's pretty shattering, believe me."

"But why Diane? The woman is as pure as the driven ice."

"I don't think so. I think underneath all that there's a volcano."

"A volcano," Bunyan said. "As much as all that. A volcano."

"She's everything I want."

"She's a predatory cunt," Bunyan said.

"She's your best friend," Rick said, with some surprise.

"I adore predatory cunts. I can afford to, because they can't do anything to hurt me. But you, darling boy. What would happen to you in the gaping yaw of a predatory cunt. I shudder to think. Papier-mâché or no papier-mâché, she will still chew them up and spit them out for breakfast. You can't sew them on again, as Thomas Wolfe might say if he could appraise the situation."

"I don't think she'd do that, not if she once . . . not if we were once together. Really together."

"Are you that good?" Bunyan said.

"It isn't just me. It's . . . what I feel for her, what I have to offer."

"Yes, I see what you mean. So what do you want from me in all this? It's all right, I don't mind if you need something. It's sweet to be needed. Makes one feel so Audrey Hepburn."

"Speak to her for me . . ."

"Oh, come . . ."

"No, I mean it. I can't talk to her myself because there have been . . . too many misunderstandings between us. Let her know how I really feel, deep down. And then if she still doesn't want me . . ."

"Yes?"

"Then I'll go away, with my tail between my legs."

"I can't think of a better place for it," Bunyan said. "Unless . . . oh but I suppose it's too early to discuss that possibility now. So you want me to play Pandarus to your Criseyde."

"Pardon?" Rick said.

"I rather love it, it's so . . . medieval. So few things nowadays are authentically medieval, except for Spoleto, of course, and they will keep putting up those neon signs. It's all we can do every spring to run over and tear them down in time for the Festival. All right, fair Troilus. I will plead your cause."

"I can't thank you enough," Rick said, and got to his feet, tugging at his trousers where they pulled into his crotch.

"Do you always dress to the left?" Bunyan said, his eyes following Rick's fingers.

"Pardon?"

"Most creative people sling their cock to the right of their fly, but military men tend to tuck it left. I suppose it goes back to some sort of hopeful tradition that it's less easily shot off that way. Considering your aversion to the military, I'm surprised to see you're in that category. Or is it because you're a good little soldier?"

"I never . . . I never really paid much attention," Rick said, reddening. "One way or the other."

"Oh but you should. You have an admirable basket."

"You will speak to Diane?"

"Constantly," Bunyan said. "It's my favorite thing, minus one. Her husband will be out of town the next few weeks, so the timing is splendid, since we can't widow her like fair Criseyde. And a tight little ass. I can see every muscular knot in those cute pants. Do you always buy them so small?"

"I have to be going," Rick said. "Thank you again."

"Well you surely don't wear them so tight for the benefit of the ladies. Ladies aren't turned on by shapely little asses. You don't have to run, Ricky Ticky. I assure you I am not after your pink little behind. I am not a punker. I prefer being punked, and I'd never ask you to do that, you're such a straight. Do you mind my speaking so frankly."

"No, of course not," Rick said, his face flaming. "What else are friends for?"

"Exactly," said Bunyan. "What I would like, though, is to suck you off. I don't mean to be offensive, but we all have our little, what, foibles, and I haven't blown a movie star since my showing on La Cienaga. And he was already doing features for television, so it wasn't really the same. Echelonwise. Do I offend you?"

"No," Rick said. "It's honest. You can't put down honesty. But of course, under the circumstances, it's impossible."

"What circumstances. You mean Diane?"

"I love her," Rick said.

"And you're saving yourself." Bunyan clapped his hands together. "Oh I can't stand it, it's so moving, as if Greer and Walter were still making pictures. I shall set about my darling task right away."

"Thank you," Rick said, and put his hand on the garden wood-framed glass door, leading out to the roof. "I'll be in constant touch."

"You have no idea," said Bunyan.

After Rick left, Bunyan stood silent for several moments, the sun brightening his silver hair, cut in the style of Caesar, and Jay Sebring, who had redesigned him on the Coast. His little belly paunched out the checkered velour shirt, and he patted it and tried to pull it in. Then he smiled and went back to his easel, and turned on the phone.

There were those who maintained that Bunyan Reis had oral diarrhea, and that if it were not for his work, his painting and his collages, he might never stop talking at all. The people who thought his work an interruption did not know him very well, and certainly had not been to his studio. Directly to the right of his easel was a small stand with a speakerphone that Bunyan could set into action with one flick of a

365

switch, while continuing to paint with his left hand. (Artistically, Bunyan was ambidextrous, which Alfredo, his secretary from Spoleto, thought the funniest joke he had ever heard, no matter how often Bunyan repeated it, and under what circumstances.) In front of the speakerphone was a file of IBM-punched index cards, which, when placed into the back of the phone, self-dialed the number. So there was no waste motion involved in any of Bunyan's activities. He could paint, wander the studio, spray-wipe the glass walls, and even urinate in the rubber plant he kept in the corner without for a moment interrupting his conversations.

The first card he placed in the dialing register was Louise Felder's. Her column that morning had been quite dull, discussing a fashion feud between Gernreich and Molly Parnis, the arrival of the Duke and Duchess of Winsdor (the last who looked just *wonderful,* poor Louise had said, being still very impressed with genuine aristocracy), the further details of Maggie Bolin Piner's refurbishing of Harry Bell's house. It was, in all, totally lacking in anything nasty, for an unwelcome change: Bunyan liked to start the day, along with orange juice and chorizos (Alfredo's mother had been Spanish) with some nice juicy printed scandal, preferably one started by himself.

Louise sounded delighted to hear his voice and asked that she be taken off the speakerphone and put to his ear because it made her very nervous to hear herself echoing. But he explained that he was in the midst of a very important collage and would not have interrupted his work if it hadn't been truly important and libelous. They both laughed.

"You know our fair-haired boy of the concert world, the pianist?" Bunyan said.

"Marshall?"

"Exactly. Well, you know he's been pussyfooting around with Millie Phelps, Maggie Bolin's cousin. Of course she only gets a zillionth of the estate, but it's still family, and a very lofty pile. Well, Millie is hopeless doe-eyed over said pianist, and their engagement is being planned even as we speak, according to Diane."

"Well that's very sweet news," Louise said. "It's not my usual style, but I guess I can fit it in as a gesture."

"So it would be, it would be sweet, if it weren't for one little tidbit. For six months yon piano player has been sneaking into a loft on Twenty-seventh Street where he is not keeping Fannie Hurst."

"Who?"

"A charming young, blue-eyed blond thing, who answers to the name of Stephen."

366

"What a shame. Poor Millie."

"You haven't heard a thing yet," Bunyan laid a leaf from Maggie's bridal bouquet (which he had caught) over the square of bridesmaid's gown. "So tight is the attachment between would-be groom and hidden Stephen that the piano player had Miss Millie put an ad in the *New York Times* for a gardener, for their little estate in Rye, and told Stephen to answer it. And of all the people who showed up for interviews, the one Marshall told her they should hire is Stephen. So they will be moving into their honeymoon hideaway, and guess who will be stashed in the gardener's cottage."

"Oh that's terrible," Louise said. "That poor Millie. What a switch on Lady Chatterley."

"Heaven!" Bunyan said. "You must say just that. If only D. H. Lawrence were here to write this most interesting variation."

"Can I really use it?" Louise said. "It's so vicious, I love it, I love it."

"Just make everything blind, darling, who is that person that what where, you know how, you do it all the time."

"That poor girl."

"Stop identifying, and just get juicy. If you don't use it, someone else will. That bitch Peter Daisy knows all about it, and he's very jealous because Stephen was his discovery, so he'll probably yak it all over town, and the next thing you know it'll be in Suzy."

"You've convinced me," Louise said. "You are a love."

"Speaking of love, darling, how is that cute slab of beef . . . what's his name. Are you still living together?"

"Don't be cunty, darling," Louise said. "I still love you better."

Bunyan giggled, switched off the phone, and reset it with Diane's card.

The phone dialed itself, and Diane answered, her voice heavy with sleep, and, Bunyan was sure he could detect, boredom. They made a date for lunch, at the Colony. Usually Bunyan saved his little activities for the cocktail hour, when the light was gone, and there was nothing much to do around the apartment. But he had had such a full morning and had accomplished so much that he felt he was entitled to some diversion in the middle of the day.

The usual people sat at their usual tables. smiling and nodding to each other in the usual fashion, while pretending to ignore each other's conversations, carried quiet easily from table to table, and, where acoustics were particularly good, across the room. Bunyan had asked the maître d' for the banquette to the left of the pillar. Though it was not as good a vantage point from which to be seen as those tables closer to the door, people would know he was there, especially since he was lunching with Diane, and so would be willing to go out of their way to greet him. The pillar did serve as an absorbent to conversation; the words of actual secrecy he had to whisper would not be spread to the world until and unless he was ready.

"But m'lord weeps and moans, have pity, lady, or he will surely die," Bunyan said, after the waiter had removed the Scotch salmon.

"What are you talking about, Bunyan," Diane's eyes darted nervously about the restaurant. "Do stop babbling and try to look enchanted with me. Laugh and do all those things, like I'm being charming and witty."

"But you are charming and witty, Diane dear. Why are you so nervous."

"It's that bitch from WWD, the one who gave me that review last summer. She's watching me and taking notes."

"Then you mustn't lose your cool," Bunyan said. "Just be absorbed in what I say, and she'll flow over you, like the dishwater she is."

"All right," Diane said, and fixed her gaze intensely on the spot where silver bangs met his gray eyes. "What were you saying?"

"You know what a beautiful woman you are, how many people admire you, worship you, even, including me."

"I'm grateful for that," Diane said, and patted his hand across the table.

"Don't be patronizing," Bunyan said. "I'm trying to be quite serious. You're an exceptional woman, and you know it, but I don't think you're an exceptionally cruel woman. At least if you are, I don't think you're intentionally cruel and spiteful."

"Cruel and spiteful?" Diane said. "Who said that? Did somebody say that about me?"

"No one's said it," Bunyan said, and looked at the tablecloth. "Not yet. But what you're doing, unintentional as it may be, is unforgivable. Especially as it's starting to show in your face."

"What? Tell me what. What have I done?"

"It isn't what you've done. It's what you're making him do."

"Who? Really Bunny, after all these years of being my friend it isn't like you to talk in such lavish circles."

"Well, I don't think it's like you, Di Di, to behave so cruelly and bitchily. Not to someone who worships you as much as Rick."

"He told you about the bathtub?" Diane said.

"Of course," Bunyan said, averting his gaze so she wouldn't know he was lying.

"He had his nerve, telling you about that. It wouldn't have

happened if he wasn't so damned insistent, hanging around my room, following me everywhere. He deserved it."

"What?"

She looked at him carefully. "Don't you know? Are you just saying you know about it?"

"Well what do you want the poor boy to do? He's half crazy, out of his mind with loving you. You should see him, his poor little ass hardly fills out his pants, tight as they are, he's lost so much weight. I'm afraid for what he might do to himself."

"Oh don't be ridiculous, this is the twentieth century. People don't perish anymore from love. Do they?"

"When they love as deeply as Rick does, they could."

"You really think he cares about me that much?"

"I know he does. He was weeping when I left him."

"Isn't that funny. And I always thought he was just another little movie star on the make."

"Oh no. Not Rick. He's filled with depths. Deep ones."

"Well that's his problem," Diane said. "What am I supposed to do?"

"You could at least talk to him."

"I've talked to him. He isn't interested in talking. I have nothing more to say. I'm a married woman."

"Oh come now, Di Di."

"It just so happens I'm very much in love with my husband. He may seem a little stick-in-the-muddy to you, but in his own way, he's a fascinating man. If you only knew," she said, and smiled.

"Why don't you tell me?"

"Don't be so sneaky, Bunyan, there are some things I won't discuss even with you."

"So what are we going to do about Mr. Flinders?"

"I'm sure I don't know. Ah, the soufflé," she said delightedly, and sat back as the waiter put it in front of her. "Isn't it gorgeous. Are you sorry now you didn't order the soufflé?"

"I felt like an omelet," Bunyan said. "I'm not sorry."

"Of course you are, I can see it in your eyes, they're practically watering that you didn't order the soufflé, confess it, confess."

"All right, I confess. I'm sorry, I didn't order the soufflé."

"You may have some of mine," Diane said.

"You see!" Bunyan set down his fork. "You see the kind of woman you are, I knew I was right about you. How can you be so gentle and giving about a soufflé, and deny this poor boy when he's dying."

"You're hopeless," she said, and moved her fork into the casserole. "I thought I adored you because you were such a romantic, but now it's melodrama, sheer melodrama. You go too far."

"Come some of the way with me, Diane, I beg of you. If not for his sake, for your own."

"Why mine?" she said warily.

"I don't like to see what's happening to you."

"Why? What is?"

"You're getting very hard. Unfeeling."

"I am not, no one could say that about me. Could they? Is it really starting to show? How could it show when I'm not even doing anything?"

"What will you feel when he kills himself?"

"Silly," Diane said. "Because he won't."

"Wait and see," said Bunyan, and attacked his omelet. "It's terrible. I'm sorry I didn't order the soufflé."

She did not offer hers again.

When they ate dessert, after the third glass of white wine she looked at Bunyan carefully. "You really think he loves me."

"Completely. I know he does. I've never seen anyone in greater pain."

"That's a shame," she said. "I suppose I treated him rather badly."

"Then you will see him?"

"Maybe just to talk," Diane said. "Maybe I could talk to him, and straighten him out."

When she finished her exercise class at Kounovsky's she was standing at the bar in front of the mirror that went the full length of the wall, to show everyone in the class, but she did not see who else was there. A woman behind her in black leotards with a cluster of diamonds above her sagging breasts asked Diane how she was, but Diane didn't hear her. She noticed only that there was a line at the corner of her mouth where she had never noticed one before, and she wondered if it was from being cruel and spiteful. On the way to her vocal coach she stopped at Arden's and picked up some extra-rich night cream, and, back inside the taxi, rubbed a little in at the corner of her lips. Her lesson that day was dull and unsatisfactory, in spite of the fact that Rosa, the coach, said her voice was getting fuller with every passing week, and there was expression in it Rosa had never heard before.

"Madame has found pain," Rosa said. "That is a good thing."

"Is that what it is?" Diane said, and stuffed her music back into her shoulder-chain bag.

It was five forty by the time she found a taxi, and she was already late for the planning committee tea at the Sherry. She had been to several luncheons that month, and lent her name and her photo, reprinted in the *New York Times*, to the committee cocktail party for the charity. In a way she had done as much for the Liver Foundation as she could, short of getting all her friends to buy tickets to the ball, which she intended to do. Besides, she was not up to all those women, doing whatever they could to fill their day, because they had no wish to be home, as she did. She gave the driver her home address, and pressed her head back against the seat, absently rubbing a little of the cream into the corner of her mouth.

After she had finished a long hot soak in the tub and rubbed herself briskly, and covered every inch of her body with talcum, she tried to put in a call to her husband. But there was a six-hour wait for overseas. She lay back, her red hair loosed against the pillow, and closed her eyes. It was hopeless. She swung her legs over the side of the bed, reached for the phone, and dialed Bunyan's number.

"I'm bored," she said. "Can we do something?"

"You told me you were all booked for the rest of the day. Why aren't you with the Liver Ladies?"

"I wasn't up to it. Can we go somewhere or something?"

"Caravelle?"

"Caravelle will be fine."

"Do you mind if I bring a friend?" Bunyan said.

"Oh Bunny, you wouldn't, it would look so obvious, everybody would know you were bearding. No reflection on you, darling, but wouldn't it be a bit pushy?"

"Yes, that's right," Bunyan said. "He's sitting right here."

"Oh."

"Maybe we could come over to your place? You could have Fritzie whip up a little sauerbraten. Does she still do that?"

"I've given them the evening off."

"Then why don't we stop Au Casserole and get some Bourguignonne to go; that might be kicky."

"I don't want him to come here. I know how good your intentions are, but I only said I would talk. If I let him come here, he might get the wrong idea."

"Very wise, Di Di. A little stuffy, but very wise."

"I could come there. We could send out for something from there, or maybe we could go out and have deli, no one would spot us having deli."

"I'll send out for it," Bunyan said.

"But you promise not to leave us alone? Not even for a minute."

"Now why would I do that," Bunyan said. "It isn't as if you wanted anything to happen, is it."

CHAPTER TWO

LOUISE never discussed Harry Bell with Charley. Sometimes she would start to bring it up, tentatively, but he avoided any prolonged discussion just as he did when she tried to speak of those men with whom she had had affairs in fact.

"But aren't you at all curious?" she asked him, when she was dressing for her appointment with Miriam Bell. "I mean he was one of your top twentieth-century people. Don't you want to know about my relationship with him?"

"No," Charley said.

"I wish you had more definite reactions," Louise said. "If there's one thing I can't stand, it's a wishy-washy attitude."

"Why are you getting dressed up?" He bent his elbows back against the headboard of the bed, so she could see the rich darkness of the hair under his arms, and she had to fight the temptation to dive into his armpits, and lose the whole morning. Saturday mornings they usually spent in bed, keeping it lazy, because Sundays she had at least one brunch to cover, and an art opening or a cocktail party. As often as not, lately, she would take Charley with her, but they could not really spend time together. He knew she had to circulate, picking up gossip, checking out hearsay; but he no longer seemed to mind her leaving him alone at any of the gatherings. He could handle himself quite nicely, either talking to the few guests he knew, or sitting alone in a corner, watching, with a detached, amused expression. Bunyan was right about him. She could take him anywhere. The place she still enjoyed taking him most was to bed, and it embarrassed her, discovering that she was such a sensualist. It had to be a low-class thing, taking so much pleasure from pleasure alone, no matter what Dr. Ehrens said.

She saw Charley watching her in the mirror, and actually caught herself blushing.

"I asked you why you're getting dressed up?" he said again.

"You know I have to go meet Harry's mother."

"I didn't say what for, I said why? Why don't you just rip off that little Peter Pan collar and jump back into bed."

"Don't tempt me," Louise said, and returned his smile in the mirror. "You know I have an obligation to Harry."

"Do you?" he said.

"I thought you said you didn't want to know about him and me."

"I don't. Not about him and you. But I am interested in you. Now. Why don't you slip out of your Goody Two Shoes, and run barefoot through my hair."

"I really did know him, you know."

"I'm not interested."

"No matter what Kate and David told you."

"They didn't tell me anything. I've made it very clear I'm not interested in stories about you, only you, the way you are now."

"And you're not even curious about him and me?"

"Not even curious."

"I never actually did anything with him, Charley, but we did go out."

"I'm sure you made a stunning couple," Charley said, and pulled the sheet up over his eyes.

She could see his chest moving up and down beneath the quilt, and tried to rivet her attention on her own reflection. The outfit was perfect, there was no doubt about that. Soft brown, not the deep black of mourning, but somber enough to be respectful, with the touch of whiteness around her throat to bring full focus up to the pink-cheeked innocence of her face. Any other mother but her own would have to fight the impulse to pinch one of those kewpie cheeks: Harry Bell's mother was as good as in her pocket.

"I should have always stayed a child," Louise said. "Then everybody would have loved me."

"Either that or go all the way to woman," Charley said. "Then somebody really could."

"I'm sorry if I don't meet with your approval."

"Oh but you do," Charley said. "I can't wait for you to start meeting with your own."

In the taxi on the way to the Ritz Towers, Louise tried not to think about him. She was happy with Charley, and she knew she was happy. But she also knew that it could be over at any time for a number of reasons: he could stop working, or he could get tired of her, or he could really love her but turn out to be a loser, in which case she would need even more to be a winner so she would be able to take care of him, if she still wanted to. She was almost sure she would. But it was nothing she had to make a move about. The important thing was to preserve all positions, just in case. The first position to be preserved, of course, was the one as Harry's fiancée; she would warm the decrepit cockles of his old mother's heart, and at the same time help her friends, Chet and Ron Abbate, who had made so much possible. And, of course, Harry, poor dear Harry, from whence all postmortem blessings had flowed.

She smiled, and leaning forward checked her reflection in the mirror above the driver's head. She had never been more honey blond and sweet-faced. In her mind she went over the details of her last telephone conversation with Ron Abbate. She was to say nothing specific about Harry's wish for a memorial building, only let it fall subtly on the old lady that he had been working out details for one. Mostly she was to concentrate on being as warm and sweet as possible, making Miriam Bell into an ally.

"I don't know her myself," Ron Abbate had said. "But I understand she's quite an unusual woman. If we can get her on your side, the brothers would probably go along with whatever she says. You sure you want to meet with her now? If you'd rather pass, we can make some excuse."

"Little old ladies are mother's milk to me," Louise said, and laughed. "Consider her won."

In the elevator on the way up to the tower apartment, Louise blotted her lipstick on a Kleenex. She was wearing a very gentle, beigey shade, so the pinkness of her natural color came through the translucence. All the same she didn't want her makeup to be in the least aggressive in case Harry's mother was orthodox as well as aged.

When the door to the tower apartment opened, Louise was quite stunned. The woman who stood in front of her seemed to be in her early fifties at most. The remarkable tight face showed a minimum of lines and almost no indication of wear or emotion. Only the hands, extending long-fingered and heavily veined from the flowing sleeves of the bronze caftan, gave any indication of a lengthy history.

"Oh but of course," Louise said. "You must be her niece or something."

"That's very charming," Miriam Bell said. "Come in."

"Her companion?" Louise followed her into the living room of the suite. "I didn't realize she had a companion."

"Well if she did, dear, she wouldn't show her to you." Miriam Bell smiled tightly. Her lips did not move very much, but the smile was in her eyes, so Louise knew it was acceptable to smile back.

"But it isn't possible. You know it isn't possible. I'm not just trying to flatter you, you must have heard it before. You couldn't possibly be his mother."

"Why not?" Miriam said, and poured a drink from the decanter on the bar into a crystal glass. "They do remarkable things with plastic surgery nowadays, even an unworldly little thing like you must realize that. Scotch?"

"No thank you, I don't drink."

"Sweet," Miriam Bell said, and dropped some ice in her glass. "Of course when I first had it done they weren't quite as clever about the scars, and I had to wear wigs for a while, but Converse finally did away with those the last time he did my eyes. See?" She pulled her straight-cut dark hair away from the front of her ears. "You can hardly tell."

"It's still incredible," Louise said. "It isn't your face, it's . . . well—everything. Your figure, and the way you move."

"Diet and exercise," Miriam said. "There's nothing you can't accomplish with diet and exercise. You should try it, dear. Cigarette?" She extended a thin gold case.

"No thank you," Louise said. "I don't smoke."

"Well that's sweet, too," Miriam said. "Only maybe you should, I notice a tendency to put on a couple of pounds if I try cutting down."

Louise looked at the floor, and felt her cheeks reddening.

"Not that you're not attractive, Miss Felder. You have a lovely face and exquisite legs. You'd be terribly pretty if you took off a few pounds. Maybe not a true beauty, but astonishingly pretty."

"Well, not all of us were born to be true beauties."

"Why not?" Miriam Bell clinked the ice in her glass, and sat on the bergère opposite Louise, leaning over and staring intently into her face. "There are so many advances in health and aesthetics, why shouldn't everyone become the most they can, and not surrender to some mystical idea of destiny. Don't you agree?"

"I don't know."

"You don't know if we should become the most we can be?"

"I don't know if it isn't very presumptuous to want to be more than we are." Louise looked at her squarely.

"You think I'm presumptuous?" Miriam smiled.

"Not at all. I think you're remarkable."

"That's very flattering. You're a clever girl, to say exactly what an ancient old lady wants to hear." She saw Louise looking around over her shoulder and under the olive cushions of the couch. "Are you looking for something?"

"The ancient old lady," Louise said, smiling. "Where is she. Who are you, really? Stop putting me on."

Miriam Bell smiled, and leaning forward, cupped her hand under Louise's chin. "Pretty. Really very pretty. And nice, too. I wouldn't be at all surprised if you were really a very nice girl."

375

"I try to be," Louise said.

"Then what's all this crap about you and Harry?" The fingers tightened under Louise's chin, until Miriam let go.

It took Louise a moment to recover. "Don't you think I was good enough for him, Mrs. Bell."

"Oh don't be a goddammed fool. You seem like you're bright enough, and you have a certain . . . subtle feminine quality. Harry had about as much appreciation of subtlety as a rhinoceros."

"Did you spend much time with him the last few years?" Louise said when she managed to catch her breath.

"I knew him most of his life," Miriam said. "So don't try to hand me any of that swill about his changing. Values don't change, people like Harry don't mellow because they're growing old. They just overindulge appetites they don't even have anymore to prove that they're not losing them. Are you a whore, Louise?"

"I won't even answer that."

"Harry only liked whores. Whatever else you are, you're not a whore."

"Well, thank you for that, anyway," Louise said.

"You needn't be too grateful," Miriam got up and went to the bar, refilling her crystal tumbler. "It takes a certain amount of innocent guts to be a whore. Obviously what guts you have aren't innocent. You sure you won't have a drink, now?"

"If you're trying to make me uncomfortable, Mrs. Bell, I promise you you're succeeding."

"Well, good. How kind of you to indulge an old lady." She smiled, and poured a drink for Louise. "Don't you just love this apartment? Of course it's a little frayed around the edges like most of us, and they've redone it since I lived here. It used to be all white satins and blue brocades, but earth tones are nice, don't you think? Soft. They show less wear. I'm thinking of redoing my hair a light chestnut. How do you think that would look?"

"Lovely, I'm sure."

"Your hair's a wonderful color," Miriam handed Louise the drink, and reached over to touch her hair. "Soft. You do have a certain lively quality. Is it possible he was getting some sense?"

"He seemed really to care about me, if that's what you mean, Mrs. Bell."

"Why don't you call me Miriam. You did say you liked this apartment?"

Louise looked around, trying to avoid the cold scrutiny of the eyes. "It's very attractive."

"I used to live here, you know. Downstairs from this very room, Mary Elizabeth Craig tried to kill herself over Harry. I don't suppose you're old enough to remember that?"

"I heard about it."

"And how is it you never tried to kill yourself over my wonderful, handsome son?"

"Maybe I better go."

Miriam put a hand on her arm. "I'm sorry. Am I being too hard on you? I don't mean to be. I have so few pleasures left in life, you understand. I suppose I like to test people. Perhaps I shouldn't be so cynical. Harry tried to tell me that once, in French I believe it was. Why don't you tell me how it was with the two of you. Come. Indulge an old woman."

"I had fun with him," Louise said slowly. "I really did. Oh I know a lot of it had to do with his being Harry Bell, but I hadn't known many people like that, and he did have a certain . . . well, style, I suppose you could say. Gusto."

"Oh, yes," Miriam said. "Great gusto. And style, yes. I remember once I tried to explain to him that gambling required elegance, and he thought that meant he had to buy a tuxedo."

"Well, you've obviously been a lot more places than I have, Mrs. Bell, and seen a lot more things."

"You can't imagine," Miriam said. "I understand you do a column?"

"That's right."

"Then I take it you can write. I'm not talking literarily, you understand, I mean you can put letters on paper with a pencil so they make words."

Louise laughed. "I guess you could say that."

"That would also seem to imply that you can read. Is that how you whiled away the long winter evenings with my lovely boy, exchanging passages from Tolstoy, aloud?"

"Listen, Mrs. Bell, I don't know what I've done to offend you, but . . ."

"Offend me? For Christ's sake, you don't offend me at all, so how can I possibly believe you had anything to do with Harry. Harry was a cretin. An ape. It was impossible to feel anything for him."

"I've never felt more for him than I feel now," Louise said.

"Oh, is your heart breaking because his mother didn't love him? You really believe that hogwash that a mother has to love her children? Why? Doesn't it ever occur to anyone that the anguish and the disappointment can work the other way, when there's nothing there to love."

"I have to go," Louise got unsteadily to her feet.

"Don't leave," Miriam said. "I'm enjoying myself. There

are few people left that I can talk to. I don't even have many living enemies anymore. My only real enemy is time, and how long can I fight time?"

"If you get really lonely, I'll give you my mother's number," Louise said. "You ought to get along just fine."

"Sit down, dammit. I like you."

"Well, as eager as I am for your approval, Mrs. Bell, I'm afraid it's a little late for Harry and me to ask your blessing. Pity."

"You do have guts," Miriam said. "You really do. Now tell me what you *do* want. You've gone this far, you might as well tell me what you hoped to accomplish by coming here."

"It wasn't anything for myself. I suppose you'll find it hard to believe that. I wasn't coming here for myself. I was coming here for Harry."

"He asked you to kiss me good-bye?" Miriam said, smiling.

"He wanted a memorial building," Louise said. "I won't bother you with the details, but he desperately wanted to be remembered."

"I find it almost impossible to forget him," Miriam said. "He was a blot on the earth when he was alive. I don't want any reminder that he ever existed."

"You're all heart," Louise said, and left.

When she got home, she took off her clothes, got into bed beside Charley without saying a word, snuggled her face on his chest, and started to cry. She cried with rage and humiliation, and sudden surprising pity for Harry Bell. When Charley didn't ask what had happened, but continued softly, rhythmically, cupping the back of her head, she allowed herself to cry openly for Louise.

Maggie could hear them, in the night. Sometimes, at three or four o'clock in the morning, she could feel George moving toward her in the bed, and her insides would contract. But he would never reach farther than the front of her mouth, waving his hand in front of it like a flag, checking her breathing. And Maggie would reward him with a snore, in case the air was not being blown from her nostrils with enough regularity to convince him she was deeply, unhearingly asleep. Shortly after that he would get out of bed, slowly, and then she could hear him padding barefooted along the uncarpeted parquet corridors, and up the stairs to Wendy's room.

She could see him, through sound, as clearly as if she followed him in fact. The house, for all the money that Harry Bell had lavished on its construction, had the acoustics of an empty museum. There would always be a slight squeak as he opened Wendy's door, and then Maggie could hear him moving toward the bed. Then a slightly surprised murmur, followed by George's hushing instruction. The sound of Wendy's bare feet, as she got up from the bed and went to brush her teeth, slosh, slosh. Spit.

George was always very careful about things like that. In the beginning, before he and Maggie had gotten married, after the first fevered sortie on the couch, they never made love unless both of them were clean, according to George's specific wish. After he was finished showering, he would leave the water running, so she would know it was her turn. Most of the time she only stuck her hand in under the shower, and wet her breasts and under her arms and between her legs. But she was careful to sing a lot and make very elaborate noises, staying in a long time, so he would be happy.

She did not feel like doing that anymore. She did not feel like doing any number of things, foremost among which was letting George inside her. She had fenced with him rather brilliantly, she thought, by using the commonest of female ploys, her pregnancy; plus, she thought, smiling, the rather uncommon ploy, at least in America, of providing him with easy access to a mistress. Moving Wendy into the house, that had been a veritable stroke.

She listened to them now, jamming away upstairs, the little metal feet of the daybed she had bought from the Salvation Army screeching against the bare floors as their movements propelled the bed away from the wall. She heard the muffled groans and imprecations as they pledged themselves into each other's throats, and necks. And she realized, lying there, that she had done more than accommodate his needs; she had actually performed a great service for him. He had never been so passionate, so often, for such lengths of time with her. Nor, she suspected, had he ever been such a regular and loyal lover of Wendy's in the old days. It was as if the mere furtiveness of the affair lent him a fire he had never before possessed. As if the mere act of sneaking around corridors to an adulterous bed, with his wife lying below, so fast asleep that she could never hear (ha!), got his sexual dander up.

In spite of herself, Maggie, listening, felt a little sad and a little angry. The same reaction in anyone else she would have branded jealousy, but of course with her and George, that was impossible. She was a human being, that was all, and aside from the truth that she didn't want him, and was pleased that he was relieving himself elsewhere, she could not help but feel resentment that he was enjoying himself more with another woman than he had with her. At least from the sound of it. And from the sound of Wendy, who sighed and groaned with a lavishness that would have befitted a high-school ingenue playing Juliet. But that was fake, probably, Wendy's old training as a whore serving her in a romantic situation. George at his best was never more than almost satisfactory, giving a few clinical flips to the clitoris before plunging in and ramming away, because he had read once that that was where the seat of woman's pleasure lay, and much as he hated to believe it, was willing to defer to the textbooks. He was hardly a lover to inspire hushed groans and sighs, at least to the extent they were offered by Wendy, who was such an old pro, in spite of her title of "nurse-receptionist" that mileage alone would have hardened and insensitized the equipment. No, she was faking, Maggie was sure. Just as Maggie was faking to have pretended needing anything more from him than the single act of fathering her child.

She curled up and wound herself, now, around her own center. The child, according to the book on expectant motherhood that Algernon had given her (in a basket of daisies), was at this point almost six and a half inches long, and weighed about four ounces. Four ounces, Maggie thought, a regular patty at Phoebe's Whamburger, not counting the cheese. Not very much really, but already it was a perfectly formed miniature baby, with membranes for fingernails and toenails, and buds in its mouth for teeth, and everything it would need to be born, except time to develop to full size. A miracle. A rudimentary miracle of perfection.

She could feel it moving around inside her, even though the books said that most movements at that time were so faint as to be indistinguishable to the mother. Some mothers, perhaps, but not Maggie. With her hand inside her nightgown, on her belly, she felt a pulse that had never been there before. Her fingers clasped across the slight roundness, and felt a distant, undulating wave, the distant, blurred reverberation of orgasm.

Naturally it didn't say that in the book on expectant motherhood. All the book spoke of was "stirrings" and "quickenings," and other euphemisms for life itself, and feeling it. But she would not write a letter to Dr. Eastman setting him straight, anymore than she would go to an obstetrician. Algernon had agreed with her about that. She had been to see him at the Function Center two days before, when she told George she was going to the doctor. It was not altogether a lie. One of Algernon's closest friends was Dr. Kunyadi, who had dropped out of Columbia Medical School in his third year to take his Ph.D. in Oriental philosophy at Yale, and had left that university eight years before, in order to write an as yet unfinished historical analysis of the growth of Transcendentalism in America. Kunyadi, for all his idealism, was somewhat disillusioned with all great figures he had turned to in his time, except Algernon. But he was as aware and as healing as anyone around with their diplomas hung cockeyed on the wall, Algernon said, and that was the only reason he permitted Kunyadi to examine Maggie.

Naturally they didn't even do that until Algernon found out she hadn't been to anyone. "Why not," he said, as he sat on the terrazzoed floor of the garden room of the Function Center, next to the kitchen.

"I don't like pressure," Maggie said. "I don't like people checking on me as if I were a child, I'm not a child, I can't stand how George keeps pestering me. They probably just make you go all that often so they can build up their fees."

"Hear hear," said Eric Kunyadi, from his mat in the corner of the room.

"I still think you should see someone," Algernon said, crossing his bare ankles, bending his face down to touch the knee of his white chinos. He was still tanned from the brief trip to Paradise Island, and his chest where the white shirt was opened to accommodate the beads was brown. "Just to make sure everything's okay, Mag."

"Everything's marvelous, Nonny, can't you see by just looking at me? Have I ever looked better in my life?"

"Never," Algernon said, staring across at her through a private mist.

"I haven't known you all your life, Maggie," Kunyadi said, sitting up slightly. "But from a professional point of view I'd say you looked groovy."

"What about Dr. Wilcox?" Algernon said.

"He's with my mother, on death row."

"Maybe you'd like me to take a look at her, Alger." Kunyadi was on his feet, moccasined beneath the kurta and punjabees.

"Are you a medical doctor?" Maggie said. "I always thought you were a philosophy kind."

"I didn't finish, if labels mean everything to you."

"I don't care about labels."

"None of us cares about labels," Algernon said. "We just don't have the setup here, Doctor, maybe it isn't such a good idea."

"Naturally I wasn't planning on giving her an internal. If she's four months along, an internal isn't necessary. I can tell how everything is from the outside. If you want me to, Al, I will."

"It might be all right," Algernon said. "It might be a good

thing, to keep it a secret from the Establishment. If they don't know about your baby, they can't get your baby. They can't label it and file it, and send it to their schools, and call it up in the draft. Shall we, Mag? Can we keep it a name, and not let it be a number?"

"Can we do that?" Maggie said.

"But of course we can. If you have it at home, and there's no record in the hospital, how can it be a truant from a life it was never announced to."

"George would never let me do it, would he, do you think he would? He'd make me have it in the hospital, he's so madly antiseptic."

"Ah yes," Algernon squeezed her neck. "But he's also a sucker for the tradition he never had. If you explained to him that you wanted the baby born in the very place where you were born, and your mother before you . . ."

"But we live in Harry Bell's house."

"All the better," Algernon said. "He'd love having his baby born at Harry's."

He hugged her then, and Maggie felt dizzy from the strength of him. "Oh yes," she whispered. "It's a fine idea."

"You want me to take a look at her," Kunyadi said.

"All right," said Algernon. "But I want to be in the room."

They took her into the kitchen and shut the doors, and placed a sheet over the old cutting table in the center of the room. Dr. Kunyadi said she was fine. She was better than fine, she was perfect, he said, as she had known all along she was. Her breasts, enlarged, with darkening nipples and blue veins against her dark skin strengthening the milk ducts, were perfect to feed the child. Her uterus was soft, and supple, and growing, and the life inside her would thrive. "The size of the uterus corresponds with the duration of gestation," Kunyadi said. He was not sure whether or not he had his stethoscope, but even if he could find it, it would be too early to hear the fetal heartbeat.

"Soon," he said. "Soon we will be able to hear that."

"I want to hear it now," said Algernon. "Excuse us, please."

Kunyadi shut the door behind him, and Algernon came toward her on the table. She raised herself on her elbow, smiling, and reached out her arm. Algernon kissed her fingertips, and then pressed his ear against her belly. She touched his hair, softly at first, and then pressed him hard against her.

"Shh," he whispered. "Shh. I can hear it. Yes. Swimming in a distant warm sea."

"Yes, that's the way it always seems to me."

"On this," he placed his hand flat against her belly. "On

this will I build my church. An authentically free spirit, because he won't be captured in the beginning. He won't have to unlearn the fake, phony values of the system, because they'll never get him to index, and break. It's beautiful, Maggie. It's beautiful. You're my Madonna, don't you see?"

"I see," Maggie said. "Make love to me."

"You better get dressed," Algernon said. "I don't want you to miss your train."

Before she left, they had a cup of Algernon's special tea. He did not give her too much, only enough to carry her through the day, and the night. She told George to take Wendy to the cabaret, she didn't feel like being with a lot of people.

She woke up to a grayly glittering day, tired and happy, and too lazy to do anything but lie in bed and watch television, and, during the commercials, feel her baby and listen to it grow. Sometime during the afternoon she answered the phone by mistake. It was Andre Sherman, apologizing for disturbing her, apologizing again for having to call her, but explaining that he had an incredibly hot tip on a new stock issue, and knew where he could get a hundred thousand shares, fantastically cheap.

"Oh, that's very sweet of you, Andre," Maggie said, "but I never make any investments. My executors are so madly efficient, what, they handle all that."

"I assumed so," Andre said. "I wasn't trying to hype you on stock, Maggie, believe me. It's just, I can get them so fantastically cheap, and all my cash right now is tied up in real estate deals, I wondered—please excuse how this must sound, but I was wondering if, in addition to the Utrillo, of course, the Utrillo is still a gift, I was wondering if you'd be interested in buying the Cézanne, or the Corot. At cost, of course. At exactly the price I paid for them."

"Oh, I'd love to," Maggie said. "I'd just love to. It's such a big house, and the walls are so bare, like the floors."

"Well that's fine," he said. "How would you like to arrange it? The Corot is sixty-eight thousand, and the Cézanne is . . ."

"I'd just love to buy them, but naturally I have no money."

"Pardon me?" Andre said.

"I'm madly strapped for cash, I haven't a farthing. Normally I'd go to my executors, but I know they wouldn't let me have a cent now for anything, what with buying the house and all, we'll be in debt for a year."

"You poor thing," Andre said.

"Well, good luck with the stock, darling, I hope you make scads of money, and then maybe you can lend some to us."

"Thank you for your good wishes," Andre said.

The rest of the day Maggie spent in bed. Wendy brought her supper on a tray, and said how sorry she was that Maggie wasn't coming along to the new hospital dedication with her and George. Before George left, he kissed her gently, and took her blood pressure and her pulse, and said she seemed to be fine. She assured him she was, that she was just a lazy pregnant lady, happy to wallow.

She still felt that way now, lying in bed, staring at the ceiling. She was wallowing, she knew it, but she didn't mind. Wallowing in disgust at the noises upstairs, wallowing in joy at the growing burden inside her.

The noise upstairs stopped. The padding on the stairs and the hallways to her door sounded again. She closed her eyes and snored long enough for him to tiptoe past her, to the bathroom. In a moment she could hear the water running, and George washing out his mouth, and soaping off his hands, and lathering his cock, probably.

Maggie closed her eyes and smiled into the pillow. She was ridiculous for even listening, for feeling the least bit of womanly resentment. It was a plan made in heaven, Wendy and George. He had given all of himself to Maggie that she could ever use.

The rest was noises.

Sometime, about four o'clock in the afternoon, Andre stopped sweating. It was forty-two degrees outside, and he had most of the windows in his apartment open, and the heat turned off. Even so, he was still sweating. He turned the air-conditioners on while he made a few calls, as he had done so fruitlessly the past few weeks. All he had managed to turn up so far, with all his wheeling, was sixty thousand from a savings and loan in the Bronx, and to get it he had to take a second mortgage on the one piece of property he owned that was still worth something. He forwarded the sixty thousand to Parke-Bernet via a friend who mailed the check from Boston, with a typewritten note explaining he was still tied up out of town on business, and on his return, would settle in full. Meanwhile, the sixty thousand would serve as the deposit and sign of his good faith. In the intervening weeks he had been unable to get any more cash, so there was nothing to do now but call the rich people.

It was amazing how poor the rich people were. Not even that cunt Maggie Bolin with her two billion dollars had a fucking farthing. Privilege, he remembered wryly: the ability to afford costly errors. There was no way in the world he could come out of it ahead, or even. He would at least have the grace to die like a gentleman.

He picked up the phone and dialed Rolf Orlovsky, who sounded like he had been waiting. "All right," Andre said, "I've already sent the gallery sixty. You give me five hundred twenty-six thousand, and they're yours, all of them."

"You sound like you're making an enormous sacrifice," Orlovsky said.

"I paid five hundred eighty-six thousand," Andre said. "You're getting them for sixty thousand under price."

"*Your* price, Mr. Sherman. Your price which you are unable to pay. I'd hardly call that a fair open-market deal."

"What do you want from me?" Andre eased his face next to the blower, and the open window, sending chilled air gusting through the drapes. "What do you want?"

"I'll give you four hundred thousand, for all of them, and that's it."

"That's almost two hundred thousand below cost. I'll forfeit them, first, you son-of-a-bitch. I'll tell them I can't pay."

"If you were going to do that, you would have done that weeks ago. No, I'm sure you already know what that would mean, the public exposure, the humiliation. You couldn't take that, Mr. Sherman. You're not a big enough man to handle shame."

"Please," Andre said, and he was crying. In less than a second he convinced himself that the tears were phony, that he was putting the bastard on.

"I won't subject myself to this," Orlovsky said. "Neither should you."

"I'm sorry. But please . . ."

"I'll give you four and a quarter, and that's it. The other hundred is your problem."

"Thank you," Andre said. "Oh thank you." And then he hung up the phone so he could dry his phony tears. He was genuinely surprised when he found they would not stop.

There was a way, there would be a time, when Andre would be able to get even with Orlovsky, but he put that out of his mind. Right now his brain was clicking with other things, how to make up the deficit, how to even himself out for the hundred thousand. It was like the old days, when he would go to Vegas for the weekend, flush with cash, and stay too long, blowing ten, fifteen, twenty thousand at the crap table. For nights afterward he would lie awake and figure out how if he went without breakfast for a year and dinners at Sardi's, if he used regular gas in his Lincoln instead of Supreme, if he picked up the car in Detroit, and kept the Michigan plates so he didn't have to pay New York state taxes on the car, if he fired his housekeeper and remarried Marianne so he didn't have to pay alimony, in three years he would be even for what he had dropped. The naive remorse of a gambler, Andre thought. He didn't gamble anymore. Not so the world could see him at an actual crap table, throwing away his brains. He hadn't gambled for three years, not since Harry Bell had told him that only morons gambled. But Harry Bell couldn't pass judgment on him now, because at least Andre was alive, and alive was smarter than dead.

He picked up the morning's *Times,* and turned to the sports pages, and started to read, hard, as he hadn't read the sports page in years. It was a dumb thing to do, but he hadn't turned out exactly smart, trying to deal on the lofty planes, with the high rollers like Orlovsky. It couldn't be worse, getting back down to his old, own low level.

There were six pro football games scheduled for Sunday. The college games he wouldn't consider; if you put too big a bet on a college game they'd figure you knew something, and take it off the boards. But a game that would determine a championship, there was a lot of action riding on a game like that, and a hundred thousand bet wouldn't be that conspicuous. Well it might not be exactly inconspicuous, but he knew someone who would take it. Had taken it, many times, in the old days, when Andre had been a promoter, maybe, but at least won once in a while, and didn't come up empty, losers, like he was now that he was a gentleman among gentlemen, like Orlovsky.

He called Red Tully, an old sportswriter friend of his on the *News,* a beer-drinking amiable redneck from Miami who was good for highly educated guesses, and more. Not that there were fixes in on the pro games, but the coaches and the scouts usually knew, could smell from the way the team was working, from the steam the boys were working up, the injuries that were sustained, what the chances were. And they usually told Red, because they liked him.

"What looks good in the Baltimore game?"

"I thought you didn't do that anymore," Red said.

"I thought I'd just get a little something down for Sunday, just to have a rooting interest in the weekend."

"It must be very boring being rich," Red said. "We certainly miss you down at the farm."

"Yeah, well we'll get together soon, buddy. I'll blow you to an evening one night next week."

"Great," said Red. "Only no concerts. My butt goes to sleep."

Andre laughed.

The Baltimore game that weekend was the Colts against

the Los Angeles Rams. In Baltimore championship fever was running very high, Andre knew that even before Red told him, so there was a lot of easy money riding on the game. Both teams were in sensational shape, Red told him, but he had a hunch the Colts had a slight edge, what with being in first place, and undefeated, and the game being in Baltimore. But the Rams were hot, so it would probably be easy to pick up a bet on the Colts, for a couple of points. The bets the bookies were giving right now was the Colts to be a two-point favorite.

"Is that a good bet?" Andre said. "Baltimore by two points."

"As good as a bet can be," Red said. "If you want to go back to your black and wily ways."

They said again they would get together soon, and hung up. Andre went to get dressed, to go spend Friday night with his mother, for the first time in four years.

Bernie Kolodny was a better son than Andre. Bernie Kolodny, beneath his white on white shirt and his white tie, had a heart that bled at regular intervals for those he loved, and a soul that pulled him back to his parents for dinner every Friday night of his life. There were those who said that it was a guilty conscience that made him such a good son, because he gave his mother so much heartache with what he did. He ignored the censure in her eyes when she opened the door to him, and ate her dinner with such gusto that she loved him all over again by the time he took a cab back to Manhattan. Friday evenings at the Kolodny home were silent, except for the reverential sound of good food being eaten with pleasure. And an occasional reference to the other boys from the neighborhood who had gotten married, and had children, and were decent people. Bernie ignored her not so subtle implications, just as he had ignored her boring discussions of right and wrong when he was in high school, and discovered that he made ten times the money running numbers as he would have jerking sodas after school. He loved his mother very much, but he also loved himself, and the feel of silk suits that cost two hundred dollars, and being able to run with the guys and spend forty, fifty a night on dinner with expensive girls that he loved to be with but wouldn't have dreamed of bringing home to Brooklyn on Friday.

He was also willing to spend his money on his family. He had offered several times a year to move his mother and father to a better apartment, in a better neighborhood. But she said she wouldn't have his blood money, which was hardly fair. He never hurt anybody, there was no blood on it, except in certain extreme cases, when somebody welshed, and badly, and it was a bet that Bernie had laid off in Cincinnati and Cleveland; but he wasn't responsible for what happened, you just didn't mess around with those people.

None of these things was discussed over Friday night dinner, at least not at length. Bernie asked his mother if she was willing to move yet, there was a beautiful bunch of apartments going up in Rego Park, and she said no thank you.

"I would rather live with a clean conscience in a filthy neighborhood," she said, and spooned out some more cabbage.

"Suit yourself," said Bernie, and winked at his father.

"I'm not the only one. There are some of us who still take pride in the neighborhood, who could move."

"Like who?"

"Like Yetta Sherman. She could move in a minute. Her son Andre is all the time asking them to come move in with him on Park Avenue."

"She told you that?" Bernie said, and smiled.

"She told me that all the time. Why, you know better?"

"I know Andre Sherman," Bernie said. "He can't stand his mother."

"He's a wonderful son, and a very important man. You read the papers?"

"I read the papers. And I know Andre. I knew him when he was Arnold. Yes, he's a very important man." Bernie bit into his food. "Great cabbage, Ma."

"I see his name all the time in those columns. I read the columns, while I'm looking for other news in the paper, with fear in my heart."

"Could I have more potatoes?" Bernie said, and held out his plate.

"Countesses he runs with. Princesses and millionaires."

"Well, he always aimed very high," Bernie said. "More gravy too, Ma, straight off the stuffed cabbage, it's delicious."

"How high does a person have to aim, not to want to run with gangsters?"

"And a little more carrots," Bernie said. "It's a sensational dinner. Don't you think so, Pop?"

Bernie's father nodded, and wiped up the gravy with a piece of bread.

"His mother can be very proud of him," Mrs. Kolodny said.

"Even though she never sees him?"

"It so happens he's having dinner there this very minute."

"How do you know?"

"She ran over to tell me while I was preparing."

"Well it must be quite an unusual event if she had to make an announcement. I wonder what made him come?"

"Maybe he loves his mother."

"Okay," Bernie said. "Whatever you say."

"Maybe it pleases him that a mother could take pride."

"Okay," Bernie said. "Okay."

"Did I upset you?"

"No," Bernie said. "No."

"Then eat," Mrs. Kolodny said. "Have a good time."

After dinner, Bernie sat with them, watching television for a few hours, not saying anything, just offering an appreciative belch every once in a while, and smiling when they looked at him. At ten o'clock he got up and kissed his mother good-bye, and walked with his father to the hallway, where he slipped him two fresh clean bills. The two men embraced, and Bernie walked along down the old, tiled steps, not looking at the graffiti on the walls.

When he reached the streets, he saw the big black Lincoln parked at the curb. From the doorway opposite came Andre Sherman.

"Hey pal!" Andre said, and raised his arm in greeting. "What are you doing here?"

"I come home every Friday for dinner."

"I didn't know that," Andre said. "Come on, I'll give you a lift back to town."

The two men got into the front seat of the Lincoln, and Andre reached over and squeezed his old friend's arm. "Hey, it's nice running into you. No kidding. Want to stop by the candy store and see if there's any action?"

Bernie laughed. "How's everything?"

"Great," Andre said. "Just great. Never been better. How's everything with you?"

"Never better," Bernie said. "You getting married again this year?"

"Maybe next," Andre said, and laughed. "It's great seeing you, no kidding. We never see each other anymore."

"Not since you stopped betting. What's it like in the world of high finance?"

"Very smooth," Andre said. "Hey, how come we don't get together more?"

"In the crowds you run with? My mother didn't stop all during dinner. She's been reading about you."

"No kidding," Andre said. "How is she?"

"Fine. Just fine. Yours?"

"Fine," Andre said. "Now that we've run into each other like this, we'll have to get together more."

It was not until they were over the bridge that Andre said

anything about the game. "Who you figure on to win in Baltimore?"

"I like the Rams," Bernie said. "The Colts are favored a little, but I like the Rams. They're getting very hot."

"That's got to be a pretty exciting game. Maybe you'd like to come over my place, Sunday, watch it in color."

"I've got color," Bernie said. "Thank you. Anyway, I'll be a little busy, tuning in on the rest of the results. I got six radios now, I can pick up the West Coast, Texas, anyplace."

"No kidding," Andre said.

"I got my mother one that picks up police calls."

Andre laughed. He was silent as the last lights on the bridge spotting the air around them, reflecting in the water under them, were absorbed into the gray glow of Manhattan.

"I guess it will be a pretty exciting game, Bern. If I were still a betting man, I'd pick Baltimore."

"They're favored by two points."

"Is that the bet?"

"That's what they're giving," Bernie said.

"Maybe I ought to put a bet down just to have a rooting interest."

"That's up to you," Bernie said. "I don't want to encourage you to go back to it. Not after you made such a big speech about giving it up."

"Well, I got a lot of cash to play with," Andre said. "What's the harm."

"Okay. If you want to place a bet, I'll take it. Only don't tell your mother. She'll tell mine, and she'll say I'm corrupting you."

Andre laughed. "Okay. Put me down for a hundred on the Colts."

"That's a very mild bet for you," Bernie said. "I guess you really are reformed."

"I meant a hundred thousand," Andre said, after a moment.

"You got to be crazy," Bernie said, and turned sideways in the seat. "I mean really crazy. When you were the world's worst gambler, you never bet more than fifty grand, and I thought then you were crazy."

"I was always good for it, wasn't I?"

"Nobody's saying you aren't good for it, Arnie, but you shouldn't sweat yourself like that. That's a hell of a big bet."

"So I can afford to lose it now. Why not make it?"

"I don't think I should handle it," Bernie said.

"Look. When everything you touch turns to gold, you have to take a chance at the big loss to make the win exciting. Like the stock market. But even that is so good to me I can't get hurt. I'm not afraid of getting hurt, Bernie, so you don't have to look out for me. It's like my building projects. I can't lose, and if I do, so what?"

"You building out on the Island? I think I saw your name on a building off the parkway—letters in the sky."

"I got a great new development in Rego Park. Why? You thinking of moving the folks out there."

"I been trying to talk my mother into it, but she doesn't want to move."

"Maybe if I talked to her," Andre said. "She always used to like me."

"She still does. She talks all the time about how happy your mother must be with you."

"Yes," Andre said, and was silent for a while. "Maybe that's how we'll do it. Maybe I can convince my mom to move to Rego Park, and then your mother will go, so they'll feel like they're not being deserted, if their friends are going along."

"Good idea," Bernie said.

"You want to come up to my place, we'll have a drink and talk about it?"

"No, I got a date," Bernie said. "Just drop me at Fifty-second and Third."

"*Kourveh?*" Andre said.

"Is there any other kind? Except maybe in the bunches you run with."

"They got them there too," Andre said. "Only with husbands, and titles."

Bernie laughed. "I'd still like to have one of those. Just once. An aristocrat."

"Well, maybe we can work that out too." Andre pulled over to the curb. "So what do you say, Bernie? You want to take my action, or do I give it to a stranger?"

Bernie hesitated. "You really made up your mind?"

"Why not," Andre said. "The worst that can happen is I lose."

"Okay, I'll take it, but I'll have to lay it off. I can't handle that much myself."

"Do what you have to do."

"That means Cleveland, Arnie. And Cincinnati. You can't mess around with those guys."

"Have I ever not been good for it?"

"No."

"So that's what you'll have to tell them."

"Yeah," Bernie said. "Yeah, I guess so."

When he got home to his apartment on Fifty-fifth Street,

Bernie told the girl to go in the bedroom and get undressed, he had to make a call. He sat for a moment on the arm of his print-covered couch, unloosening his white tie, and wiping his big dark forehead with his silk handkerchief. He had had a lot to drink, and he didn't feel so well, and something was bothering him, but he wasn't sure what it was. He reviewed the events of the evening in his somewhat fogged-up brain, and thought about his mother, and Andre. Not going home for years, coming tonight. Saying he didn't know Bernie came home for dinner every Friday, when there wasn't a mother alive who wouldn't scream at a son who never came home that Mrs. Kolodny's Bernie came every Friday. Andre coming out of the doorway, just at the moment Bernie was leaving. The fuss Andre had made at the coincidence. And then the casual way he had led into the bet.

It was all too pat. For all the suit with the brocade vest that matched the handkerchief in his pocket, and the custom Lincoln, and the Park Avenue apartment, and all the stories in the paper, it was all too pat; Andre with his casual approach was maybe too eager. Maybe he really needed the money. Maybe he didn't really have money to lose at all. Maybe Bernie was being a goddammed fool for putting his head on the block, vouching for him.

No. He was just looking for an excuse. He couldn't stand it because little Arnie Sherman was still the smartest kid on the block, and had pulled himself out of there by the bootstraps, and was straight and rich and successful, and his mother didn't have to be ashamed. And Bernie's mother did. He was jealous, it was that simple.

He picked up the phone and put in the call to Cincinnati.

For the first time since the incident in the bathtub at Paradise Island, they were alone. Every night that week they had been together, but always Bunyan was along, clucking his approval at the relationship that was growing between them, leading them like a giggling conductor of symphony into conversation; about Vietnam, about various miscellaneous stories of Mafia and riot control and the occurrence of breast cancer in transsexuals who had had mammaplasty—whatever they had managed to pick up in the *New York Times* that morning so as to have something to say at night. It was Diane, finally, who tired of the game.

"All right," she said to Rick. "I trust you. Let's take Bunyan home."

They were in the bar of the Carlyle Hotel, having coffee and an after-dinner drink. There were several people there that Diane knew, but she smiled at them with no embarrassment, through the vague, gold lighting, and even greeted them on her way out of the room. She knew how innocent the relationship was, and if they wanted to think otherwise, they could just as easily imagine that Bunyan and Rick were the twosome, and she was the coverup.

Besides, she felt good about herself, as good as she had felt in years. Her thick red hair was brushed to one side and gathered with a ribbon beneath her left ear, so it hung softly, like a schoolgirl's, over her shoulder. And a schoolgirl was what she was, beneath the trimness of her Dior. It was nice being courted. Especially since Rick wanted so badly to take her to the prom, he never mentioned dancing.

It was the only way she would agree to seeing him. She had been very clear about that to Bunyan. "If he says one personal word, I'll walk out. If he's really so mad for me that he's expiring of love, then it should be enough for him to be close enough to smell."

So every night that week they had spoken of purely impersonal matters. It was a strain for both of them, especially Diane, who detested meaningful silences. But Bunyan kept the conversational bubble afloat, as he was permitted to talk gossip and scandal along with the better things. Rick managed to control everything but his eyes.

His eyes were without doubt his most irresistible feature, Diane had to go along with *Photoplay* on that. His eyes were so deep-set and dark blue and framed so luxuriously with lashes that in closeup they might have belonged to Elizabeth Taylor. But that was forgivable, even marvelous, because the rest of his face was unmistakably masculine, strong straight nose slashing the face into two perfect halves, and slightly craggy jaw giving the lie to the gentleness of his smile. And she already knew about the rest of him, the best of him, at full staff. But the eyes were extraordinary, and as *Harper's Bazaar* had pointed out, they spoke volumes.

Tonight they had spoken of adoration, and worship, and passion, and sadness, all the while that his lips pursued the national news and the Hollywood banal. Adoration and worship Diane was used to, but not always from someone who had so little cause to put up with what she was handing out. There was no trace of resentment in his eyes, only admiration for the new way she was doing her hair (which of course he couldn't tell her because of the ground rules), respect for the fine legs she crossed so obviously as she sat down at the table, commenting on the shortness of her own skirt, and total appreciation of everything she did, from smoking her cigarette, to sipping her Galliano. Because there was no anger at the treatment to which she was subjecting him, because being so near to someone he wanted so badly, without being able to say a word, or touch her fingertips, must have been, for him, the equivalent of the rack, she decided she had gone far enough. She made up her mind, as they left the Carlyle, to forgive him for wanting her.

After they dropped Bunyan at his apartment, she gave the cab-driver her address. "Do you want to come upstairs?" she said to Rick, when the cab came to a stop.

"I don't know," he said. "I've about exhausted everything but the stock market pages, and I'm sure you know more about that than I do."

"It's all right. I'm lifting the ban. You can say anything you want to."

"Only say?"

"We'll see," said Diane.

When they were inside her apartment, she smiled and said she wanted to slip into something more comfortable. "Do you mind?" she said.

"Not if it's what you want."

"I'll only be a minute. Why don't you make yourself a drink. It's over there on the bar, everything you want."

"No it isn't." He settled himself into the one comfortable chair in the living room, and smiled.

She found, to her surprise, that she was slightly out of breath as she got out of her clothes. Opening one of the crystal bottles on her mirrored dressing table, she poured some rosewater into her palms and rubbed her breasts until they glowed pink. Then she slipped into a transparent yellow negligee and stood in front of the mirror. Her breasts looked like pale oranges through the material, and the dark red of her pubic hair glowed bronze. She smiled and drew open the satin ribbons at her neck, and lifted her arms wide to reveal herself. She did not blame him anymore. No one could blame him at all.

She tied the ribbons again, and went into the living room. "Well," she said, and sat down opposite him, lifting her legs over the side of the chair and letting her thighs open. "What will we talk about?"

He did not look away, as she expected him to. He followed the whitness of her inner thighs up to the dark triangle of polished copper, and his glance stayed there. She could feel him more strongly than when he had actually touched her.

"Whatever you like," he said.

"Well then, why don't we talk about love."

"I'm not very good at talking about it."

"Are you very good at making it?"

"I don't think that's for me to judge."

"That's almost a modest answer," she said. "I'm surprised."

"I'm sorry if we got off on the wrong foot," Rick said, and his eyes moved up to her breasts, and then her face. "I really am. I never knew I could feel this way about anybody, and I'm sorry we had such a bad start."

"What way?" Diane said. "What way do you feel."

"I love you."

"And just what does that entail."

"Everything there is, I guess."

"You'll have to get down to something a little more specific." She reached for a cigarette from the end table, and her arm brushed away the folds of the negligee from her opened thighs, so her mons veneris was completely exposed, and the petals that lay within. She did not move to cover herself, and he did not look away.

"I want to make you happy," he said.

"I am happy." She held the silver lighter to the tip of the cigarette, and pulled in the flame. "No one can possibly imagine how happy I am. You musn't believe *Cosmopolitan.* What do you really want?"

"I want to make myself happy, then."

"Well, that's honest," Diane said. "That's a little more like it. How would you make yourself happy?"

"By loving you."

"But you already said you did. If you love me so much, you must be loving me every minute, isn't it like that? Aren't you loving me with your whole heart? Aren't you loving me with your eyes?"

"Yes."

"Well what else have you got to love me with."

"This." He stood up.

"Well, that's very impressive, it certainly is very impressive, but don't forget I've already seen that, and under the best possible circumstances, you might say, in its natural habitat. Not jutting out from a pair of pants. What else."

"My hands. My arms. My tongue."

"Does it embarrass you saying things like that?"

"No."

"It's funny. You look a little embarrassed. You really shouldn't have any shame about talking these things. It isn't as if talking does any harm, or any good for that matter. I don't know anyone who really gets excited by dirty talk." She slid her legs from the side of the chair, and stood up.

"Come," she said. "We might as well get it over with."

"No."

"I beg your pardon."

"It's not anything that I want gotten over with. It isn't a dentist's appointment."

"But that's exactly what it is, Rick. It's inevitable, I realize that now, no matter how often I brush my teeth." She laughed. "So let's just have done with it, and then we can relax, for another six months at least."

"You really think I'd be as easy to dismiss as that?"

"Wouldn't you?"

"I don't know."

"Then maybe it's me," she said. "Maybe I'm just a cold cold woman, and nothing you could do could change that. So we ought to get it over with."

"I could change it," he said. "You wouldn't be cold."

"Ah, now that sounds more like my cocky, presumptuous Rick. You had me a little worried before when you were so self-effacing. Tell me how you'd do it."

"There are a lot of ways to turn women on. Even women who can't get turned on regular ways. And you're not one of them."

"Really?" She moved into the bedroom, and he followed her. She sat at the dressing table and started taking off her makeup. "Tell me about it. The ways you mention. It's interesting."

"I don't know if I should."

"Don't be silly, Rick, it isn't as if talking about these things ever caused any real harm, or got anybody excited. And nothing is wrong between two people that love each other, as long as it's between them, is it?"

"You love me?"

"I might. Go on."

"Well, you know the kind of things I mean. The magazines with the ads in them, and you send away to those mysterious addresses, and then get three kinds of vibrators in the mail."

"Really." Diane pulled off her eyelashes. "They have three kinds?"

"You can get vibrators in any drugstore, you know. And on the Coast they sell them in men's stores. With clothing. But the ones you send away for, well . . . Two of them are standard-type dildos, one rubber, shaped like a cock and balls, and one with a metallic spring inside, but the third one has an extra little triangle at the top that shimmies the clitty. I have a poor friend that sent for them, out of curiosity, she said, and she expressed great loathing when she got them in the mail. But she sneaks into the toilet every morning at two o'clock and jiggles herself to death."

"How disgusting," Diane said. "Do they really have attachments like that?"

"Like what?"

"With an extra little triangle?"

"Of course. It practically makes a man obsolete, going the male penis one better."

"Does anything really?" Diane said, and slipped the robe from her shoulders, and opened her arms to him, as she had done to herself earlier in front of the mirror.

"No," he said. "Not here. I've waited too long. I've wanted you too much to have it be anything but the way it should be. And this isn't the place."

"Oh for heaven's sake," Diane said. "I'm the one who's taking the chance, here in my apartment, with the servants sleeping. Why are you suddenly getting so prim?"

"I want you to come with me."

"Where? To the Regency? At twelve thirty in the morning?"

"I'm not at the Regency. I've rented an apartment."

"For me? You've taken an apartment just so you could be with me? Wasn't that a little presumptuous."

"Yes," he said, and fell to his knees, and rubbed his thick blond hair between her legs.

"Why can't we stay here?" she said. "Here and now."

"The lighting is red in my apartment. Have you ever made love by infrared light? Everything has a very soft glow. Everything. Have you ever done that?"

"It'll only take me a minute to get dressed," she said.

He had not told her the entire truth. He hadn't rented the apartment. He had arranged with a friend to borrow it for two weeks, and had set up the infrared lighting in the bedroom, and mounted the photographic equipment in the headboard of the bed, and at various points on the ceiling. It was something he had been planning ever since Paradise Island, when she had destroyed, forever, his chance at innocence.

"What a beautiful room," Diane said, although she could not see it clearly, because of the ethereal, almost nonexistence of the infrared light. But the bed glowed satin purple, and there were cupids on the headboard, and a huge French mirror to the left of the bed so she could watch him dimly as he stood undressing her.

"You really do love me," she said, as his head bent and his lips absorbed her naked nipple in the reflected glow.

"How could you doubt it." She could not see his head anymore, obscured as it was by her breast, but it was quite a lovely vignette, her extraordinary body, and an anonymous man loving it. He was naked to the waist, and his muscles traced fluorescently the line of his back.

"I think," she said. "I think it would be better if you were altogether naked."

"Then do it," he said.

She reached down and undid his button and zipper, and grasped his erection as his pants slid to the floor. It was a pink ivory rod in her hand, in the glow of the light. In a moment she had made it disappear, not inside her, but between her legs, so the effect in the mirror was that she had taken it away from him, but not to his advantage.

"Come," he said, and urged her toward the bed.

"I like it, standing here."

"You'll like it better on the bed."

"You really do love me?"

"Just see," he said, and danced himself between her legs. "Just feel how I do."

"You know," she said, as he laid her flat on the satin coverlet and started tracing the lines of her body with his tongue, "even if you told anybody about this, they'd never believe you."

"Why would I tell anybody? After all, I love you, don't I?"

"Do you?" she said.

"Well, what do you think?" he grinned at her and then his face was gone, and his tongue was darting fire between her legs.

"Oh," she said, as his movements urged her backward toward the headboard. "Oh," she said, as she almost thought she heard a clicking sound inside her brain.

"Now?" he said, turning her over on her stomach. "Now are you ready for me? The rest of me."

"Maybe," she said. "Maybe in a minute."

He raised her on her knees, and entered her slowly from behind, his fingers spreading her as easily as rose petals, while he penetrated her. He reached up and turned her face to the side on the pillow, so her profile showed.

"Why'd you do that?" she whispered.

"So you can breathe." He jolted her forward, and touched the headboard and smiled at the click.

"No, I don't like that. Turn me over, Rick."

"With pleasure," he said, and fell back onto his haunches, and plowed into her as he pulled the string on the side of the bed. "Now?"

"No. Not yet. Not quite . . . yet."

"Well, what would you like, my darling Diane. Speak up. Don't be ashamed. Nothing is embarrassing between two people who really love each other, is it?"

"You mean that?"

"What do you think."

"And you won't ever tell anybody?"

"I won't have to. What is it. Tell me." His fingers toyed with her clitoris, and he smiled. "Or do you want me to guess?"

"Yes, please. Guess."

"You'd like to know if I have one of those things. The vibrators."

"Do you?"

"I think I could manage to find one."

Sometime, early Sunday afternoon, when Maggie got back from church, George came in to the bedroom to see her, an eager, apple-like expression on his face. He always had a healthy glow about him, but with the help of the sunlamp in the private gymnasium, he had managed to keep up, and even deepen, his honeymoon tan, so his cheeks this day were particularly rosy. She felt quite sick, seeing his color next to her own pallor, so she looked away.

"Sweetheart," he said, and kissed the back of her hand, while his finger searched out her pulse. "How was church?"

"Lovely." Church that particular morning had been held in a basement on East Twelfth Street, with services conducted by Algernon assisted by Dr. Kunyadi. Communion had consisted of seaweed and macrobiotic food, with a supplemental vitamin and a glass of goat's milk for Maggie, because of her condition. The goat's milk had not mixed with the seaweed, and Maggie did not feel too well, but she saw no point in telling that to her husband, anymore than she would have told him she hadn't exactly gone to St. Vincent's.

"I have a wonderful surprise for you," George said.

"Really? I can hardly wait to hear it."

"Wendy's going away for a few days, and . . ."

"Going away?" Maggie said. "Why, is something wrong?"

"Not at all, not at all, but Chet Oppenheim and a few people are going skiing in Quebec, and they've invited her along."

"That isn't very considerate of her, is it, leaving you like that, going away without even asking, after all you need her, George, you've got a very thriving spa starting out, and I think it's madly inconsiderate of her to go without asking you, yes?"

"Not at all," George said. "She asked me, and I said it was fine."

"Why? Why would you say it was fine, she hadn't been with you that long to deserve a vacation. She's being outrageously selfish."

"But I told her to go," George said. "After all, she's a young woman . . ."

"And beautiful . . ."

"Yes, of course, Maggie. But she is young, and she is entitled to a life of her own. Besides, I wanted her to go."

"You did. Why?"

"Well, Maggie . . ." he grinned, and she closed her eyes. "Do you realize we haven't been together, *really* together, since we came back from Paradise Island? There's always someone around, Mary Elizabeth helping you with the house, or Wendy helping me with the clinic. And with her staying here . . . well I haven't felt—really alone with you in weeks."

"I've felt alone with you."

"I'm glad she's going. I encouraged her to go. And tomorrow night, I have plans for us."

"Plans?"

"Lovely plans. We're going to go someplace exquisite and romantic for dinner, and then we'll go to Lincoln Center, I've ordered tickets for the concert, and then afterward . . ."

"Oh what a shame," Maggie said.

"Shame?" said George.

"Tomorrow night. I suppose I should have told you sooner. We're having a party."

"Party? Party? But we don't even have any furniture downstairs."

"Well it's not that kind of party, George. We're going to play games. It's the perfect setup downstairs for games without the furniture. It should be fantastic fun, what?"

"I'm no good at games," George said. "I wanted to take you to dinner, and the concert, and afterward . . ."

"Of course I'd much rather do that, George, but I'm helpless. You must see that I'm helpless, yes?"

"Couldn't you call people and cancel?"

"Well I would in a second, darling, but I asked them all weeks ago, and you know how the games bunch are, they take their playing very seriously. They've really been looking forward to it, and you wouldn't want me to disappoint them, would you?"

"No," George said. "No, of course not."

She waited until he was in the shower, where he couldn't hear her, and where he would stay for at least a half hour, before she began telephoning people frantically, and trying to get them to come.

Outside, it was beginning to snow. The wide boulevard that was Park Avenue with its mid-islands of greens might as well

400

have been a back alley in Brooklyn, for the silence of the street, and the grayness of the day, and all it did to cheer Andre Sherman. He got no pleasure from staring down at it. The clouds were so low, and so heavy with threat, that he could all but feel them pressing. And in spite of the snow, the windows thrown wide against the dismal air, and every air-conditioner in his apartment blasting out full, he was sweating.

It made him feel even warmer and more uncomfortable, pacing back and forth in his living room, the way he was doing, but there was no way he could sit down. Sitting and watching the bright-colored course of the game on television made it seem even more torturous, as if he was actually out there in the stands of Baltimore, freezing his ass, instead of being safe in his apartment, with his ass about to be broken.

From the beginning, the game had gone against him, with the Rams making the first two touchdowns, and Baltimore seeming unable to keep the ball. At the end of the first quarter, Baltimore finally managed a touchdown, but it was not until just before the half that they managed the second, and then the Rams got a last-minute field goal. So Andre wasn't even to be allowed to enjoy the half, with the score tied, making him the maybe (please God) winner by two points. He sat, fiddling with the knobs, turning to see the other teams that were playing, the ones it would have made sense to bet on, and not be such a madman as to bet a team he didn't even care about, who cared nothing about him, who were joining in the conspiracy to give him a heart attack, before he could be killed like an honorable man, for losing a bet he couldn't pay.

When the call came in from Maggie Bolin Piner, he told her he couldn't talk to her, he was in the midst of a very important business discussion. She said she would only be a minute and was he free the following evening to come over to the house.

"Nine o'clock, don't get dressed up, you know where we are, Harry's house, and we have no furniture so you better wear levis or something so you're comfortable, what? And there's no dinner or anything, I'm sorry, I suppose I could send out for sandwiches, but there's no table to put them on, sort of a games plus picnic, yes? we could spread napkins on our knees, oh what fun. And you're the best one at games, you know you are. You will come?"

"If I'm alive," Andre said.

"Oh you are droll, and that is a coincidence, because I think we'll have to play Murder, yes? I'm not sure we even have paper and pencils, what? so Dictionary and Truth are out, and I'm not sure there's any good hiding places, what with no furniture and drapes and nothing on the walls, have you managed to do anything about your paintings? So Camouflage is out of the question, you can't play Camouflage with nothing but bare walls and bare floors, do you think? Unless you're only camouflaging a piece of plaster, no it's too good a chance to miss, all these big empty rooms, we'll have to play Murder, do you mind my thinking aloud?"

"Not at all," Andre said, as the second half started. "I have to go."

"That's all right, you've been fantastically helpful. See you at nine." She hung up the phone.

The second half started well, as if those bastards had listened to his imprecations over long-distance psychic waves. Baltimore got a third touchdown and started holding the ball nicely, so the Rams looked locked and defeated. The score was twenty-one to seventeen, favor of the Colts, and the Rams offensive team was tired. They were facing champions.

Thank God.

Andre went into the kitchen, and took out a water-glass tumbler, and a bottle of Napoleon brandy. He sat down in the red velvet couch opposite the Louis XVI cabinet of his television set and prepared to enjoy himself for the first time in weeks. The Colts held them beautifully, nicely, keeping the Rams out of scoring position, while Andre poured, and drank, and finally even closed a few windows.

And then the Rams broke away. He wasn't even sure that there had been a fumble, he didn't know in his finally relaxing brain what had taken place on the field. They were just there with their little horns painted over their ears, crashing across the goal line for a touchdown, getting the extra point, with only four minutes left to play.

The score was twenty-four to twenty-one, favor of the Rams.

And three and a half minutes left to play.

He stood there in his own apartment, screaming like the people in the stands of Baltimore, yelling like a madman at the sons of bitches to move their asses, do something. Something.

"Punt, you bastards," he shrieked. "For Christ's sake, get a field goal. I'm dying, you hear me? You're going to kill me."

He was still magic: he knew that, because it was as if they heard. They got the ball into field-goal position, and he was going to be okay, he was still a winner, no matter what it had done to him, aiming too high, going into areas where he didn't know the ground rules, where he didn't understand what the people really were, no matter how much he wanted to be like them, and knew he had more than any of them on the ball, that was where he had it, on the ball, and he wouldn't be killed, he wouldn't be dead, he would come out even from the game, and maybe even a little ahead, so they could all go fuck themselves, next time he would be smarter. Next time he would work from a starting position of contempt, like they did, the Orlovsky sons of bitches of the world, and he would get them all by the short hairs.

Because the game would end with a tie score, and that meant that Baltimore would win, the two points leverage would be added on to Baltimore, and he would come out ahead by two points, as soon as they made the lousy field goal.

They lined up. And Michaels got ready to kick. And he was the best kicker in the league, so he couldn't miss, there was no way.

He was in perfect position, and he couldn't miss. He didn't miss.

But Los Angeles blocked the ball.

Andre laughed, aloud. It was obviously a mistake. It was ridiculous. It couldn't possibly have happened that way. He was so worked up, and so fearful, that he had imagined the field goal had been blocked. But it couldn't possibly have happened.

He switched on the radio, because the radio made more sense, radio didn't confuse you with commercials and flashes of color and all the experimental camera work the networks were trying, so sometimes they were so busy watching the line you missed what was really going on. In the back of his mind he heard the gun go off, but he wasn't going to pay any attention. Maybe the gun was in his own head, like the dummy blocked field goal.

"We have a final on Baltimore and the Los Angeles Rams," the radio announcer said. "Los Angeles took it, twenty-four, twenty-one."

They had probably been watching the televised game, Andre thought, and switched it off before they could confuse him anymore. He sat down and looked at the set, and they showed him the play again, after the commercial. They showed him again how he had lost by one point, with a play that couldn't possibly have happened.

"No way," he muttered. "There's just no way."

He shook his head, sitting there, shook his head like an old man who talked to himself, like his own father, with his hand over his mouth, in his undershirt, an old man, dying, shaking his head because life wasn't really like that, it couldn't be, things like that just didn't happen. "I'm finished," he said. "I'm wiped out."

When the phone rang, Andre didn't answer it. He didn't have to; he knew who it was. He didn't answer it the next five times it rang either, and by the sixth time he was too drunk to pick it up even if he had wanted to. He looked at the sword-canes in the umbrella stand by the door and wondered if he should fall on one, if that wasn't an impressive way to go, and then wouldn't they all be sorry. He laughed. The way his luck was going he'd probably miss whatever vital was in his body and just end up in the hospital for a year, and who was going to pay the bills.

Sure, of course, Bernie Kolodny.

He laughed again, aloud, and hard so that the tears started streaming down his cheeks, blurring the vision of Park Avenue five stories below. Thirteen years he had managed it, thirteen years he had been on this street, while the seekers and the promoters and the *gonifs* broke their balls to get there, once, finally, at last, he had had it all, all along. Except that he had played a game when he wasn't really eligible. He had tried to do it on their level, with class, with elegance. With paintings, of all things. With the luxuries of the very rich. And it had turned out to be as dirty an alley fight as he had ever had in Brooklyn.

He leaned out his window and saw the lights going on in all the apartments along the avenue, saw the cooks in their various kitchens pause in their early evening ritual of preparation and come to the windows to look out at the softly falling snow. Some, arms folded, smoked cigarettes, and some just stared, probably at other cooks on his side of the street, who worked for people so rich they didn't even give Sundays off. A few cabs moved up and down the slick, darkly wet streets, and there were the echoes of doormen blowing whistles. There were cars, and the crisp echoes of footsteps. But Andre couldn't lean out to see whose feet were coming toward his building, not without falling, and he had no wish to crack his head on concrete, not with his luck, he probably would just fracture his skull and live. Besides, Bernie couldn't come on foot. Whenever he came, he would come by cab, or by black car, probably belonging to somebody from Cincinnati. For a hundred thousand dollars that by midnight, or maybe tomorrow morning, he would realize he wasn't going to get.

Andre looked out at the cooks and the maids and the doormen, and all the clean bright lights. "Listen," he yelled out to all of Park Avenue. "As long as we're here, why don't we have a party?"

CHAPTER THREE

THE game was not easy to set up. Twice Maggie had played Murder, once at Bunyan Reis' penthouse and once at Luke Benjamin's. They had the elaborate fag imagination to make the game complex and intellectual, as well as frightening fun, whereas she had only herself to work out the details. And Algernon, of course, but Algernon didn't particularly care for games, and was only coming because she had wept on the telephone, and explained that she had only nine people to play, and it was too late to get anyone else. A good Murder game, like the one at Bunyan's, took weeks to work out. He had bought old print housedresses at the thrift shop for everyone to put on, as well as terrible ratty wigs and old rubber masks; so that everyone was hideously, terrifyingly in drag when the flashlight beams caught them in the darkness, going about their business of looking for clues to unmask the murderer. But there was no time for Maggie to get as complicated as all that. She tried to rent ten pairs of coveralls and masks from Hertz, who seemed unable to understand what she wanted. In desperation, she phoned George's medical supply company and arranged for the delivery of ten surgical gowns, caps and surgical masks, and didn't even try to explain why she wanted them.

There was a novelty store on Eighty-sixth Street and Third where she found a hand buzzer for the murderer to use (that she stole from Bunyan—she had never experienced anything more horrifying in her life than the sound and feel of that murderer's hand with its staccato vibration on the back of her neck, in the blackness, signifying that she was dead and had to fall down where she had been struck, or rather, buzzed). At the same shop she got a balloon and a mama doll that was the right size for dismembering. Right across the street was a drugstore where she bought flaming red nail polish for blood (catsup she already had in the pantry, but she thought nail polish would be more effective, provided the clues were on surfaces from which it could be removed). The pen flashlights she secured from a hardware store on Second Avenue. After checking with the proprietor how much light they had before the batteries burned out, she decided that if she left them on all day, the light stored in them would be almost gone.

That left only the records. The one of the calliope playing was comparatively easy to secure in the children's record section of a local store. But a record of a baying hound ("The Baskervilles, preferably," she told the man behind the counter) was nowhere in the neighborhood, or even downtown at Sam Goody's. In the end she checked the yellow pages, and managed to get the Lon Chaney wolf man from a sound effects company on lower Broadway.

It took most of the day. She looked at her watch in the cab going home, surprised to see that it was nearly five o'clock. For a moment she felt quiet astonishment that men with so much to do with their lives, like Luke and Bunyan, would go to so much trouble, and involve themselves in anything so time-consuming. She had always imagined that the games took an hour or so to set up; now it occurred to her that a well-worked-out murder required a great many hours, even days; especially if one considered how hard it was to think up the actual clues.

She herself had settled for a fairly simple arrangement of letters, making an anagram that would provide the solution. Part of the enjoyment for the game's players was appreciation of the ingenuity of the one who set up the game, the obscurity of the clues, the difficulty of working out the solution. But she couldn't worry about accolades, or lack of them. There wasn't time to do more, especially with no one to help her but Algernon, who wasn't due in until eight thirty. It didn't matter too much that intellectually the game wasn't as challenging as the ones she had played before. In the darkness, in the empty vastness of Harry Bell's house, fear and panic would provide enough mental paralysis so that the players would feel triumph in finding the simplest of clues.

The minute she got home, she set about dismembering the doll. The gowns and caps and masks had already been delivered and were set, waiting, on a piece of brown paper in the entrance foyer. She set aside the paper bag with the pen flashlights, and checking her watch, saw that they could be left burning for another half hour before their light would begin to fail. She set the kitchen timer for twenty-five minutes, and proceeded to cut the arms, the legs, and the head from the doll, with a large carving knife.

There was no doubt about it, she thought, smiling to herself. It was going to be madly fun.

Andre had not answered his phone all day. He did not call the service, because he knew already who the messages were from; nor did he open the door for the grocery deliveries. He was not as vagrantly brave as he had been the night before; sober, he had no wish to lie down and die. There was a way, there had to be a way, to get the money to pay off Bernie, and then another way still to make up the hundred thousand to the gallery, but he wouldn't think about that. Not yet. First hundred thousand first.

At eight o'clock in the evening he went into the kitchen and made himself breakfast. Then he went into the bathroom, avoiding his own glance in the mirror, and started to shave. He was due at Maggie's at nine. He was the best game player in New York, sharper and shrewder and faster than any of them, and there was no reason not to go and remind them of the fact and have a good time in the bargain. Life went on. For a while, anyway. When he got down to the street, he nodded to his doorman, took a deep breath of the cold night air, and seeing that the snow had almost all melted, decided it was a good night for walking. He passed the corner where his car was parked. Listening to the click of his metal-tipped heels on the sidewalk, and the tap of his cane, filled his ears with the assurance of life continuing. The door to his car opened.

"Hey, pal," Bernie Kolodny said, swinging his legs down to the curb.

"Bernie," said Andre. "Why haven't I heard from you?"

"That's funny," Bernie said. "I been calling you since eight o'clock last night."

"I must not have gotten the message. I was over at Hartford's last night for a dinner party, and I left the house at eight thirty this morning to go down to Wall Street."

"You been no place. You didn't come home from anybody's and you didn't go out today. I been waiting here since nine last night."

"Then how could you have been calling me?"

"There's a pay phone around the corner," Bernie said.

"So if you went to use the pay phone, how do you know I didn't go out and come back."

"Listen, Andre, I guess you call yourself. You don't have to show me how you're so smart. I know you're smart. There's a very easy way to show me I'm wrong. Pay me."

"Oh, that's what you're worried about," Andre laughed.

"Yeah." Bernie laughed along with him. "Funny, isn't it."

"You know I'm good for it."

"I'm not interested in discussions. I want the cash."

"You'll get it. A hundred thousand, you can't put your hands on that kind of money in five minutes, Bernie, not all of us keep our cash in brown paper bags. I have investments.

You don't just pull your money out of deals like that in a second."

"You do if you owe a hundred grand."

"I just don't have the cash on hand. You'll get it, I promise you. I just don't have it on hand."

"Then you better go back upstairs, Arn. You're not going anywhere."

"What do you think? Do you think I'm trying to skip out?"

"I don't think anything. I just know you go no place till I have the money."

"You want to search me for airline tickets?"

"I don't want any trouble. With you, with Cleveland, with nobody. You just go back upstairs."

"But I'm due at a party."

"You're breaking my heart," Bernie said.

"Listen, I can't just not go. I promised."

"You promised me a hundred thousand dollars, when I asked you, I practically pleaded with you not to make the bet, not if you couldn't pay. And it's my nuts on the line."

"I can pay," Andre said. "I just can't pay this minute. And I'm due at a party. It's not just an ordinary party, Bern. Ordinarily, I'd just call and express my regrets."

"Is that what you do. Express your regrets. That's very nice."

"This is very well worked out, this party, it's an exact number of people, and it would throw everything off if I didn't go."

"You're really upsetting me," Bernie said. "And I don't have a hanky."

"Please. It's those people. All the ones I've been seeing. You don't think I'd be running with those people if I was faking, if I was a welsher."

"I don't know. I don't know what those people expect from their friends. I never run with the elegant bunch. All I know is people in Cincinnati, and guys like you."

"Maybe you'd like to meet them," Andre said, and his breathing started to relax slightly. "Maybe you'd like to come to the party. That way I could go, and you could make sure I was really staying there, that I wasn't trying to take off."

"I haven't been invited," Bernie said, smiling. "I wouldn't like to do anything rude."

"But they'd love having you, I know they would. And you'd have a ball, Bernie. It's at Maggie Piner's, the girl who just bought Harry Bell's house. Wouldn't you like to see that?"

"Harry Bell's house? The one on Fifth Avenue?"

"Come on. The worst that can happen is you have a good

time, get a few stories to tell downtown. They'll all be there. Countess Trejinska, Rick Flinders, all the people you read about."

"Not me," Bernie said. "My mother."

"So just think, next Friday you can tell her all about them, how you met them. Don't you think she'd like that?"

"Okay," Bernie said. "Why not."

"Only one thing . . ." Andre said. "We better come in separately. Don't tell them you're with me."

"Why, Arnie, you ashamed to be seen with me? You got any reason to be ashamed? You ever hear of me welshing on a hundred grand?"

"They'll like you better on your own, Bern. The idea of a crasher, well, Maggie will think that's kicky. But if I bring you, it will just seem pushy."

"Well I certainly wouldn't want to seem pushy," Bernie said. "That's the last thing in the world I want to seem."

"It's all right, if there's any problem, I'll say you're with me."

"You are too kind," Bernie said. "You really are. Okay. Why not. I always wanted to meet one of those tightcunts. Let's go."

In the center of Harry Bell's enormous country kitchen a built-in butcher's block ten feet long and four feet wide served as a breakfast table, or an informal counter for coffee and cake. The last was all Maggie would serve to the people who were ushered to the kitchen the moment they arrived. They sat in a oddly formal rectangle, on the bar stools Maggie and Mary Elizabeth had salvaged from the Old Rumanian on First Avenue. Julia White, for one, was anxious to begin.

"Well, we're all anxious to begin," Maggie said. "But we have to wait until everyone's here, don't we, you wouldn't want us to start if you weren't here."

Louise Felder lifted her face from her palms, resting open on the counter, and let out a moan. "I'd want you to start if I weren't here," she said. "Why don't I leave, and then you could start without me. I wouldn't mind, I swear."

Rick Flinders reached over and patted her hand and smiled. "Don't be such a coward, Lulu. It's only a game."

"I hate games," Louise said. "I'm the worst one, always. What am I doing here? Where did I go wrong?"

"We could always rent ice skates and go to Rockefeller Center," Charley said.

"I assume you're putting me on," said Louise. "Nobody is that healthy."

"It's all right, sweetheart," Bunyan said. "We all know . . . Charley? . . . Charley is, and we've forgiven him."

Diane Trejinska, sitting at the end of the table, laughed. "You're not the worst one, Louise, I am.'"

"Maggie, if you had any class you'd get another plane and take us all back to Paradise Island. It's cold in New York, and Lulu's tan is all faded."

"You look better than you ever have in your life," Julia White said.

"Really?" said Louise, and seeing the genuine approval in Julia's eyes, forgave her for everything.

"Beigey blondes look very muddy when they get too dark, especially when they're not natural blondes."

"And who designed your jumpsuit?" Louise said. "Ilse Koch?"

"Oh heaven, heaven!" Bunyan Reis clapped his hands. "True hostility. It's the best possible atmosphere for a Murder game."

"I'm not hostile," Louise said. "I merely assumed from the shine of her suit, and knowing Julia, that it was made from human skin."

"It's kid," said Julia White.

"Anyone we know?" said Louise, and ate another cookie.

"I was going to get one in kid," said Dainty Lee, standing up and pulling her levis down from her crotch. "But Norman assured me that the whole fad will be finished by next spring, and then what would I do with all that old leather."

"You could always make it over into throw rugs," said Bunyan Reis.

"Or lamps," said Louise.

Julia White walked around the table, pouring coffee from the unplugged electric percolator. Diane put her hand over her cup, and shook her head. "I don't want to get bloated," she said.

"You never will," said Louise. "Bitch." They smiled at each other.

"I wish I had the ability to make friends like you girls do," Charley said.

"Funny," said Louise. "Fun-nee."

"Well come on," Algernon said, from the stove, where he sat, legs dangling, on the cold iron-topped hearth. "What do you say we get this over with."

"Hear hear," said Bunyan Reis. "My nerves are on tenter-hooks."

"Can't think of a better place for them," Charley said.

"We've got to wait for Andre," Maggie said. "He'll be here any minute. He knows how important it is to get here on time." She looked at the electric clock on the wall above the refrigerator, and stamped her foot. "But he's ten minutes late, why would he do that when he knows how important it is to start on time."

"May I have a Scotch?" Julia said.

"No drinking," said Bunyan. "Everyone's got to be very alert."

"That let's me out," Algernon said, and slid down from the stove. "You better play without me."

"Oh you can't, Nonny, please, the game's set up for ten people, I have ten flashlights and ten outfits, and ten everything."

"What about Dr. George?" Algernon said.

"He's already playing. He's part of the ten."

"Where is Dr. George?" Dainty Lee said. "Why isn't he here? Are you planning some terrible surprise, Maggie, he isn't setting up any diversionary clues, is he, that isn't fair."

"He's not setting up anything," Maggie said. "He doesn't even know what the clues are."

"You swear?" said Louise.

"Of course."

"Lulu's bad enough at these things without your throwing in any red herrings. I almost killed Bunyan when he did that last time, when he put that extra person in the game that nobody knew was there. You wouldn't do anything like that, Maggie."

"Of course not," Maggie said.

"Why are you so nervous about this," Charley said to Louise.

"I can't stand being judged, that's all. I hate looking stupid, especially when I am."

"Nobody's judging you. We're just all here for a good time," Bunyan said.

"Oh, is that why we're here," Charley said. "I'm glad somebody told me."

"You never stop judging, you know you don't," Louise said. "The first time I played Dictionary I almost got drummed out of the corps because I didn't think of any clever definitions."

"Well, this isn't the same kind of game," Bunyan said. "This is much more of an action game. And we play it for fun."

"And that's why it's called Murder," Louise said.

The doorbell rang, and Maggie went to answer it. Rick leaned over toward Diane, and put his hand in front of his face.

"I can't," Diane said softly. "Not tonight."

"They're whispering!" Louise said. "Foul! Maggie, they're cheating, they're already starting a conspiracy."

"Oh shut up, you paranoid," said Andre, from the doorway to the kitchen.

"Well well well," said Louise. "If it isn't the spirit of Christmas past."

Maggie climbed the stairs to her bedroom, and knocked on the door before entering. "Are you ready?" she said to George.

"Almost." He buttoned the collar of his shirt.

"But I told you you didn't have to get dressed. Everybody's in levis, and jumpsuits. Why must you be so madly impeccable."

"I am the host," George said.

"Nobody's the host, it's a game night."

"All right then, I'm the murderer."

"Shh," Maggie said, bringing her finger to her lips. "You're not supposed to know that. It's supposed to be chance, your getting that slip. Don't forget, the third gown from the top. And for heaven's sake, don't tell any of them you're the murderer."

"Why would I do anything as stupid as that?"

"I'm not sure," Maggie said softly, and went back downstairs.

She was almost to the kitchen when the chimes rang. Fluttering her hands angrily in the darkness of the foyer, she went to the front door. "Yes, yes, who is it, if you're the sandwiches it's much too early, I told you eleven o'clock."

"I'm not the sandwiches," Bernie said, and smiled. It was quite dark on the street and there was only one small artificial candle burning in the holy font in the foyer, but even in the darkness he had a very good smile.

"Who are you?"

"The uninvited guest. Do you mind very much?"

"Are you a friend of somebody's?" Maggie said.

"I hope so. Are you Mrs. Piner?"

"Yes."

"I'm sorry to barge in like this, sincerely. I'm a crasher. Do you mind?"

"Well ordinarily I wouldn't, but this is a very carefully arranged evening, Mr. . . ."

"Kolodny," Bernie said. "Bernie Kolodny."

"What's holding it up, Mag," Algernon said. "The sooner we get started, the sooner we get it over with."

"Oh Nonny, I . . ." She turned to him. "I'm sorry to be so long, but we have a crasher."

"Oh?" Algernon shuffled across the foyer in his moccasins. "You having any trouble? You want me to get rid of him?"

"No trouble, Nonny. He seems quite nice."

"Splendid," Algernon said, and took Bernie's arm, pulling him inside. "Then you must join the party."

"But what about the game?" Maggie said. "I have it worked out for ten people."

"Gorgeous," Algernon said. "A miracle from above. Or somewhere. He can take my place."

"Oh but Nonny, he doesn't know how to play."

"Then you'll tell him, Maggie mine. And I'll be free. Free."

"To go where?" she said anxiously.

"Why wherever you do. How's that for fine?"

"Oh," she said. "Lovely. Please come in, Mr. . . ."

"Kolodny," Bernie said.

Algernon went back to the kitchen while Maggie hung up Bernie's coat in the hall closet. Her mind was full of darkness and the silence and privacy that would belong to her and Algernon, even with the other people in the house, playing games. She could hardly remember her manners.

"I'm so sorry, Mr. . . . but may I ask you, what do you do?"

"Do?" he said.

"Not for myself you understand, I'm madly indifferent to what people do, it's what they are I always say, and you're probably very nice, but the group here tonight, well they're very concerned with doing, you understand, they don't like to play games with someone unless they're a doer. Do you do anything?"

"What do they do?"

"Well, Bunyan paints, and Julia fashions fashion, and Diane Trejinska, well she does a lot with the Liver People, besides her singing, and of course Louise Felder does a column, and George, that's my husband, he's a doctor, but you don't have to do anything like that, it doesn't really count. You do do something?"

"I'm a bookie," Bernie said.

"A what?"

"A bookie."

"You mean you actually take bets on races and things like that?"

"I actually do. Or even make book. Hence, the origin of the word."

"How heaven," Maggie said. "I've never actually met a bookie before."

"I know a lot of them," Bernie said, trying very hard to get a look at the house. It was difficult with all the lights out, except the one small electric candle in the foyer. "Next time you have a party, I'll bring over a bunch of my friends."

"How droll," Maggie said. "How absolutely droll. You think they like to play games?"

"I doubt it."

"Well I hope you do."

"I haven't for a long time, but if that's what you're doing . . . I guess I'm game. I made a little joke."

"Yes," Maggie said. "I guess you did. EVERYBODY!" she ran to the doorway of the kitchen, and called them all. "Into the foyer, into the foyer, we're ready to start."

When they were all collected in the darkened entryway, Louise huddling against the old barren marble of the wall, Bunyan jumping up and down, clapping his hands, Maggie handed them each their surgical gown, cap and mask, and told them to put them on. "Now we're playing almost the usual way," she said. "In the pocket of each gown is a slip, with either the word "Murder" or "Victim" on it, so any of you might be the murderer. Only tonight the object of the clues isn't to find the identity of the true murderer. Tonight the clues will add up to the one place in the house you can go to be safe. Whoever gets there before they get killed, wins. The murderer isn't allowed to go to that place."

"How can you trust him not to go if he's a murderer," Charley said.

"They have their code," said Bunyan Reis, slipping into the sleeves of his gown. "Don't be such a cynic."

"Also in your pockets," said Maggie, "are little pen flashlights. Now when the calliope plays you're free to roam around and look for clues. All the clues are on the ground floor. But when the dog bays everybody has to freeze, and then the murderer is free to strike. Unfortunately," Maggie giggled. "I left the flashlights burning a little too long this afternoon, so the batteries are almost gone. You'll have to be very sparing in your use of the lights."

In the darkness, faces obscured by surgical masks, everyone a sinister, anonymous figure, hands reached for the flashlights, and opened slips of paper. "Well of course," Louise muttered. "I would be a victim."

"Stop, don't tell," mewed Dainty Lee. "You're spoiling it."

Bernie Kolodny slipped the cap awkwardly over his thick black hair. "This is what they do, these people? This is how they spend their time?"

"Don't look to me for sympathy, pal," Charley said. "I don't know what I'm doing here."

Andre edged toward Bernie. "You'll see. It's a lot of fun."

"I don't want to make a fool of myself," said Bernie. "I'm not sure I understand the game. I don't even know what I'm looking for."

"Don't worry," Andre whispered in the darkness. "I'll help you."

Rick Flinders moved closer to Diane. "I think you'd better reconsider about later," he said.

"What?" said Louise.

"Oh. I thought you were someone else."

"I know," said Louise, from beneath her surgical mask. "I've never looked lovelier."

"All right now, is everybody dressed? Okay. These are the partners. You work in teams, looking for clues, so you'll feel safer. But just in case you feel too safe," Maggie giggled, "remember your partner may be the murderer."

"Adorable," said Louise.

"George, your partner is Julia White. Bunyan, you're with Diane. Rick, Dainty Lee. Charley, I hope you don't mind, we have to partner you up with a boy, is that all right?"

"Well I don't know," Charley said. "If it has to be a boy in the dark, I think I should have my choice of boy. I pick Bunyan."

"Oh you're such a bitch," Bunyan said, and giggled. "You cute thing. I'm going to steal him from you, Louise."

"Louise, your partner is Andre."

"You go too far," Louise said. "I won't play."

"Oh come on," Bunyan said. "Stop being such a spoilsport. It's all in fun."

"I want to play with Charley."

"Well, we all know that, darling," Bunyan said. "But you should wait till you get home."

"Fun-nee. Can't Charley be my partner, Mag?"

"It's too incestuous, Louise, really. You can't partner up with someone close. Besides, he doesn't know the game. You'd lose."

"Well we can't allow that to happen," Charley said.

"I won't play with Andre," Louise said firmly.

"All right," Maggie said. "Then Andre, you're with Charley, and Louise is with Bernie."

"With who?" Louise said.

"Bernie."

"Who's Bernie?"

"I'm Bernie," he said softly.

"You did it, dammit, Maggie. You swore you wouldn't and you've brought in a ringer."

"Don't be silly, Louise. Bernie is just a friend of mine and Algernon's who wants to play, so he's taking Algernon's

415

place. It's all madly innocent, but if you're upset about playing with a stranger, you can switch back to Andre."

"I'll take my chances with Jack the Ripper here," Louise said.

"All right, then are we all set?"

"I've got to go to the john," Dainty Lee said.

"Oh for Christ's sake," said Andre.

"Well, what do you want me to do, hold it in?"

"All right, go," Maggie said, "hurry. It's right over there, under the stairs."

"Right over where?" Dainty Lee said. "Who can see anything."

Maggie directed her toward the stairs. "It's just as well if anybody has to go that they go now, as a matter of fact. Don't forget, when the murderer strikes, he's free to strike anywhere, and if he kills you while you're sitting on the pot, that's where you have to stay."

"What does that mean?" Bernie said to Louise.

"It means when you get murdered you have to fall down in the exact spot you're killed, the minute you're killed."

"You people certainly know how to enjoy yourselves," Charley said.

"How do you know when you're murdered," Bernie asked Louise.

"Oh you'll know," Louise said. "Believe me."

They stood there, not quite huddled together in the darkness, partner reaching for partner's hands, some hands drawing away, as they heard the sound of a reverberating tinkle which the water Dainty Lee had left running in the sink did not quite manage to cover. "You have great acoustics here," Andre said. "Did Harry build this for a concert hall?"

"It seems like that sometimes, doesn't it," Maggie said.

"I hadn't realized the walls in the house were so thin," said Dr. George.

"No," Maggie said. "I guess you didn't."

"Come on, come on," said Bunyan. "Let's get started."

"I might as well turn out the light in the kitchen," Maggie said. "So as to get the total effect."

The one slashing ribbon of yellow across the marble floor disappeared, and they were in total darkness, except for the bulb candle in the font. Maggie turned it off.

"I hate these fucking games," Louise said. "Why do I have to stand around and shiver, and wait to be murdered. Why don't I just commit suicide."

"Why don't you just tell them you don't want to play," Charley said.

"Sometimes I don't understand you, Charley."

"All right, children," Maggie said, leading Algernon by the hand through the darkened foyer toward the closet where the stereo equipment was stored. "Now we're going to start. On your mark . . ." The door to the walk-in closet closed, and in a moment the eerie throat of a calliope opened on the dark, muffled air.

Hands reached for penlights. Small points of vague light flickered in the darkness like dying fireflies, as figures moved out from the foyer into the other rooms. Louise, stepping into the cavernous emptiness of the living room, hearing the echo of feet across the uncarpeted floors, was moved to take Bernie's hand. Remembering he was not only a stranger but the potential murderer, she contented herself with his whispered assurance that he was nearby.

Dainty Lee screamed as the tired beam of her flashlight picked out a bloodied mutilated hand in the fireplace. She dropped her flashlight, Andre standing behind her whispering "Clever girl," picked it up from the floor, and shone it directly into the small childlike palm. In the center was pasted a small cardboard "A."

"My partner," Dainty Lee whispered. "Where's my partner?"

"It's an A," Louise whispered to Bernie, when she was able to stop clutching her heart, and had made her way to the fireplace.

"So it's an A," Bernie said. "What does that mean?"

"They gave me the right partner. You're going to be a lot of help . . . The A is part of a puzzle. Now we know, or maybe we know, we're looking for letters, and put together they'll spell something, and that's the answer, okay?"

"Okay."

"There's probably no other clues in this room, so we might as well start looking other places." She switched off the light, and started to move across the empty room and collided with a someone in the darkness.

"Jesus," George said.

"Is he here too?" said Louise, as she moved into the hall.

Dainty Lee, still shaking, was steadying herself against the fireplace, when the calliope stopped. She froze and whispered Rick's name, but there was no answer in the blackness. The sound of a baying hound, or a crying wolf, she did not have time to figure which, pulled the hair on her arms, and she whispered Rick's name again.

The sound stopped on her lips, as the cold buzzer pressed into her neck, and reverberated through her skull. George whispered, "You're dead," and she slumped to the floor.

"Listen, Andre," Charley said in the darkness. "I know that this is going to upset you, but I just got killed."

"I'll manage without you," Andre said.

"But I'm heartbroken," Charley said. "I just wish I weren't out of it so soon. I could go on and on forever in the dark, just waiting to be murdered."

"If you're dead, lie down," Andre said. "I can't waste time talking to you."

When the calliope started again, Rick found Diane in the darknesss, and this time made sure it was Diane before speaking. Bunyan, her partner, had his hand in the dumbwaiter and was shining his flashlight up into the empty shaft overhead, so Rick and Diane had a moment alone.

"I think you better reconsider," Rick said.

"About what?"

"About later this evening. I have something I want to show you."

"I'm not in the mood for your goodies," Diane said.

"I think you'd better be."

"Better? Better?"

"That's right."

"Why Rick, dear, that sounds curiously like a threat."

"Does it?" he said.

"I'm not available this evening."

"I think it's to your own best interest that you make yourself available."

"I'll think about it," Diane said.

"You better," said Rick.

"Diane? Diane?" Bunyan's voice rasped in the darkness. "Is that you, Diane?"

"It's me, love."

"Come," Bunyan said, and put his arm around her, and led her away, whispering his discovery.

Andre was moving fast. He always moved fast in games, and his mind moved faster, but this particular evening the natural fear engendered by the darkness and the eeriness of the atmosphere was supplemented by a wish for survival he had never realized he possessed. Adrenalin quickened his thoughts and, curiously, struck the normal fear away, making him function as he had never functioned before. He discovered an amputated foot, bloodied, in the heating register of the den, with the cardboard A stuck between its toes. He was glad Charley was out of it. Charley would have slowed him down. It wasn't a game anymore, it was a question of survival, and when survival was involved, you didn't worry about the rules, or winning. You just beat everybody out.

That was the point, he had to find the solution before anybody else, long before anybody else, so he could help Bernie.

Two A's. It made no sense, but nothing made any sense anymore. There was nothing in the salon. Were there rooms, was there a piece of equipment with two As where somebody could hide, and be safe? The house was poorly heated, but he was still sweating, as his flashlight beamed upward, and he saw the second bloodied hand in the dining room chandelier, and the cardboard U. A. A. U. Nothing. He ripped into the center of his own brain, for all the store of anagrams and championship word games he had played in his career with these people, and nothing struck him.

The calliope stopped, and he heard Diane shriek and Bunyan sigh as they were struck down, but he did not stand still in spite of the rules. There was no time to play the right way. It was not the moment for gamesmanship. He felt his way along the walls, into the kitchen, and shone the dying light quickly around. But that was silly. They had all been congregated in the kitchen when he arrived, and Maggie wouldn't have been so foolish as to leave any clue in the one lighted room where everyone had been, where it might have been observed.

Unless.

The calliope began again.

He walked to the huge refrigerator in the darkness, and opened the door. The shaft of light split the room and revealed the body of Julia White, face down, on the butcher block. He took a quick startled breath and then looked inside. There was a split of champagne, some leftover chicken and a jar of caviar next to some of Dr. George's medicine vials. Nothing else.

He opened the freezer. Next to a pint of vanilla ice cream was a severed head.

The doll must have been quite pretty when it was alive, or at least all in one piece. But now blood striped the curly yellow hair, and one of its eyes was pushed all the way into the socket, and blood ran from its busted nose. The little white teeth dangled free, beneath the red painted cupid lips, like maggots rising from an ancient box of Valentine candies. One of the porcelain cheeks was cracked into darkness, and from the gaping hole a small piece of cardboard protruded.

He turned to make sure Julia was still dead, and her head facing away, so she couldn't watch him. He drew the slotted cardboard from the hole and shoved it into his palm.

The letter N. He put it into the pocket of his dressing gown, and made for the hall. AAUN. NASHUA. Did Maggie have a stuffed horse someplace upstairs, like the old lady in the Dakota, trying to remember her husband, who rode with Teddy Roosevelt. How many words were there in the English language that used those unhelpful vowels, or was Maggie pulling a trick, and having it in a foreign language. No, that would be too unkind to dummies like Dainty Lee. Besides, Maggie wasn't that clever herself. That was something that someone like Bunyan would try. BUNYAN. No, that was two N's, not two A's.

He was concentrating so hard he tripped over the body of Rick, who had died in the same position he did in his last picture, glamorous, immortal, a waste of beautiful life. Andre steadied himself.

NAUSEA? Was there somewhere upstairs a vomitorium? It was a misleading clue, she had said a place, she had specifically said a place, and a condition wouldn't be a fair clue to a place. Yes? No?

"Watch it," Diane said, as he bumped into her, draped over the one bench in the foyer.

"Sorry," said Andre.

"It's all right, I'm already dead."

In the darkness, his hand found the umbrella stand by the front door, and he silently drew out his cane. AAUN. NUAA. UNAA. AUAN. UANA. AUNA.

Of course.

There were five extremities to a doll, and he had found four of them, so there was only one missing. S. What else could it be. SAUNA. The gymnasium. Everybody knew about the gymnasium. Harry Bell's famous gymnasium, now the cornerstone for Dr. George's spa. And it probably had a sauna. He clutched the cane in his hand and moved to the music of the calliope.

The only problem now was finding Bernie. And getting him there. He would have to be quick about it, but he had time, he knew he had time, because he was the smartest one, nobody else would have figured it out so fast, some of them were dead already. Besides, he had taken one of the clues. How would he find Bernie?

"I'm not having a good time," Louise whined in the darkness.

Andre smiled, and made his way to the sound, and sought the tall dark figure with his hands. "Bern?" he whispered.

"Arn?"

Andre placed his lips directly next to Bernie's ear, and told him to come along. He pulled him toward the stairs, guiding him carefully around the sprawled bodies, and touched the marble balustrade.

"Where are we going?" Bernie whispered.

"I worked it out, I've got the answer. You're going to win."

"I'm not having a good time," Louise murmured again, a few moments later, in the darkness. "I can't find my partner."

"Shut up and play," Andre said, beside her.

"Oh for Christ's sake, are you still alive?" she said. "There's no fucking justice."

Behind them, the shrill empty notes of the calliope played, but there was no other movement in the darkness. "Have you looked in the kitchen?" Andre whispered.

"You're not my partner, you don't have to be helpful. You're trying to make up with me. You can't stand it because I've found someone, can you."

"I'm delighted for you," Andre said. "He seems like a very nice guy."

"You like him? There's got to be something wrong with him if you approve. Andre? . . . Don't go. Lulu's afraid . . . Andre? . . . Andre? . . . You sadistic bastard, where are you?"

He waited until he heard her moving toward the kitchen before he stepped down into the living room and cocked his head, straining for another sound. In the direction of the fireplace he detected movement, and he walked toward it, deliberately clicking his heels.

"Dainty Lee?" Andre said aloud. "Is that you?"

"Yes, my dear," said a man's voice, in falsetto. "Right over here."

He strode to the fireplace and stood still, even before the calliope stopped, and the howling began. "Where?" he said.

"Right here," said Dr. George, and pressed the buzzer into his cheek. "You're dead."

Andre slumped to the floor, and smiled.

George Piner felt his way along the walls, still unfamiliar with and baffled by the complex of big rooms, and found his way, laboriously, to the closet under the stairs. He knocked twice.

"There's no clues in here," Maggie whispered through the door. "This is out of bounds."

"It's me, Maggie. George. Your husband."

The door opened slightly. "What is it?"

"I've killed seven of them. Can we stop now?"

"Are the other two alive? Did somebody find all the clues?"

"Somebody must have found them by now, Maggie. Can we stop?"

"You're not really in the spirit of the game, George. You shouldn't rest until you've made sure you got all of them."

"Maybe we ought to check the sauna, just in case the other two are there already."

"I only have one prize," Maggie said. "I certainly hope two people didn't get there, it spoils the whole game."

The scream from upstairs cut through the air like sudden light. "Oh good," Maggie said. "Someone's found the rest of the doll."

When George and Maggie switched on the light in the gymnasium, they found Louise, sitting on the floor by the electric rower, cross-legged, her head swaying toward her knees. "There's a body in there," she whimpered.

"You are a goose, of course there's a body, how madly melodramatic, Lou. It's only the torso of the doll."

"No, I mean a body. It doesn't go with the head in the freezer at all. That's a terrible thing to do to somebody, Maggie, to set up a pretend corpse in there, I almost had a heart attack when I touched it. It's not funny. For one terrible moment I thought it was Harry, and that was where he was stashed."

"You are droll," Maggie said, and patted Louise's shoulders. "You should have switched on the light, and then you would have seen it was only the rest of the doll."

"Would that have been cricket?" Louise said. "I thought the whole purpose of the game was finding things with the lights out."

"Well, not when you win," Maggie said. "You've won, you know."

"No kidding? I beat everybody. What about George here?"

"George is the murderer," Maggie said.

"Really? I really won?"

George walked past them, and switched on the light in the sauna, and moved out of sight. Maggie helped Louise up from the floor, and kissed her cheek.

"You're the cleverest one," Maggie said.

"No shit. What's the prize? Do I get to go back to Paradise Island."

"Give her her prize, George. George?" She moved toward the sauna, smiling.

George was on one knee on the tiled floor. In front of him was Bernie's body, stretched out in white surgical garb, mask hanging loosely from slack lips, a stain darkening the back of the surgical cap. Beside it lay the mutilated torso of the doll, pink balloon jutting from its neck, with "SAFE!" scrawled in nail polish across it, matching the red stain on the surgical

422

cap. The red on the doll somehow looked more real. The man's blood was a very artificial red, Louise thought.

"This man is dead," George said.

"Honest to God," said Louise. "How corny. You people go too far for effects. It's over. Stop trying to scare me."

"But he is," George said. "He really is."

When the police came, it was a little difficult to make them understand what everyone had been doing there, and the exact purpose of the game. But it had to have been an accident, Maggie explained, a madly unfortunate accident, because nobody at the party even knew the man, he was a crasher.

In the kitchen, Bunyan Reis passed trays of sandwiches on cardboard and aluminum foil, while Louise poured coffee for everybody, including the detective sergeant. Maggie apologized for forgetting her manners, explaining that she was a little shaken.

"I suppose I should send something up to your . . . boys, Sergeant, the policemen upstairs."

"No, that's all right," the sergeant said. "They have enough to do to keep them busy."

"It had to be an accident," Bunyan said. "I saw the way the body was lying, and he probably tripped on the doll and hit his head on the wall, and had a heart attack. It's very slippery in there and it's all tiles and stones and it was a very tense game."

"When exactly did you see the body?" the sergeant said.

"Not until it was over, when we all went upstairs and saw. Goodness," Bunyan said. "I couldn't kill anybody. I'm vicious, but only with words. I promise you, if you give him an autopsy, you'll find he had a heart attack."

"I almost had a heart attack," Louise said. "And I didn't even slip on the doll."

"You're the one that found the body?"

"Yes."

"And you never saw the man before this evening?"

"Of course not, I told you."

"You play this game often, Mrs. Piner?"

"Well, not often," Maggie said. "We've played two or three times before, more or less the same group. We play other games, but Murder is very hard to set up."

"Yes," the sergeant said. "So I would imagine. You all know how the game works then."

"Of course," Maggie said. "Everybody knew. All except Mr. . . . whatever his name was, poor thing, and Charley, of course."

"Which of you is Charley?"

"I am." Charley raised his head from the table.

"You've never played before?"

"No sir," Charley said. "Jesus Christ."

"And you have no idea what happened?"

"No."

"And the dead man never played before either?"

"I don't know," Charley said. "I didn't know him."

"He said he never played before," Maggie said.

"So how do you account for his being the first one to unravel the clues."

"I have no idea, Sergeant," Maggie said. "He must have been terribly bright."

"It's a shame, really," Bunyan said. "If he had such a good aptitude for games, he would have made a great guest."

"You don't think it was prearranged for him to go to the sauna? You don't think somebody might have helped him?" the sergeant said.

"Why would anybody do that?" Maggie said. "They all want to win. The only person who's supposed to help you is your partner."

"Oh I see," the sergeant said. "And everyone's a stickler for the rules."

"Certainly," Maggie said. "What kind of people do you think we are?"

Louise, as the dead man's partner, was questioned thoroughly. She told the police that she had lost contact with him early in the game. Everyone else explained that they were murdered before they could find all the clues, the essential one being the N in the doll's head in the freezer, which nobody had found except Louise.

"Aren't you forgetting the victim?" the sergeant said. "He must have found it."

"Oh, of course," Maggie said. "Julia, weren't you here in the kitchen when you were dead? You must have seen him."

"I didn't see *him*," Julia said. "My head was turned away. I only saw the light in the freezer go on."

"Twice?" the sergeant said.

"Yes, that's right, twice. . . . No. Wait a minute. Maybe it went on three times."

"If you ask me, the essential clue is the S," said Algernon Reddy. "You could figure it out easily if you had two A's and an S. The S was in the dumbwaiter, with the doll's foot."

"But you weren't playing, is that right, Mr. Reddy?"

"That's right."

"You were . . . working the phonograph, I believe that's

what you said. With Mrs. Piner? In the closet under the stairs?"

"That's what I said."

"Really, Sergeant," Bunyan Reis bit into a ham and Swiss cheese sandwich. "You're making this all sound terribly grotesque."

"Am I really?"

"Granted, it's terribly unfortunate, what happened, but accidents will happen, and you needn't make it sound as though anyone here were doing something wrong. It happens to be a delightful game, under normal circumstances, and your attitude, frankly, astonishes me. Policemen aren't supposed to be so fraught with innuendo. You should just ask everybody direct questions, and be terse, or don't you watch *Dragnet?*"

"I apologize, ma'am," said the sergeant.

Before the guests left, they were all questioned again about their whereabouts during the evening. Although everyone admitted that it was quite difficult to swear who had been downstairs in the dark, they were all able to remember where each other's bodies had been when Maggie came rushing down the stairs and switched the lights on. They were told again not to leave town. Rick bleated something about his movie, Diane muttered angrily about Biarritz, and Dainty Lee wept about her house in Acapulco. But all agreed they would stay in New York.

"Dammit," Diane said into the cold, cloudless night, as Rick hailed a cab for her on Fifth Avenue. "How could this happen? Trapped in New York. It'll be Christmas soon, and everyone's expecting me."

"Well maybe it's just as well, pussycat," Rick said.

"How can you say that. The whole thing is too horrible. That man. Having to be landlocked. And what about your picture?"

"Some things are more important than a momentary success," Rick said. "Now I'll have full time to devote to pursuing you."

"Presumption again, Ricky Ticky. Just because I went with you once, don't think we'll make a habit of it. If I decide to be with you, it will be because *I* decide. When I decide."

"I don't think so," he said. "I think you're coming home with me now."

"You're mad as a hatter, you know that, don't you. A little sexual conquest has gone straight to your pointed head. For all you know, the police will be watching us, for heaven's sake, this is no time to get involved in anything sticky."

"You're already involved." The cab pulled up beside him, splattering the residue of the previous evening's snowstorm on his custom-made, low-heeled boots. He cursed softly and opened the door.

"Good night Mr. Flinders," she said, and offered her hand. "As far as I'm concerned, nothing ever happened between us."

"I have something to show you," he pushed her hand aside, and reaching inside her spotted leopard coat, squeezed her breast, "that might change your mind."

While Andre walked to his car, he whistled, cracking his cane against the sidewalk. Without meaning to smirk, he smirked. New York's Finest, or not New York's Finest, they had obviously been so thrown by the people involved, the setup of the game, and the sheer bizarreness of the circumstances that they hadn't made a move to arrest anybody, as he had anticipated. They hadn't even seen him take his cane from the umbrella stand in the hallway, where he had placed it after coming back downstairs, on his way out the door. Awe and confusion had blinded them as surely as the darkness had blinded the game's players, and he was free.

Eventually, he supposed, they might connect him with Bernie Kolodny. But it would take a while, and by that time he would be long gone. Out of the country, someplace warm, like Argentina. People did that all the time: it wasn't only the stock swindlers and ex-Nazis who were meant to get off free. Anybody deserved it who was clever enough not to fade away under a momentary clutch of panic.

Of course, raising the money to skip might present a bit of a problem. But he could do it, he knew that now. There was nothing he couldn't do, because he was alive, and he was brilliant. And that was enough for anybody.

He was so pleased with himself as he walked toward his car, coatless and hatless in the freezing night air, that he even managed to hum.

CHAPTER FOUR

IN spite of the lights strung through the dark green trees
flooding the fenced-in island dividing the wide lanes of Park
Avenue, in spite of the number of parties given that season
and the fact that the city had had its cleanest and softest
snows in recent years, Christmas was not a particularly happy
time for most of the group. A heaviness seemed to have settled on most of Louise's closest friends. Diane's depression
was understandable, of course, in light of the fact that she
could not go to the out-of-country spots to which she was invited. She spent a great deal of time with Rick, but the glow
seemed to have gone out of her, as it seemed to have gone
out of a lot of people.

Dainty Lee complained bitterly at six consecutive cocktail
parties that the people in Acapulco had refused to refund the
deposit on her house, which had, naturally, been a fortune—
beastly of them under the circumstances. Julia White was
fretful that the whole bloody thing might not be cleared up
by March, when she was due in Paris for the new collections,
and that *Vogue* might get the jump on *Élan* magazine. Only
Maggie seemed to be thriving, her belly blossoming along
with her spirits, as if nothing had ever happened.

Louise herself was not sure what exactly had occurred. She
was content to accept Bunyan Reis' theory that L'Affaire
Grisly, as he called it, was a ghastly accident, and simple bad
luck that they had all been present. At the same time, she felt
almost pleased to have been included, when she didn't actually remember what the man had looked like, lying there.
She was sorry he had died, naturally; but at least she had
been with her friends. Having been involved in something so
dramatic made them all feel very tightly knit. It was a memo-
rable thing to have lived through, like the sinking of the *Ti-
tanic,* she supposed: the survivors, on reaching land, would
have become very close.

It was not that she had become cold, or unfeeling. When
she remembered the actuality of the death, she felt shaken
and frightened, and extremely sorry for the man. But she had
not known him. When somebody dropped dead on a street in
New York, if you were smart you didn't go over and look
and see the blue veins popping; then you could forget about

it. So she put the entire episode somewhere in the back of her mind, and let it become a part of the nightmare it was, thinking about it not at all during the day.

"They're beautiful," Charley said, one night after they had both returned, exhausted, from a party at Dainty Lee's. "A man was killed less than ten days ago, and their only reaction is annoyance because it puts the kibosh on their social schedule."

"For God's sake, it was an accident." She slipped out of her boots and left them in the foyer so as not to track her new Savonnerie rug. "It could have happened anywhere."

"Only it happened at a murder game. A bunch of bored lunatics running around in the dark, to show how clever and inventive they are."

"And what have you ever done that's clever and inventive?" Louise said.

"Well, I haven't courted disaster," Charley said. "That makes me pretty unique in the group you run with."

"I don't want to fight with you, Charley. It's very late and we're both tired, and I don't want to say anything I'll be sorry for."

"Like what?" Charley said.

"Like I'm sorry you don't approve of my friends, but they happen to be spectacular, accomplished people . . ."

". . . who play dumb games to keep themselves amused where someone gets killed," Charley said.

". . . who can go anywhere and do anything they like, and be with anyone they choose, so you ought to consider it a privilege that they accept you."

"Because I'm not on their level?"

"For God's sake, how many people are? I'm only in on a pass."

"And for that you should be forever grateful."

"You're goddammed right," Louise said. "You don't have to be so cavalier about it. I'm in on a pass, and so are you." She threw her clothes on the bench next to her bed, and slipped under the covers without even taking off her makeup. "Turn off the light."

"You can't avoid it like that."

"Why not?" she said. "You always do. Anytime I try to talk about something that's bothering me, you say you're too tired."

"All right," he said. "What's bothering you."

"Nothing's bothering me," Louise said. "I just need sleep."

"No, that isn't what's bothering you. Why don't you come out with what's really bothering you."

"I just don't like your passing judgment, that's all. Not on

428

them, and not on me. We have a lovely relationship, we really do, Charley, I enjoy being with you, but . . ."

"But that doesn't give me a right to any opinions."

"I didn't say that. You can have opinions. Only don't foist them on me like that. Don't try to make me see things your way, because I can't. I've been a long time getting to where I am today, and I can't start playing the ingenue just because I want you to approve of me."

"Do you?"

"Well, of course I do."

"Even if I'm not clever and inventive."

"I didn't mean that," Louise said. "I only said that. You know what I meant."

"No I don't," Charley said.

"Well, let's face it, we're just not extraordinary, either of us . . ."

"You mean I'm not extraordinary, don't you."

"That isn't what I meant at all."

"You don't have to be nervous about it, Louise, I'm not insulted. I have no wish to be extraordinary."

"You don't?"

"I'm making a good living. I'm enjoying my life. What's wrong with that?"

"But what if something happens? What if something went wrong with the commercials or something, what if you couldn't earn a living."

"I could always earn a living," Charley said. "That's not what you're really worried about."

"I can't stand people who try to tell me what I'm really thinking. You're not stupid, but you're not that smart."

"That's right, sweetheart. I'm not that smart, and I'm not that extraordinary, and that clever, and that inventive. Now you've said it all."

"I don't know what you're talking about. You're being ridiculous."

"Well, there I have to take exception. Ridiculous I'm not." He went to the closet and started laying out his clothes.

"What are you doing?" Louise said. "Come on, Charley, it's almost three o'clock. Stop trying to scare me."

"I'm not trying to scare you at all. In spite of what Bunyan said, the truth of the matter is you can't take me anywhere, because there are certain places I just don't care to go. And there are some unclever and uninventive places you may not want to go with me. So maybe it's better if we split."

"You don't have to make these big decisions in the middle of the night, for God's sake," Louise said. "It isn't like it's any kind of real crisis, Charley. It isn't as if we had a real fight or anything."

"That's true," he said. "I almost wish we had."

"Just stay for the night, please. Just come to bed and you can leave tomorrow."

"I don't want you auditioning for me to show me how loving you can be in bed," Charley said. "I already know that."

"I have no intention of auditioning for you. I don't have to prove anything to you." Tears stung her eyes. "Who the hell do you think you are?"

"You mean in comparison to the rest of your friends?"

"That's right, in comparison to the rest of my friends. My only problem was worrying about whether they'd accept you, not if you'd accept them."

"Well now you won't have any problems at all." He started piling things into his suitcase.

"You're really afraid, aren't you? You're really just like Kate, no wonder you're so fond of each other. You haven't got the guts to see if you can make it with those people."

"Whatever you say," Charley said.

"You have to run out, like a loser, because you're afraid that's what you are."

"Oh no," Charley said. "You're the one who's afraid I'm a loser."

"Well I'm right to be afraid," Louise said, and blew her nose. "Where are you going to go?"

"I'll find someplace. It's a big city, they tell me."

"You've got another girl. You've been seeing someone all along."

"I'm afraid not."

"You swear?" He nodded.

"Then why are you going? Why are you being such a damned fool?"

"Maybe I'll call you and if you're not busy we can have some laughs."

"You never loved me." She started to cry, openly. "You never really loved me at all."

"I never said that."

She listened to the closing of the outer door to the apartment, and waited, in silence, for the groaning sound of the elevator ascending. There was still time to go running out after him, to plead with him to come back. But that was ridiculous. She was damned if she would beg him. If anything, she ought to laugh, and be grateful. He had only made easier a decision she would have had to come to eventually, anyway.

She reached across the bed to his night table for another

Kleenex, and her hand automatically wandered under the blanket. She drew it away from the cold emptiness, as if she had been stung.

"Oh shit," she whimpered. "Screw. Who cares."

She had more invitations that Christmas than she had received the rest of her life put together. Rolf Orlovsky invited her to join the Bahamian trip on his yacht; Chet Oppenheim asked her to join his party at Aspen. Naturally she was not able to accept either, but there were many parties in New York, and she sometimes attended as many as five in one day. She lost twelve pounds because she was so happy and so busy and wanted to show Charley that she was perfectly capable of shaping up without him, in case she ran into him, which she had no intention of doing.

Three mornings a week she set aside an hour in her den with her secretary to write the column, which was now almost writing itself because she knew so many people, all of whom were anxious to ingratiate themselves with her, so told her anything juicy they picked up in the way of gossip. She had a very full life, she told her mother that all the time on the telephone, and that was why she never had a minute to get back to Great Neck. She even had four parties to go to on New Year's Eve. The floor around the Christmas tree in her living room which Algernon and Maggie had decorated for her was piled high with an unaccustomed haul. There were expensive perfumes and lingerie from the buyers of all New York department stores, plus personal gifts from the owners of Saks and Bendel. Not that it could be in any way considered payoff: she did not mention any stores in her column because she hoped for return; it was merely that the people she wrote about did most of their shopping at Saks and Bendel, and it didn't hurt to report that in her column. Press agents and publicists sent her enormous gaily decorated baskets of liquors, fruits, caviar, delicacies and cheeses. As a rule she had enough that was exclusive and interesting about the people she was running with, and personally imparted scandal, to fill out her fifty lines, without using the standard type of press-agent plant. Christmas was deductible for people in public relations, and there was no harm in the firms' keeping her on their good side. From the motion picture studios and Broadway producers she received cases of champagne and liquor; those heads of production she now knew personally sent her expensive gold lighters and elaborate gifts from Tiffany and Cartier, with her initials inscribed. There was no doubt about it. She had awakened in a roomful of goodies and was indeed Shirley Temple. Only better.

For the first time in recent years she did not feel sad about her escort for New Year's Eve being less than a romantic suitor. Unless she thought about Charley, which she carefully avoided. Charley would probably have wanted to do something stupid and sentimental, like spend the evening alone drinking champagne and fooling around at midnight. Such things were only for people with no invitations. Her date was Bunyan Reis, who was now going with her everywhere—to parties, to openings, to charity balls, since Diane was so tied up with Rick. Louise adored Bunyan; she really did: he was every bit as witty and scintillating as people said, and he adored being with her, he told her that all the time, especially now that she was losing weight.

She was so busy being everywhere, with everyone, that she did not even have time for an occasional hour with Dr. Ehrens. She very seldom thought about anything she wasn't doing that particular moment in time. When the man came to her door and gave her the subpoena, it actually took her several minutes to remember about Harry Bell.

"You promised me," she screamed, when she got to Ron Abbate's office. "You promised me it wouldn't go this far."

He sat behind his modern semicircular formica desk, looking at the paper she had handed him. "It's only a subpoena for a deposition, Louise. It doesn't mean you'll go to court. This will all be settled a long time before it gets to court, I promise you."

"I've never been in trouble in my life. And this man came to my door, he was right out of *Journey into Fear*, I swear, with big Coca-Cola bottle glasses that made his eyes fill out his whole head, and says 'Miss Felder?' just like in the movies and he hands that to me. What am I going to do?"

"It's just for a deposition, I told you," Ron said.

"What's a deposition?"

"You go in and talk to an attorney and a court reporter, and tell them what you know. It's very informal, really."

"With a court reporter, it's informal?"

"He's just there for the record, so you can't be misquoted later on."

"Misquoted about what? What are they going to ask me? I'm not going to go through anything like I went through with his mother."

"They're not going to question your relationship with Harry. They'll only ask about the last night, what Harry told you before he died. About the monument."

"You mean, the very thing he told me that he also told you."

"That's right. About wanting to build a working memorial. Someplace that would house not only his remains but all his charities, the arts clinic, and the science clinics and the religious clinic. A Harry Bell building, right here in New York, where all the arms of his foundation would embrace."

"How very poetic," Louise said. "Maybe you're in the wrong business. You're wasting yourself in law. Naturally you'd be the administrator for this building, and its many arms."

"Naturally. Chet and myself."

"And how much would this great project cost."

"I don't think you have to remember that. After all, a man doesn't put a figure on a dream, not when he's discussing it with the girl he loves."

"Just off the record, how much would it cost? I'd like to know the price he puts on it with his executor."

"About four million," Ron Abbate said.

"Jesus, you're greedy."

"Not at all," Ron said. "Harry had very big dreams. And we're not the ones who are greedy. They are. There's plenty of money left in the estate. The foundation won't even make a dent in it."

"I can't do it," Louise said. "I'm too nervous."

"But it's all based on your story, sweetheart. You were the one who told us, and the newspapers, weren't you. You were the one who gave out the interviews, about Harry. We only confirmed what you told the press."

"I won't be put under this kind of pressure."

"I'm sorry," Ron said, and got up from behind his desk. "Did I sound like I was pressuring you? I didn't mean to. Excuse me. I guess I've been under a little pressure myself. I don't like this thing dragging on anymore than you do. But I promise you it will all be settled long before we go to court. And I'll come with you to the deposition, and . . ."

"No," Louise said. "No, you don't have to do that. If I go with an attorney, it looks like I've got something to hide."

"That's foolish; I insist on going with you. You have the right to be represented by counsel."

"Harry's counsel?" she said. "Then it has to look like it's a setup, like I'm lying. No, I have nothing to be ashamed about. I'll just go and tell them what Harry said and that's it."

"I must insist," Ron said. "I insist on going with you. We have some stake in this, too."

"And that's just what it'll look like, if you're representing me. I handle it myself, or I don't go. I have nothing to hide. It'll be fun, really, won't it? I mean, matching wits and all . . ."

"I wouldn't try to match wits. Not with Jeremy Singer."

"Is he like F. Lee Bailey? I hope he's like F. Lee Bailey."

"He's a very conservative, old-line attorney. A little stuffy, a little pompous. Very impressed with himself."

"Oh goody," Louise said. "Then I'll break him down. I'll win his heart with my sweet little face and my girlish ways. Is he married?"

"Don't get cute," Ron said.

"I love it, I love it. Lulu Singer. I'll write a book about My Life with Him and sign autographs in Doubleday's!"

"Please don't get cute," Ron said. "Just answer the questions about Harry Bell, and what he said to you the last night. And try to say something that really sounds like him."

"What does that mean?" Louise said.

"Quote him like Harry, so it rings true. Authentic Harry."

"I did know him, you know. I knew him very well. I wasn't making it up."

"I'm sure not. Just answer the questions. If Singer asks you anything you don't understand, ask him to repeat it. And don't answer anything you don't want to answer. If you're not sure about something, don't guess. Say you don't remember. But don't get cute."

"I can't help it," Louise said. "I am cute. But I'll try to control myself."

"I'm coming with you. I can't allow you to . . ."

"You come with me, I don't go," said Louise. "I'm telling the truth. That's all you have to concern yourself with, is I'm telling the truth."

She dressed for the deposition as if her designer were the casting director of *Perry Mason*. She wore a simple three-piece suit of navy blue, which served not only to minimize her hips and accentuate the slim elegance of her legs but also focused attention on the white lace collar at her throat, giving full play to the sweet expression she rehearsed at length in front of her mirror. She wore no jewelry, except for her wristwatch and a plain pair of pearl earrings that sat on the tiny lobe of her beigey pink ears, like truth. At the last moment she decided there was no longer anything slutty about false eyelashes, which even Jackie Kennedy wore, so put on a pair, and stared herself boldly down in the glass. She did, however, take off the shoulder-length golden fall she was wearing in favor of her own blunt cut, deciding the hairpiece made her look a little too much like Heidi. She was after all a successful career girl, and there was nothing wrong with being honey blond and trimly chic.

434

She took a cab to 501 Fifth Avenue. In the elevator going up to Singer's office, she removed the navy blue kid glove from her right hand, so she would be free to offer him a warm, responsive and unsweaty palm.

The offices of Jeremy Singer took up at least seven doors that she counted on her way down the corridor. Even before she opened the door to his main reception room, she was impressed. The walls were darkly paneled and hung with small, dark, framed prints depicting fox hunts and dogs. The secretary at the oak reception desk was not wearing her hair in a bun, but was otherwise serviceably prim. There was no doubt about it, Louise thought, as she gave the girl her name: she was going to be a breath of fresh air.

"Will you have a seat, please, Miss Felder?" the girl said, as she hung up the phone.

"Aren't I expected?"

"Yes, you're expected; but Mr. Singer is tied up in conference and will be a few moments."

It was obvious he was trying to unsettle her. But it was her own fault for arriving on time. She smiled, and sat down on the black leather couch in the corner, and rifled through the pile of *Life* magazines, looking for the story on Diane Trejinska. The door to the corridor opened, and a middle-aged man with sparse gray hair and a well-worn black overcoat went directly to the desk and gave his name. In his hand he carried a small rectangular black case and a tripod, like a miniature ancient camera. The court reporter, Louise reasoned. She smiled at him brightly and debated introducing herself. But that would be pushy. Besides, if all he did was take down words, there was little point in getting him on her side. So instead she filled her mind with bright opening gambits of conversation, reserved for Jeremy Singer, as she had in the past rehearsed her opening remarks to Dr. Ehrens, while sitting impatiently in his waiting room.

The door from the offices opened, and she and the court reporter were ushered inside. Spotting the paneling of the heavily carpeted corridor leading to Singer's suite were several more prints, some depicting the chase, some depicting pheasant and duck hunting. She took note of them and smiled.

He stepped from behind his desk to greet her, and she was pleased to see that he was not as old as she would have imagined, or as forbidding. He was a stockily built man in his middle forties, with thinning brown hair and gray eyes under heavy black eyebrows that nearly met over the bridge of his nose. But his face was otherwise quite pleasant, and he was nattily dressed for a conservative, with a red paisley handkerchief in the pocket of his double-breasted black pinstripe suit.

"I see from the pictures in your office that you're a patron of the hunt," she said, as he drew up a chair for her to the right of his desk. "Do you know Maggie Bolin?"

"No, I don't," Jeremy Singer said.

"She used to be on a committee for abolishing fox hunting, but now she's decided she loves it. It must be a very exciting sport."

"Maybe," Jeremy Singer said. "I don't know. I have the pictures because they're nice pictures."

"Oh . . . Well I suppose you're much too busy to be interested in that sort of thing anyway. I hear so many stories about you. You're certainly surprisingly young to be so successful."

"Do you have any questions about the procedure of the deposition, Miss Felder?"

"I don't know. I guess . . ." She leveled her most ingenuous smile. "I suppose I'm a little nervous. I've never done anything like this before. The deposition I mean."

"Well there's no need to be nervous. If you want to smoke you may, or if you'd care for some water, my secretary will be glad to get some for you."

"Thank you." Out of the corner of her eye she watched the court reporter setting up his stand, the stenographic equipment atop it like a small adding machine. The seriousness of the situation suddenly struck her, and her mouth went quite dry. "Maybe I will have some water."

Jeremy Singer buzzed his secretary and issued instructions on the intercom. In a moment the secretary was in the room, with a black and silver decanter and a glass.

"Thank you," Louise said to the woman, and then directed her smile at the attorney. "You're very kind. I don't know why everybody says you're so tough." She laughed, but it had been a mistake. She was not winning him. The hell with it. She had proved what it was she had to prove: life was no longer a popularity contest.

"Would you like anything else besides the water? Some coffee perhaps."

"No, the water is fine, thank you."

"Then, if you're feeling perfectly relaxed, we might as well begin."

"We might as well," Louise said. "As long as I'm perfectly relaxed."

436

IN THE SUPREME COURT OF THE COUNTY OF NEW
YORK STATE OF NEW YORK

Irving Bell; Seymour Bell

                      Plaintiffs.

      -vs-

Ronald S. Abbate   CASE NO. 98247

Chester W. Oppenheim

The Harold A. Bell   Defendants.

Memorial Foundation, et al.

Deposition of LOUISE GRACE FELDER, taken
on behalf of Ronald Abbate, on Monday, the 12th
day of February 1969, commencing at two   o'clock
P.M., at 501 Fifth Avenue, New York City
before LOUIS W. RANIER, Certified Shorthand Reporter.

APPEARANCES

For the Plaintiffs: Jeremy S. Singer

For the Defendants: Louise Grace Felder

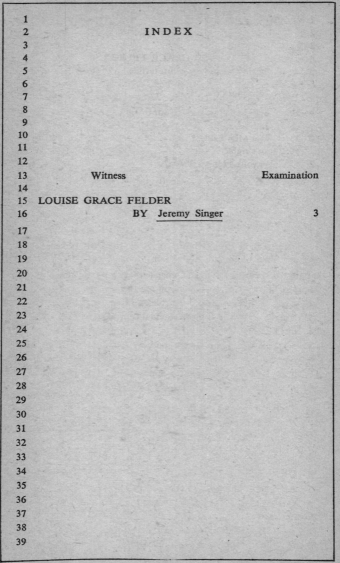

INDEX

```
1
2
3
4                LOUISE GRACE FELDER
5           having been duly sworn testified as follows:
6
7   EXAMINATION BY MR. Jeremy Singer
8   Q   Would you please state your full name?
9   A   Louise Grace Felder.
10  Q   Is that Miss Felder?
11  A   That's right.
12  Q   And your address, please?
13  A   824 Park Avenue.
14  Q   In New York—
15  A   Yes.
16  Q   —City?
17      Miss Felder, have you ever had your deposition taken
18  before?
19  A   No, I haven't.
20  Q   If I may explain, this is a legal proceeding. I will
21  pose questions to you and you are to give answers. If you
22  don't understand a question please so state. This deposi-
23  tion may be presented in the actual court proceeding in
24  this case.
25      You were advised that you have the opportunity to be
26  represented at this hearing by an attorney and I understood
27  that you have declined that opportunity; is that correct?
28  A   I don't need an attorney. I have absolutely nothing
29  to hide.
30  Q   Fine. In that regard, therefore, if there is anything
31  ambiguous or uncertain about any of my questions, please
32  advise me.
33  A   Okay.
34  Q   What is your age, please?
35  A   Do I have to answer that?
36  Q   If you don't want to answer the record will so
37  indicate.
38  A   I was only kidding. I'm thirty-three.
39  Q   What is your occupation, please?
```

1   A   I'm a columnist for a newspaper.

2   Q   Which newspaper?

3   A   Right now the New York *Sentinel* and syndication.

4   Q   And how long have you been a columnist for that
5 paper?

6   A   About eight months.

7   Q   In how many newspapers is your column to be found?

8   A   Eighteen.

9   Q   What is the name of the column?

10   A   Limelight by Louise. I've been thinking of changing
11 the name; it is really kind of tacky.

12   Q   From what college were you graduated?

13   A   I didn't go to college.

14   Q   Did you go to school in New York?

15   A   In Great Neck, yes. I went to school in Great Neck
16 and I was offered scholarships to a number of colleges but
17 I chose not to use them.

18   Q   You went straight into your work as a columnist after
19 high school?

20   A   No, I was a—I guess you could say a secretary-
21 receptionist for a public relations firm.

22   Q   Which firm was that, please?

23   A   That was Phillips and Rose.

24   Q   What is their address?

25   A   127 East Fifty-sixth Street.

26   Q   New York City?

27   A   That's right, and I worked for several public
28 relations firms after that.

29   Q   When did you first start writing a column?

30   A   Oh, about two years ago.

31   Q   It wasn't syndicated, was it?

32   A   No.

33   Q   This column, Limelight by Louise, what is its
34 subject matter?

35   A   It's more or less a general gossip column, reporting
36 on the activities of the people that everybody wants to
37 read about.

38   Q   Was this the same subject matter as in your
39 previous column?

1   A   More or less.

2   Q   What do you mean by more or less?

3   A   I just seem to know more people now than I did then.

4   Q   By "now" you mean within the last eight months?

5   A   I guess within the last year and a half. I

6   shouldn't guess, should I.

7   Q   Now, have you ever been acquainted with a Mr.

8   Harry Bell?

9   A   Yes, I was.

10   Q   Mr. Bell is now deceased; is that correct?

11   A   That's right. I believe that's what all this is

12   about.

13   Q   Just so we have no ambiguity, when I refer to Mr.

14   Bell we are referring to the Mr. Harry Bell who died on

15   July 1st last. How long had you known Mr. Bell?

16   A   For about three or four years.

17   Q   How would you characterize your relationship with

18   Mr. Bell?

19   A   We had a very close relationship.

20   Q   When did you first meet Mr. Bell?

21   A   I met him at a party, I believe it was at the

22   Harold Rankin opening for *Platinum,* the musical that

23   opened a few years ago.

24   Q   You met him at a party?

25   A   That's right.

26   Q   Who introduced you to him?

27   A   No one. He came over to talk to us.

28   Q   You had heard of Mr. Bell, you knew who he was?

29   A   I think everybody knew who Harry Bell was.

30   Q   When did you see him next after that party?

31   A   That evening we had dinner in his home.

32   Q   We?

33   A   A client of the office—I was a publicist at the

34   time. A Russian lady.

35   Q   What was the name of your client?

36   A   How quickly we forget. She never made it. Some

37   White Russian lady that was just signed by Bertram

38   Lester from behind whatever curtain that is.

39   Q   And you and this Russian lady and Mr. Bell had

1 dinner at his home?

2 A That's right.

3 Q And did you and the Russian lady go home afterward?

4 A I don't know what that has to do with anything.

5 Q I'm merely trying to have the record show the
6 nature of your relationship with Mr. Bell. I assume
7 you have no objection to that?

8 A I'm not ashamed of my relationship with Harry.
9 We had a relationship and I don't think there's anything
10 illegal about that.

11 Q I'm not accusing you of any illegality. You must
12 know that this whole lawsuit was instituted because of
13 your statement.

14 A No. No, excuse me, I did not start it. I believe
15 that it was Mr. Bell's family who were interested in
16 holding up the project that Harry wanted. I don't want
17 anything from the Harry Bell estate. I have no wish to
18 go after anything, so don't please say that it's at my
19 instigation. I was trying to—what's the word—I
20 was just trying to—

21 Q Ingratiate yourself into society?

22 A I don't even think I should answer that.

23 Q That's not a question. Let's get back to the question.

24 A I was trying to enforce whatever Harry wanted done
25 with his life—with his death. He wanted to go on meaning
26 something.

27 Q It's rather obvious that if, as is the case, your
28 story is not believed it becomes necessary to delve into
29 your relationship with Mr. Bell to determine whether on
30 a factual basis your story should be believed. Now, if
31 you do not want to continue with this deposition—

32 A I don't know why you keep saying that.

33 Q Because you're obviously afraid to answer questions.

34 A I'm not afraid to answer questions. I just think
35 some of these things are irrelevant.

36 Q If I ask you a question and you consider it
37 irrelevant you are free to answer it as it is irrelevant
38 and we'll go on to the next question or we'll dis-
39 continue this deposition and let the court decide.

1	A	All right.
2	Q	Now—
3	A	I don't want to fight with anybody. I'd like to get
4		this all straightened out and we can forget about it.
5	Q	Did you and the Russian lady leave together?
6	A	No.
7	Q	Did she leave first?
8	A	No, she did not.
9	Q	Who did?
10	A	I left first.
11	Q	Around what time did you leave?
12	A	I don't remember. It was over three years ago.
13	Q	But you and she had dinner at Mr. Bell's home?
14	A	That's right.
15	Q	And you left right after dinner?
16	A	Not right after dinner. I had coffee and brandy and
17		all the lovely things you had at Harry's house.
18	Q	Did you have intercourse with Mr. Bell that evening?
19	A	I certainly did not.
20	Q	Did the Russian lady?
21	A	I have no idea. I'm not her mother.
22	Q	When is the next time you saw Harry Bell?
23	A	I believe it was the next day or the day after that.
24	Q	What were the circumstances of that meeting?
25	A	He took me to the opening of a motion picture.
26	Q	Which motion picture?
27	A	*Ship of Fools.*
28	Q	Did he call you—
29	A	Yes.
30	Q	—for a date?
31	A	Yes, he did.
32	Q	Did he take you straight home after the movies?
33	A	No, he didn't, he took me to dinner.
34	Q	At his home?
35	A	No.
36	Q	Where did he take you to dinner?
37	A	The Sixth Avenue Delicatessen.
38	Q	That's on Sixth Avenue in New York City?
39	A	Yes. Good for you.

1 Q   Did he take you home after you were at the
2 delicatessen?
3 A   I don't remember.
4 Q   Now, if you don't remember there's no way we can
5 prove that you did remember; however, you did take an
6 oath when you began this deposition and if you lie
7 that's perjury.
8 A   I'm not lying so far.
9 Q   So far? You mean you intend to in the future?
10 A   No, but, I mean, when I say I don't remember it's
11 because I don't remember.
12 Q   You don't remember going to Mr. Bell's home that
13 evening?
14 A   Not that evening, no.
15 Q   Miss Felder, when was the first time you had
16 intercourse with Mr. Bell?
17 A   I don't know what this has to do with talking about
18 the way that Harry wanted to be buried.
19 Q   You claim that you had a close relationship with
20 Mr. Bell?
21 A   I did have a close relationship with Mr. Bell.
22 Q   And that he confided in you?
23 A   Yes, he did.
24 Q   Well, why would he confide in you? Were you a
25 lover, an acquaintance, a pickup, what were you in
26 his life?
27 A   Come on, now, you don't have to say things like
28 "pickup."
29 Q   I'm only trying to keep the record accurate.
30 A   We had a very close relationship.
31 Q   How many dates did you have with him?
32 A   I had many dates with him.
33 Q   What date was it that you had intercourse with Mr.
34 Bell?
35 A   I didn't mark it on my calendar, it was not the
36 biggest day of my life, sir.
37 Q   In other words, going to bed with someone is not a
38 big deal in your life, is that what you're saying?
39 A   I'm not a sleep-around, if that's what you mean.

1 Q I'm really not interested in your morals, I'm
2 interested—
3 A You ask very funny questions for a man who's not
4 interested in my morals.
5 Q I'm interested in your relationship with Harry Bell.
6 A You think the kourvehs . . .
7 THE REPORTER: Would you spell that, please?
8 A K-O-U-R-V-E-H-S.
9 BY MR. SINGER: I'm sorry, I don't understand that word.
10 A . . . the girls, the tramps that Harry Bell knew in
11 his life, and sometimes married, were—were of a
12 strain that is so far superior to mine that I have to
13 be subjected to this kind of questioning. If you're
14 trying to make it seem that Harry Bell wouldn't have
15 anything to do with a girl like me you can just check
16 with other people who saw Harry Bell with me, who knew
17 Harry Bell was with me. There were people that saw us
18 at the opening. You can check with the pickle man at
19 the Sixth Avenue Delicatessen.
20 Q I'm not disputing that you had a sexual relation-
21 ship with Mr. Bell. In fact, the point of this line of
22 questioning, if you want to keep pursuing a discussion,
23 is the fact that this relationship was so meaningless,
24 that Mr. Bell had so many other relationships with so
25 many girls around town that it's ludicrous that he had
26 anything of a confidential discussion with you.
27 Now, I believe this is relevant. You may not. Your
28 attorney may object to this at the trial, that's up to
29 him. As far as I'm concerned I'm going to ask the
30 questions. You may either answer or decline to answer.
31 I have no power to compel you to answer. The
32 only thing I can do is if you answer with what I
33 believe to be a fabrication and I have proof that it is,
34 at the proper time and place I will present that to
35 the court.
36 I might say that there is an adage in law that he
37 who lies in one thing will lie in another, and, so to
38 speak, if the shoe fits. Now, may we continue?
39 A I don't know. I thought you were just going to ask

1 me questions about Harry.

2 Q Let's get to the night before Harry's death. You
3 were with him?

4 A That's right.

5 Q What were the circumstances, how long had you been
6 with him?

7 A I had been with him for a few hours.

8 Q What time did you first see him?

9 A At about—oh, I don't remember, it was probably
10 about 10:00 o'clock.

11 Q In the evening?

12 A That's right.

13 Q Did he call for you?

14 A No, I came there by myself.

15 Q Was he expecting you?

16 A Yes, he was.

17 Q Did he call you to set up a date?

18 A Yes.

19 Q As best you can remember, what did he say when he
20 called you?

21 A He said he was lonesome, why didn't I come over.

22 Q Prior to that phone call when was the last time that
23 you had seen Mr. Bell?

24 A Oh, a few days before, I suppose. I don't remember exactly.

25 Q You were still going with him on and off at this
26 period of time?

27 A Yes, that's right.

28 Q You went over to his home?

29 A That's right.

30 Q At 10:00 o'clock.

31 A That's right.

32 Q Was there anyone else there?

33 A No, there wasn't.

34 Q What time did you leave his home?

35 A At 2:00 o'clock in the morning.

36 Q In which room of his home did you spend the
37 evening?

38 A We were in the downstairs study, the one to the
39 left of the foyer.

1 Q Was there anyone else in the home at this time?

2 A No. That's one of the reasons he called me

3 was that—his secretary had been ill for a few

4 days and he had given the servants some time off and I

5 guess he didn't have any place to go.

6 Q Can you remember what, if anything, he said

7 specifically about death, namely, his death?

8 A He said he wanted to be remembered. He said he

9 had made all the money that he had ever dreamed of

10 making and he knew he couldn't take it with him, and had

11 no children, and wanted to be remembered. He thought

12 maybe just instead of being put in the ground and talked

13 about for a while he'd like to have some kind of working

14 monument, not just an ordinary mausoleum, but something

15 in New York itself, which he loved and where he owned

16 a lot of property, that would house not only his remains

17 but everything that he had worked for, his interest in

18 the arts and his interest in the sciences and his

19 interest in religion and music.

20 Q What specifically did he tell you about this

21 edifice?

22 A Well, he said that—he wanted something very

23 grand. That was the word he used, grand, and operating,

24 because he had always operated in his lifetime and he

25 wanted to operate after he died and rather than spread

26 all the institutions around, or money to the

27 institutions, he'd like them all in one building and then

28 he laughed and he said kind of a Bellminster Abbey.

29 Q He was laughing at the time he said that?

30 A He laughed when he said Bellminster Abbey because

31 he always got very embarrassed by his own puns. They

32 were usually terrible, and he knew it.

33 Q So far as you know was this the first time he ever

34 mentioned this building to anyone?

35 A I don't know. I assume that he had mentioned it to

36 his attorneys and the people that he had advising him.

37 Q Was this the first time he ever mentioned building

38 an edifice after he died?

39 A I believe so, yes.

1 Q Did he discuss how much money this would cost?

2 A He said money was unimportant, especially after-
3 ward.

4 Q Did he say that he was going to take steps to see
5 that this idea of his was included in his will?

6 A He didn't mention his will but he said he certainly
7 intended to see if he couldn't do something to . . . what?
8 implement, that's the word, to take steps to implement
9 the idea. He wanted it.

10 Q What else did he discuss with you that night?

11 A I think that's a pretty broad topic, life and
12 death.

13 Q You also had intercourse with him that night, did
14 you not?

15 A No, I didn't. He wasn't feeling very well, so if
16 you're trying to imply I killed him—

17 Q I'm implying nothing. I'm just trying to find out
18 what happened. Did you stay in the study the entire
19 evening?

20 A Except when we looked at the statue. The
21 Michelangelo.

22 Q Did you have a discussion about art?

23 A Not exactly. He just said something about it.

24 Q What did he say?

25 A You really want this on the record? Well, okay, it
26 doesn't make me look bad. He said, and I remember
27 exactly, "I know what you're thinking. You're thinking
28 you'd like to ball him, right?" Doesn't that sound
29 just like Harry?

30 A Excuse me. I don't understand. What does that
31 mean, "ball"?

32 A You're putting me on.

33 Q No. Was this some pet expression that you and he
34 had?

35 A It's a pet expression a lot of people have, sir.
36 I don't know where you've been, but it means "screw."
37 Do you want me to explain what "screw" means?

38 Q No, your choice of words speaks for itself. What
39 did you answer Mr. Bell?

1 A I said, "No, that wasn't what I was thinking,
2 Harry."
3 Q Since Harry's death, has your income increased?
4 A He didn't leave me anything.
5 Q That wasn't my question.
6 A Well, there's been a natural growth in my income
7 over the past few years. I'm a very bright girl, ask
8 anybody.
9 Q I will ask some people, but the fact is that your
10 income has increased, has it not?
11 A Yes it has.
12 Q Wasn't it a direct result of your relationship with
13 Harry Bell and your exploitation of that relationship?
14 A No.
15 Q You did exploit your relationship, did you not?
16 A I don't think so.
17 Q The so-called conversation you had with Harry Bell,
18 that appeared in newspapers, did it not?
19 A I had hoped to go directly to his family.
20 Q Did you speak to his family?
21 A Only his adorable mother.
22. Q How many people do you estimate you told this story
23 to?
24 A Well, as you pointed out, it was in the paper so
25 I don't know how many people.
26 Q You're a good public relations agent, are you not?
27 A I'm not a public relations agent anymore.
28 Q But you were?
29 A Yes.
30 Q You know the business, don't you?
31 A I know the business, yes.
32 Q As a good publicist don't you think you got pretty
33 good press coverage on this?
34 A I suppose I did, yes.
35 Q You had your name in the paper frequently?
36 A I had my name in the paper before Harry died. I
37 had a column.
38 Q Did you have your name in the New York metropolitan
39 newspapers? When were you mentioned as having attended

1   any party of any import?

2   A   I don't remember.

3   Q   But you are mentioned now, are you not?

4   A   What does it matter what parties I go to? Are you
5   upset? Do you want to be on an invitation list?
6   I'll see if I can arrange something.

7   Q   My social life doesn't need any assistance from
8   you or anyone like you.

9   A   Well, my social life doesn't need any assistance,
10   either.

11   Q   Oh, but it does, does it not? It needs the
12   existence of a prefabricated story. Wasn't that what
13   started you on your career, that story?

14   A   No, it was not.

15   Q   Do you know if Mr. Bell told this same story about
16   how he wished to be buried to anyone other than you?

17   A   Well, I assume he had told it to his attorney and
18   maybe to Mr. Oppenheim.

19   Q   Have you seen his will?

20   A   No, I haven't.

21   Q   You know, of course, you aren't mentioned in that
22   will?

23   A   Yes, I know that.

24   Q   What you've said here today nowhere appears in his
25   will.

26   A   Well, Harry was a man who brainstormed a lot.
27   Maybe he got a brainstorm. I don't think he drew up his
28   will every few days.

29   Q   On the evening of the night before he died you
30   characterized your relationship as of that moment as
31   being very close; is that correct?

32   A   That's right.

33   Q   Now, in your definition of very close I assume you
34   have taken into consideration the fact you and Mr. Bell
35   had on occasion had intercourse; is that correct?

36   A   I'm not having a good time.

37   Q   You're not having a good time?

38   A   That's right.

39   Q   Now, is that an answer to a question or—

1 A It's just how I feel.
2 Q —or are you trying to be funny?
3 A It's really how I feel.
4 Q What would you like me to do to give you a good
5 time?
6 A I don't know.
7 Q Well, then, if we cannot figure out how to give you
8 a good time perhaps we can stick to the questions and
9 answers.
10 A All right. I stand corrected.
11 Q At that period of time when you considered yourself
12 a very good friend did you consider in that definition
13 of a close relationship or very good friend that you and
14 he had had intercourse together?
15 A None of your business.
16 Q Did you discuss marriage?
17 A None of your business.
18 Q For how long a period of time had you been very
19 close?
20 A On and off for over a period of years.
21 Q A period of years? Let me ask you this: for how
22 long a period back from the date of his death was it on?
23 A We had been seeing quite a bit of each other.
24 Q For how long?
25 A I don't know. A matter of months, I guess.
26 Q It's true during this period of time you were having
27 intercourse with other men, is it not?
28 A I don't think I want to answer that.
29 Q Is it not true that you had an affair with one
30 Charles Radnor?
31 A Is that his last name?
32 Q Did you have an affair with Charles Radnor?
33 A Not at the time.
34 Q It is not true?
35 A Not at the time; no, sir. I met Charley after
36 Harry was dead.
37 Q You did not know him before?
38 A No, I didn't.
39 Q Have you had intercourse with Charley?

1   A   None of your business.

2   Q   Have you ever been to the Warwick Hotel?

3   A   Don't be ridiculous. It's on the West Side.

4   Q   Have you ever been to the Warwick Hotel?

5   A   Well, it's in New York. I suppose I was there once
6 or twice.

7   Q   Who were you visiting there?

8   A   I wasn't visiting anybody. If I was there, I was
9 probably having drinks with a friend or something. You
10 stop in places and have a drink when you're in New York.

11   Q   Did you and Charles Radnor ever register at the
12 Warwick Hotel as man and wife?

13   A   Certainly not.

14   Q   But you don't deny that you visited his room in
15 the Warwick Hotel on the 8th of November and stayed
16 there for several hours.

17   A   None of your business.

18   Q   Miss Felder, I'm not going to try and trick you,
19 but I think it's fair to tell you that we have had
20 your background researched by detectives.

21   A   You're kidding.

22   Q   No, I'm not.

23   A   You really did have somebody following me?

24   Q   I told you I had. If you want to lie that's your
25 prerogative.

26   A   I don't want to lie. I have nothing to be ashamed
27 of.

28   Q   I believe the record will show that there was an
29 answer to the question, even though indirect. Did you
30 not live for a number of months with Charles Radnor? Is
31 he not still in your apartment?

32   A   There is no one living in my apartment but me.

33   Q   All right. Let's get to Andre Sherman. You know
34 Andre Sherman?

35   A   I know Andre Sherman.

36   Q   You and Mr. Sherman had an affair for a number of
37 years, had you not?

38   A   We saw each other for a long time.

39   Q   And you had intercourse with him for a number of

1 years, had you not?

2 A None of your business.

3 Q You were not seeing and dating him at the same time
4 you were seeing and dating Harry Bell?

5 A None of your business and I don't remember.

6 Q You mean you had intercourse with so many men that
7 you can't remember?

8 A No, sir; that isn't what I mean at all.

9 Q For how long have you been seeing a psychiatrist,
10 Dr. Ehrens?

11 A I haven't seen him for quite a while. I'm not crazy
12 if that's what you're insinuating.

13 Q Why don't we wait and see what I'm insinuating,
14 Miss Felder. When was the last time you saw Dr. Ehrens?

15 A I don't remember.

16 Q When did you first start seeing him?

17 A A few years ago.

18 Q Is it not a fact that you went to see him only
19 because you had heard that he was a psychiatrist for
20 Harry Bell?

21 A Dr. Ehrens was Harry Bell's psychiatrist?

22 Q You didn't know that?

23 A No, I swear, he never told me.

24 Q You didn't know that?

25 A No, I didn't. How come he never told me? I
26 shouldn't expect he would tell me. He wouldn't even
27 tell me what movies he went to.

28 Q Did you consider Harry Bell physically satisfying?

29 A None of your business.

30 Q Was it physically satisfying? Did you enjoy what he
31 did to you when you went to bed with him?

32 A You're crazy.

33 Q Wasn't he impotent?

34 A And you're really acting for his family?

35 Q The record will show whom I am representing. Did
36 he ever rip your clothes off?

37 A What's that got to do with anything?

38 Q Have you not told people the intimate details of
39 your sex life with Harry Bell?

1 A   No, I have not.

2 Q   You did not?

3 A   No.

4 Q   You did not mention that he could only, quote,
5 screw you after he raped you or in the form of raping you?

6 A   I never said that, no. Very crudely put.

7 Q   By you, wasn't it?

8 A   No, it was not.

9 Q   Are you trying to say that you have not discussed
10 the sex problems of Harry Bell with your friends,
11 because I have affidavits that I will be happy to show
12 you.

13 A   You're kidding.

14 Q   I wasn't kidding about the Warwick Hotel and I'm
15 not kidding about this.

16 A   Listen, if you're trying to scare me or upset me,
17 I am neither scared or upset. This is ridiculous. No-
18 body I know would tell you anything.

19 Q   Would you please answer the question?

20 A   No, I won't. That's it. I've had enough.

21 Q   Did you or did you not? Are you afraid to answer
22 that question?

23 A   I'm not afraid. I'm finished.

24 MR. SINGER: Let the record show that the witness, who
25 was not excused, has left the room and with that we will
26 close the deposition.

27

28

29

30

31

32

33

34

35

36

37

38

39

"I hated it," she screamed to Ron Abbate. "He hated me, I hated him and I hate you and I hate everybody, and I'm sorry I ever got involved. I never should have had anything to do with you, and I never should have gone to the fucking deposition. I thought I would be so bright and so wonderful and he started asking me all these fucking questions about my sex life."

"I told you I wanted to go with you."

"Well who knew he was going to ask me those questions? When did I fuck, who what where and when, and how did it feel. Who am I, for Christ's sake, Virginia Hill?"

"What exactly did he ask you?" Ron said.

To the best of her recollection, Louise told him. She was still shaking, angry at herself, and her stupidity in letting herself answer. "I thought all they were going to ask me was what Harry said about the fucking monument."

"That's all they should have asked you," Ron said. "That's all I would have let them ask you if you had let me come."

"What am I going to do?" Louise said. "What am I going to do."

"Don't get upset about it. There's nothing really to worry about. They won't be able to use any of it in court."

"You swear?"

"He probably only asked you to upset you, to make you think he really had the goods on you, to make you afraid."

"Yes," Louise said. "I see that now. That's all he was doing, was trying to make me afraid." She sniffled and blew her nose into the handkerchief. "Unfortunately he succeeded. I'm scared shit."

"I told you they can't use it."

"Then why did he go to all that trouble? Why did he get detectives and everything? Why did I answer any of those fucking questions. I didn't have to answer, did I? So why did I answer. I know. I wasn't just being a smart-ass, really I wasn't. I was trying to show how clever I was, how Harry really would have had to have respect for me, wasn't I, and then after that, I got scared, because I saw how much Singer really knew about me. It wasn't just that I was trying to be a smart-ass, was it?"

"I'm sure it wasn't."

"What can they do to me for perjury?"

"You're a long way from testifying in court. That's all Singer was doing, was trying to scare you off, so you'd drop out of the case."

"What can they do to me for perjury?"

"That's why he brought up the detectives. That's why he

got them in the first place, to try and get something on you to show you how dangerous he was, so you'd drop out."

"What can they do to me?" Louise said. "Goddammit, tell me something."

"I don't think this is any time to discuss it," Ron said. "Why don't we wait until you're a little calmer."

"That's funny," Louise said. "You really expect me to get over this?"

"It happens all the time. I've seen hundreds of depositions taken and hundreds of court cases, and people are always afraid they've made fools of themselves, and afterward . . ."

"Fools of themselves," she said, and drew back in the chair. "You think that's all I care about? My whole life I thought I had nothing really to be ashamed about, that I had never really done anything wrong, and he started parading everything before my eyes. Everything. Even the things in my life that I thought were sweet and meant something sounded dirty."

"He was just trying to make it seem that way," Ron said. "The only testimony that applies is the testimony about the monument and there's no way he can disprove what you said and he knows it, that's why he tried to scare you with the other things. None of it is admissible."

"I'm admissible," she said. "I'm admissible to me and I don't like it. I don't like any of it. I'm getting out."

"You can't," Ron said. "You already gave out the interview and the deposition under oath. The testimony about the memorial, that can't hurt you. That's nothing to be ashamed of, that you were with Harry the night before and he told you what he wanted. There's no shame in admitting you were with Harry."

"Obviously you never saw his wang," she said, and walked out of the office.

She took a cab uptown to Dr. Ehrens' office, and smiled at the patient in his waiting room, a nail-chewing man in worn corduroy who was reading *Listening with the Third Ear*. "Did Dr. Ehrens recommend that book to you."

"What? Oh. No," he said.

"I didn't think so. What time is your appointment?"

"Four ten," he said. "In five minutes."

She heard the outer door to Dr. Ehrens' office close, and the steps of the departing patient in the hall outside, and turned to the nail-chewer. "You'll just have to wait," she said, and opened the door to Dr. Ehrens' office.

He was sitting in his black leather revolving chair, lighting his pipe, with his back to the door. He turned slowly and saw her. His face showed no surprise. "Well, Louise. If you're ready to resume regular treatment, you know you have to phone me for an appointment."

"You miserable son of a bitch," she screamed. "Why didn't you tell me you were his analyst?"

"Who?"

"Harry Bell."

"Aside from the fact that it violates professional ethics, and is privileged information, it happens to be none of your business."

"None of my business? I told you what was going on with him, when it was going on, *really* going on. If you were my friend you could have helped me."

"What makes you think I'm not your friend."

"Why didn't you help me?"

"I tried the best I could. As a friend, and as a doctor. It had to be your decision that you were wasting your time. I couldn't tell you that."

"Why, because of professional ethics? Some professional ethics, when you told a detective and a fucking attorney what I told you about his ripping my clothes and trying to rape me."

"I never told anyone."

"Then how did they know?"

"Who else did you tell?" Dr. Ehrens said.

"Oh Jesus," she said, and lay on the couch. "I don't even remember. Big mouth."

"I'd like very much to continue this discussion, but I'm afraid I have another patient waiting, Louise. If you want to talk some more, we can——"

"Tell him to go screw," she said. "I'm having a break-down."

"I very much doubt it."

"What do you know."

"Why don't we talk about it another time?"

"Because I want to talk now. NOW! You don't know what I've been through today, and it's all your fault, and if you don't let me talk to you now, I'll burn all your *National Geographics*, honest to God I will." She looked over at him. "Please. I'm in terrible shape. They're following me with detectives. I mean, in real life."

"I'll see what I can do," he said, and went into the waiting room. In a moment he returned.

"All right," he said. "Why don't you tell me about it."

"You don't have to ask me why I did it, saying what I did about Harry, we both know why I did it. I thought it would make me important."

"Did it?"

"Of course it did."

"In what way?"

"This is a waste of time," Louise said. "I don't know why I even try talking to you. You know, that fucking attorney did more for me in one afternoon than you did in three years. My whole life, before my very eyes. Do you know what it feels like, to have it stretched before you like that, my whole life; you never did that to me in here, why didn't you ever show me that in here? Perverts, and rats, and I was grateful. I was so grateful that anybody was interested in going to bed with me that I never even stopped to consider what was so wonderful."

"What was?"

"Like it was a big fucking accomplishment, getting laid. By important people, especially. Little Lulu. I had to use a diaphragm with that squishy jelly, so I could remind myself how dirty it was."

"So if you thought it was dirty, why should it surprise you that a lawyer, with a detective's report, made it sound dirty?"

"Made it sound? You think they made it sound dirty? You don't think it was dirty?"

"Do you?"

"I don't know. I'm so mixed up. I guess everything sounds filthy if you put in those terms. Intercourse. Why is that such a terrible word. I can say fuck or screw with no problem whatsoever, and I almost fainted when he said intercourse."

"Why is that?"

"I don't know."

"Well, let's examine it."

"Let's examine intercourse," Louise said. "Next Wednesday evening's lecture at the New School. Doesn't it sound dirty to you?"

"No."

"Well I guess you're not as inhibited as I am."

"What is there about the word itself that offends you?"

"I don't know."

"Maybe it's because it's not a distortion, a colloquial joke on the word, but a description of the act itself."

"Maybe. But whatever it is, it sounds dirty. They even made Charley sound dirty. The nicest one I ever knew in my life, and they even made him sound like trash. Thank God I made him move out of the apartment. That would have been too much to bear if they were following me, and he was still living in the apartment. I'm glad he's gone. Fuck him. And fuck you. I'm wasting my time. I'm wasting my time. Where did I go wrong?" she said, giggling, and then the laughter disintegrated, with her face, like a crumbled cookie, into sobs. She cried for longer than she had cried since she was a child. When she finally managed to stop, her eyes were swollen.

"Where is he now, Charley?"

"Oh who cares," she said. "Who gives a shit. You think that really happens, that I see the error of my ways, and go running back to him, begging forgiveness and understanding, for Christ's sake, and go live in Forest Hills. You think that ever really happens? You're not so smart, life isn't really like that. Anyway he's got his own apartment on Sixty-eighth Street. He doesn't need me anymore."

"You think that's all he wanted was your apartment?"

"Did Harry ever talk about me? Did he ever say anything about me to you? You could have been so much help to me, why didn't you tell me what he said."

"Let's talk about Charley," said Dr. Ehrens.

"Please," she said. "I beg of you. It's very important to me to know. What did he say?"

"He never said anything," Dr. Ehrens lit his pipe. "He never mentioned your name."

"That son of a bitch," she said. "I spend a minimum of ten sessions on him, and he didn't think enough of me to bring up my name."

"Maybe he had more pressing things on his mind."

"You mean more important people, don't you, Doctor."

"Not necessarily important the way you mean important. Sometimes very uncelebrated people are the most important people in someone's life. Sometimes, even a mother."

"Oh, you're trying to bring me back to that. None of this has anything to do with my mother."

"I didn't say it did."

"You mean his mother? You mean he was in here crying about his mother. A sixty-five-year-old man?" She giggled. "It seems so ludicrous."

"Does it?"

"You're right, I met the lady. He was right to cry. And he never even brought it up. He never even mentioned me?"

"Well," Dr. Ehrens said. "That's show business."

"Oh funny," Louise said. "Fun-nee. I guess you've gotten very hip since you started working with me."

The phone rang. "Take it," she said. "Don't wait for me."

"The hour's almost up anyway."

"The hour's always almost up," Louise said. "We are all on death row."

CHAPTER FIVE

IT was the first night since the Murder game that they were alone together. The drapes of the living room were drawn tight against the possibility of a world outside, shimmering below. Rick told Diane that as long as she insisted on treating the room as if it were a chamber of mourning, she might as well leave the lights out. But she murmured "No thank you," and turned the key in the remodeled hurricane lamp beside the sofa.

Her fine-boned face in the yellow-soft darkness was oddly swollen, and her thick red hair in oily curly clumps on the shoulders of her dressing gown. On the brass button of the upholstery her fingers drummed in funereal rhythm, and she stared at the floor.

"You shouldn't let yourself get so depressed," Rick said. "It shows in your face, and you can't afford to let things show in your face. You must consider your future."

"What future?" Diane said.

"You're going to be a very big star. I've told everyone. It will only be a question of making a few appointments on the Coast when we're free to leave New York. I suppose you might have to go through a screen test, but it will only be a formality. Now that we know how photogenic you are."

"I hate you," she said.

"I know. Isn't it exciting?"

He got up from the wing chair and walked to the bar, pouring another brandy into the oversize snifter. He smelled it, and swirled it, and moved it to his lips.

"You're not really suave, you know," she said. "You think you do all these stagey little things so well, the lighting of other people's cigarettes, the kissing of hands, the tasting of wine. But you're obvious, Rick. You're obvious, and you're a fool. With your tight little pants and your Cardin jackets. The chic-er you think you're becoming, the more blatant it is what a hungry little peasant you are."

"Really? Then you'll have to teach me."

"You can't teach someone things like that. It has to be in-born, inbred, like it was with Tzigie. There's no substitute for breeding."

"How about money and influence? I bet that's a good start."

"You won't be able to make it. It's a fantasy you're having, like some depraved corruption of Cinderella. There's no way to force the prince into saying the slipper fits."

"Is that it, sweetheart? Do you want to be the boy?"

"I don't want to talk to you. It's bad enough I have to pretend I'm enjoying being with you in public. I won't have it within the confines of my own home."

"You'll have it. You'll have anything I want you to have. Including my cock in your mouth in the middle of the Roosevelt Grill on New Year's Eve, with Guy Lombardo playing background."

"Even your choice of nostalgia has no style," Diane said, and went into the master suite. She ran the water for her bath, and breathing in the hot unperfumed fragrance, braced herself for the touch she was sure would come. But he had not followed her. He had at least the decency to allow her a moment alone to despise him, to marshal her reserves of hatred to prepare for the next onslaught. Passing her own wardrobes, she walked to the far side of the room, and opened Tzigie's armoire. Like fleshless skeletons in a cruelly open trench, the hangers gaped at her, empty of clothes. She touched a cast-off piece of tissue paper that had once wrapped his formal hat, and raised a cast-off shoe horn to her cheek.

"Aw," said Rick, closing the door behind him. "You miss him, you really do. I find that touching. Genuinely."

"I told you I loved him. I always told you that."

"Well of course you did, angel, and he loved you too, and that's why it was the kindest thing you could have done, telling him it was over like that, that you wanted him to go away. When you really care about someone, you don't want their vision of you destroyed, do you, so it was a great and loving kindness sending him away, before he saw anything that would have desolated him."

"I made a mistake, I know I did. I should have called your bluff. He would have understood. He would have forgiven me."

"Well, if you think that, darling, why don't we send him the pictures? I've got them right here, as always, next to my heart." He reached inside his jacket, and handed them to her. "You want to look at them again, to make sure they're all here? I know how much you enjoy looking at yourself. This one, this one is my favorite, isn't it yours? Your lovely aristocratic thighs spread *so* wide, wider than they ever spread for a mere man, I would venture. And the expression on your face. So heavy-lidded, so loose-lipped, so bloated with lust and true pleasure. Do you think he ever saw you looking exactly like that? Of course, it isn't a very good picture of me, my right profile was never as perfect as my left but then it's your scene really. Yours and the lovely little friend in my hand."

"Send them to him," she said.

"This one isn't bad either, really, although you do look better right-side up than upside down, it was a distorted camera angle, I suppose. I'd do better next time."

"Send them to him."

"My only regret is that we don't have one of you blowing me. It was stupid, letting myself get carried away like that, running out of film. But then everything works out for the best, doesn't it? My unfortunate bigness cut off your mouth, and that is, after all, your best feature. I wouldn't want any pictures of you around that didn't show your mouth to its best advantage."

"SEND IT!" she screamed, and came at him, her fists beatng wildly against his chest, as he pressed her off, laughing, with one hand as he held the pictures away.

"And this one."

"SEND IT!"

"Now be careful you don't hit my face, darling, don't forget my face is our fortune. We won't be able to live off your trusts forever. Not in the style to which I intend to become accustomed."

"You've won," she said, and broke into a heap at his ankles. "You've succeeded in humiliating me. Isn't it enough for you?"

"Unzip my pants," he said.

"Send them to him," she said, and started to cry.

"All right. Don't cry. I can't stand to see you suffer. I'll do what you say. Maybe if he does love you so much, maybe if he is such an inbred gentleman, he will forgive you. Just as your mother will forgive you. And why not the magazines. Of course. You're such a heroine with the slick publications of America, I'm sure they'd forgive you too. Naturally I don't suppose they'd publish the pictures; I don't guess the newsstands are quite ready for that. But I imagine we could get quite a little private circulation out of it. No, please, don't get up; I like you there, on your knees like that. Unzip my pants."

"I'll kill you," she said. "I'll kill you without a moment's regret."

"Of course, darling. But first unzip my pants."

She did what she was told.

"Now take it. Take it in your exquisite little mouth and minister to it with the gentleness that's been so long inside you. And if you bite it again, if you try to hurt me, I swear to Christ I'll have these made into composites, and have them sent to every casting director at every major studio."

He fell silent as her hand rubbed briskly the jutting stem of his erection, and her tongue and lips pulled at the purple tip. He braced himself against the armoire, as he felt himself surging from his loins, and she tried to pull away. With both hands he grasped her open jaw and pressed her to himself, and coursed into her mouth. Then he let her go.

He listened for a moment to the gagging sounds emanating from the bathroom. Then he went inside. She was standing at the sink, gargling with mouthwash, the knuckles of her left hand white as she steadied herself against the sink.

"Oh I'm hurt," he said. "My mommy always said 'If she loves you, she'll swallow it.' "

"You pervert," she said, and spit at his reflection in the mirror. "You depraved moron."

"That's just postcoital depression talking, darling. Everyone feels a little down afterward. It'll pass. As soon as you have your bath, I'll do the same for you, and then we can start all over, Hansel and Gretel, holding hands in the woods. That's all we have, my angel. Each other."

"What do you want from me?" she said. "You're even. You've gotten back at me for Paradise Island, you've gotten back at me for every imagined sin every woman has committed. Why don't you let me go."

"Is that what you think?" Rick said, and started taking off the rest of his clothes. "You think I want to get back at you? You think I want to humiliate you? But what an unhappy view of life. What a morbid approach to sex."

"Please. I'll do anything. If you'll just go away."

"You see, you foolish girl." Rick slapped his naked belly. "You don't understand, you don't understand at all. Why don't you listen. You haven't tried to listen, that's your problem. We're going to be America's sweethearts, angel, in the style of the sixties. Flagrant lovers, living in sin, going everywhere together, all the best hotels, all over the world, flaunting ourselves in the face of society. They'll love it, don't you see, because we're both so high-toned, it has to be the right thing to do. Why we'll have offers from all over. We'll do pictures as they've never been done before. The passionate level. The free-love level. The Now People. That's who we'll be. I've made my last picture for a hundred thousand, my angel. You don't pay less than a half a mill to the conqueror of a princess."

"I can't," she said. "Please. I haven't got it in me. Let me go."

"Oh you mustn't worry, we can train you. You're beautiful, and we know you're photogenic, and we've just seen how well you take directions. You mustn't be upset about your reviews. What do they know in Steubenville about true aristocracy."

"I couldn't live like that. I'd die."

"But you'll be worshiped, saluted. Oh, maybe it's the morality of it that upsets you. All right. Very well. I'm not a hard man, really I'm not. As soon as this police business blows over, you can take a little flyer to Juarez and divorce Tzigie, so you won't feel sticky about the adultery. You see, I'm not really a hard man."

"I won't marry you. I'll kill myself first."

"Now angel, you wouldn't go that far. You couldn't. The only thing you hate more than humiliation is the idea of not having yourself to play with. Anyway, you're silly to be so concerned. I wouldn't marry you. Not right away. It's essential to the whole scheme of things, I mean if we are truly to be adored, worldwide, European grosses are so important nowadays, we have to be public immoral lovers. Maybe after a while though, maybe if you're a really good girl, I might marry you. Not until after a decent period of flaunting though. Then they can forgive us, when we do get married. Then we'll do even better, box-office-wise."

"Oh God," Diane said, and collapsed against the sink. "Oh God, oh God."

"You're tired," he said, and soothed her shaking shoulders. "Come." He slipped the robe over her arms, and let it slide to the floor, as his fingers caressed her naked back. "You'll feel much better in a nice warm tub." He led her like a grief-stricken, numb mourner to a cemetery, to the edge of the sunken marble tub, and lowered her gently to its depths. Placing the soap in her right hand, and a washcloth in her left, he pressed her right wrist toward her pudendum.

"Now scrub it up, like a good girl," he said. "Polish it and make it shiny pink and red and clean." He stripped his own shirt from his shoulders, and reached over to remove his shoes and socks. "Sweet smelling and sweet tasting is sweet living."

She raised her pale green eyes, and looked at him, a very small insect on the underside of a microscope, very far away. "What are you doing?"

"Why making myself ready for you," he said, smiling. "Not that anyone's keeping score, but you do owe me a bath."

Maggie's mother would not die. For two weeks Dr. Wilcox, and the surgeon who had performed the last operation, and the resident on the floor had been telling Maggie it would only be a matter of days, or hours. The hours and days had passed, and she would not die. Maggie sat at the side of her mother's bed, watching pain shrivel the once proud features, watching the drippings in the bag seeping into the basin turn black, watching the body shrink to an even smaller skeleton and all recognition leave the eyes. The cancer had spread from uterus to kidney to bladder, and there was no orifice of her mother's body that was not defiled with tubes or artificial bags. Maggie wished for the hundredth time that day that there really were a God of Mercy, or that someone would have the sense to listen to Algernon. Algernon had explained to Maggie at length that the desperation of the terminal patient was only a little different from that of anyone who could anticipate the possibility of death at any time, with growing certainty, the probability of death—ultimately, its inevitability. Death row was the realization in all of us that we are born to die. That was the glory of the psychedelic experience; the apprehension and anticipation, the prerequisite for the whole edifice of human civilization with its phony games of success, were dulled and dimmed. Eliminating apprehension eliminated ambition; eliminating anticipation eliminated fear of consequences. For those who were dying, it was the only way of eliminating hopelessness, the realization of doom.

Maggie tried to explain all this to Dr. Wilcox. She wished now she had brought Algernon to the hospital with her. He would be able to tell them better than she. She tried, she tried to project the truths of what Algernon said into the ears of Dr. Wilcox as she had tried for weeks. But Algernon's words, with their brilliant crystalline wisdom, became muddled in her mouth, and she had difficulty expressing herself.

"You've got to eliminate the hopelessness," she said to him, for the tenth time. He was bending over her mother's still breathing chest, listening to the dark fluids collecting, not listening to Maggie's words, she was sure. "Don't you see, I don't want her to know how desperate her situation is."

"Then why don't you stop discussing it in front of her, Maggie."

"But she knows. She must know. Her mechanism for blind optimism is destroyed. She's anticipating. That's what we have to do, is eliminate her ability to anticipate. Don't you see? Why don't you listen. How can you be so inhumane."

"We're doing everything that's humanly possible."

"On your level, don't you understand, it's so madly society-organized."

"Why don't you go home and get some sleep?" Dr. Wilcox said. "You've been here for days, Maggie. I don't want you making yourself sick in your condition."

She batted at her stomach beneath the billowing folds of silk, the gesture an assurance of strength within that did not need attending. "Why won't you let me give her something? What difference does it make?"

"She's under an extremely heavy dosage of morphine."

"I'm not talking about eliminating the pain. I know you're eliminating the pain."

The blue-veined heavy-lidded eyes fluttered open, and Mrs. Bolin breathed heavily. "She's akawe," Dr. Wilcox said. "I don't want to discuss it anymore. Not here. If you want to come out in the hall . . ."

"No," Maggie said, and reached for the wispy hand lying limp beneath the tubing dripping glucose into the wrist. "I don't want to leave her. I'm here, Mama," she whispered, and squeezed the fragile fingers, withered so they felt like pipe cleaners in her hand. There was no pressure in return. "It's all right. Just try not to anticipate anything, please, it won't help. It happens to the healthiest person, realizing he's doomed to die."

"You're making it worse," Dr. Wilcox said. "Why don't you come out in the hall? I'll have one of the nurses get you a sandwich."

"I'm not hungry," Maggie said. "Are you hungry, Mama? Shall I go out and get us a lovely basket from Poll's? Scotch salmon, and caviar, and a little champagne, and we'll have picnic, right here, like we used to in the country, wouldn't that be nice?"

The thin blue lips, a pencil line awkwardly drawn across the expanse of white face, pulled slightly and lifted at the corners. "Look," Maggie said. "She's smiling. She wants to do it, what time is it, is it after ten, if it's only nine or something like that, maybe they're still open and I could taxi over, and . . ."

"It's after midnight," Dr. Wilcox said. "I want you to go. I'll call you if there's any change."

"Midnight?" Maggie said. "Then maybe I could call him at home, he's a very pleasant man, Mr. Poll, I'm sure he wouldn't mind going back to the shop, not after all the things I've bought there, and . . ."

"Don't try to make it into a party, Maggie. She can't eat anything anyway, you know that. It's after midnight, and I want you to go home. I should have sent you home a long time ago. Visiting hours have been over since nine."

"Officially," she said. "That's all you're interested in, is what's official, don't you dare try to reprimand me, and I won't go home, not after all the money my family's donated to this hospital. And you, Dr. Wilcox, what about everything they've given to you."

"I don't think we ought to discuss this in front of your mother."

"It's all right, isn't it, dear. What was it all for, if I can't stay with you."

"Please," Dr. Wilcox said. "Please. I want to talk to you, Maggie. Come into the hall."

"No," she said, and held firm to the unfeeling hand.

"You're overwrought, I want to talk to you."

"I don't want to talk to you."

"Then do it unselfishly," he said. "For me. For a tired old man who hasn't got the ability to lose apprehension."

"Oh," Maggie said. "You're starting to have second thoughts."

"Yes. Yes I am."

She placed a kiss on the thin blue mouth, tasting of charcoal and decay. Promising she would only be a minute, she followed Dr. Wilcox down the hall to the deserted waiting room. She sat almost primly, her hands folded across her bloated stomach, like the little porcelain Dutch girl which, opened, contained a cookie jar. She smiled at him, to let him know how responsive she was to his finally listening to reason. And then she heard from his opening words, and saw from his expression, stern and fatherly, that he was going to lecture her. She let her mind, and her eyes drift.

"I'm worried, Maggie," Dr. Wilcox said. "I'd heard vaguely that you were involved with these people, but I don't like to pay attention to gossip, and your mother never discussed it with me. She didn't like to talk about you, at least not to me. She didn't even tell me you were pregnant, possibly because she thought I might be hurt, your not using me for your doctor."

"Sweet," Maggie said. "Sweet Mama." She watched herself disappearing into the center of a daisy.

"But I trust your doctor's told you the dangers of these 'harmless' drugs. I'm sure you have too much good sense to be taking them. Not during your pregnancy."

She was brought abruptly to earth, and she heard Dr. Wilcox. "What?"

"The chromosome damage, Maggie. Surely you've discussed it with him."

"Who?"

"Your obstetrician. Who are you using?"

"What chromosome damage?"

"The hallucinogens block enzymes to the brain, Maggie, that's how they work, that's what causes the psychedelic experience. I haven't read up on them thoroughly, but I do know if you block enzymes in one area, you can block them in another. They've started to investigate chromosome damage in infants born to mothers who've taken LSD."

"I don't know what you're talking about," Maggie said. "Why do you ramble so?"

"I don't want to upset you, but I just hope you've been careful with yourself. Have you discussed any of this with your doctor?"

"My baby is perfect," she said, and tears filled her eyes. "My baby has all its fingers and all its toes, and fingernails, and it's beautiful, it's a perfect baby, don't you dare try to frighten me like that just because you can't manage life, because you're jealous of life, all you understand is death, and you won't even help her out of that."

"I'm not trying to frighten you, Maggie, I . . ."

"You are, you are, that's all you know how to do is frighten people, holding their hands and telling them it's going to be all right, when all you mean is it's hopeless, everything is hopeless, we are all doomed, and you are the guide to doom, that's all you know how to be, with your oaths on the wall, and all the tribal symbols of the witch doctor, leading us down the primrose path to death. That's all you know, that, and jealousy, because I wouldn't let you take care of me, because I wouldn't put this child, this perfect child, into your death-clammy hands."

"I'm sorry," he said, and got up. "I hope . . . Well, if there's anything I can do . . . If your doctor wants to phone me . . ."

"Just go away," she said. "Just go away and leave me alone. My baby is fine, my baby is better than fine, she's perfect, I wouldn't let you get your hands on her, my baby is fine, and you won't touch her and you won't touch me. Go away. Go back where you belong, inside, with the dying."

At one o'clock that morning, when he went to the cafeteria for a cup of coffee, Dr. Wilcox tried to phone George Piner to try and advise him that perhaps Maggie needed some close professional care. The man who answered the phone said that George was away on a ski trip. Dr. Wilcox made a note to try and reach Dr. Piner later in the week. By that time, Maggie Bolin Piner's mother was beyond anticipation and apprehension; in the confusion and sadness that accompanied death, he forgot to make the call.

It was amazing, Andre could not help thinking, all the while he packed. It was amazing what the human spirit, under pressure, could conjure up out of itself, what the human brain, dazzled by urgency, could contemplate, and even create, in order to survive. Granted, his was not a brain like most people's, and if he had failed to get his due in proportion to his talent, no, his genius, all that would change. He was, after all, thirty-eight years old, and his whole life was ahead of him, even if a good part of it would have to be spent in Argentina. At least until a few things blew over. He was confident everything would.

He whistled as he folded his clothes and lay them neatly in the various compartments of his suitcase, whistled, and sometimes hummed. In the past few weeks he had been magic, the golden touch that eluded him all his life springing from his fingertips, as in the legends of Harry Bell. Two of the land developments he had despaired of ever selling had been taken over by a chemical company, as part of a living and recreational complex for its employees, at enormous profit to Andre, profit immediately reinvested in several stocks on which he had tips. For once the tips had been right. He had it, finally, the touch. Naturally he could not wait around to make as much money as he was now capable of making, but he would be able to live comfortably, and long. Perhaps *Esquire* could send one of their writers down to Argentina to talk to him, when they did their article on men under forty who could have been millionaires if they had hung around.

He laughed aloud, and thought again how stupid the world was, and how clever, how really clever under the gun he had turned out to be. It was a little puzzling to him, if he stopped to think about it, that the police hadn't connected him with Bernie. But that was just another part of the gift he had been given, the magic wrought by his change in luck. Plus the fact that they were rendered stupid and paralyzed by all the wealth and influence in that house that night, and the total implausibility of someone's being murdered, actually murdered, in the midst of New York's most elaborate mansion. Agatha Christie gone mad. He laughed again. Either that, he thought, sobering, or they were taking their time to build a really tight case against him, in which event all his precautions, the fake name on the airline reservation, the new forged passport waiting for him in New Orleans, along with the bank draft of the past weeks' profits, had been doubly wise. Brilliantly wise. Genius-wise.

His mother had been right about him all along. And he had been right about himself. He was really going to do it. He was really getting away. With murder.

He was genuinely surprised when he looked up and saw the two men in his doorway, in dark topcoats and gray felt hats; like they wore in Cincinnati.

"But it isn't happening," he shouted. "It couldn't be happening. Oh Christ," he pounded his hand on the top of his valise. "Of all the luck. Of all the lousy, rotten luck."

CHAPTER SIX

SOMETIMES, in the evenings, when she would get exceedingly depressed, Louise would take a taxi past Charley's apartment building and look up at his window. It always reassured her momentarily when the lights were on, because that meant he didn't have any place to go. At the same time she would realize that he might very well have someone there with him, so at some point during the evening she would absent herself from whatever group she was with, and call him. She never spoke but only listened to the way he said hello, to see if he were out of breath or excited, before she hung up the phone. Once in a while after a few hellos, and an angry "Who is this?" he would say, "Is that you, Louise?" and she would despise him for his presumption in thinking that she would do anything as foolish as check on him.

She also began spending a good deal of time with Kate and David. It was not, she was sure, that she had any hope of running into Charley. The social season had quieted down quite a bit, and Chet Oppenheim was already exerting a modest amount of revenge: the invitations were no longer as copious as they had been, and her column had been canceled in several papers. But she was far from an outcast, she knew that. There was more than enough to keep her busy and fulfilled. Seeing Kate and David was merely a part of her program of repair, which she had discussed at length with Dr. Ehrens. Everyone in the world did not have to be a celebrity, it seemed, and he suggested she spend time with people who led "normal," unglittering lives.

They certainly qualified as unglittering. They appeared to have settled into what Kate was always categorizing as a warm routine, although it seemed to Louise to be more routine than warm. Weekends they went to the country with their dog, and during the week they had quiet dinners in restaurants, where Louise often joined them, when she had nothing better to do. The Wednesday after Andre Sherman's disappearance was discovered, she went with them to the Café 72, where there was little likelihood of anyone seeing her.

"So what's new in the world of the glamour people?" David said. "Bring us up to date."

"Nothing spectacular," Louise said. "Do you ever see Charley?"

"He's fine," Kate said, and squeezed her hand.

"I got a new account this week," David said. "Millie Phelps. Do you know her? Maggie Bolin's cousin. How is Maggie?"

"She's fine," Louise said. "Very pregnant."

"You ought to call her, Kate, get together with her more often."

"I don't have anything to say to her," Kate said.

"Don't be silly, she's pregnant, you have a baby, you've got everything in common. You ought to have her over to the house to see the baby."

"I've had her over, she's seen the baby. I don't like to have her around."

"My lovely wife," David reached over and cupped Kate's chin, "thinks Maggie Bolin is weird. I tried to explain to her that when people are that rich, they have a right to be eccentric."

"She isn't eccentric," Kate said. "She's insane."

"She only says nice things about you," Louise said.

"You see?" David said. "What did I tell you, Kate. You ought to call her, and we should all spend some real time together. I could probably be a lot of help to Dr. Piner with his clinic, most Wall Streeters need to lose weight, and you never can tell, he might be able to throw a little business my way." The waiter came to the table offering menus, but David waved them away. "I'll order for everyone," he said. "The only thing worth eating here is the lasagna."

"I feel like having veal," Kate said.

"Three lasagnas," David said. "And a bottle of Soave. Well chilled."

"Bolla or Bertani?" the waiter said.

"Bolla, of course. So what do you think about Sherman's disappearing?"

"I don't like to think about it," Louise said. "The whole thing makes me nervous."

"You used to be pretty close to him, didn't you?" David said.

"I used to be close to a lot of people," Louise said softly.

"I spoke to him this afternoon," Kate said. "Charley."

"Excuse me," said David. "I have to go to the little boy's room."

"You see?" Louise said when he left the table. "He doesn't want to hear about it and neither do I. If Charley had anything to say to me, he'd call me and tell me himself."

"Why don't you call him."

"I do. I don't say anything. I just listen to him breathing."

Kate laughed. "He's lovely, you know. And he's really very fond of you."

"No he's not. He's fond of some male-ego idea of what I could change into, because I'm so fucking grateful to be with him."

"Aren't you?"

"No. There are too many women who confuse being dominated with being feminine. I'm not that big a fool." She looked up and saw Kate's cheeks reddening. "I mean . . ."

"It's all right," Kate said softly. "I know what you mean. I didn't think Charley was like that."

"Well he's not," Louise said. "Not exactly, I don't know what he wanted, but I wasn't it, I know that much. He kept criticizing everything I was doing, everyone I cared about, without ever coming out and really saying anything, if you know what I mean. He never said how he really felt about me. *If* he felt anything, really."

"Maybe he was waiting for you to come to some conclusion, before he let you know how serious he was."

"And maybe not all of us are meant to be loving wives and mothers."

"I don't believe that," Kate said. "I can't."

After dinner she went back with them across the street to their apartment; not, she assured herself, that she had any illusions that Charley would materialize. If he had spoken to Kate that afternoon, then he knew she would be there, and he had no wish to run into her. That was probably the only explanation for his never having appeared during all the time she forced herself to be with Kate and David. The only reason she was going back to their place tonight was because it was early, and they were her friends, and Dr. Ehrens wanted her to spend time with all kinds of people, and she had no place else to go.

On the way up in the elevator David talked a good deal about Kate's latest promotion at the agency, and Kate offered detailed accounts of how well David was doing at the brokerage firm. As a matter of fact, he had just gotten a very important new customer, Millie Phelps, or had they mentioned that already.

"No," Louise lied. "That's really very exciting."

"I'm a little excited myself," David said. "Everything's going so well, financially and career-wise. We're thinking about having another baby."

"That's marvelous," Louise said.

"Especially now that Tracy's turning into a real little girl. She's really very cute, you'll have to see."

"Will you have enough room in this apartment for another baby?"

"Well naturally such an eventuality will mean moving to larger quarters," David said. "Especially the way things are going financially and career-wise. Larger quarters, or maybe we'll even take over the apartment next door, and the children can live there, with Mrs. Hanner."

"You wouldn't mind that?" Louise said to Kate.

"Why? They'll be right next door. Oh good," Kate said, as David unlocked the door to the apartment. "I hear Tracy. That means we won't have to wake her up."

There was no doubt the child was beautiful. Her hair had changed from the soft fuzz of the early months to rich golden brown curls, her eyes had become almost black, wide-set, and alert and alive. She smiled a good deal, pink mouth stretched wide, when she was playing in the living room with them. Then, suddenly losing interest, she employed her newly mastered crawl and left the room.

"The audience is concluded," Kate said. "Miss Tracy is not amused."

"Hey," David yelled, and went after the scuttling, round-bottomed creature. "I wasn't finished with my story, kid." He scooped her into his arms, and came back with the smiling, passive bundle. "Look at my weird kid. She isn't even happy to be with her daddy. Playing hard to get, I suppose." He righted the little girl on his lap, and laughed into her face, clapping her hands together. The black eyes stared at him for a moment, then looked away, as she craned her neck backward. "Hey," David said. "Hey."

"You shouldn't have violated her privacy," Kate said. "We've been dismissed."

"I guess," David said. He called Mrs. Hanner, who came and took the baby away.

"Isn't it amazing how their personalities are already there at birth. Eight months old, and she's aloof." Kate shook her head. "Not like Albert." She reached over and patted the dog's long beige flank, and he jumped and licked at her face.

"You really believe that?" Louise said. "You really believe people are the way they're going to be, inborn?"

"Well isn't it obvious?" David said. "She'll play with you and suddenly she'll dismiss you. It's pretty sophisticated behavior for eight months old."

It bothered Louise all night, the thought that people were born the way they were going to be. That there was a possibility she might have been born vulnerable and unbalanced was terribly disturbing. Then there would be no solution.

She could hardly wait for her appointment with Dr. Ehrens the next morning. "So you see," she said, after she had resurrected the evening. "It's not their fault they aren't more responsive to the child. She's spooky. I mean, it's really spooky, a baby as small as that with its own attitudes. She's a beautiful baby, and I suppose she's darling sometimes, but she's cold. Really cold. She plays for a while, and then she 'dismisses' you, that's what Kate and David said, and they're right. She sends everybody away."

Dr. Ehrens didn't answer.

"So maybe there is such a thing as chemical schizophrenia, that people are born disturbed because there's a chemical imbalance or something."

"Probably there is."

"And that's what's wrong with Tracy?"

"I didn't say that."

"Then what did you say?"

"More important, what did you say. What did you tell me about Kate at the hospital."

"You mean that story she told me when she had just had the baby and she still had the stitches in her and she walked all the way back to the nursery, holding the baby out to the nurse saying, 'You can take her now.' "

"That's right."

"So?"

"So what was she doing?"

"Dismissing her?" Louise said.

"That's right."

"You're putting me on," Louise said. "A three-day-old baby doesn't adopt the attitude of her mother. I don't want to think about it. It's too scary."

"What frightens you?"

"It's too much of a responsibility, worrying about what's going to disturb your children, if they're going to be crazy, or what. I think I'll avoid all that by not having any."

"Well, you've certainly done your best so far," Dr. Ehrens said.

Maggie did not think about her child's being disturbed. For weeks after her mother's funeral, she tried not thinking about her child at all. She focused her waking anguish on her mother, and the black void that had swallowed her from within. Often, she cried for hours without stopping, and neither the gentle ministrations of George, with his quiet offer of sedation, nor the assurances of Algernon that a simple trip would bring her out of it could placate her. She would touch nothing, not even aspirin, because of what Dr. Wilcox had told her. But she refused to think about that at all, during the day. She lay in bed and watched old reruns, and allowed herself to drift undersea with the latest Jacques Cousteau. She would not think about her baby being defective.

Nights were not quite as easy. In spite of the insomnia which plagued her, with which she plagued herself, to avoid dreaming, her eyes, opened and shut, were filled with specters of deformed babies, limbless, eyeless, aswarm in a thalidomide sea. Once, when Maggie had contemplated an operation on her breasts, to make them conform to the smaller, more fashionable chestplates of her friends, she had visited the office of one of New York's most prominent plastic surgeons. In his waiting room she had seen a little girl with one perfect blue eye beneath blond curls and half of a charmingly pugged nose. The rest of the face was a rubber mask, punched out by a cruel, distorting hand from behind, one cheek bulging, the other collapsed. The small teeth were hideously bucked, and the lower jaw did not exist at all. After an hour of Maggie's forcing herself to look away, the little girl went inside with her mother.

"That poor child," Maggie said to the receptionist. "That poor little girl. What's wrong with her."

"Cleft face," the receptionist said.

"Oh Lord, how dreadful. How perfectly dreadful."

"You should have seen her before the doctor started working on her."

Now, in the night, in Maggie's visions and dreams, the baby's face clefted, split, melted into air, features collapsing like breath seeping out a balloon. Beside the pink satin bassinette, Maggie reached to play "this little piggy" with velvet toes; the toes broke away in her hand. Valves pumped to a twisted heart. Anus coursed blood, and vulva cracked up the center of the small torso to beneath the chin. Maggie slept little, but when she did sleep, she awoke screaming.

She would not ask George what could be involved in chromosome damage. His broad evasive answers would be worse than anything her imagined nightmares could create. Undoubtedly he did not know about the problems in detail and, not wishing to admit he didn't know, would make up things, frightening medical-sounding names to confuse her, and cloak his lack of information. Dr. Wilcox she would not call. He was too self-righteous, too opinionated; the fact that she admitted to him that she had taken anything would put her in too apologetic a position with him. He would snort and say, without words, "I always knew that about you, that you were a bad girl, and your mother was ridiculous to waste her time with you." Besides, he had refused to help her mother, at the end. Why would he want to help Maggie?

Finally, when she could not face another dreamless, or dreaming night, she made an appointment with Dr. Matthew Rady. She told his nurse on the phone that the doctor probably wouldn't remember her, but she was a friend of Kate Waller's, and she had seen the doctor once, several months before. The nurse wanted to make the appointment for a week from Thursday, but Maggie told her it was in the nature of an emergency. The nurse said she could come in at four o'clock that afternoon.

Entering the office, her belly billowing in front of her, cloaked in greatcoat and one of Kate's old maternity dresses, Maggie felt a sudden and happy conviction that she was worrying for nothing, and Dr. Rady would tell her so. Each of the faces congregated in Rady's waiting room shared her same expression of anticipatory bliss and vague anxiety. There was not an expectant mother in the world who did not have the same fears, who didn't avert her eyes from posters of retarded children, who didn't throw away the folders in the mail from cerebral palsy, birth defects, from the infantile paralysis people. She would have to speak to Diane, Maggie realized, as soon as she got home she would have to speak to Diane about marshaling the disease mail, making sure it did not find its way to expectant mothers. She would do that, right after she got home. Just as soon as Dr. Rady assured her her fears were unfounded.

She went, as instructed, into the bathroom and filled the specimen jar with urine (could they tell from that? could they stick a piece of tape into the swirling yellow and see if the baby was whole?) but would not go directly into the examination room, like all the other women waiting behind myriad doors.

"I can't just sit in there on that table, waiting," Maggie said to the nurse. "I've got to talk to him."

"Doctor's doing the best he can to work you in, Mrs. Piner. But we do have other patients, who . . ."

"I won't sit on that table, waiting," Maggie said. "Please. I need to talk to him."

"All right." The nurse opened the door to the doctor's office, and pointed out a deep leather chair. "Just make yourself comfortable."

Maggie spent the agonizing interim perusing the richly bound books on the shelves, seeking some clue in the titles. But all seemed cold and technical. If their technicality offered some article about chromosomes, she could not find it. She contented herself with glancing through the doctor's own copy of *Expectant Motherhood,* the golden hair at her neckline curling damply, her breath coming fast, as she read that her baby was about fifteen inches in length and weighed two and a half pounds. If.

"Well, well," Dr. Rady said, closing the door behind him. "How are you, Mrs. Piner. And congratulations."

"Please," she said. "Please. I've got to talk to you."

"So the nurse told me. Why don't you sit down."

"I'm very frightened about my baby," she said, as he moved behind the desk, and smiled at her, his expression gentle, impassive. "I'm afraid I've done some things—some bad things to myself, and that I've hurt the baby."

"Didn't your doctor give you a prescribed form of treatment?"

"I'm not talking about vitamins and things."

"Who is your obstetrician, Mrs. Piner?"

"A doctor in New Jersey, you wouldn't know him. It doesn't matter, I've decided not to use him anymore. Tell me about chromosome damage. What does it mean, exactly?"

"Exactly what it says. Damage to the chromosomes. They don't know exactly, and to what extent yet the damage might take place. What have you taken that makes you think you may have done damage?"

"What *kind* of damage. Will the baby have all its toes, and its face? Please, you've got to tell me."

"Why don't you sit down, Mrs. Piner. There's no point in getting yourself worked up about something we can't be sure about for several months, and maybe not even after the baby is born. If you've taken hallucinogens, I'm sorry you have, but there's no definite assurance that the baby will be hurt by them."

"Does that mean it will be all right? Can you tell me it'll be all right?"

"The greatest majority of births are normal. And the greatest majority of babies are healthy babies. It doesn't do any good to worry about these things in advance. My concern is that you do as much as you can in the last few months to ensure—"

"Stop it," Maggie screamed. "Stop it. Please. I'm not interested in platitudes. I want to know that she's all right."

"I'm sure your baby is fine."

"But you're only saying that, aren't you? You don't really know. You're pacifying me."

"We only know so much before a baby is born. Any baby. We could X-ray you to make sure that everything external was . . ."

"I won't be X-rayed. X-rays hurt the baby."

"Not in the latter part of pregnancy to that extent."

"Please," she said, and bit her lower lip to keep it from trembling. "Make it be all right."

"Why don't you come inside, and we'll have a look."

"Can you tell?" she said, as they crossed the corridor to the examining room. "Can you tell from checking me that the baby will be all right?"

"We can tell a lot of things," he said, as he helped her up on the table. "We can tell that a healthy mother is getting along fine, and will probably produce a fat, healthy baby. You look like a very healthy girl." He smiled, as he eased her backward, and his fingers lifted her skirt, and touched her bloated stomach.

"Is it?" she said. "Is everything all right?"

"When did you have your last period?" he said.

"The end of September, I think it was. Or August. I'm not sure exactly. But sometime in the early fall."

Both his hands were touching her now, and he was not looking at her, but at a point somewhere beyond her head, and the wall. Concern clouded his face, and he reached for a silver band, stethoscope attached, and placed it on his forehead. The plugs went in his ears, and he leaned over her stomach and moved the cold flat spout.

"Is everything all right?"

"Slip down your pants," Dr. Rady said. "I want to do an internal."

"Please," she said, as the rubber finger probed inside her. "Please, you have to tell me."

"Mrs. Piner." His hand came free. "Why don't you get dressed, and come inside and we'll talk."

"We've talked," she said. "We've already talked. I want you to tell me. What's wrong? Is something wrong?"

"I think it would be better if we sat down inside."

"I want to know now. Please. What's wrong with my baby? I've hurt it, haven't I? I've done something terrible to my baby."

He took her hand. "Maggie, there is in medicine, a condition known as pseudocyesis . . ."

"Don't give me medical jargon, please. I don't want to hear all these fancy names. You're just like George, you're all so madly pompous and evasive. What's wrong with my baby?"

"Nothing," Dr. Rady said. "There is no baby. You're not pregnant."

The inside of the Caravelle restaurant was unusually crowded for early in the evening; so Rick, Diane and Bunyan, who had opted out on the pre-theater cocktail party at Julia White's in favor of dinner, felt constrained to lower their voices. Even without Rick's growing celebrity and the lavish success of Bunyan's exhibition of paintings, period Paradise Island, it was obvious that people would have paid attention to them: they were without doubt the most attractive trio in the restaurant. Diane, her hair swept into a topknot of pearls, with four thick curls falling to her neck, glowing autumnally russet against the bright orange of her satin capesuit, complexion more regally pale than usual, made a stunning contrast to Rick's dark amber. Even Bunyan, who had not in the past paid too much attention to attire, was benefitting from being part of such pretty picture. His silver bangs, hanging straight to his pale gray eyes, had been copied by his tailor and incorporated into the thread of the Nehru jacket he was wearing to the opening. From time to time Bunyan would clap his hands and remark that none of them had ever looked better or been better in their lives, so the little misfortune of winter had wreaked no real hardship.

"Naturally we could all do with a weeny bit of goof-off time," Bunyan said. "It becomes so serious when you're limited to one place; treadmilly, really, one gets such a sense of purpose."

Rick lit two cigarettes and passed one to Diane, who shook her head. He passed the extra to Bunyan, who took it and inhaled. "Right after we're free again," said Bunyan, talking through unaccustomed breaths of smoke. "Methinks I shall take a little two by four in Acapulcey, and you children can come and join me. Fun, yes? I've also invited two friends of mine from the Canadian Royal Mounties, won't that be clever contrast."

"I'm not up to going anywhere," Diane said.

"We'd love to come," said Rick. "Maybe I could take some pictures of Diane in a bathing suit."

"It shouldn't be too much longer before they clear the mess, old N.Y.P.D., thinks thou?"

Rick squeezed Diane's hand. "The attorney from Marathon spoke to someone on the D.A.'s staff, and he said it ought to all be cleared up within the next few weeks. The mystery becomes less mysterious, I imagine, what with the curious disappearance of Mr. Sherman."

"You really think Andre did it?" Bunyan said. "I wouldn't have imagined he had the balls, forgive me, Diane. He's a good games player and all that, but I can't imagine him doing anything real, like murder."

"Well, we know the guy was a bookie, and apparently Andre used to do a lot of heavy betting."

"How unsporting," Bunyan said. "You mean you think he owed him money?"

"That's the theory."

"He never had it in him to be a real gentleman," Bunyan said. "To kill one's bookmaker. How chintzy. Where do you suppose Andre is?"

"Where do they go?" Rick said. "Switzerland? Argentina?"

"Oh fun, fun. All those cute ex-Nazis. Either that or maybe il Mafioso came to even el score. Do you think?"

"That never really happens," Rick said.

"Quien sabe," Bunyan said. "Even as we speak he may be a little square of compressed metal, in an abandoned-car lot in Jersey. You're not eating, Diane, my pet. Is it cold? Do you want me to send it back to the kitchen? Would you like to order something else?"

Diane shook her head.

"You'll get your appetite back, I promise you will." Bunyan reached over and patted her cheek. "You can't go around being so hangdoggy in love forever, you know. Sooner or later you'll get disenchanted with Ricky Ticky here and then you'll return to ordinary human hungers."

"I hope not," Rick said, and put his arm around her neck, squeezing her toward him. She shivered.

"My God, cover my eyes," Bunyan said. "Such unremitting passion will destroy my whole way of life. What shall we have for dessert. Cherries jubilee, yes, crepes? Something banquetty. For some reason I feel like it's a celebration."

"Funny," Rick said. "So do I."

After the play, Rick and Diane went directly to her apartment, rejecting the invitation to join the opening-night celebration at the Rainbow Room. She flung her sable onto the floor of the foyer, and walked, unspeaking, to the bedroom, where she lay face down on the blue satin spread.

"Now is that a way to behave?" Rick said. "You're going to flatten your hair, and you know you have the liver cotillion tomorrow."

"I can't," she said. "I can't go on like this."

"Not a very good reading," Rick said. "We'll have to have a dialogue coach work with you on that. Listen, angel." He sat on the bed beside her and gently stroked her back. "You're going to eat yourself up alive, keeping this up. Why don't you just relax and enjoy it, the way the man said in the movies about the Second World War."

"I despise you."

"But we know that, you and I. And since we've brought it out in the open so many times, why can't we forget about it and just live our lives, the way most people do."

"You can't do that to another human being. You can't force them to go on living in this kind of situation. You can't keep somebody against their will."

"But of course you can. I admit it's a little depraved . . ."

"And degenerate," she said. "It's degenerate."

"That too," he said. "But admit it. It's exciting. It's the kind of depravity and degeneracy you were looking for all your life, but you never knew it. I had to teach you. And to think I really believed once that you would be the solution to all my problems, all my lost longings. But you showed me. You certainly did. So I have no choice, do I, but to provide the solution for all of yours."

She turned over on her back and looked at him. Her hand came away from her face, and her look softened. "You did love me once, really loved me, didn't you?"

"Yes," he said. "You were the only one I ever really did."

"Then if you ever loved me, let me go. Please."

"Never. Not ever again. You're no better than anyone else," he said. "I thought you were a princess, but you're no better than anyone else. And you're a lot worse than some."

"You can't forgive me for being a human being?"

"I can't forgive myself for being so stupid about you."

He pinched her cheeks with thumb and forefinger, so her lips were forced open, and kissed her open mouth. She kissed him gently, fearfully in return.

"That's my girl," he said, and slapped her.

She began to cry, and he soothed her shoulders, and touched her chin with the soft back of his hand. "You know what's really wrong, don't you. You're under a strain. You have nobody you can talk to, except me. No one you can confide in. You're too smart to trust Bunyan, not with something like this, and you're too well bred to discuss anything personal with your housekeeper. That's why I hired Giselle."

"You what?"

"She's a lovely little girl, an old friend of mine, for years. German, very bright, so you can tell her things. You can talk to her and go for walks while I'm doing all these boring interviews and panel shows that take up so much of my time, and keep me away from you. I know how lonely you must get, so she can be . . . your companion."

"Don't you hire anybody. This is still my home, and I don't want anybody."

"It's our home, dearest, they've all but printed that in the *Daily News*. And she's already here. I had her bring her things this evening while we were at the theater. She's already tucked away in the guest bedroom. Would you like to meet her?"

"You bastard. You horrible . . ."

"I knew you'd be pleased about it," Rick said, going to the door. "I won't be a minute." He looked at his watch. "Maybe she's already asleep, but it shouldn't be too hard to rouse her." He smiled. "I've done it so many times before."

In a few moments the girl stood in the doorway. Her straight hair hung in silky blond shafts to her shoulders, and her skin, through the transparent chiffon of her white peignoir, was deep, glowing pink. She smiled at Diane, her white teeth radiant, as she made a curtsey.

"Isn't that adorable? She respects you," Rick said.

"That's my negligee!" Diane said.

"I know, isn't that lucky, you wear almost the same size. Of course she's a little more apple-cheeked and apple-breasted than you are, angel," he squeezed the girl's breasts to illustrate, and the nipples rose up pink in his hand. "But then that's delicious, don't you think, for contrast."

"Get her out of here."

"But that isn't like you at all, my Diane." He led Giselle to the side of the bed, and turned her around for Diane to see. "Not with how generous you are to orphans, not with all the charities you're so anxious to perform. Why when I first found Giselle she was sitting in one of those nasty little windows in Hamburg, with whips and boots and things, why it would have torn your heart out, and she was only fifteen, imagine. Is that any life for a lovely young girl?"

"Get her out."

"Look," Rick said, lifting the negligee to reveal the girl's buttocks, lightly striated with purple. "Isn't that sad, what people did to her. Luckily she hadn't got a mark anywhere else, you see?" He ran his fingers through the rich curly gold tufts of Giselle's pubis, and she looked at him lovingly. "Isn't she luxurious."

Diane closed her eyes.

"She'd give anything to be a movie star, of course, but I don't know how talented she is in other areas. And meantime she's incredibly happy just to be with people who are movie stars. I've explained to her that you're going to be a famous movie star also, so she doesn't mind if you and I spend some time together."

Diane said nothing.

"And meantime I imagine she'll be more than happy to spend some time with you. We're going to be so happy together, the three of us."

"Get out," Diane said.

"Now darling, I don't want you to think this is going to change anything in our relationship, Giselle understands that.

We are going to continue to do everything together, and I do mean everything. But a man, well you know what they say about a man's being different, and every once in a while—for variety's sake, he enjoys being wanted. Look at her. Just look." He stripped the negligee back from Giselle's shoulders, and touched her bursting nipples. "Look at that. She has her own little hard-ons, for me. Isn't that lovely. Let's see if we can find anything else." He knelt, and spread the dark pink labia wide, and found the rosy pip within. "Isn't that charming. Her own little shiny erection. Look. Goddammit, I said look." He reached over and pulled Diane's hair abruptly backward and forced her face close to Giselle's pubis. "Now isn't it lovely, tell me goddammit, isn't it lovely?"

"Yes," Diane whimpered. "Yes."

"Why it's just like a little ripe berry, bursting with juice. Have you ever seen anything so appetizing? You haven't, have you. Admit it. I said admit it."

"No. No I haven't."

"Why don't you take one little lick, just to see what it tastes like, I wouldn't mind. I see how tempting it is, I'm not selfish."

"No, please."

"Oh come on, you don't have to control yourself for me. I know what a greedy little girl you've always been. Indulge yourself. Indulge all your nasty little appetites."

She tried to wrest her head backward, but he yanked her hair. She gave a little gasp.

"Go on, sweetheart. Only one. Just one sweet little taste, and then I'll let you go, and we'll go away. A cunt shouldn't be any harder for you to tease than a cock, and that was always your favorite, wasn't it, prick-teasing? Just once, and then it'll be all over."

Diane's tongue moved slowly from her mouth, pointing into air, and Rick pressed her head forward, as Giselle moved closer to the bed. Diane closed her eyes, as tip met rosy button. Giselle sighed.

Rick let go her hair. "She likes you. She likes you very much. If I left it up to her she'd probably just as soon stay with you and finish whatever it is you girls want to do. But you'll have plenty of time to work that out. After all, she'll be free to go with us everywhere. Isn't that lucky? You just think about that, while Giselle and I are inside." He raised the peignoir back over Giselle's shoulders, and led her to the door. "Sweet dreams, honeypot," he said, and blew a kiss.

She had not told George. She had not told George or Algernon or anyone, because she knew the moment she told another human being, it would become truth, immutable. Like this, keeping it to herself, keeping the ugly words that Matthew Rady had spoken close in, like her hands on the belly that still floated in front of her, it could remain a sorrowful, imagined nightmare from which at any moment she would awaken, whole, pregnant. Maggie had spent the night lying on her back, not daring to turn on her stomach or her side for fear she might squelch whatever of life was left inside her. It wasn't true that the pregnancy was hysterical, imagined, that she had never conceived at all. The baby was there, in spite of what the doctor said, it had to be there. At ten o'clock she felt it kicking, powerfully, the little child inside struggling to assert itself against the denial. By six o'clock in the morning she was so reassured about her baby's existence, she allowed herself to fall asleep.

She was not aware of dreaming. But when she woke at eleven, Maggie knew her baby was dead. That it had never existed.

She looked down at the swollen roundness that preceded her into the bathroom, and did not weep. Instead, she drank several glasses of water and brushed her teeth in between. When she was finished, she vomited, loosing the liquid into the toilet bowl, heaving until she offered up nothing but dry, empty air. When she was finished retching she sat for a long time on the toilet, straining to rid herself of everything that was inside.

It could not come out either of those ways, Maggie realized sadly. Dr. Rady had offered her some shots to induce the renegade, unwanted period, but she had declined, saying she preferred to wait until the weekend was over, to rest in the interim. She understood now that she would have to go back to him, or someone, or it might stay inside her forever. Dead, like that. Not imaginary, the way the doctor said.

The Swiss housekeeper they had hired the week before to help her through the last, heavy months, brought her breakfast on a tray; but Maggie did not want to eat. The older woman pressed her, she had to eat, it was for the baby, strength. There was so much kindness in the woman, Maggie could not stand to disappoint her with the truth. She said nothing, and bit into the toast, beneath the warm, brown-eyed supervisory glance. When the housekeeper was gone, she went into the bathroom and vomited again.

She brushed her teeth again and dressed in the warmest of her maternity clothes, even though she could tell from the sunlight outside the diamond-paned bathroom glass that the day had a radiance, that winter was almost over. A false spring, perhaps, but spring nonetheless. Pseudo-springenesis, she supposed Dr. Rady would call it. No matter that it was ephemeral and deceptive. Those who were enjoying the day, as if it were spring finally, with whatever permanence spring afforded, should not be told it was really still winter.

She did not stop to say good-bye to George, or tell Algernon where she was going. In the downstairs hallway, she nodded her head to the housekeeper, and smiled, and said yes, she had a muffler on, and no, she wasn't going anywhere special, she just felt like taking a walk. The housekeeper told her what a good idea that was, how much better than just lying in bed. Exercise was so beneficial for the baby.

"Yes," Maggie said softly. "Yes, I'm sure it is."

She crossed the street to the Metropolitan, and walked the wide lip of the crosstown entrance, raising her shiny yellow boots into the diamond-etched pavements that ran alongside the park, and saw the bright contrast of the vinyl against sidewalk gray. The trees, cracked dark from winter, showed only the slightest buds, huddling in on themselves, and the sky, for all the blatancy of sunlight, carried a tone of neutral even in its clouds. It was still too early for bright blue. Nothing was color. New York was a gray on gray painting by Bunyan Reis, as buildings, trees and skies conformed as a backdrop to the only splash of life, of color: Maggie's boots.

And the children.

The children were red-cheeked, scarlet-coated, green mufflers floating below pink faces, purple gloves stretched out to parental hands. Gaily they paraded each other up and down the broad park sidewalk of Fifth Avenue, glowing with life and returned affection. Maggie did not try to look away. She saw them passing by her, swimming in a misty sea, part of life, and part of each other, but never to be part of her.

By the time she reached Seventy-fourth Street, she lost count of how many there were. They would not stay in ordered rows, marching up the avenue, but jumped out of hidden entranceways from the park, clambered from strollers, chased the air with little plastic windmills, leaped after lost balloons. It was impossible to keep track of them, moving around as they were. And she was tired, she was terribly tired trying to sort them all out in her mind, and decide which one was hers.

She turned the corner into the park at Seventy-second Street, and saw them grinning toothless in carriages, bouncing against the sides of their strollers, skinning their knees as they slipped from ancient skateboards, and she wished they would all behave themselves. But there was no way to tell them, because children were like that. And, of course, she wasn't really their mother. Not yet.

She leaned her weight backward as she walked the steep ramp down toward the boat lake, measuring her steps so as not to collide with the woman in front of her, heels clutching ground, holding fiercely to a baby carriage. Even from halfway down she could make out the expressions of wonder on little-boy faces, as they leaned over the cement rim of the lake, watching old men sail ancient frigates, modern yachts, polished gleaming wooden conquerors of the seas, across the tiny pond. She was glad she lived so near the park. No matter what people said about the city, and the weather, and the soot collecting in little lungs, there was not, could not be a better place for raising a child. There was no wonder that would elude hers. A miniature armada piloted by old loving hands. A carousel that played the genuine merry-go-round songs. A zoo. They would live within walking distance of fairyland.

Her eyes filled with tears of happiness as she realized how lucky she was, how fortunate her child would be. She had to steady herself against a bench at the water's edge, she felt so full. In the first flush of pretend spring, the benches were crowded with celebrants, their faces turned skyward toward the sun. There were no empty places along the green slatted benches. An old shiny-pated man, seeing the roundness beneath her coat, offered her his seat. She was about to accept, because she was so tired, so terribly tired, when she saw the carriage a few benches away.

"No," she said. "No thank you. I'm meeting friends."

She passed in front of the hot-dog stand, children, windmills, balloons, whirring around her; but she did not see any of it clearly. Only one thing was in focus. "Mrs. Hanner?" she said, to the tiny, white-haired woman, at the far side of the bench. "I'm Mrs. Piner. Maggie Piner?"

"Oh yes, of course. Mrs. Waller's friend. How are you, dear," Mrs. Hanner said, her eyes moving to Maggie's belly. "Everything coming along nicely?"

"Beautifully, thank you," Maggie said, her eyes moving to Tracy's face. The little girl sat, her white mittened hands clutching the sides of the carriage, eager face in the sunlight watching the children run. "How pretty Tracy is. She's turning into a real little girl, yes?"

"Little girls are the nicest," Mrs. Hanner said. "They're so easy. I hope you get a little girl."

"I hope so too," Maggie said. "I'm sure I will."

A little boy about four ran by the carriage, his feet kicking football, his hand dangling a balloon. The balloon smashed against Tracy's face, and she laughed.

"Be careful!" Maggie shouted angrily at the boy.

"It's all right," said Mrs. Hanner. "They're not as fragile as all that. She won't be hurt by a balloon."

"I suppose I don't know very much about babies."

"You will. Mothers do."

"Are Kate and David here at the park?"

"Oh my no. They're away in the country for the weekend. They always leave very early Friday."

"Without the baby?" Maggie started to ask, and then realized, of course, without the baby. "It's cold," Maggie said, shivering inside her coat. "The sun looks so warm, but it's really very cold."

"Would you like me to get you some coffee?" Mrs. Hanner said. "They have some nice hot coffee right back there at the boathouse. It isn't very good, but it's hot."

"That's very kind of you," Maggie opened her purse and handed the woman a bill. "Why don't you get yourself a sandwich, as long as you're there. You must be hungry, sitting out in the chill like this."

"Well how nice, Mrs. Piner. I think I will."

"Do you mind very much . . ." Maggie put her gloved hand on the cold steel of the carriage handle, and Tracy smiled. "Do you mind very much if I push her once around the pond, while you're getting the coffee."

"Well . . ." Mrs. Hanner hesitated. "No, no of course not. I suppose you can use the practice."

"Yes," Maggie said. "Yes, I can."

The water at the far side of the boat lake away from the people, away from the sunlit side, seemed darker, somehow. Maggie saw that it was speckled with old dead leaves and candy wrappers, and a wrinkled used condom. It was disgusting, really, what people did with the little dabs of loveliness offered to them in life, and she hated them for abusing beauty, and each other. She would have preferred the water clear and bluish green, the way it had been in Acapulco, or Paradise Island. But it was still water, and water was pure, no matter what people did to defile it. We sprang from water, Maggie knew, it encircled us in the womb, she had seen herself floating free inside herself so many times with Algernon, just as she had seen her child, her beautiful child swimming radiant in wet motherly sunshine.

A lone sailor awaited the coming of his miniature sailing ship on a puckish, indecisive wind, and she smiled at him as she unbuckled the baby's carriage strap, and lifted Tracy into her arms. She kissed the baby's velvet cheek, and infant hands thick and warm with mittens touched her face. The baby laughed.

"You do love me," Maggie said. "I knew you would. It's

going to be fine. It's going to be all right." She walked to the edge of the pond, past the sailor, past the curious eyes she no longer saw. Pressed close against the infant cheek, she saw only a dark heavily lashed eye, fat snub-nosed profile, blurred. And the water.

There was rebirth there. She had seen that too, more times than she remembered, could remember now. They would be sanctified, and join, and be reborn, the one inside the other, as it was meant to be. "The important thing is to die," Algernon told her all the time. "Because the hell of it is you'll probably be reborn, even within the dying. Then what you have to do, if you must be born again, is choose a groovy womb."

She smiled again, and kissed the rosy infant lips, and standing on top of the asphalt ledge, yellow boots sparkling in the sun, plunged with her tiny burden into the icy water.

They said, when all the hysteria and panic had died down, and the truck with its emergency pulmotor had gone away, they said that there was never any question that the man had tried to save her too. The infant he was sure was dead, plunging so quickly to the bottom as it did, but he had made a sincere effort to save the woman, no matter how the onlookers distorted what had happened. But she pulled away from him, and weighted herself face down in the shallow waters, as if she was trying to drink it in, all of it. And the combination, her heavy clothes floating on mucky waters, and her own eager force, were too much for him. He was no swimmer, he tried to explain. All he had ever had to do with water was sailing miniature boats, and then only when the weather was pleasant.

CHAPTER SEVEN

BECAUSE of the prominence of Maggie's family, and the distances around the globe to which they were scattered, the funeral was delayed until the following Friday, to give them all time to arrange to attend. Services for Tracy Waller had been held on Monday, and Louise genuinely regretted her decision to go. She had not anticipated the size of the white coffin, and the anguish of her friends, the sobbing sounds striking numbness into the air were too much for her. Grief, genuine grief, was not an emotion she had encountered in her lifetime. She wept because she hadn't realized the casket would be so small. She did not go to the cemetery, and it was several days before she could bring herself to visit Kate and David at home.

David's face, when he answered the door, was drained and infinitely older than Louise remembered. She averted her eyes, at the same time that she smiled weakly with her lips. "I would have come sooner," she said, "but I figured you'd have so many relatives you wouldn't want anybody else."

"Kate made them all go home," he said.

"Then maybe . . . maybe you'd rather . . . I could come back in a few days."

"No, that's all right," he said. "I'm sure she'd like to see you." He motioned her inside and headed back toward the bedroom. "Let me just see if she's awake."

"Please don't bother her . . ."

"Let him bother her," Charley said, from the far side of the living room. "She can't stay in there forever."

"Hello, Charley," Louise said, and had the grace not to smile at him. It was not a rendezvous. Life, or death, could not always be a rendezvous.

"How are you, pal," he said.

"I'm fine," said Louise. "How else would I be."

She went over to the sofa, and sat, unsurely, as far away from him as she could. "You look fine."

"Yes," he said. "It's been a regular holiday."

"You're a good person," she leaned over and squeezed his hand. "Have you been here all week?"

"Somebody had to be with David. Kate isn't."

"Are they all right?"

"They're bumping into each other. They still don't know what happened, and nobody talks. But they'll be all right. What can you do? You keep on living."

They heard the door to the bedroom open, and fell silent. "She'll be out in a minute," David said. "She's just putting on a robe."

"But she doesn't have to do that," Louise said. "I can go in . . ." But Charley was pulling on her arm.

"Let her come out," he said.

In a moment they heard Kate's footsteps, shuffling heavy on the parquet floors. She paused for a moment in the doorway, as if to practice smiling. But only a tremor pulled at the corner of her mouth, and her eyes were hollow.

"Louise," she said. "I wanted to thank you for coming to the funeral but I just wasn't up to making calls. Forgive me."

"You forgive me," Louise said. "I would have been here sooner, but I thought you'd be up to your ears in family."

Kate nodded. Slowly, painfully, she made her way to the love seat, and sat down stiffly beside David. "How are you, Lou? Is everything all right?"

"Fine," Louise said. "Are you all right?"

"Sensational." The rigidity of her face disintegrated, and Kate collapsed into sobs.

"Oh honey," David said, and reached for her shoulders.

"You stay away from me, you bastard," she screamed. "It never would have happened if it wasn't for you."

"Don't you turn against me, Kate, it had nothing to do with me."

"Why don't you call Maggie," Kate sobbed. "Why don't you spend more time with Maggie, you never can tell when somebody like that will be able to do you some good. Are you satisfied with the good, David, are you?"

"For Christ's sake, it was an accident. An insane irrational accident. She was crazy, she could have grabbed any baby."

"But it was our baby. She knew our baby and she took our baby. There are no insane accidents. It happened to our baby because you made me chase her, because you were so goddammed anxious to have Maggie Bolin for your friend."

"I better go . . ." Louise said and got up.

"No, please, don't leave," Kate wept. "I don't want to be with him."

"Don't you dare blame me," David shouted. "Maybe this wouldn't have happened, you're right maybe this wouldn't have ever happened if you spent some time with your baby, maybe if you weren't always pushing me to go away for the weekends . . ."

"Because when I was alone with you, I could stand it.

When I was alone with you I didn't have to watch you trying to ingratiate yourself with people, pushing so hard I wanted to die."

"You're lying and you know it. You were afraid of that baby, just the way you were always afraid of everything . . ."

"And so I leaned on you," Kate said. "Ha!"

"Now come on," Charley said. "Come on, both of you, cut it out. It's insane, and it happened, that's all. You've got to try to live with it."

"How," Kate whimpered. "How."

"Please," Louise whispered. "Please stop. She was crazy that's all. Maggie was crazy, and nobody knew she was crazy."

"I knew," Kate said. "I knew her ever since college. That's why I didn't want to be with her."

"You didn't want to be with her because you were afraid you couldn't make it with those people," David said. "Don't you start accusing me of anything. Do you think I wanted this to happen, that I would have let it happen . . . ?" His shoulders started to heave, and he covered his eyes.

"I have to go," Louise said. "I'm sorry."

"Maybe you both better go," David whispered hoarsely.

They walked in silence for a few blocks, along Seventy-second Street, Louise taking Charley's hand at intersections, guiding him subtly west. "What's going to happen to them?" she said finally.

"They'll be all right."

"I don't think so. You can't take back things like that once they're said. You can't get over something like this that easily."

"Not easily," he said. "But they'll get over it. They love each other."

"Do they?" Louise said. "I think she loved him because she thought he was strong. He isn't strong, you know. He's just pushy and aggressive."

"He's my friend," Charley said. "I don't want to talk about him."

"Kate talked about him," Louise said. "She finally talked about him. You can't go back on things like that. Poor Dr. Ehrens. So much for the middle-class dream."

"What's that supposed to mean?"

"Happily ever after, and all that shit. There are no happy marriages, are there?"

"That's ridiculous," he said. "Of course there are."

"You're a romantic, Charley. I wish I could be a romantic." She took his arm as they reached the corner of Madison Avenue, and steered him in the direction of uptown.

"You don't wish it hard enough, or you'd let yourself be."

"Why? So I could end up like Kate, marrying a man for his strength, and gritting my teeth against the inevitable discovery that he wasn't a giant."

"Is that what you'd marry a man for?"

"Are you proposing?" she said, and dimpled. "Why Charley, Dr. Ehrens will be so pleased, we thought you'd never ask."

"Didn't you?" Charley asked.

"I never really thought about it," Louise said. "I'm lying. I thought about it all the time. Would you have wanted to marry me?"

"I don't know. I needed to see a few things."

"I don't have to prove anything to you," Louise said.

"True," said Charley. "I was hoping you'd prove a few things to yourself."

They walked in silence, past the tiny trees in squares of earth, and hopeful tufts of spring grass. At Seventy-ninth Street he put his arm around her shoulders, and she allowed herself to lean back against him.

"It isn't that the worst of it isn't the baby, God knows," Louise said. "Nothing could be sadder than the baby. But they don't feel sorry for Maggie."

"How can they? They're so tied up with their own guilt and remorse, they can't think about anyone but themselves. And Tracy. If Maggie were alive, they'd probably kill her. They'd have to."

"But it's so sad. It wasn't her fault. She was insane, everybody knows that now, but the real sadness is nobody knew it when she was alive. Oh maybe Kate really knew it, but nobody else did, or if they knew they didn't do anything. She was so rich nobody dared tell her she was crazy. How could she possibly be helped?"

"I can't worry about her, or anyone like her. My friends are real to me. Those people aren't real."

"But they are, that's the worst of it. They have a bigger reality because of what they are, don't you see that? They have the luxury to act out what they are even if they're crazy. Don't you see how marvelous that is?"

"No," Charley said. "I'm a little surprised you still do, after everything that happened."

"Well I'm not in awe of them anymore, if that's what you mean. God, I don't know, these past—however many months it's been since Harry died, it's all been a bit much for Lulu.

Andre's running away like that, people getting killed. I'm not having a good time."

"Well that's a beginning, anyway," Charley said.

She started to cross Eighty-second Street, hoping he wouldn't ask where they were headed until they had gotten there. But his eyes suddenly took in the façade of Frank E. Campbell's parlor across the street, and he stopped.

"Where the hell are you going?"

"I have to, Charley. You know I have to. The funeral's probably nearly over, but I have to put in an appearance. Maggie was my friend. No matter what she did, she was my friend."

"And you have to see who else is there."

"No. That isn't it at all. I have to go. It's my job. And she was my friend. She was your friend, too. She liked you, she really did."

"Oh for Christ's sake," Charley said, and pulled his arm away.

"Please," Louise said. "Please come with me. Just this once. I need you, Charley, I really do. Don't make me go in there by myself. I've had enough of funerals."

"You won't change. You'll never change."

"Just help me through this. Help me through this one thing. I'm not betraying anybody by going, Charley, and neither are you. Do it for me."

He held her arm as they passed through the entrance hall. Inside, the voice of Algernon Reddy droned through the chapel. There were no seats in the rows immediately next to the doorway, so Charley and Louise stood to the side with a few other latecomers.

"Life is the issue," Algernon said from the podium behind a bank filled with flowers and Maggie's coffin. "Not death. Death is too irrational, too stupid for the living to dwell upon. Maggie is not dead. She lives in the memories, the conscious and unconscious seeking of all of us. There is nothing that any of us will perform in our lifetimes that will not be irradiated by her presence. She will be constantly resurrected in the deeds we do, in the places we are. The Function Center in New Jersey where Dr. George Piner will operate his clinic in conjunction with my work will stand as a living, pulsating monument to her. And I know that you, her beloved friends, will feel free to come, to participate, to remember, and to celebrate her. God bless you, Maggie girl. Cheers."

Afterward, on the sidewalk outside, Louise moved among the crowd, her hand pressed tight in Charley's. "Just another minute," she whispered. "I have to tell her family how sorry I am."

"I'm glad I ran into you," Chet Oppenheim said, waving Louise to one side. "I don't like your avoiding my calls. Harry's case comes up in court next week, and I want you there."

"Screw," said Louise.

Behind her, Charley laughed, and tightened his grip on her hand. Then Louise saw Diane Trejinska, sun-browned and drawn after her trip to Mexico.

"Bitch," Louise said, pushing her way through to her. "Why didn't you tell me you were going to Mexico, I had to read about it in the paper just like everyone else."

"I didn't tell anyone I was going," Diane said.

"Are you sure? Are you sure someone isn't just pressuring you not to be friendly with me anymore?"

"Why would anyone do that?" Rick said, looming up, smiling, white-teethed and perfect behind Diane.

"Oh I just thought maybe Chet or somebody . . ."

"Believe me, if there's anything to tell, you'll be the first to know," Rick said, and pinched her cheek.

"I was the last to know about the divorce."

"No you weren't," Rick said. "Tzigie was. Or hadn't you heard that the husband was always the last?" He laughed, but not too loudly. "Isn't it terrible about Maggie."

"Awful," Louise said. "So what does this mean now, does this mean the two of you will get married, or what?" Her question started to echo in Louise's own ears, and she felt a certain hollowness. She looked back and realized her hand was empty.

She turned and saw Charley making his way slowly toward the curb, away from her.

"Well, why don't you come over to Harry's house? George sent out for some food and things, and then maybe we'll have an announcement to make." Rick squeezed the back of Diane's neck, and she closed her eyes.

"Aren't they gorgeous," Bunyan squealed. "Still so much in love, and it isn't even officially spring yet, or is it. You're coming to Harry's, of course, Lulu; I haven't seen you for days."

"No," Louise said, her eyes following Charley. "No, I don't think I can."

"But you have to, love," Bunyan said. "It's the least you owe Maggie. She'd be devastated if you weren't at her wake."

"I don't think I can," Louise said starting to pull away from them. "I've got to go."

"You may miss a very important announcement," Rick said.

"Excuse me," Louise said, and started pushing through the crowd.

It was a block and a half before she managed to catch up with him, his long lean legs striding briskly along Madison Avenue. She shouted after him, not wanting to yell too loud for fear it was bad manners so close to a funeral procession.

"Why didn't you stop," she managed, out of breath. "You heard me calling you, didn't you?"

"I didn't mean to take you away from your friends."

"But you didn't, Charley. I left myself. It isn't as if I have to choose between you, is it?"

"Isn't it?"

"Sometimes you sound just like Dr. Ehrens. His office is right in the next block, why don't we stop in to see him and you can let him feel your belly."

He laughed, and hooked his hand through her arm. "Why don't we just stop in at Stark's, and I'll buy you a hamburger."

"You mean like the first time we were together. I mean really the first time?"

There was wetness in the air, in spite of the bright sun and she moved closer to him.

"I mean like having a hamburger."

"You don't want me to read more into the invitation than it is," Louise said. "Is that it?"

"Why don't we just go inside and order, and then we can talk about it."

She bit her lip, and tried to feel the warmth of him through his heavy jacket. Then she smiled. "I didn't go with them, you know."

"I know."

"Everybody's going over to Harry Bell's house. Isn't it funny how it was never really Maggie's? Rick and Diane are sounding teasingly like they're going to announce their engagement. I might be missing a very important exclusive."

"I'm thrilled for them," Charley said.

"Well you should be, you don't have to be so cynical. Not if you're really the romantic you claim to be. They're an exquisite couple, they have everything, and they're desperately in love. Everyone should envy them."

"All right," Charley said. "I envy them." He pulled open the cold glass door to Stark's, and held it for her, pointing with his arm. "Madame? . . . Unless you think the food would be better at the party."

"I want to be here. With you."

"And what happens in an hour, two hours, or a day, when you start worrying that you're missing something."

She looked at him and tried to think of the right things to

say, the honest, self-searching, grown-up thing to say. She even tried to believe she would mean it.

"Will you come in or come out," a man said from the counter of the restaurant. "But close the damned door, it's cold."

She looked inside at the bored, ordinary faces, on uninterestingly dressed, hunched-over people seated along the counter, biting without tasting into sandwiches and salads. She saw middle-aged men, reading their newspapers at cold, undecorated tables, and old ladies with dogs, leashes wound around metal table legs, and harassed young matrons with noisy children. Panic seized her.

"Well we don't have to be like them, do we," Louise said softly. "We wouldn't have to end up exactly like these people."

"I don't know," Charley said, and pulled out a chair for her, in front of an empty table. "Maybe we don't have to be exactly like anybody."